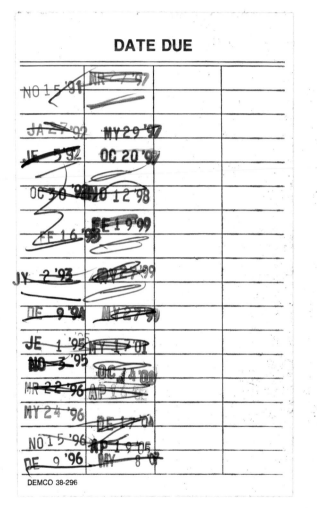

The Best Short Stories
by Black Writers

Books by LANGSTON HUGHES

Poetry

ASK YOUR MAMA
SELECTED POEMS
THE DREAM KEEPER

Fiction

NOT WITHOUT LAUGHTER
THE WAYS OF WHITE FOLKS
TAMBOURINES TO GLORY
SOMETHING IN COMMON

Autobiography

THE BIG SEA
I WONDER AS I WANDER

Humor

SIMPLE SPEAKS HIS MIND
SIMPLE STAKES A CLAIM
SIMPLE TAKES A WIFE
SIMPLE'S UNCLE SAM

Collections

THE BEST OF SIMPLE
FIVE PLAYS BY LANGSTON HUGHES
THE LANGSTON HUGHES READER

Biography and History

FAMOUS AMERICAN NEGROES
FAMOUS NEGRO MUSIC MAKERS
FAMOUS NEGRO HEROES OF AMERICA
FIGHT FOR FREEDOM: THE STORY OF THE NAACP
PICTORIAL HISTORY OF THE NEGRO IN AMERICA
(with Milton Meltzer)

Edited by LANGSTON HUGHES

AN AFRICAN TREASURY
POEMS FROM BLACK AFRICA
NEW NEGRO POETS: U.S.A.
THE BOOK OF NEGRO HUMOR
THE BOOK OF NEGRO FOLKLORE (with Arna Bontemps)
THE POETRY OF THE NEGRO (with Arna Bontemps)
THE BEST SHORT STORIES BY BLACK WRITERS

The Best Short Stories
by Black Writers

The Classic Anthology from 1899 to 1967

Edited and with an Introduction by

LANGSTON HUGHES

Little, Brown and Company • Boston • Toronto

BP

*Published simultaneously in Canada
by Little, Brown & Company (Canada) Limited*

PRINTED IN THE UNITED STATES OF AMERICA

We are grateful for permission to include the following previously copyrighted stories in this collection:

"The Checkerboard" from *Lover Man* by Alston Anderson.
Copyright © 1959 by Alston Anderson. Reprinted by permission of Doubleday & Company, Inc.

"This Morning, This Evening, So Soon" reprinted from *Going
to Meet the Man* by James Baldwin. Copyright © 1948, 1951,
1957, 1958, 1960, 1965 by James Baldwin. Used with the permission of the publisher, The Dial Press, Inc.

"A Summer Tragedy" by Arna Bontemps. Copyright 1933 by
Arna Bontemps. Reprinted by permission of the author.

"We're the Only Colored People Here" from *Maud Martha*
by Gwendolyn Brooks. Copyright 1953 by Gwendolyn Brooks
Blakely. Reprinted by permission of Harper & Row, Publishers.

"Singing Dinah's Song" by Frank London Brown. Copyright
© 1963 by Alfred A. Knopf, Inc. Reprinted by permission of
the author's widow, Evelyn M. Brown.

"The Sheriff's Children" from *The Wife of His Youth* by
Charles W. Chesnutt. Reprinted by permission of the author's
daughter, Helen M. Chesnutt.

"The Pocketbook Game" from *Like One of the Family* by
Alice Childress. Copyright © 1956 by Alice Childress. Reprinted by permission of the author.

"Santa Claus Is a White Man" by John Henrik Clarke, published in *Opportunity Magazine*, December 1939. Copyright
1939 by National Urban League. Reprinted by permission of
the author.

"The Beach Umbrella" by Cyrus Colter. Copyright © 1963
by Alfred A. Knopf, Inc. Reprinted by permission of the author
and his agent, Robert P. Mills.

"The Day the World Almost Came to an End" by Pearl Crayton, published in *Negro Digest*, August 1965. Copyright 1965
by Negro Digest. Reprinted by permission of the author.

"Come Home Early, Chile" by Owen Dodson. Copyright ©

Editor's Note

THE short stories in this volume range from those of the first famous Negro writers in this genre, Charles W. Chesnutt and Paul Laurence Dunbar, widely published at the turn of the century, to the youngest contemporary writers of creative fiction, Ronald Milner, Robert Boles and Alice Walker. Herein are all the noted names in American Negro writing, including Jean Toomer, Richard Wright, Zora Neale Hurston, Ralph Ellison, Willard Motley, John A. Williams, Frank Yerby and James Baldwin. This is, as far as I know, the most comprehensive anthology of American Negro short stories to be published anywhere.

LANGSTON HUGHES

Introduction

J UST as many Americans believe, solely from having seen *La Dolce Vita* on the screen, that Rome is one vast seraglio teeming with orgiastic vices, so many also think, from having seen *The Cool World*, that all Negroes are primitive, dirty and dangerous. White persons of the older generation add to their contemporary concepts the ancient stereotypes lazy, grinning and illiterate, drawn from memories of Stepin Fechit, Rochester and Amos and Andy. Art (and some motion pictures may be classified as art) molds the thoughts, opinions and concepts of millions of people, even before the age of reason. On one of my recent lecture tours, I was the house guest of a charming white professorial couple on a very advanced Midwestern campus of the caliber of Kenyon or Antioch. At dinner my first evening there, I was inwardly amused and not unduly surprised when the ten-year-old daughter of the house asked me [across the table], "Mr. Langston Hughes, can you teach me to shoot dice?"

Her embarrassed parents blushed deeply. "Darling, why do you ask such a thing of Mr. Hughes?"

"I see colored people all the time shooting dice in the TV movies," the child said.

I laughed. "At night they revive a lot of very old pictures, and they show a lot of old-time colored actors like Sunshine Sammy and Nicodemus and Mantan Moreland. But Negroes don't *always* shoot craps in real life and many have never even seen a pair of dice. Still, there's no harm in your learning. So if your daddy has a pair of dice, after dinner I can show you what I learned when I was in the Merchant Marine. Then if you ever go to Las Vegas — where white people shoot dice all night — you will know. Dice is a very old game, mentioned in the Bible — played by King Ahasuerus and his court. And today there's a very fashionable gambling casino at Monte Carlo where high society shoots dice."

I was talking very fast to try to keep the little girl from becoming more embroiled with her embarrassed parents: "Why did you ask such a question?" I knew why. The old stereotypes of the blackface minstrels and of Hollywood descend even unto the third and fourth generations.

Because he did not wish to be associated with similar racial stereotypes of his time, in the 1880's, the first outstanding Negro writer of fiction in the United States, Charles Waddell Chesnutt, wrote as a white man for a number of years, without revealing his ethnic identity. By hiding his color, he did not run the risk of having his material turned down by editors because of race. But after twelve years of his literary "passing," a publication called the Critic discovered his background and in a biographical note revealed Chesnutt as an author who "faces the problems of the race to which he in part belongs." Being very fair — about the complexion of Congressman Adam Clayton Powell — with only a small percentage of black blood in his family tree, Chesnutt was what anthropologists term a "voluntary" Negro. The same might be said of Jean Toomer. Shortly after the publication of Cane, he moved outside the social confines of the Negro world to live in Taos, Carmel and finally Bucks County.

Like Chesnutt, the successful contemporary novelist Frank Yerby, author of The Foxes of Harrow and a dozen other best-selling romances, revealed recently to a reporter, "I did tell my publishers at one time not to identify me as a Negro." Yerby's vast reading public today is on the whole quite unaware of his race. But the white people in the Georgia town where he was born know. When the motion picture made from The Foxes of Harrow had its highly publicized premiere in Augusta, Yerby's relatives were relegated to the Negro section of the theater. Such are the strictures of race in America even against an author whose books are translated around the world and whose earnings from writing total well over a million dollars. For almost twenty years Yerby has lived abroad where such prejudices seldom are in evidence and racial indignities such as those revealed in his early story, "Health Card," are unheard of. "I love my country," Yerby is quoted as saying. But, "Unfortunately, my country doesn't love me enough to let me live in it."

"One of the inalienable rights is that of the pursuit of happiness," Yerby says. In this anthology the themes of many of the stories concern the search for that right and how Negroes may work out the problems of their lives in order to find a modicum of happiness in America. There are drama, comedy and tragedy to be found in this fiction — so near to fact — as put down by the best of the Negro writers since 1887, when Chesnutt published his initial story in the *Atlantic Monthly*. His "The Goophered Grapevine" marked the first fiction to be published by a Negro in that highly conservative magazine. Since that time a few Negro authors have become world famous — Richard Wright, Ralph Ellison, James Baldwin. (Their stories are published here.) But none has become really rich, except Frank Yerby who, after "Health Card," put the race problem on the shelf in favor of more commercial themes. His historical romances have wonderful moviesque titles like *The Golden Hawk* and *The Saracen Blade*, but there are no noble black faces among their characters when brought to the screen. Black faces seldom sell in Hollywood.

Twenty years after publication, Ralph Ellison's *Invisible Man*, a major American novel, has not yet been filmed, and Hollywood would not touch Richard Wright's famous *Native Son*. In all its years of activity Hollywood has never made a major motion picture which portrayed with sympathy our foremost American dilemma — jampacked with drama — the Negro problem. So far as I know, exciting though many of these tales in this anthology are, only one has been filmed by Hollywood: Mary Elizabeth Vroman's charming "See How They Run" under the title of *Bright Road*. But this story is not concerned with racial problems and so offends nobody.

Ted Poston's Hopkinsonville tales or the stories of Zora Neale Hurston, Alice Childress or Lindsay Patterson would make delightful motion-picture, television, or radio comedies, much more human and real than *Amos and Andy*. (Alice Childress's off-Broadway comedy, *Trouble in Mind*, seemed to me as funny as *Born Yesterday*.) But Hollywood has not touched their work, nor have any other mass media to date. For screen-searing drama, John A. Williams's story, "Son in the Afternoon" (included here), could scarcely be surpassed. But unless times have changed greatly, Hollywood is not likely to buy it for screen treatment.

Since most Negro writers from Chesnutt to LeRoi Jones have

found it hard to make a literary living, or to derive from other labor sufficient funds to sustain creative leisure, their individual output has of necessity often been limited in quantity, and sometimes in depth and quality as well — since Negroes seldom have time to loaf and invite their souls. When a man or woman must teach all day in a crowded school, or type in an office, or write news stories, read proofs and help edit a newspaper, creative prose does not always flow brilliantly or freely at night, or during that early morning hour torn from sleep before leaving for work. Yet some people ask, "Why aren't there more Negro writers?" Or, "Why doesn't Owen Dodson produce more books?" Or how come So-and-So takes so long to complete his second novel? I can tell you why. So-and-So hasn't got the money. Unlike most promising white writers, he has never sold a single word to motion pictures, television, or radio. He has never been asked to write a single well-paying soap commercial. He is not in touch with the peripheral sources of literary income that enable others more fortunate to take a year off to go somewhere and write.

Fortunately, however, in recent years a foundation has occasionally rescued a talented black writer from the subway crush of his low-salaried job. And once in a while, one finds a patron. Writing is a time-taking task, and the living is not easy. I am in favor of national subsidies, as exist in Europe. State aid never seemed to impede good writing overseas. I do not believe it would hurt good writers here. It could hardly hurt black writers, who, so far, have had not anyone at all to subvert them. For the first national grant of a large and sizable sum, I nominate one of our solid and long esteemed writers, Arna Bontemps, who has been teaching all his literary life and who deserves release for the full flowering of his considerable talents — hitherto recognized by discriminating readers but unrecognized by money. Or if it must be a young talent as first choice for a subsidy, then why not the astounding Miss Alice Walker? Neither you nor I have ever read a story like "To Hell with Dying" before. At least, I do not think you have.

The stories in this book range geographically from South to North, East to West, from America's Panama Canal Zone to our Chicago Loop and, in point of time, from the Reconstruction through the Harlem Renaissance, the Depression, the Second

World War, the period of James Baldwin's blues in De Gaulle's Paris, to the contemporary moment of Charles Wright's "A New Day." In fiction as in life Negroes get around. They have been covering varied grounds for a considerable time via the written word. Here they reveal their thoughts, their emotions, directions and indirections over three quarters of a century — from Chesnutt and Dunbar, Wright, Ellison and Williams, to the new young writers of the sixties, Lindsay Patterson, Robert Boles, and Alice Walker; from the fright and violence of the Deep South to the tinkle of iced drinks at an interracial party in Boston; from the twisted face of a black sharecropper to the spotlighted smile of a Harlem dancer, from tragedy to comedy, laughter to tears, these stories culled from the best of Negro writing over the years, indicate how varied, complex and exciting is the milieu in which black folk live in America.

Just as once, so the saying goes, the sun never set on the British Empire (because it extended around the world), so today the sun is always rising somewhere on books by American Negro writers whose works in English and in translations are being read around the world. Wright, Ellison, Baldwin, Himes, Hughes and Yerby have all been translated into at least a dozen major languages and are to be found in the libraries and bookshops of most of the earth's large cities. Today in Japanese, French, German, Italian and Polish universities, among others, students are writing theses and working toward doctorates in various phases of Negro literature. Negro authors are beginning to reap their sunrise harvest.

September, 1966

L.H.

Contents

In approximate chronological order of the authors' birth dates

The Best Short Stories
by Black Writers

THE SHERIFF'S CHILDREN

Charles W. Chesnutt

(*The first pages of this story describe the village of Troy, county seat of Branson County, North Carolina.*)

A MURDER was a rare event in Branson County. Every well-informed citizen could tell the number of homicides committed in the county for fifty years back, and whether the slayer in any given instance had escaped, either by flight or acquittal, or had suffered the penalty of the law. So when it became known in Troy early one Friday morning in summer, about ten years after the war, that old Captain Walker, who had served in Mexico under Scott and had left an arm on the field of Gettysburg, had been foully murdered during the night, there was intense excitement in the village. Business was practically suspended, and the citizens gathered in little groups to discuss the murder and speculate upon the identity of the murderer. It transpired from testimony at the coroner's inquest held during the morning, that a strange mulatto had been met going away from Troy early Friday morning by a farmer on his way to town. Other circumstances seemed to connect the stranger with the crime. The sheriff organized a posse to search for him, and early in the evening, when most of the citizens of Troy were at supper, the suspected man was brought in and lodged in the county jail.

By the following morning the news of the capture had spread to the farthest limits of the county. A much larger number of people than usual came to town that Saturday — bearded men in straw hats and blue homespun shirts, and butternut trousers of great amplitude of material and vagueness of outline; women in homespun frocks and slat-bonnets, with faces as expressionless as the dreary sandhills which gave them a meager sustenance.

The murder was almost the sole topic of conversation. A steady stream of curious observers visited the house of mourning and gazed upon the rugged face of the old veteran, now stiff and cold in death; and more than one eye dropped a tear at the remembrance of the cheery smile, and the joke — sometimes superannuated, generally feeble, but always good-natured — with which the captain had been wont to greet his acquaintances. There was a growing sentiment of anger among these stern men toward the murderer who had thus cut down their friend, and a strong feeling that ordinary justice was too slight a punishment for such a crime.

Toward noon there was an informal gathering of citizens in Dan Ayson's store.

"I hear it 'lowed that Square Kyahtah's too sick ter hol' co'te this evenin'," said one, "an' that the purlim'nary hearin' 'll haf ter go over 'tel nex' week." A look of disappointment went round the crowd.

"Hit's the durndes', meanes' murder ever committed in this caounty," said another, with moody emphasis.

"I s'pose the nigger 'lowed the Cap'n had some greenbacks," observed a third speaker.

"The Cap'n," said another, with an air of superior information, "has left two bairls of Confedrit money, which he 'spected'd be good some day er nuther."

This statement gave rise to a discussion of the speculative value of Confederate money; but in a little while the conversation returned to the murder.

"Hangin' air too good fer the murderer," said one; "he oughter be burnt, stider bein' hung."

There was an impressive pause at this point, during which a jug of moonlight whiskey went the round of the crowd.

"Well," said a round-shouldered farmer who, in spite of his peaceable expression and faded gray eye, was known to have been one of the most daring followers of a rebel guerrilla chieftain, "what air ye gwine ter do about it? Ef you fellers air gwine ter set down an' let a wuthless nigger kill the bes' white man in Branson, an' not say nuthin' ner do nuthin', *I'll* move outen the caounty."

This speech gave tone and direction to the rest of the conversation. Whether the fear of losing the round-shouldered farmer operated to bring about the result or not is immaterial to this narrative; but at all events the crowd decided to lynch the Negro. They agreed that this was the least that could be done to avenge the death of their murdered friend, and that it was a becoming way in which to honor his memory. They had some vague notions of the majesty of the law and the rights of the citizen, but in the passion of the moment these sunk into oblivion; a white man had been killed by a Negro.

"The Cap'n was an ole sodger," said one of his friends solemnly. "He'll sleep better when he knows that a co'te-martial has be'n hilt an' jestice done."

By agreement the lynchers were to meet at Tyson's store at five o'clock in the afternoon and proceed thence to the jail, which was situated down the Lumberton Dirt Road (as the old turnpike antedating the plank-road was called) about half a mile south of the court house. When the preliminaries of the lynching had been arranged and a committee appointed to manage the affair, the crowd dispersed, some to go to their dinners and some to secure recruits for the lynching party.

It was twenty minutes to five o'clock when an excited Negro, panting and perspiring, rushed up to the back door of Sheriff Campbell's dwelling, which stood at a little distance from the jail and somewhat farther than the latter building from the court-house. A turbaned colored woman came to the door in response to the Negro's knock.

"Hoddy, Sis' Nance."

"Hoddy, Brer Sam."

"Is de shurff in?" inquired the Negro.

"Yas, Brer Sam, he's eatin' his dinner," was the answer.

"Will yer ax 'im ter step ter de do' a minute, Sis' Nance?"

The woman went into the dining room, and a moment later the sheriff came to the door. He was a tall, muscular man, of a ruddier complexion than is usual among Southerners. A pair of keen, deep-set gray eyes looked out from under bushy eyebrows, and about his mouth was a masterful expression, which a full beard, once sandy in color but now profusely sprinkled with gray, could not entirely conceal. The day was hot; the sheriff had discarded his coat and vest, and had his white shirt open at the throat.

"What do you want, Sam?" he inquired of the Negro, who

stood hat in hand, wiping the moisture from his face with a ragged shirt-sleeve.

"Shurff, dey gwine ter hang de pris'ner w'at lock' up in de jail. Dey're comin' dis a-way now. I wuz layin' down on a sack er corn down at de sto', behine a pile er flour-bairls, w'en I hearn Doc' Cain en Kunnel Wright talkin' erbout it. I slip' outen de back do', en run here as fas' as I could. I hearn you say down ter de sto' once't dat you wouldn't let nobody take a pris'ner 'way fum you widout walkin' over yo' dead body, en I thought I'd let you know 'fo' dey come, so yer could pertec' de pris'ner."

The sheriff listened calmly, but his face grew firmer, and a determined gleam lit up his gray eyes. His frame grew more erect, and he unconsciously assumed the attitude of a soldier who momentarily expects to meet the enemy face to face.

"Much obliged, Sam," he answered. "I'll protect the prisoner. Who's coming?"

"I dunno who-all *is* comin'," replied the Negro. "Dere's Mistah McSwayne, en Doc' Cain, en Maje' McDonal', and Kunnel Wright en a heap er yuthers. I wuz so skeered I done furgot mo' d'n half un em. I spec' dey mus' be mos' here by dis time, so I'll git outen de way, fer I don't want nobody fer ter think I wuz mix' up in dis business." The Negro glanced nervously down the road toward the town, and made a movement as if to go away.

"Won't you have some dinner first?" asked the sheriff.

The Negro looked longingly in at the open door, and sniffed the appetizing odor of boiled pork and collards.

"I ain't got no time fer ter tarry, Shurff," he said, "but Sis' Nance mought gin me sump'n I could kyar in my han' en eat on de way."

A moment later Nancy brought him a huge sandwich of split cornpone, with a thick slice of fat bacon inserted between the halves, and a couple of baked yams. The Negro hastily replaced his ragged hat on his head, dropped the yams in the pocket of his capacious trousers and, taking the sandwich in his hand, hurried across the road and disappeared in the woods beyond.

The sheriff reentered the house, and put on his coat and hat. He then took down a double-barreled shotgun and loaded it with buckshot. Filling the chambers of a revolver with fresh cartridges, he slipped it into the pocket of the sackcoat which he wore.

A comely young woman in a calico dress watched these proceedings with anxious surprise.

"Where are you going, Father?" she asked. She had not heard the conversation with the Negro.

"I am goin' over to the jail," responded the sheriff. "There's a mob comin' this way to lynch the nigger we've got locked up. But they won't do it," he added, with emphasis.

"Oh, Father, don't go!" pleaded the girl, clinging to his arm. "They'll shoot you if you don't give him up."

"You never mind me, Polly," said her father reassuringly, as he gently unclasped her hands from his arm. "I'll take care of myself and the prisoner, too. There ain't a man in Branson County that would shoot me. Besides, I have faced fire too often to be scared away from my duty. You keep close in the house," he continued, "and if anyone disturbs you just use the old horse-pistol in the top bureau drawer. It's a little old-fashioned, but it did good work a few years ago."

The young girl shuddered at this sanguinary allusion, but made no further objection to her father's departure.

The sheriff of Branson was a man far above the average of the community in wealth, education, and social position. His had been one of the few families in the county that before the war had owned large estates and numerous slaves. He had graduated at the State University at Chapel Hill, and had kept up some acquaintance with current literature and advanced thought. He had traveled some in his youth, and was looked up to in the county as an authority on all subjects connected wth the outer world. At first an ardent supporter of the Union, he had opposed the secession movement in his native state as long as opposition availed to stem the tide of public opinion. Yielding at last to the force of circumstances, he had entered the Confederate service rather late in the war and served with distinction through several campaigns, rising in time to the rank of colonel. After the war he had taken the oath of allegiance, and had been chosen by the people as the most available candidate for the office of sheriff, to which he had been elected without opposition. He had filled the office for several terms and was universally popular with his constituents.

Colonel or Sheriff Campbell, as he was indifferently called, as the military or civil title happened to be most important in the opinion of the person addressing him, had a high sense of the responsibility attached to his office. He had sworn to do his duty faithfully, and he knew what his duty was as sheriff perhaps more clearly than he had apprehended it in other passages of his life. It was therefore with no uncertainty in regard to his course that he prepared his weapons and went over to the jail. He had no fears for Polly's safety.

The sheriff had just locked the heavy front door of the jail behind him when a half dozen horsemen, followed by a crowd of men on foot, came round a bend in the road and drew near the jail. They halted in front of the picket fence that surrounded the building, while several of the committee of arrangements rode on a few rods farther to the sheriff's house. One of them dismounted and rapped on the door with his riding whip.

"Is the sheriff at home?" he inquired.

"No, he has just gone out," replied Polly, who had come to the door.

"We want the jail keys," he continued.

"They are not here," said Polly. "The sheriff has them himself." Then she added, with assumed indifference, "He is at the jail now."

The man turned away, and Polly went into the front room, from which she peered anxiously between the slats of the green blinds of a window that looked toward the jail. Meanwhile the messenger returned to his companions and announced his discovery. It looked as though the sheriff had learned of their design and was preparing to resist it.

One of them stepped forward and rapped on the jail door.

"Well, what is it?" said the sheriff, from within.

"We want to talk to you, Sheriff," replied the spokesman.

There was a little wicket in the door; this the sheriff opened, and answered through it.

"All right, boys, talk away. You are all strangers to me, and I don't know what business you can have." The sheriff did not think it necessary to recognize anybody in particular on such an occasion; the question of identity sometimes comes up in the investigation of these extrajudicial executions.

"We're a committee of citizens and we want to get into the jail."

"What for? It ain't much trouble to get into jail. Most people want to keep out."

The mob was in no humor to appreciate a joke, and the sheriff's witticism fell dead upon an unresponsive audience.

"We want to have a talk with the nigger that killed Cap'n Walker."

"You can talk to that nigger in the courthouse, when he's brought out for trial. Court will be in session here next week. I know what you fellows want, but you can't get my prisoner today. Do you want to take the bread out of a poor man's mouth? I get seventy-five cents a day for keeping this prisoner, and he's the only one in jail. I can't have my family suffer just to please you fellows."

One or two young men in the crowd laughed at the idea of Sheriff Campbell's suffering for want of seventy-five cents a day; but they were frowned into silence by those who stood near them.

"Ef yer don't let us in," cried a voice, "we'll bus' the do' open."

"Bust away," answered the sheriff, raising his voice so that all could hear. "But I give you fair warning. The first man that tries it will be filled with buckshot. I'm sheriff of this county; I know my duty, and I mean to do it."

"What's the use of kicking, Sheriff?" argued one of the leaders of the mob. "The nigger is sure to hang anyhow; he richly deserves it; and we've got to do something to teach the niggers their places or white people won't be able to live in the county."

"There's no use talking, boys," responded the sheriff. "I'm a white man outside, but in this jail I'm sheriff; and if this nigger's to be hung in this county, I propose to do the hanging. So you fellows might as well right-about-face, and march back to Troy. You've had a pleasant trip, and the exercise will be good for you. You know *me*. I've got powder and ball, and I've faced fire before now, with nothing between me and the enemy, and I don't mean to surrender this jail while I'm able to shoot." Having thus announced his determination, the sheriff closed and fastened the wicket and looked around for the best position from which to defend the building.

The crowd drew off a little, and the leaders conversed together in low tones.

The Branson County jail was a small, two-story brick building, strongly constructed, with no attempt at architectural ornamentation. Each story was divided into two large cells by a passage running from front to rear. A grated iron door gave entrance from the passage to each of the four cells. The jail seldom had many prisoners in it, and the lower windows had been boarded up. When the sheriff had closed the wicket, he ascended the steep wooden stairs to the upper floor. There was no window at the front of the upper passage, and the most available position from which to watch the movements of the crowd below was the front window of the cell occupied by the solitary prisoner.

The sheriff unlocked the door and entered the cell. The prisoner was crouched in a corner, his yellow face, blanched with terror, looking ghastly in the semidarkness of the room. A cold perspiration had gathered on his forehead, and his teeth were chattering with affright.

"For God's sake, Sheriff," he murmured hoarsely, "don't let 'em lynch me; I didn't kill the old man."

The sheriff glanced at the cowering wretch with a look of mingled contempt and loathing.

"Get up," he said sharply. "You will probably be hung sooner or later, but it shall not be today if I can help it. I'll unlock your fetters, and if I can't hold the jail you'll have to make the best fight you can. If I'm shot, I'll consider my responsibility at an end."

There were iron fetters on the prisoner's ankles, and handcuffs on his wrists. These the sheriff unlocked, and they fell clanking to the floor.

"Keep back from the window," said the sheriff. "They might shoot if they saw you."

The sheriff drew toward the window a pine bench which formed a part of the scanty furniture of the cell, and laid his revolver upon it. Then he took his gun in hand, and took his stand at the side of the window where he could with least exposure of himself watch the movements of the crowd below.

The lynchers had not anticipated any determined resistance. Of course they had looked for a formal protest, and perhaps a sufficient show of opposition to excuse the sheriff in the eye of any stickler for legal formalities. They had not however come prepared to fight a battle, and no one of them seemed willing to lead an attack upon the jail. The leaders of the party conferred together with a good deal of animated gesticulation, which was visible to the sheriff from his outlook, though the distance was too great for him to hear what was said. At length one of them broke away from the group and rode back to the main body of the lynchers, who were restlessly awaiting orders.

"Well, boys," said the messenger, "we'll have to let it go for the present. The sheriff says he'll shoot, and he's got the drop on us this time. There ain't any of us that want to follow Cap'n Walker jest yet. Besides, the sheriff is a good fellow and we don't want to hurt 'im. But," he added, as if to reassure the crowd, which began to show signs of disappointment, "the nigger might as well say his prayers, for he ain't got long to live."

There was a murmur of dissent from the mob, and several voices insisted that an attack be made on the jail. But pacific counsels finally prevailed, and the mob sullenly withdrew.

The sheriff stood at the window until they had disappeared around the bend in the road. He did not relax his watchfulness when the last one was out of sight. Their withdrawal might be a mere feint, to be followed by a further attempt. So closely indeed was his attention drawn to the outside, that he neither saw nor heard the prisoner creep stealthily across the floor, reach out his hand and secure the revolver which lay on the bench behind the sheriff, and creep as noiselessly back to his place in the corner of the room.

A moment after the last of the lynching party had disappeared there was a shot fired from the woods across the road; a bullet whistled by the window and buried itself in the wooden casing a few inches from where the sheriff was standing. Quick as thought, with the instinct born of a semi-guerrilla army experience, he raised his gun and fired twice at the point from which a faint puff of smoke showed the hostile to have been sent. He stood a moment watching, and then rested his gun against the window and reached behind him mechanically for the other weapon. It was not on the bench. As the sheriff realized this fact, he turned his head and looked into the muzzle of the revolver.

"Stay where you are, Sheriff," said the prisoner, his eyes glistening, his face almost ruddy with excitement.

The sheriff mentally cursed his own carelessness for allowing him to be caught in such a predicament. He had not expected anything of the kind. He had relied on the Negro's cowardice and subordination in the presence of an armed white man as a matter of course. The sheriff was a brave man, but realized that the prisoner had him at an immense disadvantage. The two men stood thus for a moment, fighting a harmless duel with their eyes.

"Well, what do you mean to do?" asked the sheriff with apparent calmness.

"To get away, of course," said the prisoner in a tone which caused the sheriff to look at him more closely, and with an involuntary feeling of apprehension; if the man was not mad, he was in a state of mind akin to madness, and quite as dangerous. The sheriff felt that he must speak to the prisoner fair and watch for a chance to turn the tables on him. The keen-eyed, desperate man before him was a different being altogether from the groveling wretch who had begged so piteously for life a few minutes before.

At length the sheriff spoke: —

"Is this your gratitude to me for saving your life at the risk of my own? If I had not done so, you would now be swinging from the limb of some neighboring tree."

"True," said the prisoner, "you saved my life, but for how long? When you came in, you said court would sit next week. When the crowd went away they said I had not long to live. It is merely a choice of two ropes."

"While there's life there's hope," replied the sheriff. He uttered this commonplace mechanically, while his brain was busy in trying to think out some way of escape. "If you are innocent you can prove it."

The mulatto kept his eye upon the sheriff. "I didn't kill the old man," he replied; "but I shall never be able to clear myself. I was at his house at nine o'clock. I stole from it the coat that was on my back when I was taken. I would be convicted even with a fair trial unless the real murderer were discovered beforehand."

The sheriff knew this only too well. While he was thinking what argument next to use, the prisoner continued: —

"Throw me the keys — no, unlock the door."

The sheriff stood a moment irresolute. The mulatto's eye glittered ominously. The sheriff crossed the room and unlocked the door leading into the passage.

"Now go down and unlock the outside door."

The heart of the sheriff leaped within him. Perhaps he might make a dash for liberty and gain the outside. He descended the narrow stairs, the prisoner keeping close behind him.

The sheriff inserted the huge iron key into the lock. The rusty bolt yielded slowly. It still remained for him to pull the door open.

"Stop!" thundered the mulatto, who seemed to divine the sheriff's purpose. "Move a muscle, and I'll blow your brain out."

The sheriff obeyed; he realized that his chance had not yet come.

"Now keep on that side of the passage and go back upstairs."

Keeping the sheriff under cover of the revolver, the mulatto followed him up the stairs. The sheriff expected the prisoner to lock him into the cell and make his own escape. He had about come to the conclusion that the best thing he could do under the circumstances was to submit quietly and take his chances of recapturing the prisoner after the alarm had been given. The sheriff had faced death more than once upon the battlefield. A few minutes before, well armed, and with a brick wall between him and them, he had dared a hundred men to fight; but he felt instinctively that the desperate man confronting him was not to be trifled with, and he was too prudent a man to risk his life against such heavy odds. He had Polly to look after and there was a limit beyond which devotion to duty would be quixotic and even foolish.

"I want to get away," said the prisoner, "and I don't want to be captured; for if I am I know I will be hung on the spot. I am afraid," he added somewhat reflectively, "that in order to save myself I shall have to kill you."

"Good God!" exclaimed the sheriff in involuntary terror; "you would not kill the man to whom you owe your own life."

"You speak more truly than you know," replied the mulatto. "I indeed owe my life to you."

The sheriff started. He was capable of surprise, even in that moment of extreme peril. "Who are you?" he asked in amazement.

"Tom, Cicely's son," returned the other. He had closed the door and stood talking to the sheriff through the gated opening. "Don't you remember Cicely — Cicely whom you sold with her child to the speculator on his way to Alabama?"

The sheriff did remember. He had been sorry for it many a time since. It had been the old story of debts, mortgages, and bad crops. He had quarreled with the mother. The price offered for her and her child had been unusually large, and he had yielded to the combination of anger and pecuniary stress.

"Good God!" he gasped; "you would not murder your own father?"

"My father?" replied the mulatto. "It were well enough for me to claim the relationship, but it comes with poor grace from you to ask anything by reason of it. What father's duty have you ever performed for me? Did you give me your name, or even your protection? Other white men gave their colored sons freedom and money, and sent them to the free states. You sold me to the rice swamps."

"I at least gave you the life you cling to," murmured the sheriff.

"Life?" said the prisoner, with a sarcastic laugh. "What kind of a life? You gave me your own blood, your own feathers — no man need look at us together twice to see that — and you gave me a black mother. Poor wretch! She died under the lash, because she had enough spirit, and you made me a slave, and crushed it out."

"But you are free now," said the sheriff. He had not doubted, could not doubt, the mulatto's word. He knew whose passions coursed beneath that swarthy skin and burned in the black eyes opposite his own. He saw in this mulatto what he himself might have become had not the safeguards of parental restraint and public opinion been thrown around him.

"Free to do what?" replied the mulatto. "Free in name, but despised and scorned and set aside by the people to whose race I belong far more than to my mother's."

"There are schools," said the sheriff. "You have been to school." He had noticed that the mulatto spoke more eloquently and used better language than most Branson County people.

"I have been to school, and dreamed when I went that it would work some marvelous change in my condition. But what did I learn? I learned to feel that no degree of learning or wisdom will change the color of my skin and that I shall always wear what in my own country is a badge of degradation. When I think about it seriously I do not care particularly for such a life. It is the animal in me, not the man, that flees the gallows. I owe you nothing," he went on, "and expect nothing of you; and it would be no more than justice if I should avenge upon you my mother's wrongs and my own. But still I have to shoot you; I have never yet taken human life — for I did *not* kill the old captain. Will you promise to give no alarm and make no attempt to capture me until morning, if I do not shoot?"

So absorbed were the two men in their colloquy and their own tumultuous thoughts that neither of them had heard the door below move upon its hinges. Neither of them had heard a light step come stealthily up the stairs, nor seen a slender form creep along the darkening passage toward the mulatto.

The sheriff hesitated. The struggle between his love of life and his sense of duty was a terrific one. It may seem strange that a man who could sell his own child into slavery should hesitate at such a moment, when his life was trembling in the balance. But the baleful influence of human slavery poisoned the very fountains of life, and created new standards of right. The sheriff was conscientious; his conscience had merely been warped by his environment. Let no one ask what his answer would have been; he was spared the necessity of a decision.

"Stop," said the mulatto, "you need not promise. I could not trust you if you did. It is your life for mine; there is but one safe way for me; you must die."

He raised his arm to fire, when there was a flash — a report from the passage behind him. His arm fell heavily at his side, and the pistol dropped at his feet.

The sheriff recovered first from his surprise, and throwing open the door secured the fallen weapon. Then seizing the prisoner he thrust him into the cell and locked the door upon him; after which he turned to Polly, who leaned half-fainting against the wall, her hands clasped over her heart.

"Oh, Father, I was just in time!" she cried hysterically and, wildly sobbing, threw herself into her father's arms.

"I watched until they all went away," she said. "I heard the shot from the woods and I saw you shoot. Then when you did not come out I feared something had happened, that perhaps you had been wounded. I got out the other pistol and ran over here. When

I found the door open I knew something was wrong, and when I heard voices I crept upstairs, and reached the top just in time to hear him say he would kill you. Oh, it was a narrow escape!"

When she had grown somewhat calmer, the sheriff left her standing there and went back into the cell. The prisoner's arm was bleeding from a flesh wound. His bravado had given place to a stony apathy. There was no sign in his face of fear or disappointment or feeling of any kind. The sheriff sent Polly to the house for cloth, and bound up the prisoner's wound with a rude skill acquired during his army life.

"I'll have a doctor come and dress the wound in the morning," he said to the prisoner. "It will do very well until then if you will keep quiet. If the doctor asks you how the wound was caused, you can say that you were struck by the bullet fired from the woods. It would do you no good to have it known that you were shot while attempting to escape."

The prisoner uttered no word of thanks or apology, but sat in sullen silence. When the wounded arm had been bandaged, Polly and her father returned to the house.

The sheriff was in an unusually thoughtful mood that evening. He put salt in his coffee at supper, and poured vinegar over his pancakes. To many of Polly's questions he returned random answers. When he had gone to bed he lay awake for several hours.

In the silent watches of the night, when he was alone with God, there came into his mind a flood of unaccustomed thoughts. An hour or two before, standing face to face with death, he had experienced a sensation similar to that which drowning men are said to feel — a kind of clarifying of the moral faculty, in which the veil of the flesh, with its obscuring passions and prejudices, is pushed aside for a moment, and all the acts of one's life stand out, in the clear light of truth, in their correct proportions and relations — a state of mind in which one sees himself as God may be supposed to see him. In the reaction following his rescue, this feeling had given place for a time to far different emotions. But now, in the silence of midnight, something of this clearness of spirit returned to the sheriff. He saw that he had owed some duty to this son of his — that neither law nor custom could destroy a responsibility inherent in the nature of mankind. He could not thus, in the eyes of God at least, shake off the consequences of his sin. Had he never sinned, this wayward spirit would never have come back from the vanished past to haunt him. As these thoughts came, his anger against the mulatto died away, and in its place there sprang up a great pity. The hand of parental authority might have restrained the passions he had seen burning in the prisoner's eyes when the desperate man spoke the words which had seemed to doom his father to death. The sheriff felt that he might have saved this fiery spirit from the sloth of slavery; that he might have sent him to the free North and given him there, or in some other land, an opportunity to turn to usefulness and honorable pursuits the talents that had run to crime, perhaps to madness; he might, still less, have given this son of his the poor simulacrum of liberty which men of his caste could possess in a slave-holding community; or least of all, but still something, he might have kept the boy on the plantation, where the burdens of slavery would have fallen lightly upon him.

The sheriff recalled his own youth. He had inherited an honored name to keep untarnished; he had had a future to make; the picture of a fair young bride had beckoned him on to happiness. The poor wretch now stretched upon a pallet of straw between the brick walls of the jail had had none of these things, no name, no father, no mother — in the true meaning of motherhood — and until the past few years no possible future, and that one vague and shadowy in its outline, and dependent for form and substance upon the slow solution of a problem in which there were many unknown quantities.

From what he might have done to what he might yet do was an easy transition for the awakened conscience of the sheriff. It occurred to him, purely as a hypothesis, that he might permit his prisoner to escape; but his oath of office, his duty as sheriff, stood in the way of such a course, and the sheriff dismissed the idea from his mind. He could, however, investigate the circumstances of the murder and move Heaven and earth to discover the real criminal, for he no longer doubted the prisoner's innocence; he could employ counsel for the accused, and perhaps influence public opinion in his favor. Acquittal once secured, some plan could be devised by which the sheriff might in some degree atone for his crime against this son of his — against society — against God.

When the sheriff had reached this conclusion he fell into an unquiet slumber, from which he awoke late the next morning.

He went over to the jail before breakfast and found the prisoner lying on his pallet, his face turned to the wall; he did not move when the sheriff rattled the door.

"Good morning," said the latter, in a tone intended to waken the prisoner.

There was no response. The sheriff looked more keenly at the recumbent figure; there was an unnatural rigidity about its attitude.

He hastily unlocked the door and, entering the cell, bent over the prostrate form. There was no sound of breathing; he turned the body over — it was cold and stiff. The prisoner had torn the bandage from his wound and bled to death during the night. He had evidently been dead several hours.

THE SCAPEGOAT

Paul Laurence Dunbar

T HE law is usually supposed to be a stern mistress, not to be
lightly wooed, and yielding only to the most ardent pursuit.
But even law, like love, sits more easily on some natures than on
others.

This was the case with Mr. Robinson Asbury. Mr. Asbury had
started life as a bootblack in the growing town of Cadgers. From
this he had risen one step and become porter and messenger in a
barbershop. This rise fired his ambition, and he was not content
until he had learned to use the shears and the razor and had a
chair of his own. From this, in a man of Robinson's temperament,
it was only a step to a shop of his own, and he placed it where it
would do the most good.

Fully one-half of the population of Cadgers was composed of
Negroes, and with their usual tendency to colonize, a tendency
encouraged, and in fact compelled, by circumstances, they had
gathered into one part of the town. Here in alleys, and streets as
dirty and hardly wider, they thronged like ants.

It was in this place that Mr. Asbury set up his shop, and he won
the hearts of his prospective customers by putting up the signifi-
cant sign, "Equal Rights Barbershop." This legend was quite
unnecessary, because there was only one race about, to patronize
the place. But it was a delicate sop to the people's vanity, and it
served its purpose.

Asbury came to be known as a clever fellow, and his business
grew. The shop really became a sort of club and, on Saturday
nights especially, was the gathering-place of the men of the whole
Negro quarter. He kept the illustrated and race journals there, and
those who cared neither to talk nor listen to someone else might

see pictured the doings of high society in very short skirts or read in the Negro papers how Miss Boston had entertained Miss Blueford to tea on such and such an afternoon. Also, he kept the policy returns, which was wise, if not moral.

It was his wisdom rather more than his morality that made the party managers after a while cast their glances towards him as a man who might be useful to their interests. It would be well to have a man — a shrewd, powerful man — down in that part of the town who could carry his people's vote in his vest pocket, and who at any time its delivery might be needed, could hand it over without hesitation. Asbury seemed that man, and they settled upon him. They gave him money, and they gave him power and patronage. He took it all silently and he carried out his bargain faithfully. His hands and his lips alike closed tightly when there was anything within them. It was not long before he found himself the big Negro of the district and, of necessity, of the town. The time came when, at a critical moment, the managers saw that they had not reckoned without their host in choosing this barber of the black district as the leader of his people.

Now, so much success must have satisfied any other man. But in many ways Mr. Asbury was unique. For a long time he himself had done very little shaving — except of notes, to keep his hand in. His time had been otherwise employed. In the evening hours he had been wooing the coquettish Dame Law, and wonderful to say, she had yielded easily to his advances.

It was against the advice of his friends that he asked for admission to the bar. They felt that he could do more good in the place where he was.

"You see, Robinson," said old Judge Davis, "it's just like this: If you're not admitted, it'll hurt you with the people; if you are admitted, you'll move uptown to an office and get out of touch with them."

Asbury smiled an inscrutable smile. Then he whispered something into the judge's ear that made the old man wrinkle from his neck up with appreciative smiles.

"Asbury," he said, "you are — you are — well, you ought to be white, that's all. When we find a black man like you we send him to State's prison. If you were white, you'd go to the Senate."

The Negro laughed confidently.

He was admitted to the bar soon after, whether by merit or by connivance is not to be told.

"Now he will move uptown," said the black community. "Well, that's the way with a colored man when he gets a start."

But they did not know Robinson Asbury yet. He was a man of surprises, and they were destined to disappointment. He did not move uptown. He built an office in a small open space next to his shop, and there hung out his shingle.

"I will never desert the people who have done so much to elevate me," said Mr. Asbury. "I will live among them and I will die among them."

This was a strong card for the barber-lawyer. The people seized upon the statement as expressing a nobility of an altogether unique brand.

They held a mass meeting and endorsed him. They made resolutions that extolled him, and the Negro band came around and serenaded him, playing various things in varied time.

All this was very sweet to Mr. Asbury, and the party managers chuckled with satisfaction and said, "That Asbury, that Asbury!"

Now there is a fable extant of a man who tried to please everybody, and his failure is a matter of record. Robinson Asbury was not more successful. But be it said that his ill success was due to no fault or shortcoming of his.

For a long time his growing power had been looked upon with disfavor by the colored law firm of Bingo & Latchett. Both Mr. Bingo and Mr. Latchett themselves aspired to be Negro leaders in Cadgers, and they were delivering Emancipation Day orations and riding at the head of processions when Mr. Asbury was blacking boots. Is it any wonder, then, that they viewed with alarm his sudden rise? They kept their counsel, however, and treated with him, for it was best. They allowed him his scope without open revolt until the day upon which he hung out his shingle. This was the last straw. They could stand no more. Asbury had stolen their other chances from them, and now he was poaching upon the last of their preserves. So Mr. Bingo and Mr. Latchett put their heads together to plan the downfall of their common enemy.

The plot was deep and embraced the formation of an opposing faction made up of the best Negroes of the town. It would have looked too much like what it was for the gentlemen to show themselves in the matter, and so they took into their confidence Mr. Isaac Morton, the principal of the colored school, and it was under his ostensible leadership that the new faction finally came into being.

Mr. Morton was really an innocent young man, and he had ideals which should never have been exposed to the air. When the wily confederates came to him with their plan he believed that his worth had been recognized, and at last he was to be what nature destined him for — a leader.

The better class of Negroes — by that is meant those who were particularly envious of Asbury's success — flocked to the new man's standard. But whether the race be white or black, political virtue is always in a minority, so Asbury could afford to smile at the force arrayed against him.

The new faction met together and resolved. They resolved, among other things, that Mr. Asbury was an enemy to his race and a menace to civilization. They decided that he should be abolished; but as they couldn't get out an injunction against him, and as he had the whole undignified but still voting black belt behind him, he went serenely on his way.

"They're after you hot and heavy, Asbury," said one of his friends to him.

"Oh, yes," was the reply, "they're after me, but after a while I'll get so far away that they'll be running in front."

"It's all the best people, they say."

"Yes. Well, it's good to be one of the best people, but your vote only counts one just the same."

The time came, however, when Mr. Asbury's theory was put to the test. The Cadgerites celebrated the first of January as Emancipation Day. On this day there was a large procession, with speechmaking in the afternoon and fireworks at night. It was the custom to concede the leadership of the colored people of the town to the man who managed to lead the procession. For two years past this honor had fallen, of course, to Robinson Asbury, and there had been no disposition on the part of anybody to try conclusions with him.

Mr. Morton's faction changed all this. When Asbury went to work to solicit contributions for the celebration, he suddenly became aware that he had a fight upon his hands. All the better-class Negroes were staying out of it. The next thing he knew was that plans were on foot for a rival demonstration.

"Oh," he said to himself, "that's it, is it? Well, if they want a fight they can have it."

He had a talk with the party managers, and he had another with Judge Davis.

"All I want is a little lift, Judge," he said, "and I'll make 'em think the sky has turned loose and is vomiting niggers."

The judge believed that he could do it. So did the party managers. Asbury got his lift. Emancipation Day came.

There were two parades. At least, there was one parade and the shadow of another. Asbury's, however, was not the shadow. There was a great deal of substance about it — substance made up of many people, many banners, and numerous bands. He did not have the best people. Indeed among his cohorts there were a good many of the pronounced ragtag and bobtail. But he had noise and numbers. In such cases, nothing more is needed. The success of Asbury's side of the affair did everything to confirm his friends in their good opinion of him.

When he found himself defeated, Mr. Silas Bingo saw that it would be policy to placate his rival's just anger against him. He called upon him at his office the day after the celebration.

"Well, Asbury," he said, "you beat us, didn't you?"

"It wasn't a question of beating," said the other calmly. "It was only an inquiry as to who were the people — the few or the many."

"Well, it was well done, and you've shown that you are a manager. I confess that I haven't always thought that you were doing the wisest thing in living down here and catering to this class of people when you might, with your ability, be much more to the better class."

"What do they base their claims of being better on?"

"Oh, there ain't any use discussing that. We can't get along without you, we see that. So I, for one, have decided to work with you for harmony."

"Harmony. Yes, that's what we want."

"If I can do anything to help you at any time, why you have only to command me."

"I am glad to find such a friend in you. Be sure, if I ever need you, Bingo, I'll call on you."

"And I'll be ready to serve you."

Asbury smiled when his visitor was gone. He smiled, and knitted his brow. "I wonder what Bingo's got up his sleeve," he said. "He'll bear watching."

It may have been pride at his triumph, it may have been gratitude at his helpers, but Asbury went into the ensuing campaign with reckless enthusiasm. He did the most daring things for the party's sake. Bingo, true to his promise, was ever at his side ready to serve him. Finally, association and immunity made danger less fearsome; the rival no longer appeared a menace.

With the generosity born of obstacles overcome, Asbury determined to forgive Bingo and give him a chance. He let him in on a deal, and from that time they worked amicably together until the election came and passed.

It was a close election and many things had had to be done, but there were men there ready and waiting to do them. They were successful, and then the first cry of the defeated party was, as usual, "Fraud! Fraud!" The cry was taken up by the jealous, the disgruntled, and the virtuous.

Someone remembered how two years ago the registration books had been stolen. It was known upon good authority that money had been freely used. Men held up their hands in horror at the suggestion that the Negro vote had been juggled with, as if that were a new thing. From their pulpits ministers denounced the machine and bade their hearers rise and throw off the yoke of a corrupt municipal government. One of those sudden fevers of reform had taken possession of the town and threatened to destroy the successful party.

They began to look around them. They must purify themselves. They must give the people some tangible evidence of their own yearnings after purity. They looked around them for a sacrifice to lay upon the altar of municipal reform. Their eyes fell upon Mr. Bingo. No, he was not big enough. His blood was too scant to wash the political stains. Then they looked into each other's eyes and turned their gaze away to let it fall upon Mr. Asbury. They really hated to do it. But there must be a scapegoat. The god from the Machine commanded them to slay him.

Robinson Asbury was charged with many crimes — with all that he had committed and some that he had not. When Mr. Bingo saw what was afoot he threw himself heart and soul into the work of his old rival's enemies. He was of incalculable use to them.

Judge Davis refused to have anything to do with the matter. But in spite of his disapproval it went on. Asbury was indicted and tried. The evidence was all against him, and no one gave more damaging testimony than his friend Mr. Bingo. The judge's charge was favorable to the defendant, but the current of popular opinion could not be entirely stemmed. The jury brought in a verdict of guilty.

"Before I am sentenced, Judge, I have a statement to make to the court. It will take less than ten minutes."

"Go on, Robinson," said the judge kindly.

Asbury started, in a monotonous tone, a recital that brought the prosecuting attorney to his feet in a minute. The judge waved him down, and sat transfixed by a sort of fascinated horror as the convicted man went on. The before-mentioned attorney drew a knife and started for the prisoner's dock. With difficulty he was restrained. A dozen faces in the courtroom were red and pale by turns.

"He ought to be killed," whispered Mr. Bingo audibly.

Robinson Asbury looked at him and smiled, and then he told a few things of him. He gave the ins and outs of some of the misdemeanors of which he stood accused. He showed who were the men behind the throne. And still, pale and transfixed, Judge Davis waited for his own sentence.

Never were ten minutes so well taken up. It was a tale of rottenness and corruption in high places told simply and with the stamp of truth upon it.

He did not mention the judge's name. But he had torn the mask from the face of every other man who had been concerned in his downfall. They had shorn him of his strength, but they had forgotten that he was yet able to bring the roof and pillars tumbling about their heads.

The judge's voice shook as he pronounced sentence upon his old ally — a year in State's prison.

Some people said it was too light, but the judge knew what it was to wait for the sentence of doom, and he was grateful and sympathetic.

When the sheriff led Asbury away the judge hastened to have a short talk with him.

"I'm sorry, Robinson," he said, "and I want to tell you that you were no more guilty than the rest of us. But why did you spare me?"

"Because I knew you were my friend," answered the convict.

"I tried to be, but you were the first man that I've ever known since I've been in politics who ever gave me any decent return for friendship."

"I reckon you're about right, Judge."

In politics, party reform usually lies in making a scapegoat of someone who is only as criminal as the rest, but a little weaker. Asbury's friends and enemies had succeeded in making him bear the burden of all the party's crimes, but their reform was hardly a success, and their protestations of a change of heart were received with doubt. Already there were those who began to pity the victim and to say that he had been hardly dealt with.

Mr. Bingo was not of these; but he found, strange to say, that his opposition to the idea went but a little way, and that even with Asbury out of his path he was a smaller man than he was before. Fate was strong against him. His poor, prosperous humanity could not enter the lists against a martyr. Robinson Asbury was now a martyr.

II

A year is not a long time. It was short enough to prevent people from forgetting Robinson, and yet long enough for their pity to grow strong as they remembered. Indeed, he was not gone a year. Good behavior cut two months off the time of his sentence, and by the time people had come around to the notion that he was really the greatest and smartest man in Cadgers he was at home again.

He came back with no flourish of trumpets, but quietly, humbly. He went back again into the heart of the black district. His business had deteriorated during his absence, but he put new blood and new life into it. He did not go to work in the shop himself but, taking down the shingle that had swung idly before his office door during his imprisonment, he opened the little room as a news- and cigar-stand.

Here anxious, pitying customers came to him and he prospered again. He was very quiet. Uptown hardly knew that he was again in Cadgers, and it knew nothing whatever of his doings.

"I wonder why Asbury is so quiet," they said to one another. "It isn't like him to be quiet." And they felt vaguely uneasy about him.

So many people had begun to say, "Well, he was a mighty good fellow after all."

Mr. Bingo expressed the opinion that Asbury was quiet because he was crushed, but others expressed doubt as to this. There are calms and calms, some after and some before the storm. Which was this?

They waited a while, and, as no storm came, concluded that this must be the afterquiet. Bingo, reassured, volunteered to go and seek confirmation of this conclusion.

He went, and Asbury received him with an indifferent, not to say impolite, demeanor.

"Well, we're glad to see you back, Asbury," said Bingo patronizingly. He had variously demonstrated his inability to lead during his rival's absence and was proud of it. "What are you going to do?"

"I'm going to work."

"That's right. I reckon you'll stay out of politics."

"What could I do even if I went in?"

"Nothing now, of course; but I didn't know —"

He did not see the gleam in Asbury's half-shut eyes. He only marked his humility, and he went back swelling with the news.

"Completely crushed — all the run taken out of him," was his report.

The black district believed this, too, and a sullen, smouldering anger took possession of them. Here was a good man ruined. Some of the people whom he had helped in his former days — some of the rude, coarse people of the low quarter who were still sufficiently unenlightened to be grateful — talked among themselves and offered to get up a demonstration for him. But he denied them. No, he wanted nothing of the kind. It would only bring him into unfavorable notice. All he wanted was that they would always be his friends and would stick by him.

They would to the death.

There were again two factions in Cadgers. The schoolmaster could not forget how once on a time he had been made a tool of by Mr. Bingo. So he revolted against his rule and set himself up as the leader of an opposing clique. The fight had been long and strong, but had ended with odds slightly in Bingo's favor.

But Mr. Morton did not despair. As the first of January and Emancipation Day approached, he arrayed his hosts, and the fight for supremacy became fiercer than ever. The schoolteacher brought the schoolchildren in for chorus singing, secured an able orator, and the best essayist in town. With all this, he was formidable.

Mr. Bingo knew that he had the fight of his life on his hands, and he entered with fear as well as zest. He, too, found an orator, but he was not sure that he was good as Morton's. There was no doubt but that his essayist was not. He secured a band, but still he felt unsatisfied. He had hardly done enough, and for the schoolmaster to beat him now meant his political destruction.

It was in this state of mind that he was surprised to receive a visit from Mr. Asbury.

"I reckon you're surprised to see me here," said Asbury, smiling.

"I am pleased, I know." Bingo was astute.

"Well, I just dropped in on our business."

"To be sure, to be sure, Asbury. What can I do for you?"

"It's more what I can do for you that I came to talk about," was the reply.

"I don't believe I understand you."

"Well, it's plain enough. They say that the schoolteacher is giving you a pretty hard fight."

"Oh, not so hard."

"No man can be too sure of winning though. Mr. Morton once did me a mean turn when he started the faction against me."

Bingo's heart gave a great leap, and then stopped for the fraction of a second.

"You were in it, of course," pursued Asbury, "but I can look over your part in it in order to get even with the man who started it."

It was true, then, thought Bingo gladly. He did not know. He wanted revenge for his wrongs and upon the wrong man. How well the schemer had covered his tracks! Asbury should have his revenge and Morton would be the sufferer.

"Of course, Asbury, you know that I did what I did innocently."

"Oh, yes, in politics we are all lambs and the wolves are only to be found in the other party. We'll pass that, though. What I want to say is that I can help you to make your celebration an overwhelming success. I still have some influence down in my district."

"Certainly, and very justly, too. Why I should be delighted with your aid. I could give you a prominent position in the procession."

"I don't want it; I don't want to appear in this at all. All I want is revenge. You can have all the credit, but let me down my enemy."

Bingo was perfectly willing, and with their heads close together, they had a long and close consultation. When Asbury was gone, Mr. Bingo lay back in his chair and laughed. "I'm a slick duck," he said.

From that hour Mr. Bingo's cause began to take on the appearance of something very like a boom. More bands were hired. The interior of the State was called upon and a more eloquent orator secured. The crowd hastened to array itself on the growing side.

With surprised eyes, the schoolmaster beheld the wonder of it, but he kept to his own purpose with dogged insistence, even when he saw that he could not turn aside the overwhelming defeat that threatened him. But in spite of his obstinacy, his hours were dark and bitter. Asbury worked like a mole, all underground, but he was indefatigable. Two days before the celebration time everything was perfected for the biggest demonstration that Cadgers had ever known. All the next day and night he was busy among his allies.

On the morning of the great day, Mr. Bingo, wonderfully caparisoned, rode down to the hall where the parade was to form. He was early. No one had yet come. In an hour a score of men all told had collected. Another hour passed, and no more had come. Then there smote upon his ear the sound of music. They were coming at last. Bringing his sword to his shoulder, he rode forward to the middle of the street. Ah, there they were. But — but — could he believe his eyes? They were going in another direction, and at their head rode — Morton! He gnashed his teeth in fury. He had been led into a trap and betrayed. The procession passing had been his — all his. He heard them cheering, and then, oh! climax of infidelity, he saw his own orator go past in a carriage, bowing and smiling to the crowd.

There was no doubting who had done this thing. The hand of Asbury was apparent in it. He must have known the truth all along, thought Bingo. His allies left him one by one for the other hall, and he rode home in a humiliation deeper than he had ever known before.

Asbury did not appear at the celebration. He was at his little newsstand all day.

In a day or two the defeated aspirant had further cause to curse his false friend. He found that not only had the people defected from him, but that the thing had been so adroitly managed that he appeared to be in fault, and three-fourths of those who knew him were angry at some supposed grievance. His cup of bitterness was full when his partner, a quietly ambitious man, suggested that they dissolve their relations.

His ruin was complete.

The lawyer was not alone in seeing Asbury's hand in his downfall. The party managers saw it too, and they met together to discuss the dangerous factor which, while it appeared to slumber, was so terribly awake. They decided that he must be appeased, and they visited him.

He was still busy at his newsstand. They talked to him adroitly, while he sorted papers and kept an impassive face. When they were all done, he looked up for a moment and replied, "You know, gentlemen, as an ex-convict I am not in politics."

Some of them had the grace to flush.

"But you can use your influence," they said.

"I am not in politics," was his only reply.

And the spring elections were coming on. Well, they worked hard, and he showed no sign. He treated with neither one party nor the other. "Perhaps," thought the managers, "he is out of politics," and they grew more confident.

It was nearing eleven o'clock on the morning of election when a cloud no bigger than a man's hand appeared upon the horizon. It came from the direction of the black district. It grew, and the managers of the party in power looked at it, fascinated by an ominous dread. Finally it began to rain Negro voters, and as one man they voted against their former candidates. Their organization was perfect. They simply came, voted, and left, but they overwhelmed everything. Not one of the party that had damned Robinson Asbury was left in power save old Judge Davis. His majority was overwhelming.

The generalship that had engineered the thing was perfect. There were loud threats against the newsdealer. But no one bothered him except a reporter. The reporter called to see just how it was done. He found Asbury very busy sorting papers. To the newspaperman's questions he had only this reply, "I am not in politics, sir."

But Cadgers had learned its lesson.

FERN

Jean Toomer

Face flowed into her eyes. Flowed in soft cream foam and plaintive ripples, in such a way that wherever your glance may momentarily have rested it immediately thereafter wavered in the direction of her eyes. The soft suggestion of down slightly darkened, like the shadow of a bird's wing might, the creamy brown color of her upper lip. Why after noticing it you sought her eyes, I cannot tell you. Her nose was aquiline, Semitic. If you have heard a Jewish cantor sing, if he has touched you and made your own sorrow seem trivial when compared with his, you will know my feeling when I follow the curves of her profile, like mobile rivers, to their common delta. They were strange eyes. In this, that they sought nothing — that is, nothing that was obvious and tangible and that one could see, and they gave the impression that nothing was to be denied. When a woman seeks, you will have observed, her eyes deny. Fern's eyes desired nothing that you could give her; there was no reason why they should withhold. Men saw her eyes and fooled themselves. Fern's eyes said to them that she was easy. When she was young, a few men took her, but got no joy from it. And then, once done, they felt bound to her (quite unlike their hit and run with other girls), felt as though it would take them a lifetime to fulfill an obligation which they could find no name for. They became attached to her, and hungered after finding the barest trace of what she might desire. As she grew up, new men who came to town felt as almost everyone did who ever saw her: that they would not be denied. Men were everlastingly bringing her their bodies. Something inside of her got tired of them, I guess, for I am certain that for the life of her she could not tell why or how she began to turn them off. A man in fever is no trifling thing to send away. They began to leave her, baffled and ashamed, yet vowing to themselves that someday they would do some fine thing for her: send her candy every week and not let her know whom it came from, watch out for her wedding day and give her a magnificent something with no name on it, buy a house and deed it to her, rescue her from some unworthy fellow who had tricked her into marrying him. As you know, men are apt to idolize or fear that which they cannot understand, especially if it be a woman. She did not deny them, yet the fact was that they were denied. A sort of superstition crept into their consciousness of her being somehow above them. Being above them meant that she was not to be approached by anyone. She became a virgin. Now a virgin in a small Sourthern town is by no means the usual thing, if you will believe me. That the sexes were made to mate is the practice of the South. Particularly, black folks were made to mate. And it is black folks whom I have been talking about thus far. What white men thought of Fern I can arrive at only by analogy. They let her alone.

Anyone of course could see her, could see her eyes. If you walked up the Dixie Pike most any time of day, you'd be most like to see her resting listless-like on the railing of her porch, back propped against a post, head tilted a little forward because there was a nail in the porch post just where her head came which for some reason or other she never took the trouble to pull out. Her eyes, if it were sunset, rested idly where the sun, molten and glorious, was pouring down between the fringe of pines. Or maybe they gazed at the gray cabin on the knoll from which an evening folksong was coming. Perhaps they followed a cow that had been turned loose to roam and feed on cotton stalks and corn leaves. Like as not they'd settle on some vague spot above the horizon, though hardly a trace of wistfulness would come to them. If it were dusk, then they'd wait for the searchlight of the evening train which you could see miles up the track before it flared across the Dixie Pike, close to her home. Wherever they looked, you'd follow them and then waver back. Like her face, the whole countryside seemed to flow into her eyes. Flowed into them with the soft listless cadence of Georgia's South. A young Negro, once, was looking at her spellbound from the road. A white man passing in a buggy had to flick him with his whip if he was to get by without running him over. I first saw her on her porch. I was passing with a fellow whose crusty numbness (I was from the North and suspected of being prejudiced and stuck-up) was melting as he found me warm. I asked him who she was. "That's Fern," was all that I could get from him. Some folks already thought I was given to nosing around; I let it go at that, so far as questions were concerned. But at first sight of her I felt as if I heard a Jewish cantor sing. As if his singing rose above the unheard chorus of a folksong. And I felt bound to her. I too had my dreams: something I would do for her. I have knocked about from town to town too much not to know the futility of mere change of place. Besides, picture if you can this cream-colored solitary girl sitting at a tenement window looking down on the indifferent throngs of Harlem. Better that she listen to folksongs at dusk in Georgia, you would say, and so would I. Or suppose she came up North and married. Even a doctor or a lawyer, say, one who would be sure to get along — that is, make money. You and I know, who have had experience in such things, that love is not a thing like prejudice which can be bettered by changes of town. Could men in Washington, Chicago, or New York, more than the men of Georgia, bring her something left vacant by the bestowal of their bodies? You and I who know men in these cities will have to say, they could not. See her out and out a prostitute along State Street in Chicago. See her move into a Southern town where white men are more aggressive. See her become a white man's concubine. . . . Something I must do for her. There was myself. What could I do for her? Talk, of course. Push back the fringe of pines upon new horizons. To what purpose? and what for? Her? Myself? Men in her case seem to lose their selfishness. I lost mine before I touched her. I ask you, friend (it makes no difference if you sit in the Pullman or the Jim Crow as the train crosses her road), what thoughts would come to you — that is, after you'd finished with the thoughts that leap into men's minds at the sight of a pretty woman who will not deny them; what thoughts would come to you, had you seen her in a quick flash, keen and intuitively, as she sat there on her porch when your train thundered by? Would you have got off at the next station and come back for her to take her, where? Would you have completely forgotten her as soon as you reached Macon, Atlanta, Augusta, Pasadena, Madison, Chicago,

Boston, or New Orleans? Would you tell your wife or sweetheart about a girl you saw? Your thoughts can help me, and I would like to know. Something I would do for her. . . .

One evening I walked up the Pike on purpose, and stopped to say hello. Some of her family were about, but they moved away to make room for me. Damn if I knew how to begin. Would you? Mr. and Miss So-and-So, people, the weather, the crops, the new preacher, the frolic, the church benefit, rabbit and possum hunting, the new soft drink they had at old Pap's store, the schedule of the trains, what kind of town Macon was, Negro's migration north, boll weevils, syrup, the Bible — to all these things she gave a yassur or nassur, without further comment. I began to wonder if perhaps my own emotional sensibility had played one of its tricks on me. "Let's take a walk," I at last ventured. The suggestion, coming after so long an isolation, was novel enough, I guess, to surprise. But it wasn't that. Something told me that men before me had said just that as a prelude to the offering of their bodies. I tried to tell her with my eyes. I think she understood. The thing from her that made my throat catch, vanished. Its passing left her visible in a way I'd thought, but never seen. We walked down the Pike with people on all the porches gaping at us. "Doesn't it make you mad?" She meant the world. Through a canebrake that was ripe for cutting, the branch was reached. Under a sweet-gum tree, and where reddish leaves had dammed the creek a little, we sat down. Dusk, suggesting the almost imperceptible procession of giant trees, settled with a purple haze about the cane. I felt strange, as I always do in Georgia, particularly at dusk. I felt that things unseen to men were tangibly immediate. It would not have surprised me had I had a vision. People have them in Georgia more often then you would suppose. A black woman once saw the mother of Christ and drew her in charcoal on the courthouse wall. . . . When one is on the soil of one's ancestors, most anything can come to one. . . . From force of habit, I suppose, I held Fern in my arms — that is, without at first noticing it. Then my mind came back to her. Her eyes, unusually weird and open, held me. Held God. He flowed in as I've seen the countryside flow in. Seen men. I must have done something — what, I don't know, in the confusion of my emotion. She sprang up. Rushed some distance from me. Fell to her knees, and began swaying, swaying.

Her body was tortured with something it could not let out. Like boiling sap it flooded arms and fingers till she shook them as if they burned her. It found her throat, and spattered inarticulately in plaintive, convulsive sounds, mingled with calls to Christ Jesus. And then she sang, brokenly. A Jewish cantor singing with a broken voice. A child's voice, uncertain, or an old man's. Dusk hid her; I could hear only her song. It seemed to me as though she were pounding her head in anguish upon the ground. I rushed to her. She fainted in my arms.

There was talk about her fainting with me in the canefield. And I got one or two ugly looks from town men who'd set themselves up to protect her. In fact, there was talk of making me leave town. But they never did. They kept a watch out for me, though. Shortly after, I came back North. From the train window I saw her as I crossed her road. Saw her on her porch, head tilted a little forward where the nail was, eyes vaguely focused on the sunset. Saw her face flow into them, the countryside and something that I call God, flowing into them. . . . Nothing ever really happened. Nothing ever came to Fern, not even I. Something I would do for her. Some fine unnamed thing. . . . And, friend, you? She is still living, I have reason to know. Her name, against the chance that you might happen down that way, is Fernie May Rosen.

MISS CYNTHIE

Rudolph Fisher

For the first time in her life somebody had called her "madam."
She had been standing, bewildered but unafraid, while innumerable redcaps appropriated piece after piece of the baggage
arrayed on the platform. Neither her brief seventy years' journey
through life nor her long two days' travel northward had dimmed
the live brightness of her eyes, which, for all their bewilderment,
had accurately selected her own treasures out of the row of luggage
and guarded them vigilantly. "These yours, madam?"

The biggest redcap of all was smiling at her. He looked for all
the world like Doc Crinshaw's oldest son back home. Her little
brown face relaxed; she smiled back at him.

"They got to be. You all done took all the others."

He laughed aloud. Then — "Carry 'em in for you?"

She contemplated his bulk. "Reckon you can manage it — puny
little feller like you?"

Thereupon they were friends. Still grinning broadly, he surrounded himself with her impedimenta, the enormous brown
extension-case on one shoulder, the big straw suitcase in the
opposite hand, the carpetbag under one arm. She herself held fast
to the umbrella. "Always like to have sump'm in my hand when I
walk. Can't never tell when you'll run across a snake."

"There aren't any snakes in the city."

"There's snakes everywhere, chile."

They began the tedious hike up the interminable platform. She
was small and quick. Her carriage was surprisingly erect, her gait
astonishingly spry. She said:

"You liked to took my breath back yonder, boy, callin' me
madam. Back home everybody call me Miss Cynthie. Even their

chillun. Black folks, white folks too. Miss Cynthie. Well, when you come up with that madam o' yourn, I say to myself, 'Now, I wonder who that chile's a-grinnin' at? Madam stands for mist'ess o' the house, and I sho' ain' mist'ess o' nothin' in this hyeh New York.' "

"Well, you see, we call everybody madam."

"Everybody? — Hm." The bright eyes twinkled. "Seem like that's worry me some — if I was a man."

He acknowledged his slip and observed, "I see this isn't your first trip to New York."

"First trip any place, son. First time I been over fifty mile from Waxhaw. Only travelin' I've done is in my head. Ain' seen many places, but I's seen a passel o' people. Reckon places is pretty much alike after people been in 'em awhile."

"Yes, ma'am. I guess that's right."

"You ain' no reg'lar bag-toter, is you?"

"Ma'am?"

"You talk too good."

"Well, I only do this in vacationtime. I'm still in school."

"You is. What you aimin' to be?"

"I'm studying medicine."

"You is?" She beamed. "Aimin' to be a doctor, huh? Thank the Lord for that. That's what I always wanted my David to be. My grandchile hyeh in New York. He's to meet me hyeh now."

"I bet you'll have a great time."

"Mussn't bet, chile. That's sinful. I tole him 'fore he left home, I say, 'Son, you the only one o' the chillun what's got a chance to amount to sump'm. Don't th'ow it away. Be a preacher or a doctor. Work yo' way up and don' stop short. If the Lord don' see fit for you to doctor the soul, then doctor the body. If you don' get to be a reg'lar doctor, be a tooth-doctor. If you jes' can't make that, be a foot-doctor. And if you don't get that fur, be a undertaker. That's the least you must be. That ain' so bad. Keep you acquainted with the house of the Lord. Always mind the house o' the Lord — whatever you do, do like a church steeple: aim high and go straight.' "

"Did he get to be a doctor?"

"Don' b'lieve he did. Too late startin', I reckon. But he's done succeeded at sump'm. Mus' be at least a undertaker, 'cause he started sendin' the homefolks money, and he come home las' year dressed like Judge Pettiford's boy what went off to school in Virginia. Wouldn't tell none of us 'zackly what he was doin', but he said he wouldn' never be happy till I come and see for myself. So hyeh I is." Something softened her voice. "His mammy died befo' he knowed her. But he was always sech a good child —" The something was apprehension. "Hope he *is* a undertaker."

They were mounting a flight of steep stairs leading to an exit-gate, about which clustered a few people still hoping to catch sight of arriving friends. Among these a tall young brown-skinned man in a light gray suit suddenly waved his panama and yelled, "Hey, Miss Cynthie!"

Miss Cynthie stopped, looked up, and waved back with a delighted umbrella. The redcap's eyes lifted too. His lower jaw sagged.

"Is that your grandson?"

"It sho' is," she said and distanced him for the rest of the climb. The grandson, with an abandonment that superbly ignored on-lookers, folded the little woman in an exultant, smothering embrace. As soon as she could, she pushed him off with breathless mock impatience.

"Go 'way, you fool, you. Aimin' to squeeze my soul out my body befo' I can get a look at this place?" She shook herself into the semblance of composure. "Well. You don't look hungry, anyhow."

"Ho-ho! Miss Cynthie in New York! Can y' imagine this? Come on. I'm parked on Eighth Avenue."

The redcap delivered the outlandish luggage into a robin's-egg-blue open Packard with scarlet wheels, accepted the grandson's dollar and smile, and stood watching the car roar away up Eighth Avenue.

Another redcap came up. "Got a break, hey, boy?"

"Dave Tappen himself — can you beat that?"

"The old lady hasn't seen the station yet — starin' at him."

"That's not the half of it, bozo. That's Dave Tappen's grand-mother. And what do you s'pose she hopes?"

"What?"

"She hopes that Dave has turned out to be a successful under-taker!"

"Undertaker? Undertaker!"

They stared at each other a gaping moment, then doubled up with laughter.

"Look — through there — that's the Chrysler Building. Oh, hellelujah! I meant to bring you up Broadway —"

"David —"

"Ma'am?"

"This hyeh wagon yourn?"

"Nobody else's. Sweet buggy, ain't it?"

"David — you ain't turned out to be one of them moonshiners, is you?"

"Moonshiners — Moon — Ho! No indeed, Miss Cynthie. I got a better racket 'n that."

"Better which?"

"Game. Business. Pickup."

"Tell me, David. What is yo' racket?"

"Can't spill it yet, Miss Cynthie. Rather show you. Tomorrow night you'll know the worst. Can you make out till tomorrow night?"

"David, you know I always wanted you to be a doctor, even if 'twasn' nothin' but a foot-doctor. The very leas' I wanted you to be was a undertaker."

"Undertaker! Oh, Miss Cynthie! — with my sunny disposition?"

"Then you ain' even a undertaker?"

"Listen, Miss Cynthie. Just forget 'bout what I am for a while. Just till tomorrow night. I want you to see for yourself. Tellin' you will spoil it. Now stop askin', you hear? — because I'm not answerin' — I'm surprisin' you. And don't expect anybody you meet to tell you. It'll mess up the whole works. Understand? Now give the big city a break. There's the elevated train going up Columbus Avenue. Ain't that hot stuff?"

Miss Cynthie looked. "Humph!" she said. "'Tain' half high as that trestle two mile from Waxhaw."

She thoroughly enjoyed the ride up Central Park West. The stagger lights, the extent of the park, the high, close, kingly buildings, remarkable because their stoves cooled them in summer as well as heated them in winter, all drew nods of mild interest. But what gave her special delight was not these: it was that David's car so effortlessly sped past the headlong drove of vehicles racing northward.

They stopped for a red light; when they started again their machine leaped forward with a triumphant eagerness that drew from her an unsuppressed, "Hot you, David! That's it."

He grinned appreciatively. "Why, you're a regular New Yorker already."

"New York nothin'! I done the same thing fifty years ago — befo' I knowed they was a New York."

"What!"

"Deed so. Didn' I use to tell you 'bout my young mare, Betty? Chile, I'd hitch Betty up to yo' grandpa's buggy and pass anything on the road. Betty never knowed what another horse's dust smelt like. No 'n deedy. Shuh, boy, this ain' nothin' new to me. Why that broke-down Fo'd yo uncle Jake's got ain' nothin' — nothin' but a sorry mess. Done got so slow I jes' won' ride in it — I declare I'd rather walk. But this hyeh thing, now, this is right nice." She settled back in complete, complacent comfort, and they sped on, swift and silent.

Suddenly she sat erect with abrupt discovery.

"David — well — bless my soul!"

"What's the matter, Miss Cynthie?"

Then he saw what had caught her attention. They were traveling up Seventh Avenue now, and something was miraculously different. Not the road; that was as broad as ever, wide, white, gleaming in the sun. Not the houses; they were lofty still, lordly, disdainful, supercilious. Not the cars; they continued to race impatiently onward, innumerable, precipitate, tumultuous. Something else, something at once obvious and subtle, insistent, pervasive, compelling.

"David — this mus' be Harlem!"

"Good Lor', Miss Cynthie — !"

"Don' use the name of the Lord in vain David."

"But I mean — gee! — you're no fun at all. You get everything before a guy can tell you."

"You got plenty to tell me, David. But don' nobody need to tell me this. Look a yonder."

Not just a change of complexion. A completely dissimilar atmosphere. Sidewalks teeming with leisurely strollers, at once strangely dark and bright. Boys in white trousers, berets, and green shirts, with slickened black heads and proud swagger. Bareheaded girls in crisp organdy dresses, purple, canary, gay scarlet. And laughter, abandoned strong Negro laughter, some falling full on the ear, some not heard at all, yet sensed — the warm life-breath of the tireless carnival to which Harlem's heart quickens in summer.

"This is it," admitted David. "Get a good eyeful. Here's One Hundred and Twenty-fifth Street — regular little Broadway. And here's the Alhambra, and up ahead we'll pass the Lafayette."

"What's them?"

"Theaters."

"Theaters? Theaters. Humph! Look, David — is that a colored folks church?" They were passing a fine gray-stone edifice.

"That? Oh. Sure it is. So's this one on this side."

"No! Well, ain' that fine? Splendid big church like that for colored folks."

Taking his cue from this, her first tribute to the city, he said, "You ain't seen nothing yet. Wait a minute."

They swung left through a side street and turned right on a boulevard. "What do you think o' that?" And he pointed to the quarter-million-dollar St. Mark's.

"That a colored church, too?"

" 'Tain' no white one. And they built it themselves, you know. Nobody's hand-me-down gift."

She heaved a great happy sigh. "Oh, yes, it was a gift, David. It was a gift from on high." Then, "Look a hyeh — which a one you belong to?"

"Me? Why, I don't belong to any — that is, none o' these. Mine's over in another section. Y'see, mine's Baptist. These are all Methodist. See?"

"M-m. Uh-huh. I see."

They circled a square and slipped into a quiet narrow street overlooking a park, stopping before the tallest of the apartment houses in the single commanding row.

Alighting, Miss Cynthie gave this imposing structure one side-wise, upward glance, and said, "Y'all live like bees in a hive, don't y'? — I boun' the women does all the work, too." A moment later, "So this is a elevator? Feel like I'm glory-bound sho' nuff."

Along a tiled corridor and into David's apartment. Rooms leading into rooms. Luxurious couches, easy chairs, a brown-walnut grand piano, gay-shaded floor lamps, paneled walls, deep rugs, treacherous glass-wood floors — and a smiling golden-skinned girl in a gingham housedress, approaching with outstretched hands.

"This is Ruth, Miss Cynthie."

"Miss Cynthie!" said Ruth.

They clasped hands. "Been wantin' to see David's girl ever since he first wrote us 'bout her."

"Come — here's your room this way. Here's the bath. Get out of your things and get comfy. You must be worn out with the trip."

"Worn out? Worn out? Shuh. How you gon' get worn out on a train? Now if 'twas a horse, maybe, or Jake's no-count Fo'd — but a train — didn' but one thing bother me on that train."

"What?"

"When the man made them beds down, I jes' couldn' manage to undress same as at home. Why, s'posin' sump'm bus' the train open — where'd you be? Naked as a jaybird in dewberry time."

David took in her things and left her to get comfortable. He returned, and Ruth, despite his reassuring embrace, whispered:

"Dave, you can't fool old folks — why don't you go ahead and tell her about yourself? Think of the shock she's going to get — at her age."

David shook his head. "She'll get over the shock if she's there looking on. If we just told her, she'd never understand. We've got to railroad her into it. Then she'll be happy."

"She's nice. But she's got the same ideas as all old folks —"

"Yea — but with her you can change 'em. Specially if everything is really all right. I know her. She's for church and all, but she believes in good times too, if they're right. Why, when I was a kid —" He broke off. "Listen!"

Miss Cynthie's voice came quite distinctly to them, singing a jaunty little rhyme:

> Oh I danced with the gal with the hole in her stockin',
> And her toe kep' a-kickin' and her heel kep' a-knockin'—
>
> Come up, Jesse, and get a drink o' gin,
> 'Cause you near to the heaven as you'll ever get ag'in.

"She taught me that when I wasn't knee-high to a cricket," David said.

Miss Cynthie still sang softly and merrily:

> *Then I danced with the gal with the dimple in her cheek,*
> *And if she'd 'a' kep' a-smilin', I'd 'a' danced for a week—*

"God forgive me," prayed Miss Cynthie as she discovered David's purpose the following night. She let him and Ruth lead her, like an early Christian martyr, into the Lafayette Theater. The blinding glare of the lobby produced a merciful self-anesthesia, and she entered the sudden dimness of the interior as involuntarily as in a dream. . . .

Attendants outdid each other for Mr. Dave Tappen. She heard him tell them, "Fix us up till we go on," and found herself sitting between Ruth and David in the front row of a lower box. A miraculous device of the devil, a motion picture that talked, was just ending. At her feet the orchestra was assembling. The motion picture faded out amid a scattered round of applause. Lights blazed and the orchestra burst into an ungodly rumpus.

She looked out over the seated multitude, scanning row upon row of illumined faces, black faces, white faces, yellow, tan, brown; bald heads, bobbed heads, kinky and straight heads; and upon every countenance, expectancy — scowling expectancy in this case, smiling in that, complacent here, amused there, commentative elsewhere, but everywhere suspense, abeyance, anticipation.

Half a dozen people were ushered down the nearer aisle to reserved seats in the second row. Some of them caught sight of David and Ruth and waved to them. The chairs immediately behind them in the box were being shifted. "Hello, Tap!" Miss Cynthie saw David turn, rise, and shake hands with two men. One of them was large, bald and pink, emanating good cheer; the other short, thin, sallow with thick black hair and a sour mien. Ruth also acknowledged their greeting. "This is my grandmother," David said proudly. "Miss Cynthie, meet my managers, Lou and Lee Goldman." "Pleased to meet you," managed Miss Cynthie. "Great lad, this boy of yours," said Lou Goldman. "Great little partner he's got, too," added Lee. They also settled back expectantly.

"Here we go!"

The curtain rose to reveal a cottonfield at dawn. Pickers in blue denim overalls, bandannas, and wide-brimmed straws, or in gingham aprons and sunbonnets, were singing as they worked. Their voices, from clearest soprano to richest bass, blended in low concordances, first simply humming a series of harmonies, until, gradually, came words, like figures forming in mist. As the sound grew, the mist cleared, the words came round and full, and the sun rose, bringing light as if in answer to the song. The chorus swelled, the radiance grew, the two, as if emanating from a single source, fused their crescendos, till at last they achieved a joint transcendence of tonal and visual brightness.

"Swell opener," said Lee Goldman.

"Ripe," agreed Lou.

David and Ruth arose. "Stay here and enjoy the show, Miss Cynthie. You'll see us again in a minute."

"Go to it, kids," said Lou Goldman.

"Yea — burn 'em up," said Lee.

Miss Cynthie hardly noted that she had been left, so absorbed was she in the spectacle. To her, the theater had always been the antithesis of the church. As the one was the refuge of righteousness, so the other was the stronghold of transgression. But this first scene awakened memories, captured and held her attention by offering a blend of truth and novelty. Having thus baited her interest, the show now proceeded to play it like the trout through swift flowing waters of wickedness. Resist as it might, her mind was caught and drawn into the impious subsequences.

The very music that had just rounded out so majestically now distorted itself into ragtime. The singers came forward and turned to dancers; boys, a crazy, swaying background, threw up their arms and kicked their legs in a rhythmic jamboree; girls, an agile, brazen foreground, caught their skirts up to their hips and displayed their copper calves, knees, thighs, in shameless, incredible steps. Miss Cynthie turned dismayed eyes upon the audience, to discover that mob of sinners devouring it all with fond satisfaction. Then the dancers separated and with final abandon flung themselves off the stage in both directions.

Lee Goldman commented through the applause, "They work easy, them babies."

"Yea," said Lou. "Savin' the hot stuff for later."

Two black-faced cotton-pickers appropriated the scene, indulging in dialogue that their hearers found uproarious.

"Ah'm tired."

"Ah'm hongry."

"Dis job jes' wears me out."

"Starves me to death."

"Ah'm so tired — you know what Ah'd like to do?"

"What?"

"Ah'd like to go to sleep and dream I was sleepin'."

"What good dat do?"

"Den I could wake up and still be 'sleep."

"Well y'know what Ah'd like to do?"

"No. What?"

"Ah'd like to swaller me a hog and a hen."

"What good dat do?"

"Den Ah'd always be full o' ham and eggs."

"Ham? Shuh. Don't you know a hog has to be smoked 'fo he's a ham?"

"Well, if I swaller him, he'll have a smoke all around him, won' he?"

Presently Miss Cynthie was smiling like everyone else, but her smile soon fled. For the comics departed, and the dancing girls returned, this time in scant travesties of their earlier voluminous costumes — tiny sunbonnets perched jauntily on one side of their glistening bobs, bandannas reduced to scarlet neck-ribbons, waists mere brassieres, skirts mere gingham sashes.

And now Miss Cynthie's whole body stiffened with a new and surpassing shock; her bright eyes first widened with unbelief, then slowly grew dull with misery. In the midst of a sudden great volley of applause her grandson had broken through that bevy of agile wantons and begun to sing.

He too was dressed as a cotton-picker, but a Beau Brummell among cotton pickers; his hat bore a pleated green band, his bandanna was silk, his overalls blue satin, his shoes black patent leather. His eyes flashed, his teeth gleamed, his body swayed, his arms waved, his words came fast and clear. As he sang, his companions danced a concerted tap, uniformly wild, ecstatic. When he stopped singing, he himself began to dance, and without sacrificing crispness of execution, seemed to absorb into himself every measure of the energy which the girls, now merely standing off and swaying, had relinquished.

"Look at that boy go," said Lee Goldman.

"He ain't started yet," said Lou.

But surrounding comment, Dave's virtuosity, the eager enthusiasm of the audience were all alike lost on Miss Cynthie. She sat with stricken eyes watching this boy whom she'd raised from a babe, taught right from wrong, brought up in the church, and endowed with her prayers, this child whom she had dreamed of seeing a preacher, a regular doctor, a tooth-doctor, a foot-doctor, at the very least an undertaker — sat watching him disport himself for the benefit of a sin-sick, flesh-hungry mob of lost souls, not one of whom knew or cared to know the loving-kindness of God; sat watching a David she'd never foreseen, turned tool of the devil, disciple of lust, unholy prince among sinners.

For a long time she sat there watching with wretched eyes, saw portrayed on the stage David's arrival in Harlem, his escape from 'old friends' who tried to dupe him; saw him working as a trapdrummer in a nightclub, where he fell in love with Ruth, a dancer; not the gentle Ruth Miss Cynthie knew, but a wild and shameless young savage who danced like seven devils — in only a girdle and breastplates; saw the two of them join in a song-and-dance act that eventually made them Broadway headliners, an act presented *in toto* as the pre-finale of this show. And not any of the melodies, not any of the sketches, not all the comic philosophy of the tired-and-hungry duo, gave her figure a moment's relaxation or brightened the dull defeat in her staring eyes. She sat apart, alone in the box, the symbol, the epitome of supreme failure. Let the rest of the theater be riotous, clamoring for more and more of Dave Tappen, "Tap," the greatest tapster of all time, idol of uptown and downtown New York. For her, they were lauding simply an exhibition of sin which centered about her David.

"This'll run a year on Broadway," said Lee Goldman.

"Then we'll take it to Paris."

Encores and curtains with Ruth, and at last David came out on the stage alone. The clamor dwindled. And now he did something quite unfamiliar to even the most consistent of his followers. Softly, delicately, he began to tap a routine designed to fit a particular song. When he had established the rhythm, he began to sing the song:

> Oh I danced with the gal with the hole in her stockin',
> And her toe kep' a-kickin' and her heel kep' a-knockin' —
>
> Come up, Jesse, and get a drink o' gin,
> 'Cause you near to the heaven as you'll ever get ag'in —

As he danced and sang this song, frequently smiling across at Miss Cynthie, a visible change transformed her. She leaned forward incredulously, listened intently, then settled back in limp wonder. Her bewildered eyes turned on the crowd, on those serried rows of shriftless sinners. And she found in their faces now an overwhelmingly curious thing: a grin, a universal grin, a gleeful and sinless grin such as not the nakedest chorus in the performance had produced. In a few seconds, with her own song, David had dwarfed into unimportance, wiped off their faces, swept out of their minds every trace of what had seemed to be sin; had reduced it all to mere trivial detail and revealed these revelers as a crowd of children, enjoying the guileless antics of another child. And Miss Cynthie whispered,

"Bless my soul! They didn' mean nothin' . . . They jes' didn' see no harm in it —"

> Then I danced with the gal with the dimple in her cheek,
> And if she'd 'a' kep' a-smilin', I'd 'a' danced for a week —
> Come up, Jesse —

The crowd laughed, clapped their hands, whistled. Someone threw David a bright yellow flower. "From Broadway!"

He caught the flower. A hush fell. He said:

"I'm really happy tonight, folks. Y'see this flower? Means success, don't it? Well, listen. The one who is really responsible for my success is here tonight with me. Now what do you think o' that?"

The hush deepened.

"Y'know folks, I'm sump'm like Adam — I never had no mother. But I've got a grandmother. Down home everybody calls her Miss Cynthie. And everybody loves her. Take that song I just did for you. Miss Cynthie taught me that when I wasn't knee-high to a cricket. But that wasn't all she taught me. Far back as I can remember, she used to always say one thing: Son, do like a church steeple — aim high and go straight. And for doin' it —" he grinned, contemplating the flower — "I get this."

He strode across to the edge of the stage that touched Miss Cynthie's box. He held up the flower.

"So y'see, folks, this isn't mine. It's really Miss Cynthie's." He leaned over to hand it to her. Miss Cynthie's last trace of doubt was swept away. She drew a deep breath of revelation; her bewilderment vanished, her redoubtable composure returned, her eyes lighted up; and no one but David, still holding the flower toward her, heard her sharply whispered reprimand:

"Keep it, you fool. Where's yo' manners — givin' 'way what somebody give you?"

David grinned:

"Take it, tyro. What you tryin' to do — crab my act?"

Thereupon Miss Cynthie, smiling at him with bright, meaningful eyes, leaned over without rising from her chair, jerked a tiny twig off the stem of the flower, then sat decisively back, resolutely folding her arms, with only a leaf in her hand.

"This'll do me," she said.

The finale didn't matter. People filed out of the theater. Miss Cynthie sat awaiting her children, her foot absently patting time to the orchestra's jazz recessional. Perhaps she was thinking, "God moves in a mysterious way," but her lips were unquestionably forming the words:

> *danced with the gal — hole in her stockin' —*
> *— toe kep' a-kickin' — heel kep' a-knockin'.*

THE WHARF RATS

Eric Walrond

Among the motley crew recruited to dig the Panama Canal were artisans from the four ends of the earth. Down in the Cut drifted hordes of Italians, Greeks, Chinese, Negroes — a hardy, sun-defying set of white, black and yellow men. But the bulk of the actual brawn for the work was supplied by the dusky peons of those coral isles in the Caribbean ruled by Britain, France and Holland.

At the Atlantic end of the Canal the blacks were herded in boxcar huts buried in the jungles of "Silver City"; in the murky tenements perilously poised on the narrow banks of Faulke's River; in the low, smelting cabins of Coco Té. The "Silver Quarters" harbored the inky ones, their wives and pickaninnies.

As it grew dark the hewers at the Ditch, exhausted, half-asleep, naked but for wormy singlets, would hum queer creole tunes, play on guitar or piccolo, and jig to the rhythm of the *coombia*. It was a *brujerial* chant, for *obeah*, a heritage of the French colonial, honeycombed the life of the Negro laboring camps. Over smoking pots, on black, death-black nights, legends of the bloodiest were recited till they became the essence of a sort of Negro Koran. One refuted them at the price of one's breath. And to question the verity of the obeah, to dismiss or reject it as the ungodly rite of some lurid, crackbrained Islander was to be an accursed paleface, dog of a white. And the obeah man in a fury of rage would throw a machete at the heretic's head or — worse — burn on his doorstep at night a pyre of Maube bark or green Ganja weed.

On the banks of a river beyond Cristobal, Coco Té sheltered a colony of Negroes enslaved to the obeah. Near a roundhouse daubed with smoke and coal ash, a river serenely flowed away and into the guava region, at the eastern tip of Monkey Hill. Across the bay from it was a sand bank — a rising out of the sea — where ships stopped for coal.

In the first of the six chinky cabins making up the family quarters of Coco Té lived a stout, potbellied St. Lucian, black as the coal hills he mended, by the name of Jean Baptiste. Like a host of the native St. Lucian emigrants, Jean Baptiste forgot where the French in him ended and the English began. His speech was the petulant patois of the unlettered French black. Still, whenever he lapsed into His Majesty's English, it was with a thick Barbadian bias.

A coal passer at the dry dock, Jean Baptiste was a man of intense piety. After work, by the glow of a red setting sun, he would discard his crusted overalls, get in starched crocus bag, aping the Yankee foreman on the other side of the track in the "Gold Quarters," and loll on his coffee-vined porch. There, dozing in a bamboo rocker, Celestin his second wife, a becomingly stout brown beauty from Martinique, chanted gospel hymns to him.

Three sturdy sons Jean Baptiste's first wife had borne him — Philip, the eldest, a good-looking, black fellow; Ernest, shifty, cunning; and Sandel, aged eight. Another boy, said to be wayward and something of a ne'er-do-well, was sometimes spoken of. But Baptiste, a proud, disdainful man, never once referred to him in the presence of his children. No vagabond son of his could eat from his table or sit at his feet unless he went to "meeting." In brief, Jean Baptiste was a religious man. It was a thrust at the omnipresent obeah. He went to "meeting." He made the boys go, too. All hands went, not to the Catholic Church, where Celestin secretly worshiped, but to the English Plymouth Brethren in the Spanish city of Colón.

Stalking about like a ghost in Jean Baptiste's household was a girl, a black ominous Trinidad girl. Had Jean Baptiste been a man given to curiosity about the nature of women, he would have viewed skeptically Maffi's adoption by Celestin. But Jean Baptiste was a man of lofty unconcern, and so Maffi remained there, shadowy, obdurate.

And Maffi was such a hardworking patois girl. From the break of day she'd be at the sink, brightening the tinware. It was she who did the chores which Madame congenitally shirked. And towards sundown, when the labor trains had emptied, it was she who scoured the beach for cockles for Jean Baptiste's epicurean palate.

And as night fell, Maffi, a long, black figure, would disappear in the dark to dream on top of a canoe hauled up on the mooning beach. An eternity Maffi'd sprawl there, gazing at the frosting of the stars and the glitter of the black sea.

A cabin away lived a family of Tortola mulattoes by the name of Boyce. The father was also a man who piously went to "meeting" — gaunt and hollow-cheeked. The eldest boy, Esau, had been a journeyman tailor for ten years; the girl next him, Ora, was plump, dark, freckled; others came — a string of ulcered girls until finally a pretty, opaque one, Maura.

Of the Bantu tribe, Maura would have been a person to turn and stare at. Crossing the line into Cristobal or Colón — a city of rarefied gaiety — she was often mistaken for a native senorita or an urbanized Chola Indian girl. Her skin was the reddish yellow of old gold and in her eyes there lurked the glint of mother-of-pearl. Her hair, long as a jungle elf's, was jettish, untethered. And her teeth were whiter than the full-blooded black Philip's.

Maura was brought up, like the children of Jean Baptiste, in the Plymouth Brethren. But the Plymouth Brethren was a harsh faith to bring hemmed-in peasant children up in, and Maura, besides, was of a gentle romantic nature. Going to the Yankee commissary at the bottom of Eleventh and Front Streets, she usually wore a leghorn hat. With flowers bedecking it, she'd look in it older, much older than she really was. Which was an impression quite flattering to her. For Maura, unknown to Philip, was in love — in love with San Tie, a Chinese half-breed, son of a wealthy canteen proprietor in Colón. But San Tie liked to go fishing and deer hunting up the Monkey Hill lagoon, and the object of his occasional visits to Coco Té was the eldest son of Jean Baptiste. And thus it was through Philip that Maura kept in touch with the young Chinese Maroon.

One afternoon Maura, at her wits' end, flew to the shed roof to Jean Baptiste's kitchen.

"Maffi," she cried, the words smoky on her lips, "Maffi, when Philip come in tonight tell 'im I want fo' see 'im particular, yes?"

"Sacre gache! All de time Philip, Philip!" growled the Trinidad girl, as Maura, in heartaching preoccupation, sped towards the lawn. "Why she no le' 'im alone, yes?" And with a spatter she flecked the hunk of lard on Jean Baptiste's stewing okras.

As the others filed up front after dinner that evening, Maffi said to Philip, pointing to the cabin across the way, "She — she want fo' see yo'."

Instantly Philip's eyes widened. Ah, he had good news for Maura! San Tie, after an absence of six days, was coming to Coco Té Saturday to hunt on the lagoon. And he'd relish the joy that'd flood Maura's face as she glimpsed the idol of her heart, the hero of her dreams! And Philip, a true son of Jean Baptiste, loved to see others happy, ecstatic.

But Maffi's curious rumination checked him. "All de time, Maura, Maura, me can't understand it, yes. But no mind, me go stop it, oui, me go stop it, so help me —"

He crept up to her, gently holding her by the shoulders.

"Le' me go, sacre!" She shook off his hands bitterly. "Le' me go — yo' go to yo' Maura." And she fled to her room, locking the door behind her.

Philip sighed. He was a generous, good-natured sort. But it was silly to try to enlighten Maffi. It wasn't any use. He could as well have spoken to the tattered torsos the lazy waves puffed up on the shores of Coco Té.

"Philip, come on, a ship is in — let's go." Ernest, the wharf rat, seized him by the arm.

"Come," he said, "let's go before it's too late. I want to get some money, yes."

Dashing out of the house the two boys made for the wharf. It was dusk. Already the Hindus in the bachelor quarters were mixing their rotie and the Negroes in their singlets were smoking and cooling off. Night was rapidly approaching. Sunset, an iridescent bit of molten gold, was enriching the stream with its last faint radiance.

The boys stole across the lawn and made their way to the pier.

"Careful," cried Philip, as Ernest slid between a prong of oyster-crusted piles to a raft below. "Careful, these shells cut wussah'n a knife."

On the raft the boys untied a rowboat they kept stowed away under the dock, got into it and pushed off. The liner still had two hours to dock. Tourists crowded its decks. Veering away from the barnacled piles the boys eased out into the churning ocean.

It was dusk. Night would soon be upon them. Philip took the oars while Ernest stripped down to loincloth.

"Come, Philip, let me paddle —" Ernest took the oars. Afar on the dusky sea a whistle echoed. It was the pilot's signal to the captain of port. The ship would soon dock.

The passengers on deck glimpsed the boys. It piqued their curiosity to see two black boys in a boat amidstream.

"All right, mistah," cried Ernest. "A penny, mistah."

He sprang at the guilder as it twisted and turned through a streak of silver dust to the bottom of the sea. Only the tips of his crimson toes — a sherbet-like foam — and up he came with the coin between his teeth.

Deep-sea gamin, Philip off yonder, his mouth noisy with coppers, gargled, "This way, sah, as far as you' like, mistah."

An old red-bearded Scot, in spats and mufti, presumably a lover of the exotic in sport, held aloft a sovereign. A sovereign! Already red, and sore by virtue of the leaps and plunges in the briny swirl, Philip's eyes bulged at its yellow gleam.

"Ovah ya, sah —"

Off in a whirlpool the man tossed it. And like a garfish Philip took after it, a falling arrow in the stream. His body, once in the water, tore ahead. For a spell the crowd on the ship held its breath. "Where is he?" "Where is the nigger swimmer gone to?" Even Ernest, driven to the boat by the race for such an ornate prize, cold, shivering, his teeth chattering — even he watched with trembling and anxiety. But Ernest's concern was of a deeper kind. For there, where Philip had leaped, was Deathpool — a spawning place for sharks, for barracudas!

But Philip rose — a brief gurgling sputter — a ripple on the sea — and the Negro's crinkled head was above the water.

"Hey!" shouted Ernest. "There, Philip! Down!"

And down Philip plunged. One — two minutes. God, how long they seemed! And Ernest anxiously waited. But the bubble on the water boiled, kept on boiling — a sign that life still lasted! It comforted Ernest.

Suddenly Philip, panting, spitting, pawing, dashed through the water like a streak of lightning.

"Shark!" cried a voice aboard ship. "Shark! There he is, a great big one! Run, boy! Run for your life!"

From the edge of the boat Philip saw the monster as twice.

thrice it circled the boat. Several times the shark made a dash for it, endeavoring to strike it with its murderous tail.

The boys quietly made off. But the shark still followed the boat. It was a pale green monster. In the glittering dusk it seemed black to Philip. Fattened on the swill of the abattoir nearby and the beef tossed from the decks of countless ships in port, it had become used to the taste of flesh and the smell of blood.

"Yo' know, Ernest," said Philip, as he made the boat fast to raft, "one time I thought he wuz rubbin' 'gainst me belly. He wuz such a big able one. But it wuz wuth it, Ernie, it wuz wuth it —"

In his palm there was a flicker of gold. Ernest emptied his loincloth and together they counted the money, dressed, and trudged back to the cabin.

On the lawn Philip met Maura. Ernest tipped his cap, left his brother, and went into the house. As he entered, Maffi, pretending to be scouring a pan, was flushed and mute as a statue. And Ernest, starved, went in the dining room and for a long time stayed there. Unable to bear it any longer, Maffi sang out, "Ernest, whey Philip dey?"

"Outside — some whey — ah talk to Maura —"

"Yo' sure yo' lie, Ernest?" she asked, suspended.

"Yes, of cose, I jes' lef' 'im 'tandin' out dey — why?"

"Nutton —"

He suspected nothing. He went on eating while Maffi tiptoed to the shed roof. Yes, confound it, there he was, near the standpipe, talking to Maura!

"Go stop ee, oui," she hissed impishly. "Go 'top ee, yes."

Low, shadowy, the sky painted Maura's face bronze. The sea, noisy, enraged, sent a blob of wind about her black, wavy hair. And with her back to the sea, her hair blew loosely about her face.

"D'ye think, d'ye think he really likes me, Philip?"

"I'm positive he do, Maura," vowed the youth.

And an aging faith shone in Maura's eyes. No longer was she a silly, insipid girl. Something holy, reverent had touched her. And in so doing it could not fail to leave an impress of beauty. It was worshipful. And it mellowed, ripened her.

Weeks she had waited for word of San Tie. And the springs of Maura's life took on a noble ecstasy. Late at night, after the others had retired, she'd sit up in bed, dreaming. Sometimes they were dreams of envy. For Maura began to look with eyes of comparison upon the happiness of the Italian wife of the boss riveter at the Dry Dock — the lady on the other side of the railroad tracks in the Gold Quarters, for whom she sewed — who got a fresh baby every year and who danced in a world of silks and satins. Yes, Maura had dreams, love dreams of San Tie, the flashy half-breed, son of a Chinese beer seller and a Jamaica Maroon, who had swept her off her feet by a playful wink of the eye.

"Tell me, Philip, does he work? Or does he play the lottery — what does he do, tell me!"

"I dunno," Philip replied with mock lassitude. "I dunno myself —"

"But it doesn't matter, Philip. I don't want to be nosy, see? I'm simply curious about everything that concerns him, see?"

Ah, but Philip wished to cherish Maura, to shield her, be kind to her. And so he lied to her. He did not tell her he had first met San Tie behind the counter of his father's saloon in the Colón tenderloin, for he would have had to tell besides why he, Philip, had gone there. And that would have led him, a youth of meager guile, to Celestin Baptiste's mulish regard for anisette, which he procured her. He dared not tell her, well-meaning fellow that he was, what San Tie, a fiery comet in the night life of the district, had said to him the day before. "She sick in de head, yes," he had said. "Ah, me no dat saht o' man — don't she know no bettah, egh, Philip?" But Philip desired to be kindly, and hid it from Maura.

"What is today?" she cogitated aloud. "Tuesday. You say he's comin' fo' hunt Saturday, Philip? Wednesday — four more days. I can wait. I can wait. I'd wait a million years fo' 'im, Philip."

But Saturday came and Maura, very properly, was shy as a duck. Other girls, like Hilda Long, a Jamaica brunette, the flower of a bawdy cabin up by the abattoir, would have been less genteel. Hilda would have caught San Tie by the lapels of his coat and in no time would have got him told.

But Maura was lowly, trepid, shy. To her he was a dream — a luxury to be distantly enjoyed. He was not to be touched. And she'd wait till he decided to come to her. And there was no fear, either, of his ever failing to come. Philip had seen to that. Had not he been the intermediary between them? And all Maura needed now was to sit back, and wait till San Tie came to her.

And besides, who knows, brooded Maura, San Tie might be a bashful fellow.

But when, after an exciting hunt, the Chinese mulatto returned from the lagoon, nodded stiffly to her, said good-bye to Philip and kept on to the scarlet city, Maura was frantic.

"Maffi," she said, "tell Philip to come here quick —"

It was the same as touching a match to the patois girl's dynamite. "Yo' mek me sick," she said. "Go call he yo'self, yo' ole hag, yo' ole fire hag yo'." But Maura, flighty in despair, had gone on past the lawn.

"Ah go stop ee, oui," she muttered diabolically. "Ah go stop it, yes. This very night."

Soon as she got through lathering the dishes she tidied up and came out on the front porch.

It was a humid dusk, and the glowering sky sent a species of fly — bloody as a tick — buzzing about Jean Baptiste's porch. There he sat, rotund and sleepy-eyed, rocking and languidly brushing the darting imps away.

"Wha' yo' gwine, Maffi?" asked Celestin Baptiste, fearing to wake the old man.

"Ovah to de Jahn Chinaman shop, mum," answered Maffi unheeding.

"Fi' what?"

"Fi' buy some wash blue, mum."

And she kept on down the road past the Hindu kiosk to the Negro mess house.

"Oh, Philip," cried Maura. "I am so unhappy. Didn't he ask about me at all? Didn't he say he'd like to visit me — didn't he give yo' any message fo' me, Philip?"

The boy toyed with a blade of grass. His eyes were downcast. Sighing heavily, he at last spoke. "No, Maura, he didn't ask about you."

"What, he didn't ask about me? Philip? I don't believe it! Oh, my God!"

She clung to Philip mutely; her face, her breath coming warm and fast.

"I wish to God I'd never seen either of you," cried Philip.

"Ah, but wasn't he your friend, Philip? Didn't yo' tell me that?" And the boy bowed his head sadly.

"Answer me!" she screamed, shaking him. "Weren't you his friend?"

"Yes, Maura —"

"But you lied to me, Philip, you lied to me! You took messages from me — you brought back — lies!" Two pearls, large as pigeon's eggs, shone in Maura's burnished face.

"To think," she cried in a hollow sepulchral voice, "That I dreamed about a ghost, a man who didn't exist. Oh, God, why should I suffer like this? Why was I ever born? What did I do, what did my people do, to deserve such misery as this?"

She rose, leaving Philip with his head buried in his hands. She went into the night, tearing her hair, scratching her face, raving.

"Oh, how happy I was! I was a happy girl! I was so young and I had such merry dreams! And I wanted so little! I was carefree —"

Down to the shore of the sea she staggered, the wind behind her, the night obscuring her.

"Maura!" cried Philip, running after her. "Maura! come back!"

Great sheaves of clouds buried the moon, and the wind bearing up from the sea bowed the cypress and palm lining the beach.

"Maura — Maura —"

He bumped into someone, a girl, black, part of the dense pattern of the tropical night.

"Maffi," cried Philip, "have you seen Maura down yondah?"

The girl quietly stared at him. Had Philip lost his mind?

"Talk, no!" he cried, exasperated.

And his quick tones sharpened Maffi's vocal anger. Thrusting him aside, she thundered, "Think I'm she keeper! Go'n look fo' she yo'self. I is not she keeper! Le' me pass, move!"

Towards the end of the track he found Maura, heartrendingly weeping.

"Oh, don't cry, Maura! Never mind, Maura!"

He helped her to her feet, took her to the standpipe on the lawn, bathed her temples and sat soothingly, uninterruptingly, beside her.

At daybreak the next morning Ernest rose and woke Philip.

He yawned, put on the loincloth, seized a "cracked licker" skillet, and stole cautiously out of the house. Of late Jean Baptiste had put his foot down on his sons' copper-diving proclivities. And he kept at the head of his bed a greased cat-o'-nine-tails which he would use on Philip himself if the occasion warranted.

"Come on, Philip, let's go —"

Yawning and scratching, Philip followed. The grass on the lawn was bright and icy with the dew. On the railroad tracks the six o'clock labor trains were coupling. A rosy mist flooded the dawn. Out in the stream the tug *Exotic* snorted in a heavy fog.

On the wharf Philip led the way to the rafters below.

"Look out fo' that crapeau, Ernest, don't step on him, he'll spit on you."

The frog splashed into the water. Prickle-backed crabs and oysters and myriad other shells spawned on the rotting piles. The boys paddled the boat. Out in the dawn ahead of them the tug puffed a path through the foggy mist. The water was chilly. Mist glistened on top of it. Far out, beyond the buoys, Philip encountered a placid, untroubled sea. The liner, a German tourist boat, was loaded to the bridge. The water was as still as a lake of ice.

"All right, Ernest, let's hurry —"

Philip drew in the oars. The *Kron Prinz Wilhelm* came near. Huddled in thick European coats, the passengers viewed from their lofty estate the spectacle of two naked Negro boys peeping up at them from a wiggly bateau.

"Penny, mistah, penny, mistah!"

Somebody dropped a quarter. Ernest, like a shot, flew after it. Half a foot down he caught it as it twisted and turned in the gleaming sea. Vivified by the icy dip, Ernest was a raving wolf and the folk aboard dealt a lavish hand.

"Ovah yah, mistah," cried Philip, "ovah yah."

For a Dutch guilder Philip gave an exhibition of "cork." Under something of a ledge on the side of the boat he had stuck a piece of cork. Now, after his and Ernest's mouths were full of coins, he could afford to be extravagant and treat the Europeans to a game of West Indian "cork."

Roughly ramming the cork down in the water, Philip, after the fifteenth ram or so, let it go, and flew back, upwards, having thus "lost" it. It was Ernest's turn now, as a sort of endman, to scramble forward to the spot where Philip had dug it down and "find" it, the first one to do so having the prerogative, which he jealously guarded, of raining on the other a series of thundering leg blows. As boys in the West Indies, Philip and Ernest had played it. Of a Sunday the Negro fishermen on the Barbados coast made a pagan rite of it. Many a Bluetown dandy got his spine cracked in a game of cork.

With a passive interest the passengers viewed the proceedings. In a game of cork, the cork after a succession of rammings is likely to drift many feet away whence it was first "lost." One had to be an expert, quick, alert, to spy and promptly seize it as it popped up on the rolling waves. Once Ernest got it, and endeavored to make much of the possession. But Philip, besides being two feet taller than he, was slippery as an eel, and Ernest, despite all the artful ingenuity at his command, was able to do no more than ineffectively beat the water about him. Again and again he tried, but to no purpose.

Becoming reckless, he let the cork drift too far away from him and Philip seized it.

He twirled it in the air like a crapshooter, and dug deep down in the water with it, "lost" it, then leaped back, briskly waiting for it to rise.

About them the water, due to the ramming and beating, grew restive. Billows sprang up; soaring, swelling waves sent the skiff nearer the shore. Anxiously Philip and Ernest watched for the cork to make its ascent.

It was all a bit vague to the whites on the deck, and an amused chuckle floated down to the boys.

And still the cork failed to come up.

"I'll go after it," said Philip at last. "I'll go and fetch it." And from the edge of the boat he leaped, his body long and resplendent in the rising tropic sun.

It was a suction sea, and down in it Philip plunged. And it was lazy, too, and willful — the water. Ebony-black, it tugged and mocked. Old brass staves — junk dumped there by the retiring French — thick, yawping mud, barrel hoops, tons of obsolete brass, a wealth of slimy steel faced him. Did a rammed cork ever go that deep?

And the water, stirring, rising, drew a haze over Philip's eyes. Had a cuttlefish, an octopus, a nest of eels been routed? It seemed

so to Philip, blindly diving, pawing. And the sea, the tide —
touching the roots of Deathpool — tugged and tugged. His gathering hands stuck in mud. Iron staves bruised his shins. It was black
down there. Impenetrable.

Suddenly, like a flash of lightning, a vision blew across Philip's
brow. It was a soaring shark's belly. Drunk on the nectar of the
deep, it soared above Philip — rolling, tumbling, rolling. It had
followed the boy's scent with the accuracy of a diver's rope.

Scrambling to the surface, Philip struck out for the boat. But
the sea, the depths of it wrested out of an aeon's slumber, had sent
it a mile from his diving point. And now, as his strength ebbed, a
shark was at his heels.

"Shark! Shark!" was the cry that went up from the ship.

Hewing a lane through the hostile sea, Philip forgot the cunning
of the doddering beast and swam noisier than he needed to. Faster
grew his strokes. His line was a straight, dead one. Fancy strokes
and dives — giraffe leaps . . . he summoned into play. He shot
out recklessly. One time he suddenly paused — and floated for a
stretch. Another time he swam on his back, gazing at the chalky
sky. He dived for whole lengths.

But the shark, a bloaty, stone-colored man-killer, took a shorter
cut. Circumnavigating the swimmer it bore down upon him with
the speed of a hurricane. Within adequate reach it turned, showed
its gleaming belly, seizing its prey.

A fiendish gargle — the gnashing of bones — as the sea once
more closed its jaws on Philip.

Someone aboard ship screamed. Women fainted. There was talk
of a gun. Ernest, an oar upraised, capsized the boat as he tried to
inflict a blow on the coursing, chop-licking man-eater.

And again the fish turned. It scraped the waters with its deadly
fins.

At Coco Té, at the fledging of the dawn, Maffi, polishing the
tinware, hummed an obeah melody.

> *Trinidad is a damn fine place*
> *But obeah down dey. . . .*

Peace had come to her at last.

A SUMMER TRAGEDY

Arna Bontemps

OLD Jeff Patton, the black share farmer, fumbled with his bow tie. His fingers trembled and the high stiff collar pinched his throat. A fellow loses his hand for such vanities after thirty or forty years of simple life. Once a year, or maybe twice if there's a wedding among his kinfolks, he may spruce up; but generally fancy clothes do nothing but adorn the wall of the big room and feed the moths. That had been Jeff Patton's experience. He had not worn his stiff-bosomed shirt more than a dozen times in all his married life. His swallow-tailed coat lay on the bed beside him, freshly brushed and pressed, but it was as full of holes as the overalls in which he worked on weekdays. The moths had used it badly. Jeff twisted his mouth into a hideous toothless grimace as he contended with the obstinate bow. He stamped his good foot and decided to give up the struggle.

"Jennie," he called.

"What's that, Jeff?" His wife's shrunken voice came out of the adjoining room like an echo. It was hardly bigger than a whisper.

"I reckon you'll have to he'p me wid this heah bow tie, baby," he said meekly. "Dog if I can hitch it up."

Her answer was not strong enough to reach him, but presently the old woman came to the door, feeling her way with a stick. She had a wasted, dead-leaf appearance. Her body, as scrawny and gnarled as a string bean, seemed less than nothing in the ocean of frayed and faded petticoats that surrounded her. These hung an inch or two above the tops of her heavy unlaced shoes and showed little grotesque piles where the stockings had fallen down from her negligible legs.

"You oughta could do a heap mo' wid a thing like that'n me — beingst as you got yo' good sight."

"Looks like I oughta could," he admitted. "But ma fingers is gone democrat on me. I get all mixed up in the looking glass an' can't tell wicha way to twist the devilish thing."

Jennie sat on the side of the bed and old Jeff Patton got down on one knee while she tied the bow knot. It was a slow and painful ordeal for each of them in this position. Jeff's bones cracked, his knee ached, and it was only after a half dozen attempts that Jennie worked a semblance of a bow into the tie.

"I got to dress maself now," the old woman whispered. "These is ma old shoes an' stockings, and I ain't so much as unwrapped ma dress."

"Well, don't worry 'bout me no mo', baby," Jeff said. "That 'bout finishes me. All I gotta do now is slip on that old coat 'n ves' an' I'll be fixed to leave."

Jennie disappeared again through the dim passage into the shed room. Being blind was no handicap to her in that black hole. Jeff heard the cane placed against the wall beside the door and knew that his wife was on easy ground. He put on his coat, took a battered top hat from the bedpost and hobbled to the front door. He was ready to travel. As soon as Jennie could get on her Sunday shoes and her old black silk dress, they would start.

Outside the tiny log house, the day was warm and mellow with sunshine. A host of wasps were humming with busy excitement in the trunk of a dead sycamore. Gray squirrels were searching through the grass for hickory nuts and blue jays were in the trees, hopping from branch to branch. Pine woods stretched away to the left like a black sea. Among them were scattered scores of log houses like Jeff's, houses of black share farmers. Cows and pigs wandered freely among the trees. There was no danger of loss. Each farmer knew his own stock and knew his neighbor's as well as he knew his neighbor's children.

Down the slope to the right were the cultivated acres on which the colored folks worked. They extended to the river, more than two miles away, and they were today green with the unmade cotton crop. A tiny thread of a road, which passed directly in front of Jeff's place, ran through these green fields like a pencil mark.

Jeff, standing outside the door, with his absurd hat in his left hand, surveyed the wide scene tenderly. He had been forty-five years on these acres. He loved them with the unexplained affection that others have for the countries to which they belong.

The sun was hot on his head, his collar still pinched his throat, and the Sunday clothes were intolerably hot. Jeff transferred the hat to his right hand and began fanning with it. Suddenly the whisper that was Jennie's voice came out of the shed room.

"You can bring the car round front whilst you's waitin'," it said feebly. There was a tired pause; then it added, "I'll soon be fixed to go."

"A'right, baby," Jeff answered. "I'll get it in a minute."

But he didn't move. A thought struck him that made his mouth fall open. The mention of the car brought to his mind, with new intensity, the trip he and Jennie were about to take. Fear came into his eyes; excitement took his breath. Lord, Jesus!

"Jeff . . . O Jeff," the old woman's whisper called.

He awakened with a jolt. "Hunh, baby?"

"What you doin'?"

"Nuthin. Jes studyin'. I jes been turnin' things round'n round in ma mind."

"You could be gettin' the car," she said.

"Oh yes, right away, baby."

He started round to the shed, limping heavily on his bad leg. There were three frizzly chickens in the yard. All his other chickens had been killed or stolen recently. But the frizzly chickens had been saved somehow. That was fortunate indeed, for these curious creatures had a way of devouring "Poison" from the yard and in that way protecting against conjure and black luck and spells. But even the frizzly chickens seemed now to be in a stupor. Jeff thought they had some ailment; he expected all three of them to die shortly.

The shed in which the old T-model Ford stood was only a grass roof held up by four corner poles. It had been built by tremulous hands at a time when the little rattletrap car had been regarded as a peculiar treasure. And, miraculously, despite wind and downpour it still stood.

Jeff adjusted the crank and put his weight upon it. The engine came to life with a sputter and bang that rattled the old car from radiator to taillight. Jeff hopped into the seat and put his foot on the accelerator. The sputtering and banging increased. The rattling became more violent. That was good. It was good banging, good sputtering and rattling, and it meant that the aged car was still in running condition. She could be depended on for this trip.

Again Jeff's thought halted as if paralyzed. The suggestion of the trip fell into the machinery of his mind like a wrench. He felt dazed and weak. He swung the car out into the yard, made a half turn and drove around to the front door. When he took his hands off the wheel, he noticed that he was trembling violently. He cut off the motor and climbed to the ground to wait for Jennie.

A few minutes later she was at the window, her voice rattling against the pane like a broken shutter.

"I'm ready, Jeff."

He did not answer, but limped into the house and took her by the arm. He led her slowly through the big room, down the step and across the yard.

"You reckon I'd oughta lock the do'?" he asked softly.

They stopped and Jennie weighed the question. Finally she shook her head.

"Ne' mind the do'," she said. "I don't see no cause to lock up things."

"You right," Jeff agreed. "No cause to lock up."

Jeff opened the door and helped his wife into the car. A quick shudder passed over him. Jesus! Again he trembled.

"How come you shaking so?" Jennie whispered.

"I don't know," he said.

"You mus' be scairt, Jeff."

"No, baby, I ain't scairt."

He slammed the door after her and went around to crank up again. The motor started easily. Jeff wished that it had not been so responsive. He would have liked a few more minutes in which to turn things around in his head. As it was, with Jennie chiding him about being afraid, he had to keep going. He swung the car into the little pencil-mark road and started off toward the river, driving very slowly, very cautiously.

Chugging across the green countryside, the small battered Ford seemed tiny indeed. Jeff felt a familiar excitement, a thrill, as they came down the first slope to the immense levels on which the cotton was growing. He could not help reflecting that the crops were good. He knew what that meant, too; he had made forty-five of them with his own hands. It was true that he had worn out nearly a dozen mules, but that was the fault of old man Stevenson, the owner of the land. Major Stevenson had the odd notion that one mule was all a share farmer needed to work a thirty-acre plot. It was an expensive notion, the way it killed mules from overwork, but the old man held to it. Jeff thought it killed a good many share farmers as well as mules, but he had no sympathy for them. He had always been strong, and he had been taught to have no patience with weakness in men. Women or children might be tolerated if they were puny, but a weak man was a curse. Of course, his own children —

Jeff's thought halted there. He and Jennie never mentioned their dead children any more. And naturally he did not wish to dwell upon them in his mind. Before he knew it, some remark would slip out of his mouth and that would make Jennie feel blue. Perhaps she would cry. A woman like Jennie could not easily throw off the grief that comes from losing five grown children within two years. Even Jeff was still staggered by the blow. His memory had not been much good recently. He frequently talked to himself. And, although he had kept it a secret, he knew that his courage had left him. He was terrified by the least unfamiliar sound at night. He was reluctant to venture far from home in the daytime. And that habit of trembling when he felt fearful was now far beyond his control. Sometimes he became afraid and trembled without knowing what had frightened him. The feeling would just come over him like a chill.

The car rattled slowly over the dusty road. Jennie sat erect and silent, with a little absurd hat pinned to her hair. Her useless eyes seemed very large, very white in their deep sockets. Suddenly Jeff heard her voice, and he inclined his head to catch the words.

"Is we passed Delia Moore's house yet?" she asked.

"Not yet," he said.

"You must be drivin' mighty slow, Jeff."

"We might just as well take our time, baby."

There was a pause. A little puff of steam was coming out of the radiator of the car. Heat wavered above the hood. Delia Moore's house was nearly half a mile away. After a moment Jennie spoke again.

"You ain't really scairt, is you, Jeff?"

"Nah, baby, I ain't scairt."

"You know how we agreed — we gotta keep on goin'."

Jewels of perspiration appeared on Jeff's forehead. His eyes rounded, blinked, became fixed on the road.

"I don't know," he said with a shiver. "I reckon it's the only thing to do."

"Hm."

A flock of guinea fowls, pecking in the road, were scattered by the passing car. Some of them took to their wings; others hid under bushes. A blue jay, swaying on a leafy twig, was annoying a roadside squirrel. Jeff held an even speed till he came near Delia's place. Then he slowed down noticeably.

Delia's house was really no house at all, but an abandoned store building converted into a dwelling. It sat near a crossroads, beneath a single black cedar tree. There Delia, a cattish old creature of Jennie's age, lived alone. She had been there more years than anybody could remember, and long ago had won the disfavor of such women as Jennie. For in her young days Delia had been gayer, yellower and saucier than seemed proper in those parts. Her ways with menfolks had been dark and suspicious. And the fact that she had had as many husbands as children did not help her reputation.

"Yonder's old Delia," Jeff said as they passed.

"What she doin'?"

"Jes sittin' in the do'," he said.

"She see us?"

"Hm," Jeff said. "Musta did."

That relieved Jennie. It strengthened her to know that her old enemy had seen her pass in her best clothes. That would give the old she-devil something to chew her gums and fret about, Jennie thought. Wouldn't she have a fit if she didn't find out? Old evil Delia! This would be just the thing for her. It would pay her back for being so evil. It would also pay her, Jennie thought, for the way she used to grin at Jeff — long ago when her teeth were good.

The road became smooth and red, and Jeff could tell by the smell of the air that they were nearing the river. He could see the rise where the road turned and ran along parallel to the stream. The car chugged on monotonously. After a long silent spell, Jennie leaned against Jeff and spoke.

"How many bale o' cotton you think we got standin'?" she said.

Jeff wrinkled his forehead as he calculated.

" 'Bout twenty-five, I reckon."

"How many you make las' year?"

"Twenty-eight," he said. "How come you ask that?"

"I's jes thinkin'," Jennie said quietly.

"It don't make a speck o' difference though," Jeff reflected. "If we get much or if we get little, we still gonna be in debt to old man Stevenson when he gets through counting up agin us. It's took us a long time to learn that."

Jennie was not listening to these words. She had fallen into a trance-like meditation. Her lips twitched. She chewed her gums and rubbed her gnarled hands nervously. Suddenly she leaned forward, buried her face in the nervous hands and burst into tears. She cried aloud in a dry cracked voice that suggested the rattle of fodder on dead stalks. She cried aloud like a child, for she had never learned to suppress a genuine sob. Her slight old frame shook heavily and seemed hardly able to sustain such violent grief.

"What's the matter, baby?" Jeff asked awkwardly. "Why you cryin' like all that?"

"I's jes thinkin'," she said.

"So you the one what's scairt now, hunh?"

"I ain't scairt, Jeff. I's jes thinkin' 'bout leavin' eve'thing like this — eve'thing we been used to. It's right sad-like."

Jeff did not answer, and presently Jennie buried her face again and cried.

The sun was almost overhead. It beat down furiously on the dusty wagon-path road, on the parched roadside grass and the tiny battered car. Jeff's hands, gripping the wheel, became wet with perspiration; his forehead sparkled. Jeff's lips parted. His mouth shaped a hideous grimace. His face suggested the face of a man being burned. But the torture passed and his expression softened again.

"You mustn't cry, baby," he said to his wife. "We gotta be strong. We can't break down."

Jennie waited a few seconds, then said, "You reckon we oughta do it, Jeff? You reckon we oughta go 'head an' do it, really?"

Jeff's voice choked; his eyes blurred. He was terrified to hear

Jennie say the thing that had been in his mind all morning. She had egged him on when he had wanted more than anything in the world to wait, to reconsider, to think things over a little longer. Now she was getting cold feet. Actually there was no need of thinking the question through again. It would only end in making the same painful decision once more. Jeff knew that. There was no need of fooling around longer.

"We jes as well to do like we planned," he said. "They ain't nothin' else for us now — it's the bes' thing."

Jeff thought of the handicaps, the near impossibility, of making another crop with his leg bothering him more and more each week. Then there was always the chance that he would have another stroke, like the one that had made him lame. Another one might kill him. The least it could do would be to leave him helpless. Jeff gasped — Lord, Jesus! He could not bear to think of being helpless, like a baby, on Jennie's hands. Frail, blind Jennie.

The little pounding motor of the car worked harder and harder. The puff of steam from the cracked radiator became larger. Jeff realized that they were climbing a little rise. A moment later the road turned abruptly and he looked down upon the face of the river.

"Jeff."

"Hunh?"

"Is that the water I hear?"

"Hm. Tha's it."

"Well, which way you goin' now?"

"Down this-a way," he said. "The road runs 'long 'side o' the water a lil piece."

She waited a while calmly. Then she said, "Drive faster."

"A'right, baby," Jeff said.

The water roared in the bed of the river. It was fifty or sixty feet below the level of the road. Between the road and the water there was a long smooth slope, sharply inclined. The slope was dry, the clay hardened by prolonged summer heat. The water below, roaring in a narrow channel, was noisy and wild.

"Jeff."

"Hunh?"

"How far you goin'?"

"Jes a lil piece down the road."

"You ain't scairt, is you, Jeff?"

"Nah, baby," he said trembling. "I ain't scairt."

"Remember how we planned it, Jeff. We gotta do it like we said. Brave-like."

"Hm."

Jeff's brain darkened. Things suddenly seemed unreal, like figures in a dream. Thoughts swam in his mind foolishly, hysterically, like little blind fish in a pool within a dense cave. They rushed, crossed one another, jostled, collided, retreated and rushed again. Jeff soon became dizzy. He shuddered violently and turned to his wife.

"Jennie, I can't do it. I can't." His voice broke pitifully.

She did not appear to be listening. All the grief had gone from her face. She sat erect, her unseeing eyes wide open, strained and frightful. Her glossy black skin had become dull. She seemed as thin, as sharp and bony, as a starved bird. Now, having suffered and endured the sadness of tearing herself away from beloved things, she showed no anguish. She was absorbed with her own thoughts, and she didn't even hear Jeff's voice shouting in her ear.

Jeff said nothing more. For an instant there was light in his cavernous brain. The great chamber was, for less than a second, peopled by characters he knew and loved. They were simple, healthy creatures, and they behaved in a manner that he could understand. They had quality. But since he had already taken leave of them long ago, the remembrance did not break his heart again. Young Jeff Patton was among them, the Jeff Patton of fifty years ago who went down to New Orleans with a crowd of country boys to the Mardi Gras doings. The gay young crowd, boys with candy-striped shirts and rouged-brown girls in noisy silks, was like a picture in his head. Yet it did not make him sad. On that very trip Slim Burns had killed Joe Beasley — the crowd had been broken up. Since then Jeff Patton's world had been the Greenbriar Plantation. If there had been other Mardi Gras carnivals, he had not heard of them. Since then there had been no time; the years had fallen on him like waves. Now he was old, worn out. Another paralytic stroke (like the one he had already suffered) would put him on his back for keeps. In that condition, with a frail blind woman to look after him, he would be worse off than if he were dead.

Suddenly Jeff's hands became steady. He actually felt brave. He slowed down the motor of the car and carefully pulled off the road. Below, the water of the stream boomed, a soft thunder in the deep channel. Jeff ran the car onto the clay slope, pointed it directly toward the stream and put his foot heavily on the accelerator. The little car leaped furiously down the steep incline toward the water. The movement was nearly as swift and direct as a fall. The two old black folks, sitting quietly side by side, showed no excitement. In another instant the car hit the water and dropped immediately out of sight.

A little later it lodged in the mud of a shallow place. One wheel of the crushed and upturned little Ford became visible above the rushing water.

THANK YOU, M'AM

Langston Hughes

S HE was a large woman with a large purse that had everything in it but a hammer and nails. It had a long strap, and she carried it slung across her shoulder. It was about eleven o'clock at night, dark, and she was walking alone, when a boy ran up behind her and tried to snatch her purse. The strap broke with the sudden single tug the boy gave it from behind. But the boy's weight and the weight of the purse combined caused him to lose his balance. Instead of taking off full blast as he had hoped, the boy fell on his back on the sidewalk and his legs flew up. The large woman simply turned around and kicked him right square in his blue-jeaned sitter. Then she reached down, picked the boy up by his shirt front, and shook him until his teeth rattled.

After that the woman said, "Pick up my pocketbook, boy, and give it here."

She still held him tightly. But she bent down enough to permit him to stoop and pick up her purse. Then she said, "Now ain't you ashamed of yourself?"

Firmly gripped by his shirt front, the boy said, "Yes'm."

The woman said, "What did you want to do it for?"

The boy said, "I didn't aim to."

She said, "You a lie!"

By that time two or three people passed, stopped, turned to look, and some stood watching.

"If I turn you loose, will you run?" asked the woman.

"Yes'm," said the boy.

"Then I won't turn you loose," said the woman. She did not release him.

"Lady, I'm sorry," whispered the boy.

"Um-hum! Your face is dirty. I got a great mind to wash your face for you. Ain't you got nobody home to tell you to wash your face?"

"No'm," said the boy.

"Then it will get washed this evening," said the large woman, starting up the street, dragging the frightened boy behind her.

He looked as if he were fourteen or fifteen, frail and willow-wild, in tennis shoes and blue jeans.

The woman said, "You ought to be my son. I would teach you right from wrong. Least I can do right now is to wash your face. Are you hungry?"

"No'm," said the being-dragged boy. "I just want you to turn me loose."

"Was I bothering *you* when I turned that corner?" asked the woman.

"No'm."

"But you put yourself in contact with *me*," said the woman. "If you think that that contact is not going to last awhile, you got another thought coming. When I get through with you, sir, you are going to remember Mrs. Luella Bates Washington Jones."

Sweat popped out on the boy's face and he began to struggle. Mrs. Jones stopped, jerked him around in front of her, put a half nelson about his neck, and continued to drag him up the street. When she got to her door, she dragged the boy inside, down a hall, and into a large kitchenette-furnished room at the rear of the house. She switched on the light and left the door open. The boy could hear other roomers laughing and talking in the large house. Some of their doors were open, too, so he knew he and the woman were not alone. The woman still had him by the neck in the middle of her room.

She said, "What is your name?"

"Roger," answered the boy.

"Then, Roger, you go to that sink and wash your face," said the woman, whereupon she turned him loose — at last. Roger looked at the door — looked at the woman — looked at the door — *and went to the sink.*

"Let the water run until it gets warm," she said. "Here's a clean towel."

"You gonna take me to jail?" asked the boy, ~~bending over the sink.~~

"Not with that face, I would not take you nowhere," said the woman. "Here I am trying to get home to cook me a bite to eat, and you snatch my pocketbook! Maybe you ain't been to your supper either, late as it be. Have you?"

"There's nobody home at my house," said the boy.

"Then we'll eat," said the woman. "I believe you're hungry — or been hungry — to try to snatch my pocketbook!"

"I want a pair of blue suede shoes," said the boy.

"Well, you didn't have to snatch *my* pocketbook to get some suede shoes," said Mrs. Luella Bates Washington Jones. "You could of asked me."

"M'am?"

The water dripping from his face, the boy looked at her. There was a long pause. A very long pause. After he had dried his face, and not knowing what else to do, dried it again, the boy turned around, wondering what next. The door was open. He could make a dash for it down the hall. He could run, run, run, *run!*

The woman was sitting on the daybed. After a while she said, "I were young once and I wanted things I could not get."

There was another long pause. The boy's mouth opened. Then he frowned, not knowing he frowned.

The woman said, "Um-hum! You thought I was going to say *but*, didn't you? You thought I was going to say, *but I didn't snatch people's pocketbooks.* Well, I wasn't going to say that." Pause. Silence. "I have done things, too, which I would not tell you, son — neither tell God, if He didn't already know. Everybody's got something in common. So you set down while I fix us something to eat. You might run that comb through your hair so you will look presentable."

In another corner of the room behind a screen was a gas plate and an icebox. Mrs. Jones got up and went behind the screen. The woman did not watch the boy to see if he was going to run now, nor did she watch her purse, which she left behind her on the daybed. But the boy took care to sit on the far side of the room, away from the purse, where he thought she could easily see him out of the corner of her eye if she wanted to. He did not trust the

~~woman *not* to trust him.~~ And he did not want to be mistrusted now.

"Do you need somebody to go to the store," asked the boy, "maybe to get some milk or something?"

"Don't believe I do," said the woman, "unless you just want sweet milk yourself. I was going to make cocoa out of this canned milk I got here."

"That will be fine," said the boy.

She heated some lima beans and ham she had in the icebox, made the cocoa, and set the table. The woman did not ask the boy anything about where he lived, or his folks, or anything else that would embarrass him. Instead, as they ate, she told him about her job in a hotel beauty shop that stayed open late, what the work was like, and how all kinds of women came in and out, blondes, redheads, and Spanish. Then she cut him a half of her ten-cent cake.

"Eat some more, son," she said.

When they were finished eating, she got up and said, "Now here, take this ten dollars and buy yourself some blue suede shoes. And next time, do not make the mistake of latching onto *my* pocketbook *nor nobody else's* — because shoes got by devilish ways will burn your feet. I got to get my rest now. But from here on in, son, I hope you will behave yourself."

She led him down the hall to the front door and opened it. "Good night! Behave yourself, boy!" she said, looking out into the street as he went down the steps.

The boy wanted to say something other than, "Thank you, m'am," to Mrs. Luella Bates Washington Jones, but although his lips moved, he couldn't even say that as he turned at the foot of the barren stoop and looked up at the large woman in the door. Then she shut the door.

THE GILDED SIX-BITS

Zora Neale Hurston

IT was a Negro yard around a Negro house in a Negro settlement that looked to the payroll of the G. and G. Fertilizer works for its support.

But there was something happy about the place. The front yard was parted in the middle by a sidewalk from gate to doorstep, a sidewalk edged on either side by quart bottles driven neck down into the ground on a slant. A mess of homey flowers planted without a plan but blooming cheerily from their helter-skelter places. The fence and house were whitewashed. The porch and steps scrubbed white.

The front door stood open to the sunshine so that the floor of the front room could finish drying after its weekly scouring. It was Saturday. Everything clean from the front gate to the privy house. Yard raked so that the strokes of the rake would make a pattern. Fresh newspaper cut in fancy edge on the kitchen shelves.

Missie May was bathing herself in the galvanized washtub in the bedroom. Her dark-brown skin glistened under the soapsuds that skittered down from her washrag. Her stiff young breasts thrust forward aggressively, like broad-based cones with the tips lacquered in black.

She heard men's voices in the distance and glanced at the dollar clock on the dresser.

"Humph! Ah'm way behind time t'day! Joe gointer be heah 'fore Ah git mah clothes on if Ah don't make haste."

She grabbed the clean meal sack at hand and dried herself hurriedly and began to dress. But before she could tie her slippers, there came the ring of singing metal on wood. Nine times.

Missie May grinned with delight. She had not seen the big tall man come stealing in the gate and creep up the walk grinning happily at the joyful mischief he was about to commit. But she knew that it was her husband throwing silver dollars in the door for her to pick up and pile beside her plate at dinner. It was this way every Saturday afternoon. The nine dollars hurled into the open door, he scurried to a hiding place behind the Cape jasmine bush and waited.

Missie May promptly appeared at the door in mock alarm.

"Who dat chunkin' money in mah do'way?" she demanded. No answer from the yard. She leaped off the porch and began to search the shrubbery. She peeped under the porch and hung over the gate to look up and down the road. While she did this, the man behind the jasmine darted to the chinaberry tree. She spied him and gave chase.

"Nobody ain't gointer be chunkin' money at me and Ah not do 'em nothin'," she shouted in mock anger. He ran around the house with Missie May at his heels. She overtook him at the kitchen door. He ran inside but could not close it after him before she crowded in and locked with him in a rough-and-tumble. For several minutes the two were a furious mass of male and female energy. Shouting, laughing, twisting, turning, tussling, tickling each other in the ribs; Missie May clutching onto Joe and Joe trying, but not too hard, to get away.

"Missie May, take yo' hand out mah pocket!" Joe shouted out between laughs.

"Ah ain't, Joe, not lessen you gwine gimme whateve' it is good you got in yo' pocket. Turn it go, Joe, do Ah'll tear yo' clothes."

"Go on tear 'em. You de one dat pushes de needles round heah. Move yo' hand, Missie May."

"Lemme git dat paper sack out yo' pocket. Ah bet it's candy kisses."

"Tain't. Move yo' hand. Woman ain't got no business in a man's clothes nohow. Go way."

Missie May gouged way down and gave an upward jerk and triumphed.

"Unhhunh! Ah got it! It 'tis so candy kisses. Ah knowed you had somethin' for me in yo' clothes. Now Ah got to see whut's in every pocket you got."

Joe smiled indulgently and let his wife go through all of his pockets and take out the things that he had hidden there for her to find. She bore off the chewing gum, the cake of sweet soap, the pocket handkerchief as if she had wrested them from him, as if they had not been bought for the sake of this friendly battle.

"Whew! dat play-fight done got me all warmed up!" Joe exclaimed. "Got me some water in de kittle?"

"Yo' water is on de fire and yo' clean things is cross de bed. Hurry up and wash yo'self and git changed so we kin eat. Ah'm hongry." As Missie said this, she bore the steaming kettle into the bedroom.

"You ain't hongry, sugar," Joe contradicted her. "Youse jes' a little empty. Ah'm de one whut's hongry. Ah could eat up camp meetin', back off 'ssociation, and drink Jurdan dry. Have it on de table when Ah git out de tub."

"Don't you mess wid mah business, man. You git in yo' clothes. Ah'm a real wife, not no dress and breath. Ah might not look lak one, but if you burn me, you won't git a thing but wife ashes."

Joe splashed in the bedroom and Missie May fanned around in the kitchen. A fresh red-and-white checked cloth on the table. Big pitcher of buttermilk beaded with pale drops of butter from the churn. Hot fried mullet, crackling bread, ham hock atop a mound of string beans and new potatoes, and perched on the windowsill a pone of spicy potato pudding.

Very little talk during the meal but that little consisted of banter that pretended to deny affection but in reality flaunted it. Like when Missie May reached for a second helping of the tater pone. Joe snatched it out of her reach.

After Missie May had made two or three unsuccessful grabs at the pan, she begged, "Aw, Joe, gimme some mo' dat tater pone."

"Nope, sweetenin' is for us menfolks. Y'all pritty lil frail eels don't need nothin' lak dis. You too sweet already."

"Please, Joe."

"Naw, naw. Ah don't want you to git no sweeter than whut you is already. We goin' down de road a lil piece t'night so you go put on yo' Sunday-go-to-meetin' things."

Missie May looked at her husband to see if he was playing some prank. "Sho nuff, Joe?"

"Yeah. We goin' to de ice cream parlor."

"Where de ice cream parlor at, Joe?"

"A new man done come heah from Chicago and he done got a place and took and opened it up for a ice cream parlor, and bein' as it's real swell, Ah wants you to be one de first ladies to walk in dere and have some set down."

"Do Jesus, Ah ain't knowed nothin' 'bout it. Who de man done it?"

"Mister Otis D. Slemmons, of spots and places — Memphis, Chicago, Jacksonville, Philadelphia and so on."

"Dat heavyset man wid his mouth full of gold teeths?"

"Yeah. Where did you see 'im at?"

"Ah went down to de sto' tuh git a box of lye and Ah seen 'im standin' on de corner talkin' to some of de mens, and Ah come on back and went to scrubbin' de floor, and he passed and tipped his hat whilst Ah was scourin' de steps. Ah thought Ah never seen *him* befo'."

Joe smiled pleasantly. "Yeah, he's up-to-date. He got de finest clothes Ah ever seen on a colored man's back."

"Aw, he don't look no better in his clothes than you do in yourn. He got a puzzlegut on 'im and he so chuckleheaded he got a pone behind his neck."

Joe looked down at his own abdomen and said wistfully: "Wisht Ah had a build on me lak he got. He ain't puzzlegutted, honey. He jes' got a corperation. Dat make 'm look lak a rich white man. All rich mens is got some belly on 'em."

"Ah seen de pitchers of Henry Ford and he's a spare-built man and Rockefeller look lak he ain't got but one gut. But Ford and Rockefeller and dis Slemmons and all de rest kin be as many-gutted as dey please, Ah's satisfied wid you jes' lak you is, baby. God took pattern after a pine tree and built you noble. Youse a pritty man, and if Ah knowed any way to make you mo' pritty still Ah'd take and do it."

Joe reached over gently and toyed with Missie May's ear. "You jes' say dat cause you love me, but Ah know Ah can't hold no light to Otis D. Slemmons. Ah ain't never been nowhere and Ah ain't got nothin' but you."

Missie May got on his lap and kissed him and he kissed back in kind. Then he went on. "All de womens is crazy 'bout 'im everywhere he go."

"How you know dat, Joe?"

"He tole us so hisself."

"Dat don't make it so. His mouf is cut crossways, ain't it? Well, he kin lie jes' lak anybody else."

"Good Lawd, Missie! You womens sho is hard to sense into things. He's got a five-dollar gold piece for a stickpin and he got a ten-dollar gold piece on his watch chain and his mouf is jes' crammed full of gold teeths. Sho wisht it wuz mine. And whut make it so cool, he got money 'cumulated. And womens give it all to 'im."

"Ah don't see whut de womens see on 'im. Ah wouldn't give 'im a wink if de sheriff wuz after 'im."

"Well, he tole us how de white womens in Chicago give 'im all dat gold money. So he don't 'low nobody to touch it at all. Not even put day finger on it. Dey tole 'im not to. You kin make 'miration at it, but don't tetch it."

"Whyn't he stay up dere where dey so crazy 'bout 'im?"

"Ah reckon dey done made 'im vast-rich and he wants to travel some. He says dey wouldn't leave 'im hit a lick of work. He got mo' lady people crazy 'bout him than he kin shake a stick at."

"Joe, Ah hates to see you so dumb. Dat stray nigger jes' tell y'all anything and y'all b'lieve it."

"Go 'head on now, honey, and put on yo' clothes. He talkin' 'bout his pritty womens — Ah want 'im to see *mine*."

Missie May went off to dress and Joe spent the time trying to make his stomach punch out like Slemmons's middle. He tried the rolling swagger of the stranger, but found that his tall bone-and-muscle stride fitted ill with it. He just had time to drop back into his seat before Missie May came in dressed to go.

On the way home that night Joe was exultant. "Didn't Ah say ole Otis was swell? Can't he talk Chicago talk? Wuzn't dat funny whut he said when great big fat ole Ida Armstrong come in? He asted me, 'Who is dat broad wid de forte shake?' Dat's a new word. Us always thought forty was a set of figgers but he showed us where it means a whole heap of things. Sometimes he don't say forty, he jes' say thirty-eight and two and dat mean de same thing. Know whut he tole me when Ah wuz payin' for our ice cream? He say, 'Ah have to hand it to you, Joe. Dat wife of yours is jes' thirty-eight and two. Yessuh, she's forte!' Ain't he killin'?"

"He'll do in case of a rush. But he sho is got uh heap uh gold on 'im. Dat's de first time Ah ever seed gold money. It lookted good on him sho nuff, but it'd look a whole heap better on you."

"Who, me? Missie May, youse crazy! Where would a po' man lak me git gold money from?"

Missie May was silent for a minute, then she said, "Us might find some goin' long de road some time. Us could."

"Who would be losin' gold money round heah? We ain't even seen none dese white folks wearin' no gold money on dey watch chain. You must be figgerin' Mister Packard or Mister Cadillac goin' pass through heah."

"You don't know whut been lost 'round heah. Maybe somebody way back in memorial times lost they gold money and went on off and it ain't never been found. And then if we wuz to find it, you could wear some 'thout havin' no gang of womens lak dat Slemmons say he got."

Joe laughed and hugged her. "Don't be so wishful 'bout me. Ah'm satisfied de way Ah is. So long as Ah be yo' husband, Ah don't keer 'bout nothin' else. Ah'd ruther all de other womens in de world to be dead than for you to have de toothache. Less we go to bed and git our night rest."

It was Saturday night once more before Joe could parade his wife in Slemmons's ice cream parlor again. He worked the night shift and Saturday was his only night off. Every other evening around six o'clock he left home, and dying dawn saw him hustling home around the lake, where the challenging sun flung a flaming sword from east to west across the trembling water.

That was the best part of life — going home to Missie May. Their whitewashed house, the mock battle on Saturday, the dinner and ice cream parlor afterwards, church on Sunday nights when Missie outdressed any woman in town — all, everything, was right.

One night around eleven the acid ran out at the G. and G. The foreman knocked off the crew and let the steam die down. As Joe rounded the lake on his way home, a lean moon rode the lake in a silver boat. If anybody had asked Joe about the moon on the lake, he would have said he hadn't paid it any attention. But he saw it with his feelings. It made him yearn painfully for Missie. Creation obsessed him. He thought about children. They had been married more than a year now. They had money put away. They ought to be making little feet for shoes. A little boy child would be about right.

He saw a dim light in the bedroom and decided to come in through the kitchen door. He could wash the fertilizer dust off himself before presenting himself to Missie May. It would be nice for her not to know that he was there until he slipped into his place in bed and hugged her back. She always liked that.

He eased the kitchen door open slowly and silently, but when he went to set his dinner bucket on the table he bumped it into a pile of dishes, and something crashed to the floor. He heard his wife gasp in fright and hurried to reassure her.

"Iss me, honey. Don't git skeered."

There was a quick, large movement in the bedroom. A rustle, a thud, and a stealthy silence. The light went out.

What? Robbers? Murderers? Some varmint attacking his helpless wife, perhaps. He struck a match, threw himself on guard and stepped over the doorsill into the bedroom.

The great belt on the wheel of Time slipped and eternity stood still. By the match light he could see the man's legs fighting with his breeches in his frantic desire to get them on. He had both chance and time to kill the intruder in his helpless condition — half in and half out of his pants — but he was too weak to take action. The shapeless enemies of humanity that live in the hours of Time had waylaid Joe. He was assaulted in his weakness. Like Samson awakening after his haircut. So he just opened his mouth and laughed.

The match went out and he struck another and lit the lamp. A howling wind raced across his heart, but underneath its fury he heard his wife sobbing and Slemmons pleading for his life. Offering to buy it with all that he had. "Please, suh, don't kill me. Sixty-two dollars at de sto'. Gold money."

Joe just stood. Slemmons looked at the window, but it was screened. Joe stood out like a rough-backed mountain between him and the door. Barring him from escape, from sunrise, from life.

He considered a surprise attack upon the big clown that stood there laughing like a chessy cat. But before his fist could travel an inch, Joe's own rushed out to crush him like a battering ram. Then Joe stood over him.

"Git into yo' damn rags, Slemmons, and dat quick."

Slemmons scrambled to his feet and into his vest and coat. As he grabbed his hat, Joe's fury overrode his intentions and he grabbed at Slemmons with his left hand and struck at him with his right. The right landed. The left grazed the front of his vest. Slemmons was knocked a somersault into the kitchen and fled through the open door. Joe found himself alone with Missie May, with the golden watch charm clutched in his left fist. A short bit of broken chain dangled between his fingers.

Missie May was sobbing. Wails of weeping without words. Joe stood, and after a while he found out that he had something in his hand. And then he stood and felt without thinking and without seeing with his natural eyes. Missie May kept on crying and Joe kept on feeling so much, and not knowing what to do with all his feelings, he put Slemmons's watch charm in his pants pocket and took a good laugh and went to bed.

"Missie May, whut you cryin' for?"

"Cause Ah love you so hard and Ah know you don't love *me* no mo'."

Joe sank his face into the pillow for a spell, then he said huskily, "You don't know de feelings of dat yet, Missie May."

"Oh Joe, honey, he said he wuz gointer give me dat gold money and he jes' kept on after me —"

Joe was very still and silent for a long time. Then he said, "Well, don't cry no mo', Missie May. Ah got yo' gold piece for you."

The hours went past on their rusty ankles. Joe still and quiet on one bed rail and Missie May wrung dry of sobs on the other. Finally the sun's tide crept upon the shore of night and drowned all its hours. Missie May with her face stiff and streaked towards the window saw the dawn come into her yard. It was day. Nothing more. Joe wouldn't be coming home as usual. No need to fling open the front door and sweep off the porch, making it nice for Joe. Never no more breakfast to cook; no more washing and starching of Joe's jumper-jackets and pants. No more nothing. So why get up?

With this strange man in her bed, she felt embarrassed to get up and dress. She decided to wait till he had dressed and gone. Then she would get up, dress quickly and be gone forever beyond reach of Joe's looks and laughs. But he never moved. Red light turned to yellow, then white.

From beyond the no-man's land between them came a voice. A strange voice that yesterday had been Joe's.

"Missie May, ain't you gonna fix me no breakfus'?"

She sprang out of bed. "Yeah, Joe. Ah didn't reckon you wuz hongry."

No need to die today. Joe needed her for a few more minutes anyhow.

Soon there was a roaring fire in the cookstove. Water bucket full and two chickens killed. Joe loved fried chicken and rice. She didn't deserve a thing and good Joe was letting her cook him some breakfast. She rushed hot biscuits to the table as Joe took his seat.

He ate with his eyes in his plate. No laughter, no banter.

"Missie May, you ain't eatin' yo' breakfus'."

"Ah don't choose none, Ah thank yuh."

His coffee cup was empty. She sprang to refill it. When she turned from the stove and bent to set the cup beside Joe's plate, she saw the yellow coin on the table between them.

She slumped into her seat and wept into her arms.

Presently Joe said calmly, "Missie May, you cry too much. Don't look back lak Lot's wife and turn to salt."

The sun, the hero of every day, the impersonal old man that beams as brightly on death as on birth, came up every morning and raced across the blue dome and dipped into the sea of fire every morning. Water ran downhill and birds nested.

Missie knew why she didn't leave Joe. She couldn't. She loved him too much, but she could not understand why Joe didn't leave her. He was polite, even kind at times, but aloof.

There were no more Saturday romps. No ringing silver dollars to stack beside her plate. No pockets to rifle. In fact, the yellow coin in his trousers was like a monster hiding in the cave of his pockets to destroy her.

She often wondered if he still had it, but nothing could have induced her to ask nor yet to explore his pockets to see for herself. Its shadow was in the house whether or no.

One night Joe came home around midnight and complained of pains in the back. He asked Missie to rub him down with liniment. It had been three months since Missie had touched his body and it all seemed strange. But she rubbed him. Grateful for the chance. Before morning youth triumphed and Missie exulted. But the next day, as she joyfully made up their bed, beneath her pillow she found the piece of money with the bit of chain attached.

Alone to herself, she looked at the thing with loathing, but look she must. She took it into her hands with trembling and saw first thing that it was no gold piece. It was a gilded half dollar. Then she knew why Slemmons had forbidden anyone to touch his gold. He trusted village eyes at a distance not to recognize his stickpin as a gilded quarter, and his watch charm as a four-bit piece.

She was glad at first that Joe had left it there. Perhaps he was through with her punishment. They were man and wife again. Then another thought came clawing at her. He had come home to buy from her as if she were any woman in the longhouse. Fifty cents for her love. As if to say that he could pay as well as Slemmons. She slid the coin into his Sunday pants pocket and dressed herself and left his house.

Halfway between her house and the quarters she met her husband's mother, and after a short talk she turned and went back home. Never would she admit defeat to that woman who prayed for it nightly. If she had not the substance of marriage she had the outside show. Joe must leave *her*. She let him see she didn't want his old gold four-bits, too.

She saw no more of the coin for some time though she knew that Joe could not help finding it in his pocket. But his health kept poor, and he came home at least every ten days to be rubbed.

The sun swept around the horizon, trailing its robes of weeks and days. One morning as Joe came in from work, he found Missie May chopping wood. Without a word he took the ax and chopped a huge pile before he stopped.

"You ain't got no business choppin' wood, and you know it."

"How come? Ah been choppin' it for de last longest."

"Ah ain't blind. You makin' feet for shoes."

"Won't you be glad to have a lil baby chile, Joe?"

"You know dat 'thout astin' me."

"Iss gointer be a boy chile and de very spit of you."

"You reckon, Missie May?"

"Who else could it look lak?"

Joe said nothing, but he thrust his hand deep into his pocket and fingered something there.

It was almost six months later Missie May took to bed and Joe went and got his mother to come wait on the house.

Missie May was delivered of a fine boy. Her travail was over when Joe came in from work one morning. His mother and the old women were drinking great bowls of coffee around the fire in the kitchen.

The minute Joe came into the room his mother called him aside.

"How did Missie May make out?" he asked quickly.

"Who, dat gal? She strong as a ox. She gointer have plenty mo'. We done fixed her wid de sugar and lard to sweeten her for de nex' one."

Joe stood silent awhile.

"You ain't ask 'bout de baby, Joe. You oughter be mighty proud cause he sho is de spittin' image of yuh, son. Dat's yourn all right, if you never git another one, dat un is yourn. And you know Ah'm mighty proud too, son, cause Ah never thought well of you marryin' Missie May cause her ma used tuh fan her foot round right smart and Ah been mighty skeered dat Missie May wuz gointer git misput on her road."

Joe said nothing. He fooled around the house till late in the day, then, just before he went to work, he went and stood at the foot of the bed and asked his wife how she felt. He did this every day during the week.

On Saturday he went to Orlando to make his market. It had been a long time since he had done that.

Meat and lard, meal and flour, soap and starch. Cans of corn and tomatoes. All the staples. He fooled around town for a while and bought bananas and apples. Way after while he went around to the candy store.

"Hello, Joe," the clerk greeted him. "Ain't seen you in a long time."

"Nope, Ah ain't been heah. Been round in spots and places."

"Want some of them molasses kisses you always buy?"

"Yessuh." He threw the gilded half dollar on the counter. "Will dat spend?"

"Whut is it, Joe? Well, I'll be doggone! A gold-plated four-bit piece. Where'd you git it, Joe?"

"Offen a stray nigger dat come through Eatonville. He had it on his watch chain for a charm — goin' round making out iss gold money. Ha ha! He had a quarter on his tiepin and it wuz all golded up too. Tryin' to fool people. Makin' out he so rich and everything. Ha! Ha! Tryin' to tole off folkses wives from home."

"How did you git it, Joe? Did he fool you, too?"

"Who, me? Naw suh! He ain't fooled me none. Know whut Ah done? He come round me wid his smart talk. Ah hauled off and knocked 'im down and took his old four-bits away from 'im. Gointer buy my wife some good ole lasses kisses wid it. Gimme fifty cents worth of dem candy kisses."

"Fifty cents buys a mighty lot of candy kisses, Joe. Why don't you split it up and take some chocolate bars, too? They eat good, too."

"Yessuh, dey do, but Ah wants all dat in kisses. Ah got a lil boy chile home now. Tain't a week old yet, but he kin suck a sugar tit and maybe eat one them kisses hisself."

Joe got his candy and left the store. The clerk turned to the next customer. "Wisht I could be like these darkies. Laughin' all the time. Nothin' worries 'em."

Back in Eatonville, Joe reached his own front door. There was the ring of singing metal on wood. Fifteen times. Missie May couldn't run to the door, but she crept there as quickly as she could.

"Joe Banks, Ah hear you chunkin' money in mah do'way. You wait till Ah got mah strength back and Ah'm gointer fix you for dat."

THE REVOLT OF THE EVIL FAIRIES

Ted Poston

THE grand dramatic offering of the Booker T. Washington Colored Grammar School was the biggest event of the year in our social life in Hopkinsville, Kentucky. It was the one occasion on which they let us use the old Cooper Opera House, and even some of the white folks came out yearly to applaud our presentation. The first two rows of the orchestra were always reserved for our white friends, and our leading colored citizens sat right behind them — with an empty row intervening, of course.

Mr. Ed Smith, our local undertaker, invariably occupied a box to the left of the house and wore his cutaway coat and striped breeches. This distinctive garb was usually reserved for those rare occasions when he officiated at the funerals of our most prominent colored citizens. Mr. Thaddeus Long, our colored mailman, once rented a tuxedo and bought a box too. But nobody paid him much mind. We knew he was just showing off.

The title of our play never varied. It was always Prince Charming and the Sleeping Beauty, but no two presentations were ever the same. Miss H. Belle LaPrade, our sixth-grade teacher, rewrote the script every season, and it was never like anything you read in the storybooks.

Miss LaPrade called it "a modern morality play of conflict between the forces of good and evil." And the forces of evil, of course, always came off second best.

The Booker T. Washington Colored Grammar School was in a state of ferment from Christmas until February, for this was the period when parts were assigned. First there was the selection of the Good Fairies and the Evil Fairies. This was very important, because the Good Fairies wore white costumes and the Evil Fairies black. And strangely enough most of the Good Fairies usually turned out to be extremely light in complexion, with straight hair and white folks' features. On rare occasions a darkskinned girl might be lucky enough to be a Good Fairy, but not one with a speaking part.

There never was any doubt about Prince Charming and the Sleeping Beauty. They were always lightskinned. And though nobody ever discussed those things openly, it was an accepted fact that a lack of pigmentation was a decided advantage in the Prince Charming and Sleeping Beauty sweepstakes.

And therein lay my personal tragedy. I made the best grades in my class, I was the leading debater, and the scion of a respected family in the community. But I could never be Prince Charming, because I was black.

In fact, every year when they started casting our grand dramatic offering my family started pricing black cheesecloth at Franklin's Department Store. For they knew that I would be leading the forces of darkness and skulking back in the shadows — waiting to be vanquished in the third act. Mamma had experience with this sort of thing. All my brothers had finished Booker T. before me.

Not that I was alone in my disappointment. Many of my classmates felt it too. I probably just took it more to heart. Rat Jointer, for instance, could rationalize the situation. Rat was not only black; he lived on Billy Goat Hill. But Rat summed it up like this:

"If you black, you black."

I should have been able to regard the matter calmly too. For our grand dramatic offering was only a reflection of our daily community life in Hopkinsville. The yallers had the best of everything. They held most of the teaching jobs in Booker T. Washington Colored Grammar School. They were the Negro doctors, the lawyers, the insurance men. They even had a "Blue Vein Society," and if your dark skin obscured your throbbing pulse you were hardly a member of the elite.

Yet I was inconsolable the first time they turned me down for Prince Charming. That was the year they picked Roger Jackson. Roger was not only dumb; he stuttered. But he was light enough to pass for white, and that was apparently sufficient.

In all fairness, however, it must be admitted that Roger had other qualifications. His father owned the only colored saloon in town and was quite a power in local politics. In fact, Mr. Clinton Jackson had a lot to say about just who taught in the Booker T. Washington Colored Grammar School. So it was understandable that Roger should have been picked for Prince Charming.

My real heartbreak, however, came the year they picked Sarah Williams for Sleeping Beauty. I had been in love with Sarah since kindergarten. She had soft light hair, bluish-gray eyes, and a dimple which stayed in her left cheek whether she was smiling or not.

Of course Sarah never encouraged me much. She never answered any of my fervent love letters, and Rat was very scornful of my one-sided love affairs. "As long as she don't call you a black baboon," he sneered, "you'll keep on hanging around."

After Sarah was chosen for Sleeping Beauty, I went out for the Prince Charming role with all my heart. If I had declaimed boldly in previous contests, I was matchless now. If I had bothered Mamma with rehearsals at home before, I pestered her to death this time. Yes, and I purloined my sister's can of Palmer's Skin Success.

I knew the Prince's role from start to finish, having played the Head Evil Fairy opposite it for two seasons. And Prince Charming was one character whose lines Miss LaPrade never varied much in her many versions. But although I never admitted it, even to myself, I knew I was doomed from the start. They gave the part to Leonardius Wright. Leonardius, of course, was yarrler.

The teachers sensed my resentment. They were almost apologetic. They pointed out that I had been such a splendid Head Evil Fairy for two seasons that it would be a crime to let anybody else try the role. They reminded me that Mamma wouldn't have to buy any more cheesecloth because I could use my same old costume. They insisted that the Head Evil Fairy was even more important than Prince Charming because he was the one who cast the spell on Sleeping Beauty. So what could I do but accept?

I had never liked Leonardius Wright. He was a goody-goody, and even Mamma was always throwing him up to me. But, above all, he too was in love with Sarah Williams. And now he got a chance to kiss Sarah every day in rehearsing the awakening scene.

Well, the show must go on, even for little black boys. So I

threw my soul into my part and made the Head Evil Fairy a character to be remembered. When I drew back from the couch of Sleeping Beauty and slunk away into the shadows at the approach of Prince Charming, my facial expression was indeed something to behold. When I was vanquished by the shining sword of Prince Charming in the last act, I was a little hammy perhaps — but terrific!

The attendance at our grand dramatic offering that year was the best in its history. Even the white folks overflowed the two rows reserved for them, and a few were forced to sit in the intervening one. This created a delicate situation, but everybody tactfully ignored it.

When the curtain went up on the last act, the audience was in fine fettle. Everything had gone well for me too — except for one spot in the second act. That was where Leonardius unexpectedly rapped me over the head with his sword as I slunk off into the shadows. That was not in the script, but Miss LaPrade quieted me down by saying it made a nice touch anyway. Rat said Leonardius did it on purpose.

The third act went on smoothly, though, until we came to the vanquishing scene. That was where I slunk from the shadows for the last time and challenged Prince Charming to mortal combat. The hero reached for his shining sword — a bit unsportsmanlike, I always thought, since Miss LaPrade consistently left the Head Evil Fairy unarmed — and then it happened!

Later I protested loudly — but in vain — that it was a case of self-defense. I pointed out that Leonardius had a mean look in his eye. I cited the impromptu rapping he had given my head in the second act. But nobody would listen. They just wouldn't believe that Leonardius really intended to brain me when he reached for his sword.

Anyway, he didn't succeed. For the minute I saw that evil gleam in his eye — or was it my own? — I cut loose with a right to the chin, and Prince Charming dropped his shining sword and staggered back. His astonishment lasted only a minute, though, for he lowered his head and came charging in, fists flailing. There was nothing yellow about Leonardius but his skin.

The audience thought the scrap was something new Miss LaPrade had written in. They might have kept on thinking so if

Miss LaPrade hadn't been screaming so hysterically from the sidelines. And if Rat Joiner hadn't decided that this was as good a time as any to settle old scores. So he turned around and took a sock at the male Good Fairy nearest him.

When the curtain rang down, the forces of Good and Evil were locked in combat. And Sleeping Beauty was wide awake and streaking for the wings.

They rang the curtain back up fifteen minutes later, and we finished the play. I lay down and expired according to specifications but Prince Charming will probably remember my sneering corpse to his dying day. They wouldn't let me appear in the grand dramatic offering at all the next year. But I didn't care. I couldn't have been Prince Charming anyway.

ALMOS' A MAN

Richard Wright

DAVE struck out across the fields, looking homeward through paling light. Whut's the usa talkin wid em niggers in the field? Anyhow, his mother was putting supper on the table. Them niggers can't understan nothing. One of these days he was going to get a gun and practice shooting, then they can't talk to him as though he were a little boy. He slowed, looking at the ground. Shucks, Ah ain scareda them even ef they are biggern me! Aw, Ah know whut Ahma do. . . . Ahm going by ol Joe's sto n git that Sears Roebuck catlog n look at them guns. Mabbe Ma will lemme buy one when she gits mah pay from ol man Hawkins. Ahma beg her t gimme some money. Ahm ol ernough to hava gun. Ahm seventeen. Almos a man. He strode, feeling his long, loose-jointed limbs. Shucks, a man oughta hava little gun aftah he done worked hard all day. . . .

He came in sight of Joe's store. A yellow lantern glowed on the front porch. He mounted steps and went through the screen door, hearing it bang behind him. There was a strong smell of coal oil and mackerel fish. He felt very confident until he saw fat Joe walk in through the rear door, then his courage began to ooze.

"Howdy, Dave! Whutcha want?"

"How yuh, Mistah Joe? Aw, Ah don wanna buy nothing. Ah jus wanted t see ef yuhd lemme look at tha ol catlog erwhile."

"Sure! You wanna see it here?"

"Nawsuh. Ah wans t take it home wid me. Ahll bring it back termorrow when Ah come in from the fiels."

"You plannin on buyin something?"

"Yessuh."

"Your ma letting you have your own money now?"

"Shucks. Mistah Joe, Ahm gittin t be a man like anybody else!"

Joe laughed and wiped his greasy white face with a red bandanna.

"Whut you plannin on buyin?"

Dave looked at the floor, scratched his head, scratched his thigh, and smiled. Then he looked up shyly.

"Ahll tell yuh, Mistah Joe, ef yuh promise yuh won't tell."

"I promise."

"Waal, Ahma buy a gun."

"A gun? Whut you want with a gun?"

"Ah wanna keep it."

"You ain't nothing but a boy. You don't need a gun."

"Aw, lemme have the catlog, Mistah Joe. Ahll bring it back."

Joe walked through the rear door. Dave was elated. He looked around at barrels of sugar and flour. He heard Joe coming back. He craned his neck to see if he were bringing the book. Yeah, he's got it! Gawddog, he's got it!

"Here, but be sure you bring it back. It's the only one I got."

"Sho, Mistah Joe."

"Say, if you wanna buy a gun, why don't you buy one from me? I gotta gun to sell."

"Will it shoot?"

"Sure it'll shoot."

"Whut kind is it?"

"Oh, it's kinda old. . . . A lefthand Wheeler. A pistol. A big one."

"Is it got bullets in it?"

"It's loaded."

"Kin Ah see it?"

"Where's your money?"

"Whut yuh wan fer it?"

"I'll let you have it for two dollars."

"Just two dollahs? Shucks, Ah could buy tha when Ah git mah pay."

"I'll have it here when you want it."

"Awright, suh. Ah be in fer it."

He went through the door, hearing it slam again behind him. Ahma git some money from Ma n buy me a gun! Only two dollahs! He tucked the thick catalogue under his arm and hurried.

"Where yuh been, boy?" His mother held a steaming dish of black-eyed peas.

"Aw, Ma, Ah jus stopped down the road t talk wid th boys."

"Yuh know bettah than t keep suppah waitin."

He sat down, resting the catalogue on the edge of the table.

"Yuh git up from there and git to the well n wash yosef! Ah ain feedin no hogs in mah house!"

She grabbed his shoulder and pushed him. He stumbled out of the room, then came back to get the catalogue.

"Whut this?"

"Aw, Ma, it's jusa catlog."

"Who yuh git it from?"

"From Joe, down at the sto."

"Waal, thas good. We kin use it around the house."

"Naw, Ma." He grabbed for it. "Gimme mah catlog, Ma."

She held onto it and glared at him.

"Quit hollerin at me! Whut's wrong wid yuh? Yuh crazy?"

"But Ma, please. It ain mine! It's Joe's! He tol me t bring it back t im termorrow."

She gave up the book. He stumbled down the back steps, hugging the thick book under his arm. When he had splashed water on his face and hands, he groped back to the kitchen and fumbled in a corner for the towel. He bumped into a chair; it clattered to the floor. The catalogue sprawled at his feet. When he had dried his eyes, he snatched up the book and held it again under his arm. His mother stood watching him.

"Now, ef yuh gonna acka fool over that ol book, Ahll take it n burn it up."

"Naw, Ma, please."

"Waal, set down n be still!"

He sat down and drew the oil lamp close. He thumbed page after page, unaware of the food his mother set on the table. His father came in. Then his small brother.

"Whutcha got there, Dave?" his father asked.

"Jusa catlog," he answered, not looking up.

"Yawh, here they is!" His eyes glowed at blue and black revolvers. He glanced up, feeling sudden guilt. His father was watching him. He eased the book under the table and rested it on his knees. After the blessing was asked, he ate. He scooped up peas and swallowed fat meat without chewing. Buttermilk helped to wash it down. He did not want to mention money before his father. He would do much better by cornering his mother when she was alone. He looked at his father uneasily out of the edge of his eye.

"Boy, how come yuh don quit foolin wid tha book n eat yo suppah."

"Yessuh."

"How yuh n ol man Hawkins gittin erlong?"

"Shuh?"

"Can't yuh hear. Why don yuh listen? Ah ast yuh how wuz yuh n ol man Hawkins gittin erlong?"

"Oh, swell, Pa. Ah plows mo lan than anybody over there."

"Waal, yuh oughta keep yo min on whut yuh doin."

"Yessuh."

He poured his plate full of molasses and sopped at it slowly with a dunk of cornbread. When all but his mother had left the kitchen he still sat and looked again at the guns in the catalogue. Lawd, ef Ah only had the pretty one! He could almost feel the slickness of the weapon with his fingers. If he had a gun like that he would polish it and keep it shining so it would never rust. N Ahd keep it loaded, by Gawd!

"Ma?"

"Hunh?"

"Ol man Hawkins give yuh mah money yit?"

"Yeah, but ain no usa yuh thinin bout thowin nona it erway. Ahm keepin tha money sos yuh kin have cloes t go to school this winter."

He rose and went to her side with the open catalogue in his palms. She was washing dishes, her head bent low over a pan. Shyly he raised the open book. When he spoke his voice was husky, faint.

"Ma, Gawd knows Ah wans one of these."

"One of whut?" she asked, not raising her eyes.

"One of these," he said again, not daring even to point. She glanced up at the page, then at him with wide eyes.

"Nigger, is yuh gone plum crazy?"

"Aw, Ma —"

"Git outta here! Don't yuh talk t me bout no gun! Yuh a fool!"

"Ma, Ah kin buy one fer two dollahs."

"Not ef Ah knows it yuh ain!"

"But yuh promised one more —"

"Ah don care whut Ah promised! Yuh ain nothing but a boy yit!"

"Ma, ef yuh lemme buy one Ahll never ast yuh fer nothing no mo."

"Ah tol yuh t git outta here! Yuh ain gonna toucha penny of tha money fer no gun! Thas how come Ah has Mistah Hawkins pay yo wages t me, cause Ah knows yuh ain got no sense."

"But Ma, we needa gun. Pa ain got no gun. We needa gun in the house. Yuh kin never tell whut might happen."

"Now don yuh try to maka fool outta me, boy! Ef we did hava gun yuh wouldn't have it!"

He laid the catalogue down and slipped his arm around her waist. "Aw, Ma, Ah done worked hard alls summer n ain ast yuh fer nothing, is Ah, now?"

"Thas whut yuh spose t do!"

"But Ma. Ah wants a gun. Yuh kin lemme have two dollah outa mah money. Please Ma. I kin give it to Pa. . . . Please, Ma! Ah loves yuh, Ma."

When she spoke her voice came soft and low.

"What yuh wan wida gun, Dave? Yuh don need no gun. Yuhll git in trouble. N ef yo Pa jus thought Ah letyuh have money t buy a gun he'd hava fit."

"Ahll hide it, Ma. It ain but two dollahs."

"Lawd, chil, whuts wrong wid yuh?"

"Ain nothing wrong, Ma. Ahm almos a man now. Ah wants a gun."

"Who gonna sell yuh a gun?"

"Ol Joe at the sto."

"N it don cos but two dollahs?"

"Thas all, Ma. Just two dollahs. Please, Ma."

She was stacking the plates away; her hands moved slowly, reflectively. Dave kept an anxious silence. Finally she turned to him.

"Ahll let yuh git the gun ef yuh promise me one thing."

"Whuts tha, Ma?"

"Yuh bring it straight back t me, yuh hear? It'll be fer Pa."

"Yessum! Lemme go now, Ma."

She stooped, turned slightly to one side, raised the hem of her dress, rolled down the top of her stocking, and came up with a slender wad of bills.

"Here," she said. "Lawd knows yuh don need no gun. But yer Pa does. Yuh bring it right back t me, yuh hear. Ahma put it up. Now ef yuh don, Ahma have yuh Pa lick yuh so hard yuh won ferget it."

"Yessum."

He took the money, ran down the steps, and across the yard.

"Dave! Yuuuuuuh Daaaaaave!"

He heard, but he was not going to stop now. "Naw, Lawd!"

The first movement he made the following morning was to reach under his pillow for the gun. In the gray light of dawn he held it loosely, feeling a sense of power. Could killa man wida gun like this. Kill anybody, black or white. And if he were holding this gun in his hand nobody could run over him; they would have to respect him. It was a big gun, with a long barrel and a heavy handle. He raised and lowered it in his hand, marveling at its weight.

He had not come straight home with it as his mother had asked; instead he had stayed out in the fields, holding the weapon in his hand, aiming it now and then at some imaginary foe. But he had not fired it; he had been afraid that his father might hear. Also he was not sure he knew how to fire it.

To avoid surrendering the pistol he had not come into the house until he knew that all were asleep. When his mother had tiptoed to his bedside late that night and demanded the gun, he had first played 'possum; then he had told her that the gun was hidden outdoors, that he would bring it to her in the morning. Now he lay turning it slowly in his hands. He broke it, took out the cartridges, felt them, and then put them back.

He slid out of bed, got a long strip of old flannel from a trunk, wrapped the gun in it, and tied it to his naked thigh while it was still loaded. He did not go in to breakfast. Even though it was not yet daylight, he started for Jim Hawkins's plantation. Just as the sun was rising he reached the barns where the mules and plows were kept.

"Hey! That you, Dave?"

He turned. Jim Hawkins stood eyeing him suspiciously.

"What're yuh doing here so early?"

"Ah didn't know Ah wuz gittin up so early, Mistah Hawkins. Ah wuz fixing hitch up of Jenny n take her t the fiels."

"Good. Since you're here so early, how about plowing that stretch down by the woods?"

"Suits me, Mistah Hawkins."

"O.K. Go to it!"

He hitched Jenny to a plow and started across the fields. Hot dog! This was just what he wanted. If he could get down by the woods, he could shoot his gun and nobody would hear. He walked behind the plow, hearing the traces creaking, feeling the gun tied tight to his thigh.

When he reached the woods, he plowed two whole rows before he decided to take out the gun. Finally he stopped, looked in all directions, then untied the gun and held it in his hand. He turned to the mule and smiled.

"Know whut this is, Jenny? Naw, yuh wouldn't know! Yuhs just ol mule! Anyhow, this is a gun, n it kin shoot, by Gawd!"

He held the gun at arm's length. Whut t hell, Ahma shoot this thing! He looked at Jenny again.

"Lissen here, Jenny! When Ah pull this ol trigger Ah don wan yuh t run n acka fool now."

Jenny stood with head down, her short ears pricked straight. Dave walked off about twenty feet, held the gun far out from him, at arm's length, and turned his head. Hell, he told himself, Ah ain afraid. The gun felt loose in his fingers; he waved it wildly for a moment. Then he shut his eyes and tightened his forefinger. Bloom! The report half-deafened him and he thought his right hand was torn from his arm. He heard Jenny whinnying and galloping over the field, and he found himself on his knees squeezing his fingers hard between his legs. His hand was numb; he jammed it into his mouth, trying to warm it, trying to stop the pain. The gun lay at his feet. He did not quite know what had happened. He stood up and stared at the gun as though it were a living thing. He gritted his teeth and kicked the gun. Yuh almos broke mah arm! He turned to look for Jenny; she was far over the fields, tossing her head and kicking wildly.

"Hol on there, ol mule!"

When he caught up with her she stood trembling, walling her big white eyes at him. The plow was far away; the traces had broken. Then Dave stopped short, looking, not believing. Jenny was bleeding. Her left side was red and wet with blood. He went closer. Lawd, have mercy! Wondah did Ah shoot this mule? He grabbed for Jenny's mane. She flinched, snorted, whirled, tossing her head.

"Hol on now! Hol on."

Then he saw the hole in Jenny's side, right between the ribs. It was round, wet, red. A crimson stream streaked down the front leg, flowing fast. Good Gawd! Ah wuzn't shootin at tha mule. He felt panic. He knew he had to stop that blood, or Jenny would bleed to death. He had never seen so much blood in all his life. He chased the mule for half a mile, trying to catch her. Finally she stopped, breathing hard, stumpy tail half arched. He caught her mane and led her back to where the plow and gun lay. Then he stooped and grabbed handfuls of damp black earth and tried to plug the bullet hole. Jenny shuddered, whinnied, and broke from him.

"Hol on! Hol on now!"

He tried to plug it again, but blood came anyhow. His fingers were hot and sticky. He rubbed dirt into his palms, trying to dry them. Then again he attempted to plug the bullet hole, but Jenny shied away, kicking her heels high. He stood helpless. He had to do something. He ran at Jenny; she dodged him. He watched a red stream of blood flow down Jenny's leg and form a bright pool at her feet.

"Jenny . . . Jenny . . ." he called weakly.

His lips trembled! She's bleeding t death! He looked in the direction of home, wanting to go back, wanting to get help. But he saw the pistol lying in the damp black clay. He had a queer feeling that if he only did something, this would not be; Jenny would not be there bleeding to death.

When he went to her this time, she did not move. She stood with sleepy, dreamy eyes; and when he touched her she gave a low-pitched whinny and knelt to the ground, her front knees slopping in blood.

"Jenny . . . Jenny . . ." he whispered.

For a long time she held her neck erect; then her head sank, slowly. Her ribs swelled with a mighty heave and she went over.

Dave's stomach felt empty, very empty. He picked up the gun and held it gingerly between his thumb and forefinger. He buried it at the foot of a tree. He took a stick and tried to cover the pool of blood with dirt — but what was the use? There was Jenny lying with her mouth open and her eyes walled and glassy. He could not tell Jim Hawkins he had shot his mule. But he had to tell him something. Yeah, Ahll tell em Jenny started gittin wil n fell on the joint of the plow. . . . But that would hardly happen to a mule. He walked across the field slowly, head down.

It was sunset. Two of Jim Hawkins's men were over near the edge of the woods digging a hole in which to bury Jenny. Dave was surrounded by a knot of people; all of them were looking down at the dead mule.

"I don't see how in the world it happened," said Jim Hawkins for the tenth time.

The crowd parted and Dave's mother, father, and small brother pushed into the center.

"Where Dave?" his mother called.

"There he is," said Jim Hawkins.

His mother grabbed him.

"Whut happened, Dave? Whut yuh done?"

"Nothing."

"C'mon, boy, talk," his father said.

Dave took a deep breath and told the story he knew nobody believed.

"Waal," he drawled. "Ah brung ol Jenny down here sos Ah could do mah plowin. Ah plowed bout two rows, just like yuh see." He stopped and pointed at the long rows of upturned earth. "Then something musta been wrong wid ol Jenny. She wouldn't ack right a-tall. She started snortin n kickin her heels. Ah tried to hol her, but she pulled erway, rearin n goin on. Then when the point of the plow was stickin up in the air, she swung erroun n twisted herself back on it. . . . She stuck herself n started t bleed. N fo Ah could do anything, she wuz dead."

"Did you ever hear of anything like that in all your life?" asked Jim Hawkins.

There were white and black standing in the crowd. They murmured. Dave's mother came close to him and looked hard into his face.

"Tell the truth, Dave," she said.

"Looks like a bullet hole ter me," said one man.

"Dave, whut yuh do wid tha gun?" his mother asked.

The crowd surged in, looking at him. He jammed his hands into his pockets, shook his head slowly from left to right, and backed away. His eyes were wide and painful.

"Did he hava gun?" asked Jim Hawkins.

"By Gawd, Ah tol yuh tha wuz a gunwound," said a man, slapping his thigh.

His father caught his shoulders and shook him till his teeth rattled.

"Tell whut happened, yuh rascal! Tell whut . . ."

Dave looked at Jenny's stiff legs and began to cry.

"Whut yuh do wid tha gun?" his mother asked.

"Come on and tell the truth," said Hawkins. "Ain't nobody going to hurt you. . . ."

His mother crowded close to him.

"Did yuh shoot tha mule, Dave?"

Dave cried, seeing blurred white and black faces.

"Ahh ddinnt gggo tt sshoooot hher. . . . Ah ssswear off Gawd Ahh ddint. . . . Ah wuz a-tryin t sssee ef the ol gggun would sshoot —"

"Where yuh git the gun from?" his father asked.

"Ah got it from Joe, at the sto."

"Where yuh git the money?"

"Ma give it t me."

"He kept worryin me, Bob. . . . Ah had t. . . . Ah tol im t bring the gun right back t me. . . . It was fer yuh, the gun."

"But how yuh happen to shoot that mule?" asked Jim Hawkins.

"Ah wuznt shootin at the mule, Mistah Hawkins. The gun jumped when Ah pulled the trigger . . . N for Ah knowed anything Jenny wuz there a-bleedin."

Somebody in the crowd laughed. Jim Hawkins walked close to Dave and looked into his face.

"Well, looks like you have bought you a mule, Dave."

"Ah swear for Gawd, Ah didn't go t kill the mule, Mistah Hawkins!"

"But you killed her!"

All the crowd was laughing now. They stood on tiptoe and poked heads over one another's shoulders.

"Well, boy, looks like yuh done bought a dead mule! Hahaha!"

"Ain tha ershame."

"Hohohohoho."

Dave stood, head down, twisting his feet in the dirt.

"Well, you needn't worry about it, Bob," said Jim Hawkins to Dave's father. "Just let the boy keep on working and pay me two dollars a month."

"Whut yuh wan fer yo mule, Mistah Hawkins?"

Jim Hawkins screwed up his eyes.

"Fifty dollars."

"Whut yuh do wid tha gun?" Dave's father demanded.

Dave said nothing.

"Yuh wan me t take a tree lim n beat yuh till yuh talk!"

"Nawsuh!"

"Whut yuh do wid it?"

"Ah thowed it erway."

"Where?"

"Ah . . . Ah thowed it in the creek."

"Waal, c mon home. N firs thing in the mawnin git to tha creek n fin tha gun."

"Yessuh."

"Whut yuh pay fer it?"

"Two dollahs."

"Take tha gun n git yo money back n carry it t Mistah Hawkins, yuh hear? N don fergit Ahma lam you black bottom good fer this! Now march yosef on home, suh!"

Dave turned and walked slowly. He heard people laughing. Dave glared, his eyes welling with tears. Hot anger bubbled in him. Then he swallowed and stumbled on.

That night Dave did not sleep. He was glad that he had gotten out of killing the mule so easily, but he was hurt. Something hot seemed to turn over inside him each time he remembered how they had laughed. He tossed on his bed, feeling his hard pillow. N

Pa says he's gonna beat me. . . . He remembered other beatings, and his back quivered. Naw, naw, Ah sho don wan im t beat me tha way no mo. . . . Dam em all! Nobody ever gave him anything. All he did was work. They treat me lika mule. . . . N then they beat me. . . . He gritted his teeth. N Ma had t tell on me.

Well, if he had to, he would take old man Hawkins that two dollars. But that meant selling the gun. And he wanted to keep that gun. Fifty dollahs fer a dead mule.

He turned over, thinking how he had fired the gun. He had an itch to fire it again. Ef other men kin shoota gun, by Gawd, Ah kin! He was still listening. Mebbe they all sleepin now. . . . The house was still. He heard the soft breathing of his brother. Yes, now! He would go down an get that gun and see if he could fire it! He eased out of bed and slipped into overalls.

The moon was bright. He ran almost all the way to the edge of the woods. He stumbled over the ground, looking for the spot where he had buried the gun. Yeah, here it is. Like a hungry dog scratching for a bone he pawed it up. He puffed his black cheeks and blew dirt from the trigger and barrel. He broke it and found four cartridges unshot. He looked around; the fields were filled with silence and moonlight. He clutched the gun stiff and hard in his fingers. But as soon as he wanted to pull the trigger, he shut his eyes and turned his head. Naw, Ah can't shoot wid mah eyes closed n mah head turned. With effort he held his eyes open; then he squeezed. Blooooom! He was stiff, not breathing. The gun was still in his hands. Dammit, he'd done it! He fired again. Bloooom! He smiled. Bloooom! Blooooom! Click, click. There! It was empty. If anybody could shoot a gun, he could. He put the gun into his hip pocket and started across the fields.

When he reached the top of a ridge he stood straight and proud in the moonlight, looking at Jim Hawkins's big white house, feeling the gun sagging in his pocket. Lawd, ef Ah had jus one mo bullet Ahd taka shot at tha house. Ahd like t scare ol man Hawkins jussa little. . . . Jussa enough t let im know Dave Sanders is a man.

To his left the road curved, running to the tracks of the Illinois Central. He jerked his head, listening. From far off came a faint hoooof-hoooof; hoooof-hoooof; hoooof-hoooof. . . . That's number eight. He took a swift look at Jim Hawkins's white house; he thought of Pa, of Ma, of his little brother, and the boys. He thought of the dead mule and heard hooof-hooof; hooof-hooof; hooof-hooof. . . . He stood rigid. Two dollahs a mont. Les see now . . . Tha means itll take bout two years. Shucks! Ahll be dam! He started down the road, toward the tracks. Yeah, here she comes! He stood beside the track and held himself stiffly. Here she comes, erroun the ben. . . . C mon, yuh slow poke! C mon! He had his hand on his gun; something quivered in his stomach. Then the train thundered past, the gray and brown boxcars rumbling and clinking. He gripped the gun tightly; then he jerked his hand out of his pocket. Ah betcha Bill wouldn't do it! Ah betcha. . . . The cars slid past, steel grinding upon steel. Ahm riding yuh ternight so hep me Gawd! He was hot all over. He hesitated just a moment; then he grabbed, pulled atop of a car, and lay flat. He felt his pocket; the gun was still there. Ahead the long rails were glinting in moonlight, stretching away, away to somewhere, somewhere where he could be a man. . . .

MARIHUANA AND A PISTOL

Chester B. Himes

"Red" Caldwell bought two "weeds" and went to the room where he lived and where he kept his pearl handled blue-steel .38 revolver in the dresser drawer and smoked them. Red was despondent because his girl friend had quit him when he didn't have any more money to spend on her. But at the height of his jag, despondency became solid to the touch and attained weight which rested so heavily upon his head and shoulders that he forgot his girl friend in the feeling of the weight.

As night came on it grew dark in the room; but the darkness was filled with colors of dazzling hue and grotesque pattern in which he abruptly lost his despondency and focused instead on the sudden, brilliant idea of light.

In standing up to turn on the light, his hand gripped the rough back of the chair. He snatched his hand away, receiving the sensation of a bruise. But the light bulb, which needed twisting, was cool and smooth and velvety and pleasing to the touch so that he lingered awhile to caress it. He did not turn it on because the idea of turning it on was gone, but he returned slowly to the middle of the floor and stood there absorbed in vacancy until the second idea came to him.

He started giggling and then began to laugh and laugh and laugh until his guts retched because it was such a swell idea, so amazingly simple and logical and perfect that it was excruciatingly funny that he had never thought of it before — he would stick up the main offices of the Cleveland Trust Company at Euclid and Ninth with two beer bottles stuck in his pockets.

His mind was not aware that the thought had come from any desire for money to win back his girl friend. In fact it was an absolutely novel idea and the completely detailed execution of it exploded in his mind like a flare, showing with a stark, livid clarity his every action from the moment of his entrance into the bank until he left it with the money from the vault. But in reviewing it, the detailed plan of execution eluded him so that in the next phase it contained a pistol and the Trust Company had turned into a theater.

Perhaps ten minutes more passed in aimless wanderings about the two-by-four room before he came upon a pistol, a pearl handled blue-steel .38. But it didn't mean anything other than a pistol, cold and sinister to the touch, and he was extremely puzzled by the suggestion it presented that he go out into the street. Already he had lost the thought of committing a robbery.

Walking down the street was difficult because his body was so light, and he became angry and annoyed because he could not get his feet down properly. As he passed the confectionery store his hand was tightly gripping the butt of the pistol and he felt its sinister coldness. All of a sudden the idea came back to him complete in every detail — only this time it was a confectionery store. He could remember the idea coming before, but he could not remember it as ever containing anything but the thought of robbing a confectionery store.

He opened the door and went inside, but by that time the idea was gone again and he stood there without knowing what for. The sensation of coldness produced by the gun made him think of his finger on the trigger, and all of a sudden the scope of the fascinating possibilities opened up before him, inspired by the feeling of his finger on the trigger of the pistol. He could shoot a man — or even two, or three, or he could go hunting and kill everybody.

He felt a dread fascination of horror growing on him which attracted him by the very essence of horror. He felt on the brink of a powerful sensation which he kept trying to capture but which kept eluding him. His mind kept returning again and again to his finger on the trigger of the pistol, so that by the time the storekeeper asked him what he wanted, he was frantic and he pulled the trigger five startling times, feeling the pressure on his finger and the kick of the gun and then becoming engulfed with stark, sheer terror at the sound of the shots.

His hands flew up, dropping the pistol on the floor. The pistol made a clanking sound, attracting his attention, and he looked down at it, recognizing it as a pistol and wondering who would leave a pistol on a store floor.

A *pistol on a store floor*. It was funny and he began to giggle, thinking, *a pistol on a store floor*, and then he began to laugh, louder and louder and harder, abruptly stopping at sight of the long pink and white sticks of peppermint candy behind the showcase.

They looked huge and desirable and delicious beyond expression and he would have died for one; and then he was eating one, and then two, reveling in the sweetish mint taste like a hog in slop, and then he was eating three, and then four, and then he was gorged and the deliciousness was gone and the taste in his mouth was bitter and brackish and sickening. He spat out what he had in his mouth. He felt like vomiting.

In bending over to vomit he saw the body of an old man lying in a puddle of blood and it so shocked him that he jumped up and ran out of the store and down the street.

He was still running when the police caught him but by that time he did not know what he was running for.

THE BEACH UMBRELLA
Cyrus Colter

T HE Thirty-first Street beach lay dazzling under a sky so blue that
Lake Michigan ran to the horizon like a sheet of sapphire silk,
studded with little barbed white sequins for sails; and the heavy
surface of the water lapped gently at the boulder "sea wall" which
had been cut into, graded, and sanded to make the beach. Saturday afternoons were always frenzied: three black lifeguards, giants
in sunglasses, preened in their towers and chaperoned the bathers
— adults, teen-agers, and children — who were going through
every physical gyration of which the human body is capable. Some
dove, swam, some hollered, rode inner tubes, or merely stood waist-
deep and pummeled the water; others — on the beach — sprinted,
did handsprings and somersaults, sucked Eskimo pies, or just
buried their children in the sand. Then there were the lollers —
extended in their languor under a garish variety of beach umbrellas.

Elijah lolled too — on his stomach in the white sand, his chin
cupped in his palm; but under no umbrella. He had none. By
habit, though, he stared in awe at those who did, and sometimes
meddled in their conversation: "It's gonna be gettin' hot pretty
soon — if it ain't careful," he said to a Bantu-looking fellow and
his girl sitting nearby with an older woman. The temperature was
then in the nineties. The fellow managed a negligent smile.
"Yeah," he said, and persisted in listening to the women. Buoyant
still, Elijah watched them. But soon his gaze wavered, and then
moved on to other lollers of interest. Finally he got up, stretched,
brushed sand from his swimming trunks, and scanned the beach
for a new spot. He started walking.

He was not tall. And he appeared to walk on his toes — his nut-colored legs were bowed and skinny and made him hobble like a jerky little spider. Next he plopped down near two men and two girls — they were hilarious about something — sitting beneath a big purple and white umbrella. The girls, chocolate brown and shapely, emitted squeals of laughter at the wisecracks of the men. Elijah was enchanted. All summer long the rambunctious gaiety of the beach had fastened on him a curious charm, a hex, that brought him gawking and twiddling to the lake each Saturday. The rest of the week, save Sunday, he worked. But Myrtle, his wife, detested the sport and stayed away. Randall, the boy, had been only twice and then without little Susan, who during the summer was her mother's own midget reflection. But Elijah came regularly, especially whenever Myrtle was being evil, which he felt now was almost always. She was getting worse, too — if that was possible. The woman was money-crazy.

"You gotta sharp-lookin' umbrella there!" he cut in on the two laughing couples. They studied him — the abruptly silent way. Then the big-shouldered fellow smiled and lifted his eyes to their spangled roof. "Yeah? . . . Thanks," he said. Elijah carried on: "I see a lot of 'em out here this summer — much more'n last year." The fellow meditated on this, but was noncommittal. The others went on gabbing, mostly with their hands. Elijah, squinting in the hot sun, watched them. He didn't see how they could be married; they cut the fool too much, acted like they'd itched to get together for weeks and just now made it. He pondered going back in the water, but he'd already had an hour of that. His eyes traveled the sweltering beach. Funny about his folks; they were every shape and color a God-made human could be. Here was a real sample of variety — pink white to jetty black. Could you any longer call that a race of people? It was a complicated complication — for some real educated guy to figure out. Then another thought slowly bore in on him: the beach umbrellas blooming across the sand attracted people — slews of friends, buddies; and gals, too. Wherever the loudest racket tore the air, a big red, or green, or yellowish umbrella — bordered with white fringe maybe — flowered in the middle of it all and gave shade to the happy good-timers.

Take, for instance, that tropical-looking pea-green umbrella over there, with the Bikinied brown chicks under it, and the portable radio jumping. A real beach party! He got up, stole over, and eased down in the sand at the fringe of the jubilation — two big thermos jugs sat in the shade and everybody had a paper cup in hand as the explosions of buffoonery carried out to the water. Chief provoker of mirth was a bulging-eyed old gal in a white bathing suit who, encumbered by big flabby overripe thighs, cavorted and pranced in the sand. When, perspiring from the heat, she finally fagged out she flopped down almost on top of him. So far he had gone unnoticed. But now, as he craned in at closer range, she brought him up: "Whatta you want, Pops?" She grinned, but with a touch of hostility.

Pops! Where'd she get that stuff? He was only forty-one, not a day older than that boozy bag. But he smiled. "Nothin'," he said brightly, "but you sure got one goin' here." He turned and viewed the noise-makers.

"An' you wanta get in on it!" she wrangled.

"Oh, I was just lookin' —"

"— You was just lookin'. Yeah, you was just lookin' at them young chicks there!" She roared a laugh and pointed at the sexy-looking girls under the umbrella.

Elijah grinned weakly.

"Beat it!" she catcalled, and turned back to the party.

He sat like a rock — the hell with her. But soon he relented, and wandered down to the water's edge — remote now from all inhospitality — to sit in the sand and hug his raised knees. Far out, the sailboats were pinned to the horizon and, despite all the close-in fuss, the wide miles of lake lay impassive under a blazing calm; far south and east down the long curving lake shore, miles in the distance, the smoky haze of the Whiting plant of the Youngstown Sheet and Tube Company hung ominously in an otherwise bright sky. And so it was that he turned back and viewed the beach again — and suddenly caught his craving. Weren't they some-thing — the umbrellas! The flashy colors of them! And the swank! No wonder folks ganged round them. Yes . . . yes, he too must have one. The thought came slow and final, and seared him. For there stood Myrtle in his mind. She nagged him now night and day, and it was always money that got her started; there was never enough — for Susan's shoes, Randy's overcoat, for new kitchen linoleum, Venetian blinds, for a better car than the old Chevy. "I just don't understand you!" she had said only night before last. "Have you got any plans at all for your family? You got a family, you know. If you could only bear to pull yourself away from that deaf old tightwad out at that warehouse, and go get yourself a real job . . . But no! Not you!"

She was talking about old man Schroeder, who owned the warehouse where he worked. Yes, the pay could be better, but it still wasn't as bad as she made out. Myrtle could be such a fool sometimes. He had been with the old man nine years now; had started out as a freight handler, but worked up to doing inventories and a little paper work. True, the business had been going down recently, for the old man's sight and hearing were failing and his key people had left him. Now he depended on him, Elijah — who of late wore a necktie on the job, and made his inventory rounds with a ball-point pen and clipboard. The old man was friendlier, too — almost "hat in hand" to him. He liked everything about the job now — except the pay. And that was only because of Myrtle. She just wanted so much; even talked of moving out of their rented apartment and buying out in the Chatham area. But one thing had to be said for her: she never griped about anything for herself; only for the family, the kids. Every payday he endorsed his check and handed it over to her, and got back in return only gasoline and cigarette money. And this could get pretty tiresome. About six weeks ago he'd gotten a ten-dollar-a-month raise out of the old man, but that had only made her madder than ever. He'd thought about looking for another job all right; but where would he go to get another white-collar job? There weren't many of them for him. She wouldn't care if he went back to the steel mills, back to pouring that white-hot ore out at Youngstown Sheet and Tube. It would be okay with her — so long as his paycheck was fat. But that kind of work was no good, undignified; coming home on the bus you were always so tired you went to sleep in your seat, with your lunch pail in your lap.

Just then two wet boys, chasing each other across the sand, raced by him into the water. The cold spray on his skin made him jump, jolting him out of his thoughts. He turned and slowly scanned the beach again. The umbrellas were brighter, gayer, bolder than ever — each a hiving center of playful people. He stood up finally, took a long last look, and then started back to the spot where he had parked the Chevy.

The following Monday evening was hot and humid as Elijah sat at home in their plain living room and pretended to read the newspaper; the windows were up, but not the slightest breeze came through the screens to stir Myrtle's fluffy curtains. At the moment she and nine-year-old Susan were in the kitchen finishing the dinner dishes. For twenty minutes now he had sat waiting for the furtive chance to speak to Randall. Randall, at twelve, was a serious, industrious boy, and did deliveries and odd jobs for the neighborhood grocer. Soon he came through — intent, absorbed — on his way back to the grocery for another hour's work.

"Gotta go back, eh, Randy?" Elijah said.

"Yes, sir." He was tall for his age, and wore glasses. He paused with his hand on the doorknob.

Elijah hesitated. Better wait, he thought — wait till he comes back. But Myrtle might be around then. Better ask him now. But Randall had opened the door. "See you later, Dad," he said — and left.

Elijah, shaken, again raised the newspaper and tried to read. He should have called him back, he knew, but he had lost his nerve — because he couldn't tell how Randy would take it. Fifteen dollars was nothing though, really — Randy probably had fifty or sixty stashed away somewhere in his room. Then he thought of Myrtle, and waves of fright went over him — to be even thinking about a beach umbrella was bad enough; and to buy one, especially now, would be to her some kind of crime; but to borrow even a part of the money for it from Randy . . . well, Myrtle would go out of her mind. He had never lied to his family before. This would be the first time. And he had thought about it all day long. During the morning, at the warehouse, he had gotten out the two big mail-order catalogues to look at the beach umbrellas; but the ones shown were all so small and dinky-looking he was contemptuous. So at noon he drove the Chevy out to a sporting-goods store on West Sixty-third Street. There he found a gorgeous assortment of yard and beach umbrellas. And there he found his prize. A beauty, a big beauty, with wide red and white stripes, and a white fringe. But oh the price! Twenty-three dollars! And he with nine.

"What's the matter with you?" Myrtle had walked in the room. She was thin, and medium brown-skinned with a saddle of freckles across her nose, and looked harried in her sleeveless housedress with her hair unkempt.

Startled, he lowered the newspaper. "Nothing," he said.

"How can you read looking over the paper?"

"Was I?"

Not bothering to answer, she sank in a chair. "Susie," she called back into the kitchen, "bring my cigarettes in here, will you, baby?"

Soon Susan, chubby and solemn, with the mist of perspiration on her forehead, came in with the cigarettes. "Only three left, Mama," she said, peering into the pack.

"Okay," Myrtle sighed, taking the cigarettes. Susan started out. "Now, scour the sink good, honey — and then go take your bath. You'll feel cooler."

Before looking at him again, Myrtle lit a cigarette. "School starts in three weeks," she said, with a forlorn shake of her head. "Do you realize that?"

"Yeah? . . . Jesus, times flies." He could not look at her.

"Susie needs dresses, and a couple of pairs of good shoes — and she'll need a coat before it gets cold."

"Yeah, I know." He patted the arm of the chair.

"Randy — bless his heart — has already made enough to get most of his things. That boy's something; he's all business — I've never seen anything like it." She took a drag on her cigarette. "And old man Schroeder giving you a ten-dollar raise! What was you thinkin' about? What'd you say to him?"

He did not answer at first. Finally he said, "Ten dollars is ten dollars, Myrtle. You know business is slow."

"I'll say it is! And there won't be any business before long — and then where'll you be? I tell you over and over again, you better start looking for something now! I been preachin' it to you for a year."

He said nothing.

"Ford and International Harvester are hiring every man they can lay their hands on! And the mills out in Gary and Whiting are going full blast — you see the red sky every night. The men make good money."

"They earn every nickel of it, too," he said in gloom.

"But they get it! Bring it home! It spends! Does that mean anything to you? Do you know what some of them make? Well, ask Hawthorne — or ask Sonny Milton. Sonny's wife says his checks some weeks run as high as a hundred twenty, hundred thirty dollars. One week! Take-home pay!"

"Yeah? . . . And Sonny told me he wished he had a job like mine."

Myrtle threw back her head with a bitter gasp. "Oh-h-h, God! Did you tell him what you made? Did you tell him that?"

Suddenly Susan came back into the muggy living room. She went straight to her mother and stood as if expecting an award. Myrtle absently patted her on the side of the head. "Now, go and run your bath water, honey," she said.

Elijah smiled at Susan. "Susie," he said, "d'you know your tummy is stickin' way out — you didn't eat too much, did you?" He laughed.

Susan turned and observed him; then looked at her mother. "No," she finally said.

"Go on now, baby," Myrtle said. Susan left the room.

Myrtle resumed. "Well, there's no use going through all this again. It's plain as the nose on your face. You got a family — a good family, I think. The only question is, do you wanta get off your hind end and do somethin' for it. It's just that simple."

Elijah looked at her. "You can talk real crazy sometimes, Myrtle."

"I think it's that old man!" she cried, her freckles contorted. "He's got you answering the phone, and taking inventory — wearing a necktie and all that. You wearing a necktie and your son mopping in a grocery store, so he can buy his own clothes." She snatched up her cigarettes, and walked out of the room.

His eyes did not follow her, but remained off in space. Finally he got up and went into the kitchen. Over the stove the plaster was thinly cracked, and in spots the linoleum had worn through the pattern; but everything was immaculate. He opened the refrigerator, poured a glass of cold water, and sat down at the kitchen table. He felt strange and weak, and sat for a long time sipping the water.

Then after a while he heard Randall's key in the front door, sending tremors of dread through him. When Randall came into the kitchen, he seemed to him as tall as himself; his glasses were steamy from the humidity outside, and his hands were dirty.

"Hi, Dad," he said gravely without looking at him, and opened the refrigerator door.

Elijah chuckled. "Your mother'll get after you about going in there without washing your hands.

But Randall took out the water pitcher and closed the door.

Elijah watched him. Now was the time to ask him. His heart was hammering. Go on — now! But instead he heard his husky voice saying, "What'd they have you doing over at the grocery tonight?"

Randall was drinking the glass of water. When he finished, he said, "Refilling shelves."

"Pretty hot job tonight, eh?"

"It wasn't so bad." Randall was matter-of-fact as he set the empty glass over the sink, and paused before leaving.

"Well . . . you're doing fine, son. Fine. Your mother sure is proud of you . . ." Purpose had lodged in his throat.

The praise embarrassed Randall. "Okay, Dad," he said, and edged from the kitchen.

Elijah slumped back in his chair, near prostration. He tried to clear his mind of every particle of thought, but the images became only more jumbled, oppressive to the point of panic.

Then before long Myrtle came into the kitchen — ignoring him. But she seemed not so hostile now as coldly impassive, exhibiting a bravado he had not seen before. He got up and went back into the living room and turned on the television. As the TV-screen lawmen galloped before him, he sat oblivious, admitting the failure of his will. If only he could have gotten Randall to himself long enough — but everything had been so sudden, abrupt; he couldn't just ask him out of the clear blue. Besides, around him Randall always seemed so busy, too busy to talk. He couldn't understand that; he had never mistreated the boy, never whipped him in his life; had shaken him a time or two, but that was long ago, when he was little.

He sat and watched the finish of the half-hour TV show. Myrtle was in the bedroom now. He slouched in his chair, lacking the resolve to get up and turn off the television.

Suddenly he was on his feet.

Leaving the television on, he went back to Randall's room in the rear. The door was open and Randall was asleep, lying on his back on the bed, perspiring, still dressed except for his shoes and glasses. He stood over the bed and looked at him. He was a good boy; his own son. But how strange — he thought for the first time — there was no resemblance between them. None whatsoever. Randy had a few of his mother's freckles on his thin brown face, but he could see none of himself in the boy. Then his musings were scattered by the return of his fear. He dreaded waking him. And he might be cross. If he didn't hurry, though, Myrtle or Susie might come strolling out any minute. His bones seemed rubbery from the strain. Finally he bent down and touched Randall's shoulder. The boy did not move a muscle, except to open his eyes. Elijah smiled at him. And he slowly sat up.

"Sorry, Randy — to wake you up like this."

"What's the matter?" Randall rubbed his eyes.

Elijah bent down again, but did not whisper. "Say, can you let me have fifteen bucks — till I get my check? . . . I need to get some things — and I'm a little short this time." He could hardly bring the words up.

Randall gave him a slow, queer look.

"I'll get my check a week from Friday," Elijah said, ". . . and I'll give it back to you then — sure."

Now instinctively Randall glanced toward the door, and Elijah knew Myrtle had crossed his thoughts. "You don't have to mention anything to your mother," he said with casual suddenness.

Randall got up slowly off the bed, and in his socks walked to the little table where he did his homework. He pulled the drawer out, fished far in the back a moment, and brought out a white business envelope secured by a rubber band. Holding the envelope close to his stomach, he took out first a ten-dollar bill, and then a five, and, sighing, handed them over.

"Thanks, old man," Elijah quivered, folding the money. "You'll get this back the day I get my check. . . . That's for sure."

"Okay," Randall finally said.

Elijah started out. Then he could see Myrtle on payday — her hand extended for his check. He hesitated, and looked at Randall, as if to speak. But he slipped the money in his trousers pocket and hurried from the room.

The following Saturday at the beach did not begin bright and sunny. By noon it was hot, but the sky was overcast and angry, the air heavy. There was no certainty whatever of a crowd, raucous or otherwise, and this was Elijah's chief concern as, shortly before twelve o'clock, he drove up in the Chevy and parked in the bumpy, graveled stretch of high ground that looked down eastward over the lake and was used for a parking lot. He climbed out of the car, glancing at the lake and clouds, and prayed in his heart it would not rain — the water was murky and restless, and only a handful of bathers had showed. But it was early yet. He stood beside the car and watched a bulbous, brown-skinned woman, in bathing suit and enormous straw hat, lugging a lunch basket down toward the beach, followed by her brood of children. And a fellow in swimming trunks, apparently the father, took a towel and sandals from his new Buick and called petulantly to his family to "just wait a minute, please." In another car, two women sat waiting, as yet fully clothed and undecided about going swimming. While down at the water's edge there was the usual cluster of dripping boys who, brash and boisterous, swarmed to the beach every day in fair weather or foul.

Elijah took off his shirt, peeled his trousers from over his swimming trunks, and started collecting the paraphernalia from the back seat of the car: a frayed pink rug filched from the house, a towel, sunglasses, cigarettes, a thermos jug filled with cold lemonade he had made himself, and a dozen paper cups. All this he stacked on the front fender. Then he went around to the rear and opened the trunk. Ah, there it lay — encased in a long, slim package trussed with heavy twine, and barely fitting athwart the spare tire. He felt prickles of excitement as he took the knife from the tool bag, cut the twine, and pulled the wrapping paper away. Red and white stripes sprang at him. It was even more gorgeous than when it had first seduced him in the store. The white fringe gave it style; the wide red fillets were cardinal and stark, and the white stripes glared. Now he opened it over his head for the full thrill of its colors, and looked around to see if anyone else agreed. Finally after a while he gathered up all his equipment and headed down for the beach, his short, nubby legs seeming more bowed than ever under the weight of their cargo.

When he reached the sand, a choice of location became a

pressing matter. That was why he had come early. From past observation it was clear that the center of gaiety shifted from day to day; last Saturday it might have been nearer the water, this Saturday, well back; or up, or down, the beach a ways. He must pick the site with care, for he could not move about the way he did when he had no umbrella; it was too noticeable. He finally took a spot as near the center of the beach as he could estimate, and dropped his gear in the sand. He knelt down and spread the pink rug, then moved the thermos jug over onto it, and folded the towel and placed it with the paper cups, sunglasses, and cigarettes down beside the jug. Now he went to find a heavy stone or brick to drive down the spike for the hollow umbrella stem to fit over. So it was not until the umbrella was finally up that he again had time for anxiety about the weather. His whole morning's effort had been an act of faith, for, as yet, there was no sun, although now and then a few azure breaks appeared in the thinning cloud mass. But before very long this brigher texture of the sky began to grow and spread by slow degrees, and his hopes quickened. Finally he sat down under the umbrella, lit a cigarette, and waited.

It was not long before two small boys came by — on their way to the water. He grinned, and called to them, "Hey, fellas, been in yet?" — their bathing suits were dry.

They stopped, and observed him. Then one of them smiled, and shook his head.

Elijah laughed. "Well, whatta you waitin' for? Go on in there and get them suits wet!" Both boys gave him silent smiles. And they lingered. He thought this a good omen — it had been different the Saturday before.

Once or twice the sun burst through the weakening clouds. He forgot the boys now in watching the skies, and soon they moved on. His anxiety was not detectable from his lazy posture under the umbrella, with his dwarfish, gnarled legs extended and his bare heels on the little rug. But then soon the clouds began to fade in earnest, seeming not to move away laterally, but slowly to recede into a lucent haze, until at last the sun came through hot and bright. He squinted at the sky and felt delivered. They would come, the folks would come! — were coming now; the beach would soon be swarming. Two other umbrellas were up already, and the diving board thronged with wet, acrobatic boys. The lifeguards were in their towers now, and still another launched his yellow rowboat. And up on the Outer Drive, the cars, one by one, were turning into the parking lot. The sun was bringing them out all right; soon he'd be in the middle of a field day. He felt a low-key, welling excitement, for the water was blue and far out the sails were starched and white.

Soon he saw the two little boys coming back. They were soaked. Their mother — a thin, brown girl in a yellow bathing suit — was with them now, and the boys were pointing to his umbrella. She seemed dignified for her youth, as she gave him a shy glance and then smiled at the boys.

"Ah, ha!" he cried to the boys. "You've been in now all right!" And then laughing to her, "I was kiddin' them awhile ago about their dry bathing suits."

She smiled at the boys again. "They like for me to be with them when they go in," she said.

"I got some lemonade here," he said abruptly, slapping the thermos jug. "Why don't you have some?" His voice was anxious.

She hesitated.

He jumped up. "Come on, sit down." He smiled at her and stepped aside.

Still she hesitated. But her eager boys pressed close behind her. Finally she smiled and sat down under the umbrella.

"You fellas can sit down under there too — in the shade," he said to the boys, and pointed under the umbrella. The boys flopped down quickly in the shady sand. He started at once serving them cold lemonade in the paper cups.

"Whew! I thought it was goin' to rain there for a while," he said, making conversation after passing out the lemonade. He had squatted on the sand and lit another cigarette. "Then there wouldn't a been much goin' on. But it turned out fine after all — there'll be a mob here before long."

She sipped the lemonade, but said little. He felt she had sat down only because of the boys, for she merely smiled and gave short answers to his questions. He learned the boys' names, Melvin and James; their ages, seven and nine; and that they were still frightened by the water. But he wanted to ask her name, and inquire about her husband. But he could not capture the courage.

Now the sun was hot and the sand was hot. And an orange and white umbrella was going up right beside them — two fellows and a girl. When the fellow who had been kneeling to drive the umbrella spike in the sand stood up, he was string-bean tall, and black, with his glistening hair freshly processed. The girl was a lighter brown, and wore a lilac bathing suit, and although her legs were thin, she was pleasant enough to look at. The second fellow was medium, really, in height, but short beside his tall, black friend. He was yellow-skinned, and fast getting bald, although still in his early thirties. Both men sported little shoestring moustaches.

Elijah — watched them in silence as long as he could. "You picked the right spot all right!" he laughed at last, putting on his sunglasses.

"How come, man?" The tall, black fellow grinned, showing his mouthful of gold teeth.

"You see everybody here!" happily rejoined Elijah. "They all come here!"

"Man, I been coming here for years," the fellow reproved, and sat down in his khaki swimming trunks to take off his shoes. Then he stood up. "But right now, in the water I goes." He looked down at the girl. "How 'bout you, Lois, baby?"

"No, Caesar," she smiled, "not yet; I'm gonna sit here awhile and relax.

"Okay, then — you just sit right there and relax. And Little Joe" — he turned and grinned to his shorter friend — "you sit there an' relax right along with her. You all can talk with this gentleman here" — he nodded at Elijah — "an' his nice wife." Then, pleased with himself, he trotted off toward the water.

The young mother looked at Elijah, as if he should have hastened to correct him. But somehow he had not wanted to. Yet too, Caesar's remark seemed to amuse her, for she soon smiled. Elijah felt the pain of relief — he did not want her to go; he glanced at her with a furtive laugh, and then they both laughed. The boys had finished their lemonade now, and were digging in the sand. Lois and Little Joe were busy talking.

Elijah was not quite sure what he should say to the mother. He did not understand her, was afraid of boring her, was desperate to keep her interested. As she sat looking out over the lake, he watched her. She was not pretty; and she was too thin. But he thought she had poise; he liked the way she treated her boys — tender, but casual; how different from Myrtle's frantic herding.

Soon she turned to the boys. "Want to go back in the water?" she laughed.

The boys looked at each other, and then at her. "Okay," James said finally, in resignation.

"Here, have some more lemonade," Elijah cut in.

The boys, rescued for the moment, quickly extended their cups. He poured them more lemonade, as she looked on smiling.

Now he turned to Lois and Little Joe sitting under their orange and white umbrella. "How 'bout some good ole cold lemonade?" he asked with a mushy smile. "I got plenty of cups." He felt he must get something going.

Lois smiled back. "No thanks," she said, fluttering her long eyelashes, "not right now."

He looked anxiously at Little Joe.

"I'll take a cup!" said Little Joe, and turned and laughed to Lois: "Hand me that bag there, will you?" He pointed to her beach bag in the sand. She passed it to him, and he reached in and pulled out a pint of gin. "We'll have some *real* lemonade," he vowed with a daredevilish grin.

Lois squealed with pretended embarrassment. "Oh, Joe!"

Elijah's eyes were big now; he was thinking of the police. But he handed Little Joe a cup and poured the lemonade, to which Joe added gin. Then Joe, grinning, thrust the bottle at Elijah. "How 'bout yourself, chief?" he said.

Elijah, shaking his head, leaned forward and whispered, "You ain't suppose to drink on the beach y'know."

"This ain't a drink, man — it's a taste!" said Little Joe, laughing and waving the bottle around toward the young mother. "How 'bout a little taste for your wife here?" he said to Elijah.

The mother laughed and threw up both hands. "No, not for me!"

Little Joe gave her a rakish grin. "What'sa matter? You 'fraid of that guy?" He jerked his thumb toward Elijah. "You 'fraid of gettin' a whippin', eh?"

"No, not exactly," she laughed.

Elijah was so elated with her his relief burst up in hysterical laughter. His laugh became strident and hoarse and he could not stop. The boys gaped at him, and then at their mother. When finally he recovered, Little Joe asked him, "Whut's so funny 'bout that?" Then Little Joe grinned at the mother. "You beat him up sometimes, eh?"

This started Elijah's hysterics all over again. The mother looked concerned now, and embarrassed; her laugh was nervous and shadowed. Little Joe glanced at Lois, laughed, and shrugged his shoulders. When Elijah finally got control of himself again he looked spent and demoralized.

Lois now tried to divert attention by starting a conversation with the boys. But the mother showed signs of restlessness and seemed ready to go. At this moment Caesar returned. Glistening beads of water ran off his long, black body; and his hair was unprocessed now. He surveyed the group and then flashed a wide, gold-toothed grin. "One big, happy family, like I said." Then he spied the paper cup in Little Joe's hand. "Whut you got there, man?"

Little Joe looked down into his cup with a playful smirk. "Lemonade, lover boy, lemonade."

"Don't hand me that jive, Joey. You ain't never had any straight lemonade in your life."

This again brought uproarious laughter from Elijah. "I got the straight lemonade here!" He beat the thermos jug with his hand. "Come on — have some!" He reached for a paper cup.

"Why, sure," said poised Caesar. He held out the cup and received the lemonade. "Now, gimme that gin," he said to Little Joe. Joe handed over the gin, and Caesar poured three fingers into the lemonade and sat down in the sand with his legs crossed under him. Soon he turned to the two boys, as their mother watched him with amusement. "Say, ain't you boys goin' in any more? Why don't you tell your daddy there to take you in?" He nodded toward Elijah.

Little Melvin frowned at him. "My daddy's workin'," he said.

Caesar's eyebrows shot up. "Oooh, la, la!" he crooned. "Hey, now!" And he turned and looked at the mother and then at Elijah, and gave a clownish little snigger.

Lois tittered before feigning exasperation at him. "There you go again," she said, "talkin' when you shoulda been listening."

Elijah laughed along with the rest. But he felt deflated. Then he glanced at the mother, who was laughing too. He could detect in her no sign of dismay. Why then had she gone along with the gag in the first place, he thought — if now she didn't hate to see it punctured?

"Hold the phone!" softly exclaimed Little Joe. "Whut is this?" He was staring over his shoulder. Three women, young, brown, and worldly looking, wandered toward them, carrying an assortment of beach paraphernalia and looking for a likely spot. They wore scant bathing suits, and were followed, but slowly, by an older woman with big, unsightly thighs. Elijah recognized her at once. She was the old gal who the Saturday before had chased him away from her beach party. She wore the same white bathing suit, and one of her girls carried the pea-green umbrella.

Caesar forgot his whereabouts ogling the girls. The older woman, observing this, paused to survey the situation. "How 'bout along in here?" she finally said to one of the girls. The girl carrying the thermos jug set it in the sand so close to Caesar it nearly touched him. He was rapturous. The girl with the umbrella had no chance to put it up, for Caesar and Little Joe instantly encumbered her with help. Another girl turned on a portable radio, and grinning, feverish Little Joe started snapping his fingers to the music's beat.

Within a half hour, a boisterous party was in progress. The little radio, perched on a hump of sand, blared out hot jazz, as the older woman — whose name turned out to be Hattie — passed around some cold, rum-spiked punch; and before long she went into her dancing-prancing act — to the riotous delight of all, especially Elijah. Hattie did not remember him from the Saturday past, and he was glad, for everything was so different today! As different as milk and ink. He knew no one realized it, but this was his party really — the wildest, craziest, funniest, and best he had ever seen or heard of. Nobody had been near the water — except Caesar, and the mother and boys much earlier. It appeared Lois was Caesar's girl friend, and she was hence more capable of reserve in face of the come-on antics of Opal, Billie, and Quanita — Hattie's girls. But Little Joe, to Caesar's tortured envy, was both free and aggressive. Even the young mother, who now volunteered her name to be Mrs. Green, got frolicsome, and twice jabbed Little Joe in the ribs.

Finally Caesar proposed they all go in the water. This met with instant, tipsy acclaim; and Little Joe, his yellow face contorted from laughing, jumped up, grabbed Billie's hand and made off with her across the sand. But Hattie would not budge. Full of rum, and stubborn, she sat sprawled with her flaccid thighs spread in an obscene V, and her eyes half shut. Now she yelled at her departing girls: "You all watch out, now! Don'tcha go in too far. . . . Just wade! None o' you can swim a lick!"

Elijah now was beyond happiness. He felt a floating, manic glee. He sprang up and jerked Mrs. Green splashing into the water, followed by her somewhat less ecstatic boys. Caesar had to paddle about with Lois and leave Little Joe unassisted to caper with Billie, Opal, and Quanita. Billie was the prettiest of the three, and despite Hattie's contrary statement, she could swim; and Little Joe, after taking her out in deeper water, waved back to Caesar in triumph. The sun was brazen now, and the beach and lake thronged with a variegated humanity. Elijah, a strong but awkward, country-style swimmer, gave Mrs. Green a lesson in floating on her back, and though she too could swim, he often felt obligated to place both his arms under her young body and buoy her up.

And sometimes he would purposely let her sink to her chin, whereupon she would feign a happy fright and utter faint simian screeches. Opal and Quanita sat in the shallows and kicked up their heels at Caesar, who, fully occupied with Lois, was a grinning, water-threshing study in frustration.

Thus the party went — on and on — till nearly four o'clock. Elijah had not known the world afforded such joy; his homely face was a wet festoon of beams and smiles. He went from girl to girl, insisting she learn to float on his outstretched arms. Once begrudging Caesar admonished him, "Man, you gonna drown one o' them pretty chicks." And Little Joe bestowed his highest accolade by calling him "lover boy," as Elijah nearly strangled from laughter.

At last they looked up to see old Hattie as she reeled down to the water's edge, coming to fetch her girls. Both Caesar and Little Joe ran out of the water to meet her, seized her by the wrists, and, despite her struggles and curses, dragged her in. "Turn me loose!

You big galoots!" she yelled and gasped as the water hit her. She was in knee-deep before she wriggled and fought herself free, with such force she sat down in the wet sand with a thud. She roared a laugh now, and spread her arms for help, as her girls came sprinting and splashing out of the water and tugged her to her feet. Her eyes narrowed to vengeful, grinning slits as she turned on Caesar and Little Joe: "I know whut you two're up to!" She flashed a glance around toward her girls. "I been watchin' both o' you studs! Yeah, yeah, but your eyes may shine, an' your teeth may grit . . ." She went limp in a sneering, raucous laugh. Everybody laughed now — except Lois and Mrs. Green.

They had all come out of the water now, and soon the whole group returned to their three beach umbrellas. Hattie's girls immediately prepared to break camp. They took down their pea-green umbrella, folded some wet towels, and donned their beach sandals, as Hattie still bantered Caesar and Little Joe.

"Well, you sure had yourself a ball today," she said to Little Joe, who was sitting in the sand.

"Coming back next Saturday?" asked grinning Little Joe.

"I jus' might at that," surmised Hattie. "We wuz here last Saturday."

"Good! Good!" Elijah broke in. "Let's all come back — next Saturday!" He searched every face.

"I'll be here," chimed Little Joe, grinning to Caesar. Captive Caesar glanced at Lois, and said nothing.

Lois and Mrs. Green were silent. Hattie, insulted, looked at them and started swelling up. "Never mind," she said pointedly to Elijah, "you jus' come on anyhow. You'll run into a slew o' folks lookin' for a good time. You don't need no certain people." But a little later, she and her girls all said friendly goodbyes and walked off across the sand.

The party now took a sudden downturn. All Elijah's efforts at resuscitation seemed unavailing. The westering sun was dipping toward the distant buildings of the city, and many of the bathers were leaving. Caesar and Little Joe had become bored; and Mrs. Green's boys, whining to go, kept a reproachful eye on their mother.

"Here, you boys, take some more lemonade," Elijah said quickly, reaching for the thermos jug. "Only got a little left —

better get while gettin's good!" He laughed. The boys shook their heads.

On Lois he tried cajolery. Smiling and pointing to her wet, but trim bathing suit, he asked, "What color would you say that is?"

"Lilac," said Lois, now standing.

"It sure is pretty! Prettiest on the beach!" he whispered.

Lois gave him a weak smile. Then she reached down for her beach bag, and looked at Caesar.

Caesar stood up. "Let's cut," he turned and said to Little Joe, and began taking down their orange and white umbrella.

Elijah was desolate. "Whatta you goin' for? It's getting cooler! Now's the time to enjoy the beach!"

"I've got to go home," Lois said.

Mrs. Green got up now; her boys had started off already. "Just a minute, Melvin," she called, frowning. Then, smiling, she turned and thanked Elijah.

He whirled around to them all. "Are we comin' back next Saturday? Come on — let's all come back! Wasn't it great! It was great! Don't you think? Whatta you say?" He looked now at Lois and Mrs. Green.

"We'll see," Lois said, smiling. "Maybe."

"Can you come?" He turned to Mrs. Green.

"I'm not sure," she said. "I'll try."

"Fine! Oh, that's fine!" He turned on Caesar and Little Joe. "I'll be lookin' for you guys, hear?"

"Okay, chief," grinned Little Joe. "An' put somethin' in that lemonade, will ya?"

Everybody laughed . . . and soon they were gone.

Elijah slowly crawled back under his umbrella, although the sun's heat was almost spent. He looked about him. There was only one umbrella on the spot now, his own, where before there had been three. Cigarette butts and paper cups lay strewn where Hattie's girls had sat, and the sandy imprint of Caesar's enormous street shoes marked his site. Mrs. Green had dropped a bobby pin. He too was caught up now by a sudden urge to go. It was hard to bear much longer — the lonesomeness. And most of the people were leaving anyway. He stirred and fidgeted in the sand, and finally started an inventory of his belongings. . . . Then his thoughts flew home, and he reconsidered. Funny — he hadn't thought of home all afternoon. Where had the time gone anyhow? . . . It seemed he'd just pulled up in the Chevy and unloaded his gear; now it was time to go home again. Then the image of solemn Randy suddenly formed in his mind, sending waves of guilt through him. He forgot where he was as the duties of his existence leapt on his back — where would he ever get Randy's fifteen dollars? He felt squarely confronted by a great blank void. It was an awful thing he had done — all for a day at the beach . . . with some sporting girls. He thought of his family and felt tiny — and him itching to come back next Saturday! Maybe Myrtle was right about him after all. Lord, if she knew what he had done . . .

He sat there for a long time. Most of the people were gone now. The lake was quiet save for a few boys still in the water. And the sun, red like blood, had settled on the dark silhouettes of the housetops across the city. He sat beneath the umbrella just as he had at one o'clock . . . and the thought smote him. He was jolted. Then dubious. But there it was — quivering, vital, swelling inside his skull like an unwanted fetus. So this was it! He mutinied inside. So he must sell it . . . his umbrella. Sell it for anything — only as long as it was enough to pay back Randy. For fifteen dollars even, if necessary. He was dogged; he couldn't do it; that wasn't the answer anyway. But the thought clawed and clung to him, rebuking and coaxing him by turns, until it finally became conviction. He must do it; it was the right thing to do; the only thing to do. Maybe then the awful weight would lift, the dull commotion in his stomach cease. He got up and started collecting his belongings; placed the thermos jug, sunglasses, towel, cigarettes, and little rug together in a neat pile, to be carried to the Chevy later. Then he turned to face his umbrella. Its red and white stripes stood defiant against the wide, churned-up sand. He stood for a moment mooning at it. Then he carefully let it down, and carrying it in his right hand, went off across the sand.

The sun now had gone down behind the vast city in a shower of crimson-golden glints, and on the beach only a few stragglers remained. For his first prospects he approached two teen-age boys, but suddenly realizing they had no money he turned away and went over to an old woman, squat and black, in street clothes — a spectator — who stood gazing eastward out across the lake. She held in her hand a little black book, with red-edged pages, which looked like the New Testament. He smiled at her. "Wanna buy a nice new beach umbrella?" He held out the collapsed umbrella toward her.

She gave him a beatific smile, but shook her head. "No, son," she said, "that ain't what I want." And she turned to gaze out on the lake again.

For a moment he still held the umbrella out, with a question mark on his face. "Okay, then," he finally said, and went on.

Next he hurried down to the water's edge, where he saw a man and two women preparing to leave. "Wanna buy a nice new beach umbrella?" His voice sounded high-pitched, as he opened the umbrella over his head. "It's brand-new. I'll sell it for fifteen dollars — it cost a lot more'n that."

The man was hostile, and glared. Finally he said, "Whatta you take me for — a fool?"

Elijah looked bewildered, and made no answer. He observed the man for a moment. Finally he let the umbrella down. As he moved away, he heard the man say to the women, "It's hot — he stole it somewhere."

Close by another man sat alone in the sand. Elijah started toward him. The man wore trousers, but was stripped to the waist, and bent over intent on some task in his lap. When Elijah reached him he looked up from half a hatful of cigarette butts he was breaking open for the tobacco he collected in a little paper bag. He grinned at Elijah, who meant now to pass on.

"No, I ain't interested either, buddy," the man insisted as Elijah passed him. "Not me. I jus' got outa jail las' week — an' ain't goin' back for no umbrella." He laughed, as Elijah kept on.

Now he saw three women, still in their bathing suits, sitting together near the diving board. They were the only people he had not yet tried — except the one lifeguard left. As he approached them, he saw that all three wore glasses and were sedate. Some schoolteachers maybe, he thought, or office workers. They were talking — until they saw him coming; then they stopped. One of them was plump, but a smooth dark brown, and sat with a towel around her shoulders. Elijah addressed them through her: "Wanna buy a nice beach umbrella?" And again he opened the umbrella over his head.

"Gee! It's beautiful," the plump woman said to the others. "But where'd you get it?" she suddenly asked Elijah, polite mistrust entering her voice.

"I bought it — just this week."

The three women looked at each other. "Why do you want to sell it so soon then?" a second woman said.

Elijah grinned. "I need the money."

"Well!" The plump woman was exasperated. "No, we don't want it." And they turned from him. He stood for a while, watching them; finally he let the umbrella down and moved on.

Only the lifeguard was left. He was a huge youngster, not over twenty, and brawny and black as he bent over cleaning out his beached rowboat. Elijah approached him so suddenly he looked up startled.

"Would you be interested in this umbrella?" Elijah said, and proffered the umbrella. "It's brand-new — I just bought it Tuesday. I'll sell it cheap." There was urgency in his voice.

The lifeguard gave him a queer stare; and then peered off toward the Outer Drive, as if looking for help. "You're lucky as hell," he finally said. "The cops just now cruised by — up on the Drive. I'd have turned you in so quick it'd make your head swim. Now you get the hell outa here." He was menacing.

Elijah was angry. "Whatta you mean? I bought this umbrella — it's mine."

The lifeguard took a step toward him. "I said you better get the hell outa here! An' I mean it! You thievin' bastard, you!"

Elijah, frightened now, gave ground. He turned and walked away a few steps; and then slowed up, as if an adequate answer had hit him. He stood for a moment. But finally he walked on, the umbrella drooping in his hand.

He walked up the gravelly slope now toward the Chevy, forgetting his little pile of belongings left in the sand. When he reached the car, and opened the trunk, he remembered; and went back down and gathered them up. He returned, threw them in the trunk and, without dressing, went around and climbed under the steering wheel. He was scared, shaken; and before starting the motor sat looking out on the lake. It was seven o'clock; the sky was waning pale, the beach forsaken, leaving a sense of perfect stillness and approaching night; the only sound was a gentle lapping of the water against the sand — one moderate hallo-o-o-o would have carried across to Michigan. He looked down at the beach. Where were they all now — the funny, proud, laughing people? Eating their dinners, he supposed, in a variety of homes. And all the beautiful umbrellas — where were they? Without their colors the beach was so deserted. Ah, the beach . . . after pouring hot ore all week out at Youngstown Sheet and Tube, he would probably be too fagged out for the beach. But maybe he wouldn't — who knew? It was great while it lasted . . . great. And his umbrella . . . he didn't know what he'd do with that . . . he might never need it again. He'd keep it, though — and see. Ha! . . . hadn't he sweat to get it! . . . and they thought he had stolen it . . . stolen it . . . ah . . . and maybe they were right. He sat for a few moments longer. Finally he started the motor, and took the old Chevy out onto the Drive in the pink-hued twilight. But down on the beach the sun was still shining.

THE RICHER, THE POORER

Dorothy West

Over the years Lottie had urged Bess to prepare for her old age.
Over the years Bess had lived each day as if there were no
other. Now they were both past sixty, the time for summing up.
Lottie had a bank account that had never grown lean. Bess had the
clothes on her back, and the rest of her worldly possessions in a
battered suitcase.

Lottie had hated being a child, hearing her parents' skimping
and scraping. Bess had never seemed to notice. All she ever wanted
was to go outside and play. She learned to skate on borrowed
skates. She rode a borrowed bicycle. Lottie couldn't wait to grow
up and buy herself the best of everything.

As soon as anyone would hire her, Lottie put herself to work.
She minded babies, she ran errands for the old.

She never touched a penny of her money, though her child's
mouth watered for ice cream and candy. But she could not bear to
share with Bess, who never had anything to share with her. When
the dimes began to add up to dollars, she lost her taste for sweets.

By the time she was twelve, she was clerking after school in a
small variety store. Saturdays she worked as long as she was wanted.
She decided to keep her money for clothes. When she entered high
school, she would wear a wardrobe that neither she nor anyone
else would be able to match.

But her freshman year found her unable to indulge so frivolous
a whim, particularly when her admiring instructors advised her to
think seriously of college. No one in her family had ever gone to
college, and certainly Bess would never get there. She would show
them all what she could do, if she put her mind to it.

She began to bank her money, and her bank became her most
private and precious possession.

In her third year high she found a job in a small but expanding restaurant, where she cashiered from the busy hour until closing. In her last year high the business increased so rapidly that Lottie was faced with the choice of staying in school or working full-time.

She made her choice easily. A job in hand was worth two in the future.

Bess had a beau in the school band, who had no other ambition except to play a horn. Lottie expected to be settled with a home and family while Bess was still waiting for Harry to earn enough to buy a marriage license.

That Bess married Harry straight out of high school was not surprising. That Lottie never married at all was not really surprising either. Two or three times she was halfway persuaded, but to give up a job that paid well for a homemaking job that paid nothing was a risk she was incapable of taking.

Bess's married life was nothing for Lottie to envy. She and Harry lived like gypsies, Harry playing in second-rate bands all over the country, even getting himself and Bess stranded in Europe. They were often in rags and never in riches.

Bess grieved because she had no child, not having sense enough to know she was better off without one. Lottie was certainly better off without nieces and nephews to feel sorry for. Very likely Bess would have dumped them on her doorstep.

That Lottie had a doorstep they might have been left on was only because her boss, having bought a second house, offered Lottie his first house at a price so low and terms so reasonable that it would have been like losing money to refuse.

She shut off the rooms she didn't use, letting them go to rack and ruin. Since she ate her meals out, she had no food at home, and did not encourage callers, who always expected a cup of tea.

Her way of life was mean and miserly, but she did not know it. She thought she lived frugally in her middle years so that she could live in comfort and ease when she most needed peace of mind.

The years, after forty, began to race. Suddenly Lottie was sixty, and retired from her job by her boss's son, who had no sentimental feeling about keeping her on until she was ready to quit.

She made several attempts to find other employment, but her dowdy appearance made her look old and inefficient. For the first time in her life Lottie would gladly have worked for nothing, to have some place to go, something to do with her day.

Harry died abroad, in a third-rate hotel, with Bess weeping as hard as if he had left her a fortune. He had left her nothing but his horn. There wasn't even money for her passage home.

Lottie, trapped by the blood tie, knew she would not only have to send for her sister, but take her in when she returned. It didn't seem fair that Bess should reap the harvest of Lottie's lifetime of self-denial.

It took Lottie a week to get a bedroom ready, a week of hard work and hard cash. There was everything to do, everything to replace or paint. When she was through the room looked so fresh and new that Lottie felt she deserved it more than Bess.

She would let Bess have her room, but the mattress was so lumpy, the carpet so worn, the curtains so threadbare that Lottie's conscience pricked her. She supposed she would have to redo that room, too, and went about doing it with an eagerness that she mistook for haste.

When she was through upstairs, she was shocked to see how dismal downstairs looked by comparison. She tried to ignore it, but with nowhere to go to escape it, the contrast grew more intolerable.

She worked her way from kitchen to parlor, persuading herself she was only putting the rooms to right to give herself something to do. At night she slept like a child after a long and happy day of playing house. She was having more fun than she had ever had in her life. She was living each hour for itself.

There was only a day now before Bess would arrive. Passing her gleaming mirrors, at first with vague awareness, then with painful clarity, Lottie saw herself as others saw her, and could not stand the sight.

She went on a spending spree from specialty shops to beauty salon, emerging transformed into a woman who believed in miracles.

She was in the kitchen basting a turkey when Bess rang the bell. Her heart raced, and she wondered if the heat from the oven was responsible.

She went to the door, and Bess stood before her. Stiffly she suffered Bess's embrace, her heart racing harder, her eyes suddenly smarting from the onrush of cold air.

"Oh, Lottie, it's good to see you," Bess said, but saying nothing about Lottie's splendid appearance. Upstairs Bess, putting down her shabby suitcase, said, "I'll sleep like a rock tonight," without a word of praise for her lovely room. At the lavish table, top-heavy with turkey, Bess said, "I'll take light and dark both," with no marveling at the size of the bird, or that there was turkey for two elderly women, one of them too poor to buy her own bread.

With the glow of good food in her stomach, Bess began to spin stories. They were rich with places and people, most of them lowly, all of them magnificent. Her face reflected her telling, the joys and sorrows of her remembering, and above all, the love she lived by that enhanced the poorest place, the humblest person.

Then it was that Lottie knew why Bess had made no mention of her finery, or the shining room, or the twelve-pound turkey. She had not even seen them. Tomorrow she would see the room as it really looked, and Lottie as she really looked, and the warmed-over turkey in its second-day glory. Tonight she saw only what she had come seeking, a place in her sister's home and heart.

She said, "That's enough about me. How have the years used you?"

"It was me who didn't use them," said Lottie wistfully. "I saved for them. I forgot the best of them would go without my ever spending a day or a dollar enjoying them. That's my life story in those few words, a life never lived.

"Now it's too near the end to try."

Bess said, "To know how much there is to know is the beginning of learning to live. Don't count the years that are left us. At our time of life it's the days that count. You've too much catching up to do to waste a minute of a waking hour feeling sorry for yourself."

Lottie grinned, a real wide open grin, "Well, to tell the truth I felt sorry for you. Maybe if I had any sense I'd feel sorry for myself, after all. I know I'm too old to kick up my heels, but I'm going to let you show me how. If I land on my head, I guess it won't matter. I feel giddy already, and I like it."

THE ALMOST WHITE BOY

Willard Motley

B Y birth he was half Negro and half white. Socially he was all
Negro. That is when people knew that his mother was a
brownskin woman with straightened hair and legs that didn't
respect the color line when it came to making men turn around to
look at them. His eyes were gray. His skin was as white as Slim
Peterson's; his blond hair didn't have any curl to it at all. His nose
was big and his lips were big — the only tip-off. Aunt Beulah-May
said he looked just like "poor white trash." Other people, black
and white, said all kinds of things about his parents behind their
backs, even if they were married. And these people, when it came
to discussing him, shook their heads, made sucking sounds with
their tongues and said, "Too bad! Too bad!" And one straggly-
haired Irish woman who had taken quite a liking to him had even
gone so far as to tell him, blissfully unmindful of his desires in the
matter, "I'd have you marry my daughter if you was white."

One thing he remembered. When he was small his dad had
taken him up in his arms and carried him to the big oval mirror in
the parlor. "Come here, Lucy," his father had said, calling Jimmy's
mother. His mother came, smiling at the picture her two men
made hugged close together; one so little and dependent, the other
so tall and serious-eyed. She stood beside him, straightening
Jimmy's collar and pushing his hair out of his eyes. Dad held him
in between them. "Look in the mirror, son," he said. And they all
looked. Their eyes were serious, not smiling, not staring, just
gloom-colored with seriousness in the mirror. "Look at your
mother. . . . Look at me." His dad gave the directions gravely.
"Look at your mother's skin." He looked. That was the dear sweet
mother he loved. "Look at the color of my skin." He looked. That

THE ALMOST WHITE BOY   135

was his daddy, the best daddy in the world. "We all love each
other, son, all three of us," his dad said, and his mother's eyes in
the mirror caught and held his father's with something shining
and proud through the seriousness; and his mother's arm stole up
around him and around his daddy. "People are just people. Some
are good and some are bad," his father said. "People are just
people. Look — and remember." He had remembered. He would
never forget.

Somehow, something of that day had passed into his life. And
he carried it with him back and forth across the color line. The
colored fellows he palled with called him "the white nigger," and
his white pals would sometimes look at him kind of funny but
they never said anything. Only when they went out on dates
together; then they'd tell him don't let something slip about
"niggers" without meaning to. Then they'd look sheepish. Jim
didn't see much difference. All the guys were swell if you liked
them; all the girls flirted and necked and went on crying jags now
and then. People were just people.

There were other things Jim remembered.

. . . On Fifty-eighth and Prairie. Lorenzo with white eyes in a
black face. With his kinky hair screwed down tight on his bald-
looking head like flies on flypaper. Ruby with her face all shiny
brown and her hair in stiff-standing braids and her pipy brown legs
Mom called razor-legs. Lorenzo saying, "You're black just like us."
Ruby singing out, "Yeah! Yeah! You're a white nigger — white
nigger!" Lorenzo taunting, "You ain't no different. My ma says so.
You're just a nigger!" Lorenzo and Ruby pushing up close to him
with threatening gestures, making faces at him, pulling his straight
blond hair with mean fists, both yelling at the same time, "White
nigger! White nigger!"

The name stuck.

. . . Women on the sidewalk in little groups. Their lips moving
when he walked past with his schoolbooks under his arm. Their
eyes lowered but looking at him. "Too bad! Too bad!" He could
see them. He knew they were talking about him. "Too bad! Too
bad!"

. . . Mom crying on the third floor of the kitchenette flat on
Thirty-ninth Street. Mom saying to Dad, "We've got to move

from here, Jim. We can't go on the street together without everybody staring at us. You'd think we'd killed somebody."

"What do we care how much they stare or what they say?"

"Even when I go out alone they stare. They never invite me to their houses. They say — they say that I think I'm better than they are — that I had to marry out of my race — that my own color wasn't good enough for me."

Dad saying, "Why can't people mind their own business? The hell with them." Mom crying. No friends. No company. Just the three of them.

. . . Then moving to the slums near Halstead and Maxwell, where all nationalities lived bundled up next door to each other and even in the same buildings. Jews. Mexicans. Poles. Negroes. Italians. Greeks. It was swell there. People changed races there. They went out on the streets together. No more staring. No more name-calling.

He grew up there.

. . . Getting older. And a lot of the white fellows not inviting him to parties at their houses when there were girls from the neighborhood. But they'd still go out of the neighborhood together and pick up girls or go on blind dates or to parties somewhere else. He didn't like to think of the neighborhood parties with the girls and the music and everything, and the door closed to him.

. . . Only once he denied it. He had been going around with Tony for a couple of weeks over on Racine Avenue. They played pool together, drank beer together on West Madison Street, drove around in Tony's old rattling Chevy. One day Tony looked at him funny and said, point-blank, "Say, what are you anyway?"

Jim got red; he could feel his face burn. "I'm Polish," he said.

He was sorry afterwards. He didn't know why he said it. He felt ashamed.

. . . Then he was finished with school and he had to go to work. He got a job in a downtown hotel because nobody knew what he really was and Aunt Beulah-May said it was all right to "pass for white" when it came to making money but he'd better never get any ideas in his head about turning his back on his people. To him it was cheating. It was denying half himself. It wasn't a straight front. He knew how hard it was for colored fellows to find decent jobs. It wasn't saying I'm a Negro and taking the same chances they took when it came to getting a job. But he did it.

Jim remembered many of these things; they were tied inside of him in hard knots. But the color line didn't exist for him and he came and went pretty much as he chose. He took the girls in stride. He went to parties on the South Side, on Thirty-fifth and Michigan, on South Park. He went dancing at the Savoy Ballroom — and the Trianon. He went to Polish hops and Italian fiestas and Irish weddings. And he had a hell of a swell time. People were just people.

He had fun with the colored girls. But some of them held off from him, not knowing what he was. These were his people. No — he didn't feel natural around them. And with white people he wasn't all himself either. He didn't have any people.

Then all of a sudden he was madly in love with Cora. This had never happened before. He had sometimes wondered if, when it came, it would be a white girl or a colored girl. Now it was here. There was nothing he could do about it. And he was scared. He began to worry, and to wonder. And he began to wish, although ashamed to admit it to himself, that he didn't have any colored blood in him.

He met Cora at a dance at the Trianon. Cora's hair wasn't as blond as his but it curled all over her head. Her skin was pink and soft. Her breasts stood erect and her red lips were parted in a queer little loose way. They were always like that. And they were always moist-looking.

Leo introduced them. Then he let them alone and they danced every dance together; and when it was time to go home Leo had disappeared. Jim asked her if he could take her home.

"I think that would be awfully sweet of you," she said. Her eyes opened wide in a baby-blue smile.

She leaned back against him a little when he helped her into her coat. He flushed with the pleasure of that brief touching of their bodies. They walked through the unwinding ballroom crowd together, not having anything to say to each other, and out onto Cottage Grove, still not having anything to say. As they passed the lighted-up plate-glass window of Walgreen's drugstore Jim asked her, "Wouldn't you like a malted milk?" She didn't answer but just smiled up at him over her shoulder and he felt the softness of her arm in the doorway.

She sipped her malted milk. He sat stirring his straw around in his glass. Once in a while she'd look up over her glass and wrinkle her lips or her eyes at him, friendly-like. Neither of them said anything. Then, when Cora had finished, he held the match for her cigarette and their eyes came together and stayed that way longer than they needed to. And her lips were really parted now, with the cigarette smoke curling up into her hair.

In front of her house they stood close together, neither of them wanting to go.

"It was a nice dance," Cora said; and her fingers played in the hedge-top.

"Yes, especially after I met you."

"I'm going to see you again, aren't I?" Cora asked, looking up at him a little.

Jim looked down at the sidewalk. He hoped he could keep the red out of his cheeks. "I might as well tell you before someone else does — I'm a Negro," he said.

There was a catch in her voice, just a little noise not made of words.

"Oh, you're fooling!" she said with a small, irritated laugh.

"No, I'm not. I told you because I like you."

She had stepped back from him. Her eyes were searching for the windows of the house to see that there was no light behind the shades.

"Please, let me see you again," Jim said.

Her eyes, satisfied, came away from the windows. They looked at the sidewalk where he had looked. Her body was still withdrawn. Her lips weren't parted now. There were hard little lines at the corners of her mouth.

"Let me meet you somewhere," Jim said.

Another furtive glance at the house; then she looked at him, unbelievingly. "You didn't mean that — about being colored?"

"It doesn't matter, does it?"

"No — only —"

"Let me meet you somewhere," Jim begged.

Her lips were parted a little. She looked at him strangely, deep into him in a way that made him tremble, then down his body and back up into his eyes. She tossed her head a little. "Well — call me up tomorrow afternoon." She gave him the number.

He watched her go into the house. Then he walked to the corner to wait for his streetcar; and he kicked at the sidewalk and clenched his fists.

Jim went to meet her in Jackson Park. They walked around. She was beautiful in her pink dress. Her lips were pouted a little bit, and her eyes were averted, and she was everything he had ever wanted. They sat on a bench far away from anybody. "You know," she said, "I never liked nig — Negroes. You're not like a Negro at all." They walked to the other end of the park. "Why do you tell people?" she asked.

"People are just people," he told her, but the words didn't sound real any more.

Twice again he met her in the park. Once they just sat talking and once they went to a movie. Both times he walked her to the car line and left her there. That was the way she wanted it.

After that it was sneaking around to meet her. She didn't like to go on dates with him when he had his white friends along. She'd never tell him why. And yet she put her body up close to him when they were alone. It was all right too when she invited some of her friends who didn't know what he was.

They saw a lot of each other. And pretty soon he thought from the long, probing looks she gave him that she must like him; from the way she'd grab his hand, tight, sometimes; from the way she danced with him. She even had him take her home now and they'd stand on her porch pressed close together. "Cora, I want you to come over to my house," he told her. "My mother and father are swell. You'll like them." He could see all four of them together. "It isn't a nice neighborhood. I mean it doesn't look good, but the people are nicer than — in other places. Gee, you'll like my mother and father."

"All right, I'll go, Jimmy. I don't care. I don't care."

Dad kidded him about his new flame, saying it must be serious, that he had never brought a girl home before. Mom made fried chicken and hot biscuits. And when he went to get Cora he saw Dad and Mom both with dust rags, shining up everything in the parlor for the tenth time; he heard Dad and Mom laughing quietly together and talking about their first date.

He hadn't told them she was a white girl. But they never batted an eye.

"Mom, this is Cora."

"How do you do, dear. Jimmy has told us so much about you." Dear, sweet Mom. Always gracious and friendly.

"Dad, this is Cora." Dad grinning, looking straight at her with eyes as blue as hers, going into some crazy story about "Jimmy at the age of three." Good old Dad. "People are just people."

Dad and Mom were at ease. Only Cora seemed embarrassed. And she was nervous, not meeting Dad's eyes, not meeting Mom's eyes, looking to him for support. She sat on the edge of her chair. "Y-y-yes, sir . . . No, Mrs. Warner." She only picked at the good food Mom had spent all afternoon getting ready. And Jim, watching her, watching Dad and Mom, hoping they wouldn't notice, got ill at ease himself and he was glad when he got her outside. Then they were themselves again.

"Mom and Dad are really swell. You'll have to get to know them," he said, looking at her appealingly, asking for approval. She smiled with expressionless eyes. She said nothing.

On Fourteenth and Halstead they met Slick Harper. Slick was as black as they come. It was sometimes hard, because of his southern dialect and his Chicago black-belt expressions, to know just what he meant in English. He practiced jitterbug steps on street corners and had a whole string of girls — black, brownskin, high-yellow. Everybody called him Slick because he handed his bevy of girls a smooth line and because he wore all the latest fashions in men's clothes — high-waisted trousers, big-brimmed hats, bright sports coats, Cuban heels and coconut straws with gaudy bands. Slick hailed Jim; his eyes gave Cora the once-over.

"Whatcha say, man!" he shouted. "Ah know they all goes when the wagon comes but where you been stuck away? And no jive! Man, ah been lookin' for you. We're throwing a party next Saturday and we want you to come."

Jim stood locked to the sidewalk, working his hands in his pockets and afraid to look at Cora. He watched Slick's big purple lips move up and down as they showed the slices of white teeth. Now Slick had stopped talking and was staring at Cora with a black-faced smirk.

"Cora, this is Slick Harper."

"How do you do." Her voice came down as from the top of a building.

"Ah'm glad to meetcha," Slick said. "You sho' got good taste, Jim." His eyes took in her whole figure. "Why don't you bring her to the party?"

"Maybe I will. Well, we've got to go." He walked fast then to keep up with Cora.

Cora never came over again.

Cora had him come over to her house. But first she prepared him a lot. "Don't ever — ever — tell my folks you're colored. Please, Jimmy. Promise me. . . . Father doesn't like colored people. . . . They aren't broad-minded like me. . . . And don't mind Father, Jimmy," she warned.

He went. There was a cream-colored car outside the house. In the parlor were smoking stands, and knickknack brackets, and a grand piano nobody played. Cora's father smoked cigars, owned a few pieces of stock, went to Florida two weeks every winter, told stories about the "Florida niggers." Cora's mother had the same parted lips Cora had, but she breathed through them heavily as if she were always trying to catch up with herself. She was fat and overdressed. And admonished her husband when he told his Southern stories through the smoke of big cigars: "Now, Harry, you mustn't talk like that. What will this nice young man think of you? There are plenty of fine upright Negroes — I'm sure. Of course I don't know any personally. . . . Now, Harry, don't be so harsh. Don't forget, you took milk from a colored mammy's breast. Oh, Harry, tell them about the little darky who wanted to watch your car — 'Two cents a awah, Mistah No'the'nah!' "

Cora sat with her hands in her lap and her fingers laced tightly together. Jim smiled at Mr. Hartley's jokes and had a miserable time. And Jim discovered that it was best not to go to anybody's house. Just the two of them.

Jim and Cora went together for four months. And they had an awful time of it. But they were unhappy apart. Yet when they were together their eyes were always accusing each other. Sometimes they seemed to enjoy hurting each other. Jim wouldn't call her up; and he'd be miserable. She wouldn't write to him or would stand him up on a date for Chuck Nelson or Fred Schultz; then she'd be miserable. Something held them apart. And something pulled them together.

Jim did a lot of thinking. It had to go four revolutions. Four times a part-Negro had to marry a white person before legally you were white. The blood had to take four revolutions. Mulatto — that's what he was — quadroon — octaroon — then it was all gone. Then you were white. His great-grandchildren maybe. Four times the blood had to let in the other blood.

Then one night they were driving out to the forest preserves in Tony's Chevy. "What are you thinking, Jimmy?"

"Oh, nothing. Just thinking."

"Do you like my new dress? How do I look in it?"

"Isn't that a keen moon, Cora?" The car slid along the dark, deserted highway. They came to a gravel road and Jim eased the car over the crushed stone in second gear. Cora put her cheek against the sleeve of his coat. The branches of trees made scraping sounds against the sides of the car. Cora was closer to him now. He could smell the perfume in her hair and yellow strands tickled the end of his nose. He stopped the motor and switched the lights off. Cora lifted his arm up over her head and around her, putting his hand in close to her waist with her hand over his, stroking his. "Let's sit here like this — close and warm," she whispered. Then her voice lost itself in the breast of his coat.

For a long time they sat like that. Then Jim said, "Let's take a walk." He opened the door and, half supporting her, he lifted her out. While she was still in his arms she bit his ear gently.

"Don't do that," he said, and she giggled.

Panting, they walked through the low scrub into the woods. The bushes scratched their arms. Twigs caught in Cora's hair. Their feet sank in the earth. Cora kept putting her fingers in Jim's hair and mussing it. "Don't. Don't," he said. And finally he caught her fingers and held them tight in his. They walked on like this. The moon made silhouettes of them, silhouettes climbing up the slow incline of hill.

Jim found a little rise of land, treeless, grassy. Far to the north-east, Chicago sprawled, row on row of dim lights growing more numerous but gentler.

The night was over them.

They sat on the little hillock, shoulder to shoulder; and Cora moved her body close to him. It was warm there against his shirt, open at the neck. They didn't talk. They didn't move. And when Cora breathed he could feel the movement of her body against him. It was almost as if they were one. He looked up at the splash of stars, and the moon clouding over. His arm went around her, shieldingly. He closed his eyes and put his face into her hair. "Cora! Cora!" The only answer she gave was the slight movement of her body.

"Cora, I love you."

"Do you, Jimmy?" she said, snuggling up so close to him that he could feel her heart beat against him.

He didn't move. But after a while she was slowly leaning back until the weight of her carried him back too and they lay full length. They lay like this a long time. He looked at her. Her eyes were closed. She was breathing hard. Her lips were parted and moist.

"Jimmy."

"What?"

"Nothing."

She hooked one of her feet over his. A slow quiver started in his shoulders, worked its way down the length of him. He sat up. Cora sat up.

"There's nobody here but us," she said. Her fingers unbuttoned the first button on his shirt, the second. Her fingers crept in on his chest, playing with the little hairs there.

"There's nobody here but us," she said, and she ran her fingers inside his shirt, over his shoulders and the back of his neck.

"We can't do this, Cora. We can't."

"Do you mean about you being colored? It doesn't matter to me, Jimmy. Honest it doesn't."

"No. Not that. It's because I love you. That's why I can't. That's why I want —"

He sat up straight then. His fingers pulled up some grass. He held it up to the light and looked at it. She had her head in his lap and lay there perfectly still. He could hear her breathing, and her breath was warm and moist on the back of his other hand where it lay on his leg. He threw the grass away, watched how the wind took it and lowered it down to the ground. He lifted her up by the shoulders, gently, until they were close together, looking into each other's eyes.

"I want it to be right for us, Cora," he said. "Will you marry me?"

The sting of red in her cheeks looked as if a blow had left it there; even the moonlight showed that. She sat up without the support of his hands. Her arms were straight and tense under her. Her eyes met his, burning angrily at the softness in his eyes. "You damn dirty nigger!" she said, and jumped up and walked away from him as fast as she could.

When she was gone he lay on his face where he had been sitting. He lay full length. The grass he had pulled stuck to his lips. "People are just people." He said it aloud. "People are just people." And he laughed, hoarsely, hollowly. "People are just people." Then it was only a half-laugh with a sob cutting into it. And he was crying, with his arms flung up wildly above his head, with his face pushed into the grass trying to stop the sound of his crying. Off across the far grass Cora was running away from him. The moon, bright now, lacquered the whiteness of his hands lying helplessly above his head; it touched the blondness of his hair.

AFTERNOON INTO NIGHT

Katherine Dunham

UMBERTO Rodriguez Morales slowly took off his elegant rented matador's vest, his tight-fitting breeches, his soiled white stockings and his low-heeled pumps and handed them to his admiring peon. He moved mechanically, trying to hold together the pieces that were bursting inside him, trying to shut out the picture of what had happened. Polero was not the first man he had seen killed in the bullring, nor were his the first entrails that Umberto had seen quivering on the angry horns of the victorious bull. But Polero had died not by accident or a slip or a weak thrust or a faulty turn but simply because at the crucial moment of the killing, when it was one or the other, Polero had given in.

From five feet away Umberto had seen it all. Automatically he had stepped forward and thrust his *escardo* into the death spot in the neck of the bull, just behind the massive skull. Then he had stood still, while the peons rushed a stretcher for what was left of Polero and the horses of the picadors dragged the dead bull in the opposite direction. The crowd, shocked, strained from the wooden seats to watch the removal of the tragedy. It was the last fight of the day. A woman broke through the guards and ran across the ring screaming after the stretcher bearers. Boys climbed walls to see more. An American woman fainted. Confused, frightened, hushed, the crowd filtered out of the arena, a lover cheated of an unnatural satisfaction.

Umberto slid into his cheap wide-shouldered zoot suit, excused his peon, and by short cuts and rear exits managed to leave the arena, unmolested by the crowds that were waiting to acclaim him the hero of the day.

Bright sun, take back your rays. How can heat and light be cold, too? When he talked to the mightiest of bulls they drank in the insults of his words and were angrier still. When he talked to women an infinite tenderness quivered between them as though he knew too well the secret fabric making up women. Polero was pure Indian, remote, sulky, sometimes cruel. Bright sun too warm to be without.

Umberto found himself in the park beside the Palacion. He sat on a bench and closed his eyes. Now he saw Polero as he knew him best. Polero ready for the kill. Umberto wondered if others who had known him felt as he did.

Always just before the kill Polero would look at his friend and pupil Umberto. In the arrested moment before the kill he would look at Umberto. A glance so hidden beneath long lashes, so much a part of his casual arrogance that Umberto could never be sure that it was for him. Sometimes he felt afraid, too, of what he might see there. At that moment, knowing that he should feel some recognition beyond anything he had every known, Umberto's blood stream would stand still. With another self he strained to reach out to something that he had never known. Another self made up of Mexican peasant bleakness and an arrow-like tautness that could, at a touch, shoot a clean straight line into the heavens. The killing would happen then, and swelling waves of applause would bring him back to the ring. He would follow the procession beside his hero, picking up the flowers, slippers and scarves that showered from the boxes.

This way he had stood that afternoon, a bronze statue. The late sun glinting from the shining embroidery of his bolero, superb in peacock blue satin and silver, gathering, from behind, and above, and all sides, electricity from the suspended onlookers. Polero was magnificent, standing between them and their miserable fears of impotency and destruction, uniting them with the beast in death.

A connecting link between these people and their fears, protecting them from the fury and destruction of the beast. A symbol of the triumph of the reason and skill of man against the unreason of fear. Someone had to make death fine and glorious.

A street urchin came to him with a hollowed-out bamboo full of orchids and gardenias from Xochimilco. The smell was heavy and sweet. He got up from the park bench and moved on. He quickened his step to pass Tonio's bar. It was here that all of the bull fighters gathered on Sunday night after the *correo*. There were always women waiting for them. There was one especially for Polero. The woman who had run screaming across the arena. Now he knew that he had heard her voice for the first time that afternoon. A deadened section of his brain relayed her scream and it shot out like a radio in full blast. Over and over again as she ran across the trampled earth. "No! No! Holy Virgin, he cannot! He cannot! He cannot!" Umberto could see her now, blinded by the low rays of the sun, stumbling over the trampled earth, ankle-deep in the blood-soaked sawdust; in that light, her red shoes turned shining black.

They would all ask him why Polero had died. They would all turn to him with questions that he could not answer. That woman, and other women, would cling to him and weep, because they knew that he too loved Polero. They would turn their grief on him, a thing now mixed with a great fear that settled in his stomach and his groin. Polero was looking at him, Umberto, as he died. Looking at him and smiling, and they must all have seen it.

He was about to turn into the Estrellita but a woman at a charcoal stove recognized him and started to speak. She thought better of it when she saw his face. He hurried on, hat pulled down, head bent low, trying to hunch his shoulders and walk casually, instead of with the proud chest and swaying hips of the bull-fighter. Even so they all knew him, and turned to stare as he passed. To get out of the street he slipped into a bar and went far back into a corner and ordered a drink. He turned his back to the tired band of mariachi players. "Noche de ronde," they sang, "noche de tristes. . . ." Infinite sadness of the Mexican peon. Aztec and Mayan sadness of centuries . . . In the fly-specked mirror behind the bar he saw the dregs of the night life of Mexico City. *Indios,* Spanish, *mestizas, mulatos* crowding into the mirror and in the midst of them Polero's eyes and mouth, talking to him.

Polero spoke always with the silent things; the turn of his head, his hands, the tempo of his breathing. When they were children, boys of nine and fourteen in the same village, it was always Umberto who talked. If he could release now that stream of child talk, perhaps his pain would go. Talk into the mirror to Polero.

Umberto ordered another drink. His blood was rushing **faster** now, and he felt hot and breathless and expectant. He looked in the mirror again, to see if Polero were still there. Instead the red eyes, distended nostrils, and slobbering mouth of the bull were before him. He closed his eyes and heard the sound of its breathing. He had heard it so many times before but this seemed closer, more terrifying, as though all of doom would sweep down on him if he opened his eyes. He stood waiting, feeling his own blood and his own entrails spilling on the floor of the bar. When he opened his eyes he saw that a man was behind him looking into his eyes in the mirror. A man whose head hung low and from whose lips a line of saliva drooled out to a glass held in midair. It was this man's breathing, this man's sound. He might have been the bull. Instinctively the muscles in the fingers of Umberto's right hand twitched. He stepped quickly to one side, stomach muscles tense, thighs pressed together. The red eyes continued to look into the mirror. Umberto flung fifty centavos on the counter and hurried out past the mariachi players. He threaded his way through *touristas* and natives, in real flight now, as though to save not only his body but his soul.

He treaded narrow streets, finding the back ways. There was no place to go. Before, he was moving blindly, to push out thinking from his mind. Now he was fleeing from a *thing* — an essence which he felt would mean real destruction if ever it caught up with him.

No place, in flight, to escape this thing that had become real.

He began to run, and as he ran he felt the man behind him. He turned sharply into an alleyway and waited for footsteps. The only sounds were night sounds of the quieting street, and the tight rush of his own breathing. He knew that somehow everything was drawing together into one picture. Pieces falling in place that he couldn't put into words. It was well past midnight. He stopped at a street stove and bought an oily *tostado* from one of the scrawny vendors. He had eaten nothing since early morning. As he reached to his pocket to pay her, he heard the thick drop of a coin in her tin cup and the woman thanked the man behind him. He felt his forehead suddenly cold and his throat contracted so that he could hardly swallow. He stayed there and ate the *tostado*, forcing it down his dry throat, trying to control the sound of his breathing and wondering where to turn for escape.

Mexico City is wide-awake until dawn. The Salon Mexico was just a few squares away, and Umberto sought refuge there. The man did not follow him, and upstairs, in the corner by the band, he felt a moment of real safety and relief. He had often been here to dance himself. Now he enjoyed watching the small Indians in white trousers and bright blankets jitterbug with girls in cheap satin and lace Sunday dresses. Umberto began to relax. He felt sleepy, drugged, carried away by the flashing bright colors on the dancers, and by the heat. Then one of the jitterbug dancers started across the floor to greet him. The whole room seemed to stop in suspended motion and turn toward him, and all of their faces were alive with the same question. . . . In panic again, he turned and ran down the stairway and into the street.

Outside there was no moon and the only light came from the street signs and here and there a kerosene lamp behind shutters. He stepped out of the Salon Mexico and as he turned from the door he felt a hand on his shoulder. He became suddenly rigid and then sprang around with the force of a whip. It was not his voice but he heard himself say: "What do you want?" The sound scarcely left his lips and his throat hurt even to make room for the words. The ugly soft face of the man pressed closer to him. Breath passed heavily over loose lips; in the neon light reflected from the sign above, they were wet. The man spoke, panting. Out of the head of the bull his voice soft and high, straining with tortured desire. He spoke in the familiar *tu* instead of *usted*. Disjointed words, things men say to women. Umberto stood transfixed, his entire body swept with mingled fear and revolt. The man stopped talking. Three drunken cattlemen stumbled by, and Umberto turned mechanically to continue his flight. The man held him by the arm. "Oh, no," he said, and the high sweet voice came again as a surprise. "Don't go." He moved closer to Umberto and one hand fell on the smooth hard muscles of the bullfighter's right arm. "I know what happened, I saw it all. I have watched every time he fought for years, watched you both. I know why he did it and you know too." They were walking now and Umberto was trying to shut out what he was hearing. But if the words didn't come from the man outside, they continued just the same, his own self supplying them in a steady stream feeding into his consciousness;

so that it became as though he were finally telling himself all of these things which he had always known.

They walked and turned into a stairway. It was dark and hot and the eagerness of the man filled the narrow hallway to bursting. On the third step Umberto stopped and closed his eyes and leaned his head against the wall. He heard the bellow of death agony of the bull and when he opened his eyes he saw the burning eyes of Polero, Polero's mouth smiling. This creature was really the bull and if he did not kill it he would be killed by it. Polero had been killed by it. All of the fear that had been drawing closer around Umberto in his flight from the arena came together now in this black stairway. He did not want to die, he did not want to be killed by this bull.

He was moving upward again. It was still intensely black but with a hand on each wall beside him, he continued to climb slowly, guided by the breathing of the man in front of him; then by a thick wet hand on his. He moved first like somone who was very ill, then like a very young boy. As he continued to climb in the darkness, he felt the man closer and closer to him. That afternoon in the torn arena blood gushed from the mouth of the bull, but not before Polero died, smiling, looking. Umberto's grief broke, silent and clean as an arrow released from its bow. Just as surely as that, he knew that he would never fight again.

FLYING HOME

Ralph Ellison

WHEN Todd came to, he saw two faces suspended above him in a sun so hot and blinding that he could not tell if they were black or white. He stirred, feeling a pain that burned as though his whole body had been laid open to the sun which glared into his eyes. For a moment an old fear of being touched by white hands seized him. Then the very sharpness of the pain began slowly to clear his head. Sounds came to him dimly. He done come to. Who are they? he thought. Naw he ain't, I coulda sworn he was white. Then he heard clearly:

"You hurt bad?"

Something within him uncoiled. It was a Negro sound.

"He's still out," he heard.

"Give 'im time. . . . Say, son, you hurt bad?"

Was he? There was that awful pain. He lay rigid, hearing their breathing and trying to weave a meaning between them and his being stretched painfully upon the ground. He watched them warily, his mind traveling back over a painful distance. Jagged scenes, swiftly unfolding as in a movie trailer, reeled through his mind, and he saw himself piloting a tailspinning plane and landing and landing and falling from the cockpit and trying to stand. Then, as in a great silence, he remembered the sound of crunching bone, and now, looking up into the anxious faces of an old Negro man and a boy from where he lay in the same field, the memory sickened him and he wanted to remember no more.

"How you feel, son?"

Todd hesitated, as though to answer would be to admit an inacceptable weakness. Then, "It's my ankle," he said.

"Which one?"

"The left."

With a sense of remoteness he watched the old man bend and remove his boot, feeling the pressure ease.

"That any better?"

"A lot. Thank you."

He had the sensation of discussing someone else, that his concern was with some far more important thing, which for some reason escaped him.

"You done broke it bad," the old man said. "We have to get you to a doctor."

He felt that he had been thrown into a tailspin. He looked at his watch; how long had he been here? He knew there was but one important thing in the world, to get the plane back to the field before his officers were displeased.

"Help me up," he said. "Into the ship."

"But it's broke too bad. . . ."

"Give me your arm!"

"But, son . . ."

Clutching the old man's arm he pulled himself up, keeping his left leg clear, thinking, "I'd never make him understand," as the leather-smooth face came parallel with his own.

"Now, let's see."

He pushed the old man back, hearing a bird's insistent shrill. He swayed giddily. Blackness washed over him, like infinity.

"You best sit down."

"No, I'm O.K."

"But, son. You jus' gonna make it worse. . . ."

It was a fact that everything in him cried out to deny, even against the flaming pain in his ankle. He would have to try again.

"You mess with that ankle they have to cut your foot off," he heard.

Holding his breath, he started up again. It pained so badly that he had to bite his lips to keep from crying out and he allowed them to help him down with a pang of despair.

"It's best you take it easy. We gon' git you a doctor."

Of all the luck, he thought. Of all the rotten luck, now I have done it. The fumes of high-octane gasoline clung in the heat, taunting him.

"We kin ride him into town on old Ned," the boy said.

Ned? He turned, seeing the boy point toward an ox team browsing where the buried blade of a plow marked the end of a furrow. Thoughts of himself riding an ox through the town, past streets full of white faces, down the concrete runways of the airfield made swift images of humiliation in his mind. With a pang he remembered his girl's last letter. "Todd," she had written, "I don't need the papers to tell me you had the intelligence to fly. And I have always known you to be as brave as anyone else. The papers annoy me. Don't you be contented to prove over and over again that you're brave or skillful just because you're black, Todd. I think they keep beating that dead horse because they don't want to say why you boys are not yet fighting. I'm really disappointed, Todd. Anyone with brains can learn to fly, but then what? What about using it, and who will you use it for? I wish, dear, you'd write about this. I sometimes think they're playing a trick on us. It's very humiliating. . . ." He wiped cold sweat from his face, thinking, What does she know of humiliation? She's never been down South. Now the humiliation would come. When you must have them judge you, knowing that they never accept your mistakes as your own, but hold it against your whole race — that was humiliation. Yes, and humiliation was when you could never be simply yourself, when you were always a part of this old black ignorant man. Sure, he's all right. Nice and kind and helpful. But he's not you. Well, there's one humiliation I can spare myself.

"No," he said, "I have orders not to leave the ship. . . ."

"Aw," the old man said. Then turning to the boy, "Teddy, then you better hustle down to Mister Graves and get him to come. . . ."

"No, wait!" he protested before he was fully aware. Graves might be white. "Just have him get word to the field, please. They'll take care of the rest."

He saw the boy leave, running.

"How far does he have to go?"

"Might' nigh a mile."

He rested back, looking at the dusty face of his watch. But now they know something has happened, he thought. In the ship there was a perfectly good radio, but it was useless. The old fellow would never operate it. That buzzard knocked me back a hundred years, he thought. Irony danced within him like the gnats circling the old man's head. With all I've learned I'm dependent upon this "peasant's" sense of time and space. His leg throbbed. In the plane, instead of time being measured by the rhythms of pain and a kid's legs, the instruments would have told him at a glance. Twisting upon his elbows he saw where dust had powdered the plane's fuselage, feeling the lump form in his throat that was always there when he thought of flight. It's crouched there, he thought, like the abandoned shell of a locust. I'm naked without it. Not a machine, a suit of clothes you wear. And with a sudden embarrassment and wonder he whispered, "It's the only dignity I have. . . ."

He saw the old man watching, his torn overalls clinging limply to him in the heat. He felt a sharp need to tell the old man what he felt. But that would be meaningless. If I tried to explain why I need to fly back, he'd think I was simply afraid of white officers. But it's more than fear . . . a sense of anguish clung to him like the veil of sweat that hugged his face. He watched the old man, hearing him humming snatches of a tune as he admired the plane. He felt a furtive sense of resentment. Such old men often came to the field to watch the pilots with childish eyes. At first it had made him proud; they had been a meaningful part of a new experience. But soon he realized they did not understand his accomplishments and they came to shame and embarrass him, like the distasteful praise of an idiot. A part of the meaning of flying had gone then, and he had not been able to regain it. If I were a prizefighter I would be more human, he thought. Not a monkey doing tricks, but a man. They were pleased simply that he was a Negro who could fly, and that was not enough. He felt cut off from them by age, by understanding, by sensibility, by technology and by his need to measure himself against the mirror of other men's appreciation. Somehow he felt betrayed, as he had when as a child he grew to discover that his father was dead. Now for him any real appreciation lay with his white officers; and with them he could never be sure. Between ignorant black men and condescending whites, his course of flight seemed mapped by the nature of things away from all needed and natural landmarks. Under some sealed orders, couched in ever more technical and mysterious terms, his path curved swiftly away from both the shame the old man symbolized and the cloudy terrain of white men's regard. Flying blind, he knew but one point of landing and there he would receive his wings. After that the enemy would appreciate his skill and he would assume his deepest meaning, he thought sadly, neither from those who condescended nor from those who praised without understanding, but from the enemy who would recognize his manhood and skill in terms of hate. . . .

He sighed, seeing the oxen making queer, prehistoric shadows against the dry brown earth.

"You just take it easy, son," the old man soothed. "That boy won't take long. Crazy as he is about airplanes."

"I can wait," he said.

"What kinda airplane you call this here'n?"

"An Advanced Trainer," he said, seeing the old man smile. His fingers were like gnarled dark wood against the metal as he touched the low-slung wing.

" 'Bout how fast can she fly?"

"Over two hundred an hour."

"Lawd! That's so fast I bet it don't seem like you moving!"

Holding himself rigid, Todd opened his flying suit. The shade had gone and he lay in a ball of fire.

"You mind if I take a look inside? I was always curious to see. . . ."

"Help yourself. Just don't touch anything."

He heard him climb upon the metal wing, grunting. Now the questions would start. Well, so you don't have to think to answer. . . .

He saw the old man looking over into the cockpit, his eyes bright as a child's.

"You must have to know a lot to work all these here things."

He was silent, seeing him step down and kneel beside him.

"Son, how come you want to fly way up there in the air?"

Because it's the most meaningful act in the world . . . because it makes me less like you, he thought.

But he said: "Because I like it, I guess. It's as good a way to fight and die as I know."

"Yeah? I guess you right," the old man said. "But how long you think before they gonna let you all fight?"

He tensed. This was the question all Negroes asked, put with the same timid hopefulness and longing that always opened a greater void within him than that he had felt beneath the plane the first time he had flown. He felt light-headed. It came to him suddenly that there was something sinister about the conversation, that he was flying unwillingly into unsafe and uncharted regions. If he could only be insulting and tell this old man who was trying to help him to shut up!

"I bet you one thing . . ."

"Yes?"

"That you was plenty scared coming down."

He did not answer. Like a dog on a trail the old man seemed to smell out his fears and he felt anger bubble within him.

"You sho' scared me. When I seen you coming down in that thing with it a-rollin' and a-jumpin' like a pitchin' hoss, I thought sho' you was a goner. I almost had me a stroke!"

He saw the old man grinning, "Ever'thin's been happening round here this morning, come to think of it.

"Like what?" he asked.

"Well, first thing I know, here come two white fellers looking for Mister Rudolph, that's Mister Graves's cousin. That got me worked up right away. . . ."

"Why?"

"Why? 'Cause he done broke outta the crazy house, that's why. He liable to kill somebody," he said. "They oughta have him by now though. Then here you come. First I think it's one of them white boys. Then doggone if you don't fall outta there. Lawd, I'd done heard about you boys but I haven't never seen one o' you-all. Cain't tell you how it felt to see somebody what look like me in a airplane!"

The old man talked on, the sound streaming around Todd's thoughts like air flowing over the fuselage of a flying plane. You were a fool, he thought, remembering how before the spin the sun had blazed bright against the billboard signs beyond the town, and how a boy's blue kite had bloomed beneath him, tugging gently in the wind like a strange, odd-shaped flower. He had once flown such kites himself and tried to find the boy at the end of the invisible cord. But he had been flying too high and too fast. He had climbed steeply away in exultation. Too steeply, he thought. And one of the first rules you learn is that if the angle of thrust is too steep the plane goes into a spin. And then, instead of pulling out of it and going into a dive you let a buzzard panic you. A lousy buzzard!

"Son, what made all that blood on the glass?"

"A buzzard," he said, remembering how the blood and feathers had sprayed back against the hatch. It had been as though he had flown into a storm of blood and blackness.

"Well, I declare! They's lots of 'em around here. They after dead things. Don't eat nothing what's alive."

"A little bit more and he would have made a meal out of me," Todd said grimly.

"They bad luck all right. Teddy's got a name for 'em, calls 'em jimcrows," the old man laughed.

"It's a damned good name."

"They the damnedest birds. Once I seen a hoss all stretched out like he was sick, you know. So I hollers, 'Gid up from there, suh!' Just to make sho! An' doggone, son, if I don't see two ole jimcrows come flying right up outa that hoss's insides! Yessuh! The sun was shinin' on 'em and they couldn't a been no greasier if they'd been eating barbecue."

Todd thought he would vomit, his stomach quivered.

"You made that up," he said.

"Nawsuh! Saw him just like I see you."

"Well, I'm glad it was you."

"You see lots a funny things down here, son."

"No, I'll let you see them," he said.

"By the way, the white folks round here don't like to see you boys up there in the sky. They ever bother you?"

"No."

"Well, they'd like to."

"Someone always wants to bother someone else," Todd said. "How do you know?"

"I just know."

"Well," he said defensively, "no one has bothered us."

Blood pounded in his ears as he looked away into space. He tensed, seeing a black spot in the sky, and strained to confirm what he could not clearly see.

"What does that look like to you?" he asked excitedly.

"Just another bad luck, son."

Then he saw the movement of wings with disappointment. It

was gliding smoothly down, wings outspread, tail feathers gripping
the air, down swiftly — gone behind the green screen of trees. It
was like a bird he had imagined there, only the sloping branches of
the pines remained, sharp against the pale stretch of sky. He lay
barely breathing and stared at the point where it had disappeared,
caught in a spell of loathing and admiration. Why did they make
them so disgusting and yet teach them to fly so well? It's like when
I was up in heaven, he heard, starting.

The old man was chuckling, rubbing his stubbled chin.

"What did you say?"

"Sho', I died and went to heaven . . . maybe by time I tell you
about it they be done come after you."

"I hope so," he said wearily.

"You boys ever sit around and swap lies?"

"Not often. Is this going to be one?"

"Well, I ain't so sho', on account of it took place when I was
dead."

The old man paused, "That wasn't no lie 'bout the buzzards,
though."

"All right," he said.

"Sho' you want to hear 'bout heaven?"

"Please," he answered, resting his head upon his arm.

"Well, I went to heaven and right away started to sproutin' me
some wings. Six good ones, they was. Just like them the white
angels had. I couldn't hardly believe it. I was so glad that I went
off on some clouds by myself and tried 'em out. You know, 'cause
I didn't want to make a fool outta myself the first thing. . . ."

It's an old tale, Todd thought. Told me years ago. Had forgotten. But at least it will keep him from talking about buzzards.

He closed his eyes, listening.

". . . First thing I done was to git up on a low cloud and jump
off. And doggone, boy, if them wings didn't work! First I tried the
right; then I tried the left; then I tried 'em both together. Then
Lawd, I started to move on out among the folks. I let 'em see
me. . . ."

He saw the old man gesturing flight with his arms, his face full
of mock pride as he indicated an imaginary crowd, thinking, It'll
be in the newspapers, as he heard, " . . . so I went and found me
some colored angels — somehow I didn't believe I was an angel till

I seen a real black one, ha, yes! Then I was sho' — but they tole me I better come down 'cause us colored folks had to wear a special kin' a harness when we flew. That was how come they wasn't flyin'. Oh yes, an' you had to be extra strong for a black man even, to fly with one of them harnesses. . . ."

This is a new turn, Todd thought, what's he driving at?

"So I said to myself, I ain't gonna be bothered with no harness! Oh naw! 'Cause if God let you sprout wings you oughta have sense enough not to let nobody make you wear something what gits in the way of flyin'. So I starts to flyin'. Heck, son," he chuckled, his eyes twinkling, "you know I had to let eve'ybody know that old Jefferson could fly good as anybody else. And I could too, fly smooth as a bird! I could even loop-the-loop — only I had to make sho' to keep my long white robe down roun' my ankles. . . ."

Todd felt uneasy. He wanted to laugh at the joke, but his body refused, as of an independent will. He felt as he had as a child when after he had chewed a sugar-coated pill which his mother had given him, she had laughed at his efforts to remove the terrible taste.

". . . Well," he heard, "I was doing all right 'til I got to speeding. Found out I could fan up a right strong breeze, I could fly so fast. I could do all kin'sa stunts too. I started flying up to the stars and divin' down and zooming roun' the moon. Man, I like to scare the devil outa some ole white angels. I was raisin' hell. Not that I meant any harm, son. But I was just feeling good. It was so good to know I was free at last. I accidentally knocked the tips offa some stars and they tell me I caused a storm and a coupla lynchings down here in Macon County — though I swear I believe them boys what said that was making up lies on me. . . ."

He's mocking me, Todd thought angrily. He thinks it's a joke. Grinning down at me . . . His throat was dry. He looked at his watch; why the hell didn't they come? Since they had to, why? One day I was flying down one of them heavenly streets. You got yourself into it, Todd thought. Like Jonah in the whale.

"Justa throwin' feathers in everybody's face. An' ole Saint Peter called me in. Said, 'Jefferson, tell me two things, what you doin' flyin' without a harness; an' how come you flyin' so fast?' So I tole him I was flyin' without a harness 'cause it got in my way, but I couldn'ta been flyin' so fast, 'cause I wasn't usin' but one wing.

Saint Peter said, 'You wasn't flyin' with but one wing?' 'Yessuh,' I says, scared-like. So he says, 'Well, since you got sucha extra fine pair of wings you can leave off yo' harness awhile. But from now on none of that there one-wing flyin', 'cause you gittin' up too damn much speed!' "

And with one mouth full of bad teeth you're making too damned much talk, thought Todd. Why don't I send him after the boy? His body ached from the hard ground and seeking to shift his position he twisted his ankle and hated himself for crying out.

"It gittin' worse?"

"I . . . I twisted it," he groaned.

"Try not to think about it, son. That's what I do."

He bit his lip, fighting pain with counter-pain as the voice resumed its rhythmical droning. Jefferson seemed caught in his own creation.

". . . After all that trouble I just floated roun' heaven in slow motion. But I forgot, like colored folks will do, and got to flyin' with one wing again. This time I was restin' my old broken arm and got to flyin' fast enough to shame the devil. I was comin' so fast, Lawd, I got myself called befo' ole Saint Peter again. He said, 'Jeff, didn't I warn you 'bout that speedin'?' 'Yessuh,' I says, 'but it was an accident.' He looked at me sad-like and shook his head and I knowed I was gone. He said, 'Jeff, you and that speedin' is a danger to the heavenly community. If I was to let you keep on flyin', heaven wouldn't be nothin' but uproar. Jeff, you got to go!' Son, I argued and pleaded with that old white man, but it didn't do a bit of good. They rushed me straight to them pearly gates and gimme a parachute and a map of the state of Alabama . . ."

Todd heard him laughing so that he could hardly speak, making a screen between them upon which his humiliation glowed like fire.

"Maybe you'd better stop awhile," he said, his voice unreal.

"Ain't much more," Jefferson laughed. "When they gimme the parachute ole Saint Peter ask me if I wanted to say a few words before I went. I felt so bad I couldn't hardly look at him, specially with all them white angels standin' around. Then somebody laughed and made me mad. So I tole him, 'Well, you done took my wings. And you puttin' me out. You got charge of things so's I can't do nothin' about it. But you got to admit just this: While I was up here I was the flyinest sonofabitch what ever hit heaven!"

At the burst of laughter Todd felt such an intense humiliation that only great violence would wash it away. The laughter which shook the old man like a boiling purge set up vibrations of guilt within him which not even the intricate machinery of the plane would have been adequate to transform and he heard himself screaming, "Why do you laugh at me this way?"

He hated himself at that moment, but he had lost control. He saw Jefferson's mouth fall open, "What — ?"

"Answer me!"

His blood pounded as though it would surely burst his temples and he tried to reach the old man and fell, screaming, "Can I help it because they won't let us actually fly? Maybe we are a bunch of buzzards feeding on a dead horse, but we can hope to be eagles, can't we? Can't we?"

He fell back, exhausted, his ankle pounding. The saliva was like straw in his mouth. If he had the strength he would strangle this old man. This grinning, gray-headed clown who made him feel as he felt when watched by the white officers at the field. And yet this old man had neither power, prestige, rank nor technique. Nothing that could rid him of this terrible feeling. He watched him, seeing his face struggle to express a turmoil of feeling.

"What you mean, son? What you talking 'bout . . . ?"

"Go away. Go tell your tales to the white folks."

"But I didn't mean nothing like that. . . . I . . . I wasn't tryin' to hurt your feelings. . . ."

"Please. Get the hell away from me!"

"But I didn't, son. I didn't mean all them things a-tall."

Todd shook as with a chill, searching Jefferson's face for a trace of the mockery he had seen there. But now the face was somber and tired and old. He was confused. He could not be sure that there had ever been laughter there, that Jefferson had ever really laughed in his whole life. He saw Jefferson reach out to touch him and shrank away, wondering if anything except the pain, now causing his vision to waver, was real. Perhaps he had imagined it all.

"Don't let it get you down, son," the voice said pensively.

He heard Jefferson sigh wearily, as though he felt more than he could say. His anger ebbed, leaving only the pain.

"I'm sorry," he mumbled.

"You just wore out with pain, was all. . . ."

He saw him through a blur, smiling. And for a second he felt the embarrassed silence of understanding flutter between them.

"What you was doin' flyin' over this section, son? Wasn't you scared they might shoot you for a cow?"

Todd tensed. Was he being laughed at again? But before he could decide, the pain shook him and a part of him was lying calmly behind the screen of pain that had fallen between them, recalling the first time he had ever seen a plane. It was as though an endless series of hangars had been shaken ajar in the air base of his memory and from each, like a young wasp emerging from its cell, arose the memory of a plane.

The first time I ever saw a plane I was very small and planes were new in the world. I was four-and-a-half and the only plane that I had ever seen was a model suspended from the ceiling of the automobile exhibit at the State Fair. But I did not know that it was only a model. I did not know how large a real plane was, nor how expensive. To me it was a fascinating toy, complete in itself, which my mother said could only be owned by rich little white boys. I stood rigid with admiration, my head straining backwards as I watched the gray little plane describing arcs above the gleaming tops of the automobiles. And I vowed that, rich or poor, someday I would own such a toy. My mother had to drag me out of the exhibit and not even the merry-go-round, the Ferris wheel, or the racing horses could hold my attention for the rest of the Fair. I was too busy imitating the tiny drone of the plane with my lips, and imitating with my hands the motion, swift and circling, that it made in flight.

After that I no longer used the pieces of lumber that lay about our back yard to construct wagons and autos . . . now it was used for airplanes. I built biplanes, using pieces of board for wings, a small box for the fuselage, another piece of wood for the rudder. The trip to the Fair had brought something new into my small world. I asked my mother repeatedly when the Fair would come back again. I'd lie in the grass and watch the sky, and each fighting bird became a soaring plane. I would have been good a year just to have seen a plane again. I became a nuisance to everyone with my questions about airplanes. But planes were new to the old folks, too, and there was little that they could tell me. Only my uncle knew some of the answers. And better still, he could carve propellers from pieces of wood that would whirl rapidly in the wind, wobbling noisily upon oiled nails.

I wanted a plane more than I'd wanted anything; more than I wanted the red wagon with rubber tires, more than the train that ran on a track with its train of cars. I asked my mother over and over again:

"Mamma?"

"What do you want, boy?" she'd say.

"Mamma, will you get mad if I ask you?" I'd say.

"What do you want now? I ain't got time to be answering a lot of fool questions. What you want?"

"Mamma, when you gonna get me one . . . ?" I'd ask.

"Get you one what?" she'd say.

"You know, Mamma; what I been asking you. . . ."

"Boy," she'd say, "if you don't want a spanking you better come on an' tell me what you talking about so I can get on with my work."

"Aw, Mamma, you know. . . ."

"What I just tell you?" she'd say.

"I mean when you gonna buy me a airplane."

"Airplane! Boy, is you crazy? How many times I have to tell you to stop that foolishness. I done told you them things cost too much. I bet I'm gon' wham the living daylight out of you if you don't quit worrying me 'bout them things!"

But this did not stop me, and a few days later I'd try all over again.

Then one day a strange thing happened. It was spring and for some reason I had been hot and irritable all morning. It was a beautiful spring. I could feel it as I played barefoot in the backyard. Blossoms hung from the thorny black locust trees like clusters of fragrant white grapes. Butterflies flickered in the sunlight above the short new dew-wet grass. I had gone in the house for bread and butter and coming out I heard a steady unfamiliar drone. It was unlike anything I had ever heard before. I tried to place the sound. It was no use. It was a sensation like that I had when searching for my father's watch, heard ticking unseen in a room. It made me feel as though I had forgotten to perform some task that my mother had ordered . . . then I located it, overhead. In the sky, flying quite low and about a hundred yards off was a plane! It came so slowly that it seemed barely to move. My mouth hung wide; my bread and butter fell into the dirt. I wanted to jump up and down and cheer. And when the idea struck I trembled with excitement: "Some little white boy's plane's done flew away and all I got to do is stretch out my hands and it'll be mine!" It was a little plane like that at the Fair, flying no higher than the eaves of our roof. Seeing it come steadily forward I felt the world grow warm with promise. I opened the screen and climbed over it and clung there, waiting. I would catch the plane as it came over and swing down fast and run into the house before anyone could see me. Then no one could come to claim the plane. It droned nearer. Then when it hung like a silver cross in the blue directly above me I stretched out my hand and grabbed. It was like sticking my finger through a soap bubble. The plane flew on, as though I had simply blown my breath after it. I grabbed again, frantically, trying to catch the tail. My fingers clutched the air and disappointment surged tight and hard in my throat. Giving one last desperate grasp, I strained forward. My fingers ripped from the screen. I was falling. The ground burst hard against me. I drummed the earth with my heels and when my breath returned, I lay there bawling.

My mother rushed through the door.

"What's the matter, chile! What on earth is wrong with you?"

"It's gone! It's gone!"

"What gone?"

"The airplane . . ."

"Airplane?"

"Yessum, jus' like the one at the Fair. . . . I . . . I tried to stop it an' it kep' right on going. . . ."

"When, boy?"

"Just now," I cried, through my tears.

"Where it go, boy, what way?"

"Yonder, there . . ."

She scanned the sky, her arms akimbo and her checkered apron flapping in the wind as I pointed to the fading plane. Finally she looked down at me, slowly shaking her head.

"It's gone! It's gone!" I cried.

"Boy, is you a fool?" she said. "Don't you see that there's a real airplane 'stead of one of them toy ones?"

"Real . . . ?" I forgot to cry. "Real?"

"Yass, real. Don't you know that thing you reaching for is bigger'n a auto? You here trying to reach for it and I bet it's flying 'bout two hundred miles higher'n this roof." She was disgusted with me. "You come on in this house before somebody else sees what a fool you done turned out to be. You must think these here lil ole arms of you'n is mighty long. . . ."

I was carried into the house and undressed for bed and the doctor was called. I cried bitterly, as much from the disappointment of finding the plane so far beyond my reach as from the pain.

When the doctor came I heard my mother telling him about the plane and asking if anything was wrong with my mind. He explained that I had had a fever for several hours. But I was kept in bed for a week and I constantly saw the plane in my sleep, flying just beyond my fingertips, sailing so slowly that it seemed barely to move. And each time I'd reach out to grab it I'd miss and through each dream I'd hear my grandma warning:

> Young man, young man,
> Yo' arms too short
> To box with God. . . .

"Hey, son!"

At first he did not know where he was and looked at the old man pointing, with blurred eyes.

"Ain't that one of you-all's airplanes coming after you?"

As his vision cleared he saw a small black shape above a distant field, soaring through waves of heat. But he could not be sure and with the pain he feared that somehow a horrible recurring fantasy of being split in twain by the whirling blades of a propeller had come true.

"You think he sees us?" he heard.

"See? I hope so."

"He's coming like a bat outa hell!"

Straining, he heard the faint sound of a motor and hoped it would soon be over.

"How you feeling?"

"Like a nightmare," he said.

"Hey, he's done curved back the other way!"

"Maybe he saw us," he said. "Maybe he's gone to send out the ambulance and ground crew." And, he thought with despair, maybe he didn't even see us.

"Where did you send the boy?"

"Down to Mister Graves," Jefferson said. "Man what owns this land."

"Do you think he phoned?"

Jefferson looked at him quickly.

"Aw sho'. Dabney Graves is got a bad name on accounta them killings but he'll call though. . . ."

"What killings?"

"Them five fellers . . . ain't you heard?" he asked with surprise.

"No."

"Everybody knows 'bout Dabney Graves, especially the colored. He done killed enough of us."

Todd had the sensation of being caught in a white neighborhood after dark.

"What did they do?" he asked.

"Thought they was men," Jefferson said. "An' some he owed money, like he do me. . . ."

"But why do you stay here?"

"You black, son."

"I know, but . . ."

"You have to come by the white folks, too."

He turned away from Jefferson's eyes, at once consoled and accused. And I'll have to come by them soon, he thought with despair. Closing his eyes, he heard Jefferson's voice as the sun burned blood-red upon his lips.

"I got nowhere to go," Jefferson said, "an' they'd come after me if I did. But Dabney Graves is a funny fellow. He's all the time making jokes. He can be mean as hell, then he's liable to turn right around and back the colored against the white folks. I seen him do it. But me, I hates him for that more'n anything else. 'Cause just as soon as he gits tired helping a man he don't care what happens to him. He just leaves him stone cold. And then the other white folks is double hard on anybody he done helped. For him it's just a joke. He don't give a hilla beans for nobody — but hisself. . . ."

Todd listened to the thread of detachment in the old man's voice. It was as though he held his words arm's length before him to avoid their destructive meaning.

"He'd just as soon do you a favor and then turn right around and have you strung up. Me, I stays outa his way 'cause down here that's what you gotta do."

If my ankle would only ease for a while, he thought. The closer I spin toward the earth the blacker I become, flashed through his mind. Sweat ran into his eyes and he was sure that he would never see the plane if his head continued whirling. He tried to see Jefferson, what it was that Jefferson held in his hand? It was a little black man, another Jefferson! A little black Jefferson that shook with fits of belly-laughter while the other Jefferson looked on with detachment. Then Jefferson looked up from the thing in his hand and turned to speak, but Todd was far away, searching the sky for a plane in a hot dry land on a day and age he had long forgotten. He was going mysteriously with his mother through empty streets where black faces peered from behind drawn shades and someone was rapping at a window and he was looking back to see a hand and a frightened face frantically beckoning from a cracked door and his mother was looking down the empty perspective of the street and shaking her head and hurrying him along and at first it was only a flash he saw and a motor was droning as through the sun-glare he saw it gleaming silver as it circled and he was seeing a burst like a puff of white smoke and hearing his mother yell, Come along, boy, I got no time for them fool airplanes, I got no time, and he saw it a second time, the plane flying high, and the burst appeared suddenly and fell slowly, billowing out and sparkling like fireworks and he was watching and being hurried along as the air filled with a flurry of white pinwheeling cards that caught in the wind and scattered over the rooftops and into the gutters and a woman was running and snatching a card and reading it and screaming and he darted into the shower, grabbing as in winter he grabbed for snowflakes and bounding away at his mother's, Come on here, boy! Come on, I say! and he was watching as she took the card away, seeing her face grow puzzled and turning taut as her voice quavered, "Niggers Stay From The Polls," and died to a moan of terror as he saw the eyeless sockets of a white hood staring at him from the card and above he saw the plane spiraling gracefully, agleam in the sun like a fiery sword. And seeing it soar he was caught, transfixed between a terrible horror and a horrible fascination.

The sun was not so high now, and Jefferson was calling and gradually he saw three figures moving across the curving roll of the field.

"Look like some doctors, all dressed in white," said Jefferson.

They're coming at last, Todd thought. And he felt such a release of tension within him that he thought he would faint. But no sooner did he close his eyes than he was seized and he was struggling with three white men who were forcing his arms into some kind of coat. It was too much for him, his arms were pinned to his sides and as the pain blazed in his eyes, he realized that it was a straitjacket. What filthy joke was this?

"That oughta hold him, Mister Graves," he heard.

His total energies seemed focused in his eyes as he searched their faces. That was Graves; the other two wore hospital uniforms. He was poised between two poles of fear and hate as he heard the one called Graves saying, "He looks kinda purty in that there suit, boys. I'm glad you dropped by."

"This boy ain't crazy, Mister Graves," one of the others said. "He needs a doctor, not us. Don't see how you led us way out here anyway. It might be a joke to you, but your cousin Rudolph liable to kill somebody. White folks or niggers, don't make no difference. . . ."

Todd saw the man turn red with anger. Graves looked down upon him, chuckling.

"This nigguh belongs in a straitjacket, too, boys. I knowed that the minit Jeff's kid said something 'bout a nigguh flyer. You all know you cain't let the nigguh git up that high without his going crazy. The nigguh brain ain't built right for high altitudes. . . ."

Todd watched the drawling red face, feeling that all the unnamed horror and obscenities that he had ever imagined stood materialized before him.

"Let's git outta here," one of the attendants said.

Todd saw the other reach toward him, realizing for the first time that he lay upon a stretcher as he yelled.

"Don't put your hands on me!"

They drew back, surprised.

"What's that you say, nigguh?" asked Graves.

He did not answer and thought that Graves's foot was aimed at his head. It landed on his chest and he could hardly breathe. He coughed helplessly, seeing Graves's lips stretch taut over his yellow teeth, and tried to shift his head. It was as though a half-dead fly was dragging slowly across his face and a bomb seemed to burst within him. Blasts of hot, hysterical laughter tore from his chest, causing his eyes to pop and he felt that the veins in his neck would surely burst. And then a part of him stood behind it all, watching the surprise in Graves's red face and his own hysteria. He thought he would never stop, he would laugh himself to death. It rang in his ears like Jefferson's laughter and he looked for him, centering his eyes desperately upon his face, as though somehow he had become his sole salvation in an insane world of outrage and humiliation. It brought a certain relief. He was suddenly aware that although his body was still contorted it was an echo that no longer rang in his ears. He heard Jefferson's voice with gratitude.

"Mister Graves, the Army done tole him not to leave his airplane."

"Nigguh, Army or no, you gittin' off my land! That airplane can stay 'cause it was paid for by taxpayers' money. But you gittin' off. An' dead or alive, it don't make no difference to me."

Todd was beyond it now, lost in a world of anguish.

"Jeff," Graves said, "you and Teddy come and grab holt. I want you to take this here black eagle over to that nigguh airfield and leave him."

Jefferson and the boy approached him silently. He looked away, realizing and doubting at once that only they could release him from his overpowering sense of isolation.

They bent for the stretcher. One of the attendants moved toward Teddy.

"Think you can manage it, boy?"

"I think I can, suh," Teddy said.

"Well, you better go behind then, and let yo' pa go ahead so's to keep that leg elevated."

He saw the white men walking ahead as Jefferson and the boy carried him along in silence. Then they were pausing and he felt a hand wiping his face; then he was moving again. And it was as though he had been lifted out of his isolation, back into the world of men. A new current of communication flowed between the man and boy and himself. They moved him gently. Far away he heard a mockingbird liquidly calling. He raised his eyes, seeing a buzzard poised unmoving in space. For a moment the whole afternoon seemed suspended and he waited for the horror to seize him again. Then like a song within his head he heard the boy's soft humming and saw the dark bird glide into the sun and glow like a bird of flaming gold.

COME HOME EARLY, CHILE

Owen Dodson

W<small>HAT</small> in the world was Deaconess Quick doing perching on a bar stool? Coin was startled and delighted to see all her great fat way up on high. A pillar of the church, no less, was on that artificial leather stool tasting, with relish, her beer. Well, bless her soul. As he watched her from his distance, she seemed perfectly at home taking small sips and giggling into her glass. She didn't look to left or right but worked her head to the mirror in front of her with secret smilings and panting joy. Maybe he should go out before she recognized him. As he started toward the door, the familiar voice hit his back like a syphon spraying him. He turned.

"Coin Foreman, well now you know. You mean you weren't going to say the word to me. . . . I'm ashamed, honey. Yes, I'm ashamed, you know, that you wouldn't press my heart after all these years. Come here, honey, now you know, and say a word." Coin stood at attention. "I ain't ashamed, honey, I learned long ago about the eat, drink and be merry, which is in the Bible, Lord."

The people in the room looked first at Coin and then at her and held their laughter in. She was ridiculous as an Easter hat fashioned of paper roses and colored eggs. That's what she had on too. And a violet dress flowered with poppies. She looked like a field held on high. And laughed with fat joy. Her bosoms bloomed toward the bar and settled in satisfaction when Coin walked to her. Getting down from the stool she was a parade of flirtation and arthritis. Now she held him in her arms kissing beer into his cheeks and onto his newly pressed uniform. "Home again, home again," she said. He breathed into her old softness. She patted him into childhood and sobbed the past into his chest. "Here he come, a grown man into my arms. Now you know, that's nice. A old lady is blessed to see you, to see thee. Coin, he has returned to me."

Coin tried to break the embrace gently but Mrs. Quick clung to him like a log in her drowning. "Don't go away, my honey, my dear. Stay with your Deaconess for the second, for my time. Now you realize meeting come but the once or the twice. Stay with me. Do you reckon we could get a table? I can't climb that stool the second time. Coin, get a table and let sit us down and talk now you a grown man and capable. Now you do that."

Coin got the table and they sat down with the precious past between them suspended and waiting for the belch of her news. He ordered new drinks as Deaconess Quick grinned at him foolishly and he grinned back at her. There would be other times to hurt people but not now. So he prepared to stay awhile.

"Thanks for this here beer, Coin. These old bones needs cooling in this heat. Ain't it something though. I just comes here regular and spends a little change. Not much, mind you. But beer's nearly as cheap as coffee or tea. I ain't worried about getting fat. Too late for that. Sometimes when I see the young like you, I just want to wind back my time, honey. Set my clock at eighteen years old. You how old?"

"Just about nineteen, Mrs. Quick."

"Then eighteen is my number. The woman she should always be a step behind the man." She threw back her head in laughter. Coin had to laugh with her. She was enjoying herself so much.

"First let me tell you this. Chile, they tried to put me out of the church. A year ago almost to this hour. Called a meeting of the righteous; they tried to hand my letter back and throw me out like suet, now you know. After all I done nursing the sick and bereaved, working to put my share into them collection plates. Deaconess Redmond, I am surprised at that woman, pointed her finger at me and declared that I had been drinking beer, not only in my home but also in a bar. Now, Coin, I never took a drink on the Lord's day, not that every day ain't the Lord's day but on Sundays, I mean. I stop my beers on Saturday sharp at twelve midnight and don't commence again till after twelve midnight Sunday night. Now you know there ain't nothing wrong with that!"

Coin had beckoned the waiter for two more beers.

"I told the Deacon and Deaconess Boards that even our Lord turned the water to wine. And you know, now don't you, that wine is stronger than beer? Yes it is!"

Coin nodded, "Uh, huh."

"And I ain't never disgraced myself in public. That's what I told Deaconess Redmond, and you know what that old fool shouted? 'Don't you, Mrs. Quick' — not even my title of Deaconess did she use — 'don't you ever use any word with grace in it because you done fell from grace and all the King's horses nor all of God's men can ever glue back together again.' "

Mrs. Quick was leaning across the table and got confidential, whispering: "Well, after she stomped out, I told them Boards a thing or two, not only about Deaconess Redmond but about a few of themselves. And they shut like clams and called that meeting to a close. The upshot is and was that I'm still a deaconess and" — with this she shook a finger at Coin, reached for her beer — "and truth, just as I'm sitting here, now that's that, please my precious savior. Thank you for this drink, boy." She drained her glass. Without any warning to Coin tears began down the channels of her cheeks.

"O Lord, here I am, a old lady, crying in the public eye."

"Mrs. Quick, would you like to go out for some fresh air?"

She snuffed in the tears, saying, "No, Coin Foreman, when you get as old as me, you crying one minute and laughing the next, or jest set looking at the past, now you know. Take the years you been away, why things happened so fast, you would've thought you was in some of the moving pictures, they went so crowded and so fast. Lord, I been talking so much. Let me hear your adventures. The picture you sent of that island was pretty as your soul, oh it was! Speaking about events going on. You know that old Italian woman, Mrs. Renaldo, who was always wearing black. Just dropped dead in the streets. Didn't even wait for the coma! They say she had liquor on her breath too. But that ain't so much to holler about. The police went up into that apartment, now you know what they found? Guess, son."

"Can't think."

"Well, I can tell you it were no sugar and spice. Tombstone catalogs, thousands of them, chile. She'd been collecting for years.

Some were as large as Montgomery Ward and the Sears and Roebuck's catalogs. Yellow and peeling. And a little doll, a girl doll she must've thought was real, 'cause they found changes of clothes for every description."

Coin had missed Mrs. Renaldo as much as he had missed Mrs. Quick and in the air he smelled the memory of peppermints and Chianti wine and black-dye bosom perspiration. In his mind he saw Mrs. Renaldo's black veils flapping against the doors of all the dead in his past, and her past. He was glad that she had dropped dead suddenly, not rotting away while living.

"Let me tell you about dolls, chile. When I was a girl, now you realize that was many years ago, although many a deacon wink at me even now. (Men has got filthy minds, sewer places.) When I was a girl in Mississippi my white folks gave me two wax dolls. In them days there were no hard and permanent dolls like they got now. I got to loving those children so much, I talked to them like I'm talking to you about just everything. One summer those folks who gave me them dolls decided to travel, in the heat now, to New Orleans. So naturally when we was packing, I didn't pack no dolls. I was bent and determined that I would carry them personal. My Mama said that there was no room for such foolishness, but I kicked up such a storm they let me take one. They promised to send the other, crated and in tar paper against the sun. So we traveled on. Of course I was in the Jim Crow car with the windows open and the hot air blowing in and not a fan going. The hottest day of that July I fell asleep by a window cradling that wax in my arms. I woke up in a hot dark sweat. The child's eyes had crossed each other and melted into the cheeks, the pretty pink dress was all wax and my fat doll had done grown skinny. Blond hair matted and lips smeared. I was fit to be tied in my own hair ribbons. Now you know, I wept like Jesus in the chapter. I kicked and I fussed. I cried at the foot of the cross. Let me tell you what I did when we arrived in New Orleans, immediately I asked if the twin doll had arrived and it had. It had! The white folks' houseman uncrated the body at once and delivered it to me. I was quiet as Eastertide when I went to the kitchen, frisking my black self and asked for a knife to cut something or other, I don't remember what lie I told. Went back to the room, now you recognize what I did, and took up the second doll and slashed away at her in New Orleans to make sure the same thing wouldn't happen to my second that happened to my first. Couldn't bear to go through the second grief. Ain't that strange?"

"Deaconess Quick, would you like another glass of beer?"

"Honey, I ain't gonna hop around here like a grasshopper, but I accept your offer. Doesn't come too once in a while, this offer, pain come twice or in all numbers but not a treat!" Coin signaled and presently the beer was brought.

"What brand of beer is this?"

"Draft," she echoed. "One of the best brands there is!"

"Deaconess Quick, is everything O.K.?"

"O.K. as the world, and you know how that is." A calm settled down. For a moment they were silent together. She finished up the last taste of her glass and with arms outstretched and her head bowed on the table as if it were the altar in the New Corinthian Baptist Church, Mrs. Quick slumped.

"Mrs. Quick, Mrs. Quick!"

"I am," she said as she raised her head, "a deaconess, not Mrs. Please, Coin, wash Mrs. Redmond and her vicious wart from your mind. Who's gonna wash me white as snow? Wash me in the grace? Nobody. Whilst you were away I attended Miss Lucy Horwitz. Who, now you reckon, is laying in the undertaker's, Branton's Morticians, in her deeds? She's laying there and ain't provided a cent for my nurse's care or the laundry of my uniforms, and I was always neat. That shows just how much you can get attached to nothings out of the goodness of your very heart. Now you know, I never loved that woman. She were distressed and I had to help, naturally, as you'd help anybody in distress. . . ."

"What in the world are you saying, Mrs. Quick?"

"Do I have to tell you again, I'm Deaconess . . ."

"Who" — and he held his breath — "who did you say was dead?"

"I want my proper title, do you hear me; I'm a servant of the Lord and I want to be called by my proper title and I ain't gonna say another word till you do." And she sat up righteously and called for another beer. Coin just looked at her while juices of his past life rose in him.

"Deaconess . . ."

"That's better," she shot back, "now where was I . . ."

"Somebody just died. . . ."

"Miss Lucy Horwitz refused the help of the doctors till the last minute, she refused the help of Jesus and His Father and my help at the end. She went to her death without the mercy of a coma, screaming inside a straitened jacket and her teeth turned black. . . . The funeral's tomorrow from the Branton's parlor but that's one funeral I need not attend with my smelling salts and ointments because there won't be nobody there to fall out." She drank the rest of her beer in one long gulp and began to straighten her hat and brush her bosom. She lurched to Coin's side.

"Oh my, Coin Foreman, the world has changed, since my day. I ain't got no day no more. Hypocritics and worry is about the whole story, the only thing I can tell my Jesus." The tears started again. "Boy, this beer is something. What the brand again? Draft, Drafts." Her behind pulled her down and Coin only heard her faintly as she called out: "Waiter. Bring me some drafts. And bring one for my son, I got my son now. . . ." Coin was walking toward the door as she smiled at his empty chair, saying something that sounded like a drunken prayer. "Death happen only the once to everybody, Coin; ain't that good!" He headed for the bar at Sumner and Quincy to think the news out by himself.

Once in the bar he threw his head on an empty, compassionate table, forced himself to sleep and dreamed.

So he rested on the table and half awake and asleep he tired himself in the dream. Soon he was whipped awake. When he first heard that Miss Lucy Horwitz was dead from Mrs. Quick, he refused to believe it. He had always thought that she would never die, she'd just funk away. At least that's what he had hoped for her. There would be that general decay and finally the smell of the odors of evil: like bat's shit and camel piss, polluted waters, the underground flush of sewers, the halitosis of worms, of snakes, asthmatic dogs, toe jam, uninspected prostitutes, the devil's armpits, the breath of lice and mayonnaise curdled with maggots, seedy diseases feeding on the garbage and marrow left in human bones. The agony she had made his family to suffer grew monumental in his alcoholic brain, and would give him no peace. He fidgeted. She had tried to destroy all of them each in a different way but now she was dead in an undertaker's parlor still bugging him into drink and that might bug him too.

Determination began to grow in Coin as he recovered and drank his beers at the bar on Sumner and Quincy. He had a half-pint of blended Green River whiskey in his sock and every once in a while he would go to the room marked GENTS for another taste. Then all the disrupted bowels of his life began to tell on him before he rushed again to GENTS. From upstairs the music made a horror of blanketed noise, a jukebox singer whispered a cozy, noisy song. The urinal flushed in a noisy sound. Coin rushed from the room. He had rejected everything and wished he were swimming where fish were small and the water was clean in the island, water was moving with a clean colored sound of the blue of his dreams and his mother's laugh: the cozy blessedness of his childhood. Lord have mercy, I'm drunk near my own street and lonely as a hill cat. . . . Astonished at himself, he left some bills on the bar and rushed out for the funeral parlor at a fast clip. He had had so much to drink, so, to keep from reeling and rocking, he hugged his toes in and began to march to a tune the sailors used to sing to keep in step:

> *You had a good home but you left,*
> *You left. You had a good home but you left,*
> *Left . . .*

He leaned against the nearest lamppost and doubled over in ironic laughter. He couldn't stop laughing; his stomach screwed up in a hard ball. Chile, you're on the streets, pull yourself together. "You left!" he shouted into the light overhead. "You left, like hell, you were put out, dispossessed, thrown into the tangles of the world at seventeen." The lines of his mind grew taut; the ball in his stomach began to bounce and he hugged the lamppost like Mary in those Italian pictures folding Jesus in her arms. His world had seemed so wide and open before his sister died. Now he had seen the world, some of it leastaways, and he recognized what life could be and was. But he was only in his first semester of hope and grief and here he was marching back to the last death. He wished that he had something to fold in his arms except this iron post with light at the top to search out evil in the streets.

> *You had a good home but you left,*
> *You left . . .*

He began tramping out the song, still hugging the iron search-light with might; around him night was flapping a black-blue flag of truce. He knew that there was no place for him to go but to the dead enemy of his youth, dead and vulnerable to the agony of the unheard taunts, threats, accusations. Ha, ha, death always happened to somebody else, not the dead. He loosed himself free and proceeded down the street with nothing in his arms to hold. He felt free now, silently walking to the end that had bugged him. But there was no fear in his staggering.

> *You had a good home but you left,*
> *You left, left . . .*

The dirty old bitch, dilapidated hag. Home! Hell, no. It was a house. A bent house. He never wanted to lay eyes on it again. Tipping his sailor's cap at a rakish angle, he entered the funeral home. Home! (It sure is her home now. The final horizontal home . . .)

Amber bulbs, shaped like flame, lit the entranceway. The smell of death hit him. From some unseen source a record was playing "Nearer My God to Thee." The record was cracked and at each turn the music bumped and hissed and scratched its way on through the dust of hundreds of weeping wakes held in this damp, leaky room where it seemed no sun ever came, where the spirit of God had never dwelt. Whoever was buried from this place was bound for someplace just as dilapidated, funky and hot as hell must be. The thought cheered him up a little. He sure smelled his beer, as if he had been washed in it. Beer and death, on the breath. He laughed. "Nearer my My God to Thee (click, hiss, scratch), nearer to Thee." There was a stand near the door with a sign over it asking VISITORS PLEASE SIGN HERE. He didn't hesitate but whipped out his pen and obliged. He wrote in large, clean letters: COIN FOREMAN WAS HERE. Let her put that in her pipe and smoke it. Those words preached a sermon to the wicked. He winked to himself. There were hardly any other names in the book. "Few have come to call," he whispered to himself as he approached the cheap oak coffin.

The grain was large and vulgar, the stain was cheap and still smelled, the lining was low-grade rayon sewn in gathers, making it appear that the body was lying in whipped cream. The light on the upturned lid sent out rays the color of forty-nine-cent sherry. She had given orders to save on her burial. Death wouldn't get any more of her hard-earned money than necessary. She might need it in the sweet bye and bye. He tilted his hat forward and hiked his pants. He noticed a wreath on the lower part of the casket, of pink and white gladioli. (Pink and white: the colors of spring, the colors of virgins, colors of innocence, affection, love, soft colors of ladies in gardens, colors of houses in southern Italy, where children were abundant and laughter was ready.) There were secondhand flowers from a Negro florist who bought the last and the least and sold them to secondhand people: the last and the least. A real joy shot through him as he moved closer. He would not take his hat off. Not to her. In a way he was shocked that she had never loved him but had used him and his inheritance; had got rid of him to fulfill a perverted affection for his sister which, he was sure, was never consummated. Perhaps that was why she was so bitter, was determined to destroy as much joy for others as possible, since joy or even crumbs of happiness would never come to her. Agnes's great simplicity, like his mother's, led her to trust the vultures and the bright snakes of this world — thinking that because they were God's creatures they couldn't be truly treacherous. Miss Lucy Horwitz had never known the geography of natural love or cared for it. No one had ever charted the courses of her body. She was a vagabond to love who tasted where she was tolerated but had never sat down to a full meal. Didn't dare to. For all her hardness, she had been a coward. She had been a destroyer. On his ship last year in hours off he had read the *Inferno,* but Dante's hell was a literary one and truly real; the hell Lucy had created was not to be believed by anyone but him. All her victims were dead.

No. He would not take his hat off. He had learned that much: not to bow to the destroyer, even in death. Death was not so much. Anyway it had its own immaculateness beyond all his potential courtesy. So he moved closer still with his racked hat. The beer came riding up in him like love and destruction. He was in a sudden panic and turned around swiftly to find a hiding place; instead he reached into his sock for his half-pint. There were faint noises overhead and smells seemed to ride about the room in waves: bacon frying, chitlin's, greens. A sudden crash of dishes brought him to. They're probably drunk up there too. Who wouldn't be, living with the dead forever in your parlor? There was a frantic rolling overhead and a dog began to howl. And then the barking of human voices, fighting, stoning each other with words. Well, at least Miss Horwitz was in her usual environment. Death couldn't steal her away from that. As he looked down into the sliced mouth of her death he saw that she was really dead in the virgin green of her shroud. Shriveled up in whipped cream. She was as gone as a snuffed-out cigar and the color of one. She looked chewed up, cancerous, utterly finished. She looked hard as pavement. He whispered to it: Mene, Mene Tekel Upharsin. She was dead after all. He took another big swig, and standing ten feet tall, in a porous of joy, he spat the whole drink in her dead face. What was left in the bottle he poured over that mouth, on those hands that had commanded him as a child, at puberty, in adolescence. Then he tossed the bottle in her stingy coffin; without staggering he left the foul funeral parlor, like a man.

SANTA CLAUS IS A WHITE MAN

John Henrik Clarke

W HEN he left the large house where his mother was a servant, he was happy. She had embraced him lovingly and had given him — for the first time in his life! — a quarter. "Now you go do your Chris'mus shopping," she had said. "Get somethin' for Daddy and something for Baby and something for Aunt Lil. And something for Mummy too, if it's any money left."

He had already decided how he would divide his fortune. A nickel for something for Daddy, another nickel for Baby, another for Aunt Lil. And ten whole cents for Mummy's present. Something beautiful and gorgeous, like a string of pearls, out of the ten-cent store.

His stubby legs moved fast as he headed toward the business district. Although it was mid-December, the warm southern sun brought perspiration flooding to his little, darkskinned face. He was so happy . . . exceedingly happy! Effortlessly he moved along, feeling light and free, as if the wind was going to sweep him up to the heavens, up where everybody could see him — Randolph Johnson, the happiest little colored boy in all Louisiana!

When he reached the outskirts of the business district, where the bulk of the city's poor-whites lived, he slowed his pace. He felt instinctively that if he ran, one of them would accuse him of having stolen something; and if he moved too slow, he might be charged with looking for something to steal. He walked along with quick, cautious strides, glancing about fearfully now and then. Temporarily the happiness which the prospect of going Christmas shopping had brought him was subdued.

He passed a bedraggled Santa Claus, waving a tinny bell beside a cardboard chimney. He did not hesitate even when the tall fat man smiled at him through whiskers that were obviously cotton. He had seen the one real Santa weeks ago, in a big department store downtown, and had asked for all the things he wanted. This forlorn figure was merely one of Santa's helpers, and he had no time to waste on him just at the moment.

Further down the street he could see a gang of white boys, urchins of the street, clustered about an outdoor fruit stand. They were stealing apples, he was sure. He saw the white-aproned proprietor rush out; saw them disperse in all directions like a startled flock of birds, then gather together again only a few hundred feet ahead of him.

Apprehension surged through his body as the eyes of the gang leader fell upon him. Fear gripped his heart, and his brisk pace slowed to a cautious walk. He decided to cross the street to avoid the possibility of an encounter with this group of dirty ragged white boys.

As he stepped from the curb the voice of the gang leader barked a sharp command. "Hey you, come here!"

The strange, uncomfortable fear within him grew. His eyes widened and every muscle in his body trembled with sudden uneasiness. He started to run, but before he could do so a wall of human flesh had been pushed around him. He was forced back onto the sidewalk, and each time he tried to slip through the crowd of laughing white boys he was shoved back abruptly by the red-headed youngster who led the others.

He gazed dumbfoundedly over the milling throng which was surrounding him, and was surprised to see that older persons, passersby, had joined to watch the fun. He looked back up the street, hopefully, toward the bell-ringing Santa Claus, and was surprised to find him calmly looking on from a safe distance, apparently enjoying the excitement.

He could see now that there was no chance to escape the gang until they let him go, so he just stood struggling desperately to steady his trembling form. His lips twitched nervously and the perspiration on his round black face reflected a dull glow. He could not think; his mind was heavy with confusion.

The red-headed boy was evidently the leader. He possessed a robustness that set him off from the others. They stared impatiently at him, waiting for his next move. He shifted his position awkwardly and spoke with all the scorn that he could muster:

"Whereya goin', nigger? An' don't you know we don't allow niggers in this neighborhood?"

His tone wasn't as harsh as he had meant it to be. It sounded a bit like poor play-acting.

"I'm jes' goin' to the ten-cent store," the little black boy said meekly. "Do my Chris'mus shopping."

He scanned the crowd hurriedly, hoping there might be a chance of escape. But he was completely engulfed. The wall of people about him was rapidly thickening; restless, curious people, laughing at him because he was frightened. Laughing and sneering at a little colored boy who had done nothing wrong, and harmed no one.

He began to cry. "Please, lemme go. I ain't done nothin'."

One of the boys said, "Aw, let 'im go." His suggestion was abruptly laughed down. The red-headed boy held up his hand. "Wait a minute, fellers," he said. "This nigger's goin' shoppin', he must have money, huh? Maybe we oughta see how much he's got."

The little black boy pushed his hand deeper into his pocket and clutched his quarter frantically. He looked about the outskirts of the crowd for a sympathetic adult face. He saw only the fat, sloppy-looking white man in the bedraggled Santa Claus suit that he had passed a moment earlier. This strange, cotton-bearded apparition was shoving his way now through the cluster of people, shifting his huge body along in gawky, poorly timed strides like a person cursed with a subnormal mentality.

When he reached the center of the circle within which the frightened boy was trapped, he waved the red-haired youth aside and, yanking off his flowing whiskers, took command of the situation.

"What's yo' name, niggah?" he demanded.

The colored boy swallowed hard. He was more stunned than frightened; never in his life had he imagined Santa — or even one of Santa's helpers — in a role like this.

"My name's Randolph," he got out finally.

A smile wrinkled the leathery face of the man in the tattered red suit.

"Randolph," he exclaimed, and there was a note of mockery in his tone. "Dat's no name fer er niggah! No niggah's got no business wit er nice name like dat!" Then, bringing his broad hand down forcefully on the boy's shoulder, he added, "Heahafter yo' name's Jem!"

His words boomed over the crowd in a loud, brusque tone, defying all other sound. A series of submerged giggles sprang up among the boys as they crowded closer to get a better glimpse of the unmasked Santa Claus and the little colored boy. . . .

The latter seemed to have been decreasing in size under the heavy intensity of their gaze. Tears mingled with the perspiration flooding his round black face. Numbness gripped his body.

"Kin I go on now?" he pleaded. His pitifully weak tone was barely audible. "My momma told me to go straight to the ten-cent store. I ain't been botherin' nobody."

"If you don't stop dat damn cryin', we'll send you t'see Saint Peter." The fat white man spoke with anger and disgust. The cords in his neck quivered and new color came to his rough face, lessening its haggardness. He paused as if reconsidering what he had just said, then added: "Second thought, don't think we will. . . . Don't think Saint Peter would have anything t' do with a nigger."

The boys laughed long and heartily. When their laughter diminished, the red-coated man shifted his gawky figure closer to the little Negro and scanned the crowd, impatient and undecided.

"Let's lynch 'im," one of the youths cried.

"Yeah, let's lynch 'im!" another shouted, much louder and with more enthusiasm.

As if these words had some magic attached to them, they swept through the crowd. Laughter, sneers, and queer, indistinguishable mutterings mingled together.

Anguish was written on the boy's dark face.

Desperately he looked about for a sympathetic countenance.

The words, "Let's lynch him," were a song now, and the song was floating through the December air, mingling with the sounds of tangled traffic.

"I'll get a rope!" the red-haired boy exclaimed. Wedging his way through the crowd, he shouted gleefully, "Just wait'll I get back!"

Gradually an ominous hush fell over the crowd. They stared

questioningly, first at the frightened boy, then at the fat man dressed like Santa Claus who towered over him.

"What's that you got in yo' pocket?" the fat man demanded suddenly.

Frightened, the boy quickly withdrew his hands from his pockets and put them behind his back. The white man seized the right one and forced it open. On seeing its contents, his eyes glittered with delight.

"Ah, a quarter!" he exclaimed. "Now tell me, niggah, where in th' hell did you steal this?"

"Didn't steal hit," the boy tried to explain. "My momma gived it to me."

"Momma gived it to you, heh?" The erstwhile Santa Claus snorted. He took the quarter and put it in a pocket of his red suit. "Niggahs ain't got no business wit' money whilst white folks is starving," he said. "I'll jes keep this quarter for myself."

Worry spread deep lines across the black boy's forehead. His lips parted, letting out a short, muted sob. The crowd around him seemed to blur.

As far as his eyes could see, there were only white people all about him. One and all they sided with the curiously out-of-place Santa Claus. Ill-nourished children, their dirty, freckled faces lighted up in laughter. Men clad in dirty overalls, showing their tobacco-stained teeth. Women whose rutted faces had never known cosmetics, moving their bodies restlessly in their soiled housedresses.

Here suddenly the red-coated figure held up his hand for silence. He looked down at the little black boy and a new expression was on his face. It was not pity; it was more akin to a deep irksomeness. When the crowd quieted slightly, he spoke.

"Folks," he began hesitantly, "ah think this niggah's too lil'l t' lynch. Besides, it's Christmas time. . . ."

"Well," a fat man answered slowly, "it jus' ain't late 'nuf in the season. 'Taint got cold yet round these parts. In this weather a lynched niggah would make the whole neighborhood smell bad."

A series of disappointed grunts belched up from the crowd. Some laughed; others stared protestingly at the red-coated white man. They were hardly pleased with his decision.

However, when the red-haired boy returned with a length of

rope, the "let's lynch 'im" song had died down. He handed the rope to the white man, who took it and turned it over slowly in his gnarled hands.

"Sorry, sonny," he said. His tone was dry, with a slight tremor. He was not firmly convinced that the decision he had reached was the best one. "We sided not to lynch him; he's too lil'l and it's too warm yet. And besides, what's one lil'l niggah who ain't ripe enough to be lynched? Let's let 'im live awhile . . . maybe we'll get 'im later."

The boy frowned angrily. "Aw, you guys!" he groaned. "T'think of all th' trouble I went to gettin' that rope. . . ."

In a swift, frenzied gesture his hand was raised to strike the little black boy, who curled up, more terrified than ever. But the bedraggled Santa stepped between them.

"Wait a minute, sonny," he said. "Look a here." He put his hand in the pocket of his suit and brought forth the quarter, which he handed to the red-haired boy.

A smile came to the white youth's face and flourished into jubilant laughter. He turned the quarter from one side to the other in the palm of his hand, marveling at it. Then he held it up so the crowd could see it, and shouted gleefully, "Sure there's a Santa Claus!"

The crowd laughed heartily.

Still engulfed by the huge throng, still bewildered beyond words, the crestfallen little colored boy stood whimpering. They had taken his fortune from him and there was nothing he could do about it. He didn't know what to think about Santa Claus now. About anything, in fact.

He saw that the crowd was falling back, that in a moment there would be a path through which he could run. He waited until it opened, then sped through it as fast as his stubby legs could carry him. With every step a feeling of thankfulness swelled within him.

The red-haired boy who had started the spectacle threw a rock after him. It fell short. The other boys shouted jovially, "Run, nigger, run!" The erstwhile Santa Claus began to readjust his mask.

The mingled chorus of jeers and laughter was behind the little colored boy, pushing him on like a great invisible force. Most of the crowd stood on the sidewalk watching him until his form became vague and finally disappeared around a corner. . . .

After a while he felt his legs weakening. He slowed down to a brisk walk, and soon found himself on the street that pointed toward his home.

Crestfallen, he looked down at his empty hands and thought of the shiny quarter that his mother had given him. He closed his right hand tightly, trying to pretend that it was still there. But that only hurt the more.

Gradually the fear and worry disappeared from his face. He was now among his neighbors, people that he knew. He felt bold and relieved. People smiled at him, said "Hello." The sun had dried his tears.

He decided he would tell no one, except his mother, of his ordeal. She, perhaps, would understand, and either give him a new quarter or do his shopping for him. But what would she say about that awful figure of a Santa Claus? He decided not to ask her. There were some things no one, not even mothers, could explain.

THE STICK UP

John Oliver Killens

I FELT good. I think the park had something to do with it. Trees, grass, bushes — everything in brand-new togs of shining green. The warm yellow sunlight sifting down through the trees, making my face feel alive and healthy and casting shadows on the paved walks and the unpaved walks and the wooden benches. Slight breezes tickling my nostrils, caressing my face, bringing with them a good clean odor of things new and live and dripping with greenness. Such a good feeling made me uneasy.

The park breathing with people, old and young. Playing checkers and chess, listening to portable radios — the Dodgers leading the Giants. I walked to the end of the park and stood near the wading pool where the water spurted skyward.

Little children in their underpants, splashing the water and pretending to swim, and throwing water at each other and yelling and shouting in wild childish happiness. One Negro child with a soft dark face and big brown eyes pretended to enjoy herself, but her big black eyes gave her away — anxious and uneasy. As if she were not sure that all of a sudden the other children would not turn on her and bite her like a bunch of mad dogs. I knew that feeling — even now. Barefoot women sat round the pool watching the children, reading books, trying to get brown without the expense of a Florida vacation. A little blonde-headed girl got smacked in the face and ran bawling to her black-haired mother. A double-decker Fifth Avenue bus passed to the east, with curious passengers looking from the top deck. The tall buildings of New York University looked over and down upon a noisy humanity playing in the park. *Perstando Et Praestando Utilitati* —

The kids were having loads of fun and it made me think back. I substituted a country woods for the beautiful city park. I made believe the wading pool was the swimming hole on old man Gibson's forbidden grounds. And something turned over and over in my stomach and ran like a chill through the length of my body, leaving a funny taste in my mouth. I took a sudden trip into the past. Meeting kids I had known many years ago, as if they had remained kids and had never grown up. My face tight and full now as I swallowed a mouthful of cool green air. It was the first time I had been homesick in many years. Standing there trying to recall names, faces and incidents. After a moment I shrugged it off. I could never really be homesick for the country woods and the swimming holes of Georgia. Give me the city—the up-north city.

I turned and started walking back through the park, passing women, young and old, blond and brunette, and black and brown and light brown in white uniforms, pushing various types of baby carriages. I had almost reached the other end of the park, when a big lumbering giant of a white man came toward me. I tried to walk out of his way, but he maneuvered into my path and grabbed me by the shoulders. He was unshaven, his clothes were filthy and he reeked of rot-gut whiskey and days and nights without soap and water. He towered over me and coughed in my face and said in a deep rasping voice — "This is a stick up!"

I must have looked silly and startled. What was he up to, in broad open daylight? Oh — no — he must be kidding. And yet, crazier things happen every day in this crazy world of New York City. Especially in the Village.

He jabbed his big forefinger into my side, causing me to wince. Then he nudged me playfully and said, "I'm only kidding, buddy. But cheesuz christmas, I do need just four more cents for the price of a drink. How about it, professor? It's just four lousy cents. Didn't hardly take me no time at all to hustle up the rest of it this morning, but seems to me I just can't get this last four cents don't care how hard I try. It's a goddamn shame!"

I made a show of feeling in my pockets. I had no loose change and knew it. I wanted to say, Well, you sure won't get it from me, but I said instead, "Gosh, I don't have it. I'm sorry."

I started to walk away from him. He put his big arms around me, surrounding me with his foul odor. His shirt was dirty and greasy, smelled like sour food and whiskey vomit. A deep gash started near his right eye and beat a trail down into his mouth. An awful cloud came between me and the springtime, blotting out the breeze, the sunshine, the freshness that had been everywhere.

"Look, buddy, I ain't no ordinary bum you meet on the street. I want you to know that. I'm just down on my luck — see?"

I wanted to shrug my shoulders, wanted to say, I don't give a damn what you are! Through the years I had built up a resistance against people like him; and I thought I was foolproof. He rambled on, "I know — you — you think I'm just one of them everyday bums, but it isn't so. I'm just as educated as the next feller. But I know what you think though. I —"

My nostrils quivered, my neck gathered sweat. I wanted to be away from him. "You don't know what I think!"

He leaned heavily on my shoulder. My body sagged under his enormous weight. My knees buckled. "You don't have to be that way, mate. Just because a feller is down on his luck. Can't never tell when you'll need a favor yourself. Listen, I'm an educated man. Look, I used to be a business man too."

I kept thinking angrily to myself, of all the people in the park, most of them white, why did he single me out? It wasn't the first time a thing like this had happened. Just a week before I was on the subway and a white drunk got on at Thirty-fourth Street. He looked around for a seat and there were plenty available next to other people. But he finally spied me, the only Negro in the half-empty car, and he came and sat down beside me, choosing me to be the benefactor of his infinite wisdom and his great liberal philosophy and his bad-liquored breath.

I tried to pull away from this one in the park but his huge hand held me by the shoulder. With his other hand he fumbled in his shirt pocket, then in the back pocket of his trousers. He fished out a dirty ragged snapshot. "Look," he said, "that's me and my family. I used to be a business man out west. Had a good business too. Yes indeed."

It would have been comical had it not been so tragic, the way pride gleamed in his eyes as he gazed at the picture. I suppose it was he, although you had to stare at it hard and stretch your imagination. He looked like a million dollars, posing with a wife and two fine-looking children. I began to wonder what had happened to him along the way — what had become of his family — then caught myself going soft. Oh — no — none of that sentimental stuff. I glanced at my watch deliberately. "Look, my friend," I said, "I've got —"

His eyes were like red flint marbles. He coughed like he would strangle to death and directly into my face. My entire being came up in revolt against everything about him, but still he was a human being, and he might have gotten his four cents, maybe more, if he hadn't made his next pitch the way he did.

"Look, professor, I don't think I'm any better than you or anybody else. I want you to know that. We're all fighting together against them goddamn gooks in Viet Nam, ain't we? You look like an intelligent young man. I'm an educa — How about it, professor? Just four little old lousy cents —"

All of my inner resentment pushed outward as I squirmed and wrested myself angrily from his hold. "I've got to go! Goddamnit — I don't have any four cents for you!"

I started walking away from him toward the street corner trembling with anger, but uplifted by the fresh air rushing into my entire body. I stood at the intersection waiting for the light to change. Something made me turn and look for the big man. I saw him lumbering toward me again. My body became tense. A flock of cars were passing. Why in the hell didn't the light change to green? But then he stopped and sat down heavily on the last bench in the park. Amid a fit of coughing I heard him mumble — "Damn. This is getting to be a helluva country, when you can't chisel four lousy pennies offa prosperous-looking nigger!"

My hands clenched unconsciously. I smiled with a bitter taste in my mouth. The light changed to green. I started across the street.

HEALTH CARD

Frank Yerby

JOHNNY stood under one of the street lights on the corner and tried to read the letter. The street lights down in the Bottom were so dim that he couldn't make out half the words, but he didn't need to: he knew them all by heart anyway.

"Sugar," he read, "it took a long time but I done it. I got the money to come to see you. I waited and waited for them to give you a furlough, but it look like they don't mean to. Sugar, I can't wait no longer. I got to see you. I got to. Find a nice place for me to stay — where we can be happy together. You know what I mean. With all my love, Lily."

Johnny folded the letter up and put it back in his pocket. Then he walked swiftly down the street past all the juke joints with the music blaring out and the G.I. brogans pounding. He turned down a side street, scuffing up a cloud of dust as he did so. None of the streets down in Black Bottom was paved, and there were four inches of fine white powder over everything. When it rained the mud would come up over the tops of his army shoes, but it hadn't rained in nearly three months. There were no juke joints on this street, and the Negro shanties were neatly whitewashed. Johnny kept on walking until he came to the end of the street. On the corner stood the little whitewashed Baptist Church, and next to it was the neat, well-kept home of the pastor.

Johnny went up on the porch and hesitated. He thrust his hand in his pocket and the paper crinkled. He took his hand out and knocked on the door.

"Who's that?" a voice called.

"It's me," Johnny answered; "it's a sodjer."

The door opened a crack and a woman peered out. She was

middle-aged and fat. Looking down, Johnny could see that her feet were bare.

"Whatcha want, sodjer?"

Johnny took off his cap.

"Please, ma'am, lemme come in. I kin explain it t' yuh better settin' down."

She studied his face for a minute in the darkness.

"Aw right," she said; "you kin come in, son."

Johnny entered the room stiffly and sat down on a cornshuck-bottomed chair.

"It's this way, ma'am," he said. "I got a wife up Nawth. I been tryin' an' tryin' t' git a furlough so I could go t' see huh. But they always put me off. So now she done worked an' saved enuff money t' come an' see me. I wants t' ax you t' rent me a room, ma'am. I doan' know nowheres t' ax."

"This ain't no hotel, son."

"I know it ain't. I cain't take Lily t' no hotel, not lak hotels in this heah town."

"Lily yo' wife?"

"Yes'm. She my sho' nuff, honest t' Gawd wife. Married in th' Baptist Church in Deetroit."

The fat woman sat back, and her thick lips widened into a smile.

"She a good girl, ain't she? An' you doan' wanta take her t' one o' these heah ho'houses they calls hotels."

"That's it, ma'am."

"Sho' you kin bring huh heah, son. Be glad t' have huh. Reveren' be glad t' have huh too. What yo' name, son?"

"Johnny. Johnny Green. Ma'am —"

"Yas, son?"

"You understands that I wants t' come heah too?"

The fat woman rocked back in her chair and gurgled with laughter.

"Bless yo' heart, chile, I ain't always been a ole woman! And I ain't always been th' preacher's wife neither!"

"Thank you, ma'am. I gotta go now. Time fur me t' be gettin' back t' camp."

"When you bring Lily?"

"Be Monday night, ma'am. Pays you now if you wants it."

"Monday be aw right. Talk it over with th' Reveren', so he make it light fur yuh. Know sodjer boys ain't got much money."

"No, ma'am, sho' Lawd ain't. G'night, ma'am."

When he turned back into the main street of the Negro section the doors of the joints were all open and the soldiers were coming out. The girls were clinging onto their arms all the way to the bus stop. Johnny looked at the dresses that stopped halfway between the pelvis and the knee and hugged the backside so that every muscle showed when they walked. He saw the purple lipstick smeared across the wide full lips, and the short hair stiffened with smelly grease so that it covered their heads like a black lacquered cap. They went on down to the bus stop arm in arm, their knotty bare calves bunching with each step as they walked. Johnny thought about Lily. He walked past them very fast without turning his head.

But just as he reached the bus stop he heard the whistles. When he turned around he saw the four M.P.s and the civilian policeman stopping the crowd. He turned around again and walked back until he was standing just behind the white men.

"Aw right," the M.P.s were saying, "you gals git your health cards out."

Some of the girls started digging in their handbags. Johnny could see them dragging out small yellow cardboard squares. But the others just stood there with blank expressions on their faces. The soldiers started muttering, a dark, deep-throated sound. The M.P.s started pushing their way through the crowd, looking at each girl's card as they passed. When they came to a girl who didn't have a card they called out to the civilian policemen:

"Aw right, mister, take A'nt Jemima for a little ride."

Then the city policemen would lead the girl away and put her in the Black Maria.

They kept this up until they had examined every girl except one. She hung back beside her soldier, and the first time the M.P.s didn't see her. When they came back through, one of them caught her by the arm.

"Lemme see your card, Mandy," he said.

The girl looked at him, her little eyes narrowing into slits in her black face.

"Tek yo' hands offen me, white man," she said.

The M.P.'s face crimsoned, so that Johnny could see it, even in the darkness.

"Listen, black girl," he said, "I told you to lemme see your card."

"An' I tole you t' tek yo' han' offen me, white man!"

"Gawddammit, you little black bitch, you better do like I tell you!"

Johnny didn't see very clearly what happened after that. There was a sudden explosion of motion, and then the M.P. was trying to jerk his hand back, but he couldn't, for the little old black girl had it between her teeth and was biting it to the bone. He drew his other hand back and slapped her across the face so hard that it sounded like a pistol shot. She went over backwards and her tight skirt split, so that when she got up Johnny could see that she didn't have anything on under it. She came forward like a cat, her nails bared, straight for the M.P.'s eyes. He slapped her down again, but the soldiers surged forward all at once. The M.P.s fell back and drew their guns and one of them blew a whistle.

Johnny, who was behind them, decided it was time for him to get out of there and he did; but not before he saw the squads of white M.P.s hurling around the corner and going to work on the Negroes with their clubs. He reached the bus stop and swung on board. The minute after he had pushed his way to the back behind all the white soldiers he heard the shots. The bus driver put the bus in gear and they roared off toward the camp.

It was after one o'clock when all the soldiers straggled in. Those of them who could still walk. Eight of them came in on the meat wagon, three with gunshot wounds. The colonel declared the town out of bounds for all Negro soldiers for a month.

"Dammit," Johnny said, "I gotta go meet Lily, I gotta. I cain't stay heah. I cain't!"

"Whatcha gonna do," Little Willie asked, "go A.W.O.L.?"

Johnny looked at him, his brow furrowed into a frown.

"Naw," he said, "I'm gonna go see th' colonel!"

"Whut! Man, you crazy! Colonel kick yo' black ass out fo' you gits yo' mouf open."

"I take a chanct on that."

He walked over to the little half mirror on the wall of the barracks. Carefully he readjusted his cap. He pulled his tie out of his shirt front and drew the knot tighter around his throat. Then he tucked the ends back in at just the right fraction of an inch between the correct pair of buttons. He bent down and dusted his shoes again, although they were already spotless.

"Man," Little Willie said, "you sho' is a fool!"

"Reckon I am," Johnny said; then he went out of the door and down the short wooden steps.

When he got to the road that divided the colored and white sections of the camp his steps faltered. He stood still a minute, drew in a deep breath, and marched very stiffly and erect across the road. The white soldiers gazed at him curiously, but none of them said anything. If a black soldier came over into their section it was because somebody sent him, so they let him alone.

In front of the colonel's headquarters he stopped. He knew what he had to say, but his breath was very short in his throat and he was going to have a hard time saying it.

"Whatcha want, soldier?" the sentry demanded.

"I wants t' see th' colonel."

"Who sent you?"

Johnny drew his breath in sharply.

"I ain't at liberty t' say," he declared, his breath coming out very fast behind the words.

"You ain't at liberty t' say," the sentry mimicked. "Well I'll be damned! If you ain't at liberty t' say, then I ain't at liberty t' let you see the colonel! Git tha hell outa here, nigger, before I pump some lead in you!"

Johnny didn't move.

The sentry started toward him, lifting his rifle butt, but another soldier, a sergeant, came around the corner of the building.

"Hold on there," he called. "What tha hell is th' trouble here?"

"This here nigger says he want t' see tha colonel an' when I ast him who sent him he says he ain't at liberty t' say!"

The sergeant turned to Johnny.

Johnny came to attention and saluted him. You aren't supposed to salute N.C.O.s, but sometimes it helps.

"What you got t' say fur yourself, boy?" the sergeant said, not unkindly. Johnny's breath evened.

"I got uh message fur th' colonel, suh," he said; "I ain't s'posed t' give it t' nobody else but him. I ain't even s'posed t' tell who sont it, suh."

The sergeant peered at him sharply.

"You tellin' tha truth, boy?"

"Yassuh!"

"Aw right. Wait here a minute."

He went into H.Q. After a couple of minutes he came back.

"Aw right, soldier, you kin go on in."

Johnny mounted the steps and went into the colonel's office. The colonel was a lean, white-haired soldier with a face tanned to the color of saddle leather. He was reading a letter through a pair of horn-rimmed glasses which had only one earhook left, so that he had to hold them up to his eyes with one hand. He put them down and looked up. Johnny saw that his eyes were pale blue, so pale that he felt as if he were looking into the eyes of an eagle or some other fierce bird of prey.

"Well?" he said, and Johnny stiffened into a salute. The colonel half smiled.

"At ease, soldier," he said. Then: "The sergeant tells me that you have a very important message for me."

Johnny gulped in the air.

"Beggin' th' sergeant's pardon, suh," he said, "but that ain't so."

"What!"

"Yassuh," Johnny rushed on, "nobody sent me. I come on m' own hook. I had t' talk t' yuh, Colonel, suh! You kin sen' me t' th' guardhouse afterwards, but please, suh, lissen t' me fur jes' a minute!"

The colonel relaxed slowly. Something very like a smile was playing around the corners of his mouth. He looked at his watch.

"All right, soldier," he said. "You've got five minutes."

"Thank yuh, thank yuh, suh!"

"Speak your piece, soldier; you're wasting time!"

"It's about Lily, suh. She my wife. She done worked an' slaved fur nigh onto six months t' git the money t' come an' see me. An' now you give th' order that none of th' cullud boys kin go t' town. Beggin' yo' pahdon, suh, I wasn't in none of that trouble. I ain't neber been in no trouble. You kin ax my cap'n, if you wants to. All

I wants is permission to go into town fur one week, an' I'll stay outa town fur two months if yuh wants me to."

The colonel picked up the phone.

"Ring Captain Walters for me," he said. Then: "What's your name, soldier?"

"It's Green, suh. Private Johnny Green."

"Captain Walters? This is Colonel Milton. Do you have anything in your files concerning Private Johnny Green? Oh yes, go ahead. Take all the time you need."

The colonel lit a long black cigar. Johnny waited. The clock on the wall spun its electric arms.

"What's that? Yes. Yes, yes, I see. Thank you, Captain."

He put down the phone and picked up a fountain pen. He wrote swiftly. Finally he straightened up and gave Johnny the slip of paper.

Johnny read it. It said: "Private Johnny Green is given express permission to go into town every evening of the week beginning August seventh and ending August fourteenth. He is further permitted to remain in town overnight every night during said week, so long as he returns to camp for reveille the following morning. By order of the commanding officer, Colonel H. H. Milton."

There was a hard knot at the base of Johnny's throat. He couldn't breathe. But he snapped to attention and saluted smartly.

"Thank yuh, suh," he said at last. Then: "Gawd bless you, suh!"

"Forget it, soldier. I was a young married man once myself. My compliments to Captain Walters."

Johnny saluted again and about-faced, then he marched out of the office and down the stairs. On the way back he saluted everybody — privates, N.C.O.s, and civilian visitors, his white teeth gleaming in a huge smile.

"That's sure one happy darky," one of the white soldiers said.

Johnny stood in the station and watched the train running in. The yellow lights from the windows flickered on and off across his face as the alternating squares of light and darkness flashed past. Then it was slowing and Johnny was running beside it, trying to keep abreast of the Jim Crow coach. He could see her standing up, holding each other, Johnny's arms crushing all the breath out of her, holding her so hard against him that his brass buttons hurt through her thin dress. She opened her mouth to speak but he kissed her, bending her head backward on her neck until her little hat fell off. It lay there on the ground, unnoticed.

"Sugah," she said, "sugah. It was awful."

"I know," he said. "I know."

Then he took her bags and they started walking out of the station toward the Negro section of town.

"I missed yuh so much," Johnny said, "I thought I lose m' mind."

"Me too," she said. Then: "I brought th' marriage license with me like yuh tole me. I doan' wan th' preacher's wife t' think we bad."

"Enybody kin look at yuh an' see yuh uh angel!"

They went very quietly through all the dark streets and the white soldiers turned to look at Johnny and his girl.

Lak a queen, Johnny thought, lak a queen. He looked at the girl beside him, seeing the velvety nightshade skin, the glossy black lacquered curls, the sweet, wide hips and the long, clean legs striding beside him in the darkness. I am black, but comely, O ye daughters of Jerusalem!

They turned into the Bottom where the street lights were dim blobs on the pine poles and the dust rose up in little swirls around their feet. Johnny had his head half turned so that he didn't see the two M.P.s until he had almost bumped into them. He dropped one bag and caught Lily by the arm. Then he drew her aside quickly and the two men went by them without speaking.

They kept on walking, but every two steps Johnny would jerk his head around and look nervously back over his shoulder. The last time he looked the two M.P.s had stopped and were looking back at them. Johnny turned out the elbow of the arm next to Lily so that it hooked into hers a little and began to walk faster, pushing her along with him.

"What's yo' hurry, sugah?" she said. "I be heah a whole week!"

But Johnny was looking over his shoulder at the two M.P.s. They were coming toward them now, walking with long, slow strides, their reddish-white faces set. Johnny started to push Lily along faster, but she shook off his arm and stopped still.

"I do declare, Johnny Green! You th' beatines' man! Whut you walk me so fas' fur?"

Johnny opened his mouth to answer her, but the military police were just behind them now, and the sergeant reached out and laid his hand on her arm.

"C'mon, gal," he said, "lemme see it."

"Let you see whut? Whut he mean, Johnny?"

"Your card," the sergeant growled. "Lemme see your card."

"My card?" Lily said blankly. "Whut kinda card, mister?"

Johnny put the bags down. He was fighting for breath.

"Look heah, Sarge," he said; "this girl my wife!"

"Oh yeah? I said lemme see your card, sister!"

"I ain't got no card, mister. I dunno whut you talkin' about."

"Look, Sarge," the other M.P. said, "th' soldier's got bags. Maybe she's just come t' town."

"These your bags, gal?"

"Yessir."

"Aw right. You got twenty-four hours to git yourself a health card. If you don't have it by then we hafta run you in. Git goin' now."

"Listen," Johnny shouted; "this girl my wife! She ain't no ho'! I tell you she ain't —"

"What you say, nigger —" the M.P. sergeant growled. "Whatcha say?" He started toward Johnny.

Lily swung on Johnny's arm.

"C'mon, Johnny," she said; "they got guns. C'mon, Johnny, please! Please, Johnny!"

Slowly she drew him away.

"Aw, leave 'em be, Sarge," the M.P. corporal said; "maybe she is his wife."

The sergeant spat. The brown tobacco juice splashed in the dirt not an inch from Lily's foot. Then the two of them turned and started away.

Johnny stopped.

"Lemme go, Lily," he said, "lemme go!" He tore her arm loose from his and started back up the street. Lily leaped, her two arms fastening themselves around his neck. He fought silently but she clung to him, doubling her knees so that all her weight was hanging from his neck.

"No, Johnny! Oh Jesus no! You be kilt! Oh, Johnny, listen t' me, sugah! You's all I got!"

He put both hands up to break her grip but she swung her weight sidewise and the two of them went down in the dirt. The M.P.s turned the corner out of sight.

Johnny sat there in the dust staring at her. The dirt had ruined her dress. He sat there a long time looking at her until the hot tears rose up back of his eyelids faster than he could blink them away, so he put his face down in her lap and cried.

"I ain't no man!" he said. "I ain't no man!"

"Hush, sugah," she said. "You's a man aw right. You's my man!"

Gently she drew him to his feet. He picked up the bags and the two of them went down the dark street toward the preacher's house.

WE'RE THE ONLY COLORED PEOPLE HERE

(Selection from *Maud Martha*)

Gwendolyn Brooks

WHEN they went out to the car there were just the very finest bits of white powder coming down, with an almost comical little ethereal hauteur, to add themselves to the really important, piled-up masses of their kind.

And it wasn't cold.

Maud Martha laughed happily to herself. It was pleasant out, and tonight she and Paul were very close to each other.

He held the door open for her — instead of going on round to the driving side, getting in, and leaving her to get in at her side as best she might. When he took this way of calling her "lady" and informing her of his love she felt precious, protected, delicious. She gave him an excited look of gratitude. He smiled indulgently.

"Want it to be the Owl again?"

"Oh, no, no, Paul. Let's not go there tonight. I feel too good inside for that. Let's go downtown?"

She had to suggest that with a question mark at the end, always. He usually had three protests. Too hard to park. Too much money. Too many white folks. And tonight she could almost certainly expect a no, she feared, because he had come out in his blue work shirt. There was a spot of apricot juice on the collar, too. His shoes were not shined.

. . . But he nodded!

"We've never been to the World Playhouse," she said cautiously. "They have a good picture. I'd feel rich in there."

"You really wanta?"

"Please?"

"Sure."

It wasn't like other movie houses. People from the Studebaker Theatre which, as Maud Martha whispered to Paul, was "all-locked-arms" with the World Playhouse, were strolling up and down the lobby, laughing softly, smoking with gentle grace.

"There must be a play going on in there and this is probably an intermission," Maud Martha whispered again.

"I don't know why you feel you got to whisper," whispered Paul. "Nobody else is whispering in here." He looked around, resentfully, wanting to see a few, just a few colored faces. There were only their own.

Maud Martha laughed a nervous defiant little laugh; and spoke loudly. "There certainly isn't any reason to whisper. Silly, huh."

The strolling women were cleverly gowned. Some of them had flowers or flashers in their hair. They looked — cooked. Well cared-for. And as though they had never seen a roach or a rat in their lives. Or gone without heat for a week. And the men had even edges. They were men, Maud Martha thought, who wouldn't stoop to fret over less than a thousand dollars."

"We're the only colored people here," said Paul.

She hated him a little. "Oh, hell. Who in hell cares."

"Well, what I want to know is, where do you pay the damn fares."

"There's the box office. Go on up."

He went on up. It was closed.

"Well," sighed Maud Martha, "I guess the picture has started already. But we can't have missed much. Go on up to that girl at the candy counter and ask her where we should pay our money."

He didn't want to do that. The girl was lovely and blonde and cold-eyed, and her arms were akimbo, and the set of her head was eloquent. No one else was at the counter.

"Well. We'll wait a minute. And see —"

Maud Martha hated him again. Coward. She ought to flounce over to the girl herself — show him up. . . .

The people in the lobby tried to avoid looking curiously at two shy Negroes wanting desperately not to seem shy. The white women looked at the Negro woman in her outfit with which no special fault could be found, but which made them think, some-how, of close rooms, and wee, close lives. They looked at her hair. They were always slightly surprised, but agreeably so, when they did. They supposed it was the hair that had got her that yellowish, good-looking Negro man without a tie.

An usher opened a door of the World Playhouse part and ran

quickly down the few steps that led from it to the lobby. Paul opened his mouth.

"Say, fella. Where do we get the tickets for the movie?"

The usher glanced at Paul's feet before answering. Then he said coolly, but not unpleasantly, "I'll take the money."

They were able to go in.

And the picture! Maud Martha was so glad that they had not gone to the Owl! Here was technicolor, and the love story was sweet. And there was classical music that silvered its way into you and made your back cold. And the theater itself! It was no palace, no such Great Shakes as the Tivoli out south, for instance (where many colored people went every night). But you felt good sitting there, yes, good, and as if when you left it you would be going home to a sweet-smelling apartment with flowers on little gleaming tables; and wonderful silver on night-blue velvet, in chests; and crackly sheets; and lace spreads on such beds as you saw at Marshall Field's. Instead of back to your kit'n't apt., with the garbage of your floor's families in a big can just outside your door, and the gray sound of little gray feet scratching away from it as you drag up those flights of narrow complaining stairs.

Paul pressed her hand. Paul said, "We oughta do this more often."

And again. "We'll have to do this more often. And go to plays, too. I mean at that Blackstone, and Studebaker."

She pressed back, smiling beautifully to herself in the darkness. Though she knew that once the spell was over it would be a year, two years, more, before he would return to the World Playhouse. And he might never go to a real play. But she was learning to love moments. To love moments for themselves.

When the picture was over, and the lights revealed them for what they were, the Negroes stood up among the furs and good cloth and faint perfume, looked about them eagerly. They hoped they would meet no cruel eyes. They hoped no one would look intruded upon. They had enjoyed the picture so, they were so happy, they wanted to laugh, to say warmly to the other outgoers, "Good, huh? Wasn't it swell?"

This, of course, they could not do. But if only no one would look intruded upon. . . .

THE POCKETBOOK GAME

Alice Childress

M ARGE . . . Day's work is an education! Well, I mean workin'
in different homes you learn much more than if you was
steady in one place. . . . I tell you, it really keeps your mind sharp
tryin' to watch for what folks will put over on you.

What? . . . No, Marge, I do not want to help shell no beans,
but I'd be more than glad to stay and have supper with you, and
I'll wash the dishes after. Is that all right? . . .

Who put anything over on who? . . . Oh yes! It's like this.
. . . I been working for Mrs. E . . . one day a week for several
months and I notice that she has some peculiar ways. Well, there
was only one thing that really bothered me and that was her
pocketbook habit. . . . No, not those little novels. . . . I mean
her purse — her handbag.

Marge, she's got a big old pocketbook with two long straps on
it . . . and whenever I'd go there, she'd be propped up in a chair
with her handbag double wrapped tight around her wrist, and
from room to room she'd roam with that purse hugged to her
bosom . . . yes, girl! This happens every time! No, there's nobody there but me and her. . . . Marge, I couldn't say nothin' to
her! It's her purse, ain't it? She can hold onto it if she wants to!

I held my peace for months, tryin' to figure out how I'd make
my point. . . . Well, bless Bess! Today was the day! . . . Please,
Marge, keep shellin' the beans so we can eat! I know you're
listenin', but you listen with your ears, not your hands. . . . Well,
anyway, I was almost ready to go home when she steps in the room
hangin' onto her bag as usual and says, "Mildred, will you ask the
super to come up and fix the kitchen faucet?" "Yes, Mrs. E . . ."
I says, "as soon as I leave." "Oh, no," she says, "he may be gone by

then. Please go now." "All right," I says, and out the door I went, still wearin' my Hoover apron.

I just went down the hall and stood there a few minutes . . . and then I rushed back to the door and knocked on it as hard and frantic as I could. She flung open the door sayin', "What's the matter? Did you see the super?" . . . "No," I says, gaspin' hard for breath, "I was almost downstairs when I remembered . . . I left my pocketbook!"

With that I dashed in, grabbed my purse and then went down to get the super! Later, when I was leavin' she says real timid-like, "Mildred, I hope that you don't think I distrust you because . . ." I cut her off real quick. . . . "That's all right, Mrs. E . . . , I understand. 'Cause if I paid anybody as little as you pay me, I'd hold my pocketbook too!"

Marge, you fool . . . lookout! . . . You gonna drop the beans on the floor!

THE CHECKERBOARD

Alston Anderson

"JAMES? James, you out there? Lord, I wonder where that nigger is now. James?"

"I'm right here," my father said.

"You come on in this house before I hit you up side the head. You get the corn like I asked you to?"

"Yeah, I got it."

"And the bread? I bet you anything in the world you done forgot the bread. You get the bread, James?"

"Yeah, I got the bread."

My father picked up the corn and the bread and went inside the house. We'd been playing checkers, with him sitting on a bench on the front porch, the checkerboard on a chair, and me squatting on the floor on the other side. I could hear him dump the corn on the table in the kitchen; and then the paper rattled as my mother took the bread out of it. I looked at the checkerboard and thought: If I move that piece right there he'll have to jump it, then I can move that one up and get me a king. I could hear my father coming back out to the porch. When he got to the doorway my mother said, "James?"

My father stopped. "Yes, Mary-Jane."

"You cut the wood like I asked you?"

"I cut some last night, Mary-Jane."

"That ain't nearbout enough and you know it. You go on out there and cut me some wood."

My father came out on the porch and stood looking down at the checkerboard. The muscles in his jaw always moved when he was thinking about something, and they were moving now. He leaned over the board and put his hands on his knees, but he didn't sit down. He looked at the pieces, studying them; then he moved. He jumped three of my men at once, bing-bing-bing. "Hot damn," I said, and scratched my head.

"Didn't see that, did you?"

"No, sir, I sure didn't."

I moved, and he countered it. My mother came out on the porch with both hands at her hips.

"You mean to tell me you can stand up there and play checkers with that child when I done asked you to do something? You's the laziest man I seen yet, I swear before God in heaven." She went into the front room. "Ask the man to do something and he act just like I ain't said boo. After I done worked and slaved in this house all day it look like the least you could do is have some kind of consideration for the things I got to put up with." She was in the kitchen now, talking louder. "That other no-good son of yours is up there in that pool hall gambling and that no-count bitch of a daughter of yours is up there up North making a whore of herself." She started to cry. "Lord have mercy, I don't know what I done to deserve this. If I had it to do all over again I'd marry a white man. You don't believe it? A nigger ain't worth nothing atall on God's earth, just as sure as I'm His witness."

"Your move," my father said. He sat down on the bench. The muscles in his jaw were still moving, but he didn't have nary an expression on his face. I moved a piece from the back row. "Watch this one," he said, and pointed to a piece I'd left exposed. I thanked him and put back the one I'd moved. I covered the piece my father had pointed to and as I did my mother came out on the porch again.

"James, you going do like I asked you?"

"Mary-Jane, I'm going do it just as soon as I'm through here. Now let me be."

"You shouting at me again, nigger? I done told you a million times never to shout at me. I'm a lady, you hear me? Soon's you get that through that thick head of yours the better it'll be for all of us. Now you git on out there in that yard and cut the wood like I asked you to."

My father looked up at her. I don't mean to say "up at her"; just "up." Because even sitting down like he was my father was nearbout as tall as she was standing up. I could hear him laughing to himself. He shook his head from side to side and got up, real slow-like. He went down in the yard and then around to the back of the house. My mother went inside, and I could hear her bustling around in the kitchen. She was slamming things around and muttering to herself: "No-count, no-good . . . work and slave all day . . ." Then I could hear my father chopping wood. He always hummed the same tune when he was chopping wood, and swung the axe in time to it: *Hmmm-hummm, hmmm-hmmm-CHACK! Ummm-hmmm-hmmm, hmmm-CHACK!*

When he was through he came around the side of the house with an armful of wood. I ran down from the porch and took some from him, and we went inside the house together. My mother was blowing at the fire in the stove, and the kitchen was full of smoke. We dumped the wood on the floor beside the stove and went out on the porch and finished the checker game. He won.

By the time my brother got home that evening we were sitting down at the dinner table. My mother was dishing out the food. There was a lot of steam coming up from the platter, and every once in a while she'd frown and move her head away. I had my eye on a nice big piece of fatback that was sitting right on top of the greens. When my mother helped my plate she moved the spoon all around it, but she didn't give it to me. Thomas, my brother, sat down without saying good evening. As soon as his plate was in front of him he started eating.

"Ain't you going say grace?" my mother said. "You act just like you was brung up in a pigpen." My brother stopped eating and looked at her. He put his knife and fork down and said, "Gracious Father we thank Thee —"

"You stop!" my mother said. "Can't you see I ain't finished serving yet? James, when you going teach these children some manners?"

"What you been up to?" my father said to Thomas.

"I been over at Miss Florence's."

"You're a lie," my mother said. "You been up there at that pool hall all day, that's where you been."

"What you been doing?" my father said.

"Making a bookshelf," my brother said.

"Say the grace, James," my mother said.

"She pay you for it?" my father said.

"James, I said say the grace," my mother said.

"She give me five dollars," my brother said.

"Only five?" my father said.

"James?" my mother said. "You hear what I said?"

"Gracious Father who are in Heaven we thank Thee for this food which we are about to receive for Christ's sake amen," my father said. "Only five?"

"You mean to tell me you's the deacon of the church and you say grace like that?" my mother said. "Take your foot off that chair, Aaron."

"It wasn't worth no more than that," my brother said.

"How big was it?" my father said.

"Six by five," Thomas said.

"Aaron, take your foot off that chair, I said," my mother said. I took my foot off the chair. "James, when you going get that child some shoes?"

"That wasn't too bad," my father said.

"Mutton Head ain't got no shoes neither," I said.

"He don't need none right now," my father said.

"You hush," my mother said to me. "Don't need none? You mean to tell me you going let that child start school in September without shoes?"

"He'll have some by then," my father said.

"Mutton Head ain't got —"

"Hush!" my mother said.

If I made a king I'd have whupped him.

"Yeah," my mother said. "I know. He'll have them shoes just like I had my anniversary present this year."

"Mary-Jane, you going bring that up again?"

"I'm going bring it up till you learns that you's got some 'sponsibilities in this world besides the Bible and corn liquor."

"Jesus, good sweet Christ," my father said.

"Pass the salt," my brother said.

Maybe next time I can make three kings.

"You better get that child some shoes right soon, that's all I got to say," my mother said.

"Pass the salt," my brother said.

"Don't you be yelling at me, boy," my mother said.

"Can't you leave nobody in peace?" my father said.

"Pass the salt!" my brother said, real loud. I reached way over and got the cup the salt was in and handed it to him.

"James, you going sit there and let that boy yell at me like that? What's the matter? You scared of him now that he's big as you? Is that it? Git up and wash your hands, Thomas, 'fore you salt God's food with your nasty fingers. Is that it? You scared of your own son?"

My father sighed and didn't say a word. My brother kept on salting the food with his fingers.

"Thomas, you hear what I said? You git on up and wash your hands 'fore I slap you up side the head."

"Yeah, woman," Thomas said, "and that'll be the last time you slap anybody, I swear."

"Hush, Tom," my father said, real soft-like.

"What's the matter? You scared of your own son?" my mother said.

"Mutton Head's way bigger than me," I said, "but I ain't scared of him."

"Hush!" my father said, but he looked like he was about to laugh.

"You hear the ball scores today?" my brother said.

"The Yankees won," I said.

"That all you two got to talk about?" my mother said.

"I ain't studying the Yankees," Thomas said. "What'd the Dodgers do?"

"They lost," I said. "The Cards beat 'em six-two." My brother frowned and I said, "Don't nobody root for bums but bums, noway." He hit at me and I ducked and laughed.

"Don't you be hitting at that child," my mother said.

"Jesus Christ, Mary-Jane, can't you leave nobody in peace? They weren't doing nothing but playing," my father said.

"James, I done told you one time today not to yell at me," my mother said. "That's all you ever done since the day you married me twenty-four years ago last June 3rd."

"June 4th," my father said.

"All you ever do is yell, yell, yell," my mother said. She got to crying. "And all I ever do in this Godforsaken house all day is work, work, work. I ain't only got the house to clean and food to fix and y'all's clothes to wash, but other people's clothes to wash, too. God knows what I ever done to deserve this. And you galli-vanting around with these young gals. Don't think I don't know it, James Jessup!" She got to dabbing at her eyes with her apron, but she was still crying. "A man ain't good for nothing in this whole world but to get a woman children and trouble."

My father got up from the table and went inside the bedroom. My brother got up and went out on the porch. I could hear him pulling the bench out so's he could set his feet up on it like he always did. My mother started clearing the table. Underneath the light her face looked like it was dark blue, and her eyes were red.

"Don't cry, Mamma," I said. She didn't say anything. I got up and helped her with the dishes, then I went inside and went to bed.

If I got that king I could've whupped him.

The next morning when I got up my brother was already gone. I didn't know what it was that woke me at first; then I heard. It was my mother calling out "James? Lord have mercy. James? James? Jesus God in heaven. James? James . . ."

THIS MORNING, THIS EVENING, SO SOON

James Baldwin

Y ou are full of nightmares," Harriet tells me. She is in her dressing gown and has cream all over her face. She and my older sister, Louisa, are going out to be girls together. I suppose they have many things to talk about — they have me to talk about, certainly — and they do not want my presence. I have been given a bachelor's evening. The director of the film which has brought us such incredible and troubling riches will be along later to take me out to dinner.

I watch her face. I know that it is quite impossible for her to be as untroubled as she seems. Her self-control is mainly for my benefit — my benefit, and Paul's. Harriet comes from orderly and progressive Sweden and has reacted against all the advanced doctrines to which she has been exposed by becoming steadily and beautifully old-fashioned. We never fought in front of Paul, not even when he was a baby. Harriet does not so much believe in protecting children as she does in helping them to build a foundation on which they can build and build again, each time life's high-flying steel ball knocks down everything they have built.

Whenever I become upset, Harriet becomes very cheerful and composed. I think she began to learn how to do this over eight years ago, when I returned from my only visit to America. Now, perhaps, it has become something she could not control if she wished to. This morning, at breakfast, when I yelled at Paul, she averted Paul's tears and my own guilt by looking up and saying, "My God, your father is cranky this morning, isn't he?"

Paul's attention was immediately distracted from his wounds, and the unjust inflicter of those wounds, to his mother's laughter. He watched her.

"It is because he is afraid they will not like his songs in New York. Your father is an *artiste, mon chou,* and they are very mysterious people, *les artistes.* Millions of people are waiting for him in New York, they are begging him to come, and they will give him a lot of money, but he is afraid they will not like him. Tell him he is wrong."

She succeeded in rekindling Paul's excitement about places he has never seen. I was also, at once, reinvested with all my glamour. I think it is sometimes extremely difficult for Paul to realize that the face he sees on record sleeves and in the newspapers and on the screen is nothing more or less than the face of his father — who sometimes yells at him. Of course, since he is only seven — going on eight, he will be eight years old this winter — he cannot know that I am baffled, too.

"Of course, you are wrong, you are silly," he said with passion — and caused me to smile. His English is strongly accented and is not, in fact, as good as his French, for he speaks French all day at school. French is really his first language, the first he ever heard. "You are the greatest singer in France" — sounding exactly as he must sound when he makes this pronouncement to his schoolmates — "the greatest American singer" — this concession was so gracefully made that it was not a concession at all, it added inches to my stature, America being only a glamorous word for Paul. It is the place from which his father came, and to which he now is going, a place which very few people have ever seen. But his aunt is one of them and he looked over at her. "Mme. Dumont says so, and she says he is a great actor, too." Louisa nodded, smiling. "And she has seen *Les Fauves Nous Attendent* — five times!" This clinched it, of course. Mme. Dumont is our concierge and she has known Paul all his life. I suppose he will not begin to doubt anything she says until he begins to doubt everything.

He looked over at me again. "So you are wrong to be afraid."

"I was wrong to yell at you, too. I won't yell at you any more today."

"All right." He was very grave.

Louisa poured more coffee. "He's going to knock them dead in New York. You'll see."

"*Mais bien sûr,*" said Paul, doubtfully. He does not quite know what "Knock them dead" means, though he was sure, from her tone, that she must have been agreeing with him. He does not quite understand this aunt, whom he met for the first time two months ago when she arrived to spend the summer with us. Her accent is entirely different from anything he has ever heard. He does not really understand why, since she is my sister and his aunt, she should be unable to speak French.

Harriet, Louisa, and I looked at each other and smiled. "Knock them dead," said Harriet, "means *d'avoir un succès fou.* But you will soon pick up all the American expressions." She looked at me and laughed. "So will I."

"That's what he's afraid of." Louisa grinned. "We have got some expressions, believe me. Don't let anybody ever tell you America hasn't got a culture. Our culture is as thick as clabber milk."

"Ah," Harriet answered, "I know. I know."

"I'm going to be practicing later," I told Paul.

His face lit up. *"Bon."* This meant that, later, he would come into my study and lie on the floor with his papers and crayons while I worked out with the piano and the tape recorder. He knew that I was offering this as an olive branch. All things considered, we get on pretty well, my son and I.

He looked over at Louisa again. She held a coffee cup in one hand and a cigarette in the other; and something about her baffled him. It was early, so she had not yet put on her face. Her short, thick, graying hair was rougher than usual, almost as rough as my own — later, she would be going to the hairdresser's; she is fairer than I, and better-looking; Louisa, in fact, caught all the looks in the family. Paul knows that she is my older sister and that she helped to raise me, though he does not, of course, know what this means. He knows that she is a schoolteacher in the American South, which is not, for some reason, the same place as South America. I could see him trying to fit all these exotic details together into a pattern which would explain her strangeness — strangeness of accent, strangeness of manner. In comparison with the people he has always known, Louisa must seem, for all her generosity and laughter and affection, peculiarly uncertain of herself, peculiarly hostile and embattled.

I wonder what he would think of his Uncle Norman, older and much blacker than I, who lives near the Alabama town in which we were born. Norman will meet us at the boat.

Now Harriet repeats, "Nightmares, nightmares. Nothing ever turns out as badly as you think it will — in fact," she adds laughing, "I am happy to say that that would scarcely be possible."

Her eyes seek mine in the mirror — dark-blue eyes, pale skin, black hair. I had always thought of Sweden as being populated entirely by blondes, and I thought that Harriet was abnormally dark for a Swedish girl. But when we visited Sweden, I found out differently. "It is all a great racial salad, Europe, that is why I am sure that I will never understand your country," Harriet said. That was in the days when we never imagined that we would be going to it.

I wonder what she is really thinking. Still, she is right, in two days we will be on a boat, and there is simply no point in carrying around my load of apprehension. I sit down on the bed, watching her fix her face. I realize that I am going to miss this old-fashioned bedroom. For years we've talked about throwing out the old junk which came with the apartment and replacing it with less massive, modern furniture. But we never have.

"Oh, everything will probably work out," I say. "I've been in a bad mood all day long. I just can't sing any more." We both laugh. She reaches for a wad of tissues and begins wiping off the cream. "I wonder how Paul will like it, if he'll make friends — that's all."

"Paul will like any place where you are, where we are. Don't worry about Paul."

Paul has never been called any names, so far. Only, once he asked us what the word *métis* meant and Harriet explained to him that it meant mixed blood, adding that the blood of just about everybody in the world was mixed by now. Mme. Dumont contributed bawdy and detailed corroboration from her own family tree, the roots of which were somewhere in Corsica; the moral of the story, as she told it, was that women were weak, men incorrigible, and *le bon Dieu* appallingly clever. Mme. Dumont's version is the version I prefer, but it may not be, for Paul, the most utilitarian.

Harriet rises from the dressing table and comes over to sit in my lap. I fall back with her on the bed, and she smiles down into my face.

"Now, don't worry," she tells me, "please try not to worry. Whatever is coming, we will manage it all very well, you will see. We have each other and we have our son and we know what we want. So, we are luckier than most people."

I kiss her on the chin. "I'm luckier than most men."

"I'm a very lucky woman too."

And for a moment we are silent, alone in our room, which we have shared so long. The slight rise and fall of Harriet's breathing creates an intermittent pressure against my chest, and I think how, if I had never left America, I would never have met her and would never have established a life of my own, would never have entered my own life. For everyone's life begins on a level where races, armies, and churches stop. And yet everyone's life is always shaped by races, churches, and armies; races, churches, armies menace, and have taken, many lives. If Harriet had been born in America, it would have taken her a long time, perhaps forever, to look on me as a man like other men; if I had met her in America, I would never have been able to look on her as a woman like all other women. The habits of public rage and power would also have been our private compulsions, and would have blinded our eyes. We would never have been able to love each other. And Paul would never have been born.

Perhaps if I had stayed in America I would have found another woman and had another son. But that other woman, that other son are in the limbo of vanished possibilities. I might also have become something else, instead of an actor-singer, perhaps a lawyer, like my brother, or a teacher like my sister. But no, I am what I have become and this woman beside me is my wife, and I love her. All the sons I might *have* had mean nothing, since I have a son. I named him, Paul, for my father, and I love him.

I think of all the things I have seen destroyed in America, all the things that I have lost there, all the threats it holds for me and mine.

I grin up at Harriet. "Do you love me?"

"Of course not. I simply have been madly plotting to get to America all these years."

"What a patient wench you are."

"The Swedes are very patient."

She kisses me again and stands up. Louisa comes in, also in a dressing gown.

"I hope you two aren't sitting in here yakking about the subject." She looks at me. "My, you are the sorriest-looking celebrity I've ever seen. I've always wondered why people like you hired press agents. Now I know." She goes to Harriet's dressing table. "Honey, do you mind if I borrow some of that mad nail polish?"

Harriet goes over to the dressing table. "I'm not sure I know which mad nail polish you mean."

Harriet and Louisa, somewhat to my surprise, get on very well. Each seems to find the other full of the weirdest and most delightful surprises. Harriet has been teaching Louisa French and Swedish expressions, and Louisa has been teaching Harriet some of the saltier expressions of the black South. Whenever one of them is not playing straight man to the other's accent, they become involved in long speculations as to how a language reveals the history and the attitudes of a people. They discovered that all the European languages contain a phrase equivalent to "to work like a nigger." ("Of course," says Louisa, "they've had black men working for them for a long time.") "Language is experience and language is power," says Louisa, after regretting that she does not know any of the African dialects. "That's what I keep trying to tell those dicty bastards down South. They get their own experience into the language, we'll have a great language. But, no, they all want to talk like white folks." Then she leans forward grasping Harriet by the knee. "I tell them, honey, white folks ain't saying nothing. Not a thing are they saying — and some of them know it, they need what you got, the whole world needs it." Then she leans back, in disgust. "You think they listen to me? Indeed they do not. They just go right on, trying to talk like white folks." She leans forward again, in tremendous indignation. "You know some of them folks are ashamed of Mahalia Jackson? Ashamed of her, one of the greatest singers alive! They think she's common." Then she looks about the room as though she held a bottle in her hand and were looking for a skull to crack.

I think it is because Louisa has never been able to talk like this to any white person before. All the white people she has ever met needed, in one way or another, to be reassured, consoled, to have their conscience pricked but not blasted; could not, could not afford to hear a truth which would shatter, irrevocably, their image of themselves. It is astonishing the lengths to which a person, or a people, will go in order to avoid a truthful mirror. But Harriet's necessity is precisely the opposite: it is of the utmost importance that she learn everything that Louisa can tell her, and then learn more, much more. Harriet is really trying to learn from Louisa how best to protect her husband and her son. This is why they are going out alone tonight. They will have tonight, as it were, a final council of war. I may be moody, but they, thank God, are practical.

Now Louisa turns to me while Harriet rummages about on the dressing table. "What time is Vidal coming for you?"

"Oh, around seven thirty, eight o'clock. He says he's reserved tables for us in some very chic place, but he won't say where." Louisa wriggles her shoulders, raises her eyebrows, and does a tiny bump and grind. I laugh. "That's right. And then I guess we'll go out and get drunk."

"I hope to God you do. You've been about as cheerful as a cemetery these last few days. And that way your hangover will keep you from bugging us tomorrow."

"What about your hangovers? I know the way you girls drink."

"Well, we'll be paying for our own drinks," says Harriet, "so I don't think we'll have that problem. But you're going to be feted, like an international movie star."

"You sure you don't want to change your mind and come out with Vidal and me?"

"We're sure," Louisa says. She looks down at me and gives a small, amused grunt. "An international movie star. And I used to change your diapers. I'll be damned." She is grave for a moment. "Mama'd be proud of you, you know that?" We look at each other and the air between us is charged with secrets which not even Harriet will ever know. "Now, get the hell out of here, so we can get dressed."

"I'll take Paul on down to Mme. Dumont's."

Paul is to have supper with her children and spend the night there.

"For the last time," says Mme. Dumont and she rubs her hand over Paul's violently curly black hair. "*Tu vas nous manquer, tu sais?*" Then she looks up at me and laughs. "He doesn't care. He is only interested in seeing the big ship and all the wonders of New York. Children are never sad to make journeys."

"I would be very sad to go," says Paul, politely, "but my father must go to New York to work and he wants me to come with him."

Over his head, Mme. Dumont and I smile at each other. "*Il est malin, ton gosse!*" She looks down at him again. "And do you think, my little diplomat, that you will like New York?"

"We aren't only going to New York," Paul answers, "we are going to California, too."

"Well, do you think you will like California?"

Paul looks at me. "I don't know. If we don't like it, we'll come back."

"So simple. Just like that," says Mme. Dumont. She looks at me. "It is the best way to look at life. Do come back. You know, we feel that you belong to us, too, here in France."

"I hope you do," I say. "I hope you do. I have always felt — always felt at home here." I bend down and Paul and I kiss each other on the cheek. We have always done so — but will we be able to do so in America? American fathers never kiss American sons. I straighten, my hand on Paul's shoulder. "You be good. I'll pick you up for breakfast, or if you get up first you come and pick me up and we can hang out together tomorrow, while your *maman* and your Aunt Louisa finish packing. They won't want two men hanging around the house."

"*D'accord.* Where shall we hang out?" On the last two words he stumbles a little and imitates me.

"Maybe we can go to the zoo, I don't know. And I'll take you to lunch at the Eiffel Tower, would you like that?"

"Oh, yes," he says, "I'd love that." When he is pleased, he seems to glow. All the energy of his small, tough, concentrated being charges an unseen battery and adds an incredible luster to his eyes, which are large and dark brown — like mine — and to his skin, which always reminds me of the colors of honey and the fires of the sun.

"Okay, then." I shake hands with Mme. Dumont. "*Bonsoir,* madame." I ring for the elevator, staring at Paul. "*Ciao,* Pauli."

"*Bonsoir,* Papa."

And Mme. Dumont takes him inside.

Upstairs, Harriet and Louisa are finally powdered, perfumed, and jeweled, and ready to go: dry Martinis at the Ritz, supper, "in some very expensive little place," says Harriet, and perhaps the Folies-Bergère afterwards. "A real cornball, tourist evening," says Louisa. "I'm working on the theory that if I can get Harriet to act like an American now, she won't have so much trouble later."

"I very much doubt," Harriet says, "that I will be able to endure the Folies-Bergère for three solid hours."

"Oh, then we'll duck across town to Harry's New York bar and drink mint juleps," says Louisa.

I realize that, quite apart from everything else, Louisa is having as much fun as she has ever had in her life before. Perhaps she, too, will be sad to leave Paris, even though she has only known it for such a short time.

"Do people drink those in New York?" Harriet asks. I think she is making a list of the things people do or do not do in New York.

"Some people do." Louisa winks at me. "Do you realize that this Swedish chick's picked up an Alabama drawl?"

We laugh together. The elevator chugs to a landing.

"We'll stop and say good night to Paul," Harriet says. She kisses me. "Give our best to Vidal."

"Right. Have a good time. Don't let any Frenchmen run off with Louisa."

"I did not come to Paris to be protected, and if I had, this wild chick you married couldn't do it. I just might upset everybody and come home with a French count." She presses the elevator button and the cage goes down.

I walk back into our dismantled apartment. It stinks of departure. There are bags and crates in the hall, which will be taken away tomorrow, there are no books in the bookcases, the kitchen looks as though we never cooked a meal there, never dawdled there, in the early morning or late at night, over coffee. Presently I must shower and shave but now I pour myself a drink and light a cigarette and step out on our balcony. It is dusk, the brilliant light of Paris is beginning to fade, and the green of the trees is darkening.

I have lived in this city for twelve years. This apartment is on the top floor of a corner building. We look out over the trees and the rooftops to the Champ de Mars, where the Eiffel Tower stands. Beyond this field is the river, which I have crossed so often, in so many states of mind. I have crossed every bridge in Paris, I have walked along every quai. I know the river as one finally knows a friend, know it when it is black, guarding all the lights of Paris in its depths, and seeming, in its vast silence, to be communing with the dead who lie beneath it; when it is yellow, evil, and roaring, giving a rough time to tugboats and barges, and causing people to remember that it has been known to rise, it has been known to kill; when it is peaceful, a slick, dark, dirty green, playing host to rowboats and *les bateaux mouches* and throwing up from time to time an extremely unhealthy fish. The men who stand along the quais all summer with their fishing lines gratefully accept the slimy object and throw it in a rusty can. I have always wondered who eats those fish.

And I walk up and down, up and down, glad to be alone.

It is August, the month when all Parisians desert Paris and one has to walk miles to find a barbershop or a laundry open in some tree-shadowed, silent side street. There is a single person on the avenue, a paratrooper walking toward Ecole Militaire. He is also walking, almost certainly, and rather sooner than later, toward Algeria. I have a friend, a good-natured boy who was always hanging around the clubs in which I worked in the old days, who has just returned from Algeria, with a recurring, debilitating fever, and minus one eye. The government has set his pension at the sum, arbitrary if not occult, of fifty-three thousand francs every three months. Of course it is quite impossible to live on this amount of money without working — but who will hire a half-blind invalid? This boy has been spoiled forever, long before his thirtieth birthday, and there are thousands like him all over France.

And there are fewer Algerians to be found on the streets of Paris now. The rug sellers, the peanut vendors, the postcard peddlers and money changers have vanished. The boys I used to know during my first years in Paris are scattered — or corralled — the Lord knows where.

Most of them had no money. They lived three and four together in rooms with a single skylight, a single hard cot, or in buildings that seemed abandoned, with cardboard in the windows, with erratic plumbing in a wet, cobblestoned yard, in dark, dead-end alleys, or on the outer, chilling heights of Paris.

The Arab cafes are closed — those dark, acrid cafes in which I used to meet with them to drink tea, to get high on hashish, to listen to the obsessive, stringed music which has no relation to any beat, any time, that I have ever known. I once thought of the North Africans as my brothers and that is why I went to their cafes. They were very friendly to me, perhaps one or two of them remained really fond of me even after I could no longer afford to smoke Lucky Strikes and after my collection of American sport shirts had vanished — mostly into their wardrobes. They seemed to feel that they had every right to them, since I could only have wrested these things from the world by cunning — it meant nothing to say that I had had no choice in the matter; perhaps I had wrested these things from the world by treason, by refusing to be identified with the misery of my people. Perhaps, indeed, I identified myself with those who were responsible for this misery.

And this was true. Their rage, the only note in all their music which I could not fail to recognize, to which I responded, yet had the effect of setting us more than ever at a division. They were perfectly prepared to drive all Frenchmen into the sea, and to level the city of Paris. But I could not hate the French, because they left me alone. And I love Paris, I will always love it, it is the city which saved my life. It saved my life by allowing me to find out who I am.

It was on a bridge, one tremendous, April morning, that I knew I had fallen in love. Harriet and I were walking hand in hand. The bridge was the Pont Royal, just before us was the great *horloge*, high and lifted up, saying ten to ten; beyond this, the golden statue of Joan of Arc, with her sword uplifted. Harriet and I were silent, for we had been quarreling about something. Now, when I look back, I think we had reached that state when an affair must either end or become something more than an affair.

I looked sideways at Harriet's face, which was still. Her dark-blue eyes were narrowed against the sun, and her full, pink lips were still slightly sulky, like a child's. In those days, she hardly ever wore make-up. I was in my shirt-sleeves. Her face made me want to laugh and run my hand over her short dark hair. I wanted to pull her to me and say, Baby, don't be mad at me, and at that moment something tugged at my heart and made me catch my breath. There were millions of people all around us, but I was alone with Harriet. She was alone with me. Never, in all my life, until that moment, had I been alone with anyone. The world had always been with us, between us, defeating the quarrel we could not achieve, and making love impossible. During all the years of my life, until that moment, I had carried the menacing, the hostile, killing world with me everywhere. No matter what I was doing or saying or feeling, one eye had always been on the world — that world which I had learned to distrust almost as soon as I learned my name, that world on which I knew one could never turn one's back, the white man's world. And for the first time in my life I was free of it; it had not existed for me; I had been quarreling with my girl. It was our quarrel, it was entirely between us, it had nothing to do with anyone else in the world. For the first time in my life I had not been afraid of the patriotism of the mindless, in uniform or out, who would beat me up and treat the woman who was with me as though she were the lowest of untouchables. For the first time in my life I felt that no force jeopardized my right, my power, to possess and to protect a woman; for the first time, the first time, I felt that the woman was not, in her own eyes or in the eyes of the world, degraded by my presence.

The sun fell over everything, like a blessing, people were moving all about us, I will never forget the feeling of Harriet's small hand in mine, dry and trusting, and I turned to her, slowing our pace. She looked up at me with her enormous, blue eyes, and she seemed to wait. I said, "Harriet. Harriet. *Tu sais, il y a quelque chose de très grave qui m'est arrivé. Je t'aime. Je t'aime. Tu me comprends*, or shall I say it in English?"

This was eight years ago, shortly before my first and only visit home.

That was when my mother died. I stayed in America for three months. When I came back, Harriet thought that the change in me was due to my grief — I was very silent, very thin. But it had not been my mother's death which accounted for the change. I had known that my mother was going to die. I had not known what America would be like for me after nearly four years away.

I remember standing at the rail and watching the distance between myself and Le Havre increase. Hands fell, ceasing to wave, handkerchiefs ceased to flutter, people turned away, they mounted their bicycles or got into their cars and rode off. Soon, Le Havre was nothing but a blur. I thought of Harriet, already miles from me in Paris, and I pressed my lips tightly together in order not to cry.

Then as Europe dropped below the water, as the days passed and passed, as we left behind us the skies of Europe and the eyes of everyone on the ship began, so to speak, to refocus, waiting for the first glimpse of America, my apprehension began to give way to a secret joy, a checked anticipation. I thought of such details as showers, which are rare in Paris, and I thought of such things as rich, cold, American milk and heavy, chocolate cake. I wondered about my friends, wondered if I had any left, and wondered if they would be glad to see me.

The Americans on the boat did not seem to be so bad, but I was fascinated, after such a long absence from it, by the nature of their friendliness. It was a friendliness which did not suggest, and was not intended to suggest, any possibility of friendship. Unlike Europeans, they dropped titles and used first names almost at once, leaving themselves, unlike the Europeans, with nowhere thereafter to go. Once one had become "Pete" or "Jane" or "Bill" all that could decently be known was known and any suggestion that there might be further depths, a person, so to speak, behind the name, was taken as a violation of that privacy which did not, paradoxically, since they trusted it so little, seem to exist among Americans. They apparently equated privacy with the unspeakable things they did in the bathroom or the bedroom, which they related only to the analyst, and then read about in the pages of best sellers. There was an eerie and unnerving irreality about everything they said and did, as though they were all members of the same team and were acting on orders from some invincibly cheerful and tirelessly inventive coach. I was fascinated by it. I found it oddly moving, but I cannot say that I was displeased. It had not occurred to me before that Americans, who had never treated me with any respect, had no respect for each other.

On the last night but one, there was a gala in the big ballroom and I sang. It had been a long time since I had sung before so many Americans. My audience had mainly been penniless French students, in the weird, Left Bank bistros I worked in those days. Still, I was a great hit with them and by this time I had become enough of a drawing card, in the Latin Quarter and in St. Germain des Prés, to have attracted a couple of critics, to have had my picture in *France-soir,* and to have acquired a legal work permit which allowed me to make a little more money. Just the same, no matter how industrious and brilliant some of the musicians had been, or how devoted my audience, they did not know, they could not know, what my songs came out of. They did not know what was funny about it. It was impossible to translate: It damn well better be funny, or Laughing to keep from crying, or What did I do to be so black and blue?

The moment I stepped out on the floor, they began to smile, something opened in them, they were ready to be pleased. I found in their faces, as they watched me, smiling, waiting, an artless relief, a profound reassurance. Nothing was more familiar to them than the sight of a dark boy singing, and there were few things on earth more necessary. It was under cover of darkness, my own darkness, that I could sing for them of the joys, passions, and terrors they smuggled about with them like steadily depreciating contraband. Under cover of the midnight fiction that I was unlike them because I was black, they could stealthily gaze at those treasures which they had been mysteriously forbidden to possess and were never permitted to declare.

I sang "I'm Coming, Virginia," and "Take This Hammer," and "Precious Lord." They wouldn't let me go and I came back and sang a couple of the oldest blues I knew. Then someone asked me to sing "Swanee River," and I did, astonished that I could, astonished that this song, which I had put down long ago, should have the power to move me. Then, if only, perhaps, to make the record complete, I wanted to sing "Strange Fruit," but on this number no one can surpass the great, tormented Billie Holiday. So I finished with "Great Getting-up Morning" and I guess I can say that if I didn't stop the show I certainly ended it. I got a big hand and I drank at a few tables and I danced with a few girls.

After one more day and one more night, the boat landed in New York. I woke up, I was bright awake at once, and I thought, We're here. I turned on all the lights in my small cabin and I stared into the mirror as though I were committing my face to memory. I took a shower and I took a long time shaving and I dressed myself very carefully. I walked the long ship corridors to the dining room, looking at the luggage piled high before the elevators and beside the steps. The dining room was nearly half empty and full of a quick and joyous excitement which depressed me even more. People ate quickly, chattering to each other, anxious to get upstairs and go on deck. Was it my imagination or was it true that they seemed to avoid my eyes? A few people waved and smiled, but let me pass; perhaps it would have made them uncomfortable, this morning, to try to share their excitement with me; perhaps they did not want to know whether or not it was possible for me to share it. I walked to my table and sat down. I munched toast as dry as paper and drank a pot of coffee. Then I tipped my waiter, who bowed and smiled and called me "sir" and said that he hoped to see me on the boat again. "I hope so, too," I said.

And was it true, or was it my imagination, that a flash of wondering comprehension, a flicker of wry sympathy, then appeared in the waiter's eyes? I walked upstairs to the deck.

There was a breeze from the water but the sun was hot and made me remember how ugly New York summers could be. All of the deck chairs had been taken away and people milled about in the space where the deck chairs had been, moved from one side of the ship to the other, clambered up and down the steps, crowded the rails, and they were busy taking photographs — of the harbor, of each other, of the sea, of the gulls. I walked slowly along the deck, and an impulse stronger than myself drove me to the rail. There it was, the great, unfinished city, with all its towers blazing in the sun. It came toward us slowly and patiently, like some enormous, cunning, and murderous beast ready to devour, impossible to escape. I watched it come closer and I listened to the people around me, to their excitement and their pleasure. There was no doubt that it was real. I watched their shining faces and wondered if I were mad. For a moment I longed, with all my heart, to be able to feel whatever they were feeling, if only to know what such a feeling was like. As the boat moved slowly into the harbor, they were being moved into safety. It was only I who was being floated into danger. I turned my head, looking for

Europe, but all that stretched behind me was the sky, thick with gulls. I moved away from the rail. A big, sandy-haired man held his daughter on his shoulders, showing her the Statue of Liberty. I would never know what this statue meant to others; she had always been an ugly joke for me. And the American flag was flying from the top of the ship, above my head. I had seen the French flag drive the French into the most unspeakable frenzies, I had seen the flag which was nominally mine used to dignify the vilest purposes: now I would never, as long as I lived, know what others saw when they saw a flag. "There's no place like home," said a voice close by, and I thought, There damn sure isn't. I decided to go back to my cabin and have a drink.

There was a cablegram from Harriet in my cabin. It said: Be good. Be quick. I'm waiting. I folded it carefully and put it in my breast pocket. Then I wondered if I would ever get back to her. How long would it take me to earn the money to get out of this land? Sweat broke out on my forehead and I poured myself some whisky from my nearly empty bottle. I paced the tiny cabin. It was silent. There was no one down in the cabins now.

I was not sober when I faced the uniforms in the first-class lounge. There were two of them; they were not unfriendly. They looked at my passport, they looked at me. "You've been away a long time," said one of them.

"Yes," I said, "it's been a while."

"What did you do over there all that time?" — with a grin meant to hide more than it revealed, which hideously revealed more than it could hide.

I said, "I'm a singer," and the room seemed to rock around me. I held on to what I hoped was a calm, open smile. I had not had to deal with these faces in so long that I had forgotten how to do it. I had once known how to pitch my voice precisely between curtness and servility, and known what razor's edge of a picka-ninny's smile would turn away wrath. But I had forgotten all the tricks on which my life had once depended. Once I had been an expert at baffling these people, at setting their teeth on edge, and dancing just outside the trap laid for me. But I was not an expert now. These faces were no longer merely the faces of two white men who were my enemies. They were the faces of two white people whom I did not understand, and I could no longer plan my moves in accordance with what I knew of their cowardice and their needs and their strategy. That moment on the bridge had undone me forever.

"That's right," said one of them, "that's what it says, right here on the passport. Never heard of you, though." They looked up at me. "Did you do a lot of singing over there?"

"Some."

"What kind — concerts?"

"No." I wondered what I looked like, sounded like. I could tell nothing from their eyes. "I worked a few nightclubs."

"Nightclubs, eh? I guess they liked you over there."

"Yes," I said, "they seemed to like me all right."

"Well" — and my passport was stamped and handed back to me — "let's hope they like you over here."

"Thanks." They laughed — was it at me, or was it my imagination? — and I picked up the one bag I was carrying and threw my trench coat over one shoulder and walked out of the first-class lounge. I stood in the slow-moving, murmuring line which led to the gangplank. I looked straight ahead and watched heads, smiling faces, step up to the shadow of the gangplank awning and then swiftly descend out of sight. I put my passport back in my breast pocket — Be quick. I'm waiting — and I held my landing card in my hand. Then, suddenly, there I was, standing on the edge of the boat, staring down the long ramp to the ground. At the end of the plank, on the ground, stood a heavy man in a uniform. His cap was pushed back from his gray hair and his face was red and wet. He looked up at me. This was the face I remembered, the face of my nightmares; perhaps hatred had caused me to know this face better than I would ever know the face of any lover. "Come on, boy," he cried, "come on, come on!"

And I almost smiled. I was home. I touched my breast pocket. I thought of a song I sometimes sang, When will I ever get to be a man? I came down the gangplank, stumbling a little, and gave the man my landing card.

Much later in the day, a customs inspector checked my baggage and waved me away. I picked up my bags and started walking down the long stretch which led to the gate, to the city.

And I heard someone call my name.

I looked up and saw Louisa running toward me. I dropped my bags and grabbed her in my arms and tears came to my eyes and rolled down my face. I did not know whether the tears were for joy at seeing her, or from rage, or both.

"How are you? How are you? You look wonderful, but, oh, haven't you lost weight? It's wonderful to see you again."

I wiped my eyes. "It's wonderful to see you, too, I bet you thought I was never coming back."

Louisa laughed. "I wouldn't have blamed you if you hadn't. These people are just as corny as ever, I swear I don't believe there's any hope for them. How's your French? Lord, when I think that it was I who studied French and now I can't speak a word. And you never went near it and you probably speak it like a native."

I grinned. *"Pas mal. Te me défends pas mal."* We started down the wide steps into the street. "My God," I said. "New York." I was not aware of its towers now. We were in the shadow of the elevated highway but the thing which most struck me was neither light nor shade, but noise. It came from a million things at once, from trucks and tires and clutches and brakes and doors; from machines shuttling and stamping and rolling and cutting and pressing; from the building of tunnels, the checking of gas mains, the laying of wires, the digging of foundations; from the chattering of rivets, the scream of the pile driver, the clanging of great shovels; from the battering down and the raising up of walls; from millions of radios and television sets and jukeboxes. The human voices distinguished themselves from the roar only by their note of strain and hostility. Another fleshy man, uniformed and red-faced, hailed a cab for us and touched his cap politely but could only manage a peremptory growl: "Right this way, miss. Step up, sir." He slammed the cab door behind us. Louisa directed the driver to the New Yorker Hotel.

"Do they take us there?"

She looked at me. "They got laws in New York, honey, it'd be the easiest thing in the world to spend all your time in court. But over at the New Yorker, I believe they've already got the message." She took my arm. "You see? In spite of all this chopping and booming, this place hasn't really changed very much. You still can't hear yourself talk."

And I thought to myself, Maybe that's the point.

Early the next morning we checked out of the hotel and took the plane for Alabama.

I am just stepping out of the shower when I hear the bell ring. I dry myself hurriedly and put on a bathrobe. It is Vidal, of course, and very elegant he is too, with his bushy gray hair quite lustrous, his swarthy, cynical, gypsy-like face shaved and lotioned. Usually he looks just any old way. But tonight his brief bulk is contained in a dark-blue suit and he has an ironical pearl stickpin in his blue tie.

"Come in, make yourself a drink. I'll be with you in a second."

"I am, *hélas!*, on time. I trust you will forgive me for my thoughtlessness."

But I am already back in the bathroom. Vidal puts on a record: Mahalia Jackson, singing "I'm Going to Live the Life I Sing About in My Song."

When I am dressed, I find him sitting in a chair before the open window. The daylight is gone, but it is not exactly dark. The trees are black now against the darkening sky. The lights in windows and the lights of motorcars are yellow and ringed. The street lights have not yet been turned on. It is as though, out of deference to the departed day, Paris waited a decent interval before assigning her role to a more theatrical but inferior performer.

Vidal is drinking a whisky and soda. I pour myself a drink. He watches me.

"Well. How are you, my friend? You are nearly gone. Are you happy to be leaving us?"

"No." I say this with more force than I had intended. Vidal raises his eyebrows, looking amused and distant. "I never really intended to go back there. I certainly never intended to raise my kid there —"

"*Mais, mon cher,*" Vidal says, calmly, "you are an intelligent man, you must have known that you would probably be returning one day." He pauses. "And, as for Pauli — did it never occur to you that he might wish one day to see the country in which his father and his father's father were born?"

"To to do that, really, he'd have to go to Africa."

"America will always mean more to him than Africa, you know that."

"I don't know." I throw my drink down and pour myself another. "Why should he want to cross all that water just to be called a nigger? America never gave him anything."

"It gave him his father."

I look at him. "You mean, his father escaped."

Vidal throws back his head and laughs. If Vidal likes you, he is certain to laugh at you and his laughter can be very unnerving. But the look, the silence which follow this laughter can be very unnerving, too. And now, in the silence, he asks me, "Do you really think that you have escaped anything? Come. I know you for a better man than that." He walks to the table which holds the liquor. "In that movie of ours which has made you so famous and, as I now see, so troubled, what are you playing, after all? What is the tragedy of this half-breed troubadour if not, precisely, that he has taken all the possible roads to escape and that all these roads have failed him?" He pauses, with the bottle in one hand, and looks at me. "Do you remember the trouble I had to get a performance out of you? How you hated me, you sometimes looked as though you wanted to shoot me! And do you remember when the role of Chico began to come alive?" He pours his drink. "Think back, remember. I am a very great director, *mais pardon!* I could not have got such a performance out of anyone but you. And what were you thinking of, what was in your mind, what nightmare were you living with when you began, at last, to play the role — truthfully?" He walks back to his seat.

Chico, in the film, is the son of a Martinique woman and a French colon who hates both his mother and his father. He flees from the island to the capital, carrying his hatred with him. This hatred has now grown, naturally, to include all dark women and all white men, in a word, everyone. He descends into the underworld of Paris, where he dies. *Les fauves* — the wild beasts — refers to the life he has fled and to the life which engulfs him. When I agreed to do the role, I felt that I could probably achieve it by bearing in mind the North Africans I had watched in Paris for so long. But this did not please Vidal. The blowup came while we were rehearsing a fairly simple, straightforward scene. Chico goes into a sleazy Pigalle dance hall to beg the French owner for a particularly humiliating job. And this Frenchman reminds him of his father.

"You are playing this boy as though you thought of him as the noble savage," Vidal said, icily. "*Ça vient d'où* — all these ghastly mannerisms you are using all the time?"

Everyone fell silent, for Vidal rarely spoke this way. This silence told me that everyone, the actor with whom I was playing the scene and all the people in the "dance hall," shared Vidal's opinion of my performance and was relieved that he was going to do something about it. I was humiliated and too angry to speak; but perhaps I also felt, at the very bottom of my heart, a certain relief, an unwilling respect.

"You are doing it all wrong," he said, more gently. Then, "Come, let us have a drink together."

We walked into his office. He took a bottle and two glasses out of his desk. "Forgive me, but you put me in mind of some of those English lady actresses who love to play *putain* as long as it is always absolutely clear to the audience that they are really ladies. So perhaps they read a book, not usually *hélas!*, *Fanny Hill*, and they have their chauffeurs drive them through Soho once or twice — and they come to the stage with a performance so absolutely loaded with detail, every bit of it meaningless, that there can be no doubt that they are acting. It is what the British call a triumph." He poured two cognacs. "That is what you are doing. Why? Who do you think this boy is, what do you think he is feeling, when he asks for this job?" He watched me carefully and I bitterly resented his look. "You come from America. The situation is not so pretty there for boys like you. I know you may not have been as poor as — as some — but is it really impossible for you to understand what a boy like Chico feels? Have you never, yourself, been in a similar position?"

I hated him for asking the question because I knew he knew the answer to it. "I would have had to be a very lucky black man not to have been in such a position."

"You would have had to be a very lucky man."

"Oh, God," I said, "please don't give me any of this equality-in-anguish business."

"It is perfectly possible," he said, sharply, "that there is not another kind."

Then he was silent. He sat down behind his desk. He cut a cigar and lit it, puffing up clouds of smoke, as though to prevent us from seeing each other too clearly. "Consider this," he said. "I am a French director who has never seen your country. I have never done you any harm except, perhaps, historically — I mean, because I am white — but I cannot be blamed for that —"

"But I can be," I said, "and I am! I've never understood why, if I have to pay for the history written in the color of my skin, you should get off scot-free!" But I was surprised at my vehemence, I had not known I was going to say these things, and by the fact that I was trembling, and from the way he looked at me I knew that, from a professional point of view anyway, I was playing into his hands.

"What makes you think I do?" His face looked weary and stern. "I am a Frenchman. Look at France. You think that I — we — are not paying for our history?" He walked to the window, staring out at the rather grim little town in which the studio was located. "If it is revenge that you want, well, then, let me tell you, you will have it. You will probably have it whether you want it or not, our stupidity will make it inevitable." He turned back into the room. "But I beg you not to confuse me with the happy people of your country, who scarcely know that there is such a thing as history and so, naturally, imagine that they can escape, as you put it, scot-free. That is what you are doing, that is what I was about to say. I was about to say that I am a French director and I have never been in your country and I have never done you any harm — but you are not talking to that man, in this room, now. You are not talking to Jean Luc Vidal, but to some other white man, whom you remember, who has nothing to do with me." He paused and went back to his desk. "Oh, most of the time you are not like this, I know. But it is there all the time, it must be, because when you are upset, this is what comes out. So you are not playing Chico truthfully, you are lying about him, and I will not let you do it. When you go back, now, and play this scene again, I want you to remember what has just happened in this room. That is what Chico does when he walks into the dance hall. The Frenchman whom he begs for a job is not merely a Frenchman — he is the father who disowned and betrayed him and all the Frenchmen whom he hates." He smiled and poured me another cognac. "Ah! If it were not for my history, I would not have so much trouble to get the truth out of you." He looked into my face, half smiling. "And you, you are angry — are you not? — that I ask you for the truth. You think I have no right to ask." Then he said something which he knew would enrage me. "Who are you then, and what good has it done you to come to France, and how will you raise your son? Will you teach him never to tell the truth to anyone?"

And he moved behind his desk and looked at me, as though from behind a barricade.

"You have no right to talk to me this way."

"Oh, yes, I do," he said. "I have a film to make and a reputation to maintain and I am going to get a performance out of you." He looked at his watch. "Let us go back to work."

I watch him now, sitting quietly in my living room, tough, cynical, crafty old Frenchman, and I wonder if he knows that the nightmare at the bottom of my mind, as I played the role of Chico, was all the possible fates of Paul. This is but another way of saying that I relived the disasters which had nearly undone me; but because I was thinking of Paul, I discovered that I did not want my son ever to feel toward me as I had felt toward my own father. He had died when I was eleven, but I had watched the humiliations he had to bear, and I had pitied him. But was there not, in that pity, however painfully and unwillingly, also some contempt? For how could I know what he had borne? I knew only that I was his son. However he had loved me, whatever he had borne, I, his son, was despised. Even had he lived, he could have done nothing to prevent it, nothing to protect me. The best that he could hope to do was to prepare me for it; and even at that he had failed. How can one be prepared for the spittle in the face, all the tireless ingenuity which goes into the spite and fear of small, unutterably miserable people, whose greatest terror is the singular identity, whose joy, whose safety, is entirely dependent on the humiliation and anguish of others?

But for Paul, I swore it, such a day would never come. I would throw my life and my work between Paul and the nightmare of the world. I would make it impossible for the world to treat Paul as it had treated my father and me.

Mahalia's record ends. Vidal rises to turn it over. "Well?" He looks at me very affectionately. "Your nightmares, please!"

"Oh, I was thinking of that summer I spent in Alabama, when my mother died." I stop. "You know, but when we finally filmed that bar scene, I was thinking of New York. I was scared in Alabama, but I almost went crazy in New York. I was sure I'd never make it back here — back here to Harriet. And I knew if I didn't, it was going to be the end of me." Now Mahalia is singing "When the Saints Go Marching In." "I got a job in the town as an elevator boy, in the town's big department store. It was a special favor, one of my father's white friends got it for me. For a long time, in the South, we all — depended — on the — kindness — of white friends." I take out a handkerchief and wipe my face. "But this man didn't like me. I guess I didn't seem grateful enough, wasn't enough like my father, what he thought my father was. And I couldn't get used to the town again, I'd been away too long, I hated it. It's a terrible town, anyway, the whole thing looks as though it's been built around a jailhouse. There's a room in the courthouse, a room where they beat you up. Maybe you're walking along the street one night, it's usually at night, but it happens in the daytime, too. And the police car comes up behind you and the cop says, Hey, boy. Come on over here. So you go on over. He says, Boy, I believe you drunk. And you see, if you say, No, no sir, he'll beat you because you're calling him a liar. And if you say anything else, unless it's something to make him laugh, he'll take you in and beat you, just for fun. The trick is to think of some way for them to have their fun without beating you up."

The street lights of Paris click on and turn all the green leaves silver. "Or to go along with the ways they dream up. And they'll do anything, anything at all, to prove that you're no better than a dog and to make you feel like one. And they hated me because I'd been North and I'd been to Europe. People kept saying, I hope you didn't bring no foreign notions back here with you, boy. And I'd say, No sir, or No ma'am, but I never said it right. And there was a time, all of them remembered it, when I had said it right. But now they could tell that I despised them — I guess, no matter what, I wanted them to know that I despised them. But I didn't despise them any more than everyone else did, only the others never let it show. They knew how to keep the white folks happy, and it was easy — you just had to keep them feeling like they were God's favor to the universe. They'd walk around with great, big, foolish grins on their faces and the colored folks loved to see this, because they hated them so much. 'Just look at So-and-So,' somebody'd say. 'His white is on him today.' And when we didn't hate them, we pitied them. In America that's usually what it means to have a white friend. You pity the poor bastard because he was born believing the world's a great place to be, and you know it's not, and you can see that he's going to have a terrible time getting used to this idea, if he ever gets used to it."

Then I think of Paul again, those eyes which still imagine that I can do anything, that skin, the color of honey and fire, his jet-black, curly hair. I look out at Paris again, and I listen to Mahalia. "Maybe it's better to have the terrible times first. I don't know. Maybe, then, you can have, if you live, a better life, a real life, because you had to fight so hard to get it away — you know? — from the mad dog who held it in his teeth. But then your life has all those tooth marks, too, all those tatters, and all that blood." I walk to the bottle and raise it. "One for the road?"

"Thank you," says Vidal.

I pour us a drink, and he watches me. I have never talked so much before, not about those things anyway. I know that Vidal has nightmares, because he knows so much about them, but he has never told me what his are. I think that he probably does not talk about his nightmares any more. I know that the war cost him his wife and his son, and that he was in prison in Germany. He very rarely refers to it. He has a married daughter who lives in England, and he rarely speaks of her. He is like a man who has learned to live on what is left of an enormous fortune.

We are silent for a moment.

"Please go on," he says, with a smile. "I am curious about the reality behind the reality of your performance."

"My sister Louisa never married," I say, abruptly, "because once, years ago, she and the boy she was going with and two friends of theirs were out driving in a car and the police stopped them. The girl who was with them was very fair and the police pretended not to believe her when she said she was colored. They made her get out and stand in front of the headlights of the car and pull down her pants and raise her dress — they said that was the only way they could be sure. And you can imagine what they said, and what they did — and they were lucky, at that, that it didn't go any further. But none of the men could do anything about it. Louisa couldn't face that boy again, and I guess he couldn't face her." Now it is really growing dark in the room and I cross to the light switch. "You know, I know what that boy felt, I've felt it. They want you to feel that you're not a man, maybe that's the only way they can feel like men, I don't know. I walked around New York with Harriet's cablegram in my pocket as though it were some atomic secret, in code, and they'd kill me if they ever found out what it meant. You know, there's something wrong with people like that. And thank God Harriet was here, she proved that the world was bigger than the world they wanted me to live in, I had to get back here, get to a place where people were too busy with their own lives, their private lives, to make fantasies about mine, to set up walls around mine." I look at him. The light in the room has made the night outside blue-black and golden and the great searchlight of the Eiffel Tower is turning in the sky. "That's what it's like in America, for me, anyway. I always feel that I don't exist there, except in someone else's — usually dirty — mind. I don't know if you know what that means, but I do, and I don't want to put Harriet through that and I don't want to raise Paul there."

"Well," he says at last, "you are not required to remain in America forever, are you? You will sing in that elegant club which apparently feels that it cannot, much longer, so much as open its doors without you, and you will probably accept the movie offer, you would be very foolish not to. You will make a lot of money. Then one day you will remember that airlines and steamship companies are still in business and that France still exists. That will certainly be cause for astonishment."

Vidal was a Gaullist before De Gaulle came to power. But he regrets the manner of De Gaulle's rise and he is worried about De Gaulle's regime. "It is not the fault of *mon général*," he sometimes says, sadly. "Perhaps it is history's fault. I suppose it must be history which always arranges to bill a civilization at the very instant it is least prepared to pay."

Now he rises and walks out on the balcony, as though to reassure himself of the reality of Paris. Mahalia is singing "Didn't It Rain?" I walk and stand beside him.

"You are a good boy — Chico," he says. I laugh. "You believe in love. You do not know all the things love cannot do, but" — he smiles — "love will teach you that."

We go, after dinner, to a Left Bank discothèque which can charge outrageous prices because Marlon Brando wandered in there one night. By accident, according to Vidal. "Do you know how many people in Paris are becoming rich — to say nothing of those, *hélas!*, who are going broke — on the off-chance that Marlon Brando will lose his way again?"

He has not, presumably, lost his way tonight, but the discothèque is crowded with those strangely faceless people who are part of the night life of all great cities, and who always arrive, moments, hours, or decades late, on the spot made notorious by an event or a movement or a handful of personalities. So here are American boys, anything but beardless, scratching around for Hemingway; American girls, titillating themselves with Frenchmen and existentialism, while waiting for the American boys to shave off their beards; French painters, busily pursuing the revolution which ended thirty years ago; and the young, bored, perverted, American *arrivistes* who are buying their way into the art world via flattery and liquor, and the production of canvases as arid as their greedy little faces. Here are boys, of all nations, one step above the pimp, who are occasionally walked across a stage or trotted before a camera. And the girls, their enemies, whose faces are sometimes seen in ads, one of whom will surely have a tantrum before the evening is out.

In a corner, as usual, surrounded, as usual, by smiling young men, sits the drunken blonde woman who was once the mistress of a famous, dead painter. She is a figure of some importance in the art world, and so rarely has to pay for either her drinks or her lovers. An older Frenchman, who was once a famous director, is playing quatre cent vingt-et-un with the woman behind the cash register. He nods pleasantly to Vidal and me as we enter, but makes no move to join us, and I respect him for this. Vidal and I are obviously cast tonight in the role vacated by Brando: our entrance justifies the prices and sends a kind of shiver through the room. It is marvelous to watch the face of the waiter as he approaches, all smiles and deference and grace, not so much honored by our presence as achieving his reality from it; excellence, he seems to be saying, gravitates naturally toward excellence. We order two whisky and sodas. I know why Vidal sometimes comes here. He is lonely. I do not think that he expects ever to love one woman again, and so he distracts himself with many.

Since this is a discothèque, jazz is blaring from the walls and record sleeves are scattered about with a devastating carelessness. Two of them are mine and no doubt, presently, someone will play the recording of the songs I sang in the film.

"I thought," says Vidal, with a malicious little smile, "that your farewell to Paris would not be complete without a brief exposure to the perils of fame. Perhaps it will help prepare you for America, where, I am told, the populace is yet more carnivorous than it is here."

I can see that one of the vacant models is preparing herself to come to our table and ask for an autograph, hoping, since she is pretty — she has, that is, the usual female equipment, dramatized in the usual, modern way — to be invited for a drink. Should the maneuver succeed, one of her boyfriends or girlfriends will contrive to come by the table, asking for a light or a pencil or a lipstick, and it will be extremely difficult not to invite this person to join us, too. Before the evening ends, we will be surrounded. I don't, now, know what I expected of fame, but I suppose it never occurred to me that the light could be just as dangerous, just as killing, as the dark.

"Well, let's make it brief," I tell him. "Sometimes I wish that you weren't quite so fond of me."

He laughs. "There are some very interesting people here tonight. Look."

Across the room from us, and now staring at our table, are a group of American Negro students, who are probably visiting Paris for the first time. There are four of them, two boys and two girls, and I suppose that they must be in their late teens or early twenties. One of the boys, a gleaming, curly-haired, golden-brown type — the color of his mother's fried chicken — is carrying a guitar. When they realize we have noticed them, they smile and wave — wave as though I were one of their possessions, as, indeed, I am. Golden-brown is a mime. He raises his guitar, drops his shoulders, and his face falls into the lugubrious lines of Chico's face as he approaches death. He strums a little of the film's theme music, and I laugh and the table laughs. It is as though we were all back home and had met for a moment, on a Sunday morning, say, before a church or a poolroom or a barbershop.

And they have created a sensation in the discothèque, naturally, having managed, with no effort whatever, to outwit all the gleaming boys and girls. Their table, which had been of no interest only a moment before, has now become the focus of a rather pathetic attention; their smiles have made it possible for the others to smile, and to nod in our direction.

"Oh," says Vidal, "he does that far better than you ever did, perhaps I will make him a star."

"Feel free, *m'sieu, le bon Dieu,* I got mine." But I can see that his attention has really been caught by one of the girls, slim, tense, and dark, who seems, though it is hard to know how one senses such things, to be treated by the others with a special respect. And in fact the table now seems to be having a council of war, to be demanding her opinion or her cooperation. She listens, frowning, laughing; the quality, the force of her intelligence causes her face to keep changing all the time, as though a light played on it. And presently, with a gesture she might once have used to scatter feed to chickens, she scoops up from the floor one of those dangling ragbags women love to carry. She holds it loosely by the draw-strings, so that it is banging somewhere around her ankle, and walks over to our table. She has an honest, forthright walk, entirely unlike the calculated, pelvic workout by means of which most women get about. She is small, but sturdily, economically, put together.

As she reaches our table, Vidal and I rise, and this throws her for a second. (It has been a long time since I have seen such an attractive girl.)

Also, everyone, of course, is watching us. It is really a quite curious moment. They have put on the record of Chico singing a sad, angry Martinique ballad; my own voice is coming at us from the walls as the girl looks from Vidal to me, and smiles.

"I guess you know," she says, "we weren't about to let you get out of here without bugging you just a little bit. We've only been in Paris just a couple of days and we thought for sure that we wouldn't have a chance of running into you anywhere, because it's in all the papers that you're coming home."

"Yes," I say, "yes. I'm leaving the day after tomorrow."

"Oh!" She grins. "Then we really are lucky." I find that I have almost forgotten the urchin-like grin of a colored girl. "I guess, before I keep babbling on, I'd better introduce myself. My name is Ada Holmes."

We shake hands. "This is Monsieur Vidal, the director of the film."

"I'm very honored to meet you, sir."

"Will you join us for a moment? Won't you sit down?" And Vidal pulls a chair out for her.

But she frowns contritely. "I really ought to get back to my friends." She looks at me. "I really just came over to say, for myself and all the kids, that we've got your records and we've seen your movie, and it means so much to us" — and she laughs, breathlessly, nervously, it is somehow more moving than tears — "more than I can say. Much more. And we wanted to know if you and your friend" — she looks at Vidal — "your director, Monsieur Vidal, would allow us to buy you a drink? We'd be very honored if you would."

"It is we who are honored," says Vidal, promptly, "and grateful. We were getting terribly bored with one another, thank God you came along."

The three of us laugh, and we cross the room.

The three at the table rise, and Ada makes the introductions. The other girl, taller and paler than Ada, is named Ruth. One of the boys is named Talley — "short for Talliafero" — and Golden-brown's name is Pete. "Man," he tells me, "I dig you the most. You tore me up, baby, tore me up."

"You tore up a lot of people," Talley says, cryptically, and he and Ruth laugh. Vidal does not know, but I do, that Talley is probably referring to white people.

They are from New Orleans and Tallahassee and North Carolina; are college students, and met on the boat. They have been in Europe all summer, in Italy and Spain, but are only just getting to Paris.

"We meant to come sooner," says Ada, "but we could never make up our minds to leave a place. I thought we'd never pry Ruth loose from Venice."

"I resigned myself," says Pete, "and just sat in the Piazza San Marco, drinking gin fizz and being photographed with the pigeons, while Ruth had herself driven all up and down the Grand Canal." He looks at Ruth. "Finally, thank heaven, it rained."

"She was working off her hostilities," says Ada, with a grin. "We thought we might as well let her do it in Venice, the opportunities in North Carolina are really terribly limited."

"There are some very upset people walking around down there," Ruth says, "and a couple of tours around the Grand Canal might do them a world of good."

Pete laughs. "Can't you just see Ruth escorting them to the edge of the water?"

"I haven't lifted my hand in anger yet," Ruth says, "but oh, Lord," and she laughs, clenching and unclenching her fists.

"You haven't been back for a long time, have you?" Talley asks me.

"Eight years. I haven't really lived there for twelve years."

Pete whistles. "I fear you are in for some surprises, my friend. There have been some changes made." Then, "Are you afraid?"

"A little."

"We all are," says Ada, "that's why I was so glad to get away for a little while."

"Then you haven't been back since Black Monday," Talley says. He laughs. "That's how it's gone down in Confederate history." He turns to Vidal. "What do people think about it here?"

Vidal smiles, delighted. "It seems extraordinarily infantile behavior, even for Americans, from whom, I must say, I have never expected very much in the way of maturity."

Everyone at the table laughs. Vidal goes on. "But I cannot really talk about it, I do not understand it. I have never really understood Americans; I am an old man now, and I suppose I never will. There is something very nice about them, something very winning, but they seem so ignorant — so ignorant of life. Perhaps it is strange, but the only people from your country with whom I have ever made contact are black people — like my good friend, my discovery, here," and he slaps me on the shoulder. "Perhaps it is because we in Europe, whatever else we do not know, or have forgotten, know about suffering. We have suffered here. You have suffered, too. But most Americans do not yet know what anguish is. It is too bad, because the life of the West is in their hands." He turns to Ada. "I cannot help saying that I think it is a scandal — and we may all pay very dearly for it — that a civilized nation should elect to represent it a man who is so simple that he thinks the world is simple." And silence falls at the table and the four young faces stare at him.

"Well," says Pete, at last, turning to me, "you won't be bored, man, when you get back there."

"It's much too nice a night," I say, "to stay cooped up in this place, where all I can hear is my own records." We laugh. "Why don't we get out of here and find a sidewalk cafe?" I tap Pete's guitar. "Maybe we can find out if you've got any talent."

"Oh, talent I've got," says Pete, "but character, man, I'm lacking."

So, after some confusion about the bill, for which Vidal has already made himself responsible, we walk out into the Paris night. It is very strange to feel that, very soon now, these boulevards will not exist for me. People will be walking up and down, as they are tonight, and lovers will be murmuring in the black shadows of the plane trees, and there will be these same still figures on the benches or in the parks — but they will not exist for me, I will not be here. For a long while Paris will no longer exist for me, except in my mind; and only in the minds of some people will I exist any longer for Paris. After departure, only invisible things are left, perhaps the life of the world is held together by invisible chains of memory and loss and love. So many things, so many people, depart! and we can only repossess them in our minds. Perhaps this is what the old folks meant, what my mother and my father meant, when they counseled us to keep the faith.

We have taken a table at the Deux Magots and Pete strums on his guitar and begins to play this song:

> Preach the word, preach the word, preach the word!
> If I never, never see you any more.
> Preach the word, preach the word.
> And I'll meet you on Canaan's shore.

He has a strong, clear, boyish voice, like a young preacher's, and he is smiling as he sings his song. Ada and I look at each other and grin, and Vidal is smiling. The waiter looks a little worried, for we are already beginning to attract a crowd, but it is a summer night, the gendarmes on the corner do not seem to mind, and there will be time, anyway, to stop us.

Pete was not there, none of us were, the first time this song was needed; and no one now alive can imagine what that time was like. But the song has come down the bloodstained ages. I suppose this to mean that the song is still needed, still has its work to do.

The others are all, visibly, very proud of Pete; and we all join him, and people stop to listen:

> Testify! Testify!
> If I never, never see you any more!
> Testify! Testify!
> I'll meet you on Canaan's shore!

In the crowd that has gathered to listen to us, I see a face I know, the face of a North African prizefighter who is no longer in the ring. I used to know him well in the old days, but have not seen him for a long time. He looks quite well, his face is shining, he is quite decently dressed. And something about the way he holds himself, not quite looking at our table, tells me that he has seen me, but does not want to risk a rebuff. So I call him. "Boona!"

And he turns, smiling, and comes loping over to our table, his hands in his pockets. Pete is still singing and Ada and Vidal have taken off on a conversation of their own. Ruth and Talley look curiously, expectantly, at Boona. Now that I have called him over, I feel somewhat uneasy. I realize that I do not know what he is doing now, or how he will get along with any of these people, and I can see in his eyes that he is delighted to be in the presence of two young girls. There are virtually no North African women in Paris, and not even the dirty, rat-faced girls who live, apparently, in cafes are willing to go with an Arab. So Boona is always looking for a girl, and because he is so deprived and because he is not Western, his techniques can be very unsettling. I know he is relieved that the girls are not French and not white. He looks briefly at Vidal and Ada. Vidal, also, though for different reasons, is always looking for a girl.

But Boona has always been very nice to me. Perhaps I am sorry that I called him over, but I do not want to snub him.

He claps one hand to the side of my head, as is his habit. "*Comment vas-tu, mon frère?* I have not see you, oh, for long time." And he asks me, as in the old days, "You all right? Nobody bother you?" And he laughs. "Ah! *Tu as fait le chemin, toi!* Now you are *vedette*, big star — wonderful!" He looks around the table, made a little uncomfortable by the silence that has fallen now that Pete had stopped singing. "I have seen you in the movies — you know? — and I tell everybody, I know him!" He points to me, and laughs, and Ruth and Talley laugh with him. "That's right, man, you make me real proud, you make me cry!"

"Boona, I want you to meet some friends of mine." And I go round the table: "Ruth, Talley, Ada, Pete" — and he bows and shakes hands, his dark eyes gleaming with pleasure — "*et Monsieur Vidal, le metteur en scène du film qui t'a arraché des larmes.*"

"*Enchanté.*" But his attitude toward Vidal is colder, more distrustful. "Of course I have heard of Monsieur Vidal. He is the director of many films, many of them made me cry." This last statement is utterly, even insolently, insincere.

But Vidal, I think, is relieved that I will now be forced to speak to Boona and will leave him alone with Ada.

"Sit down," I say, "have a drink with us, let me have your news. What's been happening with you, what are you doing with yourself these days?"

"Ah," he sits down, "nothing very brilliant, my brother." He looks at me quickly, with a little smile. "You know, we have been having hard times here."

"Where are you from?" Ada asks him.

His brilliant eyes take her in entirely, but she does not flinch. "I am from Tunis." He says it proudly, with a little smile.

"From Tunis. I have never been to Africa, I would love to go one day."

He laughs. "Africa is a big place. Very big. There are many countries in Africa, many" — he looks briefly at Vidal — "different kinds of people, many colonies."

"But Tunis," she continues, in her innocence, "is free? Freedom is happening all over Africa. That's why I would like to go there."

"I have not been back for a long time," says Boona, "but all the news I get from Tunis, from my people, is not good."

"Wouldn't you like to go back?" Ruth asks.

Again he looks at Vidal. "That is not so easy."

Vidal smiles. "You know what I would like to do? There's a wonderful Spanish place not far from here, where we can listen to live music and dance a little." He turns to Ada. "Would you like that?"

He is leaving it up to me to get rid of Boona, and it is, of course, precisely for this reason that I cannot do it. Besides, it is no longer so simple.

"Oh, I'd love that," says Ada, and she turns to Boona. "Won't you come, too?"

"Thank you, mam'selle," he says, softly, and his tongue flicks briefly over his lower lip, and he smiles. He is very moved, people are not often nice to him.

In the Spanish place there are indeed a couple of Spanish

guitars, drums, castanets, and a piano, but the uses to which these are being put carry one back, as Pete puts it, to the levee. "These are the wailingest Spanish cats I ever heard," says Ruth. "They didn't learn how to do this in Spain, no, they didn't, they been rambling. You ever hear anything like this going on in Spain?" Talley takes her out on the dance floor, which is already crowded. A very handsome Frenchwoman is dancing with an enormous, handsome black man, who seems to be her lover, who seems to have taught her how to dance. Apparently they are known to the musicians, who egg them on with small cries of "Olé!" It is a very good-natured crowd, mostly foreigners, Spaniards, Swedes, Greeks. Boona takes Ada out on the dance floor while Vidal is answering some questions put to him by Pete on the entertainment situation in France. Vidal looks a little put out, and I am amused.

We are there for perhaps an hour, dancing, talking, and I am, at last, a little drunk. In spite of Boona, who is a very good and tireless dancer, Vidal continues his pursuit of Ada, and I begin to wonder if he will make it and I begin to wonder if I want him to.

I am still puzzling out my reaction when Pete, who had disappeared, comes in through the front door, catches my eye, and signals to me. I leave the table and follow him into the streets.

He looks very upset. "I don't want to bug you, man," he says, "but I fear your boy has goofed."

I know he is not joking. I think he is probably angry at Vidal because of Ada, and I wonder what I can do about it and why he should be telling me.

I stare at him gravely, and he says, "It looks like he stole some money."

"Stole money? Who, Vidal?"

And then, of course, I get it, in the split second before he says, impatiently, "No, are you kidding? Your friend, the Tunisian."

I do not know what to say or what to do, and so I temporize with questions. All the time I am wondering if this can be true and what I can do about it if it is. The trouble is, I know that Boona steals, he would probably not be alive if he didn't, but I cannot say so to these children, who probably still imagine that everyone who steals is a thief. But he has never, to my knowledge, stolen from a friend. It seems unlike him. I have always thought of him as being better than that, and smarter than that. And so I cannot believe it, but neither can I doubt it. I do not know anything about Boona's life, these days. This causes me to realize that I do not really know much about Boona.

"Who did he steal it from?"

"From Ada. Out of her bag."

"How much?"

"Ten dollars. It's not an awful lot of money, but" — he grimaces — "none of us have an awful lot of money."

"I know." The dark side street on which we stand is nearly empty. The only sound on the street is the muffled music of the Spanish club. "How do you know it was Boona?"

He anticipates my own unspoken rejoinder. "Who else could it be? Besides — somebody saw him do it."

"Somebody saw him?"

"Yes."

I do not ask him who this person is, for fear that he will say it is Vidal.

"Well," I say, "I'll try to get it back." I think that I will take Boona aside and then replace the money myself. "Was it in dollars or in francs?"

"In francs."

I have no dollars and this makes it easier. I do not know how I can possibly face Boona and accuse him of stealing money from my friends. I would rather give him the benefit of even the faintest doubt. But, "Who saw him?" I ask.

"Talley. But we didn't want to make a thing about it —"

"Does Ada know it's gone?"

"Yes." He looks at me helplessly. "I know this makes you feel pretty bad, but we thought we'd better tell you, rather than" — lamely — "anybody else."

Now, Ada comes out of the club, carrying her ridiculous handbag, and with her face all knotted and sad. "Oh," she says, "I hate to cause all this trouble, it's not worth it, not for ten lousy dollars." I am astonished to see that she has been weeping, and tears come to her eyes now.

I put my arm around her shoulder. "Come on, now. You're not causing anybody any trouble and, anyway, it's nothing to cry about."

"It isn't your fault, Ada," Pete says, miserably.

"Oh, I ought to get a sensible handbag," she says, "like you're always telling me to do," and she laughs a little, then looks at me. "Please don't try to do anything about it. Let's just forget it."

"What's happening inside?" I ask her.

"Nothing. They're just talking. I think Mr. Vidal is dancing with Ruth. He's a great dancer, that little Frenchman."

"He's a great talker, too," Pete says.

"Oh, he doesn't mean anything," says Ada, "he's just having fun. He probably doesn't get a chance to talk to many American girls."

"He certainly made up for lost time tonight."

"Look," I say, "if Talley and Boona are alone, maybe you better go back in. We'll be in in a minute. Let's try to keep this as quiet as we can."

"Yeah," he says, "okay. We're going soon anyway, okay?"

"Yes," she tells him, "right away."

But as he turns away, Boona and Talley step out into the street, and it is clear that Talley feels that he has Boona under arrest. I almost laugh, the whole thing is beginning to resemble one of those mad French farces with people flying in and out of doors; but Boona comes straight to me.

"They say I stole money, my friend. You know me, you are the only one here who knows me, you know I would not do such a thing."

I look at him and I do not know what to say. Ada looks at him with her eyes full of tears and looks away. I take Boona's arm.

"We'll be back in a minute," I say. We walk a few paces up the dark, silent street.

"She say I take her money," he says. He, too, looks as though he is about to weep — but I do not know for which reason. "You know me, you know me almost twelve years, you think I do such a thing?"

Talley saw you, I want to say, but I cannot say it. Perhaps Talley only thought he saw him. Perhaps it is easy to see a boy who looks like Boona with his hand in an American girl's purse.

"If you not believe me," he says, "search me. Search me!" And he opens his arms wide, theatrically, and now there are tears standing in his eyes.

I do not know what his tears mean, but I certainly cannot search him. I want to say, I know you steal, I know you have to steal. Perhaps you took the money out of this girl's purse in order to eat tomorrow, in order not to be thrown into the streets tonight, in order to stay out of jail. This girl means nothing to you, after all, she is only an American, an American like me. Perhaps, I suddenly think, no girl means anything to you, or ever will again, they have beaten you too hard and kept you in the gutter too long. And I also think, If you would steal from her, then of course you would lie to me, neither of us means anything to you; perhaps, in your eyes, we are simply luckier gangsters in a world which is run by gangsters. But I cannot say any of these things to Boona. I cannot say, Tell me the truth, nobody cares about the money any more.

So I say, "Of course I will not search you." And I realize that he knew that I would not.

"I think it is that Frenchman who say I am a thief. They think we all are thieves." His eyes are bright and bitter. He looks over my shoulder. "They have all come out of the club now."

I look around and they are all there, in a little dark knot on the sidewalk.

"Don't worry," I say. "It doesn't matter."

"You believe me? My brother?" And his eyes look into mine with a terrible intensity.

"Yes," I force myself to say, "yes, of course, I believe you. Someone made a mistake, that's all."

"You know, the way American girls run around, they have their sack open all the time, she could lose the money anywhere. Why she blame me? Because I come from Africa?" Tears are glittering on his face. "Here she come now."

And Ada comes up the street with her straight, determined walk. She walks straight to Boona and takes his hand. "I am sorry," she says, "for everything that happened. Please believe me. It isn't worth all this fuss. I'm sure you're a very nice person, and" — she falters — "I must have lost the money, I'm sure I lost it." She looks at him. "It isn't worth hurting your feelings, and I'm terribly sorry about it."

"I no take your money," he says. "Really, truly, I no take it. Ask him" — pointing to me, grabbing me by the arm, shaking me — "he know me for years, he will tell you that I never, never steal!"

"I'm sure," she says. "I'm sure."

I take Boona by the arm again. "Let's forget it. Let's forget it all. We're all going home now, and one of these days we'll have a drink again and we'll forget all about it, all right?"

"Yes," says Ada, "let us forget it." And she holds out her hand.

Boona takes it, wonderingly. His eyes take her in again. "You are a very nice girl. Really. A very nice girl."

"I'm sure you're a nice person, too." She pauses. "Good night."

"Good night," he says, after a long silence.

Then he kisses me on both cheeks. "*Au revoir, mon frère.*"

"*Au revoir,* Boona."

After a moment we turn and walk away, leaving him standing there.

"Did he take it?" asks Vidal.

"I tell you I saw him," says Talley.

"Well," I say, "it doesn't matter now." I look back and see Boona's stocky figure disappearing down the street.

"No," says Ada, "it doesn't matter." She looks up. "It's almost morning."

"I would gladly," says Vidal, stammering, "gladly —"

But she is herself again. "I wouldn't think of it. We had a wonderful time tonight, a wonderful time, and I wouldn't think of it." She turns to me with that urchin-like grin. "It was wonderful meeting you. I hope you won't have too much trouble getting used to the States again."

"Oh, I don't think I will," I say. And then, "I hope you won't."

"No," she says, "I don't think anything they can do will surprise me any more."

"Which way are we all going?" asks Vidal. "I hope someone will share my taxi with me."

But he lives in the sixteenth arrondissement, which is not in anyone's direction. We walk him to the line of cabs standing under the clock at Odeon.

And we look each other in the face, in the growing morning light. His face looks weary and lined and lonely. He puts both hands on my shoulders and then puts one hand on the nape of my neck. "Do not forget me, Chico," he says. "You must come back and see us, one of these days. Many of us depend on you for many things."

"I'll be back," I say. "I'll never forget you."

He raises his eyebrows and smiles. "*Alors, adieu.*"

"*Adieu,* Vidal."

"I was happy to meet all of you," he says. He looks at Ada. "Perhaps we will meet again before you leave."

"Perhaps," she says. "Good-bye, Monsieur Vidal."

"Good-bye."

Vidal's cab drives away. "I also leave you now," I say. "I must go home and wake up my son and prepare for our journey."

I leave them standing on the corner, under the clock, which points to six. They look very strange and lost and determined, the four of them. Just before my cab turns off the boulevard, I wave to them and they wave back.

Mme. Dumont is in the hall, mopping the floor.

"Did all my family get home?" I ask. I feel very cheerful, I do not know why.

"Yes," she says, "they are all here. Paul is still sleeping."

"May I go in and get him?"

She looks at me in surprise. "Of course."

So I walk into her apartment and walk into the room where Paul lies sleeping. I stand over his bed for a long time.

Perhaps my thoughts travel — travel through to him. He opens his eyes and smiles up at me. He puts a fist to his eyes and raises his arms. "*Bonjour,* Papa."

I lift him up. "*Bonjour.* How do you feel today?"

"Oh, I don't know yet," he says.

I laugh. I put him on my shoulder and walk out into the hall. Mme. Dumont looks up at him with her radiant, aging face.

"Ah," she says, "you are going on a journey! How does it feel?"

"He doesn't know yet," I tell her. I walk to the elevator door and open it, dropping Paul down to the crook of my arm.

She laughs again. "He will know later. What a journey! *Jusqu'au nouveau monde!*"

I open the cage and we step inside. "Yes," I say, "all the way to the new world." I press the button and the cage, holding my son and me, goes up.

SEE HOW THEY RUN

Mary Elizabeth Vroman

A BELL rang. Jane Richards squared the sheaf of records decisively in the large manila folder, placed it in the right-hand corner of her desk, and stood up. The chatter of young voices subsided, and forty-three small faces looked solemnly and curiously at the slight young figure before them. The bell stopped ringing.

I wonder if they're as scared of me as I am of them. She smiled brightly.

"Good morning, children, I am Miss Richards." As if they don't know — the door of the third-grade room had a neat new sign pasted above it with her name in bold black capitals; and anyway, a new teacher's name is the first thing that children find out about on the first day of school. Nevertheless she wrote it for their benefit in large white letters on the blackboard.

"I hope we will all be happy working and playing together this year." Now why does that sound so trite? "As I call the roll will you please stand, so that I may get to know you as soon as possible, and if you like to you may tell me something about yourselves, how old you are, where you live, what your parents do, and perhaps something about what you did during the summer."

Seated, she checked the names carefully. "Booker T. Adams."

Booker stood, gangling and stoop-shouldered: he began to recite tiredly. "My name is Booker T. Adams, I'se ten years old." Shades of Uncle Tom! "I live on Painter's Path." He paused, the look he gave her was tinged with something very akin to contempt. "I didn't do nothing in the summer," he said deliberately.

"Thank you, Booker." Her voice was even. "George Allen." Must remember to correct that stoop. . . . Where is Painter's Path? . . . How to go about correcting those speech defects?

. . . Go easy, Jane, don't antagonize them. . . . They're clean enough, but this is the first day. . . . How can one teacher do any kind of job with a load of forty-three? . . . Thank heaven the building is modern and well built even though it is overcrowded, not like some I've seen — no potbellied stove.

"Sarahlene Clover Babcock." Where do these names come from? . . . Up from slavery. . . . How high is up. Jane smothered a sudden desire to giggle. Outside she was calm and poised and smiling. Clearly she called the names, listening with interest, making a note here and there, making no corrections — not yet.

She experienced a moment of brief inward satisfaction: I'm doing very well, this is what is expected of me . . . Orientation to Teaching . . . Miss Murray's voice beat a distant tattoo in her memory. Miss Murray with the Junoesque figure and the moon face . . . "The ideal teacher personality is one which, combining in itself all the most desirable qualities, expresses itself with quiet assurance in its endeavor to mold the personalities of the students in the most desirable patterns." . . . Dear dull Miss Murray.

She made mental estimates of the class. What a cross section of my people they represent, she thought. Here and there signs of evident poverty, here and there children of obviously well-to-do parents.

"My name is Rachel Veronica Smith. I am nine years old. I live at Six-oh-seven Fairview Avenue. My father is a Methodist minister. My mother is a housewife. I have two sisters and one brother. Last summer Mother and Daddy took us all to New York to visit my Aunt Jen. We saw lots of wonderful things. There are millions and millions of people in New York. One day we went on a ferryboat all the way up the Hudson River — that's a great big river as wide across as this town, and —"

The children listened wide-eyed. Jane listened carefully. She speaks good English. Healthy, erect, and even perhaps a little smug. Immaculately well dressed from the smoothly braided hair, with two perky bows, to the shiny brown oxfords . . . Bless you, Rachel, I'm so glad to have you.

"— and the buildings are all very tall, some of them nearly reach the sky."

"Haw-haw" — this from Booker, cynically.

"Well, they are too." Rachel swung around, fire in her eyes and insistence in every line of her round, compact body.

"Ain't no building as tall as the sky, is dere, Miz Richards?"

Crisis No. 1. Jane chose her answer carefully. As high as the sky . . . mustn't turn this into a lesson in science . . . all in due time. "The sky is a long way out, Booker, but the buildings in New York are very tall indeed. Rachel was only trying to show you how very tall they are. In fact, the tallest building in the whole world is in New York City."

"They call it the Empire State Building," interrupted Rachel, heady with her new knowledge and Jane's corroboration.

Booker wasn't through. "You been dere, Miz Richards?"

"Yes, Booker, many times. Someday I shall tell you more about it. Maybe Rachel will help me. Is there anything you'd like to add, Rachel?"

"I would like to say that we are glad you are our new teacher, Miss Richards." Carefully she sat down, spreading her skirt with her plump hands, her smile angelic.

Now I'll bet me a quarter her reverend father told her to say that. "Thank you, Rachel."

The roll call continued. . . . Tanya, slight and pinched, with the toes showing through the very white sneakers, the darned and faded but clean blue dress, the gentle voice like a tinkling bell, and the beautiful sensitive face. . . . Boyd and Lloyd, identical in their starched overalls, and the slightly vacant look. . . . Marjorie Lee, all of twelve years old, the well-developed body moving restlessly in the childish dress, the eyes too wise, the voice too high. . . . Joe Louis, the intelligence in the brilliant black eyes gleaming above the threadbare clothes. Lives of great men all remind us — Well, I have them all . . . Frederick Douglass, Franklin Delano, Abraham Lincoln, Booker T., Joe Louis, George Washington. . . . What a great burden you bear, little people, heirs to all your parents' stillborn dreams of greatness. I must not fail you. The last name on the list . . . C. T. Young. Jane paused, small lines creasing her forehead. She checked the list again.

"C. T., what is your name? I only have your initials on my list."

"Dat's all my name, C. T. Young."

"No, dear, I mean what does C. T. stand for? Is it Charles or Clarence?"

"No'm, jest C. T."

"But I can't put that in my register, dear."

Abruptly Jane rose and went to the next room. Rather timidly she waited to speak to Miss Nelson, the second-grade teacher, who had the formidable record of having taught all of sixteen years. Miss Nelson was large and smiling.

"May I help you, dear?"

"Yes, please. It's about C. T. Young. I believe you had him last year."

"Yes, and the year before that. You'll have him two years too."

"Oh? Well, I was wondering what name you registered him under. All the information I have is C. T. Young."

"That's all there is, honey. Lots of these children only have initials."

"You mean . . . can't something be done about it?"

"What?" Miss Nelson was still smiling, but clearly impatient.

"I . . . well . . . thank you." Jane left quickly.

Back in Room 3 the children were growing restless. Deftly Jane passed out the rating tests and gave instructions. Then she called C. T. to her. He was as small as an eight-year-old, and hungry-looking, with enormous guileless eyes and a beautifully shaped head.

"How many years did you stay in the second grade, C. T.?"

"Two."

"And in the first?"

"Two."

"How old are you?"

" 'Leven."

"When will you be twelve?"

"Nex' month."

And they didn't care . . . nobody ever cared enough about one small boy to give him a name.

"You are a very lucky little boy, C. T. Most people have to take the name somebody gave them whether they like it or not, but you can choose your very own."

"Yeah?" The dark eyes were belligerent. "My father named me C. T. after hisself, Miz Richards, an' dat's my name."

Jane felt unreasonably irritated. "How many children are there in your family, C. T.?"

" 'Leven."

"How many are there younger than you?" she asked.

"Seven."

Very gently, "Did you have your breakfast this morning, dear?"

The small figure in the too-large trousers and the too-small shirt drew itself up to full height. "Yes'm, I had fried chicken, and rice, and coffee, and rolls, and oranges too."

Oh, you poor darling. You poor proud lying darling. Is that what you'd like for breakfast?

She asked, "Do you like school, C. T.?"

"Yes'm," he told her suspiciously.

She leafed through the pile of records. "Your record says you haven't been coming to school very regularly. Why?"

"I dunno."

"Did you ever bring a lunch?"

"No'm, I eats such a big breakfast, I doan git hungry at lunchtime."

"Children need to eat lunch to help them grow tall and strong, C. T. So from now on you'll eat lunch in the lunchroom" — an after-thought: Perhaps it's important to make him think I believe him — "and from now on maybe you'd better not eat such a big breakfast."

Decisively she wrote his name at the top of what she knew to be an already too large list. "Only those in absolute necessity," she had been told by Mr. Johnson, the kindly, harassed principal. "We'd like to feed them all, so many are underfed, but we just don't have the money." Well, this was absolute necessity if she ever saw it.

"What does your father do, C. T.?"

"He work at dat big factory cross-town, he make plenty money, Miz Richards." The record said "Unemployed."

"Would you like to be named Charles Thomas?"

The expressive eyes darkened, but the voice was quiet. "No'm."

"Very well." Thoughtfully Jane opened the register; she wrote firmly C. T. Young.

October is a witching month in the Southern United States. The richness of the golds and reds and browns of the trees forms an enchanted filigree through which the lilting voices of children at play seem to float, embodied like so many nymphs of Pan.

Jane had played a fast-and-furious game of tag with her class and now she sat quietly under the gnarled old oak, watching the tireless play, feeling the magic of the sun through the leaves warmly dappling her skin, the soft breeze on the nape of her neck like a lover's hands, and her own drowsy lethargy. Paul, Paul my darling . . . how long for us now? She had worshiped Paul Carlyle since they were freshmen together. On graduation day he had slipped the small circlet of diamonds on her finger. . . . "A teacher's salary is small, Jane. Maybe we'll be lucky enough to get work together, then in a year or so we can be married. Wait for me, darling, wait for me!"

But in a year or so Paul had gone to war, and Jane went out alone to teach. . . . Lansing Creek — one year . . . the leaky roof, the potbellied stove, the water from the well. . . . Mary-weather Point — two years . . . the tight-lipped spinster principal with the small, vicious soul. . . . Three hard lonely years and then she had been lucky.

The superintendent had praised her. "You have done good work, Miss — ah — Jane. This year you are to be placed at Center-town High — that is, of course, if you care to accept the position."

Jane had caught her breath. Centertown was the largest and best equipped of all the schools in the county, only ten miles from home and Paul — for Paul had come home, older, quieter, but still Paul. He was teaching now more than a hundred miles away, but they went home every other weekend to their families and each other. . . . "Next summer you'll be Mrs. Paul Carlyle, darling. It's hard for us to be apart so much. I guess we'll have to be for a long time till I can afford to support you. But, sweet, these little tykes need us so badly." He had held her close, rubbing the nape of the neck under the soft curls. "We have a big job, those of us who teach," he had told her, "a never-ending and often thankless job, Jane, to supply the needs of these kids who lack so much." Dear, warm, big, strong, gentle Paul.

They wrote each other long letters, sharing plans and problems. She wrote him about C. T. "I've adopted him, darling. He's so pathetic and so determined to prove that he's not. He learns nothing at all, but I can't let myself believe that he's stupid, so I keep trying."

"Miz Richards, please, ma'am." Tanya's beautiful amber eyes sought hers timidly. Her brown curls were tangled from playing, her cheeks a bright red under the tightly stretched olive skin. The elbows jutted awkwardly out of the sleeves of the limp cotton dress, which could not conceal the finely chiseled bones in their pitiable fleshlessness. As always when she looked at her, Jane thought, What a beautiful child! So unlike the dark, gaunt, morose mother, and the dumpy, pasty-faced father who had visited her that first week. A fairy's changeling. You'll make a lovely angel to grace the throne of God, Tanya! Now what made me think of that?

"Please, ma'am, I'se sick."

Gently Jane drew her down beside her. She felt the parchment skin, noted the unnaturally bright eyes. Oh, dear God, she's burning up! "Do you hurt anywhere, Tanya?"

"My head, ma'am and I'se so tired." Without warning she began to cry.

"How far do you live, Tanya?"

"Two miles."

"You walk to school?"

"Yes'm."

"Do any of your brothers have a bicycle?"

"No'm."

"Rachel!" Bless you for always being there when I need you. "Hurry, dear, to the office and ask Mr. Johnson please to send a big boy with a bicycle to take Tanya home. She's sick."

Rachel ran.

"Hush now, dear, we'll get some cool water, and then you'll be home in a little while. Did you feel sick this morning?"

"Yes'm, but Mot Dear sent me to school anyway. She said I just wanted to play hooky." Keep smiling, Jane. Poor, ambitious, well-meaning parents, made bitter at the seeming futility of dreaming dreams for this lovely child . . . willing her to rise above the drabness of your own meager existence . . . too angry with life to see that what she needs most is your love and care and right now medical attention.

Jane bathed the child's forehead with cool water at the fountain. Do the white schools have a clinic? I must ask Paul. Do they have a lounge or a couch where they can lay one wee sick head? Is there anywhere in this town free medical service for one small child . . . born black?

The boy with the bicycle came. "Take care of her now, ride slowly and carefully, and take her straight home. . . . Keep the newspaper over your head, Tanya, to keep out the sun, and tell your parents to call the doctor." But she knew they wouldn't because they couldn't.

The next day Jane went to see Tanya.

"She's sho' nuff sick, Miz Richards," the mother said. "She's always been a puny child, but this time she's took real bad, throat's all raw, talk all out her haid las' night. I been using a poultice and some herb brew but she ain't got no better."

"Have you called a doctor, Mrs. Fulton?"

"No'm, we cain't afford it, an' Jake, he doan believe in doctors nohow."

Jane waited till the tide of high bright anger welling in her heart and beating in her brain had subsided. When she spoke her voice was deceptively gentle. "Mrs. Fulton, Tanya is a very sick little girl. She is your only little girl. If you love her, I advise you to have a doctor for her, for if you don't . . . Tanya may die."

The wail that issued from the thin figure seemed to have no part in reality.

Jane spoke hurriedly. "Look, I'm going into town. I'll send a doctor out. Don't worry about paying him. We can see about that later." Impulsively she put her arms around the taut, motionless shoulders. "Don't you worry, honey, it's going to be all right."

There was a kindliness in the doctor's weather-beaten face that warmed Jane's heart, but his voice was brusque. "You sick, girl? Well?"

"No, sir. I'm not sick." What long sequence of events has caused even the best of you to look on even the best of us as menials? "I am a teacher at Centertown High. There's a little girl in my class who is very ill. Her parents are very poor. I came to see if you would please go to see her."

He looked at her, amused.

"Of course I'll pay the bill, Doctor," she added hastily.

"In that case . . . well . . . where does she live?"

Jane told him. "I think it's diphtheria, Doctor."

He raised his eyebrows. "Why?"

Jane sat erect. Don't be afraid, Jane! You're as good a teacher as he is a doctor, and you made an A in that course in childhood diseases. "High fever, restlessness, sore throat, headache, croupy cough, delirium. It could, of course, be tonsillitis or scarlet fever, but that cough — well, I'm only guessing, of course," she finished lamely.

"Hmph." The doctor's face was expressionless. "Well, we'll see. Have your other children been inoculated?"

"Yes, sir, Doctor, if the parents ask, please tell them that the school is paying for your services."

This time he was wide-eyed.

The lie haunted her. She spoke to the other teachers about it the next day at recess.

"She's really very sick, maybe you'd like to help?"

Mary Winters, the sixth-grade teacher, was the first to speak. "Richards, I'd like to help, but I've got three kids of my own, and so you see how it is?"

Jane saw.

"Trouble with you, Richards, is you're too emotional." This from Nelson. "When you've taught as many years as I have, my dear, you'll learn not to bang your head against a stone wall. It may sound hardhearted to you, but one just can't worry about one child more or less when one has nearly fifty."

The pain in the back of her eyes grew more insistent. "I can," she said.

"I'll help, Jane," said Marilyn Andrews, breathless, bouncy, newlywed Marilyn.

"Here's two bucks. It's all I've got, but nothing's plenty for me." Her laughter pealed echoing down the hall.

"I've got a dollar, Richards" — this from mousy, severe, little Miss Mitchell — "though I'm not sure I agree with you."

"Why don't you ask the high-school faculty?" said Marilyn. "Better still, take it up in teachers' meeting."

"Mr. Johnson has enough to worry about now," snapped Nelson. Why, she's mad, thought Jane, mad because I'm trying to give a helpless little tyke a chance to live, and because Marilyn and Mitchell helped.

The bell rang. Wordlessly Jane turned away. She watched the children troop in noisily, an ancient nursery rhyme running through her head:

> *Three blind mice,*
> *three blind mice,*
> *See how they run,*
> *see how they run,*
> *They all ran after*
> *the farmer's wife,*
> *She cut off their tails*
> *with a carving knife.*
> *Did you ever see*
> *such a sight in your life*
> *As three blind mice?*

Only this time it was forty-three mice. Jane giggled. Why, I'm hysterical, she thought in surprise. The mice thought the sweet-smelling farmer's wife might have bread and a wee bit of cheese to offer poor blind mice; but the farmer's wife didn't like poor, hungry, dirty blind mice. So she cut off their tails. Then they couldn't run any more, only wobble. What happened then? Maybe they starved, those that didn't bleed to death. Running round in circles. Running where, little mice?

She talked to the high-school faculty, and Mr. Johnson. All together, she got eight dollars.

The following week she received a letter from the doctor:

Dear Miss Richards:

I am happy to inform you that Tanya is greatly improved, and with careful nursing will be well enough in about eight weeks to return to school. She is very frail, however, and will require special care. I have made three visits to her home. In view of the peculiar circumstances, I am donating my services. The cost of the medicines, however, amounts to the sum of fifteen dollars. I am referring this to you as you requested. What a beautiful child!

Yours sincerely,
JONATHAN H. SINCLAIR, M.D.

P.S. She had diphtheria.

Bless you forever and ever, Jonathan H. Sinclair, M.D. For all your long Southern heritage, "a man's a man for a' that . . . and a' that!"

Her heart was light that night when she wrote to Paul. Later she made plans in the darkness. You'll be well and fat by Christmas, Tanya, and you'll be a lovely angel in my pageant. . . . I must get the children to save pennies. . . . We'll send you milk and oranges and eggs, and we'll make funny little get-well cards to keep you happy.

But by Christmas Tanya was dead!

The voice from the dark figure was quiet, even monotonous. "Jake an' me, we always work so hard, Miz Richards. We didn't neither one have no schooling much when we was married — our folks never had much money, but we was happy. Jake, he tenant farm. I tuk in washing — we plan to save and buy a little house and farm of our own someday. Den the children come. Six boys, Miz Richards — all in a hurry. We both want the boys to finish school, mabbe go to college. We try not to keep them out to work the farm, but sometimes we have to. Then come Tanya. Just like a little yellow rose she was, Miz Richards, all pink and gold . . . and her voice like a silver bell. We think when she grow up an' finish school she take voice lessons — be like Marian Anderson. We think mabbe by then the boys would be old enough to help. I was kinda feared for her when she get sick, but then she start to get better. She was doing so well, Miz Richards. Den it get cold, an' the fire so hard to keep all night long, an' eben the newspapers in the cracks doan keep the win' out, an' I give her all my kivvers; but one night she jest tuk to shivering an' talking all out her haid — sat right up in bed, she did. She call your name onc't or twice, Miz Richards, then she say, 'Mot Dear, does Jesus love me like Miz Richards say in Sunday school?' I say, 'Yes, honey.' She say, 'Effen I die will I see Jesus?' I say, 'Yes, honey, but you ain't gwine die.' But she did, Miz Richards . . . jest smiled an' laid down — jest smiled an' laid down."

It is terrible to see such hopeless resignation in such tearless eyes. . . . One little mouse stopped running. . . . You'll make a lovely angel to grace the throne of God, Tanya!

Jane did not go to the funeral. Nelson and Rogers sat in the first pew. Everyone on the faculty contributed to a beautiful wreath. Jane preferred not to think about that.

C. T. brought a lovely potted rose to her the next day. "Miz Richards, ma'am, do you think this is pretty enough to go on Tanya's grave?"

"Where did you get it, C. T.?"

"I stole it out Miz Adams's front yard, right out of that li'l glass house she got there. The door was open, Miz Richards, she got plenty, she won't miss this li'l one."

You queer little bundle of truth and lies. What do I do now? Seeing the tears blinking back in the anxious eyes, she said gently, "Yes, C. T., the rose is nearly as beautiful as Tanya is now. She will like that very much."

"You mean she will know I put it there, Miz Richards? She ain't daid at all?"

"Maybe she'll know, C. T. You see, nothing that is beautiful ever dies as long as we remember it."

So you loved Tanya, a little mouse? The memory of her beauty is yours to keep now forever and always, my darling. Those things money can't buy. They've all been trying, but your tail isn't off yet, is it, brat? Not by a long shot. Suddenly she laughed aloud.

He looked at her wonderingly. "What you laughing at, Miz Richards?"

"I'm laughing because I'm happy, C. T.," and she hugged him.

Christmas with its pageantry and splendor came and went. Back from the holidays, Jane had an oral English lesson.

"We'll take this period to let you tell about your holidays, children."

On the weekends that Jane stayed in Centertown she visited different churches, and taught in the Sunday schools when she was asked. She had tried to impress on the children the reasons for giving at Christmastime. In class they had talked about things they could make for gifts, and ways they could save money to buy them. Now she stood by the window, listening attentively, reaping the fruits of her labors.

"I got a bicycle and a catcher's mitt."

"We all went to a party and had ice cream and cake."

"I got —"

"I got —"

"I got —"

Score one goose egg for Jane. She was suddenly very tired. "It's your turn, C. T." Dear God, please don't let him lie too much. He tears my heart. The children never laugh. It's funny how polite they are to C. T. even when they know he's lying. Even that day when Boyd and Lloyd told how they had seen him take food out of the garbage cans in front of the restaurant, and he said he was taking it to some poor hungry children, they didn't laugh. Sometimes children have a great deal more insight than grownups.

C. T. was talking. "I didn't get nothin' for Christmas, because Mamma was sick, but I worked all that week before for Mr. Bondel what owns the store on Main Street. I ran errands an' swep' up an' he give me three dollars, and so I bought Mamma a real pretty handkerchief an' a comb, an' I bought my father a tie pin, paid a big ole fifty cents for it too . . . an' I bought my sisters an' brothers some candy an' gum an' I bought me this whistle. Course I got what you give us, Miz Richards" (she had given each a small gift) "an' Mamma's white lady give us a whole crate of oranges, an' Miz Smith what live nex' door give me a pair of socks. Mamma she was so happy she made a cake with eggs an' butter an' everything; an' then we ate it an' had a good time."

Rachel spoke wonderingly. "Didn't Santa Claus bring you anything at all?"

C. T. was the epitome of scorn. "Ain't no Santa Claus," he said and sat down.

Jane quelled the age-old third-grade controversy absently, for her heart was singing. C. T. . . . . C. T., son of my own heart, you are the bright new hope of a doubtful world, and the gay new song of a race unconquered. Of them all — Sarahlene, sole heir to the charming stucco home on the hill, all fitted for gracious living; George, whose father is a contractor; Rachel, the minister's daughter; Angela, who has just inherited ten thousand dollars — of all of them who got, you, my dirty little vagabond, who have never owned a coat in your life, because you say you don't get cold; you, out of your nothing, found something to give, and in the dignity of giving found that it was not so important to receive. . . . Christ Child, look down in blessing on one small child made in Your image and born black!

Jane had problems. Sometimes it was difficult to maintain

discipline with forty-two children. Busy as she kept them, there were always some not busy enough. There was the conference with Mr. Johnson.

"Miss Richards, you are doing fine work here, but sometimes your room is a little . . . well — ah — well, to say the least, noisy. You are new here, but we have always maintained a record of having fine discipline here at this school. People have said that it used to be hard to tell whether or not there were children in the building. We have always been proud of that. Now take Miss Nelson. She is an excellent disciplinarian." He smiled. "Maybe if you ask her she will give you her secret. Do not be too proud to accept help from anyone who can give it, Miss Richards."

"No, sir, thank you, sir, I'll do my best to improve, sir." Ah, you dear, well-meaning, shortsighted, round, busy little man. Why are you not more concerned about how much the children have grown and learned in these past four months than you are about how much noise they make? I know Miss Nelson's secret. Spare not the rod and spoil not the child. Is that what you want me to do? Paralyze these kids with fear so that they will be afraid to move? afraid to question? afraid to grow? Why is it so fine for people not to know there are children in the building? Wasn't the building built for children? In her room Jane locked the door against the sound of the playing children, put her head on the desk, and cried.

Jane acceded to tradition and administered one whipping docilely enough, as though used to it; but the sneer in his eyes that had almost gone returned to haunt them. Jane's heart misgave her. From now on I positively refuse to impose my will on any of these poor children by reason of my greater strength. So she had abandoned the rod in favor of any other means she could find. They did not always work.

There was a never-ending drive for funds. Jane had a passion for perfection. Plays, dances, concerts, bazaars, suppers, parties followed one on another in staggering succession.

"Look here, Richards," Nelson told her one day, "it's true that we need a new piano, and that science equipment, but, honey, these drives in a colored school are like the poor: with us always. It doesn't make too much difference if Suzy forgets her lines, or if the ice cream is a little lumpy. Cooperation is fine, but the way you tear into things you won't last long."

"For once in her life Nelson's right, Jane," Elise told her later. "I can understand how intense you are because I used to be like that; but, pet, Negro teachers have always had to work harder than any others and till recently have always got paid less, so for our own health's sake we have to let up wherever possible. Believe me, honey, if you don't learn to take it easy, you're going to get sick."

Jane did. Measles!

"Oh, no," she wailed, "not in my old age!" But she was glad of the rest. Lying in her own bed at home, she realized how very tired she was.

Paul came to see her that weekend and sat by her bed, and read aloud to her the old classic poems they both loved so well. They listened to their favorite radio programs. Paul's presence was warm and comforting. Jane was reluctant to go back to work.

What to do about C. T. was a question that daily loomed larger in Jane's consciousness. Watching Joe Louis's brilliant development was a thing of joy, and Jane was hard pressed to find enough outlets for his amazing abilities. Jeanette Allen was running a close second, and even Booker, so long a problem, was beginning to grasp fundamentals, but C. T. remained static.

"I always stays two years in a grade, Miz Richards," he told her blandly. "I does better the second year.

"I don't keer." His voice had been cheerful. Maybe he really is slow, Jane thought. But one day something happened to make her change her mind.

C. T. was possessed of an unusually strong tendency to protect those he considered to be poor or weak. He took little Johnny Armstrong, who sat beside him in class, under his wing. Johnny was nearsighted and nondescript, his one outstanding feature being his hero-worship of C. T. Johnny was a plodder. Hard as he tried, he made slow progress at best.

The struggle with multiplication tables was a difficult one, in spite of all the little games Jane devised to make them easier for the children. On this particular day there was the uneven hum of little voices trying to memorize. Johnny and C. T. were having a whispered conversation about snakes.

Clearly Jane heard C. T.'s elaboration. "Man, my father caught a moccasin long as that blackboard, I guess, an' I held him while he was live right back of his ugly head — so."

Swiftly Jane crossed the room. "C. T. and Johnny, you are supposed to be learning your tables. The period is nearly up and you haven't even begun to study. Furthermore, in more than five months you haven't even learned the two-times table. Now you will both stay in at the first recess to learn it, and every day after this until you do."

Maybe I should make up some problems about snakes, Jane mused, but they'd be too ridiculous. . . . Two nests of four snakes — Oh, well, I'll see how they do at recess. Her heart smote her at the sight of the two little figures at their desks, listening wistfully to the sound of the children at play, but she busied herself and pretended not to notice them. Then she heard C. T.'s voice:

"Lissen, man, these tables is easy if you really want to learn them. Now see here. Two times one is two. Two times two is four. Two times three is six. If you forgit, all you got to do is add two like she said."

"Sho' nuff, man?"

"Sho'. Say them with me . . . two times one —" Obediently Johnny began to recite. Five minutes later they came to her. "We's ready, Miz Richards."

"Very well. Johnny, you may begin."

"Two times one is two. Two times two is four. Two times three is. . . . Two times three is —"

"Six," prompted C. T.

In sweat and pain, Johnny managed to stumble through the two-times table with C. T.'s help.

"That's very poor, Johnny, but you may go for today. Tomorrow I shall expect you to have it letter perfect. Now it's your turn, C. T."

C. T.'s performance was a fair rival to Joe Louis's. Suspiciously she took him through in random order.

"Two times nine?"

"Eighteen."

"Two times four?"

"Eight."

"Two times seven?"

"Fourteen."

"C. T., you could have done this long ago. Why didn't you?"

"I dunno. . . . May I go to play now, Miz Richards?"

"Yes, C. T. Now learn your three-times table for me tomorrow."

But he didn't, not that day or the day after that or the day after that. . . . Why doesn't he? Is it that he doesn't want to? Maybe if I were as ragged and deprived as he I wouldn't want to learn either.

Jane took C. T. to town and bought him a shirt, a sweater, a pair of dungarees, some underwear, a pair of shoes and a pair of socks. Then she sent him to the barber to get his hair cut. She gave him the money so he could pay for the articles himself and figure up the change. She instructed him to take a bath before putting on his new clothes, and told him not to tell anyone but his parents that she had bought them.

The next morning the class was in a dither.

"You seen C. T.?"

"Oh, boy, ain't he sharp!"

"C. T., where'd you get them new clothes?"

"Oh, man, I can wear new clothes any time I feel like it, but I can't be bothered with being a fancypants all the time like you guys."

C. T. strutted in new confidence, but his work didn't improve.

Spring came in its virginal green gladness and the children chafed for the out-of-doors. Jane took them out as much as possible on nature studies and excursions.

C. T. was growing more and more mischievous, and his influence began to spread throughout the class. Daily his droll wit became more and more edged with impudence. Jane was at her wit's end.

"You let that child get away with too much, Richards," Nelson told her. "What he needs is a good hiding."

One day Jane kept certain of the class in at the first recess to do neglected homework, C. T. among them. She left the room briefly. When she returned C. T. was gone.

"Where is C. T.?" she asked.

"He went out to play, Miz Richards. He said couldn't no ole teacher keep him in when he didn't want to stay."

Out on the playground C. T. was standing in a swing gently swaying to and fro, surrounded by a group of admiring youngsters. He was holding forth.

"I gets tired of stayin' in all the time. She doan pick on nobody but me, an' today I put my foot down. 'From now on,' I say, 'I ain't never goin' to stay in, Miz Richards.' Then I walks out." He was enjoying himself immensely. Then he saw her.

"You will come with me, C. T." She was quite calm except for the telltale veins throbbing in her forehead.

"I ain't comin'." The sudden fright in his eyes was veiled quickly by a nonchalant belligerence. He rocked the swing gently.

She repeated, "Come with me, C. T."

The children watched breathlessly.

"I done told you I ain't comin', Miz Richards." His voice was patient as though explaining to a child. "I ain't . . . comin' . . . a . . . damn . . . tall!"

Jane moved quickly, wrenching the small but surprisingly strong figure from the swing. Then she bore him bodily, kicking and screaming, to the building.

The children relaxed, and began to giggle. "Oh boy! Is he goin' to catch it!" they told one another.

Panting, she held him, still struggling, by the scruff of his collar before the group of teachers gathered in Marilyn's room. "All right, now you tell me what to do with him!" she demanded. "I've tried everything." The tears were close behind her eyes.

"What'd he do?" Nelson asked.

Briefly she told them.

"Have you talked to his parents?"

"Three times I've had conferences with them. They say to beat him."

"That, my friend, is what you ought to do. Now he never acted like that with me. If you'll let me handle him, I'll show you how to put a brat like that in his place."

"Go ahead," Jane said wearily.

Nelson left the room, and returned with a narrow but sturdy leather thong. "Now, C. T." — she was smiling, tapping the strap in her open left palm — "go to your room and do what Miss Richards told you to."

"I ain't gonna, an' you can't make me." He sat down with absurd dignity at a desk.

Still smiling, Miss Nelson stood over him. The strap descended without warning across the bony shoulders in the thin shirt. The whip became a dancing demon, a thing possessed, bearing no relation to the hand that held it. The shrieks grew louder. Jane closed her eyes against the blurred fury of a singing lash, a small boy's terror and a smiling face.

Miss Nelson was not tired. "Well, C. T.?"

"I won't, Yer can kill me but I won't!"

The sounds began again. Red welts began to show across the small arms and through the clinging sweat-drenched shirt.

"Now will you go to your room?"

Sobbing and conquered, C. T. went. The seated children stared curiously at the little procession. Jane dismissed them.

In his seat C. T. found pencil and paper.

"What's he supposed to do, Richards?" Jane told her.

"All right, now write!"

C. T. stared at Nelson through swollen lids, a curious smile curving his lips. Jane knew suddenly that come hell or high water, C. T. would not write. I mustn't interfere. Please, God, don't let her hurt him too badly. Where have I failed so miserably? . . . Forgive us our trespasses. The singing whip and the shrieks became a symphony from hell. Suddenly Jane hated the smiling face with an almost unbearable hatred. She spoke, her voice like cold steel.

"That's enough, Nelson."

The noise stopped.

"He's in no condition to write now anyway."

C. T. stood up. "I hate you. I hate you all. You're mean and I hate you." Then he ran. No one followed him. Run, little mouse! They avoided each other's eyes.

"Well, there you are," Nelson said as she walked away. Jane never found out what she meant by that.

The next day C. T. did not come to school. The day after that he brought Jane the fatal homework, neatly and painstakingly done, and a bunch of wild flowers. Before the bell rang, the children surrounded him. He was beaming.

"Did you tell yer folks you got a whipping, C. T.?"

"Naw! I'd 'a' only got another."

"Where were you yesterday?"

"Went fishin'. Caught me six cats long as your haid, Sambo."

Jane buried her face in the sweet-smelling flowers. Oh, my brat, my wonderful resilient brat. They'll never get your tail, will they?

It was seven weeks till the end of term, when C. T. brought Jane a model wooden boat.

Jane stared at it. "Did you make this? It's beautiful, C. T."

"Oh, I make them all the time . . . an' airplanes an' houses too. I do 'em in my spare time," he finished airily.

"Where do you get the models, C. T.?" she asked.

"I copies them from pictures in the magazine."

Right under my nose . . . right there all the time, she thought wonderingly. "C. T., would you like to build things when you grow up? Real houses and ships and planes?"

"Reckon I could, Miz Richards," he said confidently.

The excitement was growing in her.

"Look, C. T. You aren't going to do any lessons at all for the rest of the year. You're going to build ships and houses and airplanes and anything else you want to."

"I am, huh?" He grinned. "Well, I guess I wasn't goin' to get promoted nohow."

"Of course if you want to build them the way they really are, you might have to do a little measuring, and maybe learn to spell the names of the parts you want to order. All the best contractors have to know things like that, you know."

"Say, I'm gonna have real fun, huh? I always said lessons wussent no good nohow. Pop say too much study eats out yer brains anyway."

The days went by. Jane ran a race with time. The instructions from the model companies arrived. Jane burned the midnight oil planning each day's work.

Learn to spell the following words: ship, sail, steamer — boat, anchor, airplane wing, fly.

Write a letter to the lumber company, ordering some lumber.

The floor of our model house is ten inches long. Multiply the length by the width and you'll find the area of the floor in square inches.

Read the story of Columbus and his voyages.

Our plane arrives in Paris in twenty-eight hours. Paris is the capital city of a country named France across the Atlantic Ocean.

Long ago sailors told time by the sun and the stars. Now, the earth goes around the sun —.

Work and pray, Jane, work and pray!

C. T. learned. Some things vicariously, some things directly. When he found that he needed multiplication to plan his models to scale, he learned to multiply. In three weeks he had mastered simple division.

Jane bought beautifully illustrated stories about ships and planes. He learned to read.

He wrote for and received his own materials.

Jane exulted.

The last day! Forty-two faces waiting anxiously for report cards. Jane spoke to them briefly, praising them collectively, and admonishing them to obey the safety rules during the holidays. Then she passed out the report cards.

As she smiled at each childish face, she thought, I've been wrong. The long arm of circumstance, environment and heredity is the farmer's wife that seeks to mow you down, and all of us who touch your lives are in some way responsible for how successful she is. But you aren't mice, my darlings. Mice are hated, hunted pests. You are normal, lovable children. The knife of the farmer's wife is double-edged for you, because you are Negro children, born mostly in poverty. But you are wonderful children, nevertheless, for you wear the bright protective cloak of laughter, the strong shield of courage, and the intelligence of children everywhere. Some few of you may indeed become as the mice — but most of you shall find your way to stand fine and tall in the annals of man. There's a bright new tomorrow ahead. For every one of us whose job it is to help you grow that is insensitive and unworthy, there are hundreds who daily work that you may grow straight and whole. If it were not so, our world could not long endure.

She handed C. T. his card.

"Thank you, ma'm."

"Aren't you going to open it?"

He opened it dutifully. When he looked up his eyes were wide with disbelief. "You didn't make no mistake?"

"No mistake, C. T. You're promoted. You've caught up enough to go to the fourth grade next year."

She dismissed the children. They were a swarm of bees released from a hive. " 'By, Miss Richards." . . . "Happy holidays, Miss Richards."

C. T was the last to go.

"Well, C. T.?"

"Miz Richards, you remember what you said about a name being important?"

"Yes, C. T."

"Well, I talked to Mamma, and she said if I wanted a name it would be all right, and she'd go to the courthouse about it."

"What name have you chosen, C. T.?" she asked.

"Christopher Turner Young."

"That's a nice name, Christopher," she said gravely.

"Sho' nuff, Miz Richards?"

"Sure enough, C. T."

"Miz Richards, you know what?"

"What, dear?"

"I love you."

She kissed him swiftly before he ran to catch his classmates.

She stood at the window and watched the running, skipping figures, followed by the bold mimic shadows. I'm coming home, Paul. I'm leaving my forty-two children, and Tanya there on the hill. My work with them is finished now. The laughter bubbled up in her throat. But Paul, oh Paul. See how straight they run!

THE BLUES BEGINS

(From the novel *Trouble, Blues, n' Trouble*)

Sylvester Leaks

MONDAY morning came and the blues began: Rent Man Blues, Insurance Man Blues, Washday Blues, White Folks Blues, and Got-damn-it-don'tcha-mess-wit-me Blues!

Winter had come and was overstaying its welcome. January had borrowed the winds of March and was using them overtime. Ice spewed out of the ground. Rags and paper were wrapped around faucets to keep them from freezing. Broken window panes were stuffed with rags; window cracks were jammed with paper. Beds were weighted down with homemade quilts and old overcoats and clothes. Men and boys wore two pairs of trousers; girls and old ladies bundled up like babes.

To Gabriel Coker, winter, like his father, always caused him misery. Last night he went to bed with all of his clothes on because coals in the Cokers' household were existent only in the imagination; wood, what little there was, must be saved for cooking. Even so, he knew his ma would blister his hide if she knew he slept in the overalls he had to wear to school today. So now he was easing out of bed before she came into the room.

"All right, Gabriel, I hear that spring squeaking! Let's hit it! Your pa done done it again! And you know I ain't got no time to be messin' around this morning. Now let's hit the floor! There's bills to be paid and nothin' to pay 'em with."

He eased out of bed. Yeah, Pa had done it again. He was always doing it again. And she was always taking up for him. Talking 'bout he didn't understand. Honh! he understood all right. Wonder if she understood him hitting her Sattday night!

"Is you up, Gabriel?"

"I'm up." It was a good thing he didn't hit her no more though. Would've hit 'im 'cross the head with that iron poker. Every Sadday he comes home broke as a haint. Done lost every nickel and boasting 'bout what he's gonna do. Honh!

When Gabriel was through making up the bed he took his old worn out shoes, which were bought originally second-hand, removed the paper and cardboard from inside them which served as a sole. Then he took the scissors from the mantelpiece, tore off a flap from the cardboard box in the corner and cut out new soles and wrapped them with paper and placed them inside. Then he went into the kitchen.

She was tall, brown-skinned, statuesque, handsome and stern looking. He could feel her watching his lanky body and sulky face and tried to avoid her stare.

"Gitta move on you, boy!"

"Yeah'm."

"I've gotta git outa heanh and git the white folks' clothes! Don't you know that?"

"Yeah'm."

"And you've gotta git ready for school. Now stop that slow pokin'! I mean it. Now go wash your mouth out and scrub your face! And take this kettle of hot water and pour it over the faucet to unfreeze it."

"Yeah'm." He took the kettle of boiling water and went down the steps into the backyard. He returned.

"When you've had your breakfast, clean out from under the wash pot and put a fire under it. Don't light it, jes prepare it."

"Yeah'm." He sat down to the table and poured fried meat grease over six biscuits and saturated them with syrup and had himself a sopping good time.

Then, just like that, that knock on the door came. It was not loud and it was not soft. It was just enough for you to hear it. And if you heard it you knew who it was. THE RENT MAN. Gabriel watched his mother from under his eyes, sitting across the table, holding her head. She jumped at the sound of the knock. Then she took a deep breath, as if to calm herself, adjusted the head rag on her head and sighed to herself: "Well . . . stick wit me, Jesus."

All of a sudden Gabriel's appetite was gone. He got up from the table and stood in the middle of the room and watched her open the door, wondering if this would be IT.

"Rent Man." It was the voice and person of a friendly faced white man. He stood there in the middle of the door with a receipt book and pencil in his hand.

"Good morning, Mr. Bates. . . . Er . . . Ah . . . you'll have to wait till Sadday for your rent." The smile on the man's face vanished.

"That's the same thing you've been saying for three weeks now, Martha. We've gotta have our money, not excuses and promises."

"I know, Mr. Bates. The Lord knows you've been good and patient but jes bear 'long wit us till Sadday. The Lord is my secret Judge, you'll gitcha money." The way she had to plead made Gabriel feel a salty watery taste in his mouth which had surged up from the bottom of his stomach. It was the kind of feeling you get when you have a sour stomach, or getting sick or something. And it was a good thing Pa was not around. 'Cause if he wuz Gabriel felt mad enough to fight him like a natural man and then run him away from home and dare 'im to ever come back.

"What's the matter, Martha, don't your husband support you and your boy? Take 'im to court for nonsupport." She almost exploded in the man's face, but caught herself, realizing that she was at his mercy. So she choked back her fury and remained silent.

"All right so it's none of my business. . . . That's a mighty big boy you got there." He nodded appreciatively toward Gabriel. She snapped her head around, gripped her jaws together tightly in anguish, despair, and embarrassment and screamed frantically:

"Boy, what is you doing in heanh!" Then, just like that, she realized that her fright and desperation must not make her lose control of herself nor embarrass herself and Gabriel before this white man. She took a deep breath, sighed wearily, and said:

"Son, now why aintcha cleaning up the kitchen like your ma told you . . .? Yes, sir, he's done fourteen now. Going to high school," she said proudly.

"Very nice, very nice, but I'll be by Saturday and will expect my money or my house." The Rent Man left. Gabriel went into the kitchen, dejectedly, wondering what would it be next. Last week the furniture man took the bedspread off the bed and left her crying and Pa still came home broke Sadday. Now they just might be put outdoors this coming Sadday or freeze to death before then. And Pa, as usual, would come home broke as a haint. She came into the kitchen.

"Ma, why don'tcha put Pa out! Shucks! I don't see whatcha want wit 'im noway! He don't do nothing but make you cry all the time!" It was a bitter and angry explosion of words.

"Whatttttttt! What did you say, boy! C'mere to me! Don't you ever . . . !" She shook him violently and slapped him hard across the face. "Don't you ever let me hear you talk like that again! Ever EVER! NEVER! NEVER! You heanh? Of all the . . . confounded nerve!" She shook and slapped him again. And the blood came from his mouth. And her heart bled a little too at the sight of it all on his little face that looked just like his daddy. Suddenly she had the urge to just grab him and hug him and kiss the blood and tears and drink them down, to share the pains she had caused him. But he was wrong for talking like that. The Lord knows he's wrong 'bout his pa. She knew why his pa gambled. Oh! if she could only tell her son! But he was too young to understand. Slowly she released Gabriel and turned her head to choke back the tears. Jesus! what was she gonna do . . . ?

Pa was always home before dark. But somehow it seemed that this particular Monday he brought darkness with him. He was a big powerful man. Tall, broad, smooth black skin, good looking. He had a wide nose. And when he smiled his lips would slide behind his evenly set teeth and reveal pink gums that lit up his face. His big flashing eyes sat back in their sockets.

All was quiet at the table. Gabriel watched his father's every move as they sat across the table from each other having supper. At each swallow of food his father took, at each rise and fall of his Adam's apple — gliding down and up his throat like an elevator — something tightened in Gabriel. His father chewed so heartily and enjoyed the black-eyed peas and cornbread so immensely, as if he had bought them! Oh! if he wuz only a man like his father! He would show 'im!

"Josh, you want some more peas?"

"Yeahhh! Pour a few more of 'em on heanh. Now ain't that

right? Yeah, sir!" Josh stretched and yawned and looked at Gabriel. "Boy, what's the matter wit' you?"

"Nothing."

"Gabriel, you want some more peas?"

"No'm."

"Ahhh Lord, woman, you sho can cook. Great God Almighty! One of these days! Woman, one of these days Josh Coker is gonna pay you back for making such fine cooking. Yeah, sir! gonna stop you from washing and ironing and sweating over white folks' clothes. Yeah, sir! I'm gonna buy you one of dem houses like that white woman you wash for and invite her to do our washing." Josh laughed uproariously at his remarks about getting a white wash-woman, clapped his hands and said, "Ain't that right, boy."

Gabriel remained silent.

"Just stop me from worryin' 'bout the rent money." Martha did not smile.

"Don't worry 'bout it! It'll git paid! Yeah, sir!"

Martha wiped her hands with the dishrag and stood on the side of the table where he was.

"Josh?"

"What is it?"

"I'm gonna ask you something, to do something for me. And I want you to cross your heart to God you'll do it."

"What is it?"

"Lemme meetcha Sadday to pick up your pay to make sho the rent is paid and some food is in the house." The words fell like crashing timber in the forest. The spoon fell from Josh's hand, his back straightened up, his bottom lip fell, and he backed away from the table in his chair.

"Whatttt? Honh! Watcha think I is — your child? Josh Coker don't need NOBODY to pick up my money! You think I'm gonna have all the men down there laughing at me 'cause you come n' git my pay? Nawwwwww!"

"It's better they laugh atcha 'cause I PICK IT UP than to laugh atcha 'cause THEY pick it up at some old no-good skin game!"

"Don't worry 'bout it! Ain't that right, boy?"

". . . . ."

"Aintcha gonna worry 'bout us eating? Aintcha gonna worry

bout a roof over our heads? Aintcha gonna worry 'bout insurance for us if we git sick?"

"It'll git paid! EVERYTHING'LL git paid! Ain't that right, boy?"

Gabriel just stared at the plate, with anger, hate, and resentment boiling to the explosion point in his belly. Then he thought about the surprise he had for Ma and the boiling in his belly calmed down a little. For he just knew when she saw what he had she would think more of him than she did Pa. He would wait until things quieted down; then he would be the center of attraction with his surprise.

"What's the matter wit you, boy, you suckin' wind or something?"

"Naw, suh."

"Then whatcha so quiet for?"

"Nothing."

"You wanna read the old man somethin' from the Good Book?"

Silence. Naw! He never wanted to read him nothing again!

"Honh?"

"Suh?"

"You heanh me, boy! You wanna read to me from the Good Book?"

"Yeah, suh." The words came out of his mouth as though they were being dragged. Slow and hard.

"Josh, whyntcha lemme meetcha. I don't have to come to the Mill. I can meetcha . . ."

"Nawwwww! I done tole you! Naw! I ain't no child!"

"And sometimes you ain't a man neither!" She came around the table and stood in front of him, defiantly, flat footed, with her arms akimbo, swayed back. "Well, I'll tell you this, Josh Coker. There had just better be some food and some money in this house Sadday night! Or the hosts of hell will know the reason why!"

Now was the time to do it, Gabriel thought. He felt proud of himself, as he moved towards the front room.

"Don't worry 'bout it! Honh! Gonna come pick up my money. Now ain't that some up the country? You ready with the Good Book, boy?" Gabriel pretended he didn't hear, although he was only five steps away from his father.

"Honh, boy?"

"Suh?"

"Boy, you got wind in your jaws or somethin'? What you suckin' wind fer? Honh?"

"I ain't suckin' no wind."

"Then why cain't nobody git no answer outa you when they talkin' to ya, honh?"

"Well, start gittin' ready to read the Good Book to me then!"

"Yeah, suh."

Gabriel walked slowly towards the middle room, watching them — imagining the glee and joy which would erase the anguish on his mother's face when she saw what he had. Just then Josh walked over to her and smiled and threw his arm around her shoulder whispering softly to her, "Don't worry 'bout it!" Then he smiled that great big hearty smile of his that disarmed her every time. Gabriel turned away and went to get his surprise, mad with her for letting him get the best of her like that.

"Howya like that! My own woman don't trust me wit my own pay." He nudged Martha in the ribs with his elbow and smacked her on the cheek with a kiss. Then he pinched the nipple of her bosom and sort of let his hand roam.

"Gwone 'way from me, Josh! I ain't got no time for none of your foolishness." She turned her head away, trying to avoid him seeing her smiling. Yes, he had done it again. Her man sho had a way wit a woman.

Just before Josh came into the front room, Gabriel sat a sack of coals in the middle of the floor which he had dragged from under the house where he had hidden them. Josh came in.

"BRRRR! Colder than a witch's britches!" Josh said, sitting down in the rocking chair, sighing heavily. "Ahhh Lord, the bones is kinda tired tonight."

Gabriel stood in the middle of the room, letting his body camouflage the sack of coal. "Ma, c'mere!" he called excitedly. "I got somethin' to show you!"

Eagerly, with enthusiasm, he waited to see the proud expression on her face and to receive her praise. She came to the doorway and stood, staring piercingly at him and the hunk of gleaming black coal in his hand. She didn't speak; just stared. But the stare did more talking than a whole lot of words. The gladness left Gabriel's eyes, a void opened up in his chest. Something was wrong. His heart sank when she asked:

"Where'd you git 'em from?" She didn't bat an eye and her stare just kept on talking and asking unnecessary questions.

"Well looka heanh! Whattttt? Coals! Well let's put 'em on the fire! Now ain't that right?" Josh leaped up from the chair to put the coals on the fire.

"Naw, it aint right! Don't you put one piece of that coal on that fire till he tells me where he got 'em from!"

"Whatta you mean, where he got 'em from? What difference do it make where he got 'em from? Who cares? He got 'em! Let's put the coals on the fire, boy." Josh reached for the sack.

"Onh onnnh! Naw you don't! Just leave them coals right where they is! Where'd you git 'em from, boy?"

Gabriel didn't answer.

"You hear me talkin' to you, boy?"

"Yeah'm."

"Where'd you git them coals from?"

"The coal yard."

"Now ain't that some up the country! Where'd you think he got 'em from — the sawdust pile? Now what kinda question is that? Where'd he git 'em from! Hunh!" Josh sat down disgustedly.

"Now you jes shet your mouth, Josh Coker! I know what I'm doing!"

"Now looka heanh! Wait jest a minute! This heanh aintcha child you talkin' to now!" He turned from her biting, talking stare and looked at the floor.

"How much did you pay for 'em? And where did you git the money from?"

"Mam?" Gabriel squirmed and scratched places that hadn't itched for six months or more.

"Boy, you heard me! How much did you pay for them coals?"

"Awwwww, Ma, shux!"

"Boy, don'tcha come aw shuxin' me! Did you and Bopeet steal them coals?" Her words jerked his head upwards. With a shocked and surprised expression on his face, he wondered how she knew about Bopeet.

"Mam?" He lowered his head again.

"You heard me, boy! Y'all thought nobody saw you sneakin' up the back alley. I wuz jes wondering how long it would take you to bring 'em out. Look me dead in the eye!" Slowly he raised his head and looked beyond her stare.

"Look me in the eye, boy! You stole them coals, didn'tcha?"

Silence.

"Didn'tcha?"

"Well . . . awwwwww, Ma! Well . . . you see . . . I mean . . . awwww, Ma, we ain't the only ones. Somebody cut a hole in the fence . . . and . . . and a lot of folks do it."

"I don't care if everybody in Barleyville is doin' it. You ain't-a-gonna do it! You heanh?"

"Mam?"

"You gonna take 'em back! Right now! TONIGHT!"

"Woman, is you done lost your infernal mind? Take what back? Put the damn coals on the fire and forget about 'em! Burn the damn coals!"

"Looka heanh! Don't you say nothin' to me! That's all we have to do is be caught wit these coals in this house and can't prove we bought 'em! Didn't Sarah Fitzgerald's boy, C. J., git sont away for stealin' a can of sardines and a loaf of bread when they found it in her house and she couldn't prove where she bought it?"

"Awwwwwww! Burn the damn coals. Burn the evidence! Shux! If Sarah Fitzgerald had et the sardines instead of keepin' 'em around for the white folks to find 'em C. J. wouldn't've got sont away!"

"Josh Coker, sir, do you realize you're encouraging your son to be a rogue?"

"Awww, woman, put all the coals on the fire, in the stove and forget about it! Shux!"

She looked at Gabriel and stared at Josh. "Instead of going to a skin game Sadday, you go out and bring home a sack of coal! That's what you do! THEN HE WON'T HAVE TO GO OUT HEAH STEAL-ING!"

"Honh! That's right! That's right! Blame me! Blame me! You don't blame me when I win!"

"I don't blame you when you win 'cause you NEVER WIN!" Josh sucked his teeth and waved her away with disgust.

"A GAMBLER IS ENOUGH IN THIS FAMILY! I ain't-a-gonna have a gambler and a THIEF in this house! Naw, suh! I can't break you out of the habit of gambling but I sho can break him out of the habit of stealing or break his neck instead! Putcha clothes on! I'm gonna break you out of this habit right now!! I'm going witcha! You'll never have me bring you cigarettes to some chain gang cell for stealing. Naw, suh!

"I'm gonna whup your ass when we git back heanh too. I don't care if there wuz icicles dangling from every shingle on the roof and every brick in that fireplace. It ain't enough to make you steal! In this house we do the best we can wit the best we got!"

She began getting her coat out of the closet. Josh sighed resignedly and started putting his shoes on.

"Where you gwine?" She asked Josh.

"Now ain't that a ign'ant question! Where you think I'm gwine? You think I'm gonna sit heanh while y'all go out yonder by yerself in the night?"

Gabriel felt as though he had just been gutted. Couldn't she see he was only trying to help her, to stop her from crying and worrying and praying to God and never getting anything? It was funny; suddenly, just that moment, for the first time in his life, a doubt arose in his mind as to the existence of God. Then, too, he was convinced that if his pa had brought home the coals, told her he stoled 'em, she wouldn't have said a mumblin' word. She would've been bragging to Miss Caroline 'bout "My Josh this, my Josh that!" He didn't care if she didn't never brag about him.

The streets were cold, dark, and silent. There was something ghostly, haunting, frightening that pervaded the silence and darkness; as if one were passing through enemy territory being observed by unseen eyes every step of the way.

A chilly wind ripped through Gabriel's clothes and wrapped him in its icy embrace. Just as quickly the wind released its embrace and swept them forcefully down the alley. Then suddenly the wind, as if made privy to a profound secret and wanted to warn them of some impending danger, reversed itself and tried to sweep them back up the hill and into their home. With each step they took, the wind howled and wailed in distress and whipped up a fury — stomping and kicking against the tin rooftops, slamming shutters and screen doors; it flapped its tail through the naked branches of the trees, lapped up paper and dead grass and spat it out against their feet — as if it were trying to build a wall which they couldn't scale and would be forced back into the safe confines of home. It even blew sand in their eyes. But they just kept on walking, wiping their eyes, stepping over paper.

On they trudged — three bundled-up shadows in the night — through the streets, bracing cold and warning wind. A cat MEEOOWED; a dog replied with a bark. Here and there dimly lighted windows speckled the darkness with faded yellow squares.

Now the wind had lowered the register of its voice from a howl to a moan. Into the depth of darkness and the unknown, side by side, past the wood yard, past the grocery store, past everything except the echoes of their feet grinding sand and gravel beneath, they traveled heedlessly.

Gabriel glanced at her from the corner of his eyes; she just looked straight ahead, penetrating the awesome darkness with her stare. It didn't matter what he did to please her, it only mattered if Pa did it! Last night she wuz crying about how cold it wuz. Now she gets coals and gets holy and comes talking about "take 'em back!" They didn't steal the coal noway. They were there and people just took them. He would bet that right now there were people filling up their sacks. . . . Then, like a thunder clap, the thought burst through his brain and sent tremors through his flesh! SUPPOSING THEY GOT CAUGHT. The words hung in his conscience like red-hot coals of fire, burning their way into the fiber of his being. The icy wind which had chilled his body faded and he was now flushed with a heat wave. Warm water burst out of his skin and dripped down his arm. ALL OF Y'ALL COULD GO TO JAIL. His mind was just trying to play a trick on him. Who would be out there, cold as it is? NOBODY. They wouldn't get caught. Yet his teeth chattered in panic; blood bubbled through his veins so hard and fast till it made him dizzy. THEY SENT C. J. AWAY FOR THREE YEARS FOR STEALING SARDINES AND BREAD. Three years for a can of sardines and a loaf of bread.

But they found the stuff in his house though. They wouldn't get arrested for taking the coals back. Of course not. NAWWWW! Then why was his heart halfway up his throat; why was his mouth so dry and gooey? C. J. WAS STILL AWAY FOR THEM SARDINES! Wuuuu! Weeeeee!

It was so scary quiet that their footsteps exploded with a deafening blast. With each step he took, his feet got heavier and heavier and heavier. And a voice within him tried to break out of the shackled prison of his conscience, and rip through his chattering teeth to plead: Don't, Ma! Let's go back, Ma! My legs won't take me no further! Please turn around! Please turn around. But his voice had the lockjaw and his tongue was in a deep freeze.

Now they were walking down the railroad tracks. Everything was too quiet, too dark. Yeah! she had plenty of nerve except to when it came to Pa. Always taking up for him. Bet she wouldn't have made him take 'em back!

They were like three kites, severed from their cords, falling relentlessly and inexorably through space to some awaiting but unknown fate. An obliging wind lapped up the steam from his nostrils and muffled momentarily his uncontrollably loud breathing. Now his legs were dead weight, without blood, without nerves, without anything.

At last the tall mounds of coal could be seen jutting up through the blurred distance. C. J. WAS STILL AWAY. It wouldn't be long now and it would be all over. Forgotten! Their steps got slower. He tried to stretch his neck beyond the darkness to see if just in case or by chance somebody just happened to be there. And they came closer and closer and slower and slower. Then they were there. He felt a partial relief. A little slack came to his nerves; the heart pumped a few beats slower. Nothing was seen. Nothing was heard. They should have brought a lantern or something. And the screws which bolted down his nerves relaxed their grip a little more. Shux, he knew he wuz getting scared for nothing all the while. He sneaked a look over the left side of the track and down and around the fence. Not a sound! Now what wuz he getting scared for in the first place! Even the wind had stopped moaning. HUSH! What was that? He thought he heard something. Awwwwwww shux! My imagination is just trying to tease me. That's all. Pa didn't seem to hear nothing. Neither did Ma.

They took the sack of coal down the bank. It was done. A heavy weight fell from his shoulders and body and mind. They started back up the bank. Soon they would be home. Maybe it was his nerves; maybe it was his imagination; it could've been a rabbit breaking through bushes or snakes just making it to a hole, but whatever it was he heard it. And it came from right over there.

But how come Ma, Pa, didn't seem to hear anything? SOMETHING MOVED AGAIN!

His voice tried to cry out: Wait, Ma, don'tcha hear it!! THREE YEARS! Let's fall down; let's run. Now he felt eyes on him; he felt pistols and gun barrels aimed at his body. Suddenly heavy feet trampled through bushes, crushed sticks and crunched gravels beneath their feet. The sounds locked him in his tracks, speechless, dissolving like a cake of ice in broiling sun. Then Ma turned around; then Pa turned around. Then flashlights and lanterns shattered and splintered the darkness with yellow patches of light. A voice roared loud and clear. "GITCHA HANDS UP! YAWL'S UNDER ARREST."

SON IN THE AFTERNOON

John A. Williams

IT was hot. I tend to be a bitch when it's hot. I goosed the little
Ford over Sepulveda Boulevard toward Santa Monica until I
got stuck in the traffic that pours from L.A. into the surrounding
towns. I'd had a very lousy day at the studio.

I was — still am — a writer and this studio had hired me to
check scripts and films with Negroes in them to make sure the
Negro moviegoer wouldn't be offended. The signs were already
clear one day the whole of American industry would be racing pell-
mell to get a Negro, showcase a spade. I was kind of a pioneer. I'm
a *Negro* writer, you see. The day had been tough because of a
couple of verbs — slink and walk. One of those Hollywood hippies
had done a script calling for a Negro waiter to slink away from the
table where a dinner party was glaring at him. I said the waiter
should walk, not slink, because later on he becomes a hero. The
Hollywood hippie, who understood it all because he had some
colored friends, said that it was essential to the plot that the waiter
slink. I said you don't slink one minute and become a hero the
next; there has to be some consistency. The Negro actor I was
standing up for said nothing either way. He had played Uncle
Tom roles so long that he had become Uncle Tom. But the
director agreed with me.

Anyway . . . hear me out now. I was on my way to Santa
Monica to pick up my mother, Nora. It was a long haul for such a
hot day. I had planned a quiet evening: a nice shower, fresh
clothes, and then I would have dinner at the Watkins and talk
with some of the musicians on the scene for a quick taste before
they cut to their gigs. After, I was going to the Pigalle down on
Figueroa and catch Earl Grant at the organ, and still later, if

nothing exciting happened, I'd pick up Scottie and make it to the Lighthouse on the Beach or to the Strollers and listen to some of the white boys play. I liked the long drive, especially while listening to Sleepy Stein's show on the radio. Later, much later of course, it would be home, back to Watts.

So you see, this picking up Nora was a little inconvenient. My mother was a maid for the Couchmans. Ronald Couchman was an architect, a good one I understood from Nora who has a fine sense for this sort of thing; you don't work in some hundred-odd houses during your life without getting some idea of the way a house should be laid out. Couchman's wife, Kay, was a playgirl who drove a white Jaguar from one party to another. My mother didn't like her too much; she didn't seem to care much for her son, Ronald, junior. There's something wrong with a parent who can't really love her own child, Nora thought. The Couchmans lived in a real fine residential section, of course. A number of actors lived nearby, character actors, not really big stars.

Somehow it is very funny. I mean that the maids and butlers knew everything about these people, and these people knew nothing at all about the help. Through Nora and her friends I knew who who was laying whose wife; who had money and who *really* had money; I knew about the wild parties hours before the police, and who smoked marijuana, when, and where they got it.

To get to Couchman's driveway I had to go three blocks up one side of a palm-planted center strip and back down the other. The driveway bent gently, then swept back out of sight of the main road. The house, sheltered by slim palms, looked like a transplanted New England Colonial. I parked and walked to the kitchen door, skirting the growling Great Dane who was tied to a tree. That was the route to the kitchen door.

I don't like kitchen doors. Entering people's houses by them, I mean. I'd done this thing most of my life when I called at places where Nora worked to pick up the patched or worn sheets or the half-eaten roasts, the battered, tarnished silver—the fringe benefits of a housemaid. As a teen-ager I'd told Nora I was through with that crap; I was not going through anyone's kitchen door. She only laughed and said I'd learn. One day soon after, I called for her and without knocking walked right through the front door of this house and right on through the living room. I was almost out of the room when I saw feet behind the couch. I leaned over and there was Mr. Jorgensen and his wife making out like crazy. I guess they thought Nora had gone and it must have hit them sort of suddenly and they went at it like the hell-bomb was due to drop any minute. I've been that way too, mostly in the spring. Of course, when Mr. Jorgensen looked over his shoulder and saw me, you know what happened. I was thrown out and Nora right behind me. It was the middle of winter, the old man was sick and the coal bill three months overdue. Nora was right about those kitchen doors: I learned.

My mother saw me before I could ring the bell. She opened the door. "Hello," she said. She was breathing hard, like she'd been running or something. "Come in and sit down. I don't know *where* that Kay is. Little Ronald is sick and she's probably out gettin' drunk again." She left me then and trotted back through the house, I guess to be with Ronnie. I hated the combination of her white nylon uniform, her dark brown face and the wide streaks of gray in her hair. Nora had married this guy from Texas a few years after the old man had died. He was all right. He made out okay. Nora didn't have to work, but she just couldn't be still; she always had to be doing something. I suggested she quit work, but I had as much luck as her husband. I used to tease her about liking to be around those white folks. It would have been good for her to take an extended trip around the country visiting my brothers and sisters. Once she got to Philadelphia, she could go right out to the cemetery and sit awhile with the old man.

I walked through the Couchman home. I liked the library. I thought if I knew Couchman I'd like him. The room made me feel like that. I left it and went into the big living room. You could tell that Couchman had let his wife do that. Everything in it was fast, dart-like, with no sense of ease. But on the walls were several of Couchman's conceptions of buildings and homes. I guess he was a disciple of Wright. My mother walked rapidly through the room without looking at me and said, "Just be patient, Wendell. She should be here real soon."

"Yeah," I said, "with a snootful." I had turned back to the drawings when Ronnie scampered into the room, his face twisted with rage.

"Nora!" he tried to roar, perhaps the way he'd seen the parents of some of his friends roar at their maids. I'm quite sure Kay didn't shout at Nora, and I don't think Couchman would. But then no one shouts at Nora. "Nora, you come right back here this minute!" the little bastard shouted and stamped and pointed to a spot on the floor where Nora was supposed to come to roost. I have a nasty temper. Sometimes it lies dormant for ages and at other times, like when the weather is hot and nothing seems to be going right, it's bubbling and ready to explode. "Don't talk to *my* mother like that, you little — !" I said sharply, breaking off just before I cursed. I wanted him to be large enough for me to strike. "How'd you like for me to talk to *your* mother like that?"

The nine-year-old looked up at me in surprise and confusion. He hadn't expected me to say anything. I was just another piece of furniture. Tears rose in his eyes and spilled out onto his pale cheeks. He put his hands behind him, twisted them. He moved backwards, away from me. He looked at my mother with a "Nora, come help me" look. And sure enough, there was Nora, speeding back across the room, gathering the kid in her arms, tucking his robe together. I was too angry to feel hatred for myself.

Ronnie was the Couchman's only kid. Nora loved him. I suppose that was the trouble. Couchman was gone ten, twelve hours a day. Kay didn't stay around the house any longer than she had to. So Ronnie had only my mother. I think kids should have someone to love, and Nora wasn't a bad sort. But somehow when the six of us, her own children, were growing up we never had her. She was gone, out scuffling to get those crumbs to put into our mouths and shoes for our feet and praying for something to happen so that all the space in between would be taken care of. Nora's affection for us took the form of rushing out into the morning's five o'clock blackness to wake some silly bitch and get her coffee; took form in her trudging five miles home every night instead of taking the streetcar to save money to buy tablets for us, to use at school, we said. But the truth was that all of us liked to draw and we went through a writing tablet in a couple of hours every day. Can you imagine? There's not a goddamn artist among us. We never had the physical affection, the pat on the head, the quick, smiling kiss, the "gimmee a hug" routine. All of this Ronnie was getting.

Now he buried his little blond head in Nora's breast and sobbed.

"There, there now," Nora said. "Don't you cry, Ronnie. Ol' Wendell is just jealous, and he hasn't much sense either. He didn't mean nuthin'."

I left the room. Nora had hit it of course, hit it and passed on. I looked back. It didn't look so incongruous, the white and black together, I mean. Ronnie was still sobbing. His head bobbed gently on Nora's shoulder. The only time I ever got that close to her was when she trapped me with a bearhug so she could whale the daylights out of me after I put a snowball through Mrs. Grant's window. I walked outside and lit a cigarette. When Ronnie was in the hospital the month before, Nora got me to run her way over to Hollywood every night to see him. I didn't like that worth a damn. All right, I'll admit it: it did upset me. All that affection I didn't get nor my brothers and sisters going to that little white boy who, without a doubt, when away from her called her the names he'd learned from adults. Can you imagine a nine-year-old kid calling Nora a "girl," "our girl?" I spat at the Great Dane. He snarled and then I bounced a rock off his fanny. "Lay down, you bastard," I muttered. It was a good thing he was tied up.

I heard the low cough of the Jaguar slapping against the road. The car was throttled down, and with a muted roar it swung into the driveway. The woman aimed it for me. I was evil enough not to move. I was tired of playing with these people. At the last moment, grinning, she swung the wheel over and braked. She bounded out of the car like a tennis player vaulting over a net.

"Hi," she said, tugging at her shorts.

"Hello."

"You're Nora's boy?"

"I'm Nora's son." Hell, I was as old as she was; besides, I can't stand "boy."

"Nora tells us you're working in Hollywood. Like it?"

"It's all right."

"You must be pretty talented."

We stood looking at each other while the dog whined for her attention. Kay had a nice body and it was well tanned. She was high, boy, was she high. Looking at her, I could feel myself going into my sexy bastard routine; sometimes I can swing it great.

Maybe it all had to do with the business inside. Kay took off her sunglasses and took a good look at me. "Do you have a cigarette?"

I gave her one and lit it. "Nice tan," I said. Most white people I know think it's a great big deal if a Negro compliments them on their tans. It's a large laugh. You have all this volleyball about color and come summer you can't hold the white folks back from the beaches, anyplace where they can get some sun. And of course the blacker they get, the more pleased they are. Crazy. If there is ever a Negro revolt, it will come during the summer and Negroes will descend upon the beaches around the nation and paralyze the country. You can't conceal cattle prods and bombs and pistols and police dogs when you're showing your birthday suit to the sun.

"You like it?" she asked. She was pleased. She placed her arm next to mine. "Almost the same color," she said.

"Ronnie isn't feeling well," I said.

"Oh, the poor kid. I'm so glad we have Nora. She's such a charm. I'll run right in and look at him. Do have a drink in the bar. Fix me one too, will you?" Kay skipped inside and I went to the bar and poured out two strong drinks. I made hers stronger than mine. She was back soon. "Nora was trying to put him to sleep and she made me stay out." She giggled. She quickly tossed off her drink. "Another, please?" While I was fixing her drink she was saying how amazing it was for Nora to have such a talented son. What she was really saying was that it was amazing for a servant to have a son who was not also a servant. "Anything can happen in a democracy," I said. "Servants' sons drink with madames and so on."

"Oh, Nora isn't a servant," Kay said. "She's part of the family."

Yeah, I thought. Where and how many times had I heard *that* before?

In the ensuing silence, she started to admire her tan again. "You think it's pretty good, do you? You don't know how hard I worked to get it." I moved close to her and held her arm. I placed my other arm around her. She pretended not to see or feel it, but she wasn't trying to get away either. In fact she was pressing closer and the register in my brain that tells me at the precise moment when I'm in, went off. Kay was very high. I put both arms around her and she put both hers around me. When I kissed her, she responded completely.

"Mom!"

"Ronnie, come back to bed," I heard Nora shout from the other room. We could hear Ronnie running over the rug in the outer room. Kay tried to get away from me, push me to one side, because we could tell that Ronnie knew where to look for his Mom: he was running right for the bar, where we were. "Oh, please," she said, "don't let him see us." I wouldn't let her push me away. "Stop!" she hissed. "He'll *see* us!" We stopped struggling just for an instant, and we listened to the echoes of the word *see*. She gritted her teeth and renewed her efforts to get away.

Me? I had the scene laid right out. The kid breaks into the room, see, and sees his mother in this real wriggly clinch with this colored guy who's just shouted at him, see, and no matter how his mother explains it away, the kid has the image — the colored guy and his mother — for the rest of his life, see?

That's the way it happened. The kid's mother hissed under her breath, "*You're crazy!*" and she looked at me as though she were seeing me or something about me for the very first time. I'd released her as soon as Ronnie, romping into the bar, saw us and came to a full, open-mouthed halt. Kay went to him. He looked first at me, then at his mother. Kay turned to me, but she couldn't speak.

Outside in the living room my mother called, "Wendell, where are you? We can go now."

I started to move past Kay and Ronnie. I felt many things, but I made myself think mostly, *There you little bastard, there.*

My mother thrust her face inside the door and said, "Good-bye, Mrs. Couchman. See you tomorrow. 'Bye, Ronnie."

"Yes," Kay said, sort of stunned. "Tomorrow." She was reaching for Ronnie's hand as we left, but the kid was slapping her hand away. I hurried quickly after Nora, hating the long drive back to Watts.

SINGING DINAH'S SONG

Frank London Brown

A GYPSY woman once told me. She said: "Son, beware of the song
that will not leave you."

But then I've never liked gypsy women no way, which is why I
was so shook when my buddy Daddy-o did his number the other
day. I mean his natural number.

You see, I work at Electronic Masters, Incorporated, and well,
we don't make much at this joint although if you know how to
talk to the man you might work up to a dollar and a half an
hour.

Me, I work on a punch press. This thing cuts steel sheets and
molds them into shells for radio and television speakers. Sometimes when I'm in some juice joint listening to Dinah Washington
and trying to get myself together, I get to thinking about all that
noise that that big ugly punch press makes, and me sweating and
scuffing, trying to make my rates, and man I get eeevil!

This buddy of mine though, he really went for Dinah Washington; and even though his machine would bang and scream all over
the place and all those high-speed drills would whine and cry like a
bunch of sanctified soprano church-singers, this fool would be in the
middle of all that commotion just singing Dinah Washington's
songs to beat the band. One day I went up and asked this fool
what in the world he was singing about; and he looked at me and
tucked his thumbs behind his shirt collar and said: "Baby, I'm
singing Dinah's songs. Ain't that broad mellow?"

Well, I. Really, all I could say was: "Uh, why yes."

And I went back to my machine.

It was one of those real hot days when it happened: about ten-
thirty in the morning. I was sweating already. Me and that big

ugly scoundrel punch press. Tussling. Lord, I was so beat. I felt like singing Dinah's songs myself. I had even started thinking in rhythm with those presses banging down on that steel: *sh-bang boom bop! Sh, bang boom bop, sh'bang boom bop.* Then all of a sudden:

In walks Daddy-o!

My good buddy. Sharp? You'd better believe it: dark-blue single breast, a white on white shirt, and a black and yellow rep tie! Shoes shining like new money. And that pearl-gray hat kinda pulled down over one eye. I mean to tell you, that Negro was sharp.

I was way behind on my quota because, you see, fooling around with those machines is not no play thing. You just get tired sometimes and fall behind. But I just had to slow down to look at my boy.

James, that was his real name. We call him Daddy-o because he's so. I don't know; there just ain't no other name would fit him. Daddy-o's a long, tall, dark cat with hard eyes and a chin that looks like the back end of a brick. Got great big arms and a voice like ten lions. Actually, sometimes Daddy-o scares you.

He walked straight to his machine. Didn't punch his time card or nothing. I called him: "Hey, Daddy-o, you must have had a good one last night. What's happening?"

Do you know that Negro didn't open his mouth?

"Hey, Daddy-o, how come you come strolling in here at ten-thirty? We start at seven-thirty around this place!"

Still no answer.

So this cat walks over to his machine and looks it up and down and turns around and heads straight for the big boss's office. Well, naturally I think Daddy-o's getting ready to quit, so I kind of peeps around my machine so that I can see him better.

He walked to the big boss's office and stopped in front of the door and lit a cigarette smack-dab underneath the "No Smoking" sign. Then he turned around like he had changed his mind about quitting and headed back to his machine. Well, I just started back to work. After all it's none of my business if a man wants to work in his dark-blue suit and a white on white shirt with his hat on.

By this time Charlie walked up just as Daddy-o started to stick his hand into the back of the machine.

Charlie liked to busted a blood vessel. "Hey, what the hell are you doing? You want to 'lectrocute yourself?"

Now I don't blame Charlie for hollering. Daddy-o knows that you can get killed sticking your hand in the back of a machine. Everybody in the plant knows that.

Daddy-o acted like he didn't hear Charlie, and he kept right on reaching into the hole. Charlie ran up and snatched Daddy-o's hand back. Daddy-o straightened up, reared back and filled his chest with a thousand pounds of air: one foot behind him and both of those oversized fists doubled up. Charlie cleared his throat and started feeling around in his smock like he was looking for something, which I don't think he was.

Pretty soon Mr. Grobber, the big boss, walked up. One of the other foremen came up and then a couple of setup men from another department. They all stood around Daddy-o and he just stood there cool, smoking one of those long filter-tips. He started to smile, like he was bashful. But whenever anyone went near the machine, he filled up with more air and got those big ham-fists ready.

Well after all, Daddy-o was my buddy and I couldn't just let all those folks surround him without doing something, so I turned my machine off and walked over to where they were crowding around him.

"Daddy-o, what's the matter, huh? You mad at somebody, Daddy-o?"

Mr. Grobber said: "James, if you don't feel well, why don't you just go home and come in tomorrow?"

All Daddy-o did was to look slowly around the plant. He looked at each one of us. A lot of the people in the shop stopped working and were looking back at him. Others just kept on working. But he looked at them, kind of smiling, like he had a feeling for each and every one of them.

Then quick like a minute, he spread his legs out, and stretched his arms in front of the machine like it was all he had in this world.

I tried once again to talk to him.

"Aww come on, Daddy-o. Don't be that way."

That Negro's nose started twitching. Then he tried to talk but his breath was short like he had been running or something.

"Ain't nobody getting this machine. I own this machine, baby. This is mine. Ten years! On this machine. Baby, this belongs to me."

"I know it do, Daddy-o. I know it do."

Charlie Wicowycz got mad hearing him say that, so he said, "Damn," and started into Daddy-o. Daddy-o's eyes got big and he drew his arm back and kind of stood on his toes and let out a holler like, like I don't know what.

"Doonnnn't you touch this machiiinnneeee!"

Naturally Charlie stopped, then he started to snicker and play like he was tickled except his face was as white as a fish belly. I thought I would try, so I touched Daddy-o's arm. It was hard like brick. I let his arm go.

"Daddy-o man, I know how you feel. Let me call your wife so she can come and get you. You'll be all right tomorrow. What's your phone number, Daddy-o? I'll call your wife for you, hear?"

His eyes started twitching and he started blinking like he was trying to keep from crying. Still he was smiling that little baby-faced smile.

"Daddy-o, listen to me. Man, I ain't trying to do nothing to you. Give me your number and your wife will know what to do."

His lips started trembling. Big grown man, standing there with his lips trembling. He opened his mouth. His whole chin started trembling as he started to speak: "Drexel."

I said: "Okay, Drexel. Now Drexel what?"

"Drexel."

"Drexel what else, Daddy-o?"

"Drexel seven-two-three."

"Seven-two-three. What else, Daddy-o? Man, I'm trying to help you. I'm going to call your wife. She'll be here in a few minutes. Drexel seven-two-three-what else? What is the rest of your phone number. Daddy-o! I'm talkin' to you!"

"Eight-eight-eight-eight-nine."

"Drexel seven-two-three-eight-nine? That it, Daddy-o?"

Mr. Grobber started walking around scratching his stomach. He stopped in front of Charlie Wicowycz. "Call the police, Charlie."

Charles left.

The other foremen went back to their departments. The setup

men followed them. Mr. Grobber, seeing that he was being left alone with Daddy-o, went back to his office.

Daddy-o just stood there smiling.

I ran to the office and called the number he had given me. Daddy-o's wife wasn't home, but a little girl who said that she was Daddy-o's "Babygirl" answered and said that she would tell her mother as soon as she came home from work.

When I walked out of the office, the police were there. I thought about the time I had to wait three hours for the police to get to my house the time somebody broke in and took every stitch I had. One of the cops, a big mean-looking something with ice-water eyes, moved in on Daddy-o with his club out and Daddy-o just shuffled his feet, doubled up his fists and waited for him.

I started talking up for my boy.

"Officer, please don't hurt him. He's just sick. He won't do no harm."

"Who are you? Stay outa."

I tried to explain to him. "Look, Officer, just let me talk to him. I . . . I'm his friend."

"All right. Talk to him. Tell him to get into the wagon."

I touched Daddy-o's arm again. He moved it away, still smiling. I said: "Man, Daddy-o, come on now. Come on, go with me. I know how it is. I know how it is."

He still had that smile. I swear I could have cried.

I started walking, pulling his arm a bit.

"Come on, Daddy-o."

He came along easy, still smiling, and walking with a kind of strut. Looking at each and every one of us like we were his best friends. When we got to the door, he stopped and looked back at his machine. Still smiling. When we got outside, I led him right up to the wagon. The back door was open and it was dark in there. Some dusty light scooted through a little window at the back of the wagon that had a wire grating in it. It didn't look very nice in there. I turned to Daddy-o.

"Come on, Daddy-o. The man said you should get in. Ain't nothing going to git you, Daddy-o. Come on, man. Get in."

I felt like anybody's stoolie.

"Come on, get in."

He started moving with me, then he stopped and looked back at the plant. One of the officers touched his arm. And that's when he did his natural number.

He braced his arms against the door. And started to scream to bust his lungs: "That is my machine. I own. Me and this machine is blood kin. Don't none of you somitches touch it. You heah? You, you heah?"

The water-eyed policeman started to agree with Daddy-o.

"Sure, kid. You know it. Lotsa machines. You got lots of 'em."

Daddy-o turned to look at him at the same time his partner gave him a shove. The water-eyed policeman shoved him too. Daddy-o swung at him and missed. When he did that, the water-eyed policeman chunked him right behind the ear and Daddy-o fell back into the wagon. Both policemen grabbed his feet and pushed him past the door and the water-eye slammed it.

They jumped in and started to drive away. Daddy-o was up again and at the window. He was hollering, and his voice got mixed up with the trucks and cars that went by. I watched the wagon huff out of sight and I went back into the plant.

Inside, I got to think about how sharp Daddy-o was. I was real proud of that. I caught sight of Daddy-o's machine. You know that thing didn't look right without Daddy-o working on it.

I got to think about my machine and how I know that big ugly thing better than I know most live people. Seemed funny to think that it wasn't really mine. It sure seemed like mine.

Ol' Daddy-o was sure crazy about Dinah Washington. Last few days that's all he sang: her songs. Like he was singing in place of crying; like being in the plant made him sing those songs and like finally the good buddy couldn't sing hard enough to keep up the dues on his machine and then. . . . Really.

You know what? Looking around there thinking about Daddy-o and all, I caught myself singing a song that had been floating around in my head.

It goes: *I got bad news, baby, and you're the first to know.*

That's one of Dinah Washington's songs.

DUEL WITH THE CLOCK

Junius Edwards

BRAD had never seen a dead man before. Now he had seen one die in the same room with him. He had seen a body that was once full of life; that breathed and walked and ran — dead. Dead. Dead! Right before his eyes. Dead. Dead. No breath. No heartbeat. No pulse. No sound. Death. Nothing but death. Death and its ghastly silence. Walker is dead. Walker is dead. Walker is! Oh, you're kidding. Yes, he is. Walker is dead, I tell you. Dead. Dead. Dead! You hear me? Dead! — High, you mean. He is high. Real high. He is not dead. Not Walker. Not him. He's in the Medics. He knows how to take care of himself. He wouldn't take an overdose. He is not dead, ha! That son o'bitch is just in his world. Way, way up there in his world. You see. That's it. Ha! Walker, dead? You're nuts!

Walker is dead.

Brad knew it. He didn't want it to be true, but he knew. Walker is dead. He saw it. He saw it happen. He saw Walker turn that awful green color and he saw him fall to the floor, dead. How did Motts put it? — "Dead as last night's fix." — Walker is dead. Brad could still see him. There he lay, with drying red blood coming out of his eyes, ears, mouth, nose and turning brown on his green face. Walker is gone from this world. Gone. But Brad wondered about that. Gone where? What about that? They had left him back there in that cold room all alone with his blood and his green face and silence, waiting for the Japanese night. But where had Walker gone? Brad thought of all the things he had heard about the hereafter. Why is it called *hereafter*? Why not *thereafter* or *whatafter* or just plain *after*? Oh sisters and brothers live a good life if you want to have it good in the hereafter. If you want to live in the hereafter. If you want to go to heaven. If you want to escape hell's fire. How many times had he heard that? How many Sundays had he been to church to listen? How many Sundays in eighteen years? Be ready, boy. Be ready to go to heaven. How many times had Ma and Pa said that?

What about Walker? Was he ready? How did it feel to die? How did it feel to drop dead? Drop dead? *Drop* dead? You trying to be funny? Drop dead? Do you have to think of it like that? Drop dead? Drop dead. Well, that's what he did. That's what the bastard did. He dropped dead. He didn't die. You die like they do in the movies. You die like the hero. You know you're dying. You talk about it or about something and you lie down, you stretch out and wait for it in comfort, preferably with a doll's arms about you and your head on her soft breasts. That's the way to die. You don't drop dead. You have a nice little conversation; tell everyone good-bye; you'll see them in the hereafter.

But that's not the way Walker died. He just dropped dead, poor bastard. There wasn't a Moosie Mae around, not even that ugly bitch, Masako. He just dropped dead. He didn't say a word. He didn't even know he had taken an overdose. He didn't even know it was his time. Death sneaked up and sprang on him and kicked life out. It didn't even give Walker a chance to lie down. It made no appointment. It just reached out and got that poor, poor bastard.

But was he ready? Did he know about the hereafter? Did he believe in that religion business? Brad would never know. He would never know whether Walker would have prayed or cried or laughed or waited in silence. Oh, death was a monster and a sneaky bastard.

But, Brad thought, when it comes to me, I hope it's as quick. He wondered whether it was lonely in the hereafter.

Brad got back to his barracks at ten minutes to six. It was empty and quiet and he was glad of it. He fell across his bed, still thinking about Walker. Then he remembered that he was supposed to see Sgt. Eaton at six o'clock in order to get his pass. He wouldn't do it. He would lay right there on his bed and not see Eaton at all. Eaton could keep his pass. Brad didn't need it now. He wouldn't dare go out now. Walker is dead. Walker is dead. Walker is dead.

Brad heard someone come into the barracks. He didn't turn his head to see who it was. He didn't care. The footsteps got nearer and he heard the voice singing a song to the tune of "The Star Spangled Banner" and he knew it was Doc:

> *Oh, say, can you see*
> *Any bedbugs on me?*
> *If you do, take a few*
> *'Cause I got them from you. . . .*

Brad heard him stop singing and start humming the same tune and then he heard him say:

"Let's go up on the hill."

Brad said nothing.

"Let's go up on the hill."

Brad said nothing. He heard Doc walk closer and he felt the bed shake from Doc's kick. "Let's go up on the hill."

"Get out of here."

"Let's go up on the hill."

"Get out of here, will you?"

"What's the matter with you."

"Get out of here."

"What's eating you?"

"Leave me alone, will you?"

"You sick?"

"Yeah, yeah. I'm sick. Now, leave me alone, will you?"

"What's the matter?"

"Come on, Doc."

"You need some pussy. Come on, let's go up to the whorehouse on the hill."

"Come on. Get out of here, Doc."

"That's what you need."

"Come on, Doc!"

"Let's go up to the hill."

"Leave me alone, Doc, will you?"

"OK, OK." And he heard Doc tramp off down the aisle, singing his song.

Oh, these bastards, these bastards. This God damned Army and the bastards in it. The sons of bitches!

Walker is dead. Dead as last night's fix. Fix. Fix. Fix, fix, fix! He hadn't had a fix! As soon as he thought of it he felt the craving pains running wild in his chest. He turned over and lay on his back and put his right arm across his face and tried not to think of the pain. Walker is dead. Then Brad remembered. He took his arm off his face and stared up at the curved roof of the quonset hut barracks. Brad remembered. Death had saved him. Spared *him!* What else? Why had it come to Walker at that particular moment? Why not ten minutes later? Why not tomorrow? He could think of only one answer. Death had come to Walker in order to spare James Bradley. If it had come two minutes later, or even one, it would have been too late. But it hadn't. It hadn't. It had come in the nick of time. Brad and Motts had slipped out of camp and gone to the room to meet Walker. Brad was to get his first pop. He was to go over from smoke to the needle. Just two minutes later and Motts would have sunk the needle into Brad's vein and the needle would have sucked up his blood and his blood would have mixed with the heroin and Motts would have pushed the syringe and sent the mixture back into Brad's veins. Two minutes later and death might have claimed him, too.

Brad turned over and lay on his stomach again. He didn't know whether to laugh or cry or shout.

Brad felt the hand on the back of his right thigh, squeezing gently and he smelled perfume and Mennens and stink; the smell of Sgt. Eaton. Brad hadn't heard him come. Sneaky queer bastard!

"Say, young one. After six."

Brad felt the bed sink down with Butterball Eaton's added weight and felt that hand still on his thigh.

"Young one. You wake?" Eaton's voice squeaking and whispering. Brad knew that a grin was spread over Eaton's face, his yellow teeth making his skin look milk white. He didn't bother to look up.

"Yeah, Sarge."

"You wake?"

"Yeah, Sarge."

"You forgot about your pass?"

"No."

"Yes, you did, too."

"No, I didn't."

"Don't you want it, honey?"

"Don't care."

"Aren't you coming?"

Brad felt Eaton squeeze his thigh, gently.

"Don't you want to hear some records?"

"No."

"It's after six. You wake?"

"I don't feel like hearing any records, Sarge."

"Don't you want your pass?"

"You going to give it to me?"

"That's for you to find out when you come."

"Didn't you make up your mind yet?"

"Come on to my room," Eaton said, and stood.

Brad lay still.

"Young one . . ,"

"Leave me alone, Sarge."

"But . . ,"

"Come on, Sarge, leave me alone."

"Don't you want to get your pass?"

"Come on Sarge, leave me alone, will you?"

"Don't you want your pass?"

"Come on, Sarge."

"Don't you want to go to the library? You told me today you wanted your pass so you could go down to the library. Don't you want to go?"

"Sarge, will you please leave me alone?"

"Wait a minute, soldier."

"Jesus Christ, Sarge!"

"Don't go raising your voice at me, soldier."

Brad was silent. Eaton stood there.

"What's the matter?"

Brad shifted restlessly on his bed and said nothing. Leave me alone, you queer smelly bastard. Leave me alone. Leave me alone! for once, leave me alone! Oh, this Army. This God damned Army and the bastards in it. Leave me alone!

"Young one."

"Leave me alone!"

"What's the matter?"

"I told you today I was sick, Sarge."

"What's the matter?"

"I just feel awful."

"What'd you eat?"

"I couldn't eat."

"You should have ate."

Brad was silent.

"Come on to my room. I got something to eat."

"I don't want to eat."

"Come on. It'll do you good."

"I don't want to eat, Sarge."

"Where do you hurt?"

"All over."

"You need a drink. A drink will fix you up fine. Come on, I'll give you a drink."

"Don't want a drink." Can't you give up? "Thanks Sarge."

"Why don't you go down to the dispensary?"

"I don't want any pills."

"Come on to my room, just a few minutes."

Brad was silent.

"Can't you, just for a few minutes?"

"No."

"Come on, huh?"

"I said 'no' Sarge. Can't you understand that? I said 'no.' So don't ask me any more. Leave me alone!"

"I just want to help you."

"Get out of here, Sarge."

"Wait a minute, soldier."

Suddenly, Brad sprang up and sat on his bed and he saw Eaton jump, just a little bit, but it was enough to tell Brad that Eaton had been frightened.

"You heard me, Sarge. I said I didn't want to go to your God damned room and I don't want to talk to you. It's after duty hours and I want to lay on my bed. Now, leave me alone, God damn it!"

"Who, who're you cursing at, soldier?"

"You, Sarge, you!"

"Watch it, soldier. Be careful."

"You better be careful. You know what's good for you, you better be careful."

"What's the matter with you?"

"Come on, Sarge, get out of here."

"You want your pass back? You want it back? You might not never git it back."

"You know what, Sarge? You know what? I don't give a damn. I don't give a good God damn. You can take that pass and go to hell. Ram it!"

Brad laid back down on his stomach.

"You better go on sick call, that's what you better do."

Brad was silent, but he moved, restlessly. Then Eaton surprised him. He laid his pass down on his bed right before his eyes.

"Here's your pass. You can go out."

"I don't want to go out."

"You really mean it."

"I said it."

"Take it, but next time I might not give it to you so easy. You better go down to the dispensary. You hear me?"

"I will, Sarge, if it gets worse."

Eaton left. Brad didn't hear him leave, but he knew he was gone. He knew because the smell wasn't so strong any more.

The pass lay there, three inches away from his eyes. It lay there, majestically, in all its whiteness and magic. It lay there, a small rectangular piece of paper, so small he could hold it in the palm of his hand. He looked at it and thought about it. Magic, that's what it was, magic. He could take that little rectangular piece of paper with his name on it, printed in big black letters, he could take it and walk out the gate and go on out to his pad and tell Fumi to make up one joint and light it for him so he could chase the pain away, the pain that was even now pounding and running wild through his chest. After that, after the pain was gone, after he was high, way up there, after he was in his world, he could take that same small piece of paper and go on down to the bridge outside the Lympic Cabaret and stand there and wait for the woman, the real woman, Sumiko, and he could smile when the M.P.s came because they couldn't touch him, they couldn't touch him at all. He had all the authority he needed. The God damned M.P.s couldn't touch him. They couldn't lay a hand on him. He had his pass.

He lay there and kept his eyes on the pass. It got whiter and wider and longer and whiter and . . . He closed his eyes. He couldn't go. He couldn't go. He couldn't move. Mustn't move. He didn't dare. Walker is dead. Walker is dead. He was there and he saw it all. The bastard dropped dead and he saw it and that meant he had to stay in camp so he could in no way be placed at the scene. With all the suffering in his chest and sorrow in his heart for Walker, he had to stay right there in the barracks, right there on his bed so he could prove to anyone who wanted to know, the C.O., the First Sgt., the M.P.s, the C.I.D., anyone, he could prove he was nowhere near the scene. He was sick that night, he would say, he was sick, so sick he couldn't move, he didn't feel like moving. There were Doc and Eaton and he hoped there would be others to prove to whoever wanted to know, that he was there sick, sick, sick, all night long. Sick.

Now he opened his eyes and there was the pass again. It lay there and he thought it was staring at him, laughing at him, daring him to go. Grab it and go! Go! Go! Grab it and go. It would be so easy, so easy. There it lay, there it lay, all he needed to end the pain and feel good and in his world and high and way up and away and soaring and without pain and feeling good good good again.

It was so hard, so hard. Just lay here, just lay here and wait for the time to pass. Time is slow sometimes, so slow. When time is slow there is nothing slower. Just lay here and hold out until twelve, until midnight when the pass wouldn't be good any more, when he couldn't possibly go out. Hold out!

Brad tried to push his body deeper into the bed, become a part of it. He wanted the bed to swallow him up and hold him and never let him go, hold him all night long.

Brad reached out and his hand touched the pass. He picked it up and stared at it and turned it over and stared at the blank side of it and turned it back over and stared at his name again and then he raised his body from the bed and closed his eyes and fell to the bed again and crushed the pass in his right hand and dropped the wad of paper to the floor and wept.

BARBADOS

Paule Marshall

D AWN, like the night which had preceded it, came from the sea.
In a white mist tumbling like spume over the fishing boats
leaving the island and the hunched, ghost shapes of the fishermen.
In a white, wet wind breathing over the villages scattered amid the
tall canes. The cabbage palms roused, their high headdresses
solemnly saluting the wind, and along the white beach which
ringed the island the casuarina trees began their moaning — a
sound of women lamenting their dead within a cave.

The wind, smarting of the sea, threaded a wet skein through
Mr. Watford's five hundred dwarf coconut trees and around his
house at the edge of the grove. The house, Colonial American in
design, seemed created by the mist — as if out of the dawn's
formlessness had come, magically, the solid stone walls, the blind,
broad windows and the portico of fat columns which embraced
the main story. When the mist cleared, the house remained —
pure, proud, a pristine white — disdaining the crude wooden
houses in the village outside its high gate.

It was not the dawn settling around his house which awakened
Mr. Watford, but the call of his Barbary doves from their hutch in
the yard. And it was more the feel of that sound than the sound
itself. His hands had retained, from the many times a day he held
the doves, the feel of their throats swelling with that murmurous,
mournful note. He lay abed now, his hands — as cracked and
callused as a cane cutter's — filled with the sound, and against the
white sheet which flowed out to the white walls he appeared
profoundly alone, yet secure in loneliness, contained. His face was
fleshless and severe, his black skin sucked deep into the hollow of
his jaw, while under a high brow, which was like a bastion raised

against the world, his eyes were indrawn and pure. It was as if during all his seventy years, Mr. Watford had permitted nothing to sight which could have affected him.

He stood up, and his body, muscular but stripped of flesh, appeared to be absolved from time, still young. Yet each clenched gesture of his arms, of his lean shank as he dressed in a faded shirt and work pants, each vigilant, snapping motion of his head betrayed tension. Ruthlessly he spurred his body to perform like a younger man's. Savagely he denied the accumulated fatigue of the years. Only sometimes when he paused in his grove of coconut trees during the day, his eyes tearing and the breath torn from his lungs, did it seem that if he could find a place hidden from the world and himself he would give way to exhaustion and weep from weariness.

Dressed, he strode through the house, his step tense, his rough hand touching the furniture from Grand Rapids which crowded each room. For some reason, Mr. Watford had never completed the house. Everywhere the walls were raw and unpainted, the furniture unarranged. In the drawing room with its coffered ceiling, he stood before his favorite piece, an old mantel clock which eked out the time. Reluctantly it whirred five and Mr. Watford nodded. His day had begun.

It was no different from all the days which made up the five years since his return to Barbados. Downstairs in the unfinished kitchen, he prepared his morning tea — tea with canned milk and fried bakes — and ate standing at the stove while lizards skittered over the unplastered walls. Then, belching and snuffling the way a child would, he put on a pith helmet, secured his pants legs with bicycle clasps and stepped into the yard. There he fed the doves, holding them so that their sound poured into his hands and laughing gently — but the laugh gave way to an irritable grunt as he saw the mongoose tracks under the hutch. He set the trap again.

The first heat had swept the island like a huge tidal wave when Mr. Watford, with that tense, headlong stride, entered the grove. He had planted the dwarf coconut trees because of their quick yield and because, with their stunted trunks, they always appeared young. Now as he worked, rearranging the complex of pipes which irrigated the land, stripping off the dead leaves, the trees were like cool, moving presences; the stiletto fronds wove a protective dome above him and slowly, as the day soared toward noon, his mind filled with the slivers of sunlight through the trees and the feel of earth in his hands, as it might have been filled with thoughts.

Except for a meal at noon, he remained in the grove until dusk surged up from the sea; then returning to the house, he bathed and dressed in a medical doctor's white uniform, turned on the lights in the parlor and opened the tall doors to the portico. Then the old women of the village on their way to church, the last hawkers caroling, "Fish, flying fish, a penny, my lady," the roistering saga-boys lugging their heavy steel drums to the crossroad where they would rehearse under the street lamp — all passing could glimpse Mr. Watford, stiff in his white uniform and with his head bent heavily over a Boston newspaper. The papers reached him weeks late but he read them anyway, giving a little savage chuckle at the thought that beyond his world that other world went its senseless way. As he read, the night sounds of the village welled into a joyous chorale against the sea's muffled cadence and the hollow, haunting music of the steel band. Soon the moths, lured in by the light, fought to die on the lamp, the beetles crashed drunkenly against the walls and the night — like a woman offering herself to him — became fragrant with the night-blooming cactus.

Even in America Mr. Watford had spent his evenings this way. Coming home from the hospital, where he worked in the boiler room, he would dress in his white uniform and read in the basement of the large rooming house he owned. He had lived closeted like this, detached, because America — despite the money and property he had slowly accumulated — had meant nothing to him. Each morning, walking to the hospital along the rutted Boston streets, through the smoky dawn light, he had known — although it had never been a thought — that his allegiance, his place, lay elsewhere. Neither had the few acquaintances he had made mattered. Nor the women he had occasionally kept as a younger man. After the first months their bodies would grow coarse to his hand and he would begin edging away. . . . So that he had felt no regret when, the year before his retirement, he resigned his job, liquidated his properties and, his fifty-year exile over, returned home.

The clock doled out eight and Mr. Watford folded the news-paper and brushed the burnt moths from the lamp base. His lips still shaped the last words he had read as he moved through the rooms, fastening the windows against the night air, which he had dreaded even as a boy. Something palpable but unseen was always, he believed, crouched in the night's dim recess, waiting to snare him. . . . Once in bed in his sealed room, Mr. Watford fell asleep quickly.

The next day was no different except that Mr. Goodman, the local shopkeeper, sent the boy for coconuts to sell at the racetrack and then came that evening to pay for them and to herald — although Mr. Watford did not know this — the coming of the girl.

That morning, taking his tea, Mr. Watford heard the careful tap of the mule's hoofs and looking out saw the wagon jolting through the dawn and the boy, still lax with sleep, swaying on the seat. He was perhaps eighteen and the muscles packed tightly beneath his lustrous black skin gave him a brooding strength. He came and stood outside the back door, his hands and lowered head performing the small, subtle rites of deference.

Mr. Watford's pleasure was full, for the gestures were those given only to a white man in his time. Yet the boy always nettled him. He sensed a natural arrogance like a pinpoint of light within his dark stare. The boy's stance exhumed a memory buried under the years. He remembered, staring at him, the time when he had worked as a yard boy for a white family, and had had to assume the same respectful pose while their flat, raw, Barbadian voices assailed him with orders. He remembered the muscles in his neck straining as he nodded deeply and a taste like alum on his tongue as he repeated the "Yes, please," as in a litany. But because of their whiteness and wealth, he had never dared hate them. Instead his rancor, like a boomerang, had rebounded, glancing past him to strike all the dark ones like himself, even his mother with her spindled arms and her stomach sagging with a child who was, invariably, dead at birth. He had been the only one of ten to live, the only one to escape. But he had never lost the sense of being pursued by the same dread presence which had claimed them. He had never lost the fear that if he lived too fully he would tire and death would quickly close the gap. His only defense had been a cautious life and work. He had been almost broken by work at the age of twenty when his parents died, leaving him enough money for the passage to America. Gladly had he fled the island. But nothing had mattered after his flight.

The boy's foot stirred the dust. He murmured, "Please, sir, Mr. Watford, Mr. Goodman at the shop send me to pick the coconut."

Mr. Watford's head snapped up. A caustic word flared, but died as he noticed a political button pinned to the boy's patched shirt with "Vote for the Barbados People's Party" printed boldly on it, and below that the motto of the party: "The Old Shall Pass." At this ludicrous touch (for what could this boy, with his splayed and shigoed feet and blunted mind, understand about politics?) he became suddenly nervous, angry. The button and its motto seemed, somehow, directed at him. He said roughly, "Well, come then. You can't pick any coconuts standing there looking foolish!" — and he led the way to the grove.

The coconuts, he knew, would sell well at the booths in the center of the track, where the poor were penned in like cattle. As the heat thickened and the betting grew desperate, they would clamor: "Man, how you selling the water coconuts?" and hacking off the tops they would pour rum into the water within the hollow centers, then tilt the coconuts to their heads so that the rum-sweetened water skimmed their tongues and trickled bright down their dark chins. Mr. Watford had stood among them at the track as a young man, as poor as they were, but proud. And he had always found something unutterably graceful and free in their gestures, something which had roused contradictory feelings in him: admiration, but just as strong, impatience at their easy ways, and shame. . . .

That night, as he sat in his white uniform reading, he heard Mr. Goodman's heavy step and went out and stood at the head of the stairs in a formal, proprietary pose. Mr. Goodman's face floated up into the light — the loose folds of flesh, the skin slick with sweat as if oiled, the eyes scribbled with veins and mottled, bold — as if each blemish there was a sin he proudly displayed or a scar which proved he had met life head-on. His body, unlike Mr. Watford's, was corpulent and, with the trousers caught up around his full crotch, openly concupiscent. He owned the one shop in the village which gave credit and a booth which sold coconuts at the race track, kept a wife and two outside women, drank a rum with each customer at his bar, regularly caned his fourteen children, who still followed him everywhere (even now they were waiting for him in the darkness beyond Mr. Watford's gate) and bet heavily at the races, and when he lost gave a loud hacking laugh which squeezed his body like a pain and left him gasping.

The laugh clutched him now as he flung his pendulous flesh into a chair and wheezed, "Watford, how? Man, I near lose house, shop, shirt and all at races today. I tell you, they got some horses from Trinidad in this meet that's making ours look like they running backwards. Be Jese, I wouldn't bet on a Bajan horse tomorrow if Christ heself was to give me the top. Those bitches might look good but they's nothing 'pon a track."

Mr. Watford, his back straight as the pillar he leaned against, his eyes unstained, his gaunt face planed by contempt, gave Mr. Goodman his cold, measured smile, thinking that the man would be dead soon, bloated with rice and rum — and somehow this made his own life more certain.

Sputtering with his amiable laughter, Mr. Goodman paid for the coconuts, but instead of leaving then as he usually did, he lingered, his eyes probing for a glimpse inside the house. Mr. Watford waited, his head snapping warily; then, impatient, he started toward the door and Mr. Goodman said, "I tell you, your coconut trees bearing fast enough even for dwarfs. You's lucky, man."

Ordinarily Mr. Watford would have waved both the man and his remark aside, but repelled more than usual tonight by Mr. Goodman's gross form and immodest laugh, he said — glad of the cold edge his slight American accent gave the words — "What luck got to do with it? I does care the trees properly and they bear, that's all. Luck! People, especially this bunch around here, is always looking to luck when the only answer is a little brains and plenty of hard work. . . ." Suddenly remembering the boy that morning and the political button, he added in loud disgust, "Look that half-foolish boy you does send here to pick the coconuts. Instead of him learning a trade and going to England where he might find work he's walking about with a political button. He and all in politics now! But that's the way with these down here. They'll do some of everything but work. They don't want work!"

He gestured violently, almost dancing in anger. "They too busy spreeing."

The chair creaked as Mr. Goodman sketched a pained and gentle denial. "No, man," he said, "you wrong. Things is different to before. I mean to say, the young people nowadays is different to how we was. They not just sitting back and taking things no more. They not so frighten for the white people as we was. No, man. Now take that said same boy, for an example. I don't say he don't like a spree, but he's serious, you see him there. He's a member of this new Barbados People's Party. He wants to see his own color running the government. He wants to be able to make a living right here in Barbados instead of going to any cold England. And he's right!" Mr. Goodman paused at a vehement pitch, then shrugged heavily. "What the young people must do, nuh? They got to look to something . . ."

"Look to work!" And Mr. Watford thrust out a hand so that the horned knuckles caught the light.

"Yes, that's true — and it's up to we that got little something to give them work," Mr. Goodman said, and a sadness filtered among the dissipations in his eyes. "I mean to say we that got little something got to help out. In a manner of speaking, we's responsible . . ."

"Responsible!" The work circled Mr. Watford's head like a gnat and he wanted to reach up and haul it down, to squash it underfoot.

Mr. Goodman spread his hands; his breathing rumbled with a sigh. "Yes, in a manner of speaking. That's why, Watford man, you got to provide little work for some poor person down in here. Hire a servant at least! 'Cause I gon tell you something . . ." And he hitched forward his chair, his voice dropped to a wheeze. "People talking. Here you come back rich from big America and build a swell house and plant 'nough coconut trees and you still cleaning and cooking and thing like some woman. Man, it don't look good!" His face screwed in emphasis and he sat back. "Now, there's this girl, the daughter of a friend that just dead, and she need work bad enough. But I wouldn't like to see she working for these white people 'cause you know how those men will take advantage of she. And she'd make a good servant, man. Quiet and quick so, and nothing a-tall to feed and she can sleep anywhere about the place. And she don't have no boys always around her either. . . ." Still talking, Mr. Goodman eased from his chair and reached the stairs with surprising agility. "You need a servant," he whispered, leaning close to Mr. Watford as he passed. "It don't look good, man, people talking. I gon send she."

Mr. Watford was overcome by nausea. Not only from Mr. Goodman's smell — a stench of salt fish, rum and sweat — but from an outrage which was like a sediment in his stomach. For a long time he stood there almost kecking from disgust, until his clock struck eight, reminding him of the sanctuary within — and suddenly his cold laugh dismissed Mr. Goodman and his proposal. Hurrying in, he locked the doors and windows against the night air and, still laughing, he slept.

The next day, coming from the grove to prepare his noon meal, he saw her. She was standing in his driveway, her bare feet like strong dark roots amid the jagged stones, her face tilted toward the sun — and she might have been standing there always waiting for him. She seemed of the sun, of the earth. The folktale of creation might have been true with her: that along a riverbank a god had scooped up the earth — rich and black and warmed by the sun — and molded her poised head with its tufted braids and then with a whimsical touch crowned it with a sober brown felt hat which should have been worn by some stout English matron in a London suburb, had sculptured the passionless face and drawn a screen of gossamer across her eyes to hide the void behind. Beneath her bodice her small breasts were smooth at the crest. Below her waist, her hips branched wide, the place prepared for its load of life. But it was the bold and sensual strength of her legs which completely unstrung Mr. Watford. He wanted to grab a hoe and drive her off.

"What it 'tis you want?" he called sharply.

"Mr. Goodman send me."

"Send you for what?" His voice was shrill in the glare.

She moved. Holding a caved-in valise and a pair of white sandals, her head weaving slightly as though she bore a pail of water there or a tray of mangoes, she glided over the stones as if they were smooth ground. Her bland expression did not change, but her eyes, meeting his, held a vague trust. Pausing a few feet away, she curtsied deeply. "I's the new servant."

Only Mr. Watford's cold laugh saved him from anger. As always it raised him to a height where everything below appeared senseless and insignificant — especially his people, whom the girl embodied. From this height, he could even be charitable. And thinking suddenly of how she had waited in the brutal sun since morning without taking shelter under the nearby tamarind tree, he said, not unkindly, "Well, girl, go back and tell Mr. Goodman for me that I don't need no servant."

"I can't go back."

"How you mean can't?" His head gave its angry snap.

"I'll get lashes," she said simply. "My mother say I must work the day and then if you don't wish me, I can come back. But I's not to leave till night falling, if not I get lashes."

He was shaken by her dispassion. So much so that his head dropped from its disdaining angle and his hands twitched with helplessness. Despite anything he might say or do, her fear of the whipping would keep her there until nightfall, the valise and shoes in hand. He felt his day with its order and quiet rhythms threatened by her intrusion — and suddenly waving her off as if she were an evil visitation, he hurried into the kitchen to prepare his meal.

But he paused, confused, in front of the stove, knowing that he could not cook and leave her hungry at the door, nor could he cook and serve her as though he were the servant.

"Yes, please."

They said nothing more. She entered the room with a firm step and an air almost of familiarity, placed her valise and shoes in a corner and went directly to the larder. For a time Mr. Watford stood by, his muscles flexing with anger and his eyes bounding ahead of her every move, until feeling foolish and frighteningly useless, he went out to feed his doves.

The meal was quickly done and as he ate he heard the dry slap of her feet behind him — a pleasant sound — and then silence. When he glanced back she was squatting in the doorway, the sunlight aslant the absurd hat and her face bent to a bowl she held in one palm. She ate slowly, thoughtfully, as if fixing the taste of each spoonful in her mind.

It was then that he decided to let her work the day and at nightfall to pay her a dollar and dismiss her. His decision held when he returned later from the grove and found tea awaiting him, and then through the supper she prepared. Afterward, dressed in his white uniform, he patiently waited out the day's end on the portico, his face setting into a grim mold. Then just as dusk etched the first dark line between the sea and sky, he took out a dollar and went downstairs.

She was not in the kitchen, but the table was set for his morning tea. Muttering at her persistence, he charged down the corridor, which ran the length of the basement, flinging open the doors to the damp, empty rooms on either side, and sending the lizards and the shadows long entrenched there scuttling to safety.

He found her in the small slanted room under the stoop, asleep on an old cot he kept there, her suitcase turned down beside the bed, and the shoes, dress and the ridiculous hat piled on top. A loose nightshift muted the outline of her body and hid her legs, so that she appeared suddenly defenseless, innocent, with a child's trust in her curled hand and in her deep breathing. Standing in the doorway, with his own breathing snarled and his eyes averted, Mr. Watford felt like an intruder. She had claimed the room. Quivering with frustration, he slowly turned away, vowing that in the morning he would shove the dollar at her and lead her like a cow out of his house. . . .

Dawn brought rain and a hot wind which set the leaves rattling and swiping at the air like distraught arms. Dressing in the dawn darkness, Mr. Watford again armed himself with the dollar and, with his shoulders at an uncompromising set, plunged downstairs. He descended into the warm smell of bakes and this smell, along with the thought that she had been up before him, made his hand knot with exasperation on the banister. The knot tightened as he saw her, dust swirling at her feet as she swept the corridor, her face bent solemn to the task. Shutting her out with a lifted hand, he shouted, "Don't bother sweeping. Here's a dollar. G'long back."

The broom paused and although she did not raise her head, he sensed her groping through the shadowy maze of her mind toward his voice. Behind the dollar which he waved in her face, her eyes slowly cleared. And, surprisingly, they held no fear. Only anticipation and a tenuous trust. It was as if she expected him to say something kind.

"G'long back!" His angry cry was a plea.

Like a small, starved flame, her trust and expectancy died and she said, almost with reproof, "The rain falling."

To confirm this, the wind set the rain stinging across the windows and he could say nothing, even though the words sputtered at his lips. It was useless. There was nothing inside her to comprehend that she was not wanted. His shoulders sagged under the weight of her ignorance, and with a futile gesture he swung away, the dollar hanging from his hand like a small sword gone limp.

She became as fixed and familiar a part of the house as the stones — and as silent. He paid her five dollars a week, gave her Mondays off and in the evenings, after a time, even allowed her to sit in the alcove off the parlor, while he read with his back to her, taking no more notice of her than he did the moths on the lamp.

But once, after many silent evenings together, he detected a sound apart from the night murmurs of the sea and village and the metallic tuning of the steel band, a low, almost inhuman cry of loneliness which chilled him. Frightened, he turned to find her leaning hesitantly toward him, her eyes dark with urgency, and her face tight with bewilderment and a growing anger. He started, not understanding, and her arm lifted to stay him. Eagerly she bent closer. But as she uttered the low cry again, as her fingers described her wish to talk, he jerked around, afraid that she would be foolish enough to speak and that once she did they would be brought close. He would be forced then to acknowledge something about her which he refused to grant; above all, he would be called upon to share a little of himself. Quickly he returned to his newspaper, rustling it to settle the air, and after a time he felt her slowly, bitterly, return to her silence. . . .

Like sand poured in a careful measure from the hand, the weeks flowed down to August and on the first Monday, August Bank holiday, Mr. Watford awoke to the sound of the excursion buses leaving the village for the annual outing, their backfire pelleting the dawn calm and the ancient motors protesting the overcrowding. Lying there, listening, he saw with disturbing clarity his mother dressed for an excursion — the white headtie wound above her dark face and her head poised like a dancer's under the heavy outing basket of food. That set of her head had haunted his years, reappearing in the girl as she walked toward him the first day. Aching with the memory, yet annoyed with himself for remembering, he went downstairs.

The girl had already left for the excursion, and although it was her day off, he felt vaguely betrayed by her eagerness to leave him. Somehow it suggested ingratitude. It was as if his doves were suddenly to refuse him their song or his trees their fruit, despite the care he gave them. Some vital past which shaped the simple mosaic of his life seemed suddenly missing. An alien silence curled like coal gas throughout the house. To escape it he remained in the grove all day and, upon his return to the house, dressed with more care than usual, putting on a fresh, starched uniform, and solemnly brushing his hair until it lay in a smooth bush above his brow. Leaning close to the mirror, but avoiding his eyes, he cleaned the white rheum at their corners, and afterward pried loose the dirt under his nails.

Unable to read his papers, he went out on the portico to escape the unnatural silence in the house, and stood with his hands clenched on the balustrade and his taut body straining forward. After a long wait he heard the buses return and voices in gay shreds upon the wind. Slowly his hands relaxed, as did his shoulders under the white uniform; for the first time that day his breathing was regular. She would soon come.

But she did not come and dusk bloomed into night, with a fragrant heat and a full moon which made the leaves glint as though touched with frost. The steel band at the crossroads began the lilting songs of sadness and seduction, and suddenly — like shades roused by the night and the music — images of the girl flitted before Mr. Watford's eyes. He saw her lost amid the carousings in the village, despoiled; he imagined somone like Mr. Goodman clasping her lewdly or tumbling her in the canebrake. His hand rose, trembling, to rid the air of her; he tried to summon his cold laugh. But, somehow, he could not dismiss her as he had always done with everyone else. Instead, he wanted to punish and protect her, to find and lead her back to the house.

As he leaned there, trying not to give way to the desire to go and find her, his fist striking the balustrade to deny his longing, he saw them. The girl first, with the moonlight like a silver patina on her skin, then the boy whom Mr. Goodman sent for the coconuts, whose easy strength and the political button — "The Old Order Shall Pass" — had always mocked and challenged Mr. Watford. They were joined in a tender battle: the boy in a sport shirt riotous with color was reaching for the girl as he leaped and spun, weightless, to the music, while she fended him off with a gesture which was lovely in its promise of surrender. Her protests were little scattered bursts: "But, man, why don't you stop, nuh . . . ? But, you know, you getting on like a real-real idiot. . . ."

Each time she chided him he leaped higher and landed closer, until finally he eluded her arm and caught her by the waist. Boldly he pressed a leg between her tightly closed legs until they opened under his pressure. Their bodies cleaved into one whirling form and while he sang she laughed like a wanton, with her hat cocked over her ear. Dancing, the stones moiling underfoot, they claimed the night. More than the night. The steel band played for them alone. The trees were their frivolous companions, swaying as they swayed. The moon rode the sky because of them.

Mr. Watford, hidden by a dense shadow, felt the tendons which strung him together suddenly go limp; above all, an obscure belief which, like rare china, he had stored on a high shelf in his mind began to tilt. He sensed the familiar specter which hovered in the night reaching out to embrace him, just as the two in the yard were embracing. Utterly unstrung, incapable of either speech or action, he stumbled into the house, only to meet there an accusing silence from the clock, which had missed its eight o'clock winding, and his newspapers lying like ruined leaves over the floor.

He lay in bed in the white uniform, waiting for sleep to rescue him, his hands seeking the comforting sound of his doves. But sleep eluded him and instead of the doves, their throats tremulous with sound, his scarred hands filled with the shape of a woman he had once kept: her skin, which had been almost bruising in its softness; the buttocks and breasts spread under his hands to inspire both cruelty and tenderness. His hands closed to softly crush those forms, and the searing thrust of passion, which he had not felt for years, stabbed his dry groin. He imagined the two outside, their passion at a pitch by now, lying together behind the tamarind tree, or perhaps — and he sat up sharply — they had been bold enough to bring their lust into the house. Did he not smell their taint on the air? Restored suddenly, he rushed downstairs. As he reached the corridor, a thread of light beckoned him from her room and he dashed furiously toward it, rehearsing the angry words which would jar their bodies apart. He neared the door, glimpsed her through the small opening, and his step faltered; the words collapsed.

She was seated alone on the cot, tenderly holding the absurd felt hat in her lap, one leg tucked under her while the other trailed down. A white sandal, its strap broken, dangled from the foot and gently knocked the floor as she absently swung her leg. Her dress was twisted around her body — and pinned to the bodice, so that it gathered the cloth between her small breasts, was the political button the boy always wore. She was dreamily fingering it, her mouth shaped by a gentle, ironic smile and her eyes strangely acute and critical. What had transpired on the cot had not only, it seemed, twisted the dress around her, tumbled her hat and broken her sandal, but had also defined her and brought the blurred forms of life into focus for her. There was a woman's force in her aspect now, a tragic knowing and acceptance in her bent head, a hint about her of Cassandra watching the future wheel before her eyes.

Before those eyes which looked to another world, Mr. Watford's anger and strength failed him and he held to the wall for support. Unreasonably, he felt that he should assume some hushed and reverent pose, to bow as she had the day she had come. If he had known their names, he would have pleaded forgiveness for the sins he had committed against her and the others all his life, against himself. If he could have borne the thought, he would have confessed that it had been love, terrible in its demand, which he had always fled. And that love had been the reason for his return. If he had been honest, he would have whispered — his head bent and a hand shading his eyes — that unlike Mr. Goodman (whom he suddenly envied for his full life) and the boy with his political button (to whom he had lost the girl), he had not been willing to bear the weight of his own responsibility. . . . But all Mr. Watford could admit, clinging there to the wall, was, simply, that he wanted to live — and that the girl held life within her as surely as she held the hat in her hands. If he could prove himself better than the boy, he could win it. Only then, he dimly knew, would he shake off the pursuer which had given him no rest since birth. Hopefully, he staggered forward, his step cautious and contrite, his hands, quivering along the wall.

She did not see or hear him as he pushed the door wider. And for some time he stood there, his shoulders hunched in humility, his skin stripped away to reveal each flaw, his whole self offered in one outstretched hand. Still unaware of him, she swung her leg, and the dangling shoe struck a derisive note. Then, just as he had turned away that evening in the parlor when she had uttered her low call, she turned away now, refusing him.

Mr. Watford's body went slack and then stiffened ominously. He knew that he would have to wrest from her the strength needed to sustain him. Slamming the door, he cried, his voice cracked and strangled, "What you and him was doing in here? Tell me! I'll not have you bringing nastiness round here. Tell me!"

She did not start. Perhaps she had been aware of him all along and had expected his outburst. Or perhaps his demented eye and the desperation rising from him like a musk filled her with pity instead of fear. Whatever, her benign smile held and her eyes remained abstracted until his hand reached out to fling her back on the cot. Then, frowning, she stood up, wobbling a little on the broken shoe and holding the political button as if it was a new power which would steady and protect her. With a cruel flick of her arm she struck aside his hand and, in a voice as cruel, halted him. "But you best move and don't come holding on to me, you nasty, pissy old man. That's all you is, despite yuh big house and fancy furnitures and yuh newspapers from America. You ain't people, Mr. Watford, you ain't people!" And with a look and a lift of her head which made her condemnation final, she placed the hat atop her braids, and turning aside picked up the valise which had always lain, packed, beside the cot — as if even on the first day she had known that this night would come and had been prepared against it. . . .

Mr. Watford did not see her leave, for a pain squeezed his heart dry and the driven blood was a bright, blinding cataract over his eyes. But his inner eye was suddenly clear. For the first time it gazed mutely upon the waste and pretense which had spanned his years. Flung there against the door by the girl's small blow, his body slowly crumpled under the weariness he had long denied. He sensed that dark but unsubstantial figure which roamed the nights searching for him wind him in its chill embrace. He struggled against it, his hands clutching the air with the spastic eloquence of a drowning man. He moaned — and the anguished sound reached beyond the room to fill the house. It escaped to the yard and his doves swelled their throats, moaning with him.

THE DAY THE WORLD ALMOST CAME TO AN END

Pearl Crayton

I F you haven't had the world coming to an end on you when you're twelve years old and a sinner, you don't know how lucky you are! When it happened to me it scared the living daylights and some of the joy of sinning out of me and, in a lot of other ways, messed up my life altogether. But if I am to believe Ralph Waldo Emerson's "Compensation," I guess I got some good out of it too.

The calamity befell me back in 1936. We were living on a plantation in Louisiana at the time, close to the earth and God, and all wrapped up in religion. The church was the axis around which plantation life revolved, the Mother to whom the folks took their problems, the Teacher who taught them how the Lord wanted them to live, the Chastiser who threatened the sinful with Hell.

In spite of the fact that my parents were churchgoing Christians, I was still holding on to being a sinner. Not that I had anything against religion, it was just a matter of integrity. There was an old plantation custom that in order to be baptized into the church a sinner had to "get religion," a mystical experience in which the soul of the sinner was converted into Christian. A Christian had to live upright, and I knew I just couldn't come up to that on account of there were too many delicious sins around to get into. But a world coming to an end can be pretty hard on a sinner.

The trouble began when my cousin Rena came upon me playing in the watermelon patch, running like the devil was behind her. I was making a whole quarter of mud cabins by packing dirt over my foot in the shape of a cabin, putting a chimney on top, then pulling my foot out. The space left by my foot formed the room of the cabin. I'd broken some twigs off chinaberry and sycamore trees which I planted in the ground around the cabins to make "trees." Some blooming wild flowers that I had picked made up a flower yard in front of each cabin. It was as pretty a sight as you ever want to see before she came stepping all over everything. I let her know I didn't like it real loud, but she didn't pay what I said any attention, she just blurted out, "The end of the world is coming Saturday; you'd better go get you some religion in a hurry!"

That was on a Friday afternoon, getting late.

A picture of Hell flashed across my mind but I pushed it back into the subconscious. "The world's NOT coming to an end!" The confidence I tried to put in my voice failed; it quaked a little. "Who told you the world is coming to an end?"

"I heard Mama and Miss Daya talking about it just now. There's going to be an eclipse Sunday. You know what an eclipse is, don't you?"

I didn't know but I nodded anyhow.

"That's when the sun has a fight with the moon. If the sun whips, the world goes on; if the moon whips, then the world comes to an end. Well, they say that Sunday the moon is going to whip the sun!"

I wasn't going to be scared into giving up my sinning that easily. "How do they know the moon is going to whip?" I asked.

"They read it in the almanac. And it's in the Bible too, in Revelation. It says in Revelation that the world is supposed to end this year. Miss Daya is a missionary sister and she knows all about things like that."

"Nobody knows anything about Revelation, my daddy says so," I rebutted. "Ain't never been nobody born smart enough to figure out Revelation since that Mister John wrote it. He's just going to have to come back and explain it himself."

She acted like she didn't hear that. "And Reverend Davis said in church last Sunday that time is winding up," she said.

"He's been saying that for years now, and time hasn't wound up yet."

"That's what I know, he's been saying it for years, and all the while he's been saying it time's been winding right along, and now it's just about all wound up!"

That made sense to me and I began to consider that maybe she could be right. Then that Miss Daya happened by.

"Lord bless you down there on your knees, baby! Pray to the Lord 'cause it's praying time!"

I hadn't gotten up from where I'd been making mud cabins, but I jumped up quick to let her know I wasn't praying.

"Both of you girls got religion?" she asked, and without waiting for an answer, "That's good. You're both big girls, big enough to go to Hell. You all be glad you all got religion 'cause the Lord is coming soon! He said he was coming and he's coming SOON!" And she went on towards our cabin before I could ask her about the world ending Sunday.

Rena just stood there and looked at me awhile, shaking her head in an "I told you so," and advised me again to get some religion in a hurry. Then she ran off to warn someone else.

Although I was a sinner, I was a regular churchgoing sinner and at our church we had a hellfire-preaching pastor. He could paint pictures of Hell and the Devil in his sermons horrible enough to give a sinner a whole week of nightmares. Nobody with a dime's worth of sense wanted to go to a hot, burning Hell where a red, horned Devil tormented folks with a pitchfork, but I'd been taking a chance on enjoying life another thirty years or so before getting some religion — getting just enough to keep me out of Hell. I hadn't figured on time running out on me so soon, and I still wasn't taking anybody's word before asking my daddy about it first. But it was plowing time and Daddy was way back in the cornfield where I'd already run across a rattlesnake, so I figured even the world coming to an end could wait until suppertime.

I went around the rest of that day with my mind loaded down. Now I didn't exactly believe that the world was coming to an end, but I didn't exactly believe it wasn't either. About two years before, I'd went and read the worst part of Revelation and it had taken my daddy two weeks to convince me that I didn't understand what I had read, which still didn't keep me from having bad dreams about the moon dripping away in blood and a lot of other distressing visions aroused from misunderstood words.

Those dreams were only a vague and frightening memory the Friday I'm talking about, and Revelation an accepted mystery. Yet things like that have a way of sneaking back on you when you need it the least. I got to "supposing" the world did come to an end with earthquakes and hail and fire raining down from the sky and stars falling, exactly like it read in Revelation, and "supposing" the Devil got after me and took me to Hell like folks on the plantation said he would, and "supposing" Hell really and truly was as horrible as the preacher said it was. The way the preacher told it, in Hell a person got burned and burned up and never died, he just kept on burning, burning, burning. With "supposing" like that going through it, my mind was really loaded down! I figured there was no use talking to Mama about what was bothering me because that Miss Daya had stayed at our cabin for over an hour, and I was sure she had convinced Mama that the moon was going to whip the sun.

It seemed to me like it took Daddy longer than ever to come home. It was the Friday of Council Meeting at the church, and Daddy, a deacon, had to be there. I knew he wouldn't have much time to talk to me before he'd have to leave out for the church, so I started walking up the turnrow through the fields to meet him. When I finally saw him riding towards home on his slide I ran to meet him.

Daddy always hitched a plank under his plow to keep the plow blades from cutting up the turnrow when he came home from plowing the fields. The plank, which we called a slide, was long enough behind the plow for him to stand on and ride home, pulled by his plow horse. Whenever I ran to meet him he'd let me ride home with him on the slide.

"Daddy," I said as soon as he'd put me on the slide in front of him and "gee'd" the horse to go on, "is the world going to come to an end Sunday?"

"I don't know, honey," he replied. "Why do you want to know?"

I told him about Rena's prophecy. That really tickled him! He laughed and laughed like that was the funniest thing he'd ever heard! I laughed a little too, though I didn't get the joke in it.

"There's always somebody coming around prophesying that the world's coming to an end," he said after he'd laughed himself out. "Folks been doing that ever since I was a boy, they were doing it when my daddy was a boy, aw, they've been doing that for hundreds of years and the world is still here. Don't you ever pay any attention to anybody that comes around telling you the world is going to end, baby."

"But ain't the world *ever* going to end?" I wanted to know.

"Yeah, but don't anybody know when. Only the Lord knows that. Why, the world might not end for another thousand years, then again it might end tonight, we just don't know. . . ."

"TONIGHT! You mean the world might end TONIGHT!"

"Sure. I'm not saying it will but it could. A person never can tell about a thing like that. But if you let that bother you, why you'll be scared to death every day of your life looking for the world to end. You're not going to be that silly, are you?"

"Aw, shucks no," I lied. I was that silly. Right then and there I got to looking for the world to end, right there on the *spot!*

Like anybody expecting a calamity, I decided to sit up all night that night but Mama made me go to bed. My room was full of the plantation, the darkest of darkness. Before Daddy returned from church Mama put out the coal oil lamp and went to bed.

The lazy old moon was on its vacation again; there was no light anywhere, not a speck. Although my eyes couldn't see anything in that awful dark, my mind had always been very good at seeing things in the dark that weren't there. I got to "seeing" how it was going to be when the world ended, the whole drama of it paraded right before my mind. Then my imagination marched me up before the judgment seat to give account for my past sins and I tried to figure out how much burning I'd get for each offense. Counting up all the ripe plums and peaches I'd saved from going to waste on the neighbors' trees, neglecting to get the owners' permission, the fights I'd had with that sassy little Catherine who lived across the river, the domino games I'd played for penny stakes with my sinner-cousin, Sam, the times I'd handled the truth careless enough to save myself from a whipping, and other not so holy acts, I figured I'd be in for some real hot burning.

While I lay there in that pitch-black darkness worrying myself sick about burning in Hell, a distant rumbling disturbed the stillness of the night, so faint that at first I wasn't sure I'd heard it. I sat up in the bed, straining my ears listening. Sure enough there was a rumbling, far away. The rumbling wasn't thunder, I was sure of that because thunder rumbled, then died away, but this rumbling grew louder and louder and LOUDER. A slow-moving, terrible, loud rumbling that was to my scared mind the earth quaking, the sky caving in, the world ending!

I got out of there, I got out of there *fast!* I didn't even think about being dressed only in my nightgown or the awful dark outside being full of ghosts and bogeymen and other horrors, I just ran!

"The world is ending! The world is ending! Run! Run for your life!" I shouted a warning to Mama, and I just kept on hollering as I ran down the road past the other plantation cabins. "The world is ending! The world is ending! Run! Run for your life!"

Doors opened and folks came out on the cabin porches, some holding coal oil lamps in their hands. They'd look at me in my white nightgown running down the road as fast as a scared rabbit, then look up at the sky, rumbling like it was caving in, and a few of them hollered something at me as I passed by, but I couldn't make out what any of them said.

I might have run myself plumb to the ocean or death if Daddy and some other deacons hadn't been coming up the road on their way from church. Daddy caught me. He had a hard time holding me though. The fear of the Devil and Hell was stronger in me than reason. I was dead set on escaping them.

Daddy had heard my hollering about the world ending as I ran down the road towards them, so he kept telling me, "That's just an old airplane, honey, the world's not ending. That's just an old airplane making all that racket!"

When his words got through the fear that fogged my mind I calmed down a bit. "Airplane?" I'd only heard about airplanes, never had I seen one or heard one passing by.

Daddy laughed. "You were just about outrunning that old airplane and keeping up almost as much racket!" He pointed toward the sky. "Look up there, you see, it's gone now. See that light moving towards town? That's it. Those old airplanes sure have scared a lot of folks with all that racket they make."

I looked up. Sure enough there was a light that looked like a star moving across the sky. The rumbling was way off in the distance, going away slowly like it had come. And the sky was whole, not a piece of it had caved in! I broke down and cried because I was so relieved that the world wasn't coming to an end, because I'd been so scared for so long, because I'd made such a fool of myself, and just because.

Daddy pulled off his suit coat and wrapped it around me to hide the shame of my nightgown from the deacons. After I'd had a real good cry we walked home.

As we walked up the ribbon of road bordering the plantation on our way home I felt a new kind of happiness inside of me. The yellow squares of light shining from the black shapes of the plantation cabins outlined against the night made a picture that looked beautiful to me for the first time. Even the chirping of the crickets sounded beautiful, like a new song I'd never heard before. Even the darkness was beautiful, everything was beautiful. And I was alive, I felt the life within me warming me from the inside, a happy feeling I'd never had before. And the world was there all around me, I was aware of it, aware of all of it, full of beauty, full of happy things to do. Right then and there I was overwhelmed with a desire to *live*, really *live* in the world and enjoy as much of it as I could before it came to an end. And I've been doing so ever since.

AN INTERESTING SOCIAL STUDY

Kristin Hunter

CAPE May's newest summer resident settled herself as comfortably as possible in the strange stiff contours of a fanback wicker chair and awkwardly accepted a large tub-shaped glass of bourbon from her hostess.

But she was too conscious of too many things, including her wet bathing suit and bare feet, and the fine coating of sand which clung to them, to relax completely on Mrs. Powell's porch.

Noticing this, her hostess said, in her rich rumbling baritone, "You don't look a bit comfortable there." She stood up, an unusually tall and bony woman with a magnificently lined face which depicted, clearly as a graph, a mixed history of pleasure and pain.

"Here, try this rocking chair," she said in a tone less of invitation than command. "I'm sick and tired of rocking, anyway. That's all there is for an old woman like me to do in Cape May in the evenings. Sit on her porch, and rock, and get drunk."

"I always liked open porches in the summer," the new resident said. The rocking chair felt a little bit better. She began to sip the bourbon.

"Do you have a porch at your place?" Mrs. Powell's house guest inquired. She was a plump woman of vague shape and features, with wispy dyed-red hair; like her hostess, near sixty; and dressed, like her, for a city luncheon, in a silk suit, polished straw hat, and quantities of pearls. Except that Mrs. Powell's hair was uncompromisingly short and gray, and her pearls were real.

The new resident said, "Oh, no. I wish I did."

"Too bad," the house guest commiserated.

"Why on earth does she need a porch, Corinna?" Mrs. Powell

inquired sharply. "She's not a housebound old relic like us." She drained her tub of bourbon. "She's young, and young people down here spend most of their time out of doors."

"Yes, but these big verandas *are* nice, especially in the evenings," the new resident half-sighed. Extensive galleries, some of them a block long, with pools of blue light reflected from their painted ceilings to inviting deck chairs; she had been eyeing them wistfully all through her after-beach walking tour of this incredible old town. Mrs. Powell's peremptory invitation, as she passed *her* veranda, to come up for a drink had been startling, invested with an almost-magical quality, like the instant fulfillment of a wish in childhood. Even now she could not quite believe it. She had met the older woman only yesterday, in the market, while shopping for groceries on her first day in Cape May.

"A big porch is nothing but a whole lot of extra work," Mrs. Powell declared, "especially when you have to keep it clean all by yourself. I've been down here a month now, and I still can't get a cleaning woman."

"You ought to talk to some of your colored boyfriends, Mrs. Powell," her house guest said playfully. "The trash man, or the garbage man. They might be able to get you somebody."

"Never you mind about my boyfriends, Corinna," Mrs. Powell answered in the same spirit. She turned to the new resident and said, "She's just jealous because I've kept my figure, and hers has gone to hell. I may be older than she is, but the men still turn and look at me, because I've still got a shape resembling a female's. I don't turn and look back at them, of course, because I'm only half a fool. Just enough fool to enjoy it."

She indicated her house guest and gave a rich, wicked chuckle. "Now, it wouldn't do for Corinna to have any kind of a shape left at her age, because she's one hundred per cent fool. If a man ever turned to look at her, even if he was only a trash man, she'd fall on him and faint for joy."

The new resident said nothing, but smiled. She was surprised by her amusement at this byplay, and also by the memories it aroused. It reminded her of nothing so much as the incessant joshing that had gone on for forty years between her grandmother, who sewed for wealthy ladies, and her seamstress-helper, a mountain of a woman named Pettina Brown.

"Don't pay Mrs. Powell any mind," the house guest said. "She's a fool. You heard her say so yourself."

"It's all right for me to say it, Corinna. But not for you." Mrs. Powell turned her intense, somber gaze on the younger woman. "Where are you staying while you're down here?"

"I have the Kinleys' cottage for the summer," the new resident said. "The little one over on Perry Street."

"I know which one it is," Mrs. Powell declared. "There's nothing in Cape May I *don't* know."

Including me, the new resident thought, staring resentfully but not without admiration at Mrs. Powell's bright restless eyes, like a large inquisitive bird's. — Before this evening is over, you'll know everything about *me*, too. That's probably why you invited me up here on your porch. You make it your business to know everything.

"The Kinleys," the house guest mused. "Aren't they those people from New York?" She answered her own question, "Yes, of course, that's who they are. I always wondered why they picked Cape May to spend their summers. It's a long way for them to travel for a little bit of ocean. Most of the people who own property around here come from nearer by. Baltimore and Delaware and the South."

"They come from all over now, Corinna," Mrs. Powell corrected, in her booming voice of authority. "Cape May is getting some new blood in it, thank God. It's about time — It's about time I sweetened your drink, too," she said, and poured two generous slugs of whiskey into the new resident's glass before she could say, "No, thank you."

"Well, I'm new here, but even I can see the town is changing," she heard herself say instead. "Some good changes, and some bad." It had been obvious today, for instance, that there was no longer any clear pattern of segregation on Cape May's beaches. A strong tide seemed to have scattered the varicolored bodies of bathers as randomly as shells. But last night she had noticed the stately old hotels floating at the edge of the water like giant ghost ships, empty, yet lit from stem to stern. They had given her an eerie feeling, and she had turned her back on the ocean wind and hurried home, shivering.

"I think it's a shame the way no one seems to go to the big

hotels for dinner," she said. "They must have been popular once, but now everyone seems to be flocking to that ugly new nightclub down on the beach instead. The yellow one that looks like a mushroom."

"You have to consider Cape May as being two towns," Mrs. Powell explained. "The old summer people, and the new summer people. The old people are kind of wooden-headed and slow, and it takes them a long time to make up their minds about new things. But once they do make up their minds, they're set for life. The new people, now, they're like water, just flowing into any new open space that appears. Only, they don't stay anywhere very long. Just like water."

The new resident thought, And I'll bet you're the one who tells all the other old people what to think. I'll bet you run the whole town all by yourself, you old dragon.

"One thing, once the old people get to know you, there's not a thing they won't do for you," the house guest commented. "Southerners are like that. Hospitable."

"I think you're ready for another drink," Mrs. Powell announced, in that tone of a general giving incontrovertible orders.

The new resident said, with quick automatic politeness, "Oh, no. I've got to be going."

"Well, where in hell have you got to go?" Mrs. Powell demanded. "There's no place to go in Cape May."

"Well, maybe just half a drink, then."

Satisfied, Mrs. Powell nodded sharply, and snatched the glass away.

"You seem very young, child," the house guest commented while their hostess was gone. "Are you a student?"

"Yes," the new resident replied, "and thanks, but I'm not *that* young. I finished college eight years ago. Last year I went back to graduate school."

"It's so hard to get in a good school these days," the house guest complained. "When I was a young girl, it was easy. I went to *two* good schools, one right after the other. I went to Finch, and before that I went to the National Cathedral School, in Washington, D.C."

"If you went to all those schools, how come you're still so dumb,

Corinna?" Mrs. Powell demanded, returning with a bottle from which she poured two brimming tubs of bourbon for her guests.

The house guest accepted the bourbon as good-naturedly as she accepted Mrs. Powell's tyranny, as if both were divinely ordained circumstances, and replied, "When I was growing up, girls weren't supposed to train for careers. We went to school to become young ladies. Those schools I went to, National Cathedral and Finch, were mostly finishing schools."

"Well, this one's a young lady, and she's smart, besides." Mrs. Powell turned her fierce dark gaze on the new resident. "Not that anybody gives a damn around here, but where did you attend school?"

"Spelman College, in Atlanta."

The house guest reflected a moment. "I don't believe I've heard of that one. Is that a finishing school for girls?"

The new resident paused, then said in a somewhat surprised tone, "Well, yes it is, actually. It's funny, I never thought of it that way, but actually, that's what it is."

"Well, I think a finishing school education is still the best sort for a young girl. At National Cathedral, we had teas every Friday afternoon for the faculty and our guests."

"So did we, at Spelman," the new resident said eagerly. "Funny, I had forgotten all about those faculty teas. All the girls were so anxious to get away for the weekend, we hated staying around for them, but really, they were kind of nice. Everybody got all dressed up, and in good weather we were served out of doors, on a big porch."

"Well, I don't think they teach you a damn thing at those young-lady schools, especially in the South," Mrs. Powell declared. "I went to Spence, myself. And I was never allowed south of the Plaza." She elevated a stupendous column of wrinkled, warted, hairy throat, like a camel's, and laughed outrageously, adding, "I was a *brilliant* student."

The house guest winked. "Mrs. Powell means she just barely got through with passing grades. That was brilliant for *her*."

"Oh, Corinna, hush," Mrs. Powell said amiably. "Your large mouth just indicates to everybody how small your brain really is."

It was that hour in Cape May, between seven and eight in the evening, when the light turns lavender and liquid and the huge Mississippi-steamboat houses, each with two or more tiers of balconies, seem about to cast off in it and float downstream. The air was also heavy with honeysuckle, and the new resident, two days away from the city, yawned deliciously, then caught herself and returned to her stiff posture, as if she had no right to relax. "I just love these big old houses," she said.

"Well most of them are so old and run-down they're falling apart," Mrs. Powell said. "You should've seen this old wreck when I first bought it. Looked like a nigra house that hadn't been painted in forty years."

In the strangely colored twilight that falls on the southernmost point on the Jersey shore, the new resident's hands, as they caught the arms of the rocker, were tinted a soft mauve, while the faces of the older women, who had already spent a month in the sun, were deeper variations of the same shade.

"Where did you say you're attending school now?" the house guest inquired.

"Bryn Mawr, in Pennsylvania," the new resident said. She spoke now in clipped, factual phrases. "For a master's degree. In social work."

"Well, we could use some social workers down here," Mrs. Powell said. "Cape May is full of fretful old people, all useless and mostly alcoholics."

The new resident said softly, almost to herself, "I wanted a quiet place to work on my thesis this summer. That's why I picked Cape May. Besides, I heard it was a pretty town."

"Well, you came to the right place if you wanted quiet," Mrs. Powell said, pouring herself another double slug of whiskey. "This town is so damn quiet it gets on my nerves sometimes."

"Oh, no more, please, thank you," the new resident said, too late.

"If you like pretty things," the house guest said between sips, "you ought to get Mrs. Powell to show you the inside of her house. It's the prettiest house in Cape May."

"It is not," Mrs. Powell said firmly. "It's just a huge, old rundown wreck. Like me."

"Bryn Mawr's a good school, I hear," the house guest said in her weak, but pentrating voice, with a register like a piccolo's. "It's so hard to get into a good school these days. My grandson had to apply to seven schools before he got accepted into one. Princeton was one that turned him down. The other day I met a boy who had gotten accepted into Princeton, and I looked at him and said, 'Just stand still a minute and let me touch you. You're so smart, I want some of your brains to rub off on me.' "

Mrs. Powell laughed raucously. "Well, it didn't work that time, Corinna. You're still dumb as hell. But you're lucky. You've got another chance. Here's another smart one sitting right here. Why don't you touch her?"

She offered the bottle to the new resident, who shook her head.

"The damn thing's empty, anyway," Mrs. Powell observed. "I have a reserve supply in the house, though. Even if you won't have another drink, at least come inside and see my old run-down house. It's the worst wreck in Cape May, so you might find it an interesting social study."

This invitation, or command, was accompanied by a powerful tug on the young woman's hand by the other's gnarled and splendidly jeweled one.

— All right, the new resident thought, let's get it over with. I didn't come here looking to be accepted, anyway. She took a deep breath and said, "Thank you. I will."

"Welcome to my hovel," Mrs. Powell said. "Fixing it up almost broke my back, and it's still a mess. But I love it."

She flicked on an overpowering chandelier, illuminating a thirty-foot dining room with the cool, unreal beauty of an undersea cave. White curtains billowed at its tall French windows, and pale green paint had made its quantities of massive old furniture seem floating and fragile. The only ornaments were a portrait over the sideboard and, on the long, frosty-green dining table, a centerpiece of tall green candles in silver holders and bunches of real green grapes.

"Lovely," the new resident said, and caught her breath again as Mrs. Powell's enormous diamonds flashed in the light from the chandelier.

"Oh, it needs a lot more work," Mrs. Powell said, with a deprecating wave of hands like blazing claws. "But I'm too old and tired to be bothered with it any more. One of my guests said to me the other day, 'Mrs. Powell, there isn't a thing in this house to let a person know they're at the seashore. Couldn't you at least add a few seashells to that damn centerpiece?' And I told her, 'Yes, I know, it's a good idea, but by the time I've finished breaking my back cleaning around here, I'm too tired to go down to the beach and lug back any God damn shells. I'm too tired, and I'm too damn old.' — Now, if you'll excuse me, I'm going back in the kitchen for another drink. I'm the biggest lush in Cape May, but I'm so old it doesn't matter to anybody. I *love* old age."

The new resident moved closer to the long carved grape-green sideboard to study the portrait that hung above it, of a tall, gaunt man with the same deep, restless, ultimately somber eyes as Mrs. Powell's.

"That's Mrs. Powell's daddy there," the house guest piped. "I'll bet you don't know who he was. For a number of years he was the United States Senator from North Carolina." Her voice grew more shrill. "Mrs. Powell is just about the most important lady in Cape May."

"Corinna, hush," Mrs. Powell said sternly, returning with a bottle and an ice bucket and the three titanic glasses on a tray. "If there's anything I can't stand, it's big-mouthed people who go bragging about you to other people."

"Well, how would people know anything about you if other people didn't tell them, Mrs. Powell?" the house guest inquired, with shrill logic. "She's a student, she's interested in history. I thought she might like to know about your father."

"Well, maybe she's interested in history, and maybe she isn't, Corinna," Mrs. Powell rebuked her. "Here, don't stand on politeness. Help yourselves to a little nightcap."

The room seemed suddenly full of fireworks, exploding from the brilliant chandelier to the diamonds on Mrs. Powell's hands to the ice cubes she was handling with flashing silver tongs.

"Cheers," Mrs. Powell said, gulping her drink and patting her stomach. "Ah. Nothing goes down like good old country bourbon. — I'll tell her one thing about my family, though, if she's interested in history. She may not like it, but I'll tell her this one thing anyway, and maybe she'll find it interesting." She set her glass down on the sideboard and assumed a graceless stance, chin elevated and feet widely separated, like some defiant, battered colossus. "My great-grandfather was the biggest slaveholder in our state. He had over nine hundred slaves." She stared unblinking at the new resident. "I hope you don't mind hearing a thing like that about my family." Holding the pose, she looked monumental and splendid as the old beach-front hotels, and as lonely.

"Not at all," the new resident said. She set her drink back on the tray without tasting it. "I have to run home now, though."

"What's your hurry?" the house guest asked. "Finish your drink. It's only eight o'clock."

"Now, Corinna," Mrs. Powell said without moving, "let her go if she wants to. That way she won't be afraid to come back here again."

"I should have changed out of this wet bathing suit hours ago," the new resident said. She paused carefully, waiting to find out what else she wanted to say. When she knew, it surprised her, as had nearly all of her reactions on this odd evening.

"Besides," she went on, "I picked up a lot of lovely shells on the beach yesterday. It was my first day on the beach, and I was so greedy, I took home more than I can keep. I want to bring some of them back here, so Mrs. Powell can pick out the ones she likes best, for her centerpiece. That is, if she would like me to."

Mrs. Powell still held the pose, like an old edifice too proud to yield to its awful, imminent tendency to crumble.

The new resident moved quickly to the door and said, "Well, good night. Thank you for an interesting time." She was halfway outside when Mrs. Powell found her voice, a faltering croak that soon expanded to its normal bass-tuba resonance.

"Well, come back when you can," she said. "I have a lot of interesting old relics around here, if you like history, and I'm the biggest old relic of them all. Although I don't care much for history, myself."

A NEW DAY

Charles Wright

I'M caught. Between the devil and the deep blue sea." Lee
Mosely laughed and made a V for victory sign and closed the
front door against a potpourri of family voices, shouting good
wishes and tokens of warning.

The late, sharp March air was refreshing and helped cool his
nervous excitement but his large hands were tight fists in his
raincoat pockets. All morning he had been socking one fist into
the other, running around the crowded, small living room like an
impatient man waiting for a train, and had even screamed at his
mother, who had recoiled as if he had sliced her heart with a knife.
Andy, his brother-in-law, with his whine of advice. "Consider
. . . Brother . . ."

Consider your five stair-step children. Consider the sweet,
brown babe switching down the subway steps ahead of me. What
would she say? Lee wondered.

Of course, deep down in his heart, he wanted the job, wanted it
desperately. The job seemed to hold so much promise, and really
he was getting nowhere fast, not a God damn place in the year and
seven weeks that he had been shipping clerk at French-American
Hats. But that job, too, in the beginning had held such promise.
He remembered how everyone had been proud of him.

Lee Mosely was a twenty-five-year-old Negro, whose greatest
achievement had been the fact that he had graduated twenty-
fourth in his high school class of one hundred and twenty-seven.
This new job that he was applying for promised the world, at least
as much of the world as he expected to get in one hustling
lifetime. But he wouldn't wear his Ivy League suits and unloosen
his tie at ten in the morning for coffee and doughnuts. He would

have to wear a uniform, and mouth a grave Yes mam and No mam. What was worse, his future boss was a Southern white woman, and he had never said one word to a Southern white woman in his life, had never expected to either.

"It's honest work, ain't it?" his mother had said. "Mrs. Davies ain't exactly a stranger. All our people down home worked for her people. They were mighty good to us and you should be proud to work for her. Why, you'll even be going overseas and none of us ain't been overseas except Joe and that was during the big war. Lord knows, Mrs. Davies pays well."

Lee had seen her picture once in the *Daily News*, leaving the opera, furred and bejeweled, a waxen little woman with huge, gleaming eyes, who faced the camera with pouting lips as if she were on the verge of spitting. He had laughed because it seemed strange to see a society woman posing as if she were on her way to jail.

Remembering, he laughed now and rushed up the subway steps at Columbus Circle.

Mrs. Maude T. Davies had taken a suite in a hotel on Central Park South for the spring, a spring that might well be two weeks or a year. Lee's Aunt Ella in South Carolina had arranged the job, a very easy job. Morning and afternoon drives around Central Park. The hotel's room service would supply the meals, and Lee would personally serve them. The salary was one hundred and fifty dollars a week, and it was understood that Lee could have the old, custom-built Packard on days off.

"Lord," Lee moaned audibly and sprinted into the servant's entrance of the hotel.

Before ringing the doorbell, he carefully wiped his face with a handkerchief that his mother had ironed last night and inspected his fingernails, cleared his throat, and stole a quick glance around the silent, silk-walled corridor.

He rang the doorbell, whispered "damnit," because the buzzing sound seemed as loud as the sea in his ears.

"Come in," a husky female voice shouted and Lee's heart exploded in his ears. His armpits began to drip.

But he opened the door manfully, and entered like a boy who was reluctant to accept a gift, his highly polished black shoes sinking into layers of apple-green carpet.

He raised his head slowly and saw Mrs. Davies sitting in a yellow satin wing chair, bundled in a mink coat and wearing white gloves. A flowered scarf was tied neatly around her small, oval head.

"I'm Lee Mosely. Sarah's boy. I came to see about a job."

Mrs. Davies looked at him coldly and then turned toward the bedroom.

"Muffie," she called, and then sat up stiffly, clasping her gloved hands. "You go down to the garage and get the car. Muffie and I will meet you in the lobby."

"Yes mam," Lee said, executing a nod that he prayed would serve as a polite bow. He turned smartly like a soldier and started for the door.

Muffie, a Yorkshire terrier bowed in yellow satin, trotted from the bedroom and darted between Lee's legs. His bark was like an old man coughing. Lee moaned, "Lord," and noiselessly closed the door.

He parked the beige Packard ever so carefully and hopped out of the car as Mrs. Davies emerged from the hotel lobby.

Extending his arm, he assisted Mrs. Davies from the curb.

"Thank you," she said sweetly. "Now, I expect you to open and close the car door but I'm no invalid. Do you understand?"

"Yes mam. I'm sorry."

"Drive me through the park."

Muffie barked. Lee closed the door and then they drove off as the sun skirted from behind dark clouds.

There were many people in the park and it was like a spring day except for the chilled air.

"We haven't had any snow in a long time," Lee said, making conversation. "Guess spring's just around the corner."

"I know that," Mrs. Davies said curtly.

And that was the end of their conversation until they returned to the hotel, twenty minutes later.

"Put the car away," Mrs. Davies commanded. "Don't linger in the garage. The waiter will bring up lunch shortly and you must receive him."

Would the waiter ever come? Lee wondered, pacing the yellow and white tiled serving pantry. Should he or Mrs. Davies phone down to the restaurant? The silence and waiting was unbearable. Even Muffie seemed to be barking impatiently.

The servant entrance bell rang and Mrs. Davies screamed, "Lee!" and he opened the door quickly and smiled at the pale, blue-veined waiter, who did not return the smile. He had eyes like a dead fish, Lee thought, rolling in the white covered tables. There was a hastily scrawled note which read: "Miss Davies food on top. Yours on bottom."

Grinning, Lee took his tray from under the bottom shelf, and was surprised to see two bottles of German beer. He set his tray on the pantry counter and took a quick peep at Mrs. Davies's tossed salad, one baby lamp chop. There was a split of champagne in a small iced bucket.

"Lord," he marveled, and rolled the white covered table into the living room.

"Where are you eating, mam?" Lee asked, pleased because his voice sounded so professional.

"Where?" Mrs. Davies boomed. "In this room, boy!"

"But don't you have a special place?" Lee asked, relieved to see a faint smile on the thin lips.

"Over by the window. I like the view. It's almost as pretty as South Carolina. Put the yellow wing over there too. I shall always dine by the window unless I decide otherwise. Understand?"

"Yes mam." Lee bowed and rolled the table in front of the floor-to-ceiling wall of windows. Then he rushed over and picked up the wing chair as if it were a loaf of bread.

He seated Mrs. Davies and asked gravely: "Will that be all, mam?"

"Of course!"

Exiting quickly, Lee remembered what his uncle Joe had said about V-day. "Man. When they tell us the war is over, I just sat down in the foxhole and shook my head."

And Lee Mosely shook his head and entered the serving pantry, took a deep breath of relief which might well have been a prayer.

He pulled up a leather-covered fruitwood stool to the pantry counter and began eating his lunch of fried chicken, mashed potatoes, gravy and tossed salad. He marveled at the silver domes covering the hot, tasty food, amused at his distorted reflection in the domes. He thanked God for the food and the good job. True,

Mrs. Davies was sharp-tongued, a little funny, but she was nothing like the Southern women he had seen in the movies and on television and had read about in magazines and newspapers. She was not a part of Negro legends, of plots, deeds, and mockery. She was a wealthy woman named Mrs. Maude T. Davies.

Yeah, that's it, Lee mused in the quiet and luxury and warmth of the serving pantry.

He bit into a succulent chicken leg and took a long drink of the rich, clear-tasting German beer.

And then he belched. Mrs. Maude T. Davies screamed: "Nigger!"

I still have half a chicken leg left, Lee thought. He continued eating, chewing very slowly, but it was difficult to swallow. The chicken seemed to set on the valley of his tongue like glue.

So there was not only the pain of digesting but the quicksand sense of rage and frustration, and something else, a nameless something that had always started ruefully at the top of his skull like a windmill.

He knew he had heard *that* word, although the second lever of his mind kept insisting loudly that he was mistaken.

So he continued eating with difficulty his good lunch.

"Nigger boy!" Mrs. Davies repeated, a shrill command, strangely hot and tingling like the telephone wire of the imagination, the words entering through the paneled pantry door like a human being.

Lee Mosely sweated very hard summer and winter. Now, he felt his blood congeal, freeze, although his anger, hot and dry came bubbling to the surface. Saliva doubled in his mouth and his eyes smarted. The soggy chicken was still wedged on his tongue and he couldn't swallow it nor spit it out. He had never cried since becoming a man and thought very little of men who cried. But for the love of God, what could he do to check his rage, helplessness?

"Nigger!" Mrs. Davies screamed again, and he knew that some evil, white trick had come at last to castrate him. He had lived with this feeling for a long time and it was only natural that his stomach and bowels grumbled as if in protest.

And then like the clammy fear that evaporates at the crack of day, Lee's trembling left hand picked up the bottle of beer and he brought it to his lips and drank. He sopped the bread in the cold gravy. He lit a cigarette and drank the other bottle of German beer.

A few minutes later, he got up and went into the living room.

Mrs. Davies was sitting very erect and elegant in the satin chair, and had that snotty *Daily News* photograph expression, Lee thought bitterly.

"Mrs. Davies," he said politely, clearly, "did you call me?"

"Yes," Mrs. Maude T. Davies replied, like a jaded, professional actress. Her smile was warm, pleased, amused. "Lee, you and I are going to get along very well together. I like people who think before they answer."

QUIETUS

Charlie Russell

No two ways about it. Randolph, Besso Oil's first Negro salesman, knew better. Now, he can offer himself no excuse, really.
You simply don't go around acting on impulses, even good ones,
not if you want to keep your job. Twenty-seven. He is tall, dark
and thin: gray Brooks Brothers; with a thick moustache of which
he is excessively proud. Randolph sits down and slaps a fist into his
open palm: I blew, baby, I blew! If I don't ever blow another one,
I blew that one. Though a college man, he still thinks in the
language of the streets. In a less turbulent time he would tell you
he is bilingual.

"I blew, I blew!" Though released unconsciously, the expression
feels good as it leaves the rim of his mouth. But, this only paves
the way for an added agitation: Has Evelyn heard? He fingers his
heavy moustache, turns, and brings into focus Evelyn Manning.
Boss receptionist. Headquarters, Eastern Division. Her head is
bent. Engrossed in typing, apparently she has not heard. Yet he
stares. Thin face. Natural blond hair. While he is looking at her
the hair on the left side of her face unfurls itself mischievously. In
one motion there is a toss of her head and a flick of her hand, as
she artfully pushes the renegade hair back into place.

Class. Randolph decides that Evelyn has almost as much class as
his wife. He likes that, women with class. And he likes being the
company's first and only Negro salesman, too. He has just finished
a four months' training course, in which he finished first in a class
of twenty, and until a few minutes ago he looked forward to a long
and profitable career with Besso Oil.

"Damn," he curses himself. What had he been thinking about?
He has an urge to break something. Like that night when he was

fifteen, and had broken all the windows in the front of the school with rocks. Afterwards he had spent an hour ducking and dodging around corners, setting up a false trail, just in case he was hunted. But no one had followed and later in bed he was overcome with a tingling sensation that had given him a feeling of inner peace, engulfing him entirely. He had had that feeling only a few times since: once or twice hearing Charlie Parker, and when he had first entered his virginal wife, Stacey.

For one moment he almost loses control by giving way to the anger, as it swells then sweeps swiftly through his body.

"Be cool. Nerves! Be cool." Prayer-like, he repeats the phrase several times and soon he is calm. Randolph lights a cigarette, then quickly loses interest in it. Would you believe it, just ten minutes ago my world was neat as a six-pack, and now it is all gone because of some jive nigger I don't even know.

"Tch," Randolph's tongue feels heavy as it makes the sound against the roof of his mouth. Suddenly he stands and walks towards the far wall where there are pictures hanging. The room is elongated. Black wall-to-wall carpeting. The furniture, done in dull orange leather, has a contemporary motif. Heavy copper ashtrays shaped like boomerangs. The pictures are abstract originals, too. He stares.

He and Teddy discovered Charlie Parker at a party one Friday night. Hip sixteen. The party was in a dimly lit basement and they were drinking wine from paper cups, when somebody put on "Birds of Paradise." Their heads were light from the tokay, and Teddy demanded that the record be played again and again. The music was so good that even he had danced. Finally Teddy had stolen the record, and they spent the rest of the summer listening to "the Bird" weaving in and out of notes.

Stacey. Randolph has a sudden desire to talk to his wife. He walks over towards Evelyn's desk. Evelyn, the receptionist for both J. B. Nash and Larry Weeks, looks up as he approaches. "Say, look!" he hesitates. "I'm going down the hall to my office to make a phone call. If Larry should call for me, tell him I've gone to make a phone call. Tell him I'm just down the hall in my office, and I'll be right back." Now that he is finished he feels drained.

"OK," Evelyn says, returning to her typing.

Her simple dismissal adds to his anxiety. Why is she so busy all of a sudden? Most of the time, every time I look up there she is in my face. Had he missed a signal between her and Larry, and was she typing up his final papers? He almost asks her, but then decides his name is Sam, and he doesn't give a damn. He turns and walks towards the door. Where however:

It is not "Sam" but Randolph Williams V he sees reflected in the glass door. Old Randy of the drooping shoulders, scared witless, going to call his wife to tell her she must return to work because he has just made his last stand.

Randolph stands over his desk, dials his number; and wonders what Stacey will say. Beautiful Stacey who is so proper and knows what fork to use when; who comes, whispering hot obscenities into his ear. It seems only natural that he dials the wrong number. He dials again. FIVE. SIX. SEVEN. He throws the phone on the cradle, and thinks: She is either out shopping, or playing bridge, or at the beauty parlor; but wherever she is, she is doing what she does best — spending my money. He has a second thought: Maybe it is best after all, give the girl a few hours before she gets the news.

Randolph returns to the waiting room. Evelyn looks up from the typewriter, thin lips stretched into a smile, and before he can ask, she glances furtively at Larry's door, then at him and shakes her head, "No."

Randolph answers by making a silent, "Oh," with his mouth. He turns away. It seems forever he's been waiting. There is movement behind him, but even knowing it is Evelyn he jumps, anyway.

He turns. Watches her approach. Evelyn is tall, willowy and promiscuous. Head tilted slightly upwards. Simply attired: black one-piece dress. Just a dab of rouge. Nothing flashy. She is willing to try anything, but she will remain all her life below pain or joy.

Sweetly: "How is it going, Randy?"

It takes some effort, but he shrugs his shoulders. Smiles. "Fine, just fine." Such control gives him joy. He asks, "Why so busy?" indicating the typewriter.

"Oh, that," Evelyn answers matter-of-factly, "my monthly letter to the folks."

Randolph sighs deeply; he should have known. He looks into her eyes and finds in them something mysterious and hard. How could you explain a girl like her? Comes from big money, went to Wellesley, but works as a receptionist? In a real way he feels sorry for her; if he had money, he would do all his work on the French Riviera!

"You were simply wonderful in there," she says, holding his arm. A week ago she had asked him if he was weird and exotic. He had laughed and said no. She has a thing for him, he knows, but since taking this job he has been faithful and has decided that playing the role of the noble savage, or the big black buck for empty white women is no longer an adventure.

He pulls away. Gently. The smile does not leave Evelyn's lips. She is game. Discovering this about her makes him love her a second. However, when Evelyn says, "But I hadn't realized you cared so deeply about things," Randolph regrets even that second.

"Well, sometimes you have to make a stand," he explains. Softly. "You can only let them push you so far." He sees her smile broaden.

"What would you have done?" Randolph asks.

Evelyn turns from his gaze. "Frankly, I would have taken it. What does it matter, really? They can always find someone to do their dirt; but I am rather proud that you didn't." There are tears. Evelyn turns her head quickly and returns to her desk.

Randolph, resuming his pacing, returns to the picture and remembers. It had all begun two months ago and had happened because every Wednesday night he ate 'soul' food at the Red Rooster, a bar/restaurant in Harlem. Larry, after taking him on a tour of the company's service stations in Harlem, had offered to drop him off at the Rooster. Passing through his old neighborhood, he had noticed an independent station run by an elderly Negro, and observed to Larry that this man had no competitors. And did a large volume of business. "Why don't we open a station across the street?" he had suggested playfully.

This afternoon they had suddenly sprung it on him. Anyway you looked at it, it had been a tough lay and a jive scene. It had taken J. B. just twenty minutes to turn years' worth of hustling into cinders.

At lunch, Larry had casually mentioned to him that J. B., the first vice-president, wanted to see him. Routine business. Just to congratulate him for completing his training course. But Randolph had not finished top man by sleeping. From the nuance in Larry's voice he could tell there was more to it than that.

"Well, here he is," bright-eyed Larry, everybody's fat man, had bellowed. Larry, the fourth vice-president, a handshaker and a backslapper, always won at poker. He presented Randolph to J. B. as if he was a prize.

J. B., a short, slight, graying man, had shaken his hand firmly. Randolph decided that the mantle of inherited power rested easily upon J. B.'s shoulders. J. B. made a slight motion, and they had sat down.

"Well, how are things?" J. B. had begun.

Small talk.

God, these guys are cool. Power with a capital P. Sometimes he hardly remembered that they were the rulers of the world. But he knew their game: "Wonderful, sir. I envision unlimited opportunities with Besso." J. B. supposed that now that he was part of the team he and his wife would be thinking about raising a family soon. "Oh, yes sir, we were just talking about that very subject last week. Children are so wonderful." Oh, yes, he had been hip to their game.

Then, just like that it was over and J. B. had buzzed Evelyn, inviting her in for a drink.

More small talk.

And while Randolph was plotting a graceful exit, J. B. had said confidentially, "Larry here tells me you have suggested a location for a new station. Good idea. I see why Larry speaks so highly of you. How would you like to be the manager?" Before J. B. finished, the others had stopped talking.

Larry had a conspiratorial expression.

"Ah . . ., sir . . .," Randolph had faltered, as J. B. continued. "Twelve pumps, twenty by thirty garage. The whole works. Leave it open twenty-four hours a day. But I'm sure you and Larry can work out the details."

By this time Randolph's wits had returned: So that was their game. He was not only to be their Negro on display, they also meant to use him to put other Negroes out of business. Why, with him running the place, and by staying open twenty-four hours a day, the poor guy across the street wouldn't last two months. The mive mothers!

"But, why me, what about all my training?" he had asked calmly.

"Be good for you, really. Learn the business inside and out." J. B. had turned to Larry. "How long you think it'll take to set it up?"

Without giving Larry time to answer, without realizing that he was going to do it, Randolph had said:

"If I have a choice, I'd just as soon not." Though he had not meant it, his voice sounded stringent. Evelyn lifted an eyebrow, smiled; Larry, shocked, trembled; only J. B. had remained unperturbed.

"Ah, yes," J. B. seemed tired. "You take that up with Larry."

Randolph, who had not meant to venture so far, was relieved to feel Larry tugging at his sleeve.

"I think you've taken our young friend here by surprise, J. B. Let me talk to him. Ha, ha," Larry had interrupted nervously. "Ha, you didn't mention the extra thousand dollars in it for him."

"Yes, yes," J. B.'s voice sounded distant. Randolph had suddenly realized that the old man was almost asleep on his feet. He had heeded the tug and followed Larry out of the office. When they entered the waiting room, Larry had said curtly: "I'll talk to you in a minute," and had slammed his door, leaving Randolph standing alone in the waiting room. Terror had momentarily set in Randolph's eyes, leaving him with a sense of dread.

Randolph, still deep in thought, turns from the picture, walks to the window and looks down into the streets below: mid-February. Cold. Dark, dull, dank. Too cold even for love.

Randolph stands stroking his moustache thoughtfully. There is in his eyes a trace of sadness. He feels alone. No more Teddy. No more "Bird." Nothing. Teddy, over ten years ago, died in Korea in a riot with "cracker" soldiers. And in the circle in which he now travels, Charlie Parker was never in style. Once he and Stacey had some friends over, and he had put on a "Bird" record. For some reason it had been no good, and he finally made everyone happy by putting on Dave Brubeck.

"Stacey!" Unconsciously. He wants to talk to her in the worst sort of way. Why not try the number again? No. Wait. He decides to think further about his situation:

So. They want to use me to keep other Negroes down, you hip to that? Do they think I'm some kinda nut? I can get another job. I don't have to stand for this mess. Ha, ha, his laughter is profane and deep. Randolph knows the game. Why, he can even predict the line Larry will take with him:

Larry will talk to me like we're all green, as if they are not using me against another colored man. White people are good at that, boy can they talk. Always trying to hide the real issues behind some abstract or unrelated principle. And when old Larry starts talking about free enterprise, I'll tell him to shove it!

Randolph again feels the urge to smash something. To run amuck. His heart cries out that it is so unfair. You spend most of your life just fighting to get on their side. You give up Charlie Parker for them, you even cut down on chasing women and all for what? Only to be used. What right did they have to decide things among themselves and then tell him he must make a choice? Some choice! Either him, or another black man.

The yen for his wife's voice returns and Randolph finds himself standing in front of Evelyn's desk. "Look, I'm going to . . .," he begins, but the buzz of the intercom interrupts him. Evelyn, her smile erased, speaks:

"Yes, Larry." Pause. Then, tiredly: "Yes, he's standing right here, I'll send him right in." She hangs up the phone, and Randolph has no time to protest that he must call his wife. In a way he is relieved.

"Randy . . .," Evelyn begins earnestly, "you were sweet in there before. But don't do or say anything you'll be sorry for afterwards."

Gee thanks. Her attitude bugs him. Next she'd be telling him she knew just how he felt. . . . She. They had some nerve. Telling him how to fight his battle. A battle that they themselves had once been involved in, but had never completed. But out loud, Randolph says, not unkindly, "Thanks, Evelyn, I really want to thank you for that little bit of advice."

She is a sweet kid, really, and he does not resent her always. And because he feels guilty, he asks: "How do elephants make love in tall grass?" She does not know. "Successfully," he calls over his shoulder and knocks on Larry's door.

Randolph enters, and silently closes the door behind him. Larry is busy with papers. Randolph approaches his desk. Larry, he notices, is wearing his "con-artist" expression. It is a mixture of smugness and cunning; which he tries to hide behind an inoffensive smile. Randolph hesitates, then sits down. He feels giddy and tries several matches before finally lighting his cigarette.

If only I'd had time to call Stacey.

"Randy, baby, relax, relax," Larry urges in a jovial manner. "I know how you're feeling, Randy. You're probably thinking it's all some kind of conspiracy between me and J. B. But let me assure you, I was just as surprised at J. B. as you were." Larry pauses as if weighing his words, and Randolph notices a certain detachment about his manner as he adds, "I guess old J. B. caught you by surprise, eh, fellow?"

I got your "eh, fellow" hanging, baby. Randolph checks this impulsive response; he had had enough of that today. Out loud he says: "Yes, he did sort of catch me off guard. I know what J. B. said, but still the idea of putting an old man out of business . . ."

"Come on, Randy," Larry urges. "You're a bright fellow. You know what way the wind is blowing. Everything is big now, from the government on up. Somebody has to do it. If we didn't, Standard would do it," he snaps a finger, "just like that. Free Enterprise! It's the law of supply and demand, fellow, the law that our system is based on," Larry finishes, obviously pleased with himself.

Now, he knows, is the time to tell Larry to go to hell. That the real issue is his being used. That he does not mind being the "quota-Negro," but does mind very much indeed being used against other Negroes. However, Randolph finds himself unable to speak. Stacey, Stacey! Suddenly he realizes that he has known all along what Stacey would say; just as he knows that he will follow the voice that even now cries out inside him:

They got you in a cross, baby. And they can beat you in so many ways. From your first breath the odds are against you. And they get to you early, they start you out with Mickey Mouse, and you are hooked by the time you are three. Yea, baby, everybody's got a number, and you have to play the game whether you want to or not. When you think about it you don't really have a choice. You just got to go for yourself.

Randolph stirs uncomfortably in his chair.

"Randy, baby, why the long face?" Larry asks, lightly, yet firmly, "I know that this is all sort of sudden. You want some time to think it over? Maybe J. B. wouldn't mind. He probably likes a man who takes his time. You wanna talk it over with your wife?"

"No, no, that's all right," Randolph raises his head with a jerk. "Ha, my wife goes along with anything I say. Yeah. It just doesn't seems right, that's all." He sounds unreasonable he knows.

But Larry cries out in genuine surprise, "Why, Randy, you old slickster, you amaze me, really. Holding out for more money. Amazing. All right, you got yourself a deal. I'll tell J. B. to make it fifteen hundred. Randy, fellow, I can see you are going far with Besso, you're gonna make a lot of money."

"Yes, I'll make a lot of money," Randolph agrees, not caring whether Larry has deliberately misunderstood him or not. But even as he agrees with Larry, even as he thinks of the two cars and the split-level, he feels something in him die: that part of him that had always been free. He feels the loss already. It was vital. As long as he had it, he felt somehow better and different from them.

"So, what you say, kid?" There is a certain urgency in Larry's voice.

"Yea, sure. OK, Larry, we'll get started on it right away," Randolph says, and Larry relaxes, transformed before his eyes.

Then Larry is on his feet, congratulating him warmly, and proudly. Patting his shoulders and repeating that he will go far and make tons of money. He knows this. Yet, he feels unclean, and there is a grimy taste in his mouth.

After several minutes the ritual of the backslapping and hand-shaking is done. Then Randolph's hand is on the doorknob. He can hardly believe it is over. But as his hand turns the shining knob he hears Larry call, in a friendly manner:

"There is one thing, though, that J. B. did notice, Randy, fellow, you're the only one in the outfit who has a moustache."

MOTHER TO SON

Conrad Kent Rivers

THE older officer led Minnie Peoples into a small room across from the sergeant's desk. Minnie appeared helplessly lost. The younger officer did not like the look on her face. Minnie's withdrawal reminded him of death. He remembered Korea a few years back. He recalled Vince Lombardi's face after a sniper's bullet had got him. The woman seated in front of him had that same shallow and pitiful look. The room escaped her vision. It was apparent to both officers that Minnie was in a state of shock.

"It's getting late and I've a hunch we can wrap this nasty business up if you'll cooperate," said the older officer.

"I don't think she can, Frank."

"Yes, she can!"

"If it isn't her boy then who the hell is it, huh?"

"That isn't our concern."

"Guess not, Frank."

"Let those superboys upstairs handle that."

"Yeah, you're right again, Frank."

Outside, the six-forty shift could be heard lining up for roll call. Sergeant Quinn's bass voice exploded as he bawled out the graveyard crew.

"No leave!" he screamed. "No favors! No nothing! I don't want you near a coffeehouse for months!"

"Quinn's got bookie troubles," said the younger officer, with a broad baggy-eyed grin.

"Ought to lay off those doubles and quinellas."

"Baseball pools, too." They laughed.

"That ain't Jesse!" said Minnie, rising to her feet. "Lord! I done thought it over and that ain't my Jesse!"

The officers watched her with amazement. Minnie's heavy body was graceless. Her hands were large, long, and uncared for. The two men moved around her. They approached her thoughtfully and cautiously. Her eyes shifted from one man to the other. It was as though a huge bison had emerged in their presence.

"You're quite sure that ain't your boy?" asked Frank.

"I don't know my own son?" Her eyes sent out death rays. "That ain't Jesse."

"Well, what's gonna happen if we find out that was your boy and you just made a mistake?"

"We're just doing our duty, lady."

"I don't fault you," she said.

"Sign this paper and give it to the desk sergeant as you leave."

"Don't y'all say — please?"

Frank rubbed his forehead. "If you would be so kind," he replied.

"Can I make my mark?"

"Sure!"

She pointed her finger directly in his face. "Y'all ain't gonna bother me no more, no more after this?" she demanded.

"Just give that to the desk sergeant when you go — please!" Her eyes squinted.

"What's gonna happen to him?"

Frank jumped to his feet and opened the door. "If nobody claims him the taxpayers will bury him. Well, thank you for your cooperation — good-bye now."

"Did you ever live in Kenwood?" she asked.

"No!"

"You been one of those first Negroes on the poor-lice force?"

"Twenty-one years this month."

"You's a credit to your race."

"Thank you. Now please give that to the desk sergeant as you go." She sensed his impatience. She thought for a second. "A mother don't know her own flesh . . . is y'all crazy?"

"He had your picture in his back pocket! You know we covered all of Hyde Park trying to identify you." They studied her tight face.

"When Rev. Foster had me running for that dere contest the *Defender* run every year, I must of gave a hundred of dem pictures away. That picture don't prove nothing! Think, man! Why would I deny my own flesh and blood? I'm Minnie Leola Peoples! And anybody who knows me or ever even heard 'bout me will tell ya I'm a woman! A good woman! I got a good boy! He's wild, I know. Sure he done run off agin to blow dat darn horn of his with one of dem rock and rolling bands. It'll be the third time in two years, but come next week and I'll show y'all a postal check money order made out to me."

"Check, Frank!" Frank rubbed the back of his neck as he sat down at the desk.

"Bill, call the morgue and tell 'em to haul 601 back in the unidentified cooler."

Minnie sighed as he left the room.

A LONG DAY IN NOVEMBER

Ernest J. Gaines

I

SOMEBODY is shaking me but I don't want to get up, because I'm tired and I'm sleepy and I don't want to get up now. It's warm under the cover here, but it's cold up there and I don't want to get up now.

"Sonny?" I hear. I don't know who's calling me, but it must be Mama. She's shaking me by the foot. She's got my ankle through the cover. "Wake up, honey," she says. "I want you to get up and wee-wee."

"I don't want to wee-wee, Mama," I say.

"Come on," she says, shaking me. "Come on. Get up for Mama."

"It's cold up there," I say.

"Come on," she says. "Mama won't let her baby get cold."

I pull the sheet and blanket from under my head and push them back over my shoulder. I feel the cold and I try to cover up again, but Mama grabs the cover before I get it over me. Mama is standing side the bed looking down at me smiling.

"I'm cold, Mama," I say.

"Mama go'n wrap his little coat 'round her baby," she says.

She gets my coat off the chair and puts it on me, and then she fastens some of the buttons.

"Now," she says. "See? You warm."

I gape and look at Mama. She hugs me real hard and rubs her face against my face. My mama's face is warm and soft, and it feels good.

"Come on," she says.

I get up but I can still feel that cold floor. I get on my knees and look under the bed for my pot.

"See it?" Mama says.

"Uh-uh."

"I bet you didn't bring it in," she says.

"I left it on the chicken coop," I say.

"Well, go to the back door," Mama says. "Hurry up before you get cold."

We go in the kitchen and Mama cracks open the door for me. I can see the fence back of the house and I can see the little pecan tree over by the toilet. I can see the big pecan tree over by the other fence by Miss Viola Brown's house. Miss Viola Brown must be sleeping because it's late at night. I bet you nobody else in the quarters up now. I bet you I'm the only little boy up.

I get my tee-tee and I wee-wee fast and hard, because I don't want to get cold. Mama latches the door when I get through weeweeing and we go back in the front.

"Sonny?" she says.

"Hunh?"

"Tomorrow morning when you get up, me and you leaving here, hear?"

"Where we going?" I ask.

"We going to Grandma," Mama says.

"We leaving us house?" I ask.

"Yes," she says.

"Daddy leaving too?"

"No," she says. "Just me and you."

"Daddy don't want to leave?"

"I don't know what your daddy wants," Mama says. "But he don't want me. And we leaving, hear?"

"Uh-huh," I say.

"I'm tired of it," Mama says.

"Hunh?"

"You won't understand, honey," Mama says. "You too young still."

"I'm getting cold, Mama," I say.

"All right," she says.

I get back in bed and Mama pulls the cover up over me. She leans over and kisses me on the jaw, and then she goes back to her bed. I hear the spring when she gets in the bed, then I hear her crying.

"Mama?" I call.

She don't answer me.

"Mama?" I call her.

"Go to sleep, baby," she says.

I don't call her no more but I keep listening. I listen for a long time, but I don't hear nothing no more. I feel myself going back to sleep.

Billy Joe Martin's got the tire and he's rolling it in the road, and I run to the gate to look at him. I want to go out in the road, but Mama don't want me to play out there like Billy Joe Martin and the other children. . . . Lucy's playing side the house. She's jumping rope with — I don't know who that is. I go side the house and play with Lucy. Lucy beats me jumping rope. The rope keeps on hitting me on the leg. But it don't hit Lucy on the leg. Lucy jumps too high for it. . . . Me and Billy Joe Martin shoots marbles and I beat him shooting. . . . Mama's sweeping the gallery and knocking the dust out of the broom on the side of the house. Mama keeps on knocking the broom against the wall. Got plenty dust in the broom. Somebody's beating on the door. Mama, somebody's beating on the door. Somebody's beating on the door, Mama.

"Amy, please let me in," I hear.

Somebody's beating on the door, Mama. Mama, somebody's beating on the door.

"Amy, honey? Honey, please let me in."

I push the cover back and listen. I hear Daddy beating on the door.

"Mama," I say. "Mama, Daddy's knocking on the door. He wants to come in."

"Go back to sleep, Sonny," Mama says.

"Daddy's out there," I say. "He wants to come in."

"Go back to sleep, I told you," Mama says.

It gets quiet for a little while, and then Daddy says: "Sonny?"

"Hunh?"

"Come open the door for your daddy."

"Mama go'n whip me if I get up," I say.

"I won't let her whip you," Daddy says. "Come and open the door like a good boy."

I push the cover back and I sit up and look over at Mama's bed. Mama's under the cover and she's quiet like she's sleeping. I get out of my bed real quiet and go unlatch the door for Daddy.

"Look what I brought you and your mama," he says.

"What?" I ask.

Daddy takes a paper bag out of his jumper pocket. I dip my hand down in it and get a handful of candy.

"Get back in that bed, Sonny," Mama says.

"I'm eating candy," I say.

"Get back in that bed like I told you," Mama says.

"Daddy's up with me," I say.

"You heard me, boy?"

"You can take your candy with you," Daddy says. He follows me to the bed and tucks the cover under me, then he goes back to their bed.

"Honey?" he says.

"Don't touch me," Mama says.

"Honey?" Daddy says.

"Get your hands off me," Mama says.

"Honey?" Daddy says. Then he starts crying. He cries a good little while, and then he stops. I don't chew on my candy while Daddy's crying, but when he stops I chew on another piece.

"Go to sleep, Sonny," he says.

"I want to eat my candy," I say.

"Hurry then. You got to go to school tomorrow."

I put another piece in my mouth and chew on it.

"Honey?" I hear Daddy saying. "Honey, you go'n wake me up to go to work?"

"I do hope you stop bothering me," Mama says.

"Wake me up round four-thirty, hear, honey?" Daddy says. "I can cut 'bout six tons tomorrow. Maybe seven."

Mama don't say nothing to Daddy, and I feel sleepy again. I finish chewing my last piece of candy and I turn on my side. I feel like I'm going away.

I run around the house in the mud, and I feel the mud between my toes. The mud is soft and I like to play in the mud. I try to get out the mud, but I can't get out. I'm not stuck in the mud, but I can't get out. Lucy can't come over and play in the mud because her mama don't want her to catch a cold. . . . Billy Joe Martin shows me his dime and puts it back in his pocket. Mama bought me a pretty little red coat and I show it to Lucy. But I don't let Billy Joe Martin put his hand on it. Lucy can touch it all she wants, but I don't let Billy Joe Martin put his hand on it. . . . Me and Lucy get on the horse and ride up and down the road. The horse runs fast, and me and Lucy bounce on the horse and laugh. . . . Mama and Daddy and Uncle Al and Grandma's sitting by the fire talking. I'm outside shooting marbles, but I hear them. I don't know what they talking about, but I hear them. I hear them. I hear them. I hear them.

"Honey, you let me oversleep," Daddy says. "Look here, it's going on seven."

"You ought to been thought about that last night," Mama says.

"Honey, please," Daddy says. "Don't start a fuss right off this morning."

"Then don't open your mouth," Mama says.

"Honey, the car broke down," Daddy says. "What I was suppose to do — it broke down on me. I just couldn't walk away and not try to fix it."

Mama's quiet.

"Honey," Daddy says. "Don't be mad with me. Come on, now."

"Don't touch me," Mama says.

"Honey, I got to go to work. Come on."

"I mean it," she says.

"Honey, how can I work without touching you? You know I can't do a day's work without touching you some."

"I told you not to put your hands on me," Mama says. I hear her slap Daddy on the hand. "I mean it," she says.

"Honey," Daddy says. "This is Eddie, your husband."

"Go back to your car," Mama says. "Go rub 'gainst it. You ought to be able to find a hole in it somewhere."

"Honey, you oughtn't talk like that in the house," Daddy says. "What if Sonny hear you?"

I stay quiet and I don't move because I don't want them to know I'm woke.

"Honey, listen to me," Daddy says. "From the bottom of my heart I'm sorry. Now come on."

"I told you once," Mama says. "You not getting on me. Go get on your car."

"Honey, respect the child," Daddy says.

"How come you don't respect him?" Mama says. "How come you don't come home sometime and respect him? How come you don't leave the car 'lone and come home and respect him? How come you don't respect him? You the one needs to respect him."

"I told you it broke down," Daddy says. "I was coming home when it broke down. I even had to leave it out on the road. I made it here quick as I could."

"You can go back quick as you can, for all I care."

"Honey, you don't mean that," Daddy says. "I know you don't mean that. You just saying that 'cause you mad."

Mama's quiet.

"Honey?" Daddy says.

"I hope you let me go back to sleep, Eddie," Mama says.

"Honey, don't go back to sleep," Daddy says, "when I'm in this kind of fix."

"I'm getting up," Mama says. "Damn all this."

I hear the spring mash down on the bed boards, then I hear Mama walking across the floor, going back in the kitchen.

"Oh, Lord," Daddy says. "Oh, Lord. The suffering a man got to go through in this world. Sonny?" he says.

"Don't wake that baby up," Mama says from the door.

"I got to have somebody to talk to," Daddy says. "Sonny?"

"I told you not to wake him up," Mama says.

"You don't want to talk to me," Daddy says, "I need somebody to talk to. Sonny?" he says.

"Hunh?"

"See what you did?" Mama says. "You woke him up, and he ain't going back to sleep."

Daddy comes to the bed and sits beside me. He looks down at me and passes his hand over my head.

"You love your daddy, Sonny?" he says.

"Uh-huh."

"Please love me," Daddy says.

I look up at Daddy and he looks at me, and then he just falls down on me and starts crying.

"A man needs somebody to love him," he says.

"Get love from what you give love," Mama says, back in the kitchen. "You love your car. Go let it love you back."

Daddy shakes his face in the cover.

"The suffering a man got to go through in this world," he says. "Sonny, I hope you never have to go through all this."

Daddy lays there side me a long time. I can hear Mama back in the kitchen. I hear her putting some wood in the stove, and then I hear her lighting the fire. I hear her pouring some water in the teakettle, and I hear when she sets the kettle on the stove.

Daddy raises up and wipes his eyes. He looks at me and shakes his head, and then he goes and puts on his overalls.

"It's a hard life," he says. "Hard, hard. One day, Sonny — you too young right now — but one day you'll know what I mean."

"Can I get up, Daddy?"

"Better ask your mama," Daddy says.

"Can I get up, Mama?" I call.

Mama don't answer me.

"Mama?" I call.

"Your pa standing in there," Mama says. "He the one woke you up."

"Can I get up, Daddy?"

"Sonny, I got enough troubles right now," Daddy says.

"I want get up and wee-wee," I say.

"Get up," Mama says. "You go'n worry me till I let you get up anyhow."

I push the cover back and hurry and get in my clothes. Daddy ties my shoes for me, and we go back in the kitchen and stand side the stove. When Mama sees me she just looks at me a minute, then she goes out in the yard and gets my pot. She holds it to let me wee-wee, then she carries it in the front room.

"Freezing," Daddy says. "Lord."

He rubs his hands together and pours up some water in the basin. After he washes his face, he washes my face; then me and him sit at the table and eat. Mama don't eat with us.

"You love your daddy?" Daddy says.

"Uh-huh," I say.

"That's a good boy," he says. "Always love your daddy."

"I love Mama, too. I love her more than I love you."

"You got a good little mama," Daddy says. "I love her, too. She the only thing keep me going — counting you too, of course."

I look at Mama standing side the stove, warming.

"Well, I better get going," Daddy says. "Maybe if I work hard I'll get me a couple tons."

Daddy gets up from the table and goes in the front room. He comes back with his jumper and his hat on.

"I'm leaving, honey," he says.

Mama don't answer Daddy.

"Honey, tell me 'Bye, old dog' or something," Daddy says. "Just don't stand there."

Mama still don't answer him, and Daddy jerks his cane knife out the wall and goes on out.

"Hurry up, honey," Mama says. "We going to Mama."

I finish eating and I go in the front room where Mama is. Mama's pulling a big bundle from under the bed. "What's that?" I ask.

"Us clothes," she says.

"We go'n take us clothes to Grandma?"

"I'm go'n try," Mama says. "Find your cap."

I get my cap and fasten it, and I come back and look at Mama standing in front of the looking glass. I can see her face in the glass, and look like she want cry. She comes from the dresser and looks at the big bundle of clothes on the floor.

"Where's your pot?" she says. "Get it."

I get the pot from under the bed and go and dump the wee-wee out.

"Come on," Mama says.

She drags the big bundle of clothes out on the gallery and I shut the door. Mama squats down and puts the bundle on her head, and then she stands up and me and her go down the steps. Soon's I get out in the road I can feel the wind. It's strong and it's blowing in my face. My face is cold and one of my hands is cold.

I look up and I see the tree in Grandma's yard. We go little farther and I see the house. I run up ahead of Mama and hold the gate open for her. After she goes in I let the gate slam.

Spot starts barking soon's he sees me. He runs down the steps at me and I let him smell the pot. Spot follows me and Mama back to the house.

"Grandma," I call.

"Who that out there?" Grandma asks.

"Me," I say.

"What you doing out there in all that cold for, boy?" Grandma says. I hear her coming to the door fussing. She opens the door and looks at me and Mama.

"What you doing here with all that?" she asks.

"I'm leaving him, Mama," Mama says.

"Eddie?" Grandma says. "What he done you now?"

"I'm just tired of it," Mama says.

"Come in here out that cold," Grandma says. "Walking out there in all that weather . . ."

We go inside and Mama drops the big bundle of clothes on the floor. I go to the fire and warm my hands. Mama and Grandma come to the fire and Mama stands at the other end of the fireplace and warms her hands.

"Now what that no good nigger done done?" Grandma asks.

"Mama, I'm just tired of Eddie running up and down the road in that car," Mama says.

"He beat you?" Grandma asks.

"No, he didn't beat me," Mama says. "Mama, Eddie didn't get home till after two this morning. Messing 'round with that old car somewhere out on the road all night."

"I warned you 'bout that nigger," Grandma says. "Even 'fore you married him. I sung at you and sung at you. I said, 'Amy, that nigger ain't no good. A yellow nigger with a gap like that 'tween his front teeth ain't no good.' But you wouldn't listen."

"Can me and Sonny stay here?" Mama asks.

"Where else can y'all go?" Grandma says. "I'm your mom, ain't I? You think I can put you out in the cold like he did?"

"He didn't put me out, Mama, I left," Mama says.

"You finally getting some sense in your head," Grandma says. "You ought to been left that nigger before you ever married him."

Uncle Al comes in the front room and looks at the bundle of clothes on the floor. Uncle Al's got on his overall, and got just one strap hooked. The other strap's hanging down his back.

"Fix that thing on you," Grandma says. "You not in a stable."

Uncle Al fixes his clothes and looks at me and Mama at the fire.

"Y'all had a round?" he asks Mama.

"Eddie and that car again," Mama says.

"That's all they want these days," Grandma says. "Cars. Why don't they marry them cars? No. When they got their troubles, they come running to the womenfolks. When they ain't got no troubles and when their pockets full of money they run jump in the car. I told you that when you was working to help him pay for it."

Uncle Al stands side me on the fireplace, and I lean against him and look at the steam coming out of a piece of wood. I get tired of Grandma fussing all the time.

"Y'all moving in with us?" Uncle Al asks.

"For a few days," Mama says. "Then I'll try to find another place somewhere in the quarters."

"Freddie's still there," Grandma says.

"Mama, please," Mama says.

"Why not?" Grandma says. "He always loved you."

"Not in front of him," Mama says.

Mama leaves the fireplace and goes to the bundle of clothes. I can hear her untying the bundle.

"Ain't it 'bout time you was leaving for school?" Uncle Al asks.

"I don't want to go," I say. "It's too cold."

"It's never too cold for school," Mama says. "Warm up good and let Uncle Al button your coat for you."

I get closer to the fire and I feel the fire on my pants. I turn around and warm my back. I turn again, and Uncle Al leans over and buttons up my coat. Uncle Al's smoking a pipe and it almost gets in my face.

"You want take a 'tato with you?" Uncle Al says.

"Uh-huh."

Uncle Al gets a potato out of the ashes and knocks all the ashes off it and puts it in my pocket.

"Now, you ready," he says.

"And be sure to come back here when you get out," Mama says, giving me my book. "Don't go back home now."

I go out on the gallery and feel the wind in my face. Oh, I hate the winter; oh, I hate it. Soon's I come in the road, I see Lucy. Lucy sees me and waits for me. I run where she is.

"Hi," I say.

"Hi," she says. And we walk to school together.

II

It's warm inside the schoolhouse. Bill made a big fire in the heater, and I can hear it roaring up the pipes. I look out the window and I can see the smoke flying cross the yard. Bill sure knows how to make a good fire. Bill's the biggest boy in school, and he always makes the fire for us.

Everybody's studying their lesson, but I don't know mine. I wish I knowed it, but I don't. Mama didn't teach me my lesson last night, and she didn't teach it to me this morning, and I don't know it.

Bob and Rex in the yard. Rex is barking at the cow. I don't know what all this other reading is. I see Rex again, and I see the cow again. But I don't know what all the rest of it is.

Bill comes up to the heater and I look up and see him putting another piece of wood in the fire. He goes back to his seat and sits down side Juanita. Miss Hebert looks at Bill when he goes back to his seat. I look in my book at Bob and Rex. Bob's got on a white shirt and blue pants. Rex is a German police dog. He's white and brown. Mr. Bouie's got a dog just like Rex. He don't bite though. He's a good dog. But Mr. Guerin old dog'll bite you, though. I seen him this morning when me and Mama was going down to Grandma's house.

I ain't go'n eat dinner at us house, because me and Mama don't stay there no more. I'm go'n eat at Grandma's house. I don't know where Daddy go'n eat dinner. He must be go'n cook his own dinner.

I can hear Bill and Juanita back of me. They whispering to each other, but I can hear them. Juanita's some pretty. I hope I was big so I could love her. But I better look at my lesson and don't think about other things.

"First grade," Miss Hebert says.

We go up to the front and sit down on the bench. Miss Hebert looks at us and makes a mark in her rollbook. She puts the rollbook down and comes over to the bench where we at.

"Does everyone know his lesson today?" she asks.

"Yes, ma'am," Lucy says, louder than anybody else in the whole schoolhouse.

"Good," Miss Hebert says. "And I'll start with you today, Lucy. Hold your book in one hand and begin."

" 'Bob and Rex are in the yard,' " Lucy reads. " 'Rex is barking at the cow. The cow is watching Rex.' "

"Good," Miss Hebert says. "Point to barking."

Lucy points.

"Good," Miss Hebert says. "Shirley Ann, let's see how well you can read."

I look in the book at Bob and Rex. Rex is barking at the cow. The cow is looking at Rex.

"William Joseph," Miss Hebert says.

I'm next; I'm scared. I don't know my lesson and Miss Hebert go'n whip me. Miss Hebert don't like you when you don't know your lesson. Mama ought to been teached me my lesson, but she didn't. . . . Bob and Rex . . .

"Eddie," Miss Hebert says.

I don't know my lesson. I don't know my lesson. I don't know my lesson. I feel warm. I'm wet. I hear the wee-wee dripping on the floor. I'm crying. I'm crying because I wee-wee on myself. My clothes wet. Lucy and them go'n laugh at me. Billy Joe Martin and them go'n tease me. I don't know my lesson. I don't know my lesson. I don't know my lesson.

"Oh, Eddie, look what you did," I think I hear Miss Hebert saying. I don't know if she's saying this, but I think I hear her say it. My eyes shut and I'm crying. I don't want look at none of them, because I know they laughing at me.

"It's running under that bench there now," Billy Joe Martin says. "Look out for your feet back there. It's moving fast."

"William Joseph," Miss Hebert says. "Go over there and stand in that corner. Turn your face to the wall and stay there until I tell you to move. Eddie," she says to me, "go stand by the heater."

I don't move, because I'll see them, and I don't want to see them.

"Eddie," Miss Hebert says.

But I don't answer her, and I don't move.

"Bill," Miss Hebert says.

I hear Bill coming up to the front and then I feel him taking me by the hand and leading me away. I walk with my eyes shut. Me and Bill stop at the heater, because I can feel the fire. Then Bill takes my book and leaves me standing there.

"Juanita," Miss Hebert says. "Get a mop, will you. Please."

I hear Juanita going to the back, and then I hear her coming back to the front. The fire pops in the heater, but I don't open my eyes. Nobody's saying anything, but I know they all watching me.

When Juanita gets through mopping she takes the mop back, and I hear Miss Hebert going on with the lesson. When she gets through with the first graders, she calls the second graders up here.

Bill comes up to the heater and puts another piece of wood in the fire.

"Want to turn around?" he asks me.

I don't answer him, but I got my eyes open now and I'm looking down at the floor. Bill turns me around so I can dry the back of my pants. He pats me on the shoulder and goes back to his seat.

After Miss Hebert gets through with the second graders, she tells the children they can go out for recess. I can hear them getting their coats and hats. When all of them leave, I raise my head.

"Eddie," Miss Hebert says.

I turn and see her sitting behind her desk. And I see Billy Joe Martin standing in the corner with his face to the wall.

"Come up to the front," Miss Hebert says.

I go up there looking down at the floor, because I know she's go'n whip me now.

"William Joseph," Miss Hebert says. "You may leave."

Billy Joe Martin runs and gets his coat, then he runs outside to shoot marbles. I stand in front of Miss Hebert's desk with my head down.

"Look up," she says.

I raise my head and look at Miss Hebert. She's smiling, and she don't look mad.

"Now," she says. "Did you study your lesson last night?"

"Yes, ma'am," I say.

"I want the truth now," she says. "Did you?"

I oughtn't story in the churchhouse, but I'm scared Miss Hebert go'n whip me.

"Yes, ma'am," I say.

"Did you study it this morning?" she asks.

I feel a big knot coming up in my throat and I feel like I'm go'n cry again. I'm scared Miss Hebert go'n whip me, that's why I story to her.

"You didn't study your lesson, did you?" she says.

I shake my head. "No, ma'am."

"You didn't study it last night either, did you?"

"No, ma'am," I say. "Mama didn't have time to help me. Daddy wasn't home. Mama didn't have time to help me."

"Where is your father?" Miss Hebert asks.

"Cutting cane."

"Here on the place?"

"Yes, ma'am," I say.

Miss Hebert looks at me, then she gets out a pencil and starts writing on a piece of paper. I look at her writing and I look at the clock and the strap on her desk. I can hear the clock ticking. I hear Billy Joe Martin and them shooting marbles outside. I can hear Lucy and them jumping rope, and some more children playing patty-cake.

"I want you to give this to your mother or your father when you get home," Miss Hebert says. "This is only a little note saying I would like to see them sometime when they aren't too busy."

"We don't live home no more," I say.

"Oh?" Miss Hebert says. "Did you move?"

"Me and Mama," I say. "But Daddy didn't."

Miss Hebert looks at me, then she writes some more on the note. She puts her pencil down and folds the note up.

"Be sure you give this to your mother," she says. "Put it in your pocket and don't lose it."

I take the note from Miss Hebert, but I don't leave the desk.

"Do you want to go outside?" she asks.

"Yes, ma'am."

"You may leave," she says.

I go over and get my coat and cap, and then I go out in the yard. I see Billy Joe Martin and Charles and them shooting marbles over by the gate. I don't go over there because they'll tease me. I go side the schoolhouse and look at Lucy and them jumping rope. Lucy's not jumping right now.

"Hi, Lucy," I say.

Lucy looks over at Shirley and they laugh. They look at my pants and laugh.

"You want a piece of potato?" I ask Lucy.

"No," Lucy says, "And you not my boyfriend no more, neither."

I look at Lucy and I go stand side the wall in the sun. I peel my potato and eat it. And look like soon's I get through, Miss Hebert comes to the front and says recess is over.

We go inside, and I go to the back and take off my coat and cap. Bill comes back there and hangs the things up for us. I go over to Miss Hebert's desk and Miss Hebert gives me a book. I go back to my seat and sit down side Lucy.

"Hi, Lucy," I say.

Lucy looks at Shirley and Shirley puts her hand over her mouth and laughs. I feel like getting up from there and socking Shirley in the mouth, but I know Miss Hebert'll whip me. Because I got no business socking people after I done wee-wee on myself. I open my book and look at my lesson so I don't have to look at none of them.

III

It's almost dinner time, and when I get home I'm not coming back here either, now. I'm go'n stay there. I'm go'n stay right there and sit by the fire. Lucy and them don't want play with me, and I'm not coming back up here. Miss Hebert go'n touch that little bell in a little while. She getting ready to touch it right now.

Soon's Miss Hebert touch the bell all the children run go get their hats and coats. I unhook my coat and drop it on the bench till I put my cap on. Then I put my coat on, and I get my book and leave.

I see Bill and Juanita going out the schoolyard, and I run and catch up with them. Time I get there I hear Billy Joe Martin and them coming up behind me.

"Look at that baby," Billy Joe Martin says.

"Piss on himself," Ju-Ju says.

"Y'all leave him alone," Bill says.

"Baby, baby, piss on himself," Billy Joe Martin sings.

"What'd I say?" Bill says.

"Piss on himself," Billy Joe Martin sings.

"Wait," Bill says. "Let me take my belt off."

"Good-bye, piss pot," Billy Joe Martin says. Him and Ju-Ju run down the road. They spank their hindparts with their hands and run like horses.

"They just bad," Juanita says.

"Don't pay them no mind," Bill says. "They'll leave you 'lone."

We go on down the road and Bill and Juanita hold hands. I go to Grandma's gate and open it. I look at Bill and Juanita going down the road. They walking close together, and Juanita done put her head on Bill's shoulder. I like to see Bill and Juanita like that. It makes me feel good. But when I go in the yard I don't feel good no more. I know old Grandma go'n start fussing. Spot runs down the walk with me. I put my hand on his head and me and him go back to the gallery. I make him stay on the gallery, because Grandma don't want him inside. I pull the door open and I see Grandma and Uncle Al sitting by the fire. I look for my mama, but I don't see her.

"Where Mama?" I ask Uncle Al.

"In the kitchen," Grandma says. "But she talking to somebody."

I go back to the kitchen.

"Come back here," Grandma says.

"I want see my mama now," I say.

"You'll see her when she come out," Grandma says.

"I want see my mama now," I say.

"Don't you hear me talking to you, boy?" Grandma hollers at me.

"What's the matter?" Mama asks. Mama comes out of the kitchen and Mr. Freddie Jackson comes out of there too. I hate Mr. Freddie Jackson. I never did like him. He always trying to be 'round my mama.

"That boy don't listen to nobody," Grandma says.

"Hi, Sonny," Mr. Freddie Jackson says.

I look at him standing there, but I don't speak to him. And I take the note out of my pocket and hand it to Mama.

"What's this?" Mama says.

"Miss Hebert sent it."

Mama unfolds the note and takes it to the fireplace to read it. I can see Mama's mouth working. When she gets through reading, she folds the note up again.

"She want to see me or Eddie sometime when we free," Mama says. "Sonny been doing pretty bad in his class."

"I can just see that nigger husband of yours in a schoolhouse," Grandma says.

"Mama, please," Mama says.

Mama helps me off with my coat and I go to the fireplace and stand side Uncle Al. Uncle Al pulls me between his legs and holds my hand out to the fire.

"Well?" I hear Grandma saying.

"You know how I feel 'bout her," Mr. Freddie Jackson says. "My house open to her and Sonny any time she want to come there."

"Well?" Grandma says.

"Mama, I'm still married to Eddie," Mama says.

"You mean you still love that yellow thing," Gandma says. "That's what you mean, ain't it?"

"I didn't say that," Mama says. "What would people say, out one house and in another one the same day?"

"Who care what people say?" Grandma says. "Let people say what they big 'nough to say. You looking out for yourself, not what people say."

"You understand, don't you, Freddie?" Mama says.

"I believe I do," he says. "But like I say, Amy. Any time. You know that."

"And there ain't no time like right now," Grandma says. "You can take that bundle of clothes down there for her."

"Let her make up her own mind, Rachel," Uncle Al says. "She can make up her own mind."

"If you know what's good for you, you better keep out of this," Grandma says. "She my daughter and if she ain't got sense enough to look out for herself I have. What you want to do, go out in the field cutting sugarcane in the morning?"

"I don't mind it," Mama says.

"You done forgot how hard cutting sugarcane is?" Grandma says. "You must be done forgot."

"I ain't forgot," Mama says. "But if the other women can do it, I suppose I can do it too."

"Now you talking back," Grandma says.

"I'm not talking back, Mama," Mama says. "I just feel that it ain't right to leave one house and go to another house the same day. That ain't right in nobody's book."

"Maybe she's right, Mrs. Rachel," Mr. Freddie Jackson says.

"Her trouble is she still in love with that albino," Grandma says, "That's what your trouble is. You ain't satisfied 'less he got you doing all the work while he rip and run up and down the road with his other nigger friends. No, you ain't satisfied."

Grandma goes back in the kitchen fussing. After she leaves the fire everything gets quiet. Everything stays quiet a minute, then Grandma starts singing her church hymn.

"Why did you bring your book home?" Mama says.

"Miss Hebert say I can stay home if I want," I say. "We had us lesson already."

"You sure she said that?" Mama says.

"Uh-huh."

"I'm go'n ask her, you know."

"She said it," I say.

Mama don't say no more, but I know she still looking at me, and I don't look at her. Then Spot starts barking outside and everybody looks that way. But nobody don't move. Spot keeps barking, and I go to the door to see what he's barking at. I see Daddy coming up the walk. I pull the door and go back to the fireplace.

"Daddy coming, Mama," I say.

"Wait," Grandma says, coming out the kitchen. "Let me talk to that nigger. I'll give him a piece of my mind."

Grandma goes to the door and pushes it open. She stands in the door and I hear Daddy talking to Spot. Then Daddy comes up to the gallery.

"Amy in there, Mama?" Daddy says.

"She is," Grandma says.

I hear Daddy coming up the steps.

"And where you think you going?" Grandma asks.

"I want speak to her," Daddy says.

"Well, she don't want speak to you," Grandma says. "So you

might's well go right on back down them steps and march right straight out of my yard."

"I want speak to my wife," Daddy says.

"She ain't your wife no more," Grandma says. "She left you."

"What you mean she left me?" Daddy says.

"She ain't up at your house no more, is she?" Grandma says. "That look like a good 'nough sign to me that she done left."

"Amy?" Daddy calls.

Mama don't answer. She's looking down in the fire. I don't feel good when Mama's looking like that.

"Amy?" Daddy calls.

Mama still don't answer him.

"You satisfied?" Grandma says.

"You the one trying to make Amy leave me," Daddy says. "You ain't never liked me. From the starting you didn't like me."

"That's right, I never did," Grandma says. "You yellow, you got a gap 'tween your teeth, and you ain't no good. You want me to say more?"

"You always wanted her to marry somebody else," Daddy says.

"You right again," Grandma says.

"Amy?" Daddy calls. "You can hear me, honey?"

"She can hear you," Grandma says. "She standing right there by that fireplace. She can hear you good's I can hear you. And I can hear you too good for comfort."

"I'm going in there," Daddy says. "She got somebody in there and I'm going in there and see."

"You take one more step toward my door," Grandma says, "and it'll need a undertaker to collect the pieces. So help me God I'll get that butcher knife and chop on your tail till I can't see tail to chop on. You the kind of nigger who like to rip and run up and down the road in your car long's you got a dime, but when you get broke and your belly get empty you run to your wife. You just take one more step to this door, and I bet you somebody'll be crying at your funeral. If you know anybody who care that much for you, you old yellow dog."

Daddy is quiet awhile, then I hear him crying. I don't feel good, because I don't like to hear Daddy and Mama crying. I look at Mama but she's looking down in the fire.

"You never like me," Daddy says.

"You said that before," Grandma says. "And I repeat: No, I never liked you, don't like you, and never will like you. Now get out my yard 'fore I put the dog on you."

"I want see my boy," Daddy says. "I got a right to see my boy."

"In the first place, you ain't got no right in my yard," Grandma says.

"I want see my boy," Daddy says. "You might be able to keep me from seeing my wife, but you and nobody else can keep me from seeing my son. Half of him is me."

"You ain't leaving?" Grandma asks Daddy.

"I want see my boy," Daddy says. "And I'm go'n see my boy."

"Wait," Grandma says. "Your head hard. Wait till I come back. You go'n see all kind of boys."

Grandma comes back inside and goes to Uncle Al's room. I look towards the wall and I can hear Daddy moving on the gallery. I hear Mama crying and I look at her. I don't want to see my mama crying and I lay my head on Uncle Al's knee and I want to cry.

"Amy, honey," Daddy calls. "Ain't you coming up home and cook me something to eat? It's lonely up there without you, honey. You don't know how lonely it is without you. I can't stay up there without you, honey. Please come home. . . ."

I hear Grandma coming out of Uncle Al's room and I look at her. Grandma's got Uncle Al's shotgun and she's putting a shell in it.

"Mama," Mama screams.

"Don't worry," Grandma says. "I'm go'n shoot over his head. I ain't go'n have them sending me to pen for a good-for-nothing nigger like that."

"Mama, don't," Mama says. "He might hurt himself."

"Good," Grandma says. "Save me the trouble of doing it for him."

Mama runs to the wall. "Eddie, run," she screams. "Mama got the shotgun."

I hear Daddy going down the steps. I hear Spot running after him barking. Grandma knocks the door open with the gun barrel and shoots. I hear Daddy hollering.

"Mama, you did'n?" Mama says.

"I shot two miles over that nigger head," Grandma says. "Long-legged coward.

We all run out on the gallery and I see Daddy out in the road crying. I can see the people coming out on the galleries. They looking at us and they looking at Daddy. Daddy's standing out in the road crying.

"Boy, I would've like to seen old Eddie getting out of this yard," Uncle Al says.

Daddy's walking up and down the road in front of the house and he's crying.

"Let's go back inside," Grandma says. "We won't be bothered with him for a while."

It's cold and me and Uncle Al and Grandma go back inside. Mr. Freddie Jackson and Mama come back in little later.

"Oh, Lord," Mama says.

Mama starts crying and he takes Mama in his arms. Mama lays her head on his shoulder, but she just keeps her head there a little and she moves. "Can I go lay cross your bed, Uncle Al?" she says.

"Sure," Uncle Al says.

I watch Mama going to Uncle Al's room.

"Well, I better be going," he says.

"Freddie," Grandma calls him, from the kitchen.

"Yes, ma'am?" he says.

"Come here a minute," Grandma says.

He goes back in the kitchen where Grandma is. I get between Uncle Al's legs and look at the fire. Uncle Al rubs my head with his hand. He comes out of the kitchen and goes in Uncle Al's room where Mama is. He must be sitting down on the bed because I can hear the spring.

"Y'all come on and eat," Grandma tells me and Uncle Al.

Me and Uncle Al do like she say, because if we don't she go'n start fussing. And Lord knows I don't want hear no more fussing.

When I get through eating, I tell Uncle Al I want go back to the toilet. I don't want go back there for truth; I want go out in the yard and see if Daddy's still out there.

Soon's I come on the gallery I see him. He's standing by the gate looking at the house. He beckons for me to come to the gate, and I go out there. Daddy grabs me like I might run away from him and hugs me real tight.

"You still love your daddy, Sonny?" he asks me.

"Uh-huh."

Daddy hugs me and kisses me on the face.

"I love my baby," he says, "I love my baby. Where your mama?"

"Laying cross Uncle Al bed in his room," I say. "And Mr. Freddie Jackson in there, too."

Daddy pushes me away and looks at me real hard. "Who else in there?" he asks. "Who else?"

"Just them," I say. "Uncle Al in Grandma's room by the fire, and Grandma's in the kitchen."

"Oh, Lord," Daddy says. "Oh, Lord, have mercy." He turns his head and starts crying. Then he looks at me again. "This ain't right. I bet you it ain't nobody but your grandma. It's her, ain't it?"

"Uh-huh. She sent him in there."

"Oh, Lord," Daddy says. "And right in front of her little grandson — and in daylight, too." He looks at me real sad and holds me to him again. I can feel his pocket button against my face. "Come on, Sonny," he says.

"Where we going?"

"Madame Toussaint," he says. "I hate it, but I got to."

He takes my hand and me and him walk away. When we cross the railroad tracks, I see the people cutting cane. No matter how far you look you don't see nothing but cane.

"Get me a piece of cane, Daddy," I say.

"Sonny, please," he says. "I'm thinking."

"I want a piece of two-ninety," I say.

Daddy turns my hand loose and jumps over the ditch. He finds a piece of two-ninety and jumps back over. Daddy takes out a little knife and peels the cane with it. He gives me a round and he cuts him off a round and chews it. I like two-ninety cane. It's soft and sweet and got plenty juice in it.

"I want another piece," I say.

Daddy cuts me off another round and hands it to me.

"I'll be glad when you big enough to peel your own cane," he says.

"I can peel my own cane now," I say.

Daddy breaks me off three joints and hands it to me. I peel the cane with my teeth. Two-ninety cane is soft and it's easy to peel.

Me and Daddy go round the bend, then I can see Madame

Toussaint's house. Madame Toussaint got a old house, and look like it wants to fall down any minute. I'm scared of Madame Toussaint. Billy Joe Martin say Madame Toussaint's a witch, and he said one time he seen Madame Toussaint riding a broom.

Daddy pulls Madame Toussaint little old broken-down gate open and we go in the yard. Me and Daddy go far as the steps, but we don't go up on the gallery. Madame Toussaint got plenty trees round her house — little trees and big trees; and she got moss hanging from every tree. I move closer so Daddy can hold my hand.

"Madame Toussaint?" Daddy calls.

Madame Toussaint don't answer. Like she ain't there.

"Madame Toussaint?" Daddy calls again.

"Who that?" Madame Toussaint answers.

"Me," Daddy says. "Eddie Howard and his little boy Sonny."

"What you want?" Madame Toussaint calls from in her house.

"I want talk to you," Daddy says. "I need little advise on something."

I hear a dog bark three times in the house. He must be a big dog because he sure's got a heavy voice. Madame Toussaint comes to the door and cracks it open.

"Can I come in?" Daddy says.

"Come on in," Madame Toussaint says.

Me and Daddy go up the steps and Madame Toussaint opens the door for us. Madame Toussaint's a little bitty little old lady and her face the color of cowhide. I look at Madame Toussaint and I walk close side Daddy. Me and Daddy go in the house and Madame Toussaint shuts the door and comes back to her fireplace. She sits down in her big old rocking chair and looks at me and Daddy. I look round Daddy's leg at Madame Toussaint, but I let Daddy hold my hand.

"I need some advise, Madame Toussaint," Daddy says.

"Your wife left you," Madame Toussaint says.

"How you know?" Daddy asks.

"That's all you men come back here for," Madame Toussaint says. "That's how I know."

"Yes," Daddy says. "She done left and staying with another man already."

"She left," Madame Toussaint says. "But she's not staying with another man."

"Yes, she is," Daddy says.

"She's not," Madame Toussaint says. "You trying to tell me my business?"

"No, ma'am," Daddys says.

"I should hope not," Madame Toussaint says.

Madame Toussaint ain't got but three old rotten teeth in her mouth. I bet you she can't peel no cane with them old rotten teeth. I bet you they'd break off in a hard piece of cane.

"I need advise, Madame Toussaint," Daddy says.

"You got money?" Madame Toussaint asks.

"I got some," Daddy says.

"How much?" she asks Daddy. She's looking up at Daddy like she don't believe him.

Daddy turns my hand loose and sticks his hand down in his pocket. He gets all his money out his pocket and leans over the fire to see how much he's got. I see some matches and a piece of string and some nails in Daddy's hand. I reach for the piece of string and Daddy taps me on the hand.

"I got about seventy-five cents," Daddy says. "Counting pennies and all."

"My price is three dollars," Madame Toussaint says.

"I can cut you a load of wood," Daddy says. "Or make grocery for you. I'll do anything in the world if you can help me, Madame Toussaint."

"Three dollars," Madame Toussaint says. "I got all the wood I'll need this winter. Enough grocery to last me till summer."

"But this all I got," Daddy says.

"When you get more, come back," Madame Toussaint says.

"But I want my wife back now," Daddy says. "I can't wait till I get more money."

"Three dollars is my price," Madame Toussaint says. "No more, no less."

"But can't you give me just a little advise for seventy-five cents?" Daddy says. "Seventy-five cents worth? Maybe I can start from there and figure something out."

"Give me the money," Madame Toussaint says. "But don't complain to me if you're not satisfied."

"Don't worry," Daddy says. "I won't complain. Anything to get her back home."

Daddy leans over the fire again and picks the money out of his hand. Then he reaches it to Madame Toussaint.

"Give me that little piece of string, too," Madame Toussaint says. "It might come in handy sometime in the future. Wait," she says. "Run it across the boy's face three times, then pass it to me behind your back."

"What's that for?" Daddy asks.

"Just do like I say," Madame Toussaint says.

"Yes, ma'am," Daddy says. Daddy turns to me. "Hold still a second," he says. He rubs the little old dirty piece of cord over my face, and then sticks his hand behind his back.

Madame Toussaint reaches in her pocket and takes out her pocketbook. She opens it and puts the money in. She opens another little compartment and stuffs the string down in it. Then she snaps the pocketbook and puts it back in her pocket. She picks up three little green sticks she got tied together and starts poking in the fire with them.

"What's the advise?" Daddy asks.

Madame Toussaint don't say nothing.

"Madame Toussaint?" Daddy says.

Madame Toussaint still don't answer him — she just looks down in the fire. Her face is red from the fire. I get scared of Madame Toussaint. She can ride all over the plantation on her broom. Billy Joe Martin seen her one night riding cross the houses. She was whipping her broom with three switches.

Madame Toussaint raises her head and looks at Daddy. Her eyes's big and white, and I get scared of her. I hide my face side Daddy's leg.

"Give it up," I hear her say.

"Give what up?" Daddy says.

"Give it up," she says.

"What?" Daddy says.

"Give it up," she says.

"I don't even know what you talking 'bout," Daddy says. "How can I give up something and I don't know what it is?"

"I said it three times," Madame Toussaint says. "No more, no less. Up to you now to follow it through from there."

"Follow what from where?" Daddy says. "You said three little old words. 'Give it up.' I don't know no more now than I knowed before I come here."

"I told you you wasn't go'n be satisfied," Madame Toussaint says.

"You want me to be satisfied with just three little old words?" Daddy says.

"You can leave," Madame Toussaint says.

"What?" Daddy says. "You mean I give you seventy-five cents for three words? A quarter a word? And I'm leaving? Uh-uh."

"Rollo?" Madame Toussaint says.

I see Madame Toussaint's big old black dog get up out of the corner and come where she is. Madame Toussaint starts patting him on the head.

"Two dollars and twenty-five cents more and you get all the advise you need," Madame Toussaint says.

"Can't I get you a load of wood and fix your house for you or something?" Daddy says.

"I don't want my house fixed and I don't need no more wood," Madame Toussaint says. "I got three loads of wood just three days ago from a man who didn't have money. Before I know it I'll have wood piled up all over my yard."

"Can't I do anything?" Daddy asks.

"You can leave," Madame Toussaint says. "I ought to have somebody else dropping around pretty soon. Lately I've been having men dropping in three times a day. All of them just like you. What they can do to make their wives love them more. What they can do to keep their wives from running around with some other man. What they can do to make their wives give in. What they can do to make their wives scratch their backs. What they can do to make their wives look at them when they talking. Get out of my house before I put the dog on you. You been here too long for seventy-five cents."

Madame Toussaint's big old black dog gives three loud barks that makes my head hurt. Madame Toussaint pats him on the head to calm him down.

"Come on, Sonny," Daddy says.

I let Daddy take my hand and we go out of the house. It's freezing outside.

"What was them words again?"Daddy asks me.

"Hunh?"

"What she said when she looked up out the fire?" Daddy asks.

"I was scared," I say. "Her face was red and her eyes got big and white. I was scared. I had to hide my face."

"Didn't you hear what she told me?" Daddy asks.

"She told you three dollars," I say.

"I mean when she looked up, Sonny," Daddy says.

"She said 'Give it up,' " I say.

"Yes," Daddy says. " 'Give it up.' Give what up? I don't even know what she's talking 'bout. I hope she don't mean give you and Amy up. She ain't that crazy. I don't know nothing else she can be talking 'bout. You don't know, do you?"

"Uh-uh," I say.

" 'Give it up,' " Daddy says. " 'Give it up.' I wonder who them other men was she was speaking of. Charles and his wife had a fight the other week. It might be him. Frank Armstrong and his wife had a round couple weeks back. It might be him. I wonder what kind of advise she gived them. No, I'm sure that can't help me out. I just need three dollars. Three dollars is the only thing go'n make her talk."

"I want another piece of cane," I say.

"No," Daddy says. "You'll be peeing in bed all night tonight."

"Me and Mama go'n stay at Grandma house tonight," I say.

"Please be quiet, Sonny," Daddy says. "I got enough troubles on my mind. Don't add more, please."

I stay quiet after this, and I can see people cutting cane all over the field. I can see more people loading cane on a wagon.

"Come on," Daddy says. "I got to get me a few dollars some kind of way."

Daddy carries me cross the ditch on his back. I look down at the stubbles where the people done cut the cane. Them rows some long. Plenty cane's lying on the ground. I can see cane all over the field. Me and Daddy go over where the people cutting cane.

"How come you ain't working this evening?" a man asks Daddy.

"Charlie around anywhere?" Daddy asks the man.

"Farther over," the man says. "Hi, youngster."

"Hi," I say.

Me and Daddy go cross the field, and I can hear Mr. Charlie

singing. Mr. Charlie stops his singing when he sees me and Daddy. He chops the top off a armful of cane and throws it cross the row. Mr. Charlie's cutting cane all by himself.

"Hi, Brother Howard," Mr. Charlie says.

"Hi," Daddy says. Daddy squats down and let me slide off his back.

"Hi there, little Brother Sonny," Mr. Charlie says.

"Hi," I say.

"That's good," Mr. Charlie says. "How you this beautiful day, Brother Howard?"

"I'm fine," Daddy says. "Charlie, I want to know if you can spare me 'bout three dollars till Saturday."

"Sure, Brother Howard," Mr. Charlie says. "You mind telling me just why you need it? I don't mind lending a good Brother anything long's I know he ain't throwing it away."

"I want to pay Madame Toussaint for some advise," Daddy says.

"Trouble, Brother?" Mr. Charlie asks.

"Amy done left me, Charlie," Daddy says. "I need some advise. I just got to get her back."

"I know what you mean, Brother," Mr. Charlie says. "I had to visit Madame — you won't carry this no farther, huh?"

"Of course not."

"Just the other week I had to take a little trip back there to consult her," Mr. Charlie says.

"What was wrong?" Daddy asks.

"Little misunderstanding between me and Sister Laura," Mr. Charlie says.

"She helped?" Daddy asks.

"Told me to stop spending so much time in church and little more time at home," Mr. Charlie says. "I couldn't see that. You know as far back as I can go in my family, my people been good church members."

"I know that," Daddy says.

" 'Just slack up a little bit,' she tole me. 'Go twice a week, and spend the rest of the time at home.' I'm following her advise, Brother Howard, and I wouldn't be a bit surprise if there ain't a little Charlie next summer sometime."

"Charlie, you old dog," Daddy says.

Mr. Charlie laughs.

"I'll be doggone," Daddy says. "I'm glad to hear that."

"I'll be the happiest man on the plantation," Mr. Charlie says

"I know how you feel," Daddy says. "Yes, I know how you feel. But that three, can you lend it to me?"

"Sure, Brother," Mr. Charlie says. "Anything to bring a family back together. Nothing more important in this world than family love. Yes, indeed."

Mr. Charlie unbuttons his overall pocket and takes out the money.

"The only thing I got is five, Brother Howard," he says. "You don't happen to have change, huh?"

"I don't have a dime, Charlie," Daddy says. "But I'll be more than happy if you can let me have that five. I need some grocery in the house, too."

"Sure, Brother," Mr. Charlie says. He gives Daddy the money. "Nothing looks more beautiful than a family at a table eating something the little woman just cooked. You said Saturday, didn't you, Brother?"

"Yes," Daddy says. "I'll pay you back soon as I get paid. You can't ever guess how much this mean to me, Charlie."

"Glad I can help, Brother," Mr. Charlie says. "Hope she can do likewise."

"I hope so too," Daddy says. "Anyhow, this a start."

"See you Saturday, Brother," Mr. Charlie says.

"Soon's I get paid," Daddy says. "Hop on, Sonny, and hold tight. 'Cause I might not be able to stop and pick you up if you drop off."

IV

Daddy walks up on Madame Toussaint's gallery and knocks on the door.

"Who that?" Madame Toussaint asks.

"Me. Eddie Howard," Daddy says. He squats down so I can slide off his back. I slide down and I let Daddy hold my hand.

"What you want, Eddie Howard?" Madame Toussaint asks.

"I got three dollars," Daddy says. "I still want that advise."

Madame Toussaint's big old black dog barks three times, then I hear Madame Toussaint coming to the door. Madame Toussaint peeps through the keyhole at me and Daddy. She opens the door and lets me and Daddy come in. We go to the fireplace and warm. Madame Toussaint comes to the fireplace and sits down in her big old rocking chair. She looks at Daddy.

"You got three dollars?" she asks.

"Yes," Daddy says. He takes out the money and shows it to her. Madame Toussaint reaches for it, but Daddy pulls it back. "This is five," he says.

"You go'n get your two dollar change," Madame Toussaint says.

"Come to think of it," Daddy says, "I ought to just owe you two and a quarter, since I done already gived you seventy-five cents."

"You want advise?" Madame Toussaint asks Daddy. Madame Toussaint looks like she's getting mad with Daddy now.

"Sure," Daddy says. "But since —"

"Then shut up and hand me your money," Madame Toussaint says.

"But I done already —"

"Get out my house, nigger," Madame Toussaint says. "And don't come back till you learn how to act."

"All right," Daddy says. "I'll give you three more dollars."

Madame Toussaint gets her pocketbook out her pocket. Then she leans close to the fire so she can look down in it. She sticks her hand in the pocketbook and gets two dollars. She looks at the two dollars a long time. She stands up and gets her eyeglasses off the mantelpiece and puts them on. She looks at the two dollars a long time, then she hands them to Daddy. She sticks the money Daddy gived her in the pocketbook; then she takes off her eyeglasses and puts them back on the mantelpiece. Madame Toussaint sits in her big old rocker and starts poking in the fire with the three switches again. Her face gets red from the fire. Her eyes gets big and white. I turn my head and hide behind Daddy's leg.

"Go set fire to your car," Madame Toussaint says.

"What?" Daddy says.

"Go set fire to your car," Madame Toussaint says.

"You talking to me?" Daddy asks.

"Go set fire to your car," Madame Toussaint says.

"Now, just a minute," Daddy says. "I didn't give you my hard-earned three dollars for that kind of foolishness. I dismiss that seventy-five cents you took from me, but not my three dollars that easy."

"You want your wife back?" Madame Toussaint asks Daddy.

"That's what I'm paying you for," Daddy says.

"Then go set fire to your car," Madame Toussaint says. "You can't have both."

"You must be fooling," Daddy says.

"I don't fool," Madame Toussaint says. "You paid for advise and I gived you advise."

"You mean that?" Daddy says. "You mean I got to go burn up my car for Amy to come back home?"

"If you want her back there," Madame Toussaint says. "Do you?"

"I wouldn't be standing here if I didn't," Daddy says.

"Then go and burn it up," Madame Toussaint says. "A gallon of coal oil and a penny box of matches ought to do the trick. You got any gas in it?"

"A little bit — if nobody ain't drained it," Daddy says.

"Then you can use that," Madame Toussaint says. "But if you want her back there, you got to burn it up. That's my advise to you. And if I was you I'd do it right away. You can never tell."

"Tell about what?" Daddy asks.

"She might be sleeping in another man's bed a week from now," Madame Toussaint says. "This man loves her and he's kind. And that's what a woman wants. That's what they need. You men don't know this, but you better learn it before it's too late."

"Can't I at least sell the car?" Daddy says.

"You got to burn it, nigger," Madame Toussaint says, getting mad with Daddy again. "How come your head so hard?"

"But I paid good money for that car," Daddy says. "It wouldn't look right if I just jump up and put fire to it."

"You, get out my house," Madame Toussaint says, looking up at Daddy and pointing her finger. "Go do just what you want with your car. It's yours. But don't you come back here bothering me any more."

"I don't know," Daddy says. "That just don't look right."

"I'm through talking," Madame Toussaint says. "Rollo? Come on, baby."

Big old black Rollo comes up and puts his head in Madame Toussaint's lap. Madame Toussaint pats him on the head.

"Come on," Daddy says. "I reckon we better be going."

Daddy squats down and I climb up on his back. I look to Madame Toussaint patting big old black Rollo on his head.

Daddy pushes the door open and we go outside. It's cold outside. Daddy goes down Madame Toussaint's three old broken-down steps and we go out in the road.

"I don't know," Daddy says.

"Hunh?"

"I'm talking to myself," Daddy says. "I don't know 'bout burning up my car."

"You go'n burn up your car?" I ask.

"That's what Madame Toussaint say to do," Daddy says. "But I don't know."

Daddy walks fast and I bounce on his back.

"God, I wish there was another way out," Daddy says. "Don't look like that's right for a man to just set fire to something like that. Look like I ought to be able to sell it for little something. Get some of my money back. Burning it, I don't get a red copper. That just don't sound right to me. I wonder if she was fooling. No. She say she wasn't. Maybe that wasn't my advise she seen in that fireplace. Maybe that was somebody else advise. Maybe she gived me the wrong one. Maybe it belongs to the man coming back there after me. They go there three times a day, she can get them mixed up."

I bounce on Daddy's back and I close my eyes. When I open them I see me and Daddy going cross the railroad tracks. We go up the quarters to Grandma's house. Daddy squats down and I slide off his back.

"Run in the house to the fire," Daddy says. "Tell your mama come to the door."

Soon's I come in the yard, Spot runs down the walk and starts barking. Mama and all of them come out on the gallery.

"My baby," Mama says. Mama comes down the steps and hugs me to her. "My baby," she says.

"Look at that old yellow thing standing out in that road," Grandma says. "What you ought to been done was got the law on him for kidnap."

Me and Mama go back on the gallery.

"I been to Madame Toussaint house," I say.

Mama looks at me and looks at Daddy out in the road. Daddy comes to the gate and looks at us on the gallery.

"Amy," Daddy calls. "Can I speak to you a minute? Just one minute?"

"You don't get away from my gate I'm go'n make that shotgun speak to you," Grandma says. "I didn't get you at twelve o'clock, but I won't miss you now."

"Amy, honey," Daddy calls. "Please."

"Come on, Sonny," Mama says.

"Where you going?" Grandma asks.

"Far as the gate," Mama says. "I'll talk to him. I reckon I owe him that much."

"You leave this house with that nigger, don't you ever come back here again," Grandma says.

"You oughtn't talk like that, Rachel," Uncle Al says.

"I talk like I want," Grandma says. "She's my daughter, not yours; neither his."

Me and Mama go out to the gate where Daddy is. Daddy stands outside the gate and me and Mama stand inside.

"Lord, you look good, Amy," Daddy says. "Honey, didn't you miss me? Go on and say it. Go on and say it now."

"That's all you want say to me?" Mama says.

"Honey, please," Daddy says. "Say you miss me. I been suffering all day long."

"Come on, Sonny," Mama says. "Let's go back inside."

"Honey," Daddy says, "if I burn the car like Madame Toussaint say, you'll come back home?"

"What?" Mama says.

"She say for Daddy —"

"Be still, Sonny," Mama says.

"She say for me to set fire to it and you'll come home," Daddy says. "You'll come back."

"We going home, Mama?" I ask.

"You'll come back?" Daddy asks. "Tonight?"

"I'll come back," Mama says.

"If I sold it?" Daddy says.

"Burn it," Mama says.

"I can get about fifty for it," Daddy says. "You could get a couple of dresses out of that."

"Burn it," Mama says.

Daddy looks across the gate at Mama a long time. Mama looks straight at Daddy. Daddy shakes his head.

"I can't argue with you, honey," he says. "I'll go and burn it right now. You can come too if you want."

"No," Mama says. "I'll be here when you come back."

"Couldn't you go up home and start cooking some supper?" Daddy asks. "I ain't et since breakfast."

"I'll cook after you burn it," Mama says. "Come on, Sonny."

"Can I go see Daddy burn his car, Mama?" I ask.

"No," Mama says. "You been in that cold too long already."

"I want see Daddy burn his car," I say. I start crying and stomping so Mama'll let me go.

"Let him go, honey," Daddy says. "I'll keep him warm."

"You can go," Mama says. "But don't come to me if you start coughing tonight, you hear?"

"Uh-huh," I say.

Mama makes sure all my clothes buttoned good, then she lets me go. I run out in the road where Daddy is.

"I'll be back soon as I can, honey," Daddy says. "And we'll straighten out everything, hear?"

"Just make sure you burn it," Mama says. "I'll find out."

"Honey, I'm go'n burn every bit of it," Daddy says.

"I'll be here when you come back," Mama says. "How you figuring on getting up there?"

"I'll go over and see if George Williams can't take me," Daddy says.

"I don't want Sonny in that cold too long," Mama says. "And you keep your hands in your pockets, Sonny."

"I ain't go'n take them out," I say.

Mama looks at Daddy and goes back up the walk.

"I love your mama some, boy," Daddy says, looking at Mama. "I love her so much it makes me hurt. I don't know what I'd do if she left me for good."

"Can I get on your back, Daddy?" I say.

"Can't you walk sometime?" Daddy says. "What do you think I'm is, a horse?"

V

Mr. George Williams pulls to the side of the road, then him and Daddy get out. Daddy opens the back door and I get out.

"Look like we got company," Mr. George Williams says.

We go over where the people are. They got a little fire going and some of them's sitting on the car fender. The rest of them standing round the fire.

"Welcome," somebody says.

"Thanks," Daddy says. "Since this my car you setting on."

"Oh," the man says. He jumps up and the other two men jump up. They go over to the little fire and stand round it.

"We didn't mean no harm," one of them say.

Daddy goes over and peers in the car, then he opens the door and gets in. I go over to the car where he is.

"Go stand side the fire," Daddy says.

"I want get in with you."

"Do what I tell you," Daddy says.

I go back to the fire, and I look at Daddy in the car. Daddy passes his hand all over the car, then he just sits there quiet and sad-like. All the people round the fire look at Daddy in the car. After a while he gets out and comes over to the fire.

"Well," he says, "I guess that's it. You got a rope?"

"In the trunk," Mr. George Williams says. "What you go'n do, drag it off the highway?"

"We can't burn it out here," Daddy says.

"He say he go'n burn it," somebody at the fire says.

"I'm go'n burn it," Daddy says. "It's mine."

"Easy, Eddie," Mr. George Williams says.

Daddy is mad but he don't say no more. Mr. George Williams looks at Daddy, then he goes over to his car and gets the rope.

"Ought to be strong enough," he says. He hands Daddy the rope, and he goes and turns his car around. Everybody at the fire watch his backing up to Daddy's car.

"Good," Daddy says.

Daddy gets between the cars and ties them together. Some of the people come over and watch him.

"Y'all got a side road anywhere round here?" Daddy asks.

"Right over there," the man says. "Leads off back in the field. You ain't go'n burn up that good car for real, is you?"

"Who field this is?" Daddy asks.

"Mr. Roger Medlow," the man says.

"Any colored people got fields round here?" Daddy asks.

"Old man Ned Johnson, 'bout two miles down the road," another man says.

"Why don't we just take it on back to the quarters?" Mr. George Williams says. "I doubt if Mr. Grover'll mind if we burn it there."

"All right," Daddy says. "Might as well."

Me and Daddy get in his car. Some of the people from the fire run up to Mr. George Williams's car. Mr. George Williams tells them something, and I see three of them jumping in. Mr. George Williams taps on the horn, then we start. I set back in the seat and look at Daddy. Daddy is quiet and sad-like.

We go way down the road, then we turn and go down the quarters. Soon's we get down there, I hear two of the men in Mr. George Williams's car calling to the people. I set up in the seat and look out at them. They standing on the fenders, calling to the people.

"Come on," they saying. "Come on to the car burning. Free. Free."

We go farther down the quarters, and the two men keep on calling.

"Come on everybody," one of them says.

"We having a car burning party tonight," the other one says. "No charges."

The people start coming out on the galleries to see what all the racket is. I look back and I see some out in the yard, and some already out in the road. Mr. George Williams stops in front of Grandma's house.

"You go'n tell Amy?" he calls to Daddy. "Maybe she want to go, too, since you doing it all for her."

"Go tell your mama come on," Daddy says.

I jump out the car and run in the yard. It's freezing almost.

"Come on everybody," one of them says.

"We having a car burning party tonight," the other one says. "Everybody invited."

I pull Grandma's door open and go in. Mama and Uncle Al and Grandma's sitting at the fireplace.

"Mama, Daddy say come on if you want to see the burning," I say.

"See what burning?" Grandma asks. "Don't tell me that crazy nigger going through with that."

"Come on, Mama," I say.

Mama and Uncle Al get up from the fireplace and go to the door.

"He sure got it out there," Uncle Al says.

"Come on, Mama," I say. "Come on, Uncle Al."

"Wait till I get my coat," Mama says. "Mama, you going?"

"I ain't missing this for the world," Grandma says. "I still think he's bluffing."

Grandma gets her coat and Uncle Al goes and gets his coat; then we go outside. Plenty people standing round Daddy's car now. I can see more people opening doors and coming out on the galleries.

"Get in," Daddy says. "Sorry I can't take but two. Mama, you want ride?"

"No, thanks," Grandma says. "You might just get it in your head to run off in that canal with me in there. Let your wife and child ride. I'll walk with the rest of the people."

"Get in, honey," Daddy says. "It's cold out there."

Mama takes my arm and helps me in; then she gets in and shuts the door.

"How far down you going?" Uncle Al asks.

"Near the sugarhouse," Daddy says. He taps on the horn and Mr. George Williams drives away.

"Come on, everybody," one of the men says.

"We having a car burning party tonight," the other one says. "Everybody invited."

Mr. George Williams drives his car over the railroad. I look back and I see plenty people following Daddy's car. I can't see Grandma and Uncle Al, but I know they back there too.

We keep going. We get almost to the sugarhouse, then we turn down another road. This road is rough, and I have to bounce on the seat.

"Well, I reckon this's it," Daddy says.

Mama don't say nothing to Daddy.

"You know it ain't too late to change your mind," Daddy says. "All I have to do is tap on this horn and George'll stop."

"You brought any matches?" Mama asks.

"All right," Daddy says. "All right. Don't start fussing."

We go a little farther and Daddy blows the horn. Mr. George Williams stops his car. Daddy gets out of his car and goes and talks with Mr. George Williams. Little later I see Daddy coming back.

"Y'll better get out here," he says. "We go'n take it down the field a piece."

Me and Mama get out. I look down the headland and I see Uncle Al and Grandma and all the other people coming. They come up where me and Mama's standing. I look down in the field and I see the cars going down the row. It's dark, but Mr. George Williams's car lights shine bright. The cars stop and Daddy gets out of his car and goes and unties it. Mr. George Williams comes back to the headlane and turns his lights on Daddy's car so all of us can see the burning. I see Daddy getting some gas out of the tank.

"Give me a hand down here," Daddy calls. That don't even sound like his voice. Sounds like somebody else doing the calling. The men run down the field where he is and start shaking on the car. I see the car leaning; then it goes over.

"Well," Grandma says. "I never would've believed it."

I see Daddy going all around the car with the can, then I see him splashing some gas inside the car. All the other people back away from the car. I see Daddy scratching a match and throwing it in the car. Then he throws another one in there. I see little fire; then I see plenty.

"I just do declare," Grandma says. "He's a man after all."

Everybody else is quiet. We stay there a long time and look at the fire. The fire burns down low and Daddy and them go look at the car. Daddy gets the can and pours some more gas on the fire. The fire gets big again. We look at the fire some more.

"Never thought that was in Eddie," somebody says.

"You not the only one," somebody says.

"He loved that car more than he loved anything."

The fire burns down again. Daddy and them go and look at the car. They stay there a little while; then they come out to the headlane where we standing.

"That's about it, honey," Daddy says.

"Then let's go home," Mama tells him. "Sonny?" she says to me.

Me and Mama go in Grandma's house and pull the big bundle out on the gallery, Daddy picks the bundle up and puts it on his head; then we go up the quarters to us house.

"You hungry?" Mama asks Daddy.

"I'm starving," Daddy says.

"You want eat now or after you whip me?" Mama says.

"Whip you?" Daddy asks. "What I'm go'n whip you for?"

Mama goes back in the kitchen. She don't find what she's looking for, and I hear her going outside.

"Where Mama going, Daddy?"

"Don't ask me," Daddy says. "I don't know no more than you."

Daddy gets some kindling out of the corner and puts it in the fireplace. Then he pours some coal oil on the kindling and lights a match to it. Me and Daddy squat down on the fireplace and watch the fire burning.

I hear the back door open and shut; then I see Mama coming in the front room. She's got a great big old switch with her.

"Here," she says.

"What's that for?" Daddy says.

"Here. Take it," Mama says.

"I ain't got nothing to beat you for," Daddy says.

"You whip me," Mama says. "Or I turn right around and walk out that door." Daddy stands up and looks at Mama.

"You must be crazy," Daddy says. "Stop all that foolishness and go cook me some supper, woman."

"Get your pot, Sonny," Mama says.

"Shucks," I say. "Now where we going? I'm getting tired walking in all that cold. I'm go'n catch pneumonia 'fore I know it."

"Get your pot and stop answering me back," Mama says.

I go to my bed and pick the pot up again. I ain't never picked that pot up so much in all my life.

"You ain't leaving here," Daddy says.

"You better stop me," Mama says, going to the bundle.

"All right," Daddy says. "I'll beat you if that's what you want."

Daddy picks up the switch and I start crying.

"Lord, have mercy," Daddy says. "Now what?"

"Whip me," Mama says.

"Amy, whip you for what?" Daddy says. "Amy, please, just go back there and cook me something to eat."

"Come on, Sonny," Mama says. "Let's get out of here."

"All right," Daddy says. Daddy hits Mama two times on the legs. "That's enough," he says.

"Beat me," Mama says.

I cry some more. "Don't beat my mama," I say. "I don't want you to beat my mama."

"Sonny, please," Daddy says. "What y'all trying to do to me? Run me crazy? I burnt up the car. Ain't that enough?"

"I'm just go'n tell you one more time," Mama says.

"All right," Daddy says. "I'm go'n beat you, if that's what you want."

Daddy starts beating Mama, and I cry some more. But Daddy don't stop this time.

"Beat me harder," Mama says. "I mean it. I mean it."

"Honey, please," Daddy says.

"You better do it," Mama says. "I mean it."

Daddy keeps on beating Mama, and Mama cries and goes down on her knees.

"Leave my mama alone, you old yellow dog," I say. "You leave my mama alone." I throw the pot at him but I miss, and the pot go bouncing across the floor.

Daddy throws the switch away and runs to Mama and picks her up. Mama's crying in Daddy's arms. Daddy takes Mama over to the bed and lies her on the bed. Daddy lies down side Mama.

"I didn't want hit you, honey," Daddy says. "I didn't want hit you. You made me. You made me hit you."

Daddy begs Mama to stop crying, but Mama keeps on crying. I get on my bed and cry in the blanket.

I feel somebody shaking me, and I must've been asleep.

"Wake up," I hear Daddy saying.

"I'm tired and I don't feel like getting up. I feel like sleeping some more."

"You want some supper?" Daddy asks.

"Uh-huh."

"Get up then," Daddy says.

I get up. I got all my clothes on and my shoes on.

"It's morning?" I ask.

"No," Daddy says. "Still night. Come back in the kitchen and get some supper."

I follow Daddy in the kitchen, and me and him sit down at the table. Mama brings the food to the table, and she sits down too.

"Bless this food, Father, which we're 'bout to receive, the nurse of our bodies, for Christ sakes, amen," Mama says.

I raise my head and look at Mama. I can see where Mama's been crying. Mama's face is swole. I look at Daddy and Daddy's eating. Mama and Daddy don't talk and I don't say nothing neither. I eat my food. We eating sweet potatoes and bread. I got me a glass of clabber, too.

"What a day," Daddy says.

Mama don't say nothing. Daddy don't say no more neither. Mama ain't eating much. She's just picking over her food.

"Mad?" Daddy says.

"Uh-huh," Mama says.

"Honey?" Daddy says.

Mama looks at him.

"I didn't beat you 'cause you did us thing with Freddie Jackson, did I?" Daddy says.

"No," Mama says.

"Well, why, then?" Daddy says.

" 'Cause I don't want you to be the laughing stock of the quarters," Mama says.

"Who go'n laugh at me?" Daddy says.

"Everybody," Mama says. "Mama and all. Now they don't have nothing to laugh about."

"Honey, I don't mind if they laugh at me," Daddy says.

"I do mind," Mama says.

"Did I hurt you?"

"I'm all right," Mama says.

"You ain't mad no more?" Daddy says.

"No," Mama says. "I'm not mad."

Mama picks up a little bit of food and puts it in her mouth.

"Finish eating your supper, Sonny," she says.

"I got enough," I say.

"Drink your clabber," Mama says.

I drink all my clabber and I show Mama the glass.

"Go get your book," Mama says. "It's on the dresser."

I go in the front room to get my book.

"One of us got to go to school with him tomorrow," I hear Mama saying. I see her handing Daddy the note. Daddy waves it back. "Here," she says.

"Honey, you know I don't know how to act in no place like that," Daddy says.

"Time to learn," Mama says, giving him the note. "What page your lesson on, Sonny?"

I turn to the page, and I lean on Mama's leg and let her carry me over my lesson. Mama holds the book in her hand. She carries me over my lesson two times; then she makes me point to some words and spell some words.

"He know it," Daddy says.

"I'll take you over it again tomorrow morning," Mama says. "Don't let me forget it now."

"Uh-huh."

"Your daddy'll carry you over it tomorrow night," Mama says. "One night me, one night you."

"With no car," Daddy says, "I reckon I'll be around plenty now. You think we'll ever get another one, honey?"

Daddy's picking his teeth with a broomstraw.

"When you learn how to act with one," Mama says. "I ain't got nothing 'gainst cars."

"I guess you right, honey," Daddy says. "I was going little too far."

"It's time for you to go to bed, Sonny," Mama says. "Go in the front room and say your prayers to your daddy."

Me and Daddy leave Mama there in the kitchen. I put my book on the dresser and I go to the fireplace where Daddy's at. Daddy puts another piece of wood on the fire and plenty sparks shoot up the chimney. Daddy helps me to take off my clothes, and I kneel down and lean on his leg.

"Start off," Daddy says. "I'll stop you if you miss something."

"Lay me down to sleep," I say, "I pray the Lord my soul to keep. If I should die before I wake, I pray the Lord my soul to take. God bless Mama and Daddy. God bless Grandma and Uncle Al. God bless the church. . . . God bless Miss Hebert. . . . God bless Bill and Juanita." I hear Daddy gasping. "And God bless everybody else."

I jump off my knees. Them bricks on the fireplace make my knees hurt.

"Did you tell Him to bless Madame Toussaint?" Daddy says.

"No," I say. "I'm scared of Madame Toussaint."

"That's got nothing to do with it," Daddy says. "Get back down there."

I get back on my knees. I don't get on the bricks because they make my knees hurt. I get on the floor and lean against Daddy's legs.

"And God bless Madame Toussaint," I say.

"All right," Daddy says. "Warm up good."

Daddy goes over to my bed and pulls the cover back.

"Come on," he says. "Jump in."

I run and jump in the bed. Daddy pulls the cover up to my neck.

"Good night, Daddy."

"Good night," Daddy says.

"Good night, Mama."

"Good night, Sonny," Mama says.

I turn on my side and look at Daddy at the fireplace. Mama comes out of the kitchen and goes to the fireplace. Mama warms up good and goes to the bundle.

"Leave it alone," Daddy says. "We'll get up early tomorrow morning and get it."

"I'm going to bed," Mama says. "You coming now?"

"Uh-huh," Daddy says.

Mama comes to my bed and tucks the cover under me good. She leans over and kisses me and tucks the cover some more. She goes over to the bundle and gets her nightgown; then she goes in the kitchen to put it on. She comes back and puts her clothes she took off on a chair side the wall. Mama kneels down and says her prayers; then she gets in bed and covers up. Daddy stands up and takes off his clothes. I see Daddy in his big old long white BVDs. Daddy blows out the lamp, and I hear the spring when Daddy gets in the bed. Daddy never says any prayers.

"Sleepy?" Daddy says.

"Uh-uh."

I hear the spring. I hear Mama and Daddy talking low, but I don't know what they saying. I go to sleep some, but I open my eyes. It's some dark in the room. I hear Mama and Daddy talking low. I like Mama and Daddy. I like Uncle Al, but I don't like old Grandma too much. Grandma's always talking bad about Daddy. I don't like old Mr. Freddie Jackson. I like Mr. George Williams. We went riding way up the road with Mr. George Williams. We got Daddy's car and brought it all the way back here. Daddy and them turned the car over and Daddy poured some gas on it and set it on fire. Daddy ain't got no more car now. . . . I know my lesson. I ain't go'n wee-wee on myself no more. Daddy's going to school with me tomorrow. I'm go'n show him I can beat Billy Joe Martin shooting marbles. I can shoot all over Billy Joe Martin. And I can beat him running, too. He thinks he can run fast. I'm go'n show Daddy I can beat him running. . . . I don't know why I had to say, "God bless Madame Toussaint." I don't like her. And I don't like old Rollo, neither. Rollo can bark some loud. He made my head hurt. Madame Toussaint's old house don't smell good. Us house smells good. I hear the spring on Mama and Daddy's bed. I get way under the cover. I go to sleep little bit, but I wake up. I go to sleep some more. I hear the spring on Mama and Daddy's bed — shaking, shaking. It's some dark under this cover. It's warm. I feel good way under here.

MISS LUHESTER GIVES A PARTY

Ronald Fair

L UHESTER Homan owned a frame bungalow. She was one of the most highly respected ladies in the neighborhood. She was five feet two inches tall and would have been considered not quite but almost plump. Her hair was dark brown, of course, and she was a nice even walnut without the slightest imperfection anywhere on her lovely smooth skin. She was a happy woman and had enough love for her five children and everyone in the world. She had a kind word and a pleasant smile for people she passed on the street.

Luhester had never bothered to get married and she was therefore supported by the county. And since all of the men loved her so, they felt personally responsible for each of the five children. Hers were an attractive group of children, but I'm afraid they didn't favor each other very much. However, they did all seem to have some of Luhester in them and she loved each of them equally.

The fellows in the neighborhood sort of looked after Luhester. It wasn't at all unusual to see two or three of us carrying packages of clothing every first of the month on our way to Luhester's house. The paternal instinct was so strong in all of us that we were determined that Luhester's children would be the best dressed in the neighborhood. And they were.

There was a garage at the rear of Luhester's house and Mr. Beckman (the owner of the local hardware store) stored his supplies in this garage behind four locks and five steel bars. Quite often he worked late moving supplies from the garage to the store and before he went home to his wife and children he stopped by to visit with Luhester. He was a good man. She was the kind of person you'd just automatically want to protect and Mr. Beckman began storing his supplies in her garage just because he wanted to help her earn money to afford some of the necessaries of life. As a result of his kindness, hers was the best maintained house on the block and always open for company. That is, unless Mr. Beckman was there. We didn't want to disturb him because he was such a good man.

Red Top and I passed her place one day and saw her standing on a ladder painting the trim. She was having a pretty hard time of it because the baby girl was awake and kept crying and Luhester would have to get down off the ladder and run inside to see if little Jo Jo was all right. We watched her for a while, running into the house and then walking back out, climbing the ladder, making a few strokes with the brush, then down off the ladder again and back into the house. Seeing her in such a troubled condition made us both a little uneasy so we took over the painting chores. She affected everyone about the same way. We finished the trim that first day and went on the next morning, after eating a healthy breakfast she had prepared for us, and did both porches.

Somebody else pitched in a few days later and finished the rest of the house. That spring the whole house was painted inside and out. It was probably the only house ever painted out of love.

As a token of her appreciation, Luhester gave a party for the kind men of the community. We were in the poolroom one evening at about seven o'clock sitting around watching Stick clean some sucker of all his money when Luhester's oldest daughter, Little Luhester, came in and invited the chosen few with her sweet young voice whispering in our ears, "Mama says you suppose to come right now for the party."

Now the work party has different meanings to different people, but everyone knows it means fun. When Little Luhester pulled Stick's hand away from his cue, stood on her toes and whispered the magic words in his ear, it was like the voice of providence telling him to end the game immediately and hurry to the party. He couldn't miss the party because everybody knows it's really bad luck to miss a party, especially a party you're invited to attend. Stick took the omen for what it was worth and finished the game by running the last four balls off the table and banking the eight ball three-in-the-side. He had been carrying the sucker along, beating him by only one or two balls each time. But he couldn't take the chance of ruining his luck by missing the party so he had to bring the game to an end and be happy with the eight dollars he had already won.

Jesse, too, knew the punishment for missing a party and when Little Luhester passed the message on to him he got down from his creaky stool and started turning off lights at the rear of the hall. "Okay. That's it for today. I'm closin' up early."

"What the hell you mean?" Cadillac Bill said. "I just started my game."

"Finish it tomorrow."

"Tomorrow, hell! I paid my money and I'll play the game."

Just then the bearer of sweet words whispered the same magic to Cadillac Bill.

"Well," Cadillac said to Jesse, "if you got to close, you got to close."

When Little Luhester left the poolroom, everyone who was to be invited had been contacted, and no one wanted to let it be known that there was a party for fear that the uninvited would string along and spoil the magic before it had a chance to work. Fat Man had not been invited and he wondered where everyone was hurrying to so suddenly.

"Hey, Stick," Fat Man said, "where y'all goin'?"

"I'm just headin' home, man. Ain't none of yo' business where I go noway. Why you always think somebody's goin' some place? Why don't you go on home and stop bothering people?"

With that, Fat Man knew there were pleasant happenings in the area. He left the poolroom and waited in the dark to follow Stick to the festivities.

The party was a smashing success. Luhester had been buying two gallons of wine a month for five months, planning just such an occasion as this as the time for the unscrewing of the caps. She had made potato salad and sweet potatoes and black-eyed peas and baked a ham and fried four chickens. She had her Catholic Salvage Hi-Fi going full blast when the two girls who worked at Silky Martin's came in, kicked off their shoes, helped themselves to some of the wine and started dancing.

Frenchy Coolbreeze and Randolph Beard sat at opposite corners of the room staring at each other for the first hour. By the second hour they had forgotten their anger and laughed loudly about their duel. By the third hour each was proclaming the other the world's most gifted musician and then Stick asked Randy if he still had the high-powered rifle he had brought home from Germany and Frenchy Coolbreeze returned to his corner and continued staring through the rest of the party.

Cadillac Bill was busy following Luhester around, rubbing her stomach and saying: "Magic Stomach, Magic Stomach, bring me a Little Baby Cadillac."

One of the girls went upstairs with Red Top and stayed for about forty-five minutes.

Junkie Thaddeus Popcorn Jones drank a glass of wine and vomited in his potato salad.

Stick tried to pull Luhester upstairs but she fought him off successfully without losing friendship.

Tommie Murphy watered the flowers with wine.

The girl went back upstairs with Red Rop. Red Top came down alone. The girl followed fifteen minutes later with Cadillac Bill.

Fat Man didn't crash the party until we were all feeling pretty good and by then it didn't matter. Miss Joanne Joanne arrived at 11:00 with a bottle of bourbon for the hostess, saw the two junkies sleeping in the corner and left.

By midnight Doc (the drugstore janitor) and Cadillac Bill had gotten into three fights, each of them swearing that Little Luhester was his daughter. After we stopped the last fight and they cooled off, they confessed a deep lasting love for Luhester.

These magic parties either go on until morning or end abruptly because some mysterious chain of events wills it so. This grand party could not last all night because parties that linger on to the twilight hours lose their magic when the sun comes up. Everyone knows a party has to end before morning to be a success.

Silky Martin got up from his chair to leave and nudged Fat Man who was standing over Stick. Stick was wearing his new sports jacket, a soft gold with green stripes. When he realized that Fat Man had spilled a glass of wine on him he jumped to his feet and with one punch knocked Fat Man through the living room window onto the porch. Now Luhester had gone upstairs hours before this with Doc and they had no idea that downstairs Fat Man and Stick were methodically breaking up every piece of furniture in the living room. The two girls left but got their dresses slightly torn as they tried to break away from Red Top and Tommie Murphy. Silky Martin had eased out without anyone discovering that he had started things going, and the winos from the corner left. Of course they left; both the food and wine was gone. Things were really going good, so I gathered the few records I had brought along with some of those Frenchy Coolbreeze had brought and went home to bed.

The magic had worked; the party was the best we ever had.

THE DEATH OF TOMMY GRIMES

R. J. Meaddough III

Tommy had become part of the ground. At least he felt that way as he watched the dew and the daylight make giant shiny cobwebs of the treetops. The sun had not yet risen and a mist lay over the ground, which made the forest seem rather spooky to him.

His nose itched and he longed to scratch it, maybe just nudge it a little, but Pa said don't move, don't twitch, don't even breathe hard. Not one arm, one hand, even one finger, he said. "He knows the woods," Pa told him; "you'll never know he's there; suddenly he'll just *be* there looking at you, just looking."

It started so long ago, Tommy remembered, almost a year, when he was just eleven. That night, in the hen-yard, with the weasel's eyes glistening in the flashlight. He never even fired a shot, just stood there with his mouth open, foolish, while the weasel dashed into the woods.

And Pa knocking the rifle from his hands and asking, "Why didn't you shoot? What you waiting on? What's wrong with you, boy?"

"Pa, I . . . I couldn't, Pa. I just couldn't."

Pa hunkered down and pulled on a blade of grass. He didn't say anything for a minute, just knelt there chewing on that grass.

"You never did like to kill nothing did you, boy? Even when you was small."

Tommy looked at the ground without saying anything and his father sighed, "Tommy, dammit, a man *always* dies a little when he kills something, but it just plain has to be done. Some animals just ain't no damn good and got to be *killed*. Understand?"

He nodded without answering, still looking at the ground, and

Pa stood up with a groan and they walked into the hen-house without speaking. They counted forty-three dead pullets, lying in red and white patches of feathers, blood and confusion.

So he began to practice with the rifle, shooting at moving targets, and the rifle became part of his arm. It seemed so long that Pa practiced with him, so long. Again and again he would take a deep breath, let some out, then squeeze the trigger. So long, so very long.

Tommy felt beads of sweat form on his forehead despite the chill that remained in the forest air. Soon the beads would form into droplets and run down his face and burn his eyes. There was a handkerchief in his coat pocket just a few inches away but he could not, dare not reach for it. But soon it would be over. Soon.

It got so that he could hit anything he aimed at, even things a good bit out. And sometimes, when he turned real quick, he would see pride in Pa's eyes. But then Pa would always make his face blank and say, "We-e-ell, Tommy," real grim-like, "you're getting better but you need more practice."

Pa taught him how to track animals and how to lead quail, and how to lean into the rifle to take up the recoil. And Pa showed him how to lie quiet so the forest forgot he was there and Nature went on about her business.

And the time came last night when Pa came home and mentioned that some of the men were going into the forest to get a buck; and how it might be some good shooting because bucks were fast, real fast.

He bent his head to eat his beans, yet he knew without looking that his father was watching him, way out of the corner of his eye. He knew, too, that Pa wouldn't have said a word if Ma was there — she was always saying he was too young for something or other — but she was visiting overnight up in Colliersville. And he thought how it must be for Pa when the other men bragged about their boys, and him so scared to kill a weasel, and he knew what he had to do.

"Pa," he murmered, "think maybe I could go a time at that old buck?"

"Boy, this ain't no old buck, it's a young one," Pa said, making like he was surprised. "Boy, you might get hurt."

"Some time, I think I'd like to take my turn," he answered, face even closer to the beans.

"Well I'll think about it, boy," Pa mumbled, but he couldn't hide a gleam in his eye.

Tommy slowly, ever so slowly, rubbed his forehead along his sleeve and watched the gloom in front of him. Somewhere out there Pa had circled around and was trampling through the woods, scaring everything away, away toward the clearing where he lay waiting.

He laughed in his mind when he thought of the last time when Pa had gone down to the Hut for a drink with the "boys," as he called them. And when he came out his eyes were gleaming like the mischief and he wobbled into the yard like he didn't know how to walk. He had gone downstairs in his pajamas and they sat on the back porch and listened to the crickets and looked at the stars. Maybe afterwards Pa would let him go into the Hut and talk with the men and drink liquor. But right then he had to be satisfied with listening to Pa tell stories that he had heard at the Hut and then squeeze his arm at the end and laugh, oh my, how he would laugh. Then he filled his pipe and stared out across the backyard toward the north pasture.

"Dawn in the forest is a beautiful thing, boy, beautiful. All the colors and wild flowers, fresh streams, cool breeze, you feel like, boy, feel it! Even though there ain't a sound you feel it. You see a flash of white and you know some rabbit's going home. Or you might see a chuck burrowing in. And the trees," he whispered, "they just stand there watching you. Been there before you came, be there after you gone."

"Gee, Pa," he murmured, "you make it sound so nice I don't know's I want to *hunt* tomorrow."

Pa smiled. "It *is* nice, boy, real nice, but things got to be done to keep it that way. Fox eats a rabbit, he keeps the rabbit population down, else they'd overrun the land. Same here. You hunt 'cause you hungry and got to eat, that's one reason. Then you might hunt for the sport — pit your mind against animal cunning — 'course I don't hold much with that, but some do. Some do. But there's some varmints that do damage and just plain got to be killed. Understand?"

"I . . . think so. But what about what you said about a man dying when he kills something?"

"Man kills once and he starts to get callous. Next time it ain't so hard. Then you get so's you make a decision that something's got to die and you kill it, just like that. Then you dead, boy. You got no feeling no more so you just as good as dead. You just ain't had time to lay down."

Tommy wiggled his toes and got no response. They felt like sticks of wood, stilts that somebody had glued on his legs. An ant left the ground and started climbing his arm until he blew, softly, blew the ant into some brave new world. The mist was thinning and the sun began to shine dully through the trees. Pa was right, he thought. Seems as if everything had a place in the scheme of things. Birds ate worms they found on the ground. Then they got eaten by bigger birds. Rabbits got eaten by foxes and foxes by bobcats, and bobcats by bears or something all the way up to elephants. And elephants were killed by man. Pa said that man preyed on himself, whatever that meant, but everything had a place, and when they got out of place they upset the balance. Like too many rabbits or squirrels or anything.

A twig snapped like dynamite and he froze on the ground and swiveled the gun to the left and waited. Slowly, clumsily, with three blades of grass waving like pennants ahead of him, a porcupine strolled into view, made his way through the sunlight, and vanished into the grass. Tommy laughed, out loud almost, he could hardly keep from blowing up he was so relieved, so happy. Instead he settled down again to wait.

But things had changed somehow. The sunlight was duller, almost disappearing and he felt a chill again as he had before the sun came up. And the silence somehow nettled him . . . *the silence!* Not a sound! No crickets, no chirping, no rustling, nothing. There was something out there! The happy-scared feeling ran up and down Tommy's back and his breath came in painful gasps. His chest hammered, almost pushing his lungs into his mouth with its rhythm which seemed to be saying: *Soon! Soon! Soon they would be calling him Tom Grimes like his father. Soon he would be able to go into the Hut and drink liquor with the rest of the men. Soon the waiting would be over. Soon he would be grown. Soon. Soon. Soon. Soon! Soon! Soon!*

There! In the bushes! A little pinch of color behind the bramble bush moving light and easy, so very easy, behind the bushes. He slid down still further behind the gun and spread his feet wide, toes digging into the soft earth. "Put the whole side of your body behind the gun to take the recoil," Pa had said. "Spread your legs wide to brace yourself. Make the gun, your arm, your hip, your leg into one long line." Tommy drew his breath in and nearly gagged trying to hold it, sighting along the clean black ridges of the rifle. The outline was clear behind the bush, creeping, sniffling, gliding along.

"You won't see it, or hear it, or smell it, or anything," Pa had told him. "You'll just feel it, and it'll be there."

Tommy breathed out and in, let some of the air out and chokingly began to squeeze the trigger. Would it never go off, his mind asked, reeling and stumbling and clinging desperately to reality, and the earth stuttered. The light blinked. His ears rang. His nose reacted to the smell of smoke and the taste of ink crept into his mouth. There was a rustling sound in the bushes and a thrashing, a terrible thrashing and rattling, but it stopped. Suddenly it stopped. Tommy blinked. It was over; just like that, it was over.

He got to his feet and the stiffness forced him to lean against a tree trunk. Before there had been nothing, then suddenly there was something, a small patch of color the same as Pa's jacket. Tommy blinked and listened for the crashing sound of someone coming through the forest — but there was nothing. Nothing. He strained his ears and heard new-sprung crickets and birdcalls, but no crashing, no rustling, no voice, and he started for the bush and then stopped, trembling.

"Pa?" he whispered, "Pa-a-a?" There was no sound except his own voice, twisted and shapeless and mocking, twirling through the trees like vapors in the dull, chilly air. "Pa! Pa! Pa!"

Then came the rushing and the crashing to the left and the tall husky figure coming out of the gloom saying, "Boy? What's wrong, boy?" And Tommy ran over and slammed his head against his father's chest. "Pa! I thought I killed you, Pa, I thought I killed you, Pa, I thought I killed a man!"

"Now, Tommy, it's all right, everything's all right," Pa said, walking behind the bush and kneeling and then rising and coming back.

"See?" he said. "What did I tell you? Right through the heart. Now that's good shooting. Come on over here and look; come on, now."

So he looked, and then it wasn't so bad.

Later, much later, they walked the mile from town to the Hut and walked inside together. There were some men sitting at tables and they looked up as Pa hoisted him onto the bar, running his fingers through his dark, blond hair.

"Boys, I wanna tell you my boy became a man today. Yessir, killed his first nigger."

"No!" a man said. "Who?"

"Swamp-buck got away from the chain gang yes-tidy."

"Git out!" the man said.

"Yessir, got him right through the heart."

The man grabbed Tommy and hugged him around the knees. "You a man now, boy!" he yelled, "you a real live honest-to-goodness 'fore God man!"

And Pa, his blue eyes agleam, yelled out, "Bartender! Don't just stand there! Give this man a drink!"

The man sat Tommy down on the bar and the liquor made him cough a bit as it coursed down his throat and it made his ears ring like the tolling of bells. But he smiled happily as the feeling of warmth like Mississippi sunshine spread through his insides. For now he belonged.

OLD BLUES SINGERS NEVER DIE

Clifford Vincent Johnson

Hᴇʀᴇ's one for the books: River Bottom, the blues singer, in Paris, and he isn't just here, but sporting a big fat diamond ring and wearing fine clothes to go with it . . .

I may be a GI, but I found out a long time ago that this was Paris and I try all the time to tell the other guys there's something else happening outside of Pig Alley but, no, they can't see that because goodtiming with those scroungy women is about all they can think of. Killing time, taking stuff's about the extent of their lives. I've got nothing against killing time, mind you, like I said I'm a GI, but I realize the difference between Paris and Chicago South Side. I also know that these days call for you to have at least a little something in your head; you've got to have been a few places and seen a few things. That's why when they start getting sharped-up and loaded-up with liquor set to go wild, I say no, because me, it's the Latin Quarter, St.-Michel, St.-Germain as fast as I can get there. Actually, but I don't go into all that with them, I've got my own private philcsophy; I don't see any sense in wasting time when Paris is full of all kinds of people to rub shoulders with and learn something from, do you?

Take that restaurant where I ran into Bottom for instance. They've got a lot of places like that stuck up in little streets that wouldn't even make good alleys back home; and if you're not quick you'd miss them altogether. Anyway, those places are always filled up with all kinds of students and artists and every time I go in this one place where I met Bottom I see these Africans black as sin. Back home, due to the fact that we're so mixed up with Mister Charlie, you hardly ever see anybody that black except down South, like my cousins for instance, in fact those Africans remind me a lot of my cousins — it's mostly the way they laugh and the way they walk and even when they get to talking African — how they're real free about it. Those are some alright guys though, those Africans. I remember one night after I'd been seeing them in there all the time, they started talking to me in that African they were talking to one another. To me, can you picture that?

"Wait a second," I say to them, "if you come on like that we can't get together at all. . . ."

"Ah," one of them says, "you are American."

"That's right."

"You are a student?"

"Kind of," I said and I did it smooth although I should have told him I was just a GI you see, and anyway I am a kind of student, too. "I'm not a full-time student but I try to pick up what I can."

He turns around and runs off a bunch of stuff in African to the others and they all look at me funny.

"You not go back, I think?" the one who speaks English says, shaking his head.

"Not go back home?" I say, because I don't know exactly what he means to say. "You mean not go to America?"

"Yes, you not go back to America?"

I didn't quite know if I'd understood him right but I told him sure I'd go back. I didn't have nowhere else to go. He told them what I said and they nodded to me and now I really didn't understand. But like I said before, they're good guys; they even said I should come to Africa one day before it was all over, and if they could understand English better we could probably get something even better going between us. And that taught me one thing: that that stuff they put over on you in school is a lot of junk — about how they're so different and act wild, especially since they don't look or act much different from my cousins down South.

They've got these French students, I guess they are. They try to be cool all the time: even talk cool French and not like most of the Frenchmen you see on the street who look like they want to fight every time they talk to one another; these students look as if they want to be colored. That's okay since they only act like that and don't end up getting into a fight like real colored folks back home and whenever one of them sees me he gives me a little nod, pretending to know what's happening which he doesn't really, but all the same it gives you a kick to see somebody imitating your way of life. Mostly I have to give it to them when they draw things in those big green pads that they carry with them. Some of them are sure weird though, like when this guy sitting across from me all of a sudden started staring me in the face and then he took out a pad and began drawing something and when he finished it, he showed it to me, and he had a big grin on his face. I looked at it and it had a big, flat nose spread across the face and some fat lips sticking about a mile out from the forehead. Another guy might have wanted to fight. . . . Don't get me wrong now, I'm proud as the next person of being colored; that's something I'm tough about. You don't have to be white to make it, like a lot of people think — white doesn't say anything to me — but the truth was that that just didn't look anything like me. And that's where the other guy would have made his mistake. Not me! Me, I shook my head big as you please to show him that I was really getting a kick out of it, especially since the guy himself was so serious about the way he did it and seemed like a kid with something he was real proud of having made himself. So I figured, what the hell, he knows what he's doing and besides, I didn't know too much about that far-out modern stuff anyway. So I kept it, and even if I don't flash it around where everybody can see it, I still have it.

You can imagine how surprised I was to run into somebody so down-to-earth as Bottom in that place. Everything I know about Bottom came from some very down-to-earth sources. That was before I went into the army, we were living on Kimbark Avenue, I remember. We had this regular janitor who the only thing regular about was how he would wait until snow got piled up behind-deep to a ten-foot monkey and the hawk would be whipping across the ice on Lake Michigan at about a hundred miles an hour and that's when he'd be regular about disappearing and letting the furnace go to hell. That's the reason why they had to go and look for somebody to come and fill in, usually around the taverns on Forty-seventh Street.

I remember I was watching this shabby-looking guy fighting with a snow shovel out by the back steps.

"That's a man used to be known anywhere he wanted to go," my old man told me, pointing to him as he said it.

It was pretty obvious, by the way he was scuffling, that it couldn't have been for shoveling no snow, so I asked him what did he do.

" 'Course you never heard of 'im," he said, "you was too young, fact, most of that time you wasn't even on nobody's mind especially with times being so hard as they was. That's River Bottom, one of the greatest blues singers ever was."

I couldn't see how come he didn't sing then, instead of doing what he was doing. My old man said, "He's just down on his luck, that's all."

"How you mean, down on his luck?" I asked him. "He lost his voice or something?"

"No, it ain't that. I suppose he's still got his voice, it's the ears what listened to that voice what's lost."

Now if you had known my old man, you would be used to all kinds of stuff like that. But losing ears! that was too weird for me. But my old man, you see, well, he spent most of his life down South. He knows a lot about colored history, and colored history, I'd learned, is filled with a lot of weird things, so even if it didn't make much sense at the beginning, I'd learned to listen a while longer and he'd usually explain and what he'd be saying wouldn't be so weird after all. He told me about how there had been many singers like Bottom in Bottom's day but Bottom, well, Bottom was the best. Then it wasn't like now; they had good singers, singers who had something to say and not a bunch of crap. He said that any one of them had more music in his little finger than these slick-heads of today had underneath those hairdos. That was because then our folks liked to hear about their troubles and how hard making it was. When they could hear somebody telling about his own life and talking heart to heart about his own problems, right up there before them in flesh and blood like that, they got the strength to keep on going. And that big depression, what was that? It didn't say nothing to no colored man because he hadn't known nothing but depressions. By the time the people started crying about some depression and white folks was raining out of windows all over the country, colored folks might have been crying too but you're have never known it and it was the same way with blues singers like Bottom. They could go anywhere, have any price they could name and when they shouted about hard times the people didn't cry for laughing.

Now that was my old man saying all that. I couldn't know about all that because like he said, I wasn't even born and after I was born I had all the advantages of the North (my old man was smart enough to get out when my mother got pregnant). But he made me know. When he went and dug some records out that I'd never seen before from way back in the closet and he handled them so gentle and got so still after he put them on the record player to listen, that's when I began to see what Bottom meant to him. I've got to admit that that was some other stuff, I mean I couldn't have known anything about *that* without hearing it, and even hearing it I still couldn't believe it was really like that. The way Bottom sounded, I wouldn't ever know anything about. . . . All that made me start thinking about the music we young guys had the habit of listening to, and the stuff we did, and how my old man always stayed down on me about it and I never understood why. I was thinking about us screaming and carrying on like we did at the Trianon Ballroom on South Parkway and thinking about the way the girls fought to have a piece of torn clothing, or a kiss or anything they could get from these smooth-tongued, conk-headed crooners with nothing to say but some sugary nonsense with a beat in groups called The Roaches, or The Studs, or The Stone Thrillers, or any of a hundred even more stupid names and it was listening to Bottom made me ashamed of all that.

I am not the kind of guy that likes to say I told you so, but I really did. I said right then and there, "He's going to be know again," but my old man told me no.

"Folks don't want to hear what that's about," he said. "They've got other things on their minds now. They think hard times is dead and buried. They can't get rid of their money fast enough. What Bottom's talking about ain't true for them no more, ain't nothing true for them 'cept spendin' that money and playing life for a fool."

I let him go on, but knowing this is modern times and they've got TV and jets all around the world, somebody was bound to find out about Bottom. . . .

So, here I am sitting in this little restaurant taking in all that good atmosphere, waiting to get waited on, when I hear this real country voice asking for some greens. I heard right away it wasn't GI talk and when I looked I couldn't believe it. I went up and asked him to be sure.

"If you can speak French, I'll make myself know you," he said. Then he looked at me kind of suspicious for a second and said, "Where you know me from?"

"Chicago," I told him.

"Then, since you're a home boy — sit down. I don't have to tell you how it is. I'm trying to get me some greens and maybe some ribs, but between you and me, I know that would be asking just a little too much."

"I gave up long time ago," I told him. "If they've got 'em they keep 'em well hid. But why don't you let me take you to this place across town where they sell everything, they've even got chitterlings, good as they had at that place on Forty-seventh and Drexel. . . ."

"Why you want to tell me all that?" he said. "That don't leave me much hope, I've got a show to do around the corner at the Blues Cave."

"You are here now? I mean, you got a gig in Paris?"

"I ain't no tourist, let's put it that way," he said, looking at me as though he were peeking over glasses.

"I know about you," I tried to assure him. "What I didn't know was that they could pick up on the stuff you put down."

"No," he said, making a real serious face like he was thinking about that, "but I tell you what: I don't have no trouble picking up on the stuff they put down for it. But wait a minute, how's a young fellow like you come to be knowing so much about me?"

He made me real proud so I said, "They've still got some young fellows around with some taste."

"No," he said, "it ain't that. I figured you might be knowing some other things that you ought not to be knowing." And we had a good laugh.

About that time I spy this fellow I know calls himself Moses Selassie. He's one of those guys that I'd seen hanging around all the time. I'd heard him speaking French like it was English and he seemed to have a lot of sense, so I called him to come and sit with us.

"Moses, man," I say to him, "you know River Bottom, the blues singer, don't you?"

Bottom looked him in the face and squinted.

"Moses?" he said, looking at me then back at Moses. "I thought you told me your name was Jenkins or something like that?"

"When did I tell you that?"

"You must've forgot."

"I told you my name was something else beside Moses?"

"Listen, don't tell me I'm crazy. The first night I saw you, you told me you'd just come into town and you told me your name was Jenkins Henry or Henry Jenkins, or something like that."

"No, you've got the wrong man," Moses said, pulling at his bristling, black beard. "How long ago was that?"

"I didn't write no notes, but it was a good two months ago."

"I figured you had me wrong. Two months ago I was in Israel picking up my inheritance and before that I was in Ethiopia, visiting my relatives."

"You told me then, you came from New York," Bottom said laughing, "but that's alright, us folks got to make it best we can."

"Look, my man," I say, because I don't know what to call him now, "I didn't want to put you in the trick, I just wanted you to order some greens for Bottom."

"Greens?" he says to Bottom. "Don't you know you're in Paris, France and not in Paris, Georgia?"

"I know I'm in Paris, France better than you."

"You don't act like it," Moses says. "Don't you know that they throw that stuff away over here?"

"Throw it away?" I say.

"They throw it away because those are scraps," Moses says. "All that stuff you call soul food, all that's nothing but scraps. The master threw scraps to the hogs and to the colored folks."

"How you know so much about it?" I asked him, and Bottom broke out laughing and Moses didn't go for that.

"Maybe my folks was throwing the scraps . . ." he says.

Bottom passes him off by saying, "Yeah, man, that's right, your folks was throwin' scraps."

When the waiter comes up Moses commences right off to run

down a long spiel in French and when he's through the waiter looks at him and grins and says: "Tell me in English." And Moses mumbles that he wants beef something or other and then Bottom and me order chicken and rice. And while we're sitting and waiting Moses digs in his pocket and pulls out a book and starts reading as if we aren't even there.

"Look, Bottom," I say, "I'd like to know how'd they come to hear about you way over here? I don't mean to be getting into your business but when I left to go into the army you wasn't doing any good for yourself."

"Seriously, who told you about me? You pretty young to be knowin'."

"My old man."

"They'd have to be pretty old," Moses chimes in, looking up from his book. "Bottom's about as old as water." But Bottom ignores him. "Hey," he goes on anyway, "you should be glad. Aren't you glad?"

"A lot of people have heard of him," I say.

"But there's a whole lot of people dead since then, too," Moses says.

"I just put my trust in God," Bottom says, still ignoring Moses. "He's responsible for me bein' here."

"You can call it God if you want," Moses says.

"What you call it?" Bottom says, turning on him.

"I wouldn't call it God, and you know better yourself."

"I asked you what you'd call it."

"Bottom, don't be crazy."

"I ain't crazy. You crazy if you don't know what I'm talkin' about."

"I don't know nothing about no God. Where is He?"

"You still young, boy," Bottom says. You would have expected him to be mad at Moses or Jenkins or whatever his name was, but he stayed cool — fact, he was talking soft and almost loving. "You got to walk it for yourself. Can't nobody walk it for you."

Moses shakes his head and frowns and goes back to reading and the waiter comes up and while we're eating, everything calms down.

"Yeah, baby," Bottom says after a while, "I put all that religious stuff down when I was up there. All that stuff they used to tell me 'bout. What you talkin' 'bout? I was River Bottom, I could make people laugh and if I wanted, could make 'em cry too, that's right. Had more women than you could shake a stick at. Man, I was up there and I was goin' through the gates of hell and I didn't know it."

Moses looks up from his plate and says, "That's what's kept colored folks behind for so long, all that stuff you're talking about. Why can't you be man enough to admit that you're on your own? Quit talking about hell; that's life, Bottom."

"Yeah," Bottom says, "that's just what I thought; I could make it on Bottom and Bottom knew just how the deal went down. But then, one day, yeah, baby, one day Bottom didn't have nothin', not a cent, no place to go, nothin'. Bottom wasn't sharp no more and he didn't have no more women; Bottom had him some blues and you better know it and right then and there I got to thinkin' about that stuff I'd put down long time before and I had to see that none of that belonged to Bottom; Bottom wasn't nothin', baby. Bottom wasn't no better than a speck of dirt and I woke up one mornin' and started prayin' and readin' the Bible. Nigger!, I said to myself, this earth ain't yours, the earth is the Lord's and the fullness therein. And I knew that the Lord had done sacrificed for the world His Son Jesus Christ, which must have called for a lot of sufferin' on His part, and here I was cryin' 'cause I was broke. I was still livin' and that was somethin'. And who was Bottom anyway . . ."

"You're a man, aren't you?" Jenkins says.

"I ain't nothin' before the Lord."

"That's the white man that made you believe that."

"Nigger, I ain't talkin' about no white man!" Bottom says, starting to get worked up. "Don't you go gettin' God and the white man mixed up. White man's lost 'fore he starts."

"If you weren't making it, Bottom, that was your folks' fault. Colored folks put you down. You better wake up, Bottom."

"Son, God is in everythin'. God is love, and He is buried so deep you can't see him . . ."

"O," Moses says and laughs, "so that's how you figure. God got you up off the street back home and dropped you over here."

"You sound stupid. All I'm sayin' is that havin' faith . . ."

"Having faith, shit! Your God and all that crap had thrown you down. Having some white men with money is what you're trying to say. It wasn't any praying that got you here. White people trying to do some good for humanity brought you over here to put you in a museum . . ."

"Museum!" Bottom says. "Museum, you hear that? Nigger, what you talkin' 'bout? I'm workin' at the Blues Cave, that ain't no museum."

This Moses guy should have been cool and I told him so. What'd he want to jump on Bottom for, anyway?

"I'm just trying to straighten Bottom out," he says to me, "and you, do you go for all that stuff?"

"It's no big thing what I go for."

"Don't worry 'bout the mule," Bottom says to me, "he ain't no fool."

"You may not be no fool, but you don't act like you've got good sense. Your soul's in the white man's hands. He left you with a dead horse, something worn out that he'd thrown away, just like he'd thrown away all those scraps you call soul food . . ."

"Yeah, maybe he did throw it down. Yea, suppose he did. I got it now, you hear me? I got it! Finders keepers, losers weepers. Looka here, I got nothin' to do with him not knowin' what to do with it."

"Aw, man," Moses says, "the hell with it! I don't want to go into all that anyway. You can't hear what I'm saying. You're deaf. But I'll tell you this, you may not want to hear it, but I'll tell you anyway." Moses leans up across the table with a stupid smile on his face and his coat lapels almost dipping in his plate. "You want to see where your God is? I'll tell you how: you just try to go back home with all that old-time rinky-dinky music, if you think God is everywhere. Your big rich white God's gonna get you in his booking office and have a heart to heart talk with you. And you know what he's gonna say? He's gonna say Bottom, you better get your black behind back in the Blues Cave if you know what's good for you, unless you want to come back and pull down public assistance. When he tells you that, do you think you gonna like it, you think you gonna say Lord goin' take care of me? You think you gonna pawn all them fine clothes you wearing, that diamond ring — you're too old for that."

What Moses had done to Bottom was no different from if he'd

just upped and slapped him smack in the face. Bottom just sat there, looking surprised, with his mouth half open and his lower lip hanging. Honest, it was like as if Moses had gone right up-side his head! When Bottom started talking his eyes got as big as half-dollars and the big vein welled up in his forehead.

"I don't have nothin' my way, boy!" he says, "what you mean, my own way? Don't be tellin' me that shit! You think you got somethin' you own way? Do you? Tell me, boy, do you?"

"Forget it, Bottom."

"No, you ain't finished. No, now you listen to me, young boy. . . ."

"Bottom, you've got nothing to tell me."

"I do got somethin' to tell you. Damn right I got somethin' to tell you, 'cause you think you know somethin'. I went up against Him, I crossed Him when I was young, but I knew I was crossin' Him and I could feel the evil I was doin' but I could feel Him all the while too, but you . . ."

"Okay, so I'm young, let me be young."

"Me, when I was young I could feel the devil, but you, you don't feel nothin', that's why you in worse shape, you don't come nowhere close to feelin' nothin'. And you know why? No, you don't know a goddamn thing!"

"I know enough; more than you'll know."

"You don't know nothin'," Bottom spit out, and he almost did because he was choking up on his words and spit was coming out the corners of his mouth, "I say you don't know nothin', don't none of us know nothin'. How we gonna know somethin'? Just when we git a little power in our hands that the most dangerous time. You start to thinkin' you know somethin', figurin' you can do somethin' by yourself. But there ain't no days like that, Lord no. That's evil actin', Lord know it's evil, that's the way he work, evil: sneakin' up and lettin' you get your head up just a li'l bit higher above the trees, lettin' you get some fine clothes on your back and a big, brand-new stetson on your heads, that's evil, Lord ain't that the truth, and then he just sit back there evil and he be grinnin' 'cause he know once you all dress up you ain't gonna turn back one look at the Lord, ain't that the truth Lord, and he take you and make you walk to where the Lord's light can't shine on you no more, yes Lord, and right there's when he cut out just like that and all them other things you'd been seein' cut out too, 'cause they was all a part of evil — and you's imaginin' it — and that's when you by yourself, Lord know you by yourself, you got to walk that lonesome road back, turn them fine things into somethin' to eat, turn 'em into . . ."

Moses reached over and shook Bottom by the sleeve. "Bottom, you're a bigger, more ignorant fool than I thought. . . ."

And about that time I got mad. I know I should've got mad before, before he'd hurt Bottom so bad. But when I get mad I don't say nothing, that's because I'm a regular guy and I want to wait and try to understand everybody. I learned something long time ago that came back to me while I was sitting up there watching this Moses fellow who was too proud to smell his own shit and even though I had tended to agree with some of the things Moses had said about religion, I had to agree with Bottom when he said that Moses wasn't nothing. And I was thinking how this Moses — and what was that guy's game anyway, calling himself all kinds of names — who was nobody even, had less of a right to jump on Bottom who was already somebody. . . . One time back home when I was a little kid I used to get some of the other guys and we'd go down on Cottage Grove Avenue where they've got all these storefront churches. We'd get to dancing and laughing because we thought it was really funny the way all those cool jazz musicians who worked when they could in the Sixty-third Street jazz clubs, would file into those churches the same way, carrying drums and horns and bass, everything. It was mostly funny watching those good sisters and brothers bowing and grinning all dressed in white and black, all holy-like, calling them young boys God's musicians and welcoming them in. When the service would get to rocking and moving with a good swing beat, we'd dance and cut up and even try to get people passing by to join us out on the sidewalk in front. We'd do it every night without fail until that one night my old man collared me and whipped my head all the way home. I remember a lot of people sitting out on the tenement steps because it was hot and I remember trying to dodge all them blows and them laughing and my old man saying, "Ain't you got no respect," wop! "Ain't I taught you no better," wop! And when he got home and got his razor strap he really got to teaching me how nobody had no right to be singing and dancing and cutting up like that when folks was praying, SMACK! and it didn't make no difference if you didn't understand them, SMACK! it was for them to understand, not you, that's what they had to get them through and that had well gotten them through for a long time and as long as I didn't have nothing no better, SMACK! I ought not to be cutting up when nobody was praying. . . .

I learnt that well and I knew that praying was like what Bottom was doing, he wasn't in any church, but he was praying just the same because he was saying what he believed in; and so the next time Moses opened his mouth, and it didn't make any difference that the two of them had already stopped talking, and were ignoring each other, that didn't matter, I told him he didn't believe in nothing and the next time he said something to Bottom I was going to put my foot in his behind. That was about the only thing that seemed to say something to him. He didn't say another word after that; he simply got up and went to look for the waiter and when he found him he paid him and wasted no time leaving.

I swore to Bottom that the next time I saw Moses I'd kick his behind anyway, on general principle, and make him apologize to him. But Bottom said not to worry. Bottom knew how that ass had messed up my night, that's probably why he had me come over to the Blues Cave to hear him play. Once we got there, after I got a drink of Scotch in front of me and all that good blues in my ear, I had the best night I've had since I've left stateside. Sitting up there was like me and Bottom had something going between us. All the while he was singing and playing, he kept looking over at me and I'd nod back at him and when the people saw that I could tell by the way they were smiling that they didn't know what was happening, not really — and that, for them, I was somebody too. But they couldn't begin to imagine how boss all that made me feel.

So he finishes for the night and we go across town where we can find lights and people, and everything going like it was daytime — something like on Sixty-third, if you follow me — and all the while we're drinking good liquor he's telling me stories about all kinds of old-timers he was tight with, stories about Chicago and Kansas City and St. Louis, stories about everything, and they were some good stories too.

I told Bottom the same thing I'd told my old man, I mean how he was so good and all, and how with this modern age, he'd be back up top. He didn't know what was liable to happen. It's true, you don't know, I don't care what they say. I wouldn't be surprised if Bottom gets back stateside before me. He didn't deny any of that either, Bottom's no fool; he didn't say anything, he just looked at me for a long time and finally flashed me one of those little smiles like he'd been doing in the Blues Cave. He was beat, tired as he could be, more tired than he'd been in a coon's age and had to go home. But he said I could look him up any time, any time I wanted and I said he didn't have to do all that for me but he said he did and that's when he paid up and we both went home. . . .

No, that was one night I won't forget for a long time! River Bottom, the blues singer, in Paris, France, doing all right for himself, that's something I've got to write my old man about. And you think I'm not going to tell him how for once he was wrong?

THE ONLY MAN ON LIBERTY STREET

William Melvin Kelley

S HE was squatting in the front yard, digging with an old brass spoon in the dirt, which was an ocean to the islands of short yellow grass. She wore a red and white checkered dress, which hung loosely from her shoulders and obscured her legs. It was early spring and she was barefoot. Her toes stuck from under the skirt. She could not see the man yet, riding down Liberty Street, his shoulders square, the duster he wore spread back over the horse's rump, a carpetbag tied with a leather strap to his saddle horn and knocking against his leg. She could not see him until he had dismounted and tied his horse to a small, black, iron Negro jockey and unstrapped the bag. She watched now as he opened the wooden gate, came into the yard, and stood looking down at her, his face stern, almost gray beneath the brim of his wide hat.

She knew him. Her mother called him Mister Herder and had told Jennie that he was Jennie's father. He was one of the men who came riding down Liberty Street in their fine black suits and starched shirts and large, dark ties. Each of these men had a house to go to, into which, in the evening usually, he would disappear. Only women and children lived on Liberty Street. All of them were Negroes. Some of the women were quite dark, but most were coffee-color. They were all very beautiful. Her mother was light. She was tall, had black eyes, and black hair so long she could sit on it.

The man standing over her was the one who came to her house once or twice a week. He was never there in the morning when Jennie got up. He was tall, and thin, and blond. He had a short beard that looked as coarse as the grass beneath her feet. His eyes were blue, like Jennie's. He did not speak English very well.

Jennie's mother had told her he came from across the sea and Jennie often wondered if he went there between visits to their house.

"Jeannie? Your mother tells me that you ask why I do not stay at night. Is so?"

She looked up at him. "Yes, Mister Herder." The hair under his jaw was darker than the hair on his cheeks.

He nodded. "I stay now. Go bring your mother."

She left the spoon in the dirt, and ran into the house, down the long hall, dark now because she had been sitting in the sun. She found her mother standing over the stove, a great black lid in her left hand, a wooden spoon in her right. There were beads of sweat on her forehead. She wore a full black skirt and a white blouse. Her one waist-length braid hung straight between her shoulder blades. She turned to Jennie's running steps.

"Mama? That man? My father? He in the yard. He brung a carpetbag."

First her mother smiled, then frowned, then looked puzzled. "A carpetbag, darling?"

"Yes, Mama."

She followed her mother through the house, pausing with her at the hall mirror, where the woman ran her hand up the back of her neck to smooth stray black hair. Then they went onto the porch, where the man was now seated, surveying the tiny yard and the dark green hedge that enclosed it. The carpetbag rested beside his chair.

Her mother stood with her hands beneath her apron, staring at the bag. "Mister Herder?"

He turned to them. "I will not go back this time. No matter what. Why should I live in that house when I must come here to know what home is?" He nodded sharply as if in answer to a question. "So! I stay. I give her that house. I will send her money, but I stay here."

Her mother stood silently for an instant, then turned to the door. "Dinner'll be on the table in a half hour." She opened the screen door. The spring whined and cracked. "Oh." She let go the door, and picked up the carpetbag. "I'll take this on up." She went inside. As she passed, Jennie could see she was smiling again.

After that, Jennie's mother became a celebrity on Liberty Street.

The other women would stop her to ask about the man. "And he staying for good, Josie?"

"Yes."

"You have any trouble yet?"

"Not yet."

"Well, child, you make him put that there house in your name. You don't want to be no Sissie Markham. That white woman come down the same day he died and moved Sissie and her children right into the gutter. You get that house put in your name. You hear?"

"Yes."

"How is it? It different?"

Her mother would look dazed. "Yes, it different. He told me to call him Maynard."

The other women were always very surprised.

At first, Jennie too was surprised. The man was always there in the morning and sometimes even woke her up. Her mother no longer called him Mister Herder, and at odd times, though still quite seldom, said no. She had never before heard her mother say no to anything the man ever said. It was not long before Jennie was convinced that he actually was her father. She began to call him Papa.

Daily now a white woman had been driving by their house. Jennie did not know who she was or what she wanted but, playing in the yard, would see the white woman's gray buggy turn the corner and come slowly down the block, pulled by a speckled horse that trudged in the dry dust. A Negro driver sat erect in his black uniform, a whip in his fist. The white woman would peer at the house as if looking for an address or something special. She would look at the curtained windows, looking for someone, and sometimes even at Jennie. The look was not kind or tender, but hard and angry as if she knew something bad about the child.

Then one day the buggy stopped, the Negro pulling gently on the reins. The white woman leaned forward, spoke to the driver and handed him a small pink envelope. He jumped down, opened the gate, and without looking at Jennie, his face dark and shining, advanced on the porch, up the three steps, which knocked hollow beneath his boots, opened the screen door, and twisted the polished brass bell key in the center of the open winter door.

Her mother came, drying her hands. The Negro reached out the envelope and her mother took it, looking beyond him for an instant at the buggy and the white woman, who returned her look coldly. As the Negro turned, her mother opened the letter, and read it, moving her lips slightly. Then Jennie could see the twinkling at the corners of her eyes. Her mother stood framed in the black square of the doorway, tall, fair, the black hair swept to hide her ears, her eyes glistening.

Jennie turned back to the white woman now and saw her lean deeper into her seat. Then she pulled forward, shouting shrilly, and spoke like Jennie's father. "You tell him he has got one wife! You are something different!" She leaned back again, waved her gloved hand, and the buggy lurched down the street, gained speed, and jangled out of sight around the corner.

Jennie was on her feet and pounding up the stairs. "Mama?"

"Go play, Jennie. Go on now, *play!*" Still her mother stared straight ahead, as if the buggy and the white woman remained in front of the house. She still held the letter as if to read it. The corners of her eyes were wet. Then she turned and went into the house. The screen door clacked behind her.

At nights now Jennie waited by the gate in the yard for her father to turn the corner, walking. In the beginning she had been waiting too for the one day he would not turn the corner. But each night he came, that day seemed less likely to come. Even so, she was always surprised to see him. When she did, she would wave, timidly, raising her hand only to her shoulder, wiggling only her fingers, as if to wave too wildly would somehow cause the entire picture of his advancing to collapse, as only a slight wind would be enough to disarrange a design of feathers.

That night too she waved and saw him raise his hand high over his head, greeting her. She backed away when he reached the gate so he might open it, her head thrown way back, looking up at him.

"Well, my Jennie, what kind of day did you have?"

She only smiled, then remembered the white woman. "A woman come to visit Mama. She come in a buggy and give her a letter too. She made Mama cry."

His smile fled. He sucked his tongue, angry now. "We go see what is wrong. Come." He reached for her hand.

Her mother was in the kitchen. She looked as if she did not really care what she was doing or how, walking from pump to stove, stove to cupboard in a deep trance. The pink envelope was on the table.

She turned to them. Her eyes were red. Several strands of hair stuck to her temples. She cleared her nose and pointed to the letter. "She come today."

Her father let go Jennie's hand, picked up the letter and read it. When he was finished he took it to the stove and dropped it into the flame. There was a puff of smoke before he replaced the lid. He shook his head. "She cannot make me go back, Josephine."

Her mother fell heavily into a wooden chair, beginning to cry again. "But she's white, Maynard."

He raised his eyebrows like a priest or a displeased school-teacher. "Your skin is whiter."

"My mother was a slave."

He threw up his hands, making fists. "Your mother did not ask to be a slave!" Then he went to her, crouched on his haunches before her, speaking quietly. "No one can make me go back."

"But she can get them to do what she say." She turned her gaze on Jennie, but looked away quickly. "You wasn't here after the war. But I seen things. I seen things happen to field niggers that . . . I was up in the house; they didn't bother me. My own father, General Dewey Willson, he stood on a platform in the center of town and promised to keep the niggers down. I was close by." She took his face in her hands. "Maynard, maybe you better go back, leastways —"

"I go back — dead! You hear? Dead. These children, these cowardly children in their masks will not move me! I go back dead. That is all. We do not discuss it." And he was gone. Jennie heard him thundering down the hall, knocking against the table near the stairs, going up to the second floor.

Her mother was looking at her now, her eyes even more red than before, her lips trembling, her hands active in her lap. "Jennie?"

"Yes, Mama." She took a step toward her, staring into the woman's eyes.

"Jennie, I want you to promise me something and not forget it."

"Yes, Mama." She was between her mother's knees, felt the woman's hands clutching her shoulders.

"Jennie, you'll be right pretty when you get grown. Did you know that? Promise me you'll go up North. Promise me if I'm not here when you get eighteen, you'll go North and get married. You understand?"

Jennie was not sure she did. She could not picture the North, except that she had heard once it was cold and white things fell from the sky. She could not picture being eighteen and her mother not being there. But she knew her mother wanted her to understand and she lied. "Yes, Mama."

"Repeat what I just said."

She did. Her mother kissed her mouth, the first time ever.

From the kitchen below, came their voices. Her father's voice sounded hard, cut short; Jennie knew he had made a decision and was sticking to it. Her mother was pleading, trying to change his mind. It was July the Fourth, the day of the shooting match.

She dressed in her Sunday clothes and coming downstairs heard her mother: "Maynard, please don't take her." She was frantic now. "I'm begging you. Don't take that child with you today."

"I take her. We do not discuss it. I take her. Those sneaking cowards in their masks . . ." Jennie knew now what they were talking about. Her father had promised to take her to the shooting match. For some reason, her mother feared there would be trouble if Jennie went downtown. She did not know why her mother felt that way, except that it might have something to do with the white woman, who continued to ride by their house each morning after her father had left for the day. Perhaps her mother did not want to be alone in the house when the white woman drove by in her gray buggy, even though she had not stopped the buggy since the day two months ago when the Negro had given her mother the pink envelope.

But other strange things had happened after that. In the beginning she and her mother, as always before, had gone downtown to the market to shop amid the bright stalls brimming with green and yellow vegetables and brick-red meats, tended by dark country Negroes in shabby clothes and large straw hats. It would get very quiet when they passed, and Jennie would see the Negroes look away, fear in their eyes, and knots of white men watching, sometimes giggling. But the white women in fine clothes were the most frightening; sitting on the verandas or passing in carriages, some even coming to their windows, they would stare angrily as if her mother had done something terrible to each one personally, as if all these white women could be the one who drove by each morning. Her mother would walk through it all, her back straight, very like her father's, the bun into which she wove her waist-length braid on market days gleaming dark.

In the beginning they had gone to the suddenly quiet market. But now her mother hardly set foot from the house, and the food was brought to them in a carton by a crippled Negro boy, who was coming just as Jennie and her father left the house that morning.

Balancing the carton on his left arm, he removed his ragged hat and smiled. "Morning, Mister Herder. Good luck at the shooting match, sir." His left leg was short and he seemed to tilt.

Her father nodded, "Thank you, Felix. I do my best."

"Then you a sure thing, Mister Herder." He replaced his hat and went on around the house.

Walking, her hand in her father's, Jennie could see some of the women of Liberty Street peering out at them through their curtains.

Downtown was not the same. Flags and banners draped the verandas; people wore their best clothes. The Square had been roped off, a platform set up to one side, and New Marsails Avenue, which ran into the Square, had been cleared for two blocks. Far away down the Avenue stood a row of cotton bales onto which had been pinned oilcloth targets. From where they stood, the bull's-eyes looked no bigger than red jawbreakers.

Many men slapped her father on the back and, furtively, looked at her with a kind of clinical interest. But mostly they ignored her. The celebrity of the day was her father, and unlike her mother he was very popular. Everyone felt sure he would win the match; he was the best shot in the state.

After everyone shot, the judge came running down from the targets, waving his arms. "Maynard Herder. Six shots, and you can cover them all with a good gob of spit!" He grabbed her father's elbow and pulled him toward the platform, where an old man with white hair and beard, wearing a gray uniform trimmed with yellow, waited. She followed them to the platform steps, but was afraid to go any farther because now some women had begun to look at her as they had at her mother.

The old man made a short speech, his voice deep but coarse, grainy-sounding, and gave her father a silver medal in a blue velvet box. Her father turned and smiled at her. She started up the steps toward him, but just then the old man put his hand on her father's shoulder.

People had begun to walk away down the streets leading out of the Square. There was less noise now but she could not hear the first words the old man said to her father.

Her father's face tightened into the same look she had seen the day the letter came, the same as this morning in the kitchen. She went halfway up the stairs, stopped.

The old man went on: "You know I'm no meddler. Everybody knows about Liberty Street. I had a woman down there myself . . . before the war."

"I know that." The words came out of her father's face, though his lips did not move.

The old man nodded. "But, Maynard, what you're doing is different."

"She's your own daughter."

"Maybe that's why . . ." The old man looked down the street, toward the cotton bales and the targets. "But she's a nigger. And now the talking is taking an ugly turn and the folks talking are the ones I can't hold."

Her father spoke in an angry whisper. "You see what I do to that target? You tell those children in their masks I do that to the forehead of any man . . . or woman that comes near her or my house. You tell them."

"Maynard, that wouldn't do any real good *after* they'd done something to her." He stopped, looked at Jennie, and smiled. "That's my only granddaughter, you know." His eyes clicked off her. "You're a man who knows firearms. You're a gunsmith. I knew firearms too. Pistols and rifles can do lots of things, but they don't make very good doctors. Nobody's asking you to give her up. Just go back home. That's all. Go back to your wife."

Her father turned away, walking fast, came down the stairs and grabbed her hand. His face was red as blood between the white of his collar and the straw yellow of his hair.

They slowed after a block, paused in a small park with green trees shading several benches and a statue of a stern-faced young man in uniform carrying pack and rifle. "We will sit."

She squirmed up onto the bench beside him. The warm wind smelled of salt from the Gulf of Mexico. The leaves were a dull, low tambourine. Her father was quiet for a long while.

Jennie watched birds bobbing for worms in the grass near them, then looked at the young stone soldier. Far off, but from where she viewed it, just over the soldier's hat, a gliding sea gull dived suddenly behind the rooftops. That was when she saw the white man, standing across the street from the park, smiling at her. There were other white men with him, some looking at her, others at the man, all laughing. He waved to her. She smiled at him though he was the kind of man her mother told her always to stay away from. He was dressed as poorly as any Negro. From behind his back, he produced a brown rag doll, looked at her again, then grabbed the doll by its legs, and tore it partway up the middle. Then he jammed his finger into the rip between the doll's legs. The other men laughed uproariously.

Jennie pulled her father's sleeve. "Papa? What he doing?"

"Who?" Her father turned. The man repeated the show and her father bolted to his feet, yelling: "I will kill you! You hear? I will kill you for that!"

The men only snickered and ambled away.

Her father was red again. He had clenched his fists; now his hands were white like the bottoms of fishes. He sighed, shook his head and sat down. "I cannot kill everybody." He shook his head again, then leaned forward to get up. But first he thrust the blue velvet medal box into her hand. It was warm from his hand, wet and prickly. "When you grow up, you go to the North like your mother tells you. And you take this with you. It is yours. Always remember I gave it to you." He stood. "Now you must go home alone. Tell your mother I come later."

That night Jennie tried to stay awake until he came home, until he was there to kiss her good night, his whiskers scratching her cheek. But all at once there was sun at her window and the sound of carts and wagons grating outside in the dirt street. Her mother was quiet while the two of them ate. After breakfast, Jennie went into the yard to wait for the gray buggy to turn the corner, but for the first morning in many months the white woman did not jounce by, peering at the house, searching for someone or something special.

BEAUTIFUL LIGHT
AND BLACK OUR DREAMS

Woodie King, Jr.

HIS world is all aglow today. And the day itself is beautiful; the
sun is shining. Across the street in the park, young men and
women are laughing and playing in the warm sun. Now and then
pigeons flutter; birds glide in and sing gay songs; both birds and
pigeons are drinking from the beautiful fountains. Here and there
in the warm sun people are reading their free press. Today she, as
the sun, will return after her long absence. He is in the Greek
restaurant, across from the park, waiting and dreaming.

"Everyone is so full of dreams, in the light *and* in the dark," he
is remembering her saying. And he is thinking of her in light, high
above the city in a beautiful glass office, smiling gleefully. He is
thinking that on that eleventh floor of that City Building how full
of dreams she really is; aglow, he is thinking this.

Today he is sitting again, at the same spot again, waiting for her
again. This year he is fifteen minutes early.

He is remembering.

"But what's your dream?" he wanted to ask her that last time
when she sat across from him, finishing her lunch. But he did
not — not that moment. But he wanted to. He watched her. Face
like poisonous exotic fruit. Dark gray eyes, large and always on
watch. Lips full and always in that position — that position that
caused him to know his heart *could* beat. Queenly; the woman
everyone wants. The beauty, part-time actress, secretary six hours a
day on the eleventh floor of the new City Building; only one of
that beautiful color. Joanne. Watching her finish her lunch with a
million dreams in that beautiful head. Beautiful Joanne, so serene.
One of the many women born Negro, yet are almost white inside
and outside; the kind of Negro woman that has a million dreams

of winning beauty contests in Canada or being the first Negro Miss Street & Railway, then being spotted by Stanley Kramer or somebody, anybody. The light kind with the features of the Caucasian; the kind that all men seem to love because they are, yet they are not.

And yet he is man, it is not those things that made him care for her, love her. For him, it goes farther; to the time when he first saw her.

Start at the beginning. Drift backwards, travel in slow motion through other winters and summers; through time, that element that taught her you. All the way back to the reason for her being across from you, through other tears and laughter.

The beginning.

Once there was a woman named Joanne. . . .

Go on. . . .

. . . I saw her first on the floor of a Little Theater reading her lines from a Greek tragedy. She and an Irish fellow whom she loved (Oh, how she loved him!) played there on that floor in that little white theater. So gay was her laughter, so dry was his. Talking of their trip to Palestine, talking of blue grass in the beautiful Highlands, speaking like Modjeska, saying *gee whiz,* eating pizza, laughing, getting excited, playing . . . wrestling. I would watch her often. I had to. And I wondered why she never looked at me. Was it time?

They read their lines.

And I being dark and invisible to them chose to remain that way. For in a world so white and light, so strange, I felt darkness was forbidden.

Everything about the theater was white. She blended in. I did not: I could not. Often I would pass her. Sometimes she would look up — not at me, but up. Then it changed. We would be apart and our eyes would find each other. Her smiling ceased; no words. Never . . . never words . . . never smiles . . . strange. The Irish did not look up. He looked down always when he was with her.

> He came with indifference
> And with indifference did I receive him

I dreamed one night that she would tell me I did not belong. The dream occurred in a snowstorm. Far away in a place where the snow never seemed to cease its steady fall. And I was lost in that snow desert, unable to find my way. Then I saw her . . . and the falling snow . . . and she was in a sort of transparent night-gown. I asked her if she was cold; I wanted to protect her from the cold snow, wanted her warm. Her mouth moved. I could hear her voice in an echo, resounding, away . . . away . . . go away . . . away. Then the dream changed. I disappeared, and a gigantic black man in chains, sweat glistening on his back and face, walked slowly towards her singing *any day now*. And his presence made the snow melt, made the sun shine, made her smile. And they danced to songs of Leadbelly, they danced until she became exhausted, until Belafonte sang, until Leadbelly cried. I reappeared and the snow returned and the echo. Away . . . away . . . go away . . . away.

I went away.

A long interval of dream-filled days and nights.

The middle.

Once there was a store downtown. . . .

Slowly . . .

I went in out of the cold white snow. A feeling hit me; something wonderful, more wonderful than life itself in that store. Something as wonderful as the sudden return of summer after a snow-filled winter. My body became fervent. I looked for the cause throughout the large store. It had to be there. It was there, I felt it. Up from the basement, all through it until I saw that black and white checked coat far away, descending.

I saw her. I looked at her across the store, she looked at me. No words. A smile. I found her that winter morning and she saved my summers. Then we knew. We had to know.

I returned.

Winters and summers of tears and laughter, searching.

The end.

The end?

Yes.

Life stops sometimes. And in those times pain is the only

substitute. For me, there have been many. I believe this day will bring another.

He cares for her and loves her because time caused it. Time . . . time that puts beginnings, middles, and endings to life and love.

Still remembering.

She turned, flashing glances through every face within the huge immaculate restaurant, then out the large glass window facing Circus Park, the church, the Institute of Technology, North, and a city filled with pure white snow.

"Look at them," she said. "See how they move? They don't know where they are going, none of them, do they?"

He smiled, glad to be with her, nodded his head, agreeing.

"Look at that funny-looking couple with the poodle," he said finally.

They both laughed.

"I know they are cold. I just know it," she said. "Why do they pretend they are warm? It's freezing out there."

"I'm hip," he said. "But I can't really think of anything outside. You're it today."

"Love you," she said.

Silence while they looked at each other.

He wanted to ask her, have your dreams changed since the last ones? He could not — not now.

"They don't even know. One of these days they are going to know who we are, 'ay man?"

He nodded and sipped the hot black coffee.

"We are going to be famous, man, you and I," she said. But not as serious as it had been said in happier winters and summers.

And he thought he knew then.

"Yes. We are going to be famous," he said. "One of these days."

He looked at her long.

"What's your dream now, Joanne Labold?"

"My dream?" she said. "I want to get off the eleventh floor of that damned building. I want to be somebody; want things. Want so much." She turned the spoon in the black coffee. "Sometimes I look from my glass and I want to fly down and kiss my fate. But there will have to be revolutions before my dream comes true. And I can't wait that long. Look at me, my face. Where do I belong? What's my dream? What's your dream? Am I your dream?" She looked at him long, then out the window, North.

"Will my dream end here? Joanne?" He placed his dark hand on her light face. Gently . . . gently . . . gently he moved her face opposite his. And the black porters in white jackets and black ties gazed; the white men in black suits glanced. And all the white blonds, all white and starch, sat rigid while the knives and forks and spoons tinkled and clashed. But he could not hear them. He, in that moment of black agony, heard only the soft white snow, falling.

"Will my dream end *again?*" he repeated himself. And the minute she took to answer seemed like an hour.

"We have some time to talk," she said. "He will meet me here in a short while." She moved the dark hand away from her face slowly. She held it tightly with both hands. "I won't be seeing you again, honest. But I love you, I love you, *love you* . . ."

. . . *won't be seeing you again* . . .

He knew then. He felt it. It was there. All the turmoil before an erupting emotion; all the rushing to the head of the inside of his soul, leaving the boiling deep, deep, far away in the head, then changing to hot tears — tears that lingered within his hot burning eyes; not coming out to be seen, never coming out to be seen . . . tears . . . tears . . . and he fought them. He noticed her mouth — ugly now — moving, trying to say something. Not hearing her, not wanting to, he looked out the glass into the white, white snow — North. At the cathedral. At the bell that would chime, then the Te Deums that, for him, would never mean glory. After them he would be alone again, without Joanne again; viduity again . . . feeling like a single falling leaf late in the dawn again.

Is this what he had feared?

Her mouth moved. "I had to see you, tell you."

The seconds of silence seemed like years.

"What can I say? He's very nice, you will like him. Anyway, you know him. He's Irish."

"Yes, I know him," he said. His voice was a whisper.

"I know," she whispered. She turned and looked out the glass.

And that day she remembered.

She is remembering.

Saturday night, Sunday morning, the end of summer. We attended the play *Long Day's Journey into Night*. How beautifully O'Neill recreates the feeling of impending doom. And I knew there would be a sense of doom in me that night. For I had been searching in a strange black world. And that world had refused me when I needed it most. I wanted to destroy it by becoming a part of the white, blending with the white. The tragedy of nature, he would call it.

Had already told him I loved Alexandros, that he wanted to take me to Paris and Ireland. And as I remember, it was the first time we had ever really talked. Strange. Our first conversation had to be about someone white, about what that someone wanted to do for me. He was hurt because he did not want me to love Alexandros, did not want me to tell him what white could do for me. He tried desperately not to show it. I believe I convinced him that that love was a different love, not like the feeling for him. But I don't think I convinced him. Anyway he took me to see Alexandros in the O'Neill play; he took me to the after-party. He wanted me to be near Alexandros, it seemed. We stayed at the party until four A.M. I glanced at him often, watched him moving through the white party, dark and invisible to them. He never looked at me. I talked to Alexandros all that time. We exhausted ourselves talking about nothing. And when we couldn't think of anything else to say, we made a date for Sunday night. I did not tell him. He knew. We made the date at four A.M. At four A.M. he looked at me across the room through the white crowd.

Sunday morning . . . mourning . . . far away . . . the Te Deums.

We talked. We kissed for the first time that Sunday morning between darkness and dawn. So gentle. Gently . . . gently. Oh God! How wonderful I felt! I felt more love than Dido must have felt. And I fell in love's abyss for the first time. Everything around me was so strange: the darkness and the dawn, the sun and the night, the coldness and the heat, all together at the same time. All my life I had been told. and I felt that I *should* go beyond darkness. And I could. I could change with the seasons. But everything about me changed when we caught the darkness and the dawn. Every little thing became a beautiful phallic symbol, made me think of him, dark and invisible, melting the pretty, pretty snow.

"I know," she said again.

"You shouldn't have told him to meet you here," he said.

"We tried, you know that."

"Tried?" He tried to say something else; no words came. Even his lips felt heavy, thick. He prayed to be what she wanted, but he knew he could never be. "Let's talk about something else. How's your family?"

She looked at him long. Her eyes and pretty face expressionless. Everything about her serene, as if she was at rest, as if she was . . . was . . . inertia.

"I wanted to tell you how it came about; I wanted you to understand."

"I understand," he says. "But do you understand?"

"Don't make me cry," she said. "This had to be."

"Do YOU UNDERSTAND?" he said louder, bitter.

The black porters in white jackets and black ties turned; the blond people, all white and starch, showed signs of life. And he was slowly dying, again.

"All my life," she said, "I have had to protect myself, be on guard."

"From what?" he shouted.

"The pimps, hustlers, lesbians, and others trying to misuse me." She paused, rubbed his hand, continued without looking at him. "I look unusual —"

"Go on; what else?" he asked.

"More than anything else it is the Negro man."

"I am Negro man," he said, "and I never attempted to misuse you."

"How could I know that? Tell me how could I have known? How could I be sure you were *real*? I always guess at what you are feeling, never knowing where you are, never."

He looked at a white blond, snow white, crisp.

"Are you listening?"

"Yes."

The seconds seemed like hours.

"And man I have been misused!" She lit a cigarette. "Some tell me of movie contracts. And I say, 'Well, Miss Labold, this is *it*.' I spend weeks, sometimes months making sure. Disillusioned. Some tell me they can make me a star in the Ebony Fashion Fairs or put me on the cover or in the center of *Jet* magazine. Always it seemed like the break, my chance. Some seem truthful. And God knows I try, I try to find out. But it's always the same: to them I am an illusion. They want that day and night dream — me. But they don't want the *real* me; they don't want the me that breathes, cries, wakes up in the morning, goes to the bathroom. Men don't want me. They want an illusion."

"Joanne —" he tried to say something.

"Please listen. Please," she continued. "It made me feel like half a woman, not complete in the way I want to be complete. Long ago, Iarbas, I think I discovered — and it may sound funny as hell — men are spiritually weak. They believe in God and nature." She smiled. "You too, man, you too."

"Joanne," he said, "you are trying to get outside your world. The Irish one is not for you. He will never be; he cannot be. Nature and God forbid it. Don't you see? Don't you understand?"

They could find nothing to say for a long time.

"Just as nature and God forbid snow to fall twelve months of the year, summer must return. You are my summers, Joanne. And if you are leaving because of disillusions, feeling I think you are an illusion, you will return. Like summer."

"So full of dreams," she said. "Love you."

"In light *and* darkness?"

"I think, maybe yes," she said.

The seconds lingered.

"Don't leave me, Joanne," he whispered. "Don't take it away."

"I can never be complete with you bridge people; I cannot make your dream come true. I am human."

"Don't you know you will return, again? Don't you know you cannot — he cannot — take away what is *mine*? By birth you are mine. I know it, he knows it, you know it . . . mine . . . mine . . . mine . . ."

"I love you I love you I love you I love you, Iarbas, I love . . ."

"Don't, Joanne," he remembered saying.

The bell in the church rang. One-two-three-four . . . His heart must have skipped a beat, he felt his chest once, looked out the glass. Hearing the bell sounding in his ears, feeling his heart hitting his chest, feeling his mouth becoming dry; still looking out the glass, looking for that face — looking — searching for that face that would blend with the snow. And she, flashing glances as if really frightened, regaining her composure; putting on her lipstick or looking at herself in her small mirror. And he, still looking out into the snow, hearing the bell, hoping it would cease. Then both looking out the glass; both seeing Alexandros approaching from the far end of the park; approaching, dressed in a black topcoat. And sitting there he could not hear chains dragging from afar, and he could not hear *him* singing *any day now*, but he could hear music from the psaltery. And the music sounded so beautiful in that glen of blue grass in the Highlands far away where he could never be but where she might go and leave him forever. And she could dance her dance to the music of the psaltery; she could play in the blue grass of the high places as she played on that floor in that little theater long ago, she could stop and listen to the bell. The bell. The bell. One-two-three . . . The Te Deums . . . bong-bong-bong-bong-I love you-bong-love you-bong-love-bong-you-bong . . . bong . . .

Alexandros approaching *with indifference*.

She rose, looked at him. "See you."

"See you."

Alexandros there.

She smiling up to him.

. . . *and with indifference did I receive him.*

Both leaving.

He is alone.

Both crossing the snow-filled park. Her checked black and white coat's collar turned up. He, holding her arm, going north. And she speaking something to Alexandros.

He, still sitting in the restaurant, watching her ugly back; watching the tracks of her black overshoes sink deeper and deeper into the pretty, pretty snow. Watching and hoping; hearing her voice, *see you . . . see you . . .* Wishing he could be what she wanted.

He turns and looks into the sun-filled park; at the couples laughing; at the birds and pigeons that lounge and linger there; at

the beautiful water fountains that emit all colors of waters —
waters that spring so misty and settle so clear; at the cut green
grass, so green that it appears blue. And the feeling he holds at this
moment should be a bequeathal to the world. It is everyman's.

He sees her. She is running towards him, calling his name. He
stands; he smiles. She waves. And watching her he is thinking that
winters cannot last forever, but he is also thinking that neither can
the warm summers.

There are so many things that nature and God forbid.

RED BONNET

Lindsay Patterson

Granma Jo just upped and walked one day. That she did. She never learnt walking like other people, for she hadn't walked a day in her life, that is, till right 'fore she just vanished into thin air. 'Course I know it ain't so, 'cause I see her sometimes, just sittin'.

I was there the day she suddenly popped herself out of her lopsided old black rocker and just walked on down the street as if she had been walking all her life. I scooted in the house to tell Ma and nearly got tore up with the big razor strap she kept handy over the kitchen sink 'fore I persuaded her to go look for herself. She did, and we could see Granma promenading so straight and proud down the street and nodding her head and saying good morning like she did it every day; and people so flabbergasted that they could hardly speak. And then she came back and sat down in her old rocker like she always did and stayed there till her daughter and her husband came from work and picked up chair and all and carried her into the house like they always did about dusk.

When people tole the daughter and her husband about Granma walking the daughter tole 'em they were all crazy and jealous. Jealous she meant of the new car she had sent all the way from across the ocean, and when she passed by in it kicking up dust 'cause she was going so fast and our eyes popping out of our heads; I guess she thought we were jealous all right.

The next morning everybody sat in his yard not minding the sun beaming down so hard it'd dry up a Jersey cow, or that the folks cross town were howling for their breakfasts and dinners, and all mad 'cause they never had to take care of their brats before and finally getting a taste of how awful their little monsters really were. Nobody had to wait long. Close to an hour after the daughter and her husband went to work, Granma pushed herself up from her ole rocker and started walking again. We kids followed after her, and our folks was so busy watching her walk they didn't notice us running behind the old lady shouting, "One-two, one-two, and look at Granma Jo GO!" WHEW! She didn't go slow. She was like Boots Hatcher, the time he came running so hard into home plate that the only thing that could stop him was the big Pea-con tree in Mister Laske's cotton patch cross the road, and if Boots's head hadn't been so goshdang tough it'd kilt him right then and there.

Granma didn't just walk up and down the block like she did the day before, she went over to Peach Street and walked around for a while and then came back to our street and walked. Twenty-seven times she walked up and down Peach Street, and no countin' the times she walked our street. By the time Granma was through walking we kids were all pooped out, but Granma looked as if she didn't want to quit. But she finally did, and got in her rocker just in time, too. Her daughter and her husband came sailing down the road in their new car, kicking up a dust storm the likes of which we never seen in these parts. Even the rich white folks never drive so fast. They hardly raise a speck.

The daughter really got mad when she was tole that Granma was walking again. She threatened to move and she said that we were not genteel people anyways and she didn't know why she lived on this ugly street anyway. I guess the reason she didn't ask Granma had she been walking again was that Granma just sat there with that sweet smile on her face and her big black eyes shining as if they were close to tears. And then they carried her in like they always did about dusk and put her to bed. They didn't haft to change her clothes like Ma did me years ago being that she wore her going-to-bed clothes all the time, but she did, like me, get a change of clean ones every week. Only I got mine every Saturday night. There was never any set day when they'd change Granma's. Just one morning you'd see her sittin' in her rocker looking so fresh and clean you'd think she was an angel down from heaven.

A delegation of women from our street decided to go over and see the daughter 'cause they didn't want anybody calling them liars. Besides, they didn't think much of the daughter anyways. Her and that new car, even if she did work for the richest white family in town she only got five dollars more a week than most of the ladies, and that wouldn't buy a new car like the folks' she worked for, even with her husband working at the sawmill like all the other men.

Well, the delegation didn't get anywhere with the daughter. I know, I heared it all. We lived next door to Granma. Our house being only about ten feet away, and when anybody raised their voice we could hear everything. Shucks, I heared something every night between the daughter and her husband. Ma and Pa had their room on the other side of the house and they couldn't hear a thing. Well, anyways, it seem that the husband didn't know how the daughter could afford the car, either.

Anyways. Mrs. Goodfellow, President of the AME Zion Church Women's Missionary Society, headed the delegation, and if anybody could straighten out Granma's daughter she could. Mrs. Goodfellow could hold her own with anybody. She makes her husband mind her just like Ma makes me mind her. And if he talks back, like I do sometimes to Ma, she paddles him just like Ma paddles me, only she does it with her fist. But the difference is I don't cry as loud as he does.

But Mrs. Goodfellow was no match for the daughter. We found that the daughter could holler just as loud as Mrs. Goodfellow, even louder.

It's a good thing that the daughter belonged to the Baptist Church two miles from town, 'cause it's hard enough having to hear Mrs. Goodfellow getting carried away at prayer meetings every Wednesday, with the AME Church only two streets over and down a little toward Snakes' Pond.

Well, Mrs. Goodfellow said to the daughter, "You been telling lies on us and that ain't right. We ain't got nothing to lie about. We all love Granma like you do, and we all seen Granma walking. She walks better than I do, like she been walking all her life. Granma been fooling you. She could walk all the time."

At that the daughter called Mrs. Goodfellow "a bald-headed lie," and the two women started pulling out each other's hair, and Mrs. Grover, vice president of the Missionaries, got bopped on the head a couple of times before she could part them.

After that Mrs. Goodfellow started calling the daughter nasty names and telling her that she was no good and not fittin' to live in a decent neighborhood; and that she must be doing something wrong to get a new car like the folks she worked for had.

The daughter said, "I works hard and I spends my money anyway I Gawddamn please." Several of the ladies put their hands over their mouths when they heared her use the Lawd's name in vain. It was all right for the men to cuss but to hear a lady use that kind of language, and it wasn't even Saturday night, did not set well with the delegation, most of whom belonged to the Sunday Night Bible Study Group, too.

Finally the daughter said she'd stay home tomorrow and see if Granma walked, and then she ordered the delegation out of her house. Some of them didn't want to leave "poor Granma" in the house 'cause they thought the daughter would do somethin' to her. A woman using the Lawd's name like that'll do anything, they said, and them forgetting that all of their husbands met at Benny's Poolroom every Saturday night, and they went dragging them out on Sunday mornings for church, and the husbands cussing and they cussing right back.

The next day our street was like it was at circus time in the fall on the road going out by Mister Silas Adams's farm. Some of the white folks musta heared about Granma. Their big shiny cars, just like the one the daughter had, were parked all up and down the street. They carried Granma out early that morning and she had been washed and had on her clean red going-to-bed clothes, and her hair had been combed and braided just like my sister's pigtails. The street was crammed so full of people that Granma couldn't have walked if she'd wanted to.

You probably guessed it. Granma didn't budge an inch. She just sat there smiling all cherubic, like one of those figures on the big stone white Epistle Church or somethin' like that.

Along about dinnertime the people waiting for Granma to walk became restless, especially the white folks, and they began to holler at Granma, but she paid them no mind. Just smiling, I guess, at all the excitement she was causing.

At nightfall everybody went away real mad. The ladies on my street could be heared laying out Granma. They said she just had the devil in her and all the time they thinking her a woman of God. The ladies from the Bible Study Group, of which Granma was a good standing member, talked about putting her out. Mrs.

Goodfellow said that Granma did just what the white folks wanted. It just confirms to them, she said, that we all do nothing but lie. "Ain't nothing but the devil in that woman." Them was her exact words. "The Devil done come to earth in the form of that old lady."

The only body who was happy about Granma not walking was the daughter; she sat on the porch long after dark singin' like a croaked frog, "I tole 'em so and I tole 'em so."

Things just kinda went along for a while and people forgot about Granma and her daughter and her husband. As Ma said, things was duller than dull. But Ma kept saying she smelt somethin' in the air and she didn't know what it was. I didn't pay that no mind, Ma was always smelling somethin'. She claimed she smelt somethin' when old man Turner got kilt. She never tole exactly what it was she smelt, but she said she smelt it a week before he got cut in two at the sawmill. I tole her if she ever smelt anything about me to keep it to herself, 'cause I didn't want to know about it.

After what Ma said I noticed somethin' about Granma that I guess other people didn't. She smiled now like my sister does when she wants somethin' from Ma and she knows that Ma doesn't want her to have it. Sis just grins and plays up to Ma, and Ma seeing her so happy and lovable gives her what she wants. She never done me like that when I tried it.

Granma had that same smile, like she wanted somethin' and she was set on gitting it. In trying to find out what Granma wanted I'd go over and offer her a lick of my ice cream, but she'd never take it. I don't know why I did that 'cause I ain't never offered my ice cream to nobody since I let Choot Sample take a lick and he darn near took it all, and Ma seeing what he did, tole me not to never give anybody my ice cream ag'in or she'd cut off my nickel a day. But Granma wanted somethin' and it wasn't ice cream.

I hate to see August coming, 'cause it's getting too near school-time, but there's one good thing. Some days it gits a little cool, but then there're lots of bad points about it getting cool. You can't get no ice cream at the little store on Peach Street and it's quite a piece to haft to truck way uptown. 'Course you can ride the bus, but heck, ain't no sense for a fellow like me to ride it, I wouldn't have anything left over for my ice cream, it being a nickel one way.

There was that day I decided to go to town and buy me some vanilla, come hell or high water, as Pa says. It was hot as blazers that day and a fellow just got all wet if he moved a muscle. Outside of the ice cream cooling you off when you got to the place, they had some kind of thing in it that you couldn't see but it made a little humming noise and the place felt like a March wind had come and hit it. Well, anyways, I remember that day well, 'cause it was near the end of August and I was getting nervous. There had been talk around that old Miss Dalton was going to have the sixth, and I was as scared as a wildcat of her. She made you wear ties to her class and if you forgot one morning and didn't wear one, she made you put on one of her dead pa's ties, which was kinda spooky; and you'd get no peace from the other kids, they being big and crazy-colored. WOW! You could see them for a mile off. My brother wore one once and he couldn't sleep for a week after. He said it was like having a noose around your neck, and you was waiting for old man Dalton to come and choke you any minute. I heared that the father and daughter didn't get along at all.

As I was getting ready to take off for town the mailman came by. It was a good thing. Ma wasn't going to let me go. She said it was too hot and I'd catch sunstroke. Well, anyways, the mailman left a welfare check for Granma like he always did about this time of month.

I put on my big straw hat with the little green men on it. It came from Panama, that's what the man in the store said when Pa bought it. And Pa and the man talked about it, since both said they had passed through it during the war. Pa said he didn't see much of it, it being so near dinnertime and his rolls was about to burn and when he finished tending them they was way out in the ocean and all he could see was a little speck. He tole it to the white man so it must've been true, about a big ole somethin' like that looking like a speck.

Anyways. As I was about to pass Granma's I saw that she was trying to get up. She was twisting from side to side and then she put both of her hands on the chair arms and lifted herself. HOTDANG! *She was walking again.*

She came straight down the steps and headed for the mailbox without anything on her head; it being so hot and all she could've had a sunstroke right there. Well, she opened the mailbox and took the letter out and went right past me. I caught up and asked her where she was off to. She tole me she was going to town and I tole her it was too hot, that she'd catch sunstroke, and maybe die. And she tole me she wasn't. Not today anyway. I'd never heared Granma talk so clear before. Usually she said things kinda slow like all old people do. Since I couldn't talk no sense to her, I tole her I was going to town, too, and she said I'd better walk fast or I'd git left behind.

When we got to town I was dripping wet and Granma had hardly worked up a sweat. She took the shortcut through Mister Aaron Tobdy's cornfield and that was enough to work up a sweat, 'cause he'd said that if he found any "niggers" passing through his cornfield he'd fill their hide full of buckshots, but I couldn't talk no sense to Granma.

I wanted to hurry to the ice cream place and git cooled off 'fore I drowned, me being so wet and on top of that my skin prickling from the corn leaves, but Granma wanted me to go to the bank with her, telling me that she might need somebody to tell the bank people who she was. She didn't. They must've heared about her there. Pa says that white people know everything.

I left Granma in front of the bank and hurried to my place. It really was good to get inside and I felt just like somebody had poured a big hundred-pound block of ice on me all crushed up. After I got my vanilla I looked around for Granma and I saw her coming out of Herman's where we buy all of our things. She had on a big red bonnet, the reddest color I'd ever seen. Granma was smiling, and she strutted down the street like she did the first day she started walking. I declare. She sure looked swell.

I asked Granma was she ready to walk back and she tole me that she was going to take the bus, for she wasn't going to git her new bonnet all dusty and everything. She said she had always wanted a red one and now that she got it nothing was going to happen to it. I tole her I was going to walk back, and she said she would pay my way on the bus, I being so kind as to go with her to the bank. I ain't never rode a bus before, but Ma always tole me to go to the back of it. The white folks, she said, took up the front, it being their bus and all, they could sit where they please.

We got on the bus all right, but after Granma paid the man our nickels her legs gave out and she couldn't go no further, having to wheel herself on the front seat to keep from hitting the floor. Remembering what Ma had said, I tried to help Granma up. She said she couldn't go no further, and that she done done all the walking she gonna ever do. I begged her, telling her what Ma had said to me. All she could say was that she done walked out. Everybody was frowning at me and Granma, and the bus driver tole us he wasn't going to move a damn inch till we sat where we belonged. But Granma couldn't move. The driver got all red in the neck, then he got up and grabbed Granma by the arm and started draggin' her off the bus and me startin' to cry all over my vanilla just like I was a little baby, and not fightin' the man back like I was a man. He just let Granma fall on the ground and got back in the bus and drove off without even giving us our money back. Granma was asking for her red bonnet and it was nowhere in sight. She didn't say anything else, but I could see that she felt bad, 'cause I could see the water swell up in her eyes. I tried to get Granma up, but she still said she couldn't walk any more, and I'm startin' to cry ag'in, just like I was a baby, it being so hot and if Granma caught sunstroke and died, somebody'd blame me.

It's a good thing that Sister Mitchell came along with her T-Model, 'cause me and Granma might still be there and me being blamed for her sunstroke and not having anything to do with it. If Sister Mitchell hadn't been a big woman we'd never gotten Granma up those steps and into her rocker. I was scared to death to tell Ma, but she found out anyway.

Well, soon after Ma had finished with me in the kitchen I ran up to my room, and looking out of the window I could see Granma sittin' there and the sun still hot and it shining off her eyes like they was diamonds.

Soon the daughter came rushing down the road in her new car faster than a lunatic mule, and almost wound up in the ditch by the mailbox 'fore she could stop. She hopped out and ran up to Granma and started shoutin' and cryin' and carryin' on so that I couldn't make out a word she was saying. But Granma paid no attention at all. She had sort of a far-off look in her eyes, the kind Pa gets when he talks about going back across the ocean one day and living. After a while the daughter cooled down and I could make out her talk.

"You is been walking, ain't you? Getting on that bus and sittin' down in the front like you ain't had no sense. My own mama gitting me in bad before all those white folks. They don't like what you done, Mama. They think I put you up to it and I tole 'em I swear I didn't know you could walk. I ain't never seen you. Lawd knows you done got those folks all riled up ag'in."

Granma iged her like she wasn't being talked to by nobody. She just sat as she did most of the time, only she wasn't smiling like she was most of the time. She had a funny look in her eyes and once she glanced over in my yard and looked at my red wagon.

Stuff really gits around in this town. As Pa says, the white folks know everything. Before I could count to ten our street was filled with big shiny cars full of white folks and they all getting out and standin' in front of Granma's, like they was the day all of 'em came to see her walk. I ain't going to tell you what they said, 'cause I ain't heared nobody say them things to a person before. Mr. Charlie Fairflax says things like that to his mules, but they ought not have said those things to Granma. She didn't do nothing much wrong.

The daughter hearing all that was going on came out and I guess she couldn't stand them talkin' to Granma like a dog, either, and she started saying them things right back and cussing, the likes of which Pa says no black man had ever done before. They soon left. I guess they were scared of the daughter, too.

For the rest of the afternoon, our street was so quiet it seemed like you was walking through a graveyard. Ma come up to my room and tole me not to go out and she gave me a hug and kissed me on the forehead. Somethin' she never did after I got a whipping.

In the early part of the night things were really dull and I was almost screaming mad at nothing to do. My brother ain't no fun, all he does is carves things with the dirk he got for Christmas. Well, I shouldn't have talked too soon, 'cause things really got hot later.

I smelt smoke. I thought it was my brother sneaking a cigarette, but he was fast asleep. I tole myself it was my imagination. Ma says I got too much funny-book stuff in my mind and she believes that one of these days I'll go crazy. She just doesn't understand a feller like me. One of these days I want to go far away like Pa done, where a feller can have some peace and nobody to bother him.

It was smoke I smelt all right. There got to be so much of it in my room that my eyes started burning and I had to go out. I went to Ma and Pa's room and tole them about the smoke. They didn't seem at all surprised. They rushed out of the house and then rushed back grabbing my brother and sister. I tagged along behind my folks, not knowing what to expect, and there was the smoke, coming from Granma's house. Pa wanted to go in and see what he could do, but Ma held him back and tole 'em that he'd get as-phix-, well, anyways, she wouldn't let him go in. By the time the fire engine got there, the house had burnt up inside and all they could do was watch out for our house and the one on the other side. You could hardly tell from the outside that Granma's house was burnt, but inside there was nothing. They brought out the daughter and her husband and Ma wouldn't let me look. She caught me by the head and buried my face in her thigh. By this time everybody on my street had come out and they didn't seem to care nothing about the daughter and her husband gitting burnt up. They all wanted to find out about Granma. The women were wailin' and carryin' on so about Granma that I thought I'd cry, too. But the men said that there was nobody else in there. They kept looking and looking, but they couldn't find another body there. After a little while they gave up and decided to come back in the day and look, being that their lights were giving out.

They came early in the morning and searched for most of the day, but they still didn't find anything of Granma.

I ain't never tole nobody, but some nights I see Granma sittin' on the porch, her eyes shining in the moonlight and a bonnet on her head.

THE BURGLAR

Lebert Bethune

M ORE out of relief than out of any sadness, Mary Ashley switched on the ignition of her car, pressed the starter and began to cry in short quiet sobs. Out of the warm thick night-sky, the fierce scream of an airliner's jet engines faded away till only the sound of her sobs and of the idling motor remained in the car.

The woman beside Mary reached out and touched her shoulder gently.

"Come now, Mary, he'll only be gone for three weeks."

"I know . . . I'll be all right." She wiped her eyes with the back of her hand. "Tension." She tried smiling for the other woman.

"Are you sure you'll be all right? . . . You can stay with us if you like." The woman's voice sounded as if she wasn't used to soothing.

"No, I'm all right, really I am, please don't worry . . . I'll be fine in a minute."

Her grip on the wheel was tight in the darkness. The two women sat quietly. Theirs was the last remaining car in the parking area before the air terminal building.

"I'll drive you home," Mary said finally, with a forced smile.

The other woman seemed to relax, gratefully, with the note of cheery façade covering Mary's voice. "Good," she said. "I thought for a moment it was something serious." Then she added as an afterthought — confidentially — "I know how it can be sometimes . . . I'm a bit like that myself when Henry is away."

Mary reversed the car carefully out of the parking lot and began to drive slowly homeward. The other woman started to chatter, but she wasn't listening.

"I've found the most marvelous houseboy in Dar es Salaam, a real treasure. He's honest, respectful, and not at all sullen like the others."

No answer. Mary's eyes were following the white beams of her headlights to their limit and beyond. The night was only semi-dark. Moonlight covered everything in a bluish haze.

"Do you provide yours with uniforms?"

Still no answer.

Mary had cried in relief for many reasons. That her husband was on a plane winging thousands of miles from Tanganyika toward London. That she was free for a while from the task of entertaining dull expatriate technical experts like her husband, and like herself their suffering, bored, homesick wives. That a certain frustration, all the more painful when the means of satisfaction ay so near and unreachable at the same time, would be replaced by a more bearable solitude. Most of all, that maybe now she could begin to try to recover a way to love her husband. For that, his absence was ironically necessary.

At first when Henry had told her about the job in Tanganyika, she was frightened. The thought of what he had referred to as an "underdeveloped continent" still lurked in her imagination as the "dark continent." But gradually her fears had quieted, though she could never tell her husband with what she had replaced them — painted natives, colorful costumes, beads, drumming and dancing warriors. She had eventually gotten over that. Henry had helped with books and not a little of his pompous compulsive lecturing.

Finally, by the time they had left England, she was prepared for Africa. Perhaps, she thought, she could teach the native women something about home economics. She had even read up on the subject, taken notes.

As she kept the car steady on the narrow bumpy unpaved road leading toward the other woman's house, the headlights picked up a gray ill-defined shape led by two gleaming green points, drifting across the road. She shoved the brake pedal to the floorboard, jerking them both forward. The car stopped in a haze of bluish dust, the headlights blazing through it.

"What was it, did you see it?"

"Hyena . . . you run into them sometimes," Mary said without much expression in her voice.

"Oh my God! Here in the city . . . it's dreadful, isn't it?"

She didn't answer, she was still trembling. Minutes later as she guided the small car around the driveway in front of a brightly lighted, sprawling white villa, the other woman said, "I'm so glad we didn't kill it."

"Kill what?"

"The hyena, of course, that horrible beast." She shuddered as if from cold.

Mary said, "It would have been rather a mess, I suppose."

"Oh, I can't bear the thought of it." Then she added, "Mary, will you call us as soon as you get home." It was a statement rather than a request. The woman sounded relieved to be home.

"Goodnight, Carol. I'll call you."

The rain came pouring down moments after she began driving along the jumble of holes in the road leading toward her own place. It was often like that in Dar es Salaam, rain without warning. Huge drops almost as big as pebbles came down in a rush. The car was almost crawling now. Her vision was down to just a few yards ahead.

She thought about stopping and waiting it out. It was bound to stop soon, and as abruptly as it had begun. She rather liked the feeling of being besieged in a small place, isolated with the rain hammering and splashing all around her. It was only a mile straight on to her villa. So she inched the car forward in the driving rain. Already she had forgotten Henry. She felt no remorse, he would've forgotten her too.

Henry had been thoughtful and courteous when she first met him eight years before. Now he was simply courteous and she had to accept that. It could've been worse, she supposed. He could've been a bully. She would never have stood it if he'd been a bully. Thank God he wasn't.

The distance from the garage to the veranda fronting the villa was only twenty yards. She ran through the rain feeling its rough, warm wetness sting through her light dress. By the time she covered the distance to the long veranda, she was completely soaked.

The dogs were quiet. Probably sheltering with the watchman at the back of the villa. It was such a bother to have a watchman as well as dogs. They said it was necessary; provided employment too, she guessed. They all had them, all the "expatriates" living in villas outside the city in what used to be in pre-independent times, and by and large still remained, the European quarter. In fact, with the exception of a few high-ranking civil servants and one or two rich Asian merchants, only Europeans lived in these beautiful villas — some of them overlooking the Indian Ocean. The area was nicely placed, separated from the city by a sort of *cordon sanitaire* of open scrub land about two miles wide. On the other side of that the Africans lived.

As she entered the door, she realized that one of the wide French windows had been left open. The rain had blown in, soaking the lace curtains and spreading a small pool of water in which a large green beetle was swimming around. She closed the window after rescuing the beetle from drowning, or dying of fatigue, as she suddenly thought he couldn't have drowned in so little water.

Leaving her sandals in the middle of the living room, she walked slowly down the long passage leading to her bedroom, keeping close, almost brushing against the wall as she went. She could never have left her sandals where she did had Henry been there. He was a stickler for neatness. It might have had to do with his occupation as a statistician. She often felt that Henry would've made a good librarian. But, she reflected, even if he had been something as romantic as an artist, he would probably have painted small precise pictures with well-defined edges.

In the bedroom she climbed out of her soaked dress. She wore nothing underneath the bright yellow printed shift but the briefest of bikini-styled pants. She took those off as well — damp. Leaving everything in a small wet heap on the floor. She felt tonight, something she seldom if ever felt, even on the occasion of one of Henry's rare trips upcountry. She felt a strange excitement, vitality, as if — as if, she dared to think . . . the way a woman might feel just before she commits adultery. She couldn't imagine why she felt this way, but she liked it.

The rain had slowed to a quiet drizzle. It made the sound of a continuous soft wind blowing through foliage as it fell through the trees outside. After toweling her body till the flush of blood showed through her lightly tanned shoulders and legs, she began to appraise herself in front of the long mirror facing her bed.

She was being honest with herself. She wasn't a great beauty, she admitted. But she had straight firm legs and her breasts were small and upright. No doubt if she'd had children, her breasts would be hanging like little empty purses, she thought. She supposed there were some advantages to being childless. At thirty-five, the only really marked sign of aging in her body was a light tracery of wrinkles round her throat when she didn't keep her head up. She might have passed for thirty. Her backside, a trifle low normally, seemed just a little lower of late. Try as she might, she couldn't control it enough to keep that little bit up. The color of her eyes was light hazel. Her nose was small and straight enough for most men. If only her lips were a shade fuller, she felt her face with its frame of straight brown hair could almost border on beauty. If only her lips were fuller by a shade.

She began to think of lips, full lips, the lips of African women. Theirs were full enough for anyone, she felt. So was everything else about them. For no other reason, she thought, than that she wondered how she would look if she were an African woman, she tried pouting her lips as fully as she could make them. Then she arched her back so the line of her backside was exaggerated. Keeping her head absolutely straight on her neck, she began to walk slowly round in front of the mirror. She took it to be a good imitation of an African woman walking.

Funny that before she'd come to Tanganyika, she'd expected — hoped — to get to know the women. To teach them to sew, perhaps in time to embroider. The government, however, had no plans for this sort of thing and she couldn't just start it off on her own. When she brought it up to Henry, he had simply said, "We aren't missionaries, darling, these aren't colonial times." She had asked him angrily why the hell they were out here, and he had said, "We're out here because I'm an expert in my field, they need experts and they pay pretty damned well for them — that's why."

What had that got to do with wanting to help, with colonial times? It was as if something terrible had happened during colonial times, instead of people's learning to read and write and to count and wear clothes. Henry's attitude toward any interest she showed in the Africans was as cold and as arbitrary as the cryptic answer given her by the cook. One day when she'd asked him why it seemed that every third African woman she saw was pregnant, he simply said, "Since independence, Missy."

The phone rang as she walked around in her imitation. It startled her out of the pose. For a moment she became prickly with fear. As if she had been surprised by Henry in an illicit act. She picked up the receiver, heart beating rapidly.

"Mary!"

"Oh, it's you, Carol."

"Yes, it's me . . . Are you all right?" She'd heard Mary's sigh.

"Why yes, of course I'm all right."

"I thought you would call after you arrived home."

"I'm sorry, Carol, I forgot, thoughtless of me." Her mouth made a little grimace at the lie.

"George wants me to remind you to fasten the windows."

"Yes, yes I will, thank you for calling, goodnight . . . yes, tomorrow."

After she replaced the receiver she stood by the phone regarding her naked reflection in the mirror. She so resented the cozy atmosphere between all the Europeans out here. Everybody knew everybody, everybody felt as if they were responsible for, even to, everybody. She found the coziness difficult to maintain. She wasn't used to so many friends in London. Henry must be a thousand miles away. Perhaps she did miss him. For nothing else but his heavy snoring presence behind the mosquito netting above his bed. It had been months since they had tried together. Perhaps she would take a warm bath. So she took a warm bath.

The rain had stopped completely by the time she lay down under the flowing canopy of netting. She could hear the fine high buzz of a solitary mosquito on the other side. Only intermittent drips of water and now and then a chorus of crickets disturbed the silence. She thought no night must be as quiet as an African night, yet full of sound. It was cool enough for a light nightgown, but she had gone to bed naked and lay on her back sweating a little. Then she fell asleep.

The dream was an old dream but one she loved to dream. If only she could reach the end of it. She was sledding down a mountain slope in deep snow, bundled against the sharp wind, a mask to protect her face. And the fantastic sense of clean cold speed. Like flying under one's own power. The sound of the runners in the snow like rushing wind. Then halfway down the slope, she came awake. Just as the sensation seemed about to crystallize into reality, she came awake.

Lying motionless, her eyes half opened from the dream, she became first aware of the warm tense nipples of her breasts. Her hands went up gently to calm them. And then she heard a sound in the room. Not cricket, not rain, but something other. Something that was breathing in the soft darkness of the room. Strangely, she wasn't afraid. Though she lay motionless with her hands covering her breasts. Her eyes were now wide open. There was a man in a corner of the room beside the window.

Faint moonlight through the lace curtains glinted off his bare shoulders. Excitement not terror, perhaps both were the same, flowed over her body in a wave. She kept quiet, trembling a little, unable to move even if she wanted to. The man glided across the window and she saw him fully. Tall, slim as a bow, black, absolutely naked and shining as if his body had been oiled from head to toe. He would slip like a spirit from any grasp.

In profile, his penis hung like a stout tassel. She could even tell that he was circumcised. A new flow of blood surged through her from the chest downward to the tingling soles of her feet. The burglar was opening a drawer of the dresser beside Henry's bed. Now his back was toward her. Light outlined the glistening curve of his long spine. Desire began to pulse up to her throat, up up, until it cascaded. The moan escaped her. A short moan, almost a grunt as she tried to keep it back. The figure whirled.

She saw the glistening intruder leap toward the half-open window and squirm through. And briefly the sound of his footsteps drumming over the wet leaves. Then Mary began to sob. Softly, like a small girl. Still cupping her breasts, until the pressure from her sharp nails began to hurt.

JUNKIE-JOE HAD SOME MONEY

Ronald Milner

J UNKIE-Joe had some money. Nobody thought so — except those two big cats. Everybody thinks he was just a old, poor junkman — everybody but those two big cats, and me.

I mean, I *know* he had some money, I know it, I told them over and over, once — but they didn't believe me, and I'm glad they didn't.

I was just twelve, and asleep kinda', that's why they didn't believe me. When you're twelve nobody believes you know anything. And you don't know too much. You know just about what's good for you and what's not — like green apples and castor oil — and you know just about what's right and what's wrong. Sometimes you don't even know that much, and sometimes even when you know better you just go along with the rest.

I mean, like when the rest of the guys used to run after old Junkie-Joe and holler,

> Oo' JUNKIE-JOE,
> AIN'T GOT
> No DOUGH!
> Oo' JUNKIE-JOE,
> AIN'T GOT
> No PLACE TO GO!
> HE SLEEPS IN
> A BARN
> ON A
> DIRTY
> OL'
> FLO'!,

I used to run and holler that too.

I mean, I used to go by the barn old Mr. Junkie-Joe lived in when I took a shortcut to my house, and I knew it was real clean on the inside, and I knew he had a bed, and I knew he was a nice old junkman, if you just let him alone. But I used to run and holler that anyway, because the rest of the boys did. And like he would chase you with sticks and things if you followed him hollering that, and that was something to do besides watching the big dudes play ball or something, so the guys used to run after him — me too, even though I knew better. Like I said, when you're twelve you usually go along with the bunch.

Only, there wasn't no bunch that time. I don't know how it happened — I don't remember that part too good — but that time I was by myself. And it was wintertime and snowing so there wasn't even no big studs on the street for me to watch. It was getting dark and cold, and about dinnertime, so I started home.

I took that shortcut I told you about before, through the alleys. And when I got close to Junkie-Joe's barn I saw that it was on fire. I mean, I saw the little window all bright orangey and the long funny moving shadows behind it, and I don't know, I just knew it was on fire inside.

I ran and I hollered, "Hey, Mr. Junkie-Joe! Hey, Mr. Junkie-Joe!" I remember that part good — running and hollering that.

And when I got to his door, it slid open — it was one of those sideways sliding kinds — and the first big cat, the skinny one who had all those dollars in his hand and mean, mean eyes, grabbed me and snatched me inside.

"What the —— you doin' aroun' here?" he said, holding my neck too tight, his eyes real mad.

"I saw the fire! I saw the fire," I tried to tell him, but he was holding my neck too tight. I saw the other big cat, the one with the knife, and the blood all over his overcoat, putting Junkie-Joe's blanket over the little window, hurrying up because the fire was climbing all up the back wall and jumping at the ceiling.

"What the —— did you have to bring yo' little ass in here for?" The big skinny cat with the mean eyes squeezed my neck so tight I couldn't cry; he pulled me and I bumped hard against his pockets — they were hard with change. He made a fist and gritted his teeth, I felt like I was going to do something on myself, but just then the fire went *whuff* on the ceiling and he looked back at the other big cat. I wanted to cry so bad I could have prayed to cry. He was holding my neck up and I saw the fire moving wild on the ceiling and it was like I was dreaming about Hell. I twisted around and saw the other big cat coming over, and when he stepped over him I saw Junkie-Joe. He was on the floor with his eyes and his mouth open, and blood all over his raggedy shirt, and all over the floor where he was laying — the fire made him look like he wasn't real. And there was blood all over the other big cat's coat. He pushed the skinny cat and grabbed me, it was like the devil had grabbed me, I just wanted to die.

"You had to be nosy, huh? You had to see, huh? Well, you won't see nothing else, little —" it was like his voice was the fire, and I saw the knife move out to the side, and his sleeve was all ugly slimy red, and all the front of his coat was slimy ugly red, and all I could see was the knife and the blood and I knew it was going to hurt, and I opened my mouth — but I couldn't holler to save my soul.

But the skinny cat grabbed him and pushed him. "Naw, man, naw, two of 'em make 'em wonder an' check up!" he hollered.

Then he grabbed me. "You know what'll happen if you tell anybody — anybody! yo' mama, anybody! — We'll cut you up an' burn you — understand!" He bumped me against the door.

My mouth was open, but I couldn't say nothing — he had the meanest eyes in the world — I just shook my head and tried to cry.

"An' if we ever get caught — ever! — our friends'll get you — understand?!" He bumped me on the door again.

"Naw, man, we gotta' do him too — now!" The other big cat pushed him and pulled me up against the sticky wet blood, it was on my face, and the fire was hotter than in Hell, I wanted to just close my eyes and throw up.

"Naw, he knows what'll happen if he tells just one word — one word! to anybody! — don't you?" The skinny cat shook one long finger by one of his mean eyes — I could see the dollars in his hand, the fire was burning my face. I guess I shook my head, because the door slid open, and they pushed me and kicked me in the butt.

I heard the door close, I heard them running away, but I didn't look back, I just ran — God! running never felt so good! And when I got between the houses I stopped and washed the blood off my face with snow — washed it! washed it! washed it! Then I ran home.

I didn't eat much. I didn't want to eat at all, but Mama would have asked questions — Daddy was at work, Mama kept looking at me while I tried to keep my head down and eat. She kept asking me if I felt good; then the fire sirens started and she went to the window. She went to the back door and I scraped my plate in the garbage and covered it up, and told her I was going to bed because I didn't feel too good. She just said okay because she was looking for the fire. I washed up quick and got in the bed. I closed my eyes tight and covered my ears, but I could still see the blood all over his raggedy shirt, and his eyes and mouth wide open, and I could still hear the sirens screaming and hollering, like somebody getting stabbed.

I didn't eat much breakfast the next day either — Mama was telling Daddy all about poor old Junkie-Joe getting burned up in the fire. I just ate a little and ran to school.

I ran home from school too, and then I couldn't be still, I ran back out. I ran all day, all around — I ran whenever I saw my bunch because I knew they would be talking about the fire, and I ran whenever I saw some big cats. I didn't eat much that night either.

And I didn't eat much the next day either; I just ran to school, and back and out again and all around.

I didn't eat much for a long time. I ran all the time, for a long time, all day, every day, in and out, all around, everywhere I could think of. Mama said she was worried about me because I was so fidgety, but Daddy said I was just growing and told me to be still sometimes.

But I couldn't be still, I just ran and ran, and then I'd slow down and walk because I didn't want people to think I was running from them, but I'd be running again before I knew it.

I was running from school one day and I fell down and couldn't get up.

The doctors at the hospital told Mama and Daddy that I had pneumonia. And for a long time I couldn't say nothing at all. But when I started getting a little better I told them over and over that

Junkie-Joe had some money, but I was asleep kinda' and they didn't believe me.

I'm glad they didn't believe me, because I'm fourteen now, and those two big cats still look at me funny-like, quiet-like when they see me. And I keep asking my folks to move, and they keep saying that they don't have enough money for a house yet. I just turn away from them when they say that, because I don't care about money and a house, I just want to move away from here — right now! Junkie-Joe had some money, and a house — and you see what happened to him. Hell! I can't even sleep sometimes because he had some money and those two big cats knew it.

DIRECT ACTION

Mike Thelwell

W E were all sitting around the front room the night it started. The front room of the pad was pretty kooky. See, five guys lived there. It was a reconstructed basement and the landlord didn't care what we did, just so he got his rent.

Well, the five guys who lived there were pretty weird, at least so it was rumored about the campus. We didn't care too much. Lee was on a sign kick, and if he thought of anything that appeared profound or cool — and the words were synonymous with him — wham! we had another sign. See, he'd write a sign and put it up. Not only that; he was klepto about signs. He just couldn't resist lifting them, so the pad always looked like the basement of the Police Traffic Department, with all the DANGER NO STANDING signs he had in the john, and over his bed he had a sign that read WE RESERVE THE RIGHT TO DENY SERVICE TO ANYONE. Man, he'd bring in those silly freshman girls who'd think the whole place was "so-o-o bohemian," and that sign would really crack them up.

Anyway, I was telling you about the front room. Lee had put up an immense sign he'd written: IF YOU DON'T DIG KIKES, DAGOS, NIGGERS, HENRY MILLER, AND J. C., YOU AIN'T WELCOME! Across from that he had another of his prize acquisitions; something in flaming red letters issued a solemn WARNING TO SHOPLIFTERS. You've probably seen them in department stores.

Then there was the kid in art school, Lisa, who was the house artist and mascot. Man, that kid was mixed up. She was variously in love with everyone in the pad. First she was going with Dick — that's my brother. Then she found that he was a "father surrogate"; then it was Lee, but it seems he had been "only an intellectual status symbol." Later it was Doug "the innocent."

After Doug it was Art — that's our other roomie — but he had only been an expression of her "urge to self-destruction." So now that left only me. The chick was starting to project that soulful look, but hell, man, there was only one symbol left and I wasn't too eager to be "symbolized." They should ban all psychology books, at least for freshman girls.

Anyway, I was telling you about the room. When Lisa was "in love" with Dick she was in her surrealist period. She used to bring these huge, blatantly Freudian canvases, which she hung on the walls until the room looked, as Doug said, like "the pigmented expression of a demented psyche." Then Lisa started to down Dick because of his lack of "critical sensitivity and creativity." She kept this up, and soon we were all bugging Dick. He didn't say too much, but one day when he was alone in the pad, he got some tins of black, green, yellow, and red house paint, stripped the room, and started making like Jackson Pollock. The walls, the windows, and dig this, even the damn floor was nothing but one whole mess of different-colored paint. Man, we couldn't go in the front room for four days; when it dried, Dick brought home an instructor from art school to "appraise some original works."

I was sorry for the instructor. He was a short, paunchy little guy with a bald patch, and misty eyes behind some of the thickest lenses you ever saw. At first he thought Dick was joking, and he just stood there fidgeting and blinking his watery little eyes. He gave a weak giggle and muttered something that sounded like, "Great . . . uh . . . sense of humor. Hee."

But Dick was giving him this hurt-creative-spirit come-on real big. His face was all pained, and he really looked stricken and intense.

"But, sir, surely you can see some promise, some little merit?"

"Well, uh, one must consider, uh, the limitations of your medium, uh . . . hee."

"Limitations of medium, yes, but surely there must be *some* merit?"

"Well, you must realize —"

"Yes, but not even *some* spark of promise, some faint, tiny spark of promise?" Dick was really looking distraught now. The art teacher was visibly unhappy and looked at me appealingly, but I gave him a don't-destroy-this-poor-sensitive-spirit look. He mopped his face and tried again.

"Abstractionism is a very advanced genre —"

"Yes, yes, advanced," Dick said, cutting him off impatiently, "but not even the faintest glimmer of merit?" He was really emoting now, and then he started sobbing hysterically and split the scene. I gave the poor instructor a cold how-could-you-be-so-cruel look, and he began to stutter. "I had n-no idea, n-no idea. Oh, dear, so strange . . . Do you suppose he is all right? How d-do you explain . . . Oh, dear."

"Sir," I said, "I neither suppose nor explain. All I know is that my brother is very high-strung and you have probably induced a severe trauma. If you have nothing further to say, would you . . . ?" and I opened the door suggestively. He looked at the messed-up walls in bewilderment and shook his head. He took off his misty glasses, wiped them, looked at the wall, bleated something about "all insane," and scurried out. He probably heard us laughing.

Man, these white liberals are really tolerant. If Dick and I were white, the cat probably would have known right off that we were kidding. But apparently he was so anxious not to hurt our feelings that he gave a serious response to any old crap we said. Man, these people either kill you with intolerance or they turn around and overdo the tolerance bit. However, as Max Shulman says, "I digress."

The cats in our pad were kind of integrated, but we never thought of it that way. We really dug each other, so we hung around together. As Lee would say, "We related to each other in a meaningful way." (That's another thing about Lee. He was always "establishing relationships." Man, if he made a broad or even asked her the time, it was always, "Oh, I established a relationship today.") Like, if you were a cat who was hung up on this race bit, you could get awfully queered up around the pad. The place was about as mixed up as Brooklyn. The only difference, as far as I could see, was that we could all swear in different languages. Lee's folks had come from Milan, Dick and I were Negro, and Art, with his flaming red head and green Viking eyes, was Jewish.

The only cat who had adjustment problems was Doug. He was

from sturdy Anglo-Saxon Protestant stock; his folks still had the Mayflower ticket stub and a lot of bread. When he was a freshman in the dorm, some of the cats put him down because he was shy and you could see that he was well off. And those s.o.b.'s would have been so helpful if the cat had been "culturally deprived" and needed handouts. Man, people are such bastards. It's kind of a gas, you know. Doug probably could have traced his family back to Thor, and yet he had thin, almost Semitic features, dark brown hair, and deep eyes with a dark rabbinical sadness to them.

Anyway, we guys used to really swing in the pad; seems like we spent most of the time laughing. But don't get the idea that we were just kick-crazy or something out of Kerouac, beat-type stuff. All of us were doing okay in school — grades and that jazz. Take Art, for instance: most people thought that because he had a beard and was always playing the guitar and singing, and ready to party, he was just a campus beatnik-in-residence. They didn't know that he was an instructor and was working on his doctorate in anthropology. Actually, we were really more organized than we looked.

Anyway, this thing I'm telling you about happened the summer when this sit-in bit broke out all over. Since Pearl Springs was a Midwestern college town, there was no segregation of any kind around — at least, I didn't see any. But everyone was going out to picket Woolworth's every weekend. At first we went, but since there was this crowd out each week, and nobody was crossing the line anyway, we kind of lost interest. (Actually, they had more people than they needed.)

So we were all sitting around and jiving each other, when I mentioned that a guy we called "The Crusader" had said he was coming over later.

"Oh, no," Dick groaned; "that cat bugs me. Every time he sees me in the cafeteria or the union he makes a point of coming over to talk, and he never has anything to say. Hell, every time I talk to the guy I feel as if he really isn't seeing me, just a cause — a minority group."

"Yeah, I know," Art added. "Once at a party I was telling some broad that I was Jewish and he heard. You know, he just had to steer me into a corner to tell me how sympathetic he was to the

'Jewish cause' and 'Jewish problems.' The guy isn't vicious, only misguided."

Then Lee said, "So the guy is misguided, but, hell, he's going to come in here preaching all this brotherly love and Universal Brotherhood. And who wants to be a brother to bums like you?"

That started it.

Dick was reading the paper, but he looked up. "Hey, those Israelis in Tel Aviv are really getting progressive."

"Yeah, them Israelis don't mess around. What they do now?" Art asked. He was a real gung-ho Zionist, and had even spent a summer in a kibbutz in Israel.

"Oh," said Dick, "they just opened a big hydroelectric plant."

Art waded in deeper. "So what?"

"Nothing, only they ain't got no water, so they call it The Adolf Eichmann Memorial Project."

Everybody cracked up. Art said something about "niggers and flies."

"Niggers and kikes," I chimed in. "I don't like them, either, but they got rights . . . in their place."

"Rights! They got too many rights already. After all, this is a free country, and soon a real American like me won't even have breathing room," cracked Lee.

"Hey, Mike," someone shouted, "you always saying some of your best friends are dagos, but would you like your sister to marry one?"

"Hell no, she better marryink der gute Chewish boy," I replied.

"And for niggers, I should of lynched you all when I had the chance . . ." Art was saying when The Crusader entered. This was the cat who organized the pickets — or at least he used to like to think he did. A real sincere crusading-type white cat. He looked with distaste at Lee's sign about kikes and niggers.

"Well, fellas, all ready for the picket on Saturday?"

"Somebody tell him," said Lee.

"Well, you see," I ventured, "we ain't going."

"Ain't going!" The Crusader howled. "But why? Don't you think —"

"Of course not. We are all dedicated practitioners of non-think. Besides, all our Negrahs are happy. Ain't yuh happy, Mike?" Art drawled.

"Yeah, but I don' like all these immigran's, kikes, dagos, an' such. Like, I thinks —"

"And Ah purely hates niggers: they stink so," Lee announced.

The Crusader didn't get the message. "Look, guys, I know you're joking, but . . . I know you guys are awful close — hell, you room together — but you persist in using all these derogatory racial epithets. I should think that you of all people . . . I really don't think it's funny."

"Man," said Dick, "is this cat for real?"

I knew just what he meant: I can't stomach these crusading liberal types, either, who just have to prove their democracy.

"Okay, can it, guys. I think we ought to explain to this gentleman what we mean," Art said. "Look, I don't think I have to prove anything to anyone in this room. We're all in favor of the demonstrations. In fact, nearly half the community is, so we don't think we need to parade our views. Besides, you have enough people as it is. So we're supporting the students in the South, but why not go across the state line into Missouri and really do something? That's where direct action is needed."

"Oho, the same old excuse for doing nothing," The Crusader sneered.

I could see that Lee over in his corner was getting mad. Suddenly he said, "So you accuse us of doing nothing? Well, we'll show you what we mean by direct action. We mean action calculated to pressure people, to disrupt economic and social functions and patterns, to pressure them into doing something to improve racial relations."

"Very fine, Comrade Revolutionary, and just what do you propose to do, besides staying home and lecturing active people like me?" The Crusader's tone dripped sarcasm.

Lee completely lost control. "What do we propose to do?" he shouted. "We'll go across the state line and in two weeks we'll integrate some institution! That'll show you what direct action means."

"Okay, okay, just make sure you do it," said The Crusader as he left.

Man, next day it was all over campus that we had promised to integrate everything from the State of Georgia to the White House main bedroom — you know how rumors are. We were in a fix. Every time Lee blew his top we were always in a jam. Now we had to put up or shut up.

The pressure was mounting after about a week. We were all sitting around one day when Doug proclaimed to Lee, "We shall disrupt their social functions, we shall disrupt their human functions — You utter nut, what the hell are you going to do?"

Lee was real quiet, like he hadn't heard; then he jumped up. "Human functions! Doug — genius. I love you!" Then he split the scene, real excited-like.

About an hour later Lee came back still excited, and mysterious. "Look," he said, "we're cool. I have it all worked out. You know that big department store in Deershead? Well, they have segregated sanitary facilities."

Dick interrupted, "So? This is a Christian country. You expect men and women to use the same facilities?"

"Oh, shut up, you know what I mean. Anyway, we're going to integrate them. All you guys have to do is get ten girls and five other guys and I'll do the rest."

"Oh, isn't our genius smart," I snarled. "If you think that, hot as it is, I'm going to picket among those hillbillies, you're out of your cotton-chopping little mind."

"Who's going to picket?" Lee said. "Credit me with more finesse than that. I said direct action, didn't I? Well, that's what I meant. All you guys have to do is sit in the white johns and use all the seats. I'll do the rest."

"And the girls?" I asked.

"They do the same over in the women's rest rooms. Oh, is this plan a riot!" The cat cracked up and wouldn't say any more. Nobody liked it much. Lee was so damn wild at times. See, he was a real slick cat. I mean, if he had ten months with a headshrinker he'd probably end up President. But, man, most of the jams we got into were because the cat *hadn't* seen a headshrinker. Anyway, we didn't have any alternative, so we went along.

The morning we were ready to leave, Lee disappeared. Just when everyone was getting real mad, he showed, dragging two guys with him. One was The Crusader and the other cat turned out to be a photographer from the school paper. So we drove to Deershead, a hick town over in Missouri. All the way, Lee was real confident. He kept gloating to The Crusader that he was going to show him how to operate.

When we arrived at the "target," as Lee called it, he told everyone to go in and proceed with stage one. All this means is that we went and sat in the white johns. The girls did the same. Lee disappeared again. We all sat and waited. Soon he showed up grinning all over and said:

"Very good. Now I shall join you and wait for our little scheme to develop." He told The Crusader and the photographer to wait in the store for our plan to take effect. Man, we sat in that place for about an hour. It was real hot, even in there. The guys started to get restless and finally threatened to leave if Lee didn't clue us in on the plan — if he had one.

Just as he decided to tell us, two guys came into the john real quick. We heard one of them say, "Goddamn, the place is full." They waited around for a while, and more guys kept coming in. All of a sudden the place was filled with guys. They seemed real impatient, and one of them said, "Can't you fellas hurry up? There's quite a line out here."

"Wonder why everyone has such urgent business?" drawled Lee. "Must be an epidemic."

"Must be something we ate," the guy said. His voice sounded strange and tense. "Hurry up, fellas, will you?"

I peeped through the crack in the door and saw the guys outside all sweating and red in the face. One cat was doubled up, holding his middle and grimacing. I heard Lee say in a tone of real concern, "I tell you what, men, looks like we'll be here for some time. Why don't you just go down to the other rest room?"

"What!" someone shouted. "You mean the nigger john?"

Then Lee said ever so sweetly, "Oh, well . . . there's always the floor." And he started laughing softly.

The guys got real mad. Someone tried my door, but it was locked. I heard one guy mutter, "The hell with this," and he split. For a minute there was silence; then we heard something like everyone rushing for the door.

Lee said, "C'mon, let's follow them." So we all slipped out.

Man, that joint was in an uproar. There was a crowd of whites milling around the door of both colored johns. The Crusader was standing around looking bewildered. Lee went over to the photographer and told him to get some pictures. After that, we got the girls and split the scene.

In the car coming back, Lee was crowing all over the place about what a genius he was. "See," he said, "I got the idea from Doug when he was saying all that bit about 'human functions.' That was the key: all I had to do then was figure out some way to create a crisis. So what do I do? Merely find a good strong colorless laxative and introduce it into the drinking water at the white coolers — a cinch with the old-fashioned open coolers they got here. Dig? That's what I was doing while you guys were sitting in."

Just then The Crusader bleeped, "Hey — would you stop at the next service station?"

The guy did look kinda pale at that. I thought, "And this cat always peddling his brotherhood and dragging his white man's burden behind him all the time." Oh, well, I guess I might have used the cooler, too.

Well, there was quite a furor over the whole deal. The school newspaper ran the shots and a long funny story, and the local press picked it up. Deershead was the laughingstock of the whole state. The management of the store was threatening to sue Lee and all that jazz, but it was too late to prove any "willful mischief or malice aforethought," or whatever it is they usually prove in these matters. The Negro kids in Deershead got hep and started a regular picket of the store. Man, I hear some of those signs were riots: LET US SIT DOWN TOGETHER, and stuff like that. The store held out a couple of months, but finally they took down the signs over the johns. Guess they wanted to forget.

That's the true story as it happened. You'll hear all kinds of garbled versions up on campus, but that's the true story of the "sitting" as it happened. Oh, yeah, one other thing: the Deershead branch of the N.A.A.C.P. wanted to erect a little statue of either me or Dick sitting on the john, the first Negro to be so integrated in Deershead. You know how they dig this first Negro bit. We had to decline. Always were shy and retiring.

THE ENGAGEMENT PARTY

Robert Boles

SHE was not a drinker, for she held her glass too carefully. My eyes fastened to a detail. Her fingernail polish. The red was put into check by its own too-even glaze, was held, suspended.

"Yes. Well, my husband's work is similar to yours," she continued.

"Is it really?" I asked, but not quite politely enough. Had it been the lines of her eyes which projected the effect of my lack of attention? Her makeup, though not overdone, was obvious. Immediately, a sense of having played this scene before.

I turned slightly away from her as a member of the combo walked by, and noticed Helen beckoning me.

"Excuse me, please," I said.

The woman smiled with closed jaws, shifted her weight and pivoted on a heel. Her last name was Nolan. I remembered that then. I had no intention of embarrassing her. One should be accustomed to that sort of thing at a party.

Smiling now, I worked my way towards Helen.

"By God! It's George! It's George himself!" The voice belonged to Helen's younger brother. I clapped him on the shoulder. "And you don't even have to drink!"

"I left it on the mantel."

"Have you had enough already?"

"I've hardly begun," I said.

Helen appeared. Her arms were in front of her as if she were holding an imaginary purse with both hands. "There's someone you have to meet. My father's partner."

"I'm starved," I said.

She took my hand and led me across the room and into another.

The people seemed plant-like, rooted in the carpet. Their motions seemed to have been caused by winds and crosswinds. Necks bent, backs; arms gestured in conversation. I had begun to perspire.

"I hope he doesn't get drunk," she confided without moving her lips or looking at me.

"Who?"

"My brother."

I bumped into the woman who wore the brocade dress, the one I had had the conversation with a moment before. Laughter and apologies, far in excess of what was called for. It was a brief bursting of her tension.

"Here he is," Helen announced.

"So, this is the young man who's going to carry you away." The man in his late forties or early fifties took my hand and shook it vigorously.

"Yes, sir," I said, assuming the bearing of a lower responding to an upper classman.

"It's about time I met you. Engineering, isn't it?"

"Yes, sir. Aeronautical."

"That's fine. You're a good-looking young man."

"Thank you, sir."

Helen moved away from me. I felt her absence as a hollow space beside me. Someone had asked her something and I had heard her say, "Certainly, Marie." That was all. I folded my arms, turned at the waist and followed her with my eyes. She escorted a woman to the foyer. The woman was a politician of some sort, I think. I believe I had seen her picture in the paper in regards to a "Culture March" on the Negro community.

"Wonderful girl, Helen."

"Yes, I agree," I said, and turned to face him again.

"Fine family."

"Yes, sir, I know," I said.

A group of men to my right were involved in a familiar and hearty political discussion. I tried to divide my attention.

"Your family's in . . . ?"

"California."

"Right. Ken told me. I had forgotten. Doctor, is he?"

"Not an M.D. He has a doctorate in education."

"I was in California for two years, you know."

"No, I didn't," I said. It was difficult for me to keep my eyes on him. His complexion was sallow, the color of coffee with heavy cream. I watched someone take a sip of a drink and felt thirsty again.

"I was in L.A.," he continued.

"We're from San Francisco."

"And what do you think of Boston?"

"It's fine. I like it," I said without much enthusiasm.

The music began. Bass throb, brushes on cymbals, then piano, vibes and saxophone in a long chorus. People separated. We stepped back. Some danced the High-Life, others the Bossa-Nova.

"I don't intend for us to stay here," I continued. "I've taken a job in Connecticut."

"I'm sure it's best. Best to get the bride away from her parents."

I nodded, then covered my mouth while belching.

I recognized the bellowing of Tommy's voice to my right. He was, perhaps, getting drunk. "Being colored doesn't have anything to do with color! It's a question of attitudes and history and all that crap!"

"It's a good life that's yours to lead," Helen's father's partner said. "When I was your age, I had to struggle. Not like you young people today."

"Yes," I said. "I realize how hard it must have been. I know how hard my father had to work."

The entire conversation was one often repeated. A needless formality. We were knowledgeably secure in the words we spoke. I felt a little disquiet.

"You youngsters have all of the opportunities, you know. And there are new ones opening every day. No worry about finding a job. If you're qualified, you'll get one."

Although it was not altogether true, I could do nothing but nod in solemn agreement and press my lips together in a gesture akin to a pout.

I thought I heard Helen call me, but I could not see her.

"What are your hobbies, son? I heard that you were a fine trackman in school."

"I swim, of course," I said, and struggled to say naturally, "and I'm a bit of a bug on sailing." It was the truth and it seemed to offend him. I had known that it would and that he would enjoy it.

A group of people parted in laughter. Helen entered between them. She came to my side. "Excuse me, Al. I'm going to take him away from you." Her voice sounded remarkably like her mother's.

"I understand." He extended his hand immediately and shook mine again quite vigorously.

Helen's hand was cool, as if it had been in cold water.

"You look fresh," I remarked.

"I just freshened up. I was wilting. It's so warm, and all of these people," she said. "Did you have a good conversation?"

"Yes. I suppose so. He's a very interesting man."

"What time is it?"

Instead of taking my hand away from her, I stood on my toes, stretched myself, and attempted to read the clock on the mantel in the other room. My drink had disappeared from in front of the mirror. "Quarter to eleven, I think."

There was a roar of laughter that was quickly muffled.

"Little brother is acting up again," she said.

"Leave Tommy alone," I said. "He's happy and well adjusted. Let him have some fun."

"You don't know what I go through with him!"

From across the room, a woman's voice calling Helen's name. The tone of it was comparable to the surface of a highly polished piece of wood. All of us, in a dense atmosphere of movements and poses, were beneath and supportive to it. "Helen!"

She looked.

Again, "Helen!"

I saw her at the other end of the room before Helen did. She sipped at a Manhattan and waved from her wrist as women, curiously, always wave.

Between smiles, I managed to repeat myself more forcefully than before. "I am starved, Helen. Famished!"

"You told me."

"I'm beginning to get a headache," I lied. "I didn't get a chance to eat this evening." But the evening was getting to me, the sensuous fugue, the cacophony of voices, the odors and light, the smoke. But something more than that. My disquietude.

"My poor dear," she mouthed, as she stroked my forehead with her fingertips. "I'm sure the caterer has some of those . . . things left. What were those things? Cabbage leaves stuffed with something and baked. Go into the kitchen."

"I think I will."

She had not really expected me to do so. "Dance with me first."

"No," I said. "You're cruel. I'm salivating and starved and you want me to burn more of my energy."

If she had pressed me, I would have danced. But she didn't.

"I'll see you in a few minutes."

We separated. She, it seemed, with misgivings. But I was relieved. I felt at once the dissolution of the effect of the hundred small embarrassments which had occurred between myself and others throughout the evening, the seconds of arbitrary inattentiveness which inflicted wounds, pinpricks, on each of us.

Perhaps I'm lying.

The kitchen door was on spring hinges. It closed itself after I had entered. I let my smile fall and imagined myself making an entrance onto a stage. I, as an actor with a small part in a play with Strindberg overtones.

I was at ease with the noise practically shut out. I hadn't noticed how sweaty I was. With a lot of room and air, it seemed to be present all at once. The white tiles of the floor and walls, glazed, flat and hard, made me doubly aware of my body and the bodies of the caterer and the girl. All of us were dark mobile beings set into this sterile chamber. The room was filled with the odors of smoke and powder and perfume in the other rooms.

"The groom-to-be is here!" the caterer said.

"You know it, dad," I said, slipping easily into the dialect to let him know that I was a member. "And I want me some f-o-o-d!"

"I hear you talkin', baby," the caterer said.

A metal chair painted white was against one of the walls. I sat in it and stretched out my legs. The caterer took a plate and began filling it. His white uniform was badly fitted. It was large. His arms were lean. The girl stood beside him and waited to help. She was very dark. Her bones were large, her hair coarse and beautiful.

"Get some salad for the man, Celestine," he said to her.

The name was right for her. It suggested fragility. Her bearing in some remarkable way suggested the same thing. She went to the refrigerator. I pretended that I had had slightly too much to drink.

Her uniform played on my mind. The name Celestine did also. Her uniform was white. Starched. The material at the seams was doubled. Something easily noticeable for it was whiter there. The cloth played on her hips.

She looked at me briefly. I returned her glance with a smile and wondered, while I was doing so, what she thought of me. My complexion is agreeable with a black or charcoal gray suit. I am brown in the way a Mexican is brown. I had my jacket open, my vest unbuttoned part of the way.

Celestine put some salad into a wooden bowl. I raised my hand in a political gesture when enough had been placed there. She added a spoonful more and offered the words, "For your health."

"This is my daughter Celestine," the caterer said proudly.

"She's a very attractive girl."

Celestine turned away from me in modesty. It suddenly seemed right to speak of her with her father in this manner, the masculine dominant, the female subservient. I was particularly aware of the roles we had assumed and had heightened.

I noticed that the caterer continued to put food on my plate. "Enough!" I said. "Man, when I want food for next year, I'll let you know."

He accepted my criticism with gentle laughter, but I was vaguely aware that I had overstepped myself.

"And what do you want to drink with that, sir?" he asked.

"Either Scotch or bourbon on the rocks," I said, with the full, coarse, American aplomb.

"I'll have to go to the bar to get some." He put the plate on the table near me. The top of the table was porcelain.

Celestine went to a drawer, pulled it open and began to remove a table mat.

"I don't need that," I said with an unintended sharpness. I smiled idiotically afterwards.

Her father left the kitchen.

I pulled my chair to the table and began to eat.

"Sit down," I said to her after a moment. "You make me nervous standing there."

She obeyed me. My voice still had a residue of sharpness. It was her father who had gotten beneath my skin. All of us had accepted Southern attitudes in a minute.

I wanted to speak to her as I ate, but nothing seemed worth saying. It was difficult to cut through the cloth of pretension we had woven together. I ate in silence and she watched me in silence.

My thoughts turned to Helen, but it was clearly an alternative — something to compensate for my failure to communicate normally with the breathing girl seated next to me.

I ate too quickly and when I was almost done her father returned with a double light Scotch. I thanked him with a full mouth, then finished eating, and drank half of the drink slowly, with my eyes on the walls and ceiling.

I smiled to myself. I almost laughed.

In another moment I was in one of the large rooms again.

"So you're the fiancé!" a woman said, pointing her finger at my chest.

"I am," I said, and smiled.

"Well, dance with me, darling!" All of her *a*'s were broad, and her voice rasped pleasantly.

"Only the High-Life," I said. "I don't want to put my drink down."

We walked into the other room and began the lilting African dance which had gained so much favor. She danced well, if a bit stiffly, but it became her.

"You know, I just learned this," she said. "I think it's marvelous! And you must tell me about Helen. You two go so well together."

The combo ended the song. We had hardly begun. I hoped that I could separate myself from her without appearing to be rude. I excused myself but she gave no indication of having noticed. She continued as we walked to the side of the room, then she met someone I had met previously and introduced us. I slipped quietly away from her.

I wandered through groups of people as if I were looking for someone. I stopped briefly to chat with Helen's mother, and once again near a small group of men centered around a white civil rights worker who had just returned from the South. He emoted before his words as he told a story of an atrocity too vile to be printed in a newspaper.

It all seemed a circus I cared little about. Or a parade. I've never liked parades. I did something idiotic. I stamped my foot. When I did it, a little of the contents of my glass spilled out onto my thumb and fingers. There was no reason for it. Perhaps I wanted to hear the sound of my footstep beneath the carpet. And I didn't know any longer if I loved Helen. I'd marry her in any case, but I wondered if love was possible. It had disappeared in a second. It was like walking out in the middle of one of those romantic screen comedies. Of course, tomorrow I would feel differently. In all likelihood this pattern would stay with me for the next forty or fifty years.

After finishing my drink, I went to the bar and asked for a Scotch-and-quinine. I was slapped on the back.

"By Jove, it's Georgie!" Helen's brother said.

"Hello, Tommy."

"Great party, is it not?"

"It is that," I said.

He posed unwittingly against the bar. There was a serenity in the moment or him. "Who am I going to play tennis with on Saturdays when you're hooked up to Helen and in Connecticut?"

"Where is she, by the way?" I asked.

"Upstairs. Mrs. Williams spilled a drink on her dress . . . well, I kind of knocked her arm a little. You know how those things happen."

"I'll bet Helen has it in for you."

"What the hell! She's getting married in a couple of months," he said, then added, "You lucky son of a . . . So, what's going to happen to tennis and me on Saturdays?"

"You'll find a better player." I feinted a left to his jaw, bent my knees and jabbed at his stomach with my right. He jackknifed a bit. Then I mussed up his hair. "Judging by your reflexes, you haven't had as much to drink as I thought."

The bartender placed my drink on the counter. I didn't really want it, but picked it up and returned to the area in which couples danced. I watched without seeing and heard without listening. My preoccupation was with nothing. Maybe only the restlessness which had no outlet.

"Nice combo," someone said.

I tried, but not very hard, to remember his name. "Yes, they're very good."

In another moment I rested my glass and danced again. I found that this woman whose hand I had taken when I had stepped onto the floor was a fervent dancer. After our first words, all conversation stopped.

I danced with her several times. I got warm. My legs perspired. I saw Helen once and waved at her. She smiled obligingly and waved back. Tommy also danced a lot. We stopped when our foreheads and shirts were wet.

"To hell with being sedate!" he said. "I know we're supposed to, but it is a party."

Both of us went to the bar again, ordered and waited. Helen shook a finger of warning at him. I walked to her and kissed her. She recoiled from lack of privacy and said, "Not now, darling. Not here in front of all of these people. Gracious!"

"Leave your brother alone," I said. "That's an order."

"Yes, dear."

I took my glass and began to mingle half-heartedly. The alcohol had worked its miniature wonder. I was dizzy. Still, I hadn't learned anything. I wanted to go swimming. That was all. The idea of it seized me at once. I could envision and feel it. I stood still in the center of the crowded room, closed my eyes and began a process of complete imagination. The voices, the laughter, the music intruded.

Upon opening my eyes, I walked without hesitation to the French doors that led to the patio and stepped out into the open. The air was much colder than I had expected it to be, and it took me a few seconds to get used to it. I sat in a deck lounge and closed my eyes. Who would be the first to disturb me?, I wondered. Helen might come looking for me. Tommy might want to tell me the latest dirty joke.

I felt myself sinking into the pulsating deepness of intoxication that precedes sleep, but pulled myself up and out of it at the sound of footsteps. I did not look behind me. I took a swallow of my drink. I followed the motion of the person behind me with my hearing. After a moment I realized that whoever it was had no interest in me. I closed my eyes again.

The footsteps moved from here to there, stopped, moved from here to there again. There was the sound of one glass touching another. When the sound moved to the side of me and a little in front of me, I opened my eyes. It was the caterer's daughter. I couldn't remember her name right away. Celestine. I should have guessed that it might have been either she or her father. She was putting empty glasses left by guests onto a tray.

I watched her, unnoticed. There was a certain dignity in her manner I find difficult to explain. It was feminine without the feminine embellishments of gesture. It was not decadent. Her uniform, her darkness, and that she worked contributed to it. But there was much more. I was at ease. I decided to finish my drink so that she would have to take my glass.

She heard me move, turned and seemed surprised by my presence. I smiled at her. She returned the smile and continued. She picked up glasses in front and then to the right of me. When she had almost finished, I held up my glass and turned it upside down to demonstrate its emptiness. She came and took it from me.

"Sit down for a while," I said.

She looked to the patio doors before deciding to accept.

I swung my legs over and put them on the ground to make room for her.

"I meant what I said to your father," I told her. My words were sincere. "It's a bit cold out here, don't you think?"

She did not answer.

I said nothing for the next few seconds. I reached for her bare arm. The contact, though brief, was electric. She did not move and was facing away from me. I wanted very much to see her face. I put my hand to her chin and forced her to look at me. I could not read her expression. I let go of her and waited for her to get up. She sat completely still.

"This is where my engagement was announced," I said. "Everyone was assembled here and a toast was made."

The night spun softly. I was not even able to hear her breathe. She sat rigidly, with her eyes fastened to some immobile bit of shadow. My need for her then urged me. I would give her something afterwards. Money. Fifty dollars perhaps. I had that much in my wallet.

The moment seemed to lick us with a broad tongue. I felt strangely like someone from the Southern past of masters and servants. I did love her for the moment. To make love with her once would be all that I needed. I would never have to see her again.

I stood and took her arm. "Let's go into the garden," I whispered.

I pulled her gently. I beckoned. My whispering voice trembled.

She broke away from me. "No," she said firmly. Her head was lowered. Her chin touched the top of her dress, her uniform, and although I could not see her eyes I detected a look of betrayal on her face.

Had I read the moment so inaccurately? She picked up the tray of unclean glasses and walked with quick, sure steps back to the house.

I waited for a decent length of time before returning. I wanted to smoke a cigarette, but had no matches. My disquietude was inert. The guests would begin to leave in an hour or so. Then the evening could be forgotten.

TO HELL WITH DYING

Alice Walker

"To hell with dying," my father would say, "these children want Mr. Sweet!"

M R. Sweet was a diabetic and an alcoholic and a guitar player and lived down the road from us on a neglected cotton farm. My older brothers and sisters got the most benefit from Mr. Sweet, for when they were growing up he had quite a few years ahead of him and so was capable of being called back from the brink of death any number of times — whenever the voice of my father reached him as he lay expiring. . . . "To hell with dying, man," my father would say, pushing the wife away from the bedside (in tears although she knew the death was not necessarily the last one unless Mr. Sweet really wanted it to be), "the children want Mr. Sweet!" And they did want him, for at a signal from Father they would come crowding around the bed and throw themselves on the covers and whoever was the smallest at the time would kiss him all over his wrinkled brown face and begin to tickle him so that he would laugh all down in his stomach, and his moustache which was long and sort of straggly, would shake like Spanish moss and was also that color.

Mr. Sweet had been ambitious as a boy, wanted to be a doctor or lawyer or sailor, only to find that black men fare better if they are not. Since he could be none of those things he turned to fishing as his only earnest career and playing the guitar as his only claim to doing anything extraordinarily well. His son, the only one that he and his wife, Miss Mary, had, was shiftless as the day is long and spent money as if he were trying to see the bottom of the mint, which Mr. Sweet would tell him was the clean brown palm of his hand. Miss Mary loved her "baby," however, and worked hard to get him the "li'l necessaries" of life, which turned out mostly to be women.

Mr. Sweet was a tall, thinnish man with thick kinky hair going dead white. He was dark brown, his eyes were very squinty and sort of bluish, and he chewed Brown Mule tobacco. He was constantly on the verge of being blind drunk, for he brewed his own liquor and was not in the least a stingy sort of man, and was always very melancholy and sad, though frequently when he was "feelin' good" he'd dance around the yard with us, usually keeling over just as my mother came to see what the commotion was.

Toward all of us children he was very kind, and had the grace to be shy with us, which is unusual in grown-ups. He had great respect for my mother for she never held his drunkenness against him and would let us play with him even when he was about to fall in the fireplace from drink. Although Mr. Sweet would sometimes lose complete or nearly complete control of his head and neck so that he would loll in his chair, his mind remained strangely acute and his speech not too affected. His ability to be drunk and sober at the same time made him an ideal playmate, for he was as weak as we were and we could usually best him in wrestling, all the while keeping a fairly coherent conversation going.

We never felt anything of Mr. Sweet's age when we played with him. We loved his wrinkles and would draw some on our brows to be like him, and his white hair was my special treasure and he knew it and would never come to visit us just after he had had his hair cut off at the barbershop. Once he came to our house for something, probably to see my father about fertilizer for his crops, for although he never paid the slightest attention to his crops he liked to know what things would be best to use on them if he ever did. Anyhow, he had not come with his hair since he had just had it shaved off at the barbershop. He wore a huge straw hat to keep off the sun and also to keep his head away from me. But as soon as I saw him I ran up and demanded that he take me up and kiss me, with his funny beard which smelled so strongly of tobacco. Looking forward to burying my small fingers into his woolly hair I threw away his hat only to find he had done something to his hair, that it was no longer there! I let out a squall which made my mother think that Mr. Sweet had finally dropped me in the well or something and from that day I've been wary of men in hats. However, not long after, Mr. Sweet showed up with his hair grown out and just as white and kinky and impenetrable as it ever was.

Mr. Sweet used to call me his princess, and I believed it. He made me feel pretty at five and six, and simply outrageously devastating at the blazing age of eight and a half. When he came to our house with his guitar the whole family would stop whatever they were doing to sit around him and listen to him play. He liked to play "Sweet Georgia Brown," that was what he called me sometimes, and also he liked to play "Caldonia" and all sorts of sweet, sad, wonderful songs which he sometimes made up. It was from one of these songs that I learned that he had had to marry Miss Mary when he had in fact loved somebody else (now living in Chi'-ca-go, or De-stroy, Michigan). He was not sure that Joe Lee, her "baby," was also his baby. Sometimes he would cry and that was an indication that he was about to die again. And so we would all get prepared, for we were sure to be called upon.

I was seven the first time I remember actually participating in one of Mr. Sweet's "revivals" — my parents told me I had participated before, I had been the one chosen to kiss him and tickle him long before I knew the rite of Mr. Sweet's rehabilitation. He had come to our house, it was a few years after his wife's death, and he was very sad, and also, typically, very drunk. He sat on the floor next to me and my older brother, the rest of the children were grown-up and lived elsewhere, and began to play his guitar and cry. I held his woolly head in my arms and wished I could have been old enough to have been the woman he loved so much and that I had not been lost years and years ago.

When he was leaving my mother said to us that we'd better sleep light that night for we'd probably have to go over to Mr. Sweet's before daylight. And we did. For soon after we had gone to bed one of the neighbors knocked on our door and called my father and said that Mr. Sweet was sinking fast and if he wanted to get in a word before the crossover he'd better shake a leg and get over to Mr. Sweet's house. All the neighbors knew to come to our house if something was wrong with Mr. Sweet, but they did not know how we always managed to make him well, or at least stop him from dying, when he was often so near death. As soon as we heard the cry we got up, my brother and I and my mother and father, and put on our clothes. We hurried out of the house and down the road for we were always afraid that we might someday be too late and Mr. Sweet would get tired of dallying.

When we got to the house, a very poor shack really, we found the front room full of neighbors and relatives and someone met us at the door and said that it was all very sad that old Mr. Sweet Little (for Little was his family name although we mostly ignored it) was about to kick the bucket. My parents were advised not to take my brother and me into the "death-room" seeing we were so young and all, but we were so much more accustomed to the death-room than he that we ignored him and dashed in without giving his warning a second thought. I was almost in tears, for these deaths upset me fearfully, and the thought of how much depended on me and my brother (who was such a ham most of the time) made me very nervous.

The doctor was bending over the bed and turned back to tell us for at least the tenth time in the history of my family that alas, old Mr. Sweet Little was dying and that the children had best not see the face of implacable death (I didn't know what "implacable" was, but whatever it was, Mr. Sweet was not!). My father pushed him rather abruptly out of the way saying as he always did and very loudly for he was saying it to Mr. Sweet, "To hell with dying, man, these children want Mr. Sweet!" which was my cue to throw myself upon the bed and kiss Mr. Sweet all around the whiskers and under the eyes and around the collar of his nightshirt where he smelled so strongly of all sorts of things, mostly liniment.

I was very good at bringing him around, for as soon as I saw that he was struggling to open his eyes I knew he was going to be all right and could finish my revival sure of success. As soon as his eyes were open he would begin to smile and that way I knew that I had surely won. Once though I got a tremendous scare for he could not open his eyes and later I learned that he had had a stroke and that one side of his face was stiff and hard to get into motion. When he began to smile I could tickle him in earnest for I was sure that nothing would get in the way of his laughter, although once he began to cough so hard that he almost threw me off his stomach, but that was when I was very small, little more than a baby, and my bushy hair had gotten in his nose.

When we were sure he would listen to us we would ask him

why he was in bed and when he was coming to see us again and could we play with his guitar which more than likely would be leaning against the bed. His eyes would get all misty and he would sometimes cry out loud, but we never let it embarrass us for he knew that we loved him and that we sometimes cried too for no reason. My parents would leave the room to just the three of us; Mr. Sweet, by that time, would be propped up in bed with a number of pillows behind his head and with me sitting and lying on his shoulder and along his chest. Even when he had trouble breathing he would not ask me to get down. Looking into my eyes he would shake his white head and run a scratchy old finger all around my hairline, which was rather low down nearly to my eyebrows and for which some people said I looked like a baby monkey.

My brother was very generous in all this, he let me do all the revivaling — he had done it for years before I was born and so was glad to be able to pass it on to someone new. What he would do while I talked to Mr. Sweet was pretend to play the guitar, in fact pretend that he was a young version of Mr. Sweet, and it always made Mr. Sweet glad to think that someone wanted to be like him — of course we did not know this then, we played the thing by ear, and whatever he seemed to like, we did. We were desperately afraid that he was just going to take off one day and leave us.

It did not occur to us that we were doing anything special; we had not learned that death was final when it did come. We thought nothing of triumphing over it so many times, and in fact became a trifle contemptuous of people who let themselves be carried away. It did not occur to us that if our own father had been dying we could not have stopped it, that Mr. Sweet was the only person over whom we had power.

When Mr. Sweet was in his eighties I was a young lady studying away in a university many miles from home. I saw him whenever I went home, but he was never on the verge of dying that I could tell and I began to feel that my anxiety for his health and psychological well-being was unnecessary. By this time he not only had a moustache but a long flowing snow-white beard which I loved and combed and braided for hours. He was still a very heavy drinker and was like an old Chinese opium-user, very peaceful, fragile, gentle, and the only jarring note about him was his old steel guitar which he still played in the old sad, sweet, downhome blues way.

On Mr. Sweet's ninetieth birthday I was finishing my doctorate in Massachusetts and had been making arrangements to go home for several weeks' rest. That morning I got a telegram telling me that Mr. Sweet was dying again and could I please drop everything and come home. Of course I could. My dissertation could wait and my teachers would understand when I explained to them when I got back. I ran to the phone, called the airport, and within four hours I was speeding along the dusty road to Mr. Sweet's.

The house was more dilapidated than when I was last there, barely a shack, but it was overgrown with yellow roses which my family had planted many years ago. The air was heavy and sweet and very peaceful. I felt strange walking through the gate and up the old rickety steps. But the strangeness left me as I caught sight of the long white beard I loved so well flowing down the thin body over the familiar quilt coverlet. Mr. Sweet!

His eyes were closed tight and his hands, crossed over his stomach, were thin and delicate, no longer rough and scratchy. I remembered how always before I had run and jumped up on him just anywhere; now I knew he would not be able to support my weight. I looked around at my parents, and was surprised to see that my father and mother also looked old and frail. My father, his own hair very gray, leaned over the quietly sleeping old man who, incidentally, smelled still of wine and tobacco, and said as he'd done so many times, "To hell with dying, man! My daughter is home to see Mr. Sweet!" My brother had not been able to come as he was in the war in Asia. I bent down and gently stroked the closed eyes and gradually they began to open. The closed, wine-stained lips twitched a little, then parted in a warm, slightly embarrassed smile. Mr. Sweet could see me and he recognized me and his eyes looked very spry and twinkly for a moment. I put my head down on the pillow next to his and we just looked at each other for a long time. Then he began to trace my peculiar hairline with a thin, smooth finger. I closed my eyes when his finger halted above my ear (he used to rejoice at the dirt in my ears when I was little), his hand stayed cupped around my cheek. When I opened my eyes, sure I had reached him in time, his were closed.

Even at twenty-four how could I believe that I had failed? that

Mr. Sweet was really gone? He had never gone before. But when I looked up at my parents I saw that they were holding back tears. They had loved him dearly. He was like a piece of rare and delicate china which was always being saved from breaking and which finally fell. I looked long at the old face, the wrinkled forehead, the red lips, the hands that still reached out to me. Soon I felt my father pushing something cool into my hands. It was Mr. Sweet's guitar. He had asked them months before to give it to me, he had known that even if I came next time he would not be able to respond in the old way. He did not want me to feel that my trip had been for nothing.

The old guitar! I plucked the strings, hummed "Sweet Georgia Brown." The magic of Mr. Sweet lingered still in the cool steel box. Through the window I could catch the fragrant delicate scent of tender yellow roses. The man on the high old-fashioned bed with the quilt coverlet and the flowing white beard had been my first love.

BIOGRAPHICAL NOTES

ANDERSON, ALSTON (1924–   ) born in Panama Canal Zone of Jamaican parents, attended school in Kingston, but moved to the United States when he was fourteen. After serving in the U.S. Army he enrolled in North Carolina College, and later studied at Columbia University and the Sorbonne in Paris. He is the author of *Lover Man*, a book of short stories; also a novel, *All God's Children*. He lives in Majorca.

BALDWIN, JAMES (1924–   ) born in New York City, lived for a long while in Europe. Articles and stories by Mr. Baldwin have appeared in leading magazines and periodicals, and he is the recipient of a number of literary awards for his books, which include three novels, *Go Tell It on the Mountain, Giovanni's Room* and *Another Country*; short stories, *Going to Meet the Man*; essays, *Notes of a Native Son, Nobody Knows My Name* and *The Fire Next Time*. He spends a great deal of time in Turkey where, he says, he writes best.

BETHUNE, LEBERT (1937–   ) was born in Kingston, Jamaica. After secondary studies there, he joined his parents in New York, where he was graduated from New York University. He has traveled in Africa, and lived for a time in Tanzania. His first book of poems, *A Juju of My Own,* was published in Paris, where he is currently registered at the Sorbonne while completing a first novel.

BOLES, ROBERT (1943–   ) spent much of his childhood abroad while his father practiced architecture in the Foreign Service of the Department of State. Later, as a medic in the United States Air Force, Mr. Boles was stationed in France. He now lives with his family on Cape Cod.

BONTEMPS, ARNA (1902–   ) born in Alexandria, Louisiana, received his B.A. degree from Pacific Union College in 1923. He came to Harlem in the midst of the "Harlem Renaissance" and began to write; he married and supported himself by teaching school. Mr. Bontemps has been librarian at Fisk University, and is now executive assistant to the president. He has written poetry, fiction, essays, and children's books, and has edited several anthologies. Among his works are *The Story of the Negro, 100 Years of Negro Freedom, Frederick Douglass: Slave Fighter and Freeman* and *Any Place But Here.*

BROOKS, GWENDOLYN (1917–   ) born in Topeka, Kansas, has lived most of her life in Chicago. She is married and has two children. Her second volume of poetry, *Annie Allen*, received the Pulitzer Prize in 1950. Other literary and fellowship awards include two Guggenheim Fellowships and an American Academy of Arts and Letters Grant in Literature. In addition to her books of poetry, Miss Brooks has written one published novel, *Maud Martha.*

BROWN, FRANK LONDON (1927–1962) born in Kansas City, Missouri, attended Wilberforce University, Roosevelt University and the Chicago Kent College of Law. Before devoting full time to writing, he worked as a machinist, union organizer, bartender, and government employee, and as associate editor of *Ebony* magazine. His novel, *Trumbull Park*, appeared in 1959, and at the time of his death he was nearing completion of a second novel.

CHESNUTT, CHARLES W. (1858–1932) born in Cleveland, Ohio, was the first of the Negro writers to use the short story form as a serious medium for literary expression. His first story accepted by a major publication was "The Goophered Grapevine" in the *Atlantic Monthly* in 1887. Many of Mr. Chesnutt's stories were written from the point of view of a white man looking at Negro life. In fact, he lived as a white man for a number of years. His best-known books are *The House Behind the Cedars, The Conjure Woman* and *The Wife of His Youth*.

CHILDRESS, ALICE (c. 1920–   ) born in South Carolina, grew up in Harlem, where she studied acting at the American Negro Theatre. While acting and writing, Miss Childress has worked as an apprentice machinist, photo-negative retoucher, governess, saleslady and insurance agent. She has had several plays produced off-Broadway, the most notable of which are *Gold Through the Trees, Just a Little Simple*, an adaptation of Langston Hughes's *Simple Speaks His Mind*, and *Trouble in Mind*. She is the author of one book of topical humor, *Like One of the Family: Conversations from a Domestic's Life*.

CLARKE, JOHN HENRIK (1915–   ) was born in Alabama but grew up in Columbus, Georgia. He came to New York City in 1933 to study creative writing at Columbia University. His short stories, poems, articles and book reviews have been published in magazines and newspapers for over twenty years. He was co-founder and fiction editor of the *Harlem Quarterly*, book review editor of the *Negro History Bulletin*, feature writer on African and American Negro subjects for the *Pittsburgh Courier* and the *Ghana Evening News*. He is an associate editor of *Freedomways*, the author of *The Lives of Great African Chiefs* and editor of the anthology *Harlem: U.S.A.*

COLTER, CYRUS (1910–   ) born in Noblesville, Indiana, began writing fiction only in 1960 as a weekend hobby. Mr. Colter for a number of years has been a member of the Illinois Commerce Commission. His short stories have appeared in *Epoch*, the *University of Kansas City Review* and various anthologies.

CRAYTON, PEARL (c. 1930–   ) was born in Louisiana, and was for a time editor of the *Alexander News Leader*, a weekly newspaper. She has written articles on pioneer Louisiana Negroes and the leading Negro citizens of the state. Mrs. Crayton has published stories of the "confession" type, and is now working on a book.

DODSON, OWEN (1914–   ) born in Brooklyn, New York, and educated at Bates College and Yale University, is head of the Drama Department at Howard University. In addition to being a playwright, he is a poet, short story writer and novelist. His published works include a book of poems, *Powerful Long Ladder*, and a novel, *Boy at the Window*. He received the *Paris Review* prize for his short story "The Summer Fire." He has held Rosenwald and General Education Board fellowships.

DUNBAR, PAUL LAURENCE (1872–1906) the most successful of the early Negro poets, was born in Dayton, Ohio, where he worked as an elevator operator after graduating from high school. His first volume of poetry, *Oak and Ivy*, appeared in 1893. His second book, *Majors and Minors*, came to the attention of William Dean Howells, who persuaded him to combine the best poetry of his first two volumes into a third, *Lyrics of Lowly Life*. With a preface by Howells, this book made Dunbar a national literary figure. During his short lifetime, Dunbar published six collections of poetry, four collections of short stories and four novels.

DUNHAM, KATHERINE (1912–   ) is better known for her work as an international dance star and choreographer than as a writer, but Miss Dunham is the author of two books, *Journey to Accompong* and her autobiography, *A Touch of Innocence*, and has contributed stories and articles to many magazines. She supervised the Chicago City Theatre writers project on cult studies, and in 1945 she organized the Katherine Dunham School of Cultural Arts.

EDWARDS, JUNIUS (1929–   ) born in Alexandria, Louisiana, received his college education at the University of Oslo in Norway. He has written many short stories and has received both the Writer's Digest Award of 1958 and the Eugene Saxton Fellowship of 1959. At present Mr. Edwards works for a New York advertising firm and lives with his wife and four children in Westchester County. He is author of one novel, *If We Must Die*.

ELLISON, RALPH (1914–   ) was born in Oklahoma City. He majored in music at Tuskegee Institute, where he had the assistance of a scholarship from the State of Oklahoma. Mr. Ellison has been everything from shoeshine boy to first trumpeter in a jazz orchestra. He came to New York City in 1936 to study sculpture and music composition, and ended up a writer. His stories and articles have been featured in most of the best literary magazines, and he has been a writer-in-residence at many of the leading universities in this country. He is the author of *Invisible Man*, which has become a literary classic, and *Shadow and Act*, a collection of essays.

FAIR, RONALD (1933–   ) born in Chicago, began writing poetry when he was sent to a high school for problem children, and came under the influence of an inspiring teacher. In the Navy he continued to write poetry and upon his discharge enrolled in a court reporters' school. He is married and the father of two sons. His first book, a satirical novel, *Many Thousand Gone*, appeared in 1965, his second, *Hog Butcher*, in 1966.

FISHER, RUDOLPH (1897–1934) was born in Washington, D.C., and received degrees from Brown University and Howard University Medical School. He practiced roentgenology in New York City, where he published two books, *The Walls of Jericho* and *The Conjure-Man Dies*.

GAINES, ERNEST J. (1933–   ) was born on a Louisiana plantation. When he was fifteen his family moved to Vallejo, California, where he attended school until 1953, when he was drafted into the Army. On his return to civilian life, he resumed his studies at San Francisco State College. Mr. Gaines received a Wallace Stegner Creative Writing Fellowship to Stanford University in 1958 and the Joseph Henry Jackson literary award in 1959. His one novel to date is *Catherine Carmier*.

HIMES, CHESTER B. (1909–   ) was born in Jefferson City, Missouri. He studied for a time at Ohio State University and resided in Cleveland and New York until he moved to Paris, where he has lived for many years, sometimes publishing his novels there in French before they appeared in English. His books include *If He Hollers Let Him Go, Lonely Crusade, Cast the First Stone, The Third Generation, Cotton Comes to Harlem* and *Pink Toes*.

HUGHES, LANGSTON (1902–   ) born in Joplin, Missouri, lived in Kansas and Colorado in his youth. He attended Columbia College in New York and Lincoln University in Pennsylvania. He has worked as a seaman and in nightclubs in Paris, and has traveled widely, reading his poems on four continents. His books include *The Weary Blues, Not Without Laughter, Ask Your Mama, The Langston Hughes Reader, Selected Poems,* and a series of *Simple* volumes.

HUNTER, KRISTIN (1931–   ) born in Philadelphia, is the only child of schoolteacher parents. She has earned her living as a schoolteacher, newspaperwoman, secretary, advertising employee and public relations executive. In 1959 she received a John Hay Whitney Fellowship. Her first novel, *God Bless the Child*, appeared in 1964 and her second, *The Landlord*, in 1966.

HURSTON, ZORA NEALE (1903–1960) born in Eatonville, Florida, attended Morgan College, Howard University and Barnard College. Miss Hurston received many fellowships during her lifetime for creative writing and for research in Negro folklore. Her writings include the novels *Jonah's Gourd; Mules and Men; Their Eyes Were Watching God; Moses, Man of the Mountain* and *Seraph on the Suwannee*, and many articles and short stories.

JOHNSON, CLIFFORD VINCENT (1936–   ) born in Chicago, was educated in New Orleans, Louisiana, receiving his undergraduate degree from Dillard University there. He then attended graduate school at the University of Illinois and worked as a laboratory technician in Chicago. In 1961 he went to live in Paris, where he resides with his wife and five children. He is employed in biochemistry research at the Faculté de Médicine de Paris.

KELLEY, WILLIAM MELVIN (1937–   ) born in New York City, attended Harvard University, where he studied under Archibald MacLeish and John Hawkes. Mr. Kelley has been the recipient of awards from the John Hay Whitney Foundation and from the Richard and Hinda Rosenthal Foundation of the National Institute of Arts and Letters for his first novel, *A Different Drummer*. His articles and stories have appeared in the *Saturday Evening Post, Esquire*, the *Negro Digest* and *Mademoiselle*. He is also author of *Dancers on the Shore*, a book of short stories, and *A Drop of Patience*, a novel.

KILLENS, JOHN OLIVER (1916–   ) born in Macon, Georgia, is a resident of Brooklyn. During World War II for three years he was a member of an amphibian unit in the South Pacific. He has written two novels, *Youngblood* and *And Then We Heard the Thunder*; a book of essays, *Black Man's Burden* and a motion picture, *Odds Against Tomorrow*, which starred Harry Belafonte. He is a teaching fellow in creative writing at Fisk University and chairman of the Workshop of the Harlem Writers Guild.

KING, WOODIE, JR. (1937–   ) born in Detroit, attended Wayne University and the Detroit Institute of Technology. He is a playwright and actor, and one of the founders of the Concept East Theatre. He has received a John Hay Whitney Fellowship for the study of directing, and in 1965 became director of the Cultural Arts Program of Mobilization for Youth in New York City.

LEAKS, SYLVESTER (1927–   ) born in Macon, Georgia, has lived in New York City since 1947, is presently assistant director of the Creative Writing Workshop of Bedford-Stuyvesant Youth in Action (Brooklyn, New York) and president of the Harlem Writers Guild. He is also a public relations specialist for Broadway plays and movies, and lectures extensively on African and Afro-American culture and history. Currently Mr. Leaks is at work on a novel, *Trouble, Blues, n' Trouble*.

MARSHALL, PAULE (1929–   ) was born in Brooklyn during the Depression, of West Indian parents who had immigrated from Barbados to America shortly after the First World War. Mrs. Marshall, who began writing sketches and poems before she was ten years old, was graduated Phi Beta Kappa from Brooklyn College, and is the author of one novel, *Brown Girl, Brownstones*, and a volume of stories, *Soul Clap Hands and Sing*.

MEADDOUGH, R. J., III (1935–   ) was born in New York City, and graduated from New York University in 1960. After serving in the Marine Corps from 1954 to 1957, attaining the rank of sergeant, he worked at various jobs, and is presently assistant director of arts and culture for HARYOU-ACT, Inc. He is a member of the Harlem Writers Guild, has completed a collection of short stories, *A White Negro with a Button Down Mind*, and is presently working on a first novel, *We Who Are About to Die*.

MILNER, RONALD (1938–   ) born in Detroit, has received two literary grants, the John Hay Whitney Fellowship and a Rockefeller Fellowship, to continue work on a novel in progress, *The Life of the Brothers Brown*. He has had a one-act play, *Life Agony*, produced at the Unstable Theatre in Detroit and a full-length drama done on television. A new play, *Who's Got His Own*, was an American Place Theatre production in New York.

MOTLEY, WILLARD (1912–1965) was born in Chicago of middle-class parents, but he chose to live on Chicago's Skid Row and write about the derelicts there. His first novel *Knock on Any Door*, published when he was thirty-five years old, was an immediate best seller. He asked his publishers not to put his photograph on the dust jacket of his novel, because he wanted, he said, to come before the public as a writer, "not as a Negro writer." After publishing two other novels, *We Fished All Night* and *Let No Man Write My Epitaph*, Mr. Motley was nearing completion of his fourth book when he died in Mexico City, where he had made his home for twelve years.

PATTERSON, LINDSAY (1937–   ) born in Louisiana, went to college in Virginia and has lived in Mexico and Europe. In 1965 he received a fellowship to the MacDowell Colony to continue work on his first novel, *Pierian Spring*. He lives in New York.

POSTON, TED (1906–) born in Hopkinsville, Kentucky, attended Tennessee Agricultural and Industrial College and New York University. He began work as a newspaperman in 1928 on Negro weeklies and is now on the daily *New York Post*, frequently covering major news stories in the racially perturbed South. His stories have often been anthologized and are now being collected in a book.

RIVERS, CONRAD KENT (1933–) born in Atlantic City, New Jersey, graduated from Wilberforce University in Ohio and continued his studies at Indiana University and the Chicago Teachers College. After service in the armed forces, he married and settled down in Chicago, where he is a teacher. His poems have appeared in booklet form and in various literary publications, including the *Kenyon Review, Antioch Review,* and *Free Lance*.

RUSSELL, CHARLIE (1932–) born in Monroe, Louisiana, was graduated from the University of San Francisco, and is now studying for a Master's degree in social work at New York University. Currently living in Harlem, he is fiction editor of *Liberator* magazine, and is working on a first novel.

THELWELL, MIKE (1938–) was born in Jamaica, West Indies, immigrated to the United States in 1959 to attend Howard University. Active in civil rights, Mr. Thelwell has worked with the Student Non-violent Coordinating Committee and was director of the Washington office of the Mississippi Freedom Democratic Party. He has published stories in *Negro Digest, Short Story International* and *Story* magazine. He is a teaching assistant in the University of Massachusetts creative writing program.

TOOMER, JEAN (1894–) was born in Washington, D.C., and studied at the University of Wisconsin and the City College of New York. He lived for a time among the artists and writers of Carmel, California, and later in Taos, New Mexico, but finally settled down in Bucks County, Pennsylvania, where he became a Quaker and a reader of a Friends Meeting House. His one and only book, *Cane*, a collection of short stories, poems and sketches, appeared in 1923 in the early days of the Harlem "Negro Renaissance."

VROMAN, MARY ELIZABETH (1925–   ) brought up in the British West Indies, attended college at Alabama State. Two of her short stories, "See How They Run" and "And Have Not Charity," have been published in the *Ladies Home Journal*, and "See How They Run" was made into the motion picture *Bright Road* in 1953. She was the first Negro woman to be given membership in the Screen Writers Guild. Her novel, *Esther*, appeared in 1963, and *Shaped to Its Purpose*, a history of Delta Sigma Theta Sorority, in 1964.

WALKER, ALICE (1944–   ) was born in Eatonton, Georgia. She is the youngest of eight children — her parents were share-croppers — and she attended the public schools in Eatonton. She spent two years at Spelman College in Atlanta, Georgia, before she transferred to Sarah Lawrence College. She graduated from Sarah Lawrence in January 1966. She is now at work on a collection of short stories.

WALROND, ERIC (1898–   ) born in British Guiana, was edu-cated in the Panama Canal Zone, at the City College of New York, and at Columbia University. In his early years he traveled extensively throughout Europe, settled for a while in France, and now lives in London. His only published book, a volume of exotic short stories of the West Indies, *Tropic Death*, appeared in 1926 during Harlem's "Negro Renaissance," when Walrond lived in New York. He is currently working on a book about the Panama Canal.

WEST, DOROTHY (1910–   ) born in Boston, attended Girls Latin School there, Boston University and later the Columbia University School of Journalism. Afterwards, she lived for a time in New York and edited the Negro quarterlies *Challenge* and *New Challenge*, in which the early work of such well-known

Negro writers as Richard Wright, Margaret Walker and Owen Dodson appeared. During the Depression, Miss West worked as a relief investigator in Harlem and began to write short stories which were syndicated in newspapers across the country and soon enabled her to do no other work. In 1948 her novel *The Living Is Easy* appeared. She now lives on Martha's Vineyard.

WILLIAMS, JOHN A. (1925–   ) was raised in Syracuse but has lived in recent years in New York City. He is the author of three novels, *The Angry Ones, Night Song* and *Sissie,* and one non-fiction book, *This Is My Country Too,* an account of a journey across the United States in 1963. In 1965 he sailed for Europe with his wife to complete his fourth novel.

WRIGHT, CHARLES (1932–   ) was born in New Franklin, Missouri, where he left high school during his sophomore year. He has since held a variety of jobs, including that of messenger. The title of his first novel is *The Messenger* and that of his second, *The Wig.* He lives in New York City.

WRIGHT, RICHARD (1908–1960) was born on a plantation near Natchez, Mississippi, and spent his youth in Memphis, Tennessee. In his teens he journeyed to Chicago, where he worked at odd jobs while writing his first book, *Uncle Tom's Children,* which received an annual *Story* magazine award. In 1940, his novel *Native Son* became a best seller, enabling Mr. Wright to devote full time to writing. He made his home in Paris for more than a decade before his death in 1960. Other books by Wright are *Black Boy* (Book-of-the-Month Club selection), *The Outsider, The Long Dream, Eight Men* (a collection of short stories), and *White Man, Listen.*

YERBY, FRANK (1916–   ) born in Augusta, Georgia, enrolled in the Federal Writers Project in Chicago during the Depression, later taught English at various Southern colleges, and worked on the Ford assembly line in Detroit. He did not hit his stride as a writer until he began publishing lush historical romances like *The Foxes of Harrow, The Devil's Laughter, Benton's Row,* and

Odor of Sanctity. His novels have sold over two million copies and several have been filmed. The story that appears in this volume was Mr. Yerby's first published fiction. It appeared in *Harper's* magazine and was included in the *O. Henry Memorial Award Prize Stories of 1944.* He now lives in Madrid.